THE REALM
OF FICTION
74 Short Stories

4/06

Third Edition

THE REALM
OF FICTION
74 Short Stories

JAMES B. HALL
Professor of Literature
University of California, Santa Cruz

ELIZABETH C. HALL

McGraw-Hill Book Company
New York   St. Louis   San Francisco   Auckland   Bogotá
Düsseldorf   Johannesburg   London   Madrid   Mexico
Montreal   New Delhi   Panama   Paris   São Paulo
Singapore   Sydney   Tokyo   Toronto

Photo Credits
Culver Pictures, Inc. (facing page 1)
Culver Pictures, Inc. (page 202)
Culver Pictures, Inc. (page 372)
Culver Pictures, Inc. (page 373)
Wide World Photographs (page 490)

THE REALM OF FICTION
74 Short Stories

1 2 3 4 5 6 7 8 9 0 DODO 7 8 3 2 1 0 9 8 7

This book was set in Times Roman by National ShareGraphics, Inc.
The editors were Ellen B. Fuchs, Donald W. Burden, and Phyllis T. Dulan;
the cover was designed by Nicholas Krenitsky;
the photo editor was Juanita James;
the production supervisor was Charles Hess.
R. R. Donnelley & Sons Company was printer and binder.

See Acknowledgments on pages 629–634. Copyrights included on this page by reference.

Library of Congress Cataloging in Publication Data

Hall, James B   ed.
The realm of fiction.

Includes index.
1. Short Stories   I.   Hall, Elizabeth C.   II.   Title
PZ1.H16Re8   [PN6014]   823'.01   76-53745
ISBN 0-07-025594-6

Contents

MODERN MASTERS   203

EUROPE-GREAT BRITAIN

THE UNITED STATES

NEW VOICES, NEW VISIONS   489

EUROPE-GREAT BRITAIN

THE UNITED STATES

Preface

Twelve years since first publication this third edition of the *Realm of Fiction* continues as a coherent anthology which suggests in detail and in broad outline the development and future state of the short story. Using the sturdy chronological framework of prior editions but modifying the formal divisions of the book to three sections, the text continues by specific stories to suggest a literary history of the form. Three main sections—Early Masters; Modern Masters; and New Voices, New Visions—draw alike from Europe, Great Britain, and the United States, with an increased emphasis on modern and contemporary accomplishments. Authors are grouped according to their national origin, usually in order of their date of birth. A useful birth/death chart is included at the back of the book.

With the formal divisions of the third edition now more flexible, there is also a greater range and a greater diversity among the seventy-four stories. All stories were selected with the intention of helping the student to recognize literary quality in short fictions—and by extension—in all literature. At the same time, the student also should understand that the dimensions, the definitions of the form are changing and are presently pushing far beyond previously recognized frontiers.

As one indication of the thorough revision of the earlier text, the editors note that of the present seventy-four stories, forty are new selections. Of these, twenty-three are by authors not previously represented including, among others: Trollope, Garland, Wharton, Pirandello, Moravia, Pritchett, Lessing, Faulkner, Hemingway, Welty, and Clark. In addition, stories by seventeen previously included authors have been changed in order that they may be represented by work which is more memorable, more fresh, less heavily anthologized.

For the first known time in a short-story anthology intended primarily for the classroom, *Realm of Fiction* presents outstanding examples from two kinds of popular short fiction: stories of crime detection and science fiction. With their well-defined traditions and wide international appeals, these subgenres may have become more representative of literature of our age than many critics presently allow. Masters of these genres here included for the first time are: Arthur Conan Doyle, Agatha Christie, Dashiell Hammett, Isaac Asimov, Ilya Varshavsky, and J. G. Ballard.

Another distinctive feature of the third edition is the inclusion of stories of high literary quality which are also humorous in tone. A great many stories of all nations dramatize tragic situations, isolation, death; far fewer stories of literary quality occur in which the artists's attitude toward the materials produces a comic tone. The editors, therefore, include several new stories which show the comic, the farcical, the satirical possibilities of short fiction. To cite American writers only as cases in point, the editors direct attention to the stories by: O. Henry, Faulkner, Hughes, Malamud, Hall, and Sondheim.

Since the publication of the first edition in 1965, the outer limits of the short-story form have been extended so far and are so unpredictably startling that today many readers may have difficulty in recognizing examples of the form itself; a number of these "extreme," innovative stories—perhaps they should be called "presentations"—are included in New Voices, New Visions. With slight structure, little characterization, and no recognizable setting—in fact with few or none of the conventional elements of fiction— these presentations approach a pure state of nonverbal expression. For examples, see the work of Lars Görling (Sweden) and Peter Handke (West Germany). Along with these extreme stories are others of apparently more conventional techniques but which may exploit language in unusual ways, treat materials once "taboo," or present motifs and symbols not easily categorized.

In this edition, the new translation by Ben T. Clark from the Russian of Chekhov's "Gusev" joins several previous, original translations done especially for *Realm of Fiction*. The editors regret that the Peter Gontrum translation of Hesse's "The Poet" must be dropped from this edition because of copyright considerations.

As in the two prior editions, except for short biographical notes on each author with references for further reading, this text omits pedagogical apparatus which may come between the reader and a more direct experience of a story.

The dual editorship of the third edition represents accurately a true collaborative effort: virtues, errors of omission, of fact, of judgment equally to be shared.

Our work is done. The book is yours.

James B. Hall

Elizabeth C. Hall

Introduction

The short prose narrative is at once the oldest of literary forms and among the latest to receive modern definition. In its primitive state, perhaps of necessity, the prose tale was orally expressed: to entertain an audience few of which could read or write; to chronicle history or miracles believed; or even to prophesy the future. These uses of the prose tale performed a function of value to a tribe, a race, a king, and thus some prose tales survived. A few have become the literary heritage of nations. Only about 150 years ago, in widely separated countries, such literary artists as Hoffman, Mérimée, Tolstoy, Poe, and Hawthorne began to transform the eighteenth-century prose tale into an exacting, complex art form. Among other reasons, this transformation was possible because of the development of high-speed presses, newer means of book and magazine distribution, an audience more complexly educated to recognize and to value literature as a fine art. Today the short story is still in the process of dynamic change.

Of all literary art forms, the short story is the most deceptive. Its traditional focus on a single episode, its relative lack of mass—of density of character, variety of scene, and richness of detail—and its frequently casual tone all seem to suggest ease of composition, at least to the inexperienced reader. In contrast to the panorama of the novel, the short story must strike the unwary reader as an art of limited means, of modest resources. Actually, the apparent limitations of the form are a measure of its strength: all materials must come under strict artistic management or the overall effect is lost. Very possibly the deceptive nature of the short story is one reason for its evident, wide appeal; for given conscious artists and more sophisticated audiences, the form quickly became a worldwide institution. In the twentieth century the continued fecundity of short fiction is a striking fact of literary history.

The transmutation of the older prose tales into the modern short story is not difficult to understand in broad outline. The oldest known tale, *The Shipwrecked Sailor* (from Egyptian papyri, about 4000 B.C.), or the Book of Jonah (from the Old Testament, 350 to 750 B.C.), or tales from the *Decameron* (1353 A.D.) are not very different in overall literary quality from the eighteenth-century tales which immediately preceded the short story. The latest ancestors of the modern short story are fictional essays, such as "The Vision of Mirza" by Addison in the *Spectator* (1711) or digressions within a novel, such as "The Tale of the Old Man of the Hill" in Fielding's *Tom Jones* (1748). Typically, these short prose pieces lack restraint, or an economy of means; either the moral point is obtrusive and thus the artistic effect is thin, or they lack a significant plot structure, and are thus merely discursive, flat. Very possibly, the greatest difference between the older prose tale and the more recent nineteenth-century short story is a consciousness of technique on the part of later artists. Precisely this awareness and a commitment to short fiction as a demanding, distinctive art form mark Hawthorne and Poe as literary pioneers of great importance. In particular, Poe felt that the crucial element in the short story was unity of effect—this effect coming from the artistic combination of "incident" and most especially "tone." Poe was speaking of this necessary unity when he praised Hawthorne's stories by saying, "Every word *tells,* and there is not a word which does *not* tell. . . . " Other American and European writers shared an equally lofty concept of the short story as an art form and thus pointed the way for the short story of the twentieth century.

Compressed statement, the embodiment of significance at several levels of meaning, distinguishes modern short stories of the highest quality. To convey multiple meanings, the artist frequently employs language which is metaphorical, figurative; by definition this kind of language is richly connotative, allusive, freighted with suggestion. The story which is resourceful in its exploitation of language will most gracefully support symbolic detail and symbolic actions; in fact, the use of symbolism, justified by an adequate language, is the most interesting and useful advance in narrative technique of modern times. Because of heightened language many short stories approach poetry in intensity. Even in other contemporary examples wherein the tone remains casual, the action undramatic, the characterization minimal, the writer's major concern remains complexity with control.

Nor does this imply that the modern writer ignores entirely the established, received conventions of the form. As a matter of course the present-day short story comments on the quality, the nature of life; where moral issues are a factor, the artist recognizes that the implied, the suggested is always more moving, more effective, than an easy precept easily formulated. In a like manner, character (imaginative characterization) continues in importance; now, however, the focus of narration may be on the mind or on the psychic states of the protagonists. Plot structure (the largest unit of composition) is more clearly recognized as an integral part of meaning; details are rigorously selected to "tell." Although a story may have literal, allegorical, symbolical, and mythical levels of meaning, this does not imply merely an intellectual exercise, a puzzle posed by the artist and to be "solved" by an adept reader. Although close reading of a story is a useful prelude to a fuller appreciation or to the rendering of critical judgment, the story's intention and the responsible author's intention remain unchanged: to create a unified artistic statement which may give both knowledge and pleasure.

If the modern story has moved toward complexity, there is little cause for regret. After all, the influences on short fiction are of a scientific age, of a magnificently complex world in part described by Darwin, Marx, and Freud. In that world we live. If the literary artist is to render truthfully the present circumstances of life, he or she must impose new demands on the form. In any event the short story is no exception, for the identical situation prevails at the present time in all imaginative writing: in the novel, poetry, and drama.

Each in its own way, the stories in this book describe a specific vision of a complex world. In "The Last Judgment" Karel Čapek reexamines a received notion of an all-powerful God; "Check!," by the Polish author Slawomir Mrozek, dramatizes in terms of a bizarre game of chess the relationship—or lack thereof—of man to some "higher" power. Seen together, the stories bring a new kind of focus to the age-old relationship of man to— shall we say—his God. Other stories raise similar questions about the nature of the human experience, the conflicts of man and nature, or of man with the most powerful antagonist, himself. All literature, including short fiction, is read with the faith that posing such dramatic situations is the first step to a more comprehensive understanding of art, of the world, and of the self.

The concluding section, New Voices, New Visions, presents recent developments in short fiction in America and abroad. Certain stories are of a middle range of experience, the conventions almost totally familiar; in contradistinction, others rely on the extremes of technique and vision and are thus abstract and all but nonverbal in expression. Taken together, these concluding seventeen stories affirm a continued viability of the genre. Vitality, however, may be expressed in reaction *from* something: for example, the abstract fictions by Görling and Handke react against the traditional values associated with scale and with depicting "real" life; the pieces by Borges, Varshavsky, Mrozek, and Hughes deny naturalistic conventions in favor of fantasy, the dream, the visionary. The story by Robbe-Grillet denies the value of analysis, of process in fiction; the story by Sondheim is without event, and the absurd dominates any implied rationality. The works by Rosenfeld, Hall, and Ballard render an extreme vision of what is an extraordinary but still "recognizable" world.

As to the significance of the stories which make up the final section of the book, probably it is too soon after the event of composition to judge the permanency of either the trends or the individual works. Beyond doubt, however, these stories confirm certain facets of very real conditions in present society: the recurrence of despair, frustration, doubt; the prevalence of terror, the absurdity of daily occurrences, the futility of seeking absolute answers in an unstable society of shifting moral values. By being true to both the positive and the negative implications of modern life, the short-story artist fulfills his or her own most admirable calling.

If education is the attainment not only of knowledge but also of wisdom concerning the world and ourselves, the short-story form in all its manifestations provides one useful means to that end.

THE REALM OF FICTION
74 Short Stories

GUY DE MAUPASSANT

EARLY MASTERS

Fyodor Dostoevsky (1821–1881) was born in Moscow, the son of an autocratic, impoverished nobleman, a resident physician at a hospital for the indigent. Dostoevsky's mother died when he was fifteen, and he was sent to a St. Petersburg school for military engineering. During this time, his father was murdered by his own serfs, and Dostoevsky developed epilepsy, from which he suffered for the remainder of his life. In 1849, he was sentenced to death for being an ancillary member of a revolutionary group; melodramatically, at the last moment, his sentence was revoked; he was, instead, exiled by the Czar to Siberia for ten years. Eventually Dostoevsky returned to St. Petersburg, where he lived in extreme poverty and suffered great personal tragedy; nevertheless, he continued to write some of his great masterpieces, most notably Crime and Punishment *(1866) and* The Brothers Karamazov *(1880). For further reading:* White Nights and Other Stories *(translated by Constance Garnett, 1918).*

FYODOR DOSTOEVSKY

A Christmas Tree and a Wedding

*T*he other day I saw a wedding . . . but no! Better I tell you about the Christmas tree. The wedding was nice; I enjoyed it very much, but the other thing that happened was better. I do not know why, but while looking at the wedding, I thought about that Christmas tree. This was the way it happened.

On New Year's Eve, exactly five years ago, I was invited to a children's party. The host was a well-known businessman with many connections, friends and intrigues, so you might think the children's party was a pretext for the parents to meet each other and to talk things over in an innocent, casual and inadvertent manner.

I was an outsider. I did not have anything to contribute, and therefore I spent the evening on my own. There was another gentleman present who had no special family or position, but, like myself, had dropped in on this

3

family happiness. He was the first to catch my eye. He was a tall, lean man, very serious and very properly dressed. Actually he was not enjoying this family-type party in the least. If he withdrew into a corner, he immediately stopped smiling and knit his thick busy black eyebrows. Except for our host, the man had not a single acquaintance at the whole party. Obviously, he was terribly bored, but he was making a gallant effort to play the role of a perfectly happy, contented man. Afterwards I learned he was a gentleman from the provinces, with important, puzzling business in the capital; he had brought our host a letter of introduction, from a person our host did not patronize, so this man was invited to this children's party only out of courtesy. He didn't even play cards. They offered him no cigars; no one engaged him in conversation. Perhaps we recognized the bird by its feathers from a distance; that is why my gentleman was compelled to sit out the whole evening and stroke his whiskers merely to have something to do with his hands. His whiskers really were very fine, but he stroked them so diligently, you thought the whiskers came first, and were then fixed onto his face, the better to stroke them.

Besides this man—who had five well-fed boys—my attention was caught by a second gentleman. He was an important person. His name was Yulian Mastakovitch. With one glance, you saw he was a guest of honor. He looked down on the host much as the host looked down on the gentleman who stroked his whiskers. The host and hostess spoke to the important man from across a chasm of courtesy, waited on him, gave him drink, pampered him, and brought their guests to him for introductions. They did not take him to anyone.

When Yulian Mastakovitch commented, in regard to the evening, that he had seldom spent time in such a pleasant manner, I noticed tears sparkled in the host's eyes. In the presence of such a person, I was frightened, and, after admiring the children, I walked into a small deserted drawing-room and sat down beside an arbour of flowers which took up almost half of the room.

All the children were incredibly sweet. They absolutely refused to imitate their "elders," despite all the exhortations of their governesses and mothers. In an instant the children untwisted all the Christmas tree candy and broke half of the toys before they knew for whom they were intended. One small, black eyed, curly haired boy was especially nice. He kept wanting to shoot me with his wooden gun. But my attention was still more drawn to his sister, a girl of eleven, a quiet, pensive, pale little cupid with large thoughtful eyes. In some way, the children wounded her feelings, and so she came into the same room where I sat and busied herself in the corner—with her doll.

The guests respectfully pointed out one of the wealthy commissioned tax gatherers—her father. In a whisper someone said three hundred thousand roubles were already set aside for her dowry.

I swung around to look at those who were curious about such circumstances: my gaze fell on Yulian Mastakovitch. With his hands behind his back, with his head cocked a little to one side, he listened with extraordinary attention to the empty talk of the guests.

Later, I marveled at the wisdom of the host and hostess in the distribution of the children's gifts. The little girl—already the owner of three hundred thousand roubles—received the most expensive doll. Then followed presents lowering in value according to the class of the parents of these happy children. Finally, the last gift: a young boy, ten years-old; slender, small, freckled, red-haired, received only a book of stories about the marvels of nature and the tears of devotion—without pictures and even without engravings. He was the son of the governess of the hosts' children, a poor widow; he was a little boy, extremely oppressed and frightened. He wore a jacket made from a wretched nankeen. After he received his book, he walked around the other toys for a long time; he wanted to play with the other children, but he did not dare; he already felt and understood his position.

I love to watch children. They are extraordinarily fascinating in their first independent interests in life. I noticed the red-haired boy was so tempted by the costly toys of the other children, especially a theater in which he certainly wanted to take some kind of part, that he decided to act differently. He smiled and began playing with the other children. He gave away his apple to a puffy little boy, who had bound up a full handkerchief of sweets. He even went as far as to carry another boy on his back, so they would not turn him away from the theater. But a minute later, a kind of mischievous child gave him a considerable beating. The boy did not dare to cry. Here the governess, his mother, appeared and ordered him not to disturb the play of the other children. Then the boy went to the same room where the little girl was. She allowed him to join her. Very eagerly they both began to dress the expensive doll.

I had been already sitting in the ivy-covered arbour for a half an hour. I was almost asleep, yet listening to the little conversations of the red-haired boy and the little beauty with the dowry of three hundred thousand fussing over her doll.

Suddenly Yulian Mastakovitch walked into the room. Under cover of the quarreling children, he had noiselessly left the drawing-room. A minute before I noticed he was talking very fervently with the father of the future heiress, with whom he had just become acquainted. He discussed the advantages of one branch of the service over another. Now he stood deep in thought, as if he were calculating something on his fingers.

"Three hundred . . . three hundred," he whispered. "Eleven, twelve, thirteen," and so forth. "Sixteen—five years! Let us assume it is at four per cent—five times twelve is sixty, yes, to that sixty . . . now let us assume what it will be in five years—four hundred. Yes! Well . . . oh, but he won't hold to four per cent, the swindler. Maybe he can get eight or ten. Well, five hundred, let us assume five hundred thousand, the final measure, that's certain. Well, say a little extra for frills. H'm. . . ."

He ended his reflection. He blew his nose, and intended to leave the room. Suddenly he glanced at the little girl and stopped short. He did not see me behind the pots of greenery. It seemed to me that he was really disturbed. Either his calculations had affected him, or something else. He rubbed his hands and could not stand in one place. This nervousness increased to the utmost limit. And then he stopped and threw another resolute glance at the future heiress. He was about to advance, but first he looked around. On tiptoe, as if he felt guilty, he approached the children. With a half-smile, he drew near, stooped, and kissed the little girl on the head. Not expecting the attack, she cried out, frightened.

"And what are you doing here, sweet child?" he asked in a whisper, looking around and patting the girl on the cheek.

"We are playing."

"Ah, with him?" Yulian Mastakovitch looked to one side at the boy. "And you, my dear, go into the drawing-room."

The boy kept silent and stared at him with open eyes.

Yulian Mastakovitch again looked around him and again stooped to the little girl.

"And what is this you have," he asked, "A dolly, sweet child?"

"A dolly," the little girl answered, wrinkling her face, a trifle shy.

"A dolly . . . and do you know, my sweet child, from what your dolly is made?"

"I don't know . . ." answered the little girl in a whisper, hanging her head.

"From rags, darling. You'd better go into the drawing-room to your companions, little boy," said Yulian Mastakovitch, staring severely at the child. The little girl and boy made a wry face and held onto each other's hand. They did not want to be separated.

"And do you know why they gave you that doll?" asked Yulian Mastakovitch, lowering his voice more and more.

"I don't know."

"Because you have been a sweet, well-behaved child all week."

Here Yulian Mastakovitch, emotional as could be, looked around and lowered his voice more and more, and finally asked, inaudibly, almost standing completely still from excitement and with an impatient voice:

"And will you love me, sweet little girl? When I come to visit your parents?"

Having said this, Yulian Mastakovitch tried once again to kiss the sweet girl. The red-haired boy, seeing that she wanted to cry, gripped her hand and began to whimper from sheer sympathy for her. Yulian Mastakovitch became angry, and not in jest.

"Go away. Go away from here, go away!" he said to the little boy. "Go into the drawing-room! Go in there to your companions!"

"No, he doesn't have to, doesn't have to! You go away," said the little girl, almost crying, "Leave him alone, leave him alone!"

Someone made a noise at the door.

Yulian Mastakovitch immediately raised his majestic body and became frightened. But the red-haired boy was even more startled than Yulian Mastakovitch. He left the little girl and quietly, guided by the wall, passed from the drawing-room into the dining-room. To avoid arousing suspicion, Yulian Mastakovitch also went into the dining-room. He was red as a lobster. He glanced into the mirror, as if he were disconcerted. He was perhaps annoyed with himself for his fervor and his impatience. At first perhaps he was so struck by the calculations on his fingers, so enticed and inspired that in spite of all his dignity and importance, he decided to act like a little boy, and directly pursue the object of his attentions even though she could not possibly be *his* object for at least five more years.

I followed the respectable gentleman into the dining-room. I beheld a strange sight. All red from vexation and anger, Yulian Mastakovitch frightened the red-haired boy, who was walking farther and farther, and in his fear did not know where to run.

"Go away. What are you doing here? Go away, you scamp, go away! You're stealing the fruits here, ah? You're stealing the fruits here? Go away, you reprobate. Go away. You snot-nosed boy, go away. Go to your companions!"

The frightened boy tried to get under the table. Then his persecutor, flushed as could be, took out his large batiste handkerchief and began to lash under the table at the child, who remained absolutely quiet.

It must be noted that Yulian Mastakovitch was a little stout. He was a man, well-filled out, red-faced, sleek, with a paunch, with thick legs; in short, what is called a fine figure of a man, round as a nut. He was sweating, puffing and turning terribly red. Finally, he was almost in a frenzy, so great was his feeling of indignation and perhaps (who knows?) jealousy.

I burst out laughing at the top of my voice. Yulian Mastakovitch turned around, and despite all his manners, he was confounded into dust. From the opposite door at that moment came the host. The little boy climbed out from under the table and wiped his elbows and knees. Yulian Mastakovitch hurriedly blew his nose on a handkerchief, which he held in his hand by a corner.

Meanwhile, the host gave the three of us a puzzled look. But as with a man who knows life and looks at it with dead seriousness, he immediately availed himself of the chance to catch his guest in private.

"Here's the little boy," he said pointing to the red-haired boy, "for whom I was intending to intercede, your honor. . . ."

"Ah?" answered Yulian Mastakovitch, still not fully put in order.

"The son of my children's governess," the host continued with a pleading tone. "A poor woman, a widow, wife of an honest official; and therefore
. . . Yulian Mastakovitch if it were possible. . . ."

"Oh, no, no," hurriedly answered Yulian Mastakovitch, "no, excuse
me, Filip Alexyevitch, it's no way possible. I've asked, there are no vacan-
cies. If there were, there are already ten candidates—all better qualified
than he. . . . I'm very sorry. Very sorry. . . ."

"I am sorry," repeated the host. "The little boy is modest, quiet. . . ."

"A very mischievous boy, as I've noticed," answered Yulian Mastakovitch, hysterically distorting his mouth. "Go away, little boy," he said addressing the child. "Why are you staying, go to your companions!"

It seemed he could not restrain himself. He glanced at me with one eye.
In fun I could not restrain myself and burst out laughing directly in his
face.

Yulian Mastakovitch immediately turned away, and clear enough for
me to hear, he asked the host who was that strange young man. They
whispered together and left the room. Afterwards, I saw Yulian Mastakovitch listening to the host, mistrustfully shaking his head.

After laughing to my heart's content, I returned to the drawing-room.
Surrounded by the fathers and mothers of the families and the host and
hostess, the great man was uttering a mating call with warmth, towards a
lady to whom he had just been introduced.

The lady was holding by the hand the girl, with whom ten minutes ago
Yulian Mastakovitch had had the scene in the drawing-room. Now, he was
showering praise and delight about the beauty, talent, grace and good manners of the sweet child. He was fawning, obviously, over the mamma; the
mother listened to him almost in tears from delight. The father's lips made
a smile; the host rejoiced because of the general satisfaction. All the guests
were the same, and even the children stopped playing in order not to disturb the conversation. The whole atmosphere was saturated with reverence.

Later, as if touched to the depth of her heart, I heard the mother of the
interesting child beg Yulian Mastakovitch to do her the special honor of
presenting them his precious acquaintanceship; and I heard, with his kind
of unaffected delight, Yulian Mastakovitch accepting the invitation. Afterwards, the guests all dispersed in different directions, as decency demanded; they spilled out to each other touching words of praise upon the
commissioned tax gatherer who worked farmers, his wife, their daughter,
and especially Yulian Mastakovitch.

"Is that gentleman married?" I asked, almost aloud, of one of my
acquaintances, who was standing closest to Yulian Mastakovitch.

Yulian Mastakovitch threw at me a searching malicious glance.

"No!" my friend answered me, chagrined to the bottom of his heart at
my awkwardness, which I had displayed deliberately.

Recently, I walked by a certain church. The crowd, the congress of people startled me. All around they talked about the wedding. The day was cloudy, and it was starting to drizzle; I made my way through the crowd around the church and saw the bridegroom. He was a small, rotund, well-fed man with a slight paunch and highly dressed. He was running about, bustling, and giving orders. Finally, the voices of the crowd said that the bride was coming. I pushed my way through the crowd and saw a wonderful beauty, who had scarcely begun her first season. But the beauty was pale and sad. She looked distracted; it even seemed to me that her eyes were red from recent crying. The classical severity of every line of her face added a certain dignity and solemnity to her beauty. Through that severity and dignity, through that sadness, still appeared the first look of childish innocence—very naive, fluid, youthful, and yet neither asking nor entreating for mercy.

They were saying she was just sixteen years-old. Glancing carefully at the bridegroom, I suddenly recognized him as Yulian Mastakovitch, whom I had not seen for five years. I took a look at her. My God!

I began to push my way quickly out of the church. The voices of the crowd said the bride was rich: a dowry of five hundred thousand . . . and a trousseau with ever so much. . . .

"It was a good calculation, though," I thought, and made my way out into the street.

Long acknowledged as one of the world's leading novelists, Leo Tolstoy (1828–1910) was born on the family estate in the province of Tula, Russia. Educated privately, usually by French tutors, the young Count attempted—but failed—to establish what was then a progressive peasant school. A later military career saw him as a wealthy, often wastrel, artillery officer in and around Moscow and St. Petersburg. While serving as an artillery officer in the Crimea, he began to write sketches and stories based on his travels and military service. Encouraged by Ivan Turgenev, Tolstoy settled down on his very large estate and after marriage wrote the novels War and Peace *(1866) and* Anna Karenina *(1877). Perhaps because of gradual disenchantment with bourgeois, materialistic values, perhaps because of unexplained inner turmoil, after about 1876 Count Tolstoy underwent a spiritual conversion, renounced the world, and largely lived the life of a "saint." For further reading:* A Russian Proprietor; The Invaders; The Death of Ivan Ilyitch *(1899–1902).*

LEO TOLSTOY

After the Dance

"—And you say that a man cannot, of himself, understand what is good and evil; that it is all environment, that the environment swamps the man. But I believe it is all chance. Take my own case . . . ."

Thus spoke our excellent friend, Ivan Vasilievich, after a conversation between us on the impossibility of improving individual character without a change of the conditions under which men live. Nobody had actually said that one could not of oneself understand good and evil; but it was a habit of Ivan Vasilievich to answer in this way the thoughts aroused in his own mind by conversation, and to illustrate those thoughts by relating incidents in his own life. He often quite forgot the reason for his story in telling it; but he always told it with great sincerity and feeling.

He did so now.

"Take my own case. My whole life was moulded, not by environment, but by something quite different."

"By what, then?" we asked.

"Oh, that is a long story. I should have to tell you about a great many things to make you understand."

"Well, tell us then."

Ivan Vasilievich thought a little, and shook his head.

"My whole life," he said, "was changed in one night, or, rather, morning."

"Why, what happened?" one of us asked.

"What happened was that I was very much in love. I have been in love many times, but this was the most serious of all. It is a thing of the past; she has married daughters now. It was Varinka B——." Ivan Vasilievich mentioned her surname. "Even at fifty she is remarkably handsome; but in her youth, at eighteen, she was exquisite—tall, slender, graceful, and stately. Yes, stately is the word; she held herself very erect, by instinct as it were; and carried her head high, and that together with her beauty and height gave her a queenly air in spite of being thin, even bony one might say. It might indeed have been deterring had it not been for her smile, which was always gay and cordial, and for the charming light in her eyes and for her youthful sweetness."

"What an entrancing description you give, Ivan Vasilievich!"

"Description, indeed! I could not possibly describe her so that you could appreciate her. But that does not matter; what I am going to tell you happened in the forties. I was at that time a student at a provincial university. I don't know whether it was a good thing or no, but we had no political clubs, no theories in our universities then. We were simply young and spent our time as young men do, studying and amusing ourselves. I was a very gay, lively, careless fellow, and had plenty of money too. I had a fine horse, and used to go tobogganing with the young ladies. Skating had not yet come into fashion. I went to drinking parties with my comrades—in those days we drank nothing but champagne—if we had no champagne we drank nothing at all. We never drank vodka, as they do now. Evening parties and balls were my favourite amusements. I danced well, and was not an ugly fellow."

"Come, there is no need to be modest," interrupted a lady near him. "We have seen your photograph. Not ugly, indeed! You were a handsome fellow."

"Handsome, if you like. That does not matter. When my love for her was at its strongest, on the last day of the carnival, I was at a ball at the provincial marshal's, a good-natured old man, rich and hospitable, and a court chamberlain. The guests were welcomed by his wife, who was as good-natured as himself. She was dressed in puce-colored velvet, and had a diamond diadem on her forehead, and her plump, old white shoulders and bosom were bare like the portraits of Empress Elizabeth, the daughter of Peter the Great.

"It was a delightful ball. It was a splendid room, with a gallery for the orchestra, which was famous at the time, and consisted of serfs belonging to a musical landowner. The refreshments were magnificant, and the champagne flowed in rivers. Though I was fond of champagne I did not drink that night, because without it I was drunk with love. But I made up for it by dancing waltzes and polkas till I was ready to drop—of course, whenever possible, with Varinka. She wore a white dress with a pink sash, white shoes, and white kid gloves, which did not quite reach to her thin pointed elbows. A disgusting engineer named Anisimov robbed me of the mazurka with her—to this day I cannot forgive him. He asked her for the dance the minute she arrived, while I had driven to the hair-dresser's to get a pair of gloves, and was late. So I did not dance the mazurka with her, but with a German girl to whom I had previously paid a little attention; but I am afraid I did not behave very politely to her that evening. I hardly spoke or looked at her, and saw nothing but the tall, slender figure in a white dress, with a pink sash, a flushed, beaming, dimpled face, and sweet, kind eyes. I was not alone; they were all looking at her with admiration, the men and women alike, although she outshone all of them. They could not help admiring her.

"Although I was not nominally her partner for the mazurka, I did as a matter of fact dance nearly the whole time with her. She always came forward boldly the whole length of the room to pick me out. I flew to meet her without waiting to be chosen, and she thanked me with a smile for my intuition. When I was brought up to her with somebody else, and she guessed wrongly, she took the other man's hand with a shrug of her slim shoulders, and smiled at me regretfully.

"Whenever there was a waltz figure in the mazurka, I waltzed with her for a long time, and breathing fast and smiling, she would say, '*Encore*'; and I went on waltzing and waltzing, as though unconscious of any bodily existence."

"Come now, how could you be unconscious of it with your arm around her waist? You must have been conscious, not only of your own existence, but of hers," said one of the party.

Ivan Vasilievich cried out, almost shouting in anger: "There you are, moderns all over! Nowadays you think of nothing but the body. It was different in our day. The more I was in love the less corporeal was she in my eyes. Nowadays you see legs, ankles, and I don't know what. You undress the women you are in love with. In my eyes, as Alphonse Karr said—and he was a good writer—'the one I loved was always draped in robes of bronze.'

We never thought of doing so; we tried to veil her nakedness, like Noah's good-natured son. Oh, well, you can't understand."

"Don't pay any attention to him. Go on," said one of them.

"Well, I danced for the most part with her, and did not notice how time was passing. The musicians kept playing the same mazurka tunes over and over again in desperate exhaustion—you know what it is towards the end of a ball. Papas and mammas were already getting up from the card-tables in the drawing-room in expectation of supper, the men-servants were running to and fro bringing in things. It was nearly three o'clock. I had to make the most of the last minutes. I chose her again for the mazurka, and for the hundredth time we danced across the room.

" 'The quadrille after supper is mine,' I said, taking her to her place.

" 'Of course, if I am not carried off home,' she said, with a smile.

" 'I won't give you up,' I said.

" 'Give me my fan, anyhow,' she answered.

" 'I am so sorry to part with it,' I said, handing her a cheap white fan.

" 'Well, here's something to console you," she said, plucking a feather out of the fan, and giving it to me.

"I took the feather, and could only express my rapture and gratitude with my eyes. I was not only pleased and gay, I was happy, delighted; I was good, I was not myself but some being not of this earth, knowing nothing of evil. I hid the feather in my glove, and stood there unable to tear myself away from her.

" 'Look, they are urging father to dance,' she said to me, pointing to the tall, stately figure of her father, a colonel with silver epaulettes, who was standing in the doorway with some ladies.

" 'Varinka, come here!' exclaimed our hostess, the lady with the diamond *ferronnière* and with shoulders like Elizabeth, in a loud voice.

"Varinka went to the door, and I followed her.

" 'Persuade your father to dance the mazurka with you, *ma chère.*— Do, please, Peter Valdislavovich,' she said, turning to the colonel.

"Varinka's father was a very handsome, well-preserved old man. He had a good colour, moustaches curled in the style of Nicolas I., and white whiskers which met the moustaches. His hair was combed on to his forehead, and a bright smile, like his daughter's, was on his lips and in his eyes. He was splendidly set up, with a broad military chest, on which he wore some decorations, and he had powerful shoulders and long slim legs. He was that ultra-military type produced by the discipline of Emperor Nicolas I.

"When we approached the door the colonel was just refusing to dance, saying that he had quite forgotten how; but at that instant he smiled, swung his arm gracefully around to the left, drew his sword from its sheath, handed it to an obliging young man who stood near, and smoothed his suède glove on his right hand.

" 'Everything must be done according to rule,' he said with a smile. He took the hand of his daughter, and stood one-quarter turned, waiting for the music.

"At the first sound of the mazurka, he stamped one foot smartly, threw the other forward, and, at first slowly and smoothly, then buoyantly and impetuously, with stamping of feet and clicking of boots, his tall, imposing figure moved the length of the room. Varinka swayed gracefully beside him, rhythmically and easily, making her steps short or long, with her little feet in their white satin slippers.

"All the people in the room followed every movement of the couple. As for me I not only admired, I regarded them with enraptured sympathy. I was particularly impressed with the old gentleman's boots. They were not the modern pointed affairs, but were made of cheap leather, squared-toed, and evidently built by the regimental cobbler. In order that his daughter might dress and go out in society, he did not buy fashionable boots, but wore home-made ones, I thought, and his square toes seemed to me most touching. It was obvious that in his time he had been a good dancer; but now he was too heavy, and his legs had not spring enough for all the beautiful steps he tried to take. When at the end, standing with legs apart, he suddenly clicked his feet together and fell on one knee, a bit heavily, and she danced gracefully around him, smiling and adjusting her skirt, the whole room applauded.

"Rising with an effort, he tenderly took his daughter's face between his hands. He kissed her on the forehead, and brought her to me, under the impression that I was her partner for the mazurka. I said I was not. 'Well, never mind. Just go around the room once with her,' he said, smiling kindly, as he replaced his sword in the sheath.

"As the contents of a bottle flow readily when the first drop has been poured, so my love for Varinka seemed to set free the whole force of loving within me. In surrounding her it embraced the world. I loved the hostess with her diadem and her shoulders like Elizabeth, and her husband and her guests and her footmen, and even the engineer Anisimov who felt peevish towards me. As for Varinka's father, with his home-made boots and his kind smile, so like her own, I felt a sort of tenderness for him that was almost rapture.

"After supper I danced the promised quadrille with her, and though I had been infinitely happy before, I grew still happier every moment.

"We did not speak of love. I neither asked myself nor her whether she loved me. It was quite enough to know that I loved her. And I had only one fear—that something might come to interfere with my great joy.

"When I went home, and began to undress for the night, I found it quite out of the question. I held the little feather out of her fan in my hand, and one of her gloves which she gave me when I helped her into the carriage after her mother. Looking at these things, and without closing my eyes I could see her before me as she was for an instant when she had to choose between two partners. She tried to guess what kind of person was represented in me, and I could hear her sweet voice as she said, 'Pride—am I right?' and merrily gave me her hand. At supper she took the first sip from my glass of champagne, looking at me over the rim with her caressing glance. But, plainest of all, I could see her as she danced with her father, gliding along beside him, and looking at the admiring observers with pride and happiness.

"He and she were united in my mind in one rush of pathetic tenderness.

"I was living then with my brother, who has since died. He disliked going out, and never went to dances; and besides, he was busy preparing for his last university examinations, and was leading a very regular life. He was asleep. I looked at him, his head buried in the pillow and half covered with the quilt; and I affectionately pitied him—pitied him for his ignorance of the bliss I was experiencing. Our serf Petrusha had met me with a candle, ready to undress me, but I sent him away. His sleepy face and tousled hair seemed to me so touching. Trying not to make a noise, I went to my room on tiptoe and sat down on my bed. No, I was too happy; I could not sleep. Besides, it was too hot in the rooms. Without taking off my uniform, I went quietly into the hall, put on my overcoat, opened the front door and stepped out into the street.

"It was after four when I had left the ball; going home and stopping there a while had occupied two hours, so by the time I went out it was dawn. It was regular carnival weather—foggy, and the road full of water-soaked snow just melting, and water dripping from the eaves. Varinka's family lived on the edge of town near a large field, one end of which was a parade ground: at the other end was a boarding-school for young ladies. I passed through our empty little street and came to the main thoroughfare, where I met pedestrians and sledges laden with wood, the runners grating the road. The horses swung with regular paces beneath their shining yokes, their backs covered with straw mats and their heads wet with rain; while the drivers, in enormous boots, splashed through the mud beside the sledges. All this, the very horses themselves, seemed to me stimulating and fascinating, full of suggestion.

"When I approached the field near their house, I saw at one end of it, in the direction of the parade ground, something very huge and black, and I heard sounds of fife and drum proceeding from it. My heart had been full of song, and I had heard in imagination the tune of the mazurka, but this was very harsh music. It was not pleasant.

" 'What can that be?' I thought, and went towards the sound by a slippery path through the centre of the field. Walking about a hundred paces, I began to distinguish many black objects through the mist. They were evidently soldiers. 'It is probably a drill,' I thought.

"So I went along in that direction in company with a blacksmith, who wore a dirty coat and an apron, and was carrying something. He walked ahead of me as we approached the place. The soliders in black uniforms stood in two rows, facing each other motionless, their guns at rest. Behind them stood the fifes and drums, incessantly repeating the same unpleasant tune.

" 'What are they doing?' I asked the blacksmith, who halted at my side.

" 'A Tartar is being beaten through the ranks for his attempt to desert,' said the blacksmith in an angry tone, as he looked intently at the far end of the line.

"I looked in the same direction, and saw between the files something horrid approaching me. The thing that approached was a man, stripped to the waist, fastened with cords to the guns of two soldiers who were leading him. At his side an officer in overcoat and cap was walking, whose figure had a familiar look. The victim advanced under the blows that rained upon him from both sides, his whole body plunging, his feet dragging through the snow. Now he threw himself backward, and the subalterns who led him thrust him forward. Now he fell forward, and they pulled him up short; while ever at his side marched the tall officer, with firm and nervous pace. It was Varinka's father, with his rosy face and white moustache.

"At each stroke the man, as if amazed, turned his face, grimacing with pain, towards the side whence the blow came, and showing his white teeth repeated the same words over and over. But I could only hear what the words were when he came quite near. He did not speak them, he sobbed them out,—

" 'Brothers, have mercy on me! Brothers, have mercy on me!' But the brothers had no mercy, and when the procession came close to me, I saw how a soldier who stood opposite me took a firm step forward and lifting his stick with a whirr, brought it down upon the man's back. The man plunged forward, but the subalterns pulled him back, and another blow came down from the other side, then from this side and then from the other. The colonel marched beside him, and looking now at his feet and now at the man, inhaled the air, puffed out his cheeks, and breathed it out between his protruded lips. When they passed the place where I stood, I caught a glimpse between the two files of the back of the man that was being punished. It was something so many-coloured, wet, red, unnatural, that I could hardly believe it was a human body.

" 'My God!' muttered the blacksmith.

"The procession moved farther away. The blows continued to rain upon the writhing, falling creature; the fifes shrilled and the drums beat, and the tall imposing figure of the colonel moved along-side the man, just as before. Then, suddenly, the colonel stopped, and rapidly approached a man in the ranks.

" 'I'll teach you to hit him gently,' I heard his furious voice say. 'Will you pat him like that? Will You?' and I saw how his strong hand in the suède glove struck the weak, bloodless, terrified soldier for not bringing down his stick with sufficient strength on the red neck of the Tartar.

" 'Bring new sticks!' he cried, and looking round, he saw me. Assuming an air of not knowing me, and with a ferocious, angry frown, he hastily turned away. I felt so utterly ashamed that I didn't know where to look. It was as if I had been detected in a disgraceful act. I dropped my eyes, and quickly hurried home. All the way I had the drums beating and the fifes whistling in my ears. And I heard the words, 'Brothers, have mercy on me!' or 'Will you pat him? Will you?' My heart was full of physical disgust that was almost sickness. So much so that I halted several times on my way, for I had the feeling that I was going to be really sick from all the horrors that possessed me at that sight. I do not remember how I got home and got to bed. But the moment I was about to fall asleep I heard and saw again all that had happened, and I sprang up.

" 'Evidently he knows something I do not know,' I thought about the colonel. 'If I knew what he knows I should certainly grasp—understand—what I have just seen, and it would not cause me such suffering.'

"But however much I thought about it, I could not understand the thing that the colonel knew. It was evening before I could get to sleep, and then only after calling on a friend and drinking till I was quite drunk.

"Do you think I had come to the conclusion that the deed I had witnessed was wicked? Oh, no. Since it was done with such assurance, and was recognised by every one as indispensable, they doubtless knew something which I did not know. So I thought, and tried to understand. But no matter, I could never understand it, then or afterwards. And not being able to grasp it, I could not enter the service as I had intended. I don't mean only the military service: I did not enter the Civil Service either. And so I have been of no use whatever, as you can see."

"Yes, we know how useless you've been," said one of us. "Tell us, rather, how many people would be of any use at all if it hadn't been for you."

"Oh, that's utter nonsense," said Ivan Vasilievich, with genuine annoyance.

"Well, and what about the love affair?"

"My love? It decreased from that day. When, as often happened, she looked dreamy and meditative, I instantly recollected the colonel on the parade ground, and I felt so awkward and uncomfortable that I began to see her less frequently. So my love came to naught. Yes, such chances arise, and they alter and direct a man's whole life," he said in summing up. "And you say . . ."

Giovanni Verga (1840–1922) was born in Catania, Sicily, of one of the oldest families on the island. He gave up the study of law for literature; his early novels were melodramatic tales of passion. When he turned to the harsh life of the Sicilian peasant as the material of his fiction, he struck a vein of strength, simplicity, and "truth" that brought him acclaim as one of the most important naturalistic writers of the nineteenth century. His style is simple and unadorned, based upon acute observation, and focusing on stark details of his characters' lives. In spite of its tragic focus, his work holds a note of hope in his strong belief in the continuity of life. His best-known novel is The House by the Medlar Tree *(1881). For further reading:* The She Wolf and Other Stories *(translated by Giovanni Cecchetti, 1958).*

GIOVANNI VERGA

Consolation

"You'll be happy but first you'll have troubles," the fortuneteller had told Arlia.

Who would have imagined it when she married Manica, who had his fine barbershop on Fabbri Street, and she was a hairdresser too—both of them young and healthy? Only Father Calogero, her uncle, hadn't wanted to bless that marriage—had washed his hands of it like Pilate, as he said. He knew they were all consumptive in his own family, from father to son, and he had been able to put a little fat on himself by choosing the quiet life of a parish rector.

"The world is full of troubles," Father Calogero preached. "It's best to keep away from it."

The troubles had come, in fact, little by little. Arlia was always pregnant, year after year, so that her clients deserted her shop, because it was sad to see her come all out of breath and cursed with that big belly. Besides, she didn't have time to keep up to date with fashions. Her husband had dreamed of a big barbershop on the Avenue, with perfumes in the window, but in vain he could go on and on shaving beards at three *soldi* each. The children became consumptive one after the other, and before going to the cemetery gobbled up the small profit of the year.

Angiolino, who didn't want to die so young, complained during his fever:

"Mamma, why did you bring me into the world?" Just like his brothers who had died before him. The mother, thin and wan, standing before the little bed, didn't know what to answer. They had done the impossible; the children had eaten all kinds of things, cooked and raw: broths, medicines, pills as small as the head of a pin. Arlia had spent three *lire* for a Mass, and had gone to hear it on her knees in Saint Lawrence's, beating her breast for her sins. The Virgin in the picture seemed to be winking yes to her. But Manica, more sensible, would laugh with his crooked mouth, scratching his beard. Finally, the poor mother grabbed her veil like a crazy woman and ran to the fortuneteller. A countess, who had wanted to have her hair cut off out of desperation over her lover, had found consolation there.

"You'll be happy, but first you'll have troubles," answered the fortune-teller.

In vain her uncle, the priest, could say over and over again:

"It's all a fraud of Satan!"

You have to feel what it is like to have your heart black with bitterness as you wait for the verdict, while that old woman reads your whole destiny in the white of an egg. Afterward, it seemed to her that at home she would find her boy up, saying to her happily: "Mamma, I'm all better."

Instead, the boy was slowly wasting away, all skin and bones in his little bed, his eyes getting bigger and bigger. When Father Calogero, who knew about dead people, came to see his nephew, he called the mother aside and said:

"I'll take care of the funeral myself. Don't worry!"

But the unfortunate woman, beside the bed, went on hoping. Sometimes, when also Manica, with an eight-day beard and his back bent, came upstairs to see how his boy was doing, she pitied him because he didn't believe. How the poor man must have suffered! She, at least, had the words of the fortuneteller in her heart, like a burning lamp, till the moment when her uncle, the priest, sat at the foot of the bed with his stole on. Then when they carried her hope away inside her son's coffin, she felt a great darkness in her breast, and mumbled before the empty little bed:

"And what did the fortuneteller promise me?"

Because of all the heartache, her husband had taken to drinking. Finally, a great calm came slowly into her heart. Just like before. Now that all the troubles had fallen on her shoulders, happiness would come. That's the way it often is with the poor!

Fortunata, the last one of so many children, got up in the morning, pale and with rings the color of mother-of-pearl under her eyes, like her brothers who had died of consumption. The clients deserted Arlia one by one, the debts piled up, the shop became empty. Manica, her husband, waited for customers all day long, his nose against the clouded window.

Arlia asked her daughter:

"Does your heart tell you that what fate promised us will really come true?"

Fortunata didn't say anything, her eyes circled with black like her brothers', and fixed on a point that only she could see. One day her mother caught her on the stairs with a young man, who slipped away quickly when he saw somebody come, and the girl was left there all red in the face.

"Oh, poor me! . . . What are you doing here?"

Fortunata lowered her head.

"Who was that young man? What did he want?"

"Nothing."

"Tell your mother, who's your own flesh and blood. If your father knew! . . ."

The girl's only answer was to raise her forehead and fix her blue eyes on her mother's face.

"Mamma, I don't want to die like the others!"

May was in flower, but the girl wore a different look on her face and had become uneasy under the anxious eyes of her mother. The neighbors warned:

"Arlia, watch your girl."

Even her husband, frowning, one day had taken her aside face to face, in the dark little shop, in order to repeat:

"Watch your daughter, understand? Let's at least not have our flesh and blood disgraced!"

The poor woman, seeing her daughter so wild-eyed, didn't dare question her. She only fixed her eyes on her with looks that went through to the heart. One night, in front of the open window, while the song of spring came up from the street, the girl buried her face in her mother's breast and confessed everything, crying bitter tears.

The poor mother fell into a chair, as if her legs had been cut off. And she kept stammering with her colorless lips:

"Ah, what'll we do now?"

She seemed to see Manica warmed by wine, his heart hardened by misfortune. But worst of all were the eyes of the girl when she answered:

"See that window, Mamma? . . . See how high it is? . . ."

The young man, who was an honest fellow, had sent someone to see the uncle, the priest, to sound him out in order to know which way to turn. Father Calogero had purposely become a priest so that he wouldn't have to listen to the troubles of the world. It was no secret that Manica wasn't rich.

The young man understood the refrain and sent word that he was sorry that he wasn't rich himself and wouldn't be able to do without a dowry.

Then Fortunata became really sick and began to cough as her brothers had done. Holding her arm around her mother, she often whispered, with her face red, and repeated:

"See how high that window is? . . ."

And her mother had to run here and there, to comb rich women's hair for the theater, the terror of that window always before her eyes if she couldn't find a dowry for her daughter, or if her husband learned about the blunder.

From time to time the fortuneteller's words came back into her mind, like a ray of light. One evening, passing before a lottery window as she was going back home tired and discouraged, the printed numbers fell under her eyes, and for the first time she got the idea of gambling. Then, with the little yellow slip in her pocket, it seemed to her as if she had her daughter healthy, her husband rich and her home peaceful. She also thought with tenderness of Angiolino and the other children who had long been underground in the Porta Magenta cemetery. It was a Friday, a day of the afflicted, and the spring twilight was serene.

And so it was every week. By going without food, she got together the few cents needed for the lottery ticket, so that she could live with the hope of the great happiness which was to come to her all at once. The blessed souls of her children would take care of it from up above. Manica, one day when the little yellow slips jumped out of the drawer as he was secretly looking for a few *lire* to drown his ill-humor at the tavern, flew into a terrible rage:

"So that's the way the money's been going! . . ."

His wife, trembling all over, didn't know what to answer.

"But listen, what if the Lord should send us the right numbers? . . . We have to leave the door open to luck."

And in her heart she was thinking of the words of the fortuneteller.

"If that's the only hope you've got . . . ," muttered Manica with a bitter smile.

"And what hope have you got?"

"Give me two *lire*!" he answered bluntly.

"Two *lire*! Holy Virgin! . . . What do you want them for?"

"Give me just one!" insisted Manica, his face distorted.

It was a dark day with snow everywhere and dampness that you felt in your bones. That night Manica came back home with his face shining and gay. Fortunata instead kept saying:

"I'm the only one who can't find any consolation."

At times, she would have liked to have been under the grass in the cemetery, like her brothers. They, at least, weren't suffering any more, and even their parents, poor people, had become hardened.

"The Lord won't abandon us completely," stammered Arlia. "The fortuneteller told me so. And I've got an idea."

On Christmas Day they set the table with flowers and their best tablecloth, and this time they had invited her uncle, the priest, who was the only hope they had left. Manica rubbed his hands together and said:

"Today we've got to be happy and gay."

But the lamp hanging on the ceiling swayed sadly.

They had beef, roast turkey, and even a *panettone* that had a picture of the Cathedral of Milan. At dessert, the poor uncle, a good glass of *barbera* wine in his hand, seeing them lament on such a day, couldn't resist any more and had to promise the girl a dowry. The lover—Silvio Liotti, a clerk in a store, and well-informed—was heard from again: he was ready to make amends for the wrong he had done.

Manica, holding up a glass in his hand, said to Father Calogero:

"See this, sir? It cures many ills."

It was destiny, though, that where Arlia was, happiness didn't last. The son-in-law, a really fine fellow, ate up his wife's dowry, and after six months Fortunata, hungry and beaten, went back to her parents' home to tell her troubles and to show her bruises. Every year she too had a baby, just like her mother, and each one was bursting with health and ate like a horse. To the grandmother it seemed as if she were having babies again herself, because each one brought more trouble, even without dying of consumption. Having become old now, she had to run as far as Borgo Degli Ortolani and to Porta Garibaldi in order to earn four *lire* a month doing little jobs for the shopkeepers. Her husband, whose hands trembled, made hardly ten *lire* on Saturday, by cutting his customers and using spider webs to stop the blood. The rest of the week, he either sulked behind the dirty window or was at the tavern with his hat slanted over his ear.

And Arlia now spent the lottery money on brandy, drinking it secretly and hiding it under her apron; her consolation was to feel it warm her heart, as she sat before the window thinking of nothing, looking out at the wet, dripping roofs.

Guy de Maupassant (1850–1893) was born near Dieppe (Normandy); at thirteen he was a seminary student, but was expelled for irregular conduct. After service in the Franco-Prussian war, he became a clerk in the Naval Ministry. His chief influence and acknowledged master was the celebrated novelist Gustave Flaubert, to whom Maupassant apprenticed himself, informally, for almost seven years. The language of Maupassant's stories is precise, the structure unusually well controlled, and each story presents a climactic moment or scene. Within his limitations, Maupassant is a modern master of his particular kind of short story; the recurring flaws are said to be more the result of his view of life rather than defects of craftsmanship. He died in an asylum, but not before having written about 300 stories, all within a span of about ten years (1880–1890). For further reading: The House of Madam Tellier *(1881);* Mademoiselle Fifi *(1882).*

GUY DE MAUPASSANT

A Wife's Confession

*M*y friend, you have asked me to relate to you the liveliest recollections of my life. I am very old, without relatives, without children; so I am free to make a confession to you. Promise me one thing—never to reveal my name.

I have been much loved, as you know; I have often myself loved. I was very beautiful; I may say this to-day, when my beauty is gone. Love was for me the life of the soul, just as the air is the life of the body. I would have preferred to die rather than exist without affection, without having somebody always to care for me. Women often pretend to love only once with all the strength of their hearts; it has often happened to be so violent in one of my attachments that I thought it would be impossible for my transports ever to end. However, they always died out in a natural fashion, like a fire when it has no more fuel.

I will tell you to-day the first of my adventures, in which I was very innocent, but which led to the others. The horrible vengeance of that dreadful chemist of Pecq recalls to me the shocking drama of which I was, in spite of myself, a spectator.

I had been a year married to a rich man, Comte Hervé de Ker—a Breton of ancient family, whom I did not love, you understand. True love needs, I believe at any rate, freedom and impediments at the same time. The love which is imposed, sanctioned by law, and blessed by the priest— can we really call that love? A legal kiss is never as good as a stolen kiss. My husband was tall in stature, elegant, and a really fine gentleman in his manners. But he lacked intelligence. He spoke in a downright fashion, and uttered opinions that cut like the blade of a knife. He created the impression that his mind was full of ready-made views instilled into him by his father and mother, who had themselves got them from their ancestors. He never hesitated, but on every subject immediately made narrow-minded suggestions, without showing any embarrassment and without realizing that there might be other ways of looking at things. One felt that his head was closed up, that no ideas circulated in it, none of those ideas which renew a man's mind and make it sound, like a breath of fresh air passing through an open window into a house.

The château in which we lived was situated in the midst of a desolate tract of country. It was a large melancholy structure, surrounded by enormous trees, with tufts of moss on it resembling old men's white beards. The park, a real forest, was inclosed in a deep trench called the ha-ha; and at its extremity, near the moorland, we had big ponds full of reeds and floating grass. Between the two, at the edge of a stream which connected them, my husband had got a little hut built for shooting wild ducks.

We had, in addition to our ordinary servants, a keeper, a sort of brute devoted to my husband to the death, and a chambermaid, almost a friend, passionately attached to me. I had brought her back from Spain with me five years before. She was a deserted child. She might have been taken for a gypsy with her dusky skin, her dark eyes, her hair thick as a wood and always clustering around her forehead. She was at the time sixteen years old, but she looked twenty.

The autumn was beginning. We hunted much, sometimes on neighboring estates, sometimes on our own; and I noticed a young man, the Baron de C—, whose visits at the château became singularly frequent. Then, he ceased to come; I thought no more about it; but I perceived that my husband changed in his demeanor toward me.

He seemed taciturn and preoccupied; he did not kiss me; and, in spite of the fact that he did not come into my room, as I insisted on separate apartments in order to live a little alone, I often at night heard a furtive step drawing near my door, and withdrawing a few minutes after.

As my window was on the ground floor, I thought I had also often heard some one prowling in the shadow around the château. I told my husband about it, and, having looked at me intensely for some seconds, he answered:

"It is nothing—it is the keeper."

Now, one evening, just after dinner, Hervé, who appeared to be extraordinarily gay, with a sly sort of gaiety, said to me:

"Would you like to spend three hours out with the guns, in order to shoot a fox who comes every evening to eat my hens?"

I was surprised. I hesitated; but, as he kept staring at me with singular persistency, I ended by replying:

"Why, certainly, my friend." I must tell you that I hunted like a man the wolf and the wild boar. So it was quite natural that he should suggest this shooting expedition to me.

But my husband, all of a sudden, had a curiously nervous look; and all the evening he seemed agitated, rising up and sitting down feverishly.

About ten o'clock he suddenly said to me:

"Are you ready?"

I rose; and, as he was bringing me my gun himself, I asked:

"Are we to load with bullets or with deershot?"

He showed some astonishment; then he rejoined:

"Oh! only with deershot; make your mind easy! That will be enough."

Then, after some seconds, he added in a peculiar tone:

"You may boast of having splendid coolness."

I burst out laughing.

"I? Why, pray? Coolness because I go to kill a fox? What are you thinking of, my friend?"

And we quietly made our way across the park. All the household slept. The full moon seemed to give a yellow tint to the old gloomy building, whose slate roof glittered brightly. The two turrets that flanked it had two plates of light on their summits, and no noise disturbed the silence of this clear, sad night, sweet and still, which seemed in a death-trance. Not a breath of air, not a shriek from a toad, not a hoot from an owl; a melancholy numbness lay heavy on everything. When we were under the trees in the park, a sense of freshness stole over me, together with the odor of fallen leaves. My husband said nothing; but he was listening, he was watching, he seemed to be smelling about in the shadows, possessed from head to foot by the passion for the chase.

We soon reached the edges of the ponds.

Their tufts of rushes remained motionless; not a breath of air caressed them; but movements which were scarcely perceptible ran through the water. Sometimes the surface was stirred by something, and light circles gathered around, like luminous wrinkles enlarging indefinitely.

When we reached the hut, where we were to lie in wait, my husband made me go in first; then he slowly loaded his gun, and the dry cracking of the power produced a strange effect on me. He saw that I was shuddering and asked:

"Does this trial happen to be quite enough for you? If so, go back."

I was much surprised, and I replied:

"Not at all. I did not come to go back without doing anything. You seem queer this evening."

He murmured:

"As you wish." And we remained there without moving.

At the end of about half an hour, as nothing broke the oppressive stillness of this bright autumn night, I said, in a low tone:

"Are you quite sure he is passing this way?"

Hervé winced as if I had bitten him, and, with his mouth close to my ear, he said:

"Make no mistake about it! I am quite sure."

And once more there was silence.

I believe I was beginning to get drowsy when my husband pressed my arm, and his voice, changed to a hiss, said:

"Do you see him there under the trees?"

I looked in vain; I could distinguish nothing. And slowly Hervé now cocked his gun, all the time fixing his eyes on my face.

I was myself making ready to fire, and suddenly, thirty paces in front of us, appeared in the full light of the moon a man who was hurrying forward with rapid movements, his body bent, as if he were trying to escape.

I was so stupefied that I uttered a loud cry; but, before I could turn round, there was a flash before my eyes; I heard a deafening report; and I saw the man rolling on the ground, like a wolf hit by a bullet.

I burst into dreadful shrieks, terrified, almost going mad; then a furious hand—it was Hervé's—seized me by the throat. I was flung down on the ground, then carried off by his strong arms. He ran, holding me up, till he reached the body lying on the grass, and he threw me on top of it violently, as if he wanted to break my head.

I thought I was lost; he was going to kill me; and he had just raised his heel up to my forehead when, in his turn, he was gripped, knocked down, before I could yet realize what had happened.

I rose up abruptly, and saw kneeling on top of him Porquita, my maid, clinging like a wild cat to him with desperate energy, tearing off his beard, his mustache, and the skin of his face.

Then, as if another idea had suddenly taken hold of her mind, she rose up, and flinging herself on the corpse, she threw her arms around the dead man, kissing his eyes and his mouth, opening the dead lips with her own lips, trying to find in them a breath and the long, long kiss of lovers.

My husband, picking himself up, gazed at me. He understood, and, falling at my feet, said:

"Oh! forgive me, my darling, I suspected you, and I killed this girl's lover. It was my keeper that deceived me."

But I was watching the strange kisses of that dead man and that living woman, and her sobs and her writhings of sorrowing love, and at that moment I understood that I might be unfaithful to my husband.

The son of an unsuccessful grocery store owner and grandson of a serf, Anton Pavlovich Chekhov (1860–1904) first began to write humorous sketches for newspapers while earning a degree in medicine at the University of Moscow. His literary talent developed quickly and he became Russia's greatest writer of short fiction and also one of the very best Russian playwrights. Chekhov died of tuberculosis at the age of forty-four; nevertheless, he left hundreds of short stories and novellas. His fiction and plays are subtle mixtures of comedy, tragedy, and gentle irony; his characters are seen compassionately; his plot-structures are low-keyed and subdued. Chekhov's influence on Continental and American writers is immense; his best, later work continues to grow in stature. For further reading: The Tales of Chekhov *(translated by Constance Garnett, 1916–1922).*

ANTON CHEKHOV

Gusev

I

*A*lready it was dark; soon night would fall.

Gusev, a discharged private, sits up a little in his bunk and in a low voice says:

"Pavel Ivanich, are you listening? A soldier in Suchan told me that while under sail their ship ran into a big fish—it smashed a hole in the bottom."

The fellow of unknown social rank whom he was addressing said nothing, just as if he hadn't heard. In the sick-bay everyone called him Pavel Ivanich.

And once again—silence . . . the waves lash, the wind weaves about the rigging, the screw throbs, the bunks creak, but long ago the ear became accustomed to all this; now it seems everything is asleep and silent. It's dull. The two soldiers and a sailor, who played cards all day long, already are asleep and raving deliriously.

The ship seems to begin to rock. Beneath Gusev the bunk rises slowly and falls, as though it were sighing—once, twice, three times. . . . Something hits the floor with a clang. It must be a tankard that fell.

"The wind has broken loose from its chain," Gusev says, listening intently.

Pavel Ivanich coughs and answers irritably:

"First you have a ship run into a fish. Then the wind breaks loose from its chain. . . . Do you think the wind is a wild beast that breaks loose from its chain?"

"Christians say it is."

"And Christians are just as stupid as you. . . . There's no end to their babbling. You have to use your head and figure things out reasonably. You're a fool."

Pavel Ivanich gets seasick easily. When the sea is rough, he usually gets angry; the slightest trifle irritates him. But in Gusev's opinion there is nothing to get angry at whatsoever. For example, what is strange or puzzling either about that fish or about the wind breaking loose from its chain? What if the fish is as big as a mountain and has a backbone as hard as a sturgeon's? What if over there, at the edge of the world, there are huge stone walls and to the walls evil winds are chained. . . . If they don't break loose from their chains, why do they rush headlong all over the sea and strain to be free from their leash, just as dogs do? If they're not chained, where do they go when it's calm?"

Gusev thinks for a long while about fish as big as a mountain, and as heavy as rusty chains. Then he gets bored and begins to think about returning home after five years service in the Far East. He pictures the immense pond covered with snow. . . . On one side of the pond is the brick-colored ceramic factory with its tall chimney and clouds of black smoke; on the other side, the village. . . . From the fifth yard from the street's end his brother Aleksei drives out a sleigh; behind Aleksei sits Vanka, his little son, wearing big felt boots, and his daughter Akulka, also in felt boots. Aleksei has been drinking, Vanka is laughing, and because she is all muffled up, you can't see Akulka's face.

"Aleksei had better watch out . . . the children will get frostbitten," Gusev thinks. "May the good Lord grant them the sense," he muses, "to honor their parents and not be smarter than their father and mother. . . ."

The big sailor raves deliriously in a bass voice, "New soles are needed here. Yes, yes!"

Abruptly Gusev's thoughts break off; suddenly, for no reason whatsoever, instead of a pond there appears a large eyeless head of a bull. The horse and sleigh no longer drive down the road; instead they whirl around in the black smoke. Nevertheless Gusev is grateful to have seen his relatives. He is so pleased he loses his breath, his whole body is covered with goosepimples, and even his fingers tingle.

"The Lord permitted us to see one another!" deliriously he murmurs; then his eyes open, and in the dark he tries to find the water.

He drinks and lies down. Again the sleigh is moving along; once again there is the eyeless head of the bull, smoke, clouds. . . .

And so it continues until daybreak.

II

First a dark blue circle appears in the darkness—it is a porthole. Gusev begins gradually to discern Pavel Ivanich, his bunkmate. Pavel has to sleep in a sitting position; he cannot breathe lying down. His face is gray, his nose is long and sharp, and due to his emaciation, his eyes are huge; his temples are sunken, his beard sparse, his hair long. . . . His face gives no clue of his social rank: gentleman, merchant, or peasant. From his long hair and expression one might guess he was pious, perhaps a monastery lay brother; but once he speaks, you know for sure he's not a monk. Exhausted from coughing, his illness, and the hot stuffy air, he breathes with difficulty and moves his parched lips. He notices Gusev staring at him, so he turns his face and says:

"I'm beginning to guess. . . . Yes. . . . Now I understand everything . . . completely."

"You understand what, Pavel Ivanich?"

"Here's what. . . . It seemed strange. Instead of resting in a room, you seriously ill fellows turn up on a steamer; it's stifling hot, the sea is rough, in other words, everything threatens you with death. It's all clear to me now. . . . Yes. . . . Your doctors put you on the steamer to be rid of you. They got sick of dealing with you, with cattle. You don't pay them money. You're a nuisance. By your deaths you ruin their reports. . . . So, you're cattle. And that's that. But it's not difficult to get rid of you. . . . First of all, have no conscience or love for mankind; second, deceive the steamer authorities. You almost can ignore the first condition; everyone's an artist at this. With a little practice, the second always can be managed. Five sick men don't stand out in a crowd of 400 healthy soldiers and sailors. So they herded you out, put you on the steamer and mixed you with the healthy ones. The count was done in a hurry. In the confusion the steamer people didn't notice a thing. But after the ship had sailed, they saw paralytics and consumptives on their last legs lying about the deck. . . ."

Gusev did not understand Pavel Ivanich. He thought he was being reprimanded, so in his own defense he said:

"I was lying on the deck because I was tired out; when we were unloaded from the barge to the steamer I got a terrible chill."

"It's an outrage!" continued Pavel Ivanich. "What's worse, they know full well you can't possibly survive this long journey. But they put you aboard. Well, let's say you make it to the Indian Ocean. . . . Then what? I hate to think of it. . . . This is your thanks for irreproachable faithful service!"

Pavel Ivanich's eyes flash angrily, he frowns with disgust. Then, gasping, he says:

"They should be raked over the coals in the newspapers . . . until their feathers are singed!"

The two soldiers who were sick and the sailor had awakened from their sleep and already had begun playing cards. The sailor was half-reclining in his bunk; the soldiers sat on the floor beside him in the most uncomfortable positions imaginable. The bandage on the hand of one of the soldiers was so large it looked like a cap; consequently, while playing with his left hand he held his cards under his right arm or in the crook of his elbow. The ship rolled heavily. No one could stand up, or pour tea, or take medicine.

"You were an orderly?" Pavel Ivanich asks Gusev.

"That's right, an orderly."

"Good Lord, good Lord!" and Pavel Ivanich sadly shakes his head. "They tear a person from his home, drag him off 15,000 versts, then drive him till he gets consumption. Why all this, you may ask? To turn him into an orderly for some Captain Kopeikin or Midshipman Dyrka! How logical!"

"It wasn't a hard job, Pavel Ivanich. You get up in the morning, polish the boots, heat the samovar, clean the rooms; after that . . . nothing to do. The lieutenant spends his whole day drawing up plans, but if you want, you can pray. You can read books or go out. If only everyone could have such a life."

"Yes, it's just fine! The lieutenant drafts plans, while you sit all day in the kitchen and long for your native land. Plans. . . . Human life counts, not plans! You have but one life to live. You must protect it."

"Of course, Pavel Ivanich, a stupid person will not find mercy anywhere, neither at home, nor in the service, but if you live right and obey orders, then who will wish to do you wrong? The gentlemen are educated. They understand. . . . In five years I wasn't in the guard house once, and if I remember right, I was hit only one time . . ."

"What for?"

"Fighting. I have a heavy hand, Pavel Ivanich. Four Chinamen came into our yard; maybe they were carrying firewood . . . I forget now. Well, I got bored, so went for them. One of them, damn him, got a bloody nose. . . . The lieutenant saw it all through the window, got sore, and hit me on the ear."

"What a pitiful stupid fellow you are. . . ." whispered Pavel Ivanich. "You don't understand a thing."

He was utterly exhausted from the rolling of the ship, so closed his eyes; alternately his head rolled back, then fell to his chest. He tried to lie down several times, but his breath became short, and he couldn't lie down at all.

After a while he asked, "Why did you beat up the four Chinamen?"

"Well, they came into our yard. So I went for them."

And then everything was still. The card players played for an hour or so. They got angry and cursed one another, but eventually even they were overcome by the rolling of the ship and went to bed.

Once again Gusev pictures the large pond, the factory, the village. . . . Once again the sleigh moves down the street, again Vanka laughs, and silly little Akulka throws open her fur coat and sticks out her feet, as if to say: "Look, everyone, my felt boots aren't like Vanka's; mine are new!"

"Going on six, but still she doesn't have good sense!" Gusev says in his delirium. "Instead of kicking your feet you should come over here and bring your soldier uncle something to drink. I'll give you a present."

And there goes Anton with a flintlock on his shoulder, carrying a rabbit he has killed: and behind him comes the old decrepit Jew Isaac offering to trade a piece of soap for the rabbit. Look, a black calf is in the sleigh, and Domna is sewing a shirt and crying about something or other; and there again is the eyeless head of the bull, and black smoke.

Someone overhead shouts loudly. Several sailors run by. Something bulky is being dragged over the deck, or something has crashed down upon it. They run past again. Was it an accident? Gusev raises his head, listens, and then notices the two soldiers and the sailor still playing cards; Pavel Ivanich is sitting there moving his lips. It is stifling, and you don't have the strength even to breathe; the water is warm and disgusting. . . . The rolling of the ship goes on and on.

Suddenly, something strange happens to the card playing soldier. He begins to call hearts diamonds and gets confused about the score. He drops his cards. Then he gives a foolish frightened smile and looks round at all of them.

"Be right there, fellows . . . ," he says and lies down on the floor. No one knows what to do. They call him, but he does not answer.

"Stepan, what's wrong? Don't you feel well?" asks the soldier with the bandaged hand. "Should we call the priest?"

"Here, Stepan, drink some water . . . ," says the sailor. "Come on, mate, drink."

"Hey, why knock the mug against his teeth?" Gusev says angrily. "You turnip brain, can't you see?"

"See what?"

"What?" Gusev says, mocking him. "He's stopped breathing; he's dead. That's what. Good God, what stupid people. . . ."

III

The sea is calm, and Pavel Ivanich is in a good mood. He's not angry any more. It's as if he wanted to say: "Well, now I'm going to tell you a joke, a really good one. . . . You'll split your sides laughing." The round porthole is open and a soft breeze blows on Pavel Ivanich. There are voices and the splash of oars on the water. . . . Directly below the porthole, a thin unpleasant voice is heard; it must be the Chinaman singing.

"Well, now we're on the way," says Pavel Ivanich with a mocking smile. "Within a month we'll be in Russia. When I get to Odessa, I'll go straight on to Kharkov. I have a friend in Kharkov; he's a literary person. I'll go to him and say: "Well, brother, for a short while just put aside your infamous plots about women's amours and the beauties of Nature and expose the miserable two-legged wretches. . . . That's what you should be writing about."

He ponders for a minute and then says:

"Gusev, you know how I tricked them?"

"Tricked who, Pavel Ivanich?"

"Why those. . . . On this steamer, you know, there are only two classes: first and third, and the only ones allowed to travel third class are the peasants, the bums. If you're wearing a jacket and at a distance even resemble a gentleman or a bourgeois, you travel first class. You also fork over 500 rubles, no matter what. 'Why do you have such a regulation?' I ask. 'Is your plan to increase the prestige of the Russian intelligencia?' 'Not at all. We won't let you, simply because a respectable person would never make it traveling third class; it's absolutely ghastly down there.' 'Really? Well, thanks for showing so much concern for respectable people. But regardless of whether it's dreadful or nice down there, I don't have 500 rubles. I haven't robbed the treasury, exploited the natives, smuggled anything, or flogged anyone to death, so I ask you to judge for yourself: have I the right solemnly to sit in state in first class, much less to associate myself with the Russian intelligencia?' But you can't get through to them with logic, so I resorted to trickery. I put on a peasant's coat and high boots, screwed up my face like a drunk, and went to the agent. 'Give me a little ticket, your excellency.'"

"What is your social rank?" asks the sailor.

"Ecclesiastic. My father was an honest priest. Always he told the Truth to the high and mighty of this world, right to their faces. So he suffered a great deal."

Pavel Ivanich was exhaused by all this talking and gasping; nevertheless, he continued, "Always I tell people the Truth, to their faces . . . I'm not afraid of anything or anybody. In this respect I am entirely different from you. You people are ignorant, blind, crushed; you see nothing, or

what you see you don't understand. . . . They tell you the wind tears loose
from its chains, that you are cattle, Pechenegs, and you believe it. They beat
you across the neck, and you kiss their hands. Some beast in a raccoon coat
robs you, then tosses you a fifteen kopeck tip, and you say: 'Let me kiss
your hand, sir.' You're outcasts, pitiful people. . . . But I'm quite a different
type. I live in a rational way; I see everything, like an eagle or hawk flying
above the earth; and I understand everything. I am Protest Incarnate. I see
tyranny—and I protest. I see a bigot and hypocrite—and I protest. I see
swine triumphant—and I protest. No Spanish Inquisition can make me be
silent. I am invincible. That's right. . . . Cut out my tongue, and with
gestures I'll protest. Wall me up in a cellar, and I'll shout so loudly my cries
will be heard a verst away, or I'll starve myself to death—another stone to
weigh on their black consciences. Kill me, and I'll return to haunt them. My
acquaintances all tell me: 'You're a completely impossible person, Pavel
Ivanich!' And I am proud of this reputation. I served in the Far East for
three years, and they'll remember me there for one hundred. I quarreled
with everyone. From Russia my friends write, 'Don't come to see us.' So
here I come out of spite. . . . Yes . . . as I understand it, that's what life is
all about. That's what you really can call life."

Not listening, Gusev stares out the porthole. On the transparent, soft,
turquoise water, flooded with the dazzling hot sunshine, a boat sways to
and fro. In it stand naked Chinese, holding up cages with canaries and
shouting:

"It sings! It sings!"

Another boat bumps against it; quickly a steam launch passes. And
there's yet another boat; sitting in that boat is a fat Chinese eating rice with
chopsticks. Lazily the water rolls, and lazily above it white seagulls hover.

Yawning and looking at the stout Chinaman, Gusev thinks:

"That fat one there. . . . I wish I could give it to him right on the neck.
. . ."

Gusev dozes, and it seems to him that everything in nature is dozing,
too. Time passes quickly. The day passes imperceptibly, and imperceptibly
darkness approaches. . . . The ship is no longer standing still; it is moving
on.

IV

Two days pass. Pavel Ivanich is sitting up no longer; he is lying down, his
eyes closed, and his nose seems to be sharper.

"Pavel Ivanich?" Gusev calls, "Oh, Pavel Ivanich!"

Pavel Ivanich opens his eyes and moves his lips.

"Are you sick?"

"No, I'm all right . . ." answers Pavel Ivanich gasping for breath. I'm all right; in fact, I'm even . . . better. . . . See, now I can lie down. . . . I've improved."

"Well, thank the Lord, Pavel Ivanich."

"When I compare us, I feel sorry for you, you poor fellows. My lungs are still in good shape, my cough comes from the stomach. I can put up with hell; the Red Sea means nothing to me. In addition, I view my illness and medicines critically. But you . . . you are ignorant. It's hard on you, very, very hard!"

The ship is not rolling; it is quiet. To make up for it, the heat is stifling . . . hot as a steambath. It's difficult to talk, even to listen. Gusev wraps his arms around his knees, rests his head on them and thinks of home. God, it's a pleasure in this oppressively hot weather to think of snow and cold weather! You're riding in a sleigh; suddenly something frightens the horses, and they bolt. . . . Off they dash like creatures possessed through the village, paying heed neither to roads, nor canals, nor ravines . . . through the pond, past the factory, and then across the fields. . . . The factory workers and others coming towards them shout: "Hold them!" But why hold them? Let the sharp cold wind beat in your face and bite at your hands; let the lumps of snow thrown up by the horses' hooves hit against your cap, on your neck behind your collar, on your chest; let the runners whistle and tear off the traces and singletrees. To hell with them! And as the sleigh turns over, what a joy when you fly head first into a snowdrift. Then up you get, white from head to toe, with icicles on your mustache. No cap, no mittens, belt undone. . . . The people laugh and dogs bark. . . .

Pavel Ivanich half-opens one eye, looks at Gusev and asks softly:

"Gusev, your commanding officer, did he steal?"

"Who knows, Pavel Ivanich! We had no way of knowing; that sort of thing didn't reach our ears."

And then a long time passes in silence. Gusev broods, deliriously mutters, and drinks more water; it's difficult for him to speak, to listen, and he is afraid someone will try to strike up a conversation. An hour passes, two, three; evening descends, then night, but of all this he is oblivious; he sits there thinking only of freezing weather.

For a minute it sounded as if someone had come down to the sick-bay; there were voices, a minute passed, then all was silent.

"The Kingdom of Heaven and eternal peace be granted unto him," says the soldier with the bandaged hand. "He was a troubled fellow."

"What?" asks Gusev. "Who?"

"He died. They just took him up."

"Well, so be it," mutters Gusev, yawning. "The Kingdom of Heaven."

"Gusev, what do you think?" asks the soldier with the bandage after a few moments of silence. "Will he go to Heaven, or not?"

"Who are you talking about?"

"About Pavel Ivanich."

"He will. . . . He suffered a long time. . . . Also don't forget he's of the clergy. Priests have lots of relatives. They'll pray for him."

The soldier with the bandage sits down on Gusev's bunk and in a low voice says:

"You, Gusev, you aren't long for this world. You'll never make it to Russia."

"Was it the doctor said that or his assistant?"asks Gusev.

"Who said it isn't important; I can see it. . . . You can always tell when a man's about to die. You don't eat, don't drink, and you've wasted away to the point that it's awful just to look at you. Let's face it, you've got consumption. I'm not saying this to worry you. I just think you might want to take communion and have the last rites. And if you have any money, you could give it to the senior officer."

"I didn't write home," Gusev sighs. "I'll die. No one will ever know about it."

"Yes they will," the sick sailor says in a bass voice. "When you die, the steamer people make an entry in the log book; in Odessa they give a copy to the military authority. Then he sends it to your rural district or some-where. . . ."

The conversation makes Gusev feel uneasy, and a desire of some sort begins to torment him. He drinks water, but that isn't it; he drags himself over to the round porthole and breathes the hot humid air, but that isn't it; he tries to think about home, about cold weather, but that isn't it. Finally he decides that if he remains in the sick-bay one minute more he will choke to death.

"I feel terrible, fellows . . ." he says. "I'm going on deck. For Christ's sake, help me get on deck!"

"All right," agrees the soldier with the bandage. "You won't make it there on your own; I'll carry you up. Put your arm around my neck."

Gusev puts his arm around the sailor's neck, who then places his good arm around him and carries him on deck. There the discharged soldiers and sailors are sleeping side by side, so many it is hard to get through.

"Stand up," the soldier with the bandage says softly. "Hold on to my shirt and follow me slowly."

It's dark. There are lights neither on the deck, nor on the masts, nor on the sea around them. In the prow the lookout stands completely still, a statue; you might think he was asleep. It seems as if the ship is on its own, going where it wishes.

"They're throwing Pavel Ivanich into the sea . . ." says the soldier with the bandage. "Into a bag, and then into the water."

"Yes, that's the way it is. It's much better to lie at home in the ground. At least your mother will come to your grave and cry."

"That's right."

There is a smell of manure and hay. With heads hanging, some bulls stand by the rail: one, two, three . . . eight of them! Also there's a pony there, too. Gusev reaches out to pat it, but the pony shakes its head, shows its teeth, and tries to bite his sleeve.

"Damned beast . . ." says Gusev angrily.

The two of them, he and the soldier, quietly thread their way to the prow; they stand at the rail and glance silently up and down, up and down. Above the sky is vast; bright stars, peace and quiet—just like home in the village—but below is darkness and disorder. No one knows what makes the waves roar so. Which wave you look at makes no difference; each tries to rise higher than all the rest. They push and chase one another. Each in turn is attacked by a wave with a gleaming white crest that is equally fierce and outrageous.

The sea neither reasons nor pities. If a ship is small and not constructed of heavy iron, the waves will break it to pieces with no regrets whatsoever and will devour all the people without finding out if they are saints or sinners. A ship also has a senseless, cruel expression. This big-nosed monster moves forward, cutting millions of waves in its path; it fears neither darkness, nor wind, nor space, nor solitude; it cares for nothing, and if the sea were populated by people, the monster would crush them, too, without bothering to distinguish between saints and sinners.

"Where are we now?" asks Gusev.

"I don't know. We must be in the ocean."

"You can't see land. . . ."

"Oh, come on! They say we won't see land for seven days."

The two soldiers think silently and watch the white phosphorescent foam. The first to break the silence is Gusev.

"Actually there's nothing really frightening out here," he says. "It's creepy, like sitting in a dark forest. For instance, if they lowered a boat now and an officer ordered me to go off into the sea 100 versts to catch fish—I'd do it. Or, let's say, if a Christian fell into the water—I'd go right in after him. I wouldn't save a German or a Chinaman, but I'd go in after a Christian."

"Are you afraid of dying?"

"I am. I feel sorry for the family at home. My brother who is still at home isn't reliable. He's a drunkard. He beats his wife for no reason . . . doesn't respect his parents. Everything will fall apart without me, and my mother and father will have to go out and beg. But my legs won't hold me up, brother, and it's stifling here. . . . Let's go back to sleep."

V

Gusev returns to the sick-bay and lies down on his bunk. As before, an indefinable desire torments him, but he can't for the life of him say what he needs. He feels a pressure in his chest, a throbbing in his head, and his mouth is so dry that he scarcely can move his tongue. He dozes, talks deliriously, is tormented by nightmares, coughing, and the oppressive heat; towards morning he falls into a deep sleep. He dreams that they have just taken the bread out of the barrack's oven, and that he has crawled into the oven and is beating himself with birch branches.

For two days he sleeps and on the third day at noon, two sailors come below to carry him out of the sick-bay. They sew him up in a sailcloth and add two iron furnace bars for extra weight. Sewn up in a sailcloth, he is like a carrot or a radish: broad at the head and narrow at the feet. . . . Just before sunset, he is carried out onto the deck and placed on a board; one end of the board lies on the rail, the other on a box on a stool. Around him stand the discharged men and the crew with hats removed.

"Blessed be the name of the Lord," begins the priest, "as it was in the beginning, is now and ever shall be!"

Three sailors respond, "Amen."

The discharged men and crew cross themselves and look down towards the waves. It's strange that a man should be sewn up in a sailcloth and cast into the waves. Is it possible this will happen to us all?

The priest sprinkles earth on Gusev and bows down. They all sing "Eternal Memory."

The seaman on watch duty lifts one end of the board; Gusev slides off, flies down head first, twists once in the air and—splash! The foam covers him over, and for an instant he seems wrapped in lace. But a moment passes—and Gusev disappears into the waves.

He sinks quickly toward the bottom. Will he reach it? They say that it's four versts to the bottom. After eight or ten fathoms, he begins to descend more and more slowly, to sway rhythmically, obviously hesitating, carried along by the current. He moves more quickly sideways than down.

On the way he meets a school of little fish called pilot fish. Having caught sight of the dark body, the fish stop, as though transfixed, and suddenly they turn and disappear. In less than a minute once again like arrows they quickly dart at Gusev and all around him begin to pierce the water in zig-zags.

After that another dark body appears. It's a shark. Important and unconcerned, just as if it didn't notice him, it swims under Gusev. Gusev slides across the shark's back, and it turns belly up, basking in the warm transparent water; then it lazily opens its mouth which has two rows of teeth. The pilot fish are in ecstasy; they stop to watch, to see what comes next. After playing a while with the body, the shark nonchalantly puts his mouth under it, cautiously touches it with his teeth, and the sailcloth rips along the entire length of the body, from head to foot. One furnace iron falls out, and having frightened the pilot fish, hits the shark on the side. It then quickly sinks to the bottom.

And during this time, up above in the direction of the setting sun, clouds are gathering; one cloud looks like an arch of triumph, another like a lion, a third like a pair of scissors. . . . From behind the clouds a broad green shaft of light emerges and stretches all the way to the middle of the sky; a little later a violet one joins the first, then a gold, then pink. . . . The sky takes on a soft lilac hue. Looking at this enchanting magnificent sky, the sea frowns at first, but soon the sea itself takes on colors which are gentle, happy, and passionate; colors that man would find difficult to describe in words.

Son of an improvident London lawyer and a mother who wrote novels and travel sketches, Anthony Trollope (1815–1882) was later to feel he was a social "outcast," when he attended the elite schools of Harrow and Winchester. In any event, he was an indifferent student and several times withdrew from school because of waning family fortunes. Trollope spent seven impoverished, lonely years as a junior postal clerk in London; at last, a promotion to deputy postal inspector took him to a new post in Ireland. Here he wrote his first novel in 1843; thereafter, he wrote constantly to a rigorous schedule and during his life produced more than fifty novels. His work was extremely popular, and he is now remembered largely for his "Barchester" novels and for his gently satirical views of the social and political structures of Victorian England. For further reading: Lotta Schmidt and Other Stories *(1867).*

ANTHONY TROLLOPE

Malachi's Cove

*O*n the northern coast of Cornwall, between Tintagel and Bossiney, down on the very margin of the sea, there lived not long since an old man who got his living by saving seaweed from the waves, and selling it for manure. The cliffs there are bold and fine, and the sea beats in upon them from the north with a grand violence. I doubt whether it be not the finest morsel of cliff scenery in England, though it is beaten by many portions of the west coast of Ireland, and perhaps also by spots in Wales and Scotland. Cliffs should be nearly precipitous, they should be broken in their outlines, and should barely admit here and there of an insecure passage from their summit to the sand at their feet. The sea should come, if not up to them, at least very near to them, and then, above all things, the water below them should be blue, and not of that dead leaden colour which is so familiar to us in England. At Tintagel all these requisites are there, except that bright blue colour which is so lovely. But the cliffs themselves are bold and well broken, and the margin of sand at high water is very narrow—so narrow that at spring-tides there is barely a footing there.

Close upon this margin was the cottage or hovel of Malachi Trenglos, the old man of whom I have spoken. But Malachi, or old Glos, as he was commonly called by the people around him, had not built his house absolutely upon the sand. There was a fissure in the rock so great that at the top it formed a narrow ravine, and so complete from the summit to the base that it afforded an opening for a steep and rugged track from the top of the rock to the bottom. This fissure was so wide at the bottom that it had afforded space for Trenglos to fix his habitation on a foundation of rock, and here he had lived for many years. It was told of him that in the early days of his trade he had always carried the weed in a basket on his back to the top, but latterly he had been possessed of a donkey, which had been trained to go up and down the steep track with a single pannier over his loins, for the rocks would not permit of panniers hanging by his side; and for this assistant he had built a shed adjoining his own, and almost as large as that in which he himself resided.

But, as years went on, old Glos procured other assistance than that of the donkey, or, as I should rather say, Providence supplied him with other help; and, indeed, had it not been so, the old man must have given up his cabin and his independence and gone into the workhouse at Camelford. For rheumatism had afflicted him, old age had bowed him till he was nearly double, and by degrees he became unable to attend the donkey on its upward passage to the world above, or even to assist in rescuing the coveted weed from the waves.

At the time to which our story refers Trenglos had not been up the cliff for twelve months, and for the last six months he had done nothing towards the furtherance of his trade, except to take the money and keep it, if any of it was kept, and occasionally to shake down a bundle of fodder for the donkey. The real work of the business was done altogether by Mahala Trenglos, his granddaughter.

Mally Trenglos was known to all the farmers round the coast, and to all the small tradespeople in Camelford. She was a wild-looking, almost . unearthly creature, with wild-flowing, black, uncombed hair, small in stature, with small hands and bright black eyes; but people said that she was very strong, and the children around declared that she worked day and night and knew nothing of fatigue. As to her age there were many doubts. Some said she was ten, and others five-and-twenty, but the reader may be allowed to know that at this time she had in truth passed her twentieth birthday. The old people spoke well of Mally, because she was so good to her grandfather; and it was said of her that though she carried to him a little gin and tobacco almost daily, she bought nothing for herself—and as to the gin, no one who looked at her would accuse her of meddling with that. But she had no friends and but few acquaintances among people of her own age. They said that she was fierce and ill-natured, that she had not a good word for anyone, and that she was, complete at all points, a thorough little vixen. The young men did not care for her; for, as regarded dress, all days were alike with her. She never made herself smart on Sundays. She was generally without stockings and seemed to care not at all to exercise any of those feminine attractions which might have been hers had she studied to attain them. All days were the same to her in regard to dress; and, indeed, till lately, all days had, I fear, been the same to her in other respects. Old Malachi had never been seen inside a place of worship since he had taken to live under the cliff.

But within the last two years Mally had submitted herself to the teaching of the clergyman at Tintagel, and had appeared at church on Sundays, if not absolutely with punctuality, at any rate so often that no one who knew the peculiarity of her residence was disposed to quarrel with her on that subject. But she made no difference in her dress on these occasions. She took her place on a low stone seat just inside the church door, clothed as usual in her thick red serge petticoat and loose brown serge jacket, such being the apparel which she had found to be best adapted for her hard and perilous work among the waters. She had pleaded to the clergyman when he attacked her on the subject of church attendance with vigour that she had got no church-going clothes. He had explained to her that she would be received there without distinction to her clothing. Mally had taken him at his word, and had gone, with a courage which certainly deserved admiration, though I doubt whether there was not mingled with it an obstinacy which was less admirable.

For people said that old Glos was rich, and that Mally might have proper clothes if she chose to buy them. Mr. Polwarth, the clergyman, who, as the old man could not come to him, went down the rocks to the old man, did make some hint on the matter in Mally's absence. But old Glos, who had been patient with him on other matters, turned upon him so angrily when he made an allusion to money, that Mr. Polwarth found himself obliged to give that matter up, and Mally continued to sit upon the stone bench in her short serge petticoat, with her long hair streaming down her face. She did so far sacrifice to decency on such occasions to tie up her back hair with an old shoestring. So tied it would remain through the Monday and Tuesday, but by Wednesday afternoon Mally's hair had generally managed to escape.

As to Mally's indefatigable industry there could be no manner of doubt, for the quantity of seaweed which she and the donkey amassed between them was very surprising. Old Glos, it was declared, had never collected half what Mally gathered together; but then the article was becoming cheaper, and it was necessary that the exertion should be greater.

So Mally and the donkey toiled and toiled, and the seaweed came up in heaps which surprised those who looked at her little hands and light form. Was there not someone who helped her at nights, some fairy, or demon, or the like? Mally was so snappish in her answers to people that she had no right to be surprised if ill-natured things were said of her.

No one ever heard Mally Trenglos complain of her work, but about this time she was heard to make great and loud complaints of the treatment she received from some of her neighbours. It was known that she went with her plaints to Mr. Polwarth; and when he could not help her, or did not give her such instant help as she needed, she went—ah, so foolishly! to the office of a certain attorney at Camelford, who was not likely to prove himself a better friend than Mr. Polwarth.

Now the nature of her injury was as follows. The place in which she collected her seaweed was a little cove;—the people had come to call it Malachi's Cove from the name of the old man who lived there—which was so formed, that the margin of the sea therein could only be reached by the passage from the top down to Trenglos's hut. The breadth of the cove when the sea was out might perhaps be two hundred yards, and on each side the rocks ran out in such a way that both from north and south the domain of Trenglos was guarded from intruders. And this locality had been well chosen for its intended purpose.

There was a rush of the sea into the cove, which carried there large, drifting masses of seaweed, leaving them among the rocks when the tide was out. During the equinoctial winds of the spring and autumn the supply would never fail; and even when the sea was calm, the long, soft, salt-bedewed, trailing masses of the weed, could be gathered there when they could not be found elsewhere for miles along the coast. The task of getting the weed from the breakers was often difficult and dangerous—so difficult that much of it was left to be carried away by the next incoming tide.

Mally doubtless did not gather half the crop that was there at her feet. What was taken by the returning waves she did not regret; but when interlopers came upon her cove, and gathered her wealth—her grandfather's wealth, beneath her eyes, then her heart was broken. It was this interloping, this intrusion, that drove poor Mally to the Camelford attorney. But, alas, though the Camelford attorney took Mally's money, he could do nothing for her, and her heart was broken!

She had an idea, in which no doubt her grandfather shared, that the path to the cove was, at any rate, their property. When she was told that the cove, and sea running into the cove, were not the freeholds of her grandfather, she understood that the statement might be true. But what then as to the use of the path? Who had made the path what it was? Had she not painfully, wearily, with exceeding toil, carried up bits of rock with her own little hands, that her grandfather's donkey might have footing for his feet?

Had she not scraped together crumbs of earth along the face of the cliff that she might make easier to the animal the track of that rugged way? And now, when she saw big farmer's lads coming down with other donkeys— and, indeed, there was one who came with a pony; no boy, but a young man, old enough to know better than rob a poor old man and a young girl—she reviled the whole human race, and swore that the Camelford attorney was a fool.

Any attempt to explain to her that there was still weed enough for her was worse than useless. Was it not all hers and his, or, at any rate, was not the sole way to it his and hers? And was not her trade stopped and impeded? Had she not been forced to back her laden donkey down, twenty yards she said, but it had, in truth, been five, because Farmer Gunliffe's son had been in the way with his thieving pony? Farmer Gunliffe had wanted to buy her weed at his own price, and because she had refused he had set on his thieving son to destroy her in this wicked way.

"I'll hamstring the beast the next time as he's down here!" said Mally to old Glos, while the angry fire literally streamed from her eyes.

Farmer Gunliffe's small homestead—he held about fifty acres of land, was close by the village of Tintagel, and not a mile from the cliff. The seawrack, as they call it, was pretty well the only manure within his reach, and no doubt he thought it hard that he should be kept from using it by Mally Trenglos and her obstinacy.

"There's heaps of other coves, Barty," said Mally to Barty Gunliffe, the farmer's son.

"But none so nigh, Mally, nor yet none that fills 'emselves as this place."

Then he explained to her that he would not take the weed that came up close to hand. He was bigger than she was, and stronger, and would get it from the outer rocks, with which she never meddled. Then, with scorn in her eye, she swore that she could get it where he durst not venture, and repeated her threat of hamstringing the pony. Barty laughed at her wrath, jeered her because of her wild hair, and called her a mermaid.

"I'll mermaid you!" she cried. "Mermaid, indeed! I wouldn't be a man to come and rob a poor girl and an old cripple. But you're no man, Barty Gunliffe! You're not half a man."

Nevertheless, Bartholomew Gunliffe was a very fine young fellow as far as the eye went. He was about five feet eight inches high, with strong arms and legs, with light curly brown hair and blue eyes. His father was but in a small way as a farmer, but, nevertheless, Barty Gunliffe was well thought of among the girls around. Everybody liked Barty—excepting only Mally Trenglos and she hated him like poison.

Barty, when he was asked why so good-natured a lad as he persecuted a poor girl and an old man, threw himself upon the justice of the thing. It wouldn't do at all, according to his view, that any single person should take upon himself to own that which God Almighty sent as the common property of all. He would do Mally no harm, and so he had told her. But Mally was a vixen—a wicked little vixen; and she must be taught to have a civil tongue in her head. When once Mally would speak him civil as he went for weed, he would get his father to pay the old man some sort of toll for the use of the path.

"Speak him civil?" said Mally. "Never; not while I have a tongue in my mouth!" And I fear old Glos encouraged her rather than otherwise in her view of the matter.

But her grandfather did not encourage her to hamstring the pony. Hamstringing a pony would be a serious thing, and old Glos thought it might be very awkward for both of them if Mally were put into prison. He suggested, therefore, that all manner of impediments should be put in the way of the pony's feet, surmising that the well-trained donkey might be able to work in spite of them. And Barty Gunliffe on his next descent, did find the passage very awkward when he came near to Malachi's hut, but he made his way down, and poor Mally saw the lumps of rock at which she had laboured so hard pushed on one side or rolled out of the way with a steady persistency of injury towards herself that almost drove her frantic.

"Well, Barty, you're a nice boy," said old Glos, sitting in the doorway of the hut, as he watched the intruder.

"I ain't a doing no harm to none as doesn't harm me," said Barty. "The sea's free to all, Malachi."

"And the sky's free to all, but I musn't get up on the top of your big barn to look at it," said Mally, who was standing among the rocks with a long hook in her hand. The long hook was the tool with which she worked in dragging the weed from the waves. "But you ain't got no justice, nor yet no sperrit, or you wouldn't come here to vex an old man like he."

"I didn't want to vex him, nor yet to vex you, Mally. You let me be for a while, and we'll be friends yet."

"Friends!" exclaimed Mally. "Who'd have the likes of you for a friend? What are you moving them stones for? Them stones belongs to grandfather." And in her wrath she made a movement as though she were going to fly at him.

"Let him be, Mally," said the old man; "let him be. He'll get his punishment. He'll come to be drowned some day if he comes down here when the wind is in shore."

"That he may be drowned then!" said Mally, in her anger. "If he was in the big hole there among the rocks, and the sea running in at half-tide, I wouldn't lift a hand to help him out."

"Yes, you would, Mally; you'd fish me up with your hook like a big stick of seaweed."

She turned from him with scorn as he said this, and went into the hut. It was time for her to get ready for her work, and one of the great injuries done her lay in this—that such a one as Barty Gunliffe should come and look at her during her toil among the breakers.

It was an afternoon in April, and the hour was something after four o'clock. There had been a heavy wind from the north-west all the morning, with gusts of rain, and the sea-gulls had been in and out of the cove all the day, which was a sure sign to Mally that the incoming tide would cover the rocks with weed.

The quick waves were now returning with wonderful celerity over the low reefs, and the time had come at which the treasure must be seized, if it was to be garnered on that day. By seven o'clock it would be growing dark, at nine it would be high water, and before daylight the crop would be carried out again if not collected. All this Mally understood very well, and some of this Barty was beginning to understand also.

As Mally came down with her bare feet, bearing her long hook in her hand, she saw Barty's pony standing patiently on the sand, and in her heart she longed to attack the brute. Barty at this moment, with a common three-pronged fork in his hand, was standing down on a large rock, gazing forth towards the waters. He had declared that he would gather the weed only at places which were inaccessible to Mally, and he was looking out that he might settle where he would begin.

"Let 'un be, let 'un be," shouted the old man to Mally, as he saw her take a step towards the beast, which she hated almost as much as she hated the man.

Hearing her grandfather's voice through the wind, she desisted from her purpose, if any purpose she had had, and went forth to her work. As she passed down the cove, and scrambled in among the rocks, she saw Barty still standing on his perch; out beyond, the white-curling waves were cresting and breaking themselves with violence, and the wind was howling among the caverns and abutments of the cliff.

Every now and then there came a squall of rain, and though there was sufficient light, the heavens were black with clouds. A scene more beautiful might hardly be found by those who love the glories of the coast. The light for such objects was perfect. Nothing could exceed the grandeur of the colours—the blue of the open sea, the white of the breaking waves, the yellow sands, or the streaks of red and brown which gave such richness to the cliff.

But neither Mally nor Barty were thinking of such things as these. Indeed they were hardly thinking of their trade after its ordinary forms. Barty was meditating how he might best accomplish his purpose of working beyond the reach of Mally's feminine powers, and Mally was resolving that wherever Barty went she would go farther.

And, in many respects, Mally had the advantage. She knew every rock in the spot, and was sure of those which gave a good foothold, and sure also of those which did not. And then her activity had been made perfect by practice for the purpose to which it was to be devoted. Barty, no doubt, was stronger than she, and quite as active. But Barty could not jump among the waves from one stone to another as she could do, nor was he as yet able to get aid in his work from the very force of the water as she could get it. She had been hunting seaweed in that cove since she had been an urchin of six years old, and she knew every hole and corner and every spot of vantage. The waves were her friends, and she could use them. She could measure their strength, and knew when and where it would cease.

Mally was great down in the salt pools of her own cove—great, and very fearless. As she watched Barty make his way forward from rock to rock, she told herself, gleefully, that he was going astray. The curl of the wind as it blew into the cove would not carry the weed up to the northern buttresses of the cove; and then there was the great hole just there—the great hole of which she had spoken when she wished him evil.

And now she went to work, hooking up the dishevelled hairs of the ocean, and landing many a cargo on the extreme margin of the sand, from whence she would be able in the evening to drag it back before the invading waters would return to reclaim the spoil.

And on his side also Barty made his heap up against the northern buttresses of which I have spoken. Barty's heap became big and still bigger, so that he knew, let the pony work as he might, he could not take it all up that evening. But still it was not as large as Mally's heap. Mally's hook was better than his fork, and Mally's skill was better than his strength. And when he failed in some haul Mally would jeer him with a wild, weird laughter, and shriek to him through the wind that he was not half a man. At first he answered her with laughing words, but before long, as she boasted of her success and pointed to his failure, he became angry, and then he answered her no more. He became angry with himself, in that he missed so much of the plunder before him.

The broken sea was full of the long straggling growth which the waves had torn up from the bottom of the ocean, but the masses were carried past him, away from him—nay, once or twice over him; and then Mally's weird voice would sound in his ear, jeering him. The gloom among the rocks was now becoming thicker and thicker, the tide was beating in with increased strength, and the gusts of wind came with quicker and greater violence. But still he worked on. While Mally worked he would work, and he would work for some time after she was driven in. He would not be beaten by a girl.

The great hole was now full of water, but of water which seemed to be boiling as though in a pot. And the pot was full of floating masses—large treasures of seaweed which were thrown to and fro upon its surface, but lying there so thick that one would seem almost able to rest upon it without sinking.

Mally knew well how useless it was to attempt to rescue aught from the fury of that boiling caldron. The hole went in under the rocks, and the side of it towards the shore lay high, slippery, and steep. The hole, even at low water, was never empty; and Mally believed that there was no bottom to it. Fish thrown in there could escape out to the ocean, miles away—so Mally in her softer moods would tell the visitors to the cove. She knew the hole well. Poulnadioul she was accustomed to call it; which was supposed, when translated, to mean that this was the hole of the Evil One. Never did Mally attempt to make her own of weed which had found its way into that pot.

But Barty Gunliffe knew no better, and she watched him as he endeavoured to steady himself on the treacherously slippery edge of the pool. He fixed himself there and made a haul, with some small success. How he managed it she hardly knew, but she stood still for a while watching him anxiously, and then she saw him slip. He slipped, and recovered himself— slipped again, and again recovered himself.

"Barty, you fool!" she screamed, "if you get yourself pitched in there, you'll never come out no more."

Whether she simply wished to frighten him, or whether her heart relented and she had thought of his danger with dismay, who shall say? She could not have told herself. She hated him as much as ever—but she could hardly have wished to see him drowned before her eyes.

"You go on, and don't mind me," said he, speaking in a hoarse, angry tone.

"Mind you!—who minds you?" retorted the girl. And then she again prepared herself for her work.

But as she went down over the rocks with her long hook balanced in her hands, she suddenly heard a splash, and, turning quickly round saw the body of her enemy tumbling amidst the eddying waves in the pool. The tide had now come up so far that every succeeding wave washed into it and over it from the side nearest to the sea, and then ran down again back from the rocks, as the rolling wave receded, with a noise like the fall of a cataract. And then, when the surplus water had retreated for a moment, the surface of the pool would be partly calm, though the fretting bubbles would still boil up and down, and there was ever a simmer on the surface, as though, in truth, the caldron were heated. But this time of comparative rest was but a moment, for the succeeding breaker would come up almost as soon as the foam of the preceding one had gone, and then again the waters would be dashed upon the rocks, and the sides would echo with the roar of the angry wave.

Instantly Mally hurried across to the edge of the pool, crouching down upon her hands and knees for security as she did so. As a wave receded,

Barty's head and face was carried round near to her, and she could see that his forehead was covered with blood. Whether he were alive or dead she did not know. She had seen nothing but his blood, and the light-coloured hair of his head lying amidst the foam. Then his body was drawn along by the suction of the retreating wave; but the mass of water that escaped was not on this occasion large enough to carry the man out with it.

Instantly Mally was at work with her hook, and getting it fixed into his coat, dragged him towards the spot on which she was kneeling. During the half minute of repose she got him so close that she could touch his shoulder. Straining herself down, laying herself over the long bending handle of the hook, she strove to grasp him with her right hand. But she could not do it; she could only touch him.

Then came the next breaker, forcing itself on with a roar, looking to Mally as though it must certainly knock her from her resting-place, and destroy them both. But she had nothing for it but to kneel, and hold by her hook.

What prayer passed through her mind at that moment for herself or for him, or for that old man who was sitting unconsciously up at the cabin, who can say? The great wave came and rushed over her as she lay almost prostrate, and when the water was gone from her eyes, and the tumult of the foam, and the violence of the roaring breaker had passed by her, she found herself at her length upon the rock, while his body had been lifted up, free from her hook, and was lying upon the slippery ledge, half in the water and half out of it. As she looked at him, in that instant, she could see that his eyes were open and that he was struggling with his hands.

"Hold by the hook, Barty," she cried, pushing the stick of it before him, while she seized the collar of his coat in her hands.

Had he been her brother, her lover, her father she could not have clung to him with more of the energy of despair. He did contrive to hold by the stick which she had given him, and when the succeeding wave had passed by, he was still on the ledge. In the next moment she was seated a yard or two above the hole, in comparative safety, while Barty lay upon the rocks with his still bleeding head resting upon her lap.

What could she do now? She could not carry him; and in fifteen minutes the sea would be up where she was sitting. He was quite insensible, and very pale, and the blood was coming slowly—very slowly—from the wound on his forehead. Ever so gently she put her hand upon his hair to move it back from his face; and then she bent over his mouth to see if he breathed, and as she looked at him she knew that he was beautiful.

What would she not give that he might live? Nothing now was so precious to her as his life—as this life which she had so far rescued from the waters. But what could she do? Her grandfather could scarcely get himself down over the rocks, if indeed he could succeed in doing so much as that.

Could she drag the wounded man backwards, if it were only a few feet, so that he might lie above the reach of the waves till further assistance could be procured?

She set herself to work and she moved him, almost lifting him. As she did so she wondered at her own strength, but she was very strong at that moment. Slowly, tenderly, falling on the rocks herself so that he might fall on her, she got him back to the margin of the sand, to a spot which the waters would not reach for the next two hours.

Here her grandfather met them, having seen at last what had happened from the door.

"Dada," she said, "he fell into the pool yonder, and was battered against the rocks. See there at his forehead."

"Mally, I'm thinking that he's dead already," said old Glos, peering down over the body.

"No, dada; he is not dead; but mayhap he's dying. But I'll go at once up to the farm."

"Mally," said the old man, "look at his head. They'll say we murdered him."

"Who'll say so? Who'll lie like that? Didn't I pull him out of the hole?"

"What matters that? His father'll say we killed him."

It was manifest to Mally that whatever anyone might say hereafter, her present course was plain before her. She must run up the path to Gunliffe's farm and get necessary assistance. If the world were as bad as her grandfather said it would be so bad that she would not care to live longer in it. But be that as it might, there was no doubt as to what she must do now.

So away she went as fast as her naked feet could carry her up the cliff. When at the top she looked round to see if any person might be within ken, but she saw no one. So she ran with all her speed along the headland of the corn-field which led in the direction of old Gunliffe's house, and as she drew near to the homestead she saw that Barty's mother was leaning on the gate. As she approached she attempted to call, but her breath failed her for any purpose of loud speech, so she ran on till she was able to grasp Mrs. Gunliffe by the arm.

"Where's himself?" she said, holding her hand upon her beating heart that she might husband her breath.

"Who is it you mean?" said Mrs. Gunliff, who participated in the family feud against Trenglos and his granddaughter. "What does the girl clutch me for in that way?"

"He's dying then, that's all."

"Who is dying? Is it old Malachi? If the old man's bad, we'll send someone down."

"It ain't dada; it's Barty! Where's himself? Where's the master?" But by this time Mrs. Gunliffe was in an agony of despair, and was calling out for assistance lustily. Happily Gunliffe, the father, was at hand, and with him a man from the neighbouring village.

"Will you not send for the doctor?" said Mally. "Oh, man, you should send for the doctor!"

Whether any orders were given for the doctor she did not know, but in a very few minutes she was hurrying across the field again towards the path to the cove, and Gunliffe with the other man and his wife were following her.

As Mally went along she recovered her voice, for their step was not so quick as hers, and that which to them was a hurried movement, allowed her to get her breath again. And as she went she tried to explain to the father what had happened, saying but little, however, of her own doings in the matter. The wife hung behind listening, exclaiming every now and again that her boy was killed, and then asking wild questions as to his being yet alive. The father, as he went, said little. He was known as a silent, sober man, well spoken of for diligence and general conduct, but supposed to be stern and very hard when angered.

As they drew near to the top of the path the other man whispered something to him, and then he turned round upon Mally and stopped her.

"If he has come by his death between you, your blood shall be taken for his," said he.

Then the wife shrieked out that her child had been murdered, and Mally, looking round into the faces of the three, saw that her grandfather's words had come true. They suspected her of having taken the life, in saving which she had nearly lost her own.

She looked round at them with awe in her face, and then, without saying a word, preceded them down the path. What had she to answer when such a charge as that was made against her? If they chose to say that she pushed him into the pool and hit him with her hook as he lay amidst the waters, how could she show that it was not so?

Poor Mally knew little of the law of evidence, and it seemed to her that she was in their hands. But as she went down the steep track with a hurried step—a step so quick that they could not keep up with her—her heart was very full—very full and very high. She had striven for the man's life as though he had been her brother. The blood was yet not dry on her own legs and arms, where she had torn them in his service. At one moment she had felt sure that she would die with him in that pool. And now they said that she had murdered him! It may be that he was not dead, and what would he say if ever he should speak again? Then she thought of that moment when his eyes had opened, and he had seemed to see her. She had no fear for herself, for her heart was very high. But it was full also—full of scorn, disdain, and wrath.

When she had reached the bottom, she stood close to the door of the hut waiting for them, so that they might precede her to the other group, which was there in front of them, at a little distance on the sand.

"He is there, and dada is with him. Go and look at him," said Mally.

The father and mother ran on stumbling over the stones, but Mally remained behind by the door of the hut.

Barty Gunliffe was lying on the sand where Mally had left him, and old Malachi Trenglos was standing over him, resting himself with difficulty upon a stick.

"Not a move he's moved since she left him," said he; "not a move. I put his head on the old rug as you see, and I tried 'un with a drop of gin, but he wouldn't take it—he wouldn't take it."

"Oh, my boy! my boy!" said the mother, throwing herself beside her son upon the sand.

"Haud your tongue, woman," said the father, kneeling down slowly by the lad's head, "whimpering that way will do 'un no good."

Then having gazed for a minute or two upon the pale face beneath him, he looked up sternly into that of Malachi Trenglos.

The old man hardly knew how to bear this terrible inquisition.

"He would come," said Malachi; "he brought it all upon hisself."

"Who was it struck him?" said the father.

"Sure he struck hisself, as he fell among the breakers."

"Liar!" said the father, looking up at the old man.

"They have murdered him!—they have murdered him!" shrieked the mother.

"Haud your peace, woman!" said the husband again. "They shall give us blood for blood."

Mally, leaning against the corner of the hovel heard it all, but did not stir. They might say what they liked. They might make it out to be murder. They might drag her and her grandfather to Camelford gaol, and then to Bodmin, and the gallows; but they could not take from her the conscious feeling that was her own. She had done her best to save him—her very best. And she had saved him!

She remembered her threat to him before they had gone down on the rocks together, and her evil wish. Those words had been very wicked; but since that she had risked her life to save his. They might say what they pleased of her, and do what they pleased. She knew what she knew.

Then the father raised his son's head and shoulders in his arms, and called on the others to assist him in carrying Barty towards the path. They raised him between them carefully and tenderly, and lifted their burden on towards the spot at which Mally was standing. She never moved, but watched them at their work; and the old man followed them, hobbling after them with his crutch.

When they had reached the end of the hut she looked upon Barty's face, and saw that it was very pale. There was no longer blood upon the forehead, but the great gash was to be seen there plainly, with its jagged cut, and the skin livid and blue around the orifice. His light brown hair was hanging back, as she had made it to hang when she had gathered it with her hand after the big wave had passed over them. Ah, how beautiful he was in Mally's eyes with that pale face, and the sad scar upon his brow! She turned her face away, that they might not see her tears; but she did not move, nor did she speak.

But now, when they had passed the end of the hut, shuffling along with their burden, she heard a sound which stirred her. She roused herself quickly from her leaning posture, and stretched forth her head as though to listen; then she moved to follow them. Yes, they had stopped at the bottom of the path, and had again laid the body on the rocks. She heard that sound again, as of a long, long sigh, and then, regardless of any of them, she ran to the wounded man's head.

"He is not dead," she said. "There, he is not dead."

As she spoke Barty's eyes opened, and he looked about him.

"Barty, my boy, speak to me," said the mother.

Barty turned his face upon his mother, smiled, and then stared about him wildly.

"How is it with thee, lad?" said his father. Then Barty turned his face again to the latter voice, and as he did so his eyes fell upon Mally.

"Mally!" he said, "Mally!"

It could have wanted nothing further to any of those present to teach them that, according to Barty's own view of the case, Mally had not been his enemy; and, in truth, Mally herself wanted no further triumph. That word vindicated her, and she withdrew back to the hut.

"Dada," she said, "Barty is not dead, and I'm thinking they won't say anything more about our hurting him."

Old Glos shook his head. He was glad the lad hadn't met his death there; he didn't want the young man's blood, but he knew what folk would say. The poorer he was the more sure the world would be to trample on him. Mally said what she could to comfort him, being full of comfort herself.

She would have crept up to the farm if she dared, to ask how Barty was. But her courage failed her when she thought of that, so she went to work again, dragging back the weed she had saved to the spot at which on the morrow she would load the donkey. As she did this she saw Barth's pony still standing patiently under the rock; so she got a lock of fodder and threw it down before the beast.

It had become dark down in the cove, but she was still dragging back the seaweed, when she saw the glimmer of a lantern coming down the pathway. It was a most unusual sight, for lanterns were not common down in Malachi's Cove. Down came the lantern rather slowly—much more slowly than she was in the habit of descending, and then through the gloom she saw the figure of a man standing at bottom of the path. She went up to him, and saw that it was Mr. Gunliffe, the father.

"Is that Mally?" said Gunliffe.

"Yes, it is Mally; and how is Barty, Mr. Gunliffe?"

"You must come to 'un yourself, now at once," said the farmer. "He won't sleep a wink till he's seed you. You must not say but you'll come."

"Sure I'll come if I'm wanted," said Mally.

Gunliffe waited a moment, thinking that Mally might have to prepare herself, but Mally needed no preparation. She was dripping with salt water from the weed which she had been dragging, and her elfin locks were streaming wildly from her head; but, such as she was, she was ready.

"Dada's in bed, " she said, "and I can go now if you please."

Then Guliffe turned round and followed her up the path, wondering at the life which this girl led so far away from all her sex. It was now dark night, and he had found her working at the very edge of the rolling waves by herself, in the darkness, while the only human being who might seem to be her protector had already gone to his bed.

When they were at the top of the cliff Gunliffe took her by her hand, and led her along. She did not comprehend this, but she made no attempt to take her hand from his. Something he said about falling on the cliffs, but it was muttered so lowly that Mally hardly understood him. But in truth the man knew that she had saved his boy's life, and that he had injured her instead of thanking her. He was now taking her to his heart, and as words were wanting to him, he was showing his love after this silent fashion. He held her by the hand as though she were a child, and Mally tripped along at his side asking him no questions.

When they were at the farm-yard gate he stopped there for a moment.

"Mally, my girl," he said, "he'll not be content till he sees thee, but thou must not stay long wi' him, lass. Doctor says he's weak like, and wants sleep badly."

Mally merely nodded her head, and then they entered the house. Mally had never been within it before, and looked about with wondering eyes at the furniture of the big kitchen. Did any idea of her future destiny flash upon her then, I wonder? But she did not pause here a moment, but was led up to the bedroom above stairs, where Barty was lying on his mother's bed.

"Is it Mally herself?" said the voice of the weak youth.

"It's Mally herself," said the mother, "so now you can say what you please."

"Mally," said he, "Mally, it's along of you that I'm alive this moment."

"I'll not forget it on her," said the father, with his eyes turned away from her. "I'll never forget it on her."

"We hadn't a one but only him," said the mother, with her apron up to her face.

"Mally, you'll be friends with me now?" said Barty.

To have been made lady of the manor of the cove for ever, Mally couldn't have spoken a word now. It was not only that the words and presence of the people there cowed her and made her speechless, but the big bed, and the looking-glass, and the unheard-of wonders of the chamber, made her feel her own insignificance. But she crept up to Barty's side, and put her hand upon his.

"I'll come and get the weed, Mally; but it shall be all for you," said Barty.

"Indeed, you won't then, Barty dear," said the mother; "you'll never go near the awesome place again. What would we do if you were took from us?"

"He mustn't go near the hole if he does," said Mally, speaking at last in a solemn voice, and imparting the knowledge which she had kept to herself while Barty was her enemy; "'specially not if the wind's any way from the nor'rard."

"She'd better go down now," said the father.

Barty kissed the hand which he held, and Mally, looking at him as he did so, thought that he was like an angel.

"You'll come and see us tomorrow, Mally?" said he.

To this she made no answer, but followed Mrs. Gunliffe out of the room. When they were down in the kitchen the mother had tea for her, and thick milk, and a hot cake—all the delicacies which the farm could afford. I don't know that Mally cared much for the eating and drinking that night, but she began to think that the Gunliffe's were good people—very good people. It was better thus, at any rate, than being accused of murder and carried off to Camelford prison.

"I'll never forget it on her—never," the father had said.

Those words stuck to her from that moment, and seemed to sound in her ears all the night. How glad she was that Barty had come down to the cove—oh, yes, how glad! There was no question of his dying now, and as for the blow on his forehead, what harm was that to a lad like him?

"But father shall go with you," said Mrs. Gunliffe, when Mally prepared to start for the cove by herself. Mally, however, would not hear of this. She could find her way to the cove whether it was light or dark.

"Mally, thou art my child now, and I shall think of thee so," said the mother, as the girl went off by herself.

Mally thought of this too, as she walked home. How could she become Mrs. Gunliffe's child; ah, how?

I need not, I think, tell the tale any further. That Mally did become Mrs. Gunliffe's child, and how she became so the reader will understand;

and in process of time the big kitchen and all the wonders of the farm-house were her own. The people said that Barty Gunliffe had married a mermaid out of the sea; but when it was said in Mally's hearing I doubt whether she liked it; and when Barty himself would call her a mermaid she would frown at him, and throw about her black hair, and pretend to cuff him with her little hand.

Old Glos was brought up to the top of the cliff, and lived his few remaining days under the roof of Mr. Gunliffe's house; and as for the cove and right of seaweed, from that time forth all that has been supposed to attach itself to Gunliffe's farm, and I do not know that any of the neighbours are prepared to dispute the right.

Although born in Ireland, George Moore (1852–1933) lived most of his adult life in Paris and London. First he studied to be a painter; soon he turned to literature and became a well-known novelist, short-story writer, and critic. He was one of the founders of the celebrated Irish theater, and at one period of his life (1901–1910) lived in Dublin and wrote in Gaelic; through Moore, the influence of major European and Russian writers came to Ireland. For further reading see his novels: Esther Waters *(1894) and* The Lake *(1905);* Hail and Farewell *(1911–1914) is a history of the Irish literary revival. His collection of short stories is* The Untilled Field *(1903).*

GEORGE MOORE

Home Sickness

*H*e told the doctor he was due in the bar-room at eight o'clock in the morning; the bar-room was in a slum in the Bowery; and he had only been able to keep himself in health by getting up at five o'clock and going for long walks in the Central Park.

"A sea voyage is what you want," said the doctor. "Why not go to Ireland for two or three months? You will come back a new man."

"I'd like to see Ireland again."

And then he began to wonder how the people at home were getting on. The doctor was right. He thanked him, and three weeks afterwards he landed in Cork.

As he sat in the railway carriage he recalled his native village—he could see it and its lake, and then the fields one by one, and the roads. He could see a large piece of rocky land—some three or four hundred acres of headland stretching out into the winding lake. Upon this headland the peasantry had been given permission to build their cabins by former owners of the Georgian house standing on the pleasant green hill. The present owners considered the village a disgrace, but the villagers paid high rents for their plots of ground, and all the manual labour that the Big House required came from the village: the gardeners, the stable helpers, the house and the kitchen maids.

He had been thirteen years in America, and when the train stopped at his station, he looked round to see if there were any changes in it. It was just the same blue limestone station-house as it was thirteen years ago. The platform and the sheds were the same, and there were five miles of road from the station to Duncannon. The sea voyage had done him good, but five miles were too far for him to-day; the last time he had walked the road, he had walked it in an hour and a half, carrying a heavy bundle on a stick.

He was sorry he did not feel strong enough for the walk; the evening was fine, and he would meet many people coming home from the fair, some of whom he had known in his youth, and they would tell him where he could get a clean lodging. But the carman would be able to tell him that; he called the car that was waiting at the station, and soon he was answering questions about America. But Bryden wanted to hear of those who were still living in the old country, and after hearing the stories of many people he had forgotten, he heard that Mike Scully, who had been away in a situation for many years as a coachman in the King's County, had come back and built a fine house with a concrete floor. Now there was a good loft in Mike Scully's house, and Mike would be pleased to take in a lodger.

Bryden remembered that Mike had been in a situation at the Big House; he had intended to be a jockey, but had suddenly shot up into a fine tall man, and had had to become a coachman instead. Bryden tried to recall the face, but he could only remember a straight nose, and a somewhat dusky complexion. Mike was one of the heroes of his childhood, and his youth floated before him, and he caught glimpses of himself, something that was more than a phantom and less than a reality. Suddenly his reverie was broken: the carman pointed with his whip, and Bryden saw a tall, finely-built, middle-aged man coming through the gates, and the driver said:—

"There's Mike Scully."

Mike had forgotten Bryden even more completely than Bryden had forgotten him, and many aunts and uncles were mentioned before he began to understand.

"You've grown into a fine man, James," he said, looking at Bryden's great width of chest. "But you are thin in the cheeks, and you're sallow in the cheeks too."

"I haven't been very well lately—that is one of the reasons I have come back; but I want to see you all again."

Bryden paid the carman, wished him "God-speed," and he and Mike divided the luggage between them, Mike carrying the bag and Bryden the bundle, and they walked round the lake, for the townland was at the back of the demesne; and while they walked, James proposed to pay Mike ten shillings a week for his board and lodging.

He remembered the woods thick and well-frosted; now they were wind-worn, the drains were choked, and the bridge leading across the lake inlet was falling away. Their way led between long fields where herds of cattle were grazing; the road was broken—Bryden wondered how the villagers drove their carts over it, and Mike told him that the landlord could not keep it in repair, and he would not allow it to be kept in repair out of the rates, for then it would be a public road, and he did not think there should be a public road through his property.

At the end of many fields they came to the village, and it looked a desolate place, even on this fine evening, and Bryden remarked that the county did not seem to be as much lived in as it used to be. It was at once strange and familiar to see the chickens in the kitchen; and, wishing to re-knit himself to the old habits, he begged of Mrs. Scully not to drive them out, saying he did not mind them. Mike told his wife that Bryden was born in Duncannon, and when he mentioned Bryden's name she gave him her hand, after wiping it in her apron, saying he was heartily welcome, only she was afraid he would not care to sleep in a loft.

"Why wouldn't I sleep in a loft, a dry loft! You're thinking a good deal of America over here," said he, "but I reckon it isn't all you think it. Here you work when you like and you sit down when you like; but when you have had a touch of blood-poisoning as I had, and when you have seen young people walking with a stick, you think that there is something to be said for old Ireland."

"Now won't you be taking a sup of milk? You'll be wanting a drink after travelling," said Mrs. Scully.

And when he had drunk the milk Mike asked him if he would like to go inside or if he would like to go for a walk.

"Maybe it is sitting down you would like to be."

And they went into the cabin, and started to talk about the wages a man could get in America, and the long hours of work.

And after Bryden had told Mike everything about America that he thought would interest him, he asked Mike about Ireland. But Mike did not seem to be able to tell him much that was of interest. They were all very poor—poorer, perhaps, than when he left them.

"I don't think anyone except myself has a five pound note to his name."

Bryden hoped he felt sufficiently sorry for Mike. But after all Mike's life and prospects mattered little to him. He had come back in search of health; and he felt better already; the milk had done him good, and the bacon and cabbage in the pot sent forth a savoury odour. The Scullys were very kind, they pressed him to make a good meal; a few weeks of country air and food, they said, would give him back the health he had lost in the Bowery; and when Bryden said he was longing for a smoke, Mike said there was no better sign than that. During his long illness he had never wanted to smoke, and he was a confirmed smoker.

It was comfortable to sit by the mild peat fire watching the smoke of their pipes drifting up the chimney, and all Bryden wanted was to be let alone; he did not want to hear of anyone's misfortunes, but about nine o'clock a number of villagers came in, and their appearance was depressing. Bryden remembered one or two of them—he used to know them very well when he was a boy; their talk was as depressing as their appearance, and he could feel no interest whatever in them. He was not moved when he heard that Higgins the stone-mason was dead; he was not affected when he heard that Mary Kelly, who used to go to do the laundry at the Big House, had married; he was only interested when he heard she had gone to America. No, he had not met her there, America is a big place. Then one of the peasants asked him if he remembered Patsy Carabine, who used to do the gardening at the Big House. Yes, he remembered Patsy well. Patsy was in the poor-house. He had not been able to do any work on account of his arm; his house had fallen in; he had given up his holding and gone into the poor-house. All this was very sad, and to avoid hearing any further unpleasantness, Bryden began to tell them about America. And they sat round listening to him; but all the talking was on his side; he wearied of it; and looking round the group he recognised a ragged hunchback, and, turning to him, Bryden asked him if he were doing well with his five acres.

"Ah, not much. This has been a bad season. The potatoes failed; they were watery—there is no diet in them."

These peasants were all agreed that they could make nothing out of their farms. Their regret was that they had not gone to America when they were young; and after striving to take an interest in the fact that O'Connor had lost a mare and foal worth forty pounds Bryden began to wish himself back in the slum. And when they left the house he wondered if every evening would be like the present one. Mike piled fresh sods on the fire, and he hoped it would show enough light in the loft for Bryden to undress himself by.

The cackling of some geese in the road kept him awake, and the loneliness of the country seemed to penetrate to his bones, and to freeze the marrow in them. There was a bat in the loft—a dog howled in the distance—and then he drew the clothes over his head. Never had he been so unhappy, and the sound of Mike breathing by his wife's side in the kitchen added to his nervous terror. Then he dozed a little; and lying on his back he dreamed he was awake, and the men he had seen sitting round the fireside that evening seemed to him like spectres come out of some unknown region of morass and reedy tarn. He stretched out his hands for his clothes, determined to fly from this house, but remembering the lonely road that led to the station he fell back on his pillow. The geese still cackled, but he was too tired to be kept awake any longer. He seemed to have been asleep only a few minutes when he heard Mike calling him. Mike had come half way up the ladder and was telling him that breakfast was ready. "What kind of breakfast will he give me?" Bryden asked himself as he pulled on his clothes. There were tea and hot griddle cakes for breakfast, and there were fresh eggs; there was sunlight in the kitchen and he liked to hear Mike tell of the work he was going to do in the fields. Mike rented a farm of about fifteen acres, at least ten of it was grass; he grew an acre of potatoes and some corn, and some turnips for his sheep. He had a nice bit of meadow, and he took down his scythe, and as he put the whetstone in his belt Bryden noticed a second scythe, and he asked Mike if he should go down with him and help him to finish the field.

"You haven't done any mowing this many a year; I don't think you'd be of much help. You'd better go for a walk by the lake, but you may come in the afternoon if you like and help to turn the grass over."

Bryden was afraid he would find the lake shore very lonely, but the magic of returning health is the sufficient distraction for the convalescent, and the morning passed agreeably. The weather was still and sunny. He could hear the ducks in the reeds. The hours dreamed themselves away, and it became his habit to go to the lake every morning. One morning he met the landlord, and they walked together, talking of the country, of what it had been, and the ruin it was slipping into. James Bryden told him that ill health had brought him back to Ireland; and the landlord lent him his boat, and Bryden rowed about the islands, and resting upon his oars he looked at the old castles, and remembered the pre-historic raiders that the landlord had told him about. He came across the stones to which the lake dwellers had tied their boats, and these signs of ancient Ireland were pleasing to Bryden in his present mood.

As well as the great lake there was a smaller lake in the bog where the villagers cut their turf. This lake was famous for its pike, and the landlord allowed Bryden to fish there, and one evening when he was looking for a frog with which to bait his line he met Margaret Dirken driving home the cows for the milking. Margaret was the herdsman's daughter, and she lived in a cottage near the Big House; but she came up to the village whenever there was a dance, and Bryden had found himself opposite to her in the reels. But until this evening he had had little opportunity of speaking to her, and he was glad to speak to someone, for the evening was lonely, and they stood talking together.

"You're getting your health again," she said. "You'll soon be leaving us."

"I'm in no hurry."

"You're grand people over there; I hear a man is paid four dollars a day for his work."

"And how much," said James, "has he to pay for his food and for his clothes?"

Her cheeks were bright and her teeth small, white and beautifully even; and a woman's soul looked at Bryden out of her soft Irish eyes. He was troubled and turned aside, and catching sight of a frog looking at him out of a tuft of grass he said:—

"I have been looking for a frog to put upon my pike line."

The frog jumped right and left, and nearly escaped in some bushes, but he caught it and returned with it in his hand.

"It is just the kind of frog a pike will like," he said. "Look at its great white belly and its bright yellow back."

And without more ado he pushed the wire to which the hook was fastened through the frog's fresh body, and dragging it through the mouth he passed the hooks through the hind legs and tied the line to the end of the wire.

"I think," said Margaret, "I must be looking after my cows; it's time I got them home."

"Won't you come down to the lake while I set my line?"

She thought for a moment and said:—

"No, I'll see you from here."

He went down to the reedy tarn, and at his approach several snipe got up, and they flew above his head uttering sharp cries. His fishing-rod was a long hazel stick, and he threw the frog as far as he could into the lake. In doing this he roused some wild ducks; a mallard and two ducks got up, and they flew towards the larger lake. Margaret watched them; they flew in a line with an old castle; and they had not disappeared from view when Bryden came towards her, and he and she drove the cows home together that evening.

They had not met very often when she said, "James, you had better not come here so often calling to me."

"Don't you wish me to come?"

"Yes, I wish you to come well enough, but keeping company is not the custom of the country, and I don't want to be talked about."

"Are you afraid the priest would speak against us from the altar?"

"He has spoken against keeping company, but it is not so much what the priest says, for there is no harm in talking."

"But if you are going to be married there is no harm in walking out together."

"Well, not so much, but marriages are made differently in these parts; there is not much courting here."

And the next day it was known in the village that James was going to marry Margaret Dirken.

His desire to excel the boys in dancing had aroused much gaiety in the parish, and for some time past there had been dancing in every house where there was a floor fit to dance upon; and if the cottager had no money to pay for a barrel of beer, James Bryden, who had money, sent him a barrel, so that Margaret might get her dance. She told him that they sometimes crossed over into another parish where the priest was not so adverse to dancing, and James wondered. And next morning at Mass he wondered at their simple fervour. Some of them held their hands above their heads as they prayed, and all this was very new and very old to James Bryden. But the obedience of these people to their priest surprised him. When he was a lad they had not been so obedient, or he had forgotten their obedience; and he listened in mixed anger and wonderment to the priest who was scolding his parishioners, speaking to them by name, saying that he had heard there was dancing going on in their homes. Worse than that, he said he had seen boys and girls loitering about the roads, and the talk that went on was of one kind—love. He said that newspapers containing love-stories were finding their way into the people's houses, stories about love, in which there was nothing elevating or ennobling. The people listened, accepting the priest's opinion without question. And their submission was pathetic. It was the submission of a primitive people clinging to religious authority, and Bryden contrasted the weakness and incompetence of the people about him with the modern restlessness and cold energy of the people he had left behind him.

One evening, as they were dancing, a knock came to the door, and the piper stopped playing, and the dancers whispered:—

"Some one has told on us; it is the priest."

And the awe-stricken villagers crowded round the cottage fire, afraid to open the door. But the priest said that if they did not open the door he would put his shoulder to it and force it open. Bryden went towards the door, saying he would allow no one to threaten him, priest or no priest, but Margaret caught his arm and told him that if he said anything to the priest, the priest would speak against them from the altar, and they would be shunned by the neighbours. It was Mike Scully who went to the door and let the priest in, and he came in saying they were dancing their souls into hell.

"I've heard of your goings on," he said—"of your beer-drinking and dancing. I will not have it in my parish. If you want that sort of thing you had better go to America."

"If that is intended for me, sir, I will go back tomorrow. Margaret can follow."

"It isn't the dancing, it's the drinking I'm opposed to," said the priest, turning to Bryden.

"Well, no one has drunk too much, sir," said Bryden.

"But you'll sit here drinking all night," and the priest's eyes went towards the corner where the women had gathered, and Bryden felt that the priest looked on the women as more dangerous than the porter.

"It's after midnight," he said, taking out his watch.

By Bryden's watch it was only half-past eleven, and while they were arguing about the time Mrs. Scully offered Byrden's umbrella to the priest, for in his hurry to stop the dancing the priest had gone out without his; and, as if to show Bryden that he bore him no ill-will, the priest accepted the loan of the umbrella, for he was thinking of the big marriage fee that Bryden would pay him.

"I shall be badly off for the umbrella to-morrow," Bryden said, as soon as the priest was out of the house. He was going with his father-in-law to a fair. His father-in-law was learning him how to buy and sell cattle. And his father-in-law was saying that the country was mending, and that a man might become rich in Ireland if he only had a little capital. Bryden had the capital, and Margaret had an uncle on the other side of the lake who would leave her all he had, that would be fifty pounds, and never in the village of Duncannon had a young couple begun life with so much prospect of success as would James Bryden and Margaret Dirken.

Some time after Christmas was spoken of as the best time for the marriage; James Bryden said that he would not be able to get his money out of America before the spring. The delay seemed to vex him, and he seemed anxious to be married, until one day he received a letter from America, from a man who had served in the bar with him. This friend wrote to ask Bryden if he were coming back. The letter was no more than a passing wish to see Bryden again. Yet Bryden stood looking at it, and everyone wondered what could be in the letter. It seemed momentous, and they hardly believed him when he said it was from a friend who wanted to know if his health were better. He tried to forget the letter, and he looked at the worn fields, divided by walls of loose stones, and a great longing came upon him.

The smell of the Bowery slum had come across the Atlantic, and had found him out in this western headland; and one night he awoke from a dream in which he was hurling some drunken customer through the open doors into the darkness. He had seen his friend in his white duck jacket throwing drink from glass into glass amid the din of voices and strange accents; he had heard the clang of money as it was swept into the till, and his sense sickened for the bar-room. But how should he tell Margaret Dirksen that he could not marry her? She had built her life upon this marriage. He could not tell her that he would not marry her . . . yet he must go. He felt as if he were being hunted; the thought that he must tell Margaret that he could not marry her hunted him day after day as a weasel hunts a rabbit. Again and again he went to meet her with the intention of telling her that he did not love her, that their lives were not for one another, that it had all been a mistake, and that happily he had found out it was a mistake soon enough. But Margaret, as if she guessed what he was about to speak of, threw her arms about him and begged him to say he loved her, and that they would be married at once. He agreed that he loved her, and that they would be married at once. But he had not left her many minutes before the feeling came upon him that he could not marry her—that he must go away. The smell of the bar-room hunted him down. Was it for the sake of the money that he might make there that he wished to go back? No, it was not the money. What then? His eyes fell on the bleak country, on the little fields divided by bleak walls; he remembered the pathetic ignorance of the people, and it was these things he could not endure. It was the priest who came to forbid the dancing. Yes, it was the priest. As he stood looking at the line of the hills the bar-room seemed by him. He heard the politicians, and the excitement of politics was in his blood again. He must go away from this place—he must get back to the bar-room. Looking up he saw the scanty orchard, and he hated the spare road that led to the village, and he hated the little hill at the top of which the village began, and he hated more than all other places the house where he was to live with Margaret Dirken—if he married her. He could see it from where he stood—by the edge of the lake, with twenty acres of pasture land about it, for the landlord had given up part of his demesne land to them.

He caught sight of Margaret, and he called to her to come through the stile.

"I have just had a letter from America."

"About the money?" she asked.

"Yes, about the money. But I shall have to go over there."

He stood looking at her, seeking for words; and she guessed from his embarrassment that he would say to her that he must go to America before they were married.

"Do you mean, James, you will have to go at once?"

"Yes," he said, "at once. But I shall come back in time to be married in August. It will only mean delaying our marriage a month."

They walked a little way talking; every step he took James felt that he was a step nearer the Bowery slum. And when they came to the gate Bryden said:—

"I must hasten or I shall miss the train."

"But," she said, "you are not going now—you are not going to-day?"

"Yes, this morning. It is seven miles. I shall have to hurry not to miss the train."

And then she asked him if he would ever come back.

"Yes," he said, "I am coming back."

"If you are coming back, James, why not let me go with you?"

"You could not walk fast enough. We should miss the train."

"One moment, James. Don't make me suffer; tell me the truth. You are not coming back. Your clothes—where shall I send them?"

He hurried away, hoping he would come back. He tried to think that he liked the country he was leaving, that it would be better to have a farmhouse and live there with Margaret Dirken than to serve drinks behind a counter in the Bowery. He did not think he was telling her a lie when he said he was coming back. Her offer to forward his clothes touched his heart, and at the end of the road he stood and asked himself if he should go back to her. He would miss the train if he waited another minute, and he ran on. And he would have missed the train if he had not met a car. Once he was on the car he felt himself safe—the country was already behind him. The train and the boat at Cork were mere formulae; he was already in America.

The moment he landed he felt the thrill of home that he had not found in his native village, and he wondered how it was that the smell of the bar seemed more natural than the smell of the fields, and the roar of crowds more welcome than the silence of the lake's edge. However, he offered up a thanksgiving for his escape, and entered into negotiations for the purchase of the bar-room.

He took a wife, she bore him sons and daughters, the bar-room prospered, property came and went; he grew old, his wife died, he retired from business, and reached the age when a man begins to feel there are not many years in front of him, and that all he has had to do in life has been done. His children married, lonesomeness began to creep about him; in the evening, when he looked into the fire-light, a vague, tender reverie floated up, and Margaret's soft eyes and name vivified the dusk. His wife and children passed out of mind, and it seemed to him that a memory was the only real thing he possessed, and the desire to see Margaret again grew intense. But she was an old woman, she had married, maybe she was dead. Well, he would like to be buried in the village where he was born.

There is an unchanging, silent life within every man that none knows but himself, and his unchanging, silent life was his memory of Margaret Dirken. The bar-room was forgotten and all that concerned it, and the things he saw most clearly were the green hillside, and the bog lake and the rushes about it, and the greater lake in the distance, and behind it the blue lines of wandering hills.

*Arthur Conan Doyle (1859–1930) was born in Edin-
burgh, Scotland, and studied medicine in Scotland
and at Stonyhurst College, England. While practicing medicine at Southsea, he began to write. With
the publication of* A Study in Scarlet *(1887), Doyle
introduced Sherlock Holmes, a free-lance detective
with amazing powers of deduction, who became one
of the most widely known characters in modern fiction. Eventually Doyle became bored with his protagonist and devised Holmes's "death" in 1893. Because
of public demand, however, the author restored the
detective to further fictional life. For further reading:*
The Adventures of Sherlock Holmes *(1891).*

ARTHUR CONAN DOYLE

The Musgrave Ritual

*A*n anomaly which often struck me in the character of my friend Sherlock Holmes was that, although in his methods of thought he was the neatest and most methodical of mankind, and although also he affected a certain quiet primness of dress, he was none the less in his personal habits one
of the most untidy men that ever drove a fellow-lodger to distraction. Not
that I am in the least conventional in that respect myself. The rough-and-
tumble work in Afghanistan, coming on the top of a natural Bohemianism
of disposition, has made me rather more lax than befits a medical man. But
with me there is a limit, and when I find a man who keeps his cigars in the
coal-scuttle, his tobacco in the toe end of a Persian slipper, and his unan-
swered correspondence transfixed by a jack-knife into the very centre of his
wooden mantelpiece, then I begin to give myself virtuous airs. I have always
held, too, that pistol practice should distinctly be an open-air pastime; and
when Holmes in one of his queer humours would sit in an arm-chair, with
his hair-trigger and a hundred Boxer cartridges, and proceed to adorn the
opposite wall with a patriotic V.R. done in bullet-pocks, I felt strongly that
neither the atmosphere nor the appearance of our room was improved by it.

Our chambers were always full of chemicals and of criminal relics,
which had a way of wandering into unlikely positions, and of turning up in
the butterdish, or in even less desirable places. But his papers were my great

crux. He had a horror of destroying documents, especially those which were connected with his past cases, and yet it was only once in every year or two that he would muster energy to docket and arrange them, for as I have mentioned somewhere in these incoherent memoirs, the outbursts of passionate energy when he performed the remarkable feats with which his name is associated were followed by reactions of lethargy, during which he would lie about with his violin and his books, hardly moving, save from the sofa to the table. Thus month after month his papers accumulated, until every corner of the room was stacked with bundles of manuscript which were on no account to be burned, and which could not be put away save by their owner.

One winter's night, as we sat together by the fire, I ventured to suggest to him that as he had finished pasting extracts into his commonplace book he might employ the next two hours in making our room a little more habitable. He could not deny the justice of my request, so with a rather rueful face he went off to his bedroom, from which he returned presently pulling a large tin box behind him. This he placed in the middle of the floor, and squatting down upon a stool in front of it he threw back the lid. I could see that it was already a third full of bundles of paper tied up with red tape into separate packages.

"There are cases enough here, Watson," said he, looking at me with mischievous eyes. "I think that if you knew all that I had in this box you would ask me to pull some out instead of putting others in."

"These are the records of your early work, then?" I asked. "I have often wished that I had notes of those cases."

"Yes, my boy; these were all done prematurely, before my biographer had come to glorify me." he lifted bundle after bundle in a tender, caressing sort of way. "They are not all successes, Watson," said he, "but there are some pretty little problems among them. Here's the record of the Tarleton murders, and the case of Vamberry, the wine merchant, and the adventure of the old Russian woman, and the singular affair of the aluminium crutch, as well as a full account of Ricoletti of the club foot and his abominable wife. And here—ah, now! this really is something a little *recherché*."

He dived his arm down to the bottom of the chest, and brought up a small wooden box, with a sliding lid, such as children's toys are kept in. From within he produced a crumpled piece of paper, an old-fashioned brass key, a peg of wood with a ball of string attached to it, and three rusty old discs of metal.

"Well, my boy, what do you make of this lot?" he asked, smiling at my expression.

"It is a curious collection."

"Very curious, and the story that hangs round it will strike you as being more curious still."

"These relics have a history, then?"

"So much so that they *are* history."

"What do you mean by that?"

Sherlock Holmes picked them up one by one, and laid them along the edge of the table. Then he reseated himself in his chair, and looked them over with a gleam of satisfaction in his eyes.

"These," said he, "are all that I have left to remind me of the episode of the Musgrave Ritual."

I had heard him mention the case more than once, though I had never been able to gather the details.

"I should be so glad, " said I, "if you would give me an account of it."

"And leave the litter as it is?" he cried mischievously. "Your tidiness won't bear much strain, after all, Watson. But I should be glad that you should add this case to your annals, for there are points in it which make it quite unique in the criminal records of this or, I believe, of any other country. A collection of my trifling achievements would certainly be incomplete which contained no account of this very singular business.

"You may remember how the affair of the *Gloria Scott,* and my conversation with the unhappy man, whose fate I told you of, first turned my attention in the direction of the profession which has become my life's work. You see me now when my name has become known far and wide, and when I am generally recognised both by the public and by the official force as being a final court of appeal in doubtful cases. Even when you knew me first, at the time of the affair which you have commemorated in 'A Study in Scarlet,' I had already established a considerable, though not a very lucrative, connection. You can hardly realise, then, how difficult I found it at first, and how long I had to wait before I succeeded in making any headway.

"When I first came up to London I had rooms in Montague Street, just round the corner from the British Museum, and there I waited, filling in my too abundant leisure time by studying all those branches of science which might make me more efficient. Now and again cases came in my way, principally through the introduction of old fellow students, for during my last years at the university there was a good deal of talk there about myself and my methods. The third of these cases was that of the Musgrave Ritual, and it is to the interest which was aroused by that singular chain of events, and the large issues which proved to be at stake, that I trace my first stride towards the position which I now hold.

"Reginald Musgrave had been in the same college as myself, and I had some slight acquaintance with him. He was not generally popular among the undergraduates, though it always seemed to me that what was set down as pride was really an attempt to cover extreme natural diffidence. In appearance he was a man of an exceedingly aristocratic type, thin, high-nosed, and large-eyed, with languid and yet courtly manners. He was indeed a scion of one of the very oldest families in the kingdom, though his branch was a cadet one which had separated from the Northern Musgraves some time in the sixteenth century, and had established itself in western Sussex, where the manor house of Hurlstone is perhaps the oldest inhabited building in the county. Something of his birthplace seemed to cling to the man, and I never looked at his pale, keen face, or the poise of his head, without associating him with grey archways and mullioned windows and all the venerable wreckage of a feudal keep. Now and again we drifted into talk, and I can remember that more than once he expressed a keen interest in my methods of observation and inference.

"For four years I had seen nothing of him, until one morning he walked into my room in Montague Street. He had changed little, was dressed like a young man of fashion—he was always a bit of a dandy—and preserved the same quiet, suave manner which had formerly distinguished him.

" 'How has all gone with you, Musgrave?' I asked, after we had cordially shaken hands.

" 'You probably heard of my poor father's death,' said he. 'He was carried off about two years ago. Since then I have, of course, had the Hurlstone estates to manage, and as I am member for my district as well, my life has been a busy one; but I understand, Holmes, that you are turning to practical ends those powers with which you used to amaze us.'

" 'Yes,' said I, 'I have taken to living by my wits.'

" 'I am delighted to hear it, for your advice at present would be exceedingly valuable to me. We have had some very strange doings at Hurlstone, and the police have been able to throw no light upon the matter. It is really the most extraordinary and inexplicable business.'

"You can imagine with what eagerness I listened to him, Watson, for the very chance for which I had been panting during all those months of inaction seemed to have come within my reach. In my inmost heart I believed that I could succeed where others failed, and now I had the opportunity to test myself.

" 'Pray let me have the details,' I cried.

"Reginald Musgrave sat down opposite to me, and lit the cigarette which I had pushed towards him.

" 'You must know,' said he, 'that though I am a bachelor I have to keep up a considerable staff of servants at Hurlstone, for it is a rambling old place, and takes a good deal of looking after. I preserve, too, and in the pheasant months I usually have a house party, so that it would not do to be shorthanded. Altogether there are eight maids, the cook, the butler, two footmen, and a boy. The garden and the stables, of course, have a separate staff.

" 'Of these servants the one who had been longest in our service was

Brunton, the butler. He was a young schoolmaster out of place when he was first taken up by my father, but he was a man of great energy and character, and he soon became quite invaluable in the household. He was a well-grown, handsome man, with a splendid forehead, and though he has been with us for twenty years he cannot be more than forty now. With his personal advantages and his extraordinary gifts, for he can speak several languages and play nearly every musical instrument, it is wonderful that he should have been satisfied so long in such a position, but I suppose that he was comfortable and lacked energy to make any change. The butler of Hurlstone is always a thing that is remembered by all who visit us.

" 'But this paragon has one fault. He is a bit of a Don Juan, and you can imagine that for a man like him it is not a very difficult part to play in a quiet country district.

" 'When he was married it was all right, but since he has been a widower we have had no end of trouble with him. A few months ago we were in hopes that he was about to settle down again, for he became engaged to Rachel Howells, our second housemaid, but he has thrown her over since then and taken up with Janet Tregellis, the daughter of the head gamekeeper. Rachel, who is a very good girl, but of an excitable Welsh temperament, had a sharp touch of brain fever, and goes about the house now—or did until yesterday—like a black-eyed shadow of her former self. That was our first drama at Hurlstone, but a second one came to drive it from our minds, and it was prefaced by the disgrace and dismissal of butler Brunton.

" 'This is how it came about. I have said that the man was intelligent, and this very intelligence has caused his ruin, for it seems to have led to an insatiable curiosity about things which did not in the least concern him. I had no idea of the lengths to which this would carry him until the merest accident opened my eyes to it.

" 'I have said that the house is a rambling one. One night last week—on Thursday night, to be more exact—I found that I could not sleep, having foolishly taken a cup of strong *café noir* after my dinner. After struggling against it until two in the morning I felt that it was quite hopeless, so I rose and lit the candle with the intention of continuing a novel which I was reading. The book, however, had been left in the billard-room, so I pulled on my dressing-gown and started off to get it.

" 'In order to reach the billiard-room I had to descend a flight of stairs, and then to cross the head of the passage which led to the library and the gun-room. You can imagine my surprise when as I looked down this corridor I saw a glimmer of light coming from the open door of the library. I had myself extinguished the lamp and closed the door before coming to bed. Naturally, my first thought was of burglars. The corridors at Hurlstone have their walls largely decorated with trophies of old weapons. From one of these I picked a battle-axe, and then, leaving my candle behind me, I crept on tip-toe down the passage and peeped in at the open door.

" 'Brunton, the butler, was in the library. He was sitting, fully dressed, in an easy chair, with a slip of paper, which looked like a map, upon his knee, and his forehead sunk forward upon his hand in deep thought. I stood, dumb with astonishment, watching him from the darkness. A small taper on the edge of the table shed a feeble light, which sufficed to show me that he was fully dressed. Suddenly, as I looked, he rose from his chair, and walking over to a bureau at the side, he unlocked it and drew out one of the drawers. From this he took a paper, and, returning to his seat, he flattened it out beside the taper on the edge of the table, and began to study it with minute attention. My indignation at this calm examination of our family documents overcame me so far that I took a step forward, and Brunton, looking up, saw me standing in the doorway. He sprang to his feet, his face turned livid with fear, and he thrust into his breast the chart-like paper which he had been originally studying.

" 'So!' said I, 'this is how you repay the trust which we have reposed in you! You will leave my service to-morrow.'

" 'He bowed with the look of a man who is utterly crushed, and slunk past me without a word. The taper was still on the table, and by its light I glanced to see what the paper was which Brunton had taken from the bureau. To my surprise it was nothing of any importance at all, but simply a copy of the questions and answers in the singular old observance called the Musgrave Ritual. It is a sort of ceremony peculiar to our family, which each Musgrave for centuries past has gone through upon his coming of age—a thing of private interest, and perhaps of some little importance to the archæologist, like our own blazonings and charges, but of no practical use whatever.'

" 'We had better come back to the paper afterwards,' said I.

" 'If you think it really necessary,' he answered, with some hesitation. 'To continue my statement, however, I re-locked the bureau, using the key which Brunton had left, and I had turned to go, when I was surprised to find that the butler had returned and was standing before me.

" 'Mr. Musgrave, sir,' he cried, in a voice which was hoarse with emotion, 'I can't bear disgrace, sir. I've always been proud above my station in life, and disgrace would kill me. My blood will be on your head, sir—it will, indeed—if you drive me to despair. If you cannot keep me after what has passed, then for God's sake let me give you notice and leave in a month, as if of my own free will. I could stand that, Mr. Musgrave, but not to be cast out before all the folk that I know so well.'

" 'You don't deserve much consideration, Brunton,' I answered. 'Your conduct has been most infamous. However, as you have been a long time in the family, I have no wish to bring public disgrace upon you. A month, however, is too long. Take yourself away in a week, and give what reason you like for going.'

" 'Only a week, sir?' he cried in a despairing voice. 'A fortnight—say at least a fortnight.'

" 'A week,' I repeated, 'and you may consider yourself to have been very leniently dealt with.'

" 'He crept away, his face sunk upon his breast, like a broken man, while I put out the light and returned to my room.

" 'For two days after this Brunton was most assiduous in his attention to his duties. I made no allusion to what had passed, and waited with some curiosity to see how he would cover his disgrace. On the third morning, however, he did not appear, as was his custom, after breakfast to receive my instructions for the day. As I left the dining-room I happened to meet Rachel Howells, the maid. I have told you that she had only recently recovered from an illness, and was looking so wretchedly pale and wan that I remonstrated with her for being at work.

" 'You should be in bed,' I said. 'Come back to your duties when you are stronger.'

" 'She looked at me with so strange an expression that I began to suspect that her brain was affected.

" 'I am strong enough, Mr. Musgrave,' said she.

" 'We will see what the doctor says,' I answered. 'You must stop work now, and when you go downstairs just say that I wish to see Brunton.'

" 'The butler is gone,' said she.

" 'Gone! Gone where?'

" 'He is gone. No one has seen him. He is not in his room. Oh, yes, he is gone—he is gone!' She fell back against the wall with shriek after shriek of laughter, while I, horrified at this sudden hysterical attack, rushed to the bell to summon help. The girl was taken to her room, still screaming and sobbing, while I made inquiries about Brunton. There was no doubt about it that he had disappeared. His bed had not been slept in; he had been seen by no one since he had retired to his room the night before; and yet it was difficult to see how he could have left the house, as both windows and doors were found to be fastened in the morning. His clothes, his watch, and even his money were in his room—but the black suit which he usually wore was missing. His slippers, too, were gone, but his boots were left behind. Where, then, could butler Brunton have gone in the night, and what could have become of him now?

" 'Of course we searched the house from cellar to garret, but there was no trace of him. It is as I have said a labyrinth of an old house, especially the original wing, which is now practically uninhabited, but we ransacked every room and attic without discovering the least sign of the missing man. It was incredible to me that he could have gone away leaving all his property behind him, and yet where could he be? I called in the local police, but without success. Rain had fallen on the night before, and we examined the lawn and the paths all round the house, but in vain. Matters were in this state when a new development quite drew our attention away from the original mystery.

" 'For two days Rachel Howells had been so ill, sometimes delirious, sometimes hysterical, that a nurse had been employed to sit up with her at night. On the third night after Brunton's disappearance, the nurse, finding her patient sleeping nicely, had dropped into a nap in the arm-chair, when she woke in the early morning to find the bed empty, the window open, and no signs of the invalid. I was instantly aroused, and with the two footmen started off at once in search of the missing girl. It was not difficult to tell the direction which she had taken, for, starting from under her window, we could follow her footmarks easily across the lawn to the edge of the mere, where they vanished, close to the gravel path which leads out of the grounds. The lake there is eight feet deep, and you can imagine our feelings when we saw that the trail of the poor demented girl came to an end at the edge of it.

" 'Of course, we had the drags at once, and set to work to recover the remains; but no trace of the body could we find. On the other hand, we brought to the surface an object of a most unexpected kind. It was a linen bag, which contained within it a mass of old rusted and discoloured metal and several dull-coloured pieces of pebble or glass. This strange find was all that we could get from the mere, and although we made every possible search and inquiry yesterday, we know nothing of the fate either of Rachel Howells or Richard Brunton. The county police are at their wits' end, and I have come up to you as a last resource.'

"You can imagine, Watson, with what eagerness I listened to this extraordinary sequence of events, and endeavoured to piece them together, and to devise some common thread upon which they might all hang.

"The butler was gone. The maid was gone. The maid had loved the butler, but had afterwards had cause to hate him. She was of Welsh blood, fiery and passionate. She had been terribly excited immediately after his disappearance. She had flung into the lake a bag containing some curious contents. These were all factors which had to be taken into consideration, and yet none of them got quite to the heart of the matter. What was the starting-point of this chain of events? There lay the end of this tangled line.

" 'I must see that paper, Musgrave,' said I, 'which this butler of yours thought it worth his while to consult, even at the risk of the loss of his place.'

" 'It is rather an absurd business, this Ritual of ours,' he answered, 'but it has at least the saving grace of antiquity to excuse it. I have a copy of the questions and answers here, if you care to run your eye over them.'

"He handed me the very paper which I have here, Watson, and this is the strange catechism to which each Musgrave had to submit when he came to man's estate. I will read you the questions and answers as they stand:

" 'Whose was it?

" 'His who is gone.

" 'Who shall have it?

" 'He who will come.

" 'What was the month?

" 'The sixth from the first.

" 'Where was the sun?

" 'Over the oak.

" 'Where was the shadow?

" 'Under the elm.

" 'How was it stepped?

" 'North by ten and by ten, east by five and by five, south by two and by two, west by one and by one, and so under.

" 'What shall we give for it?

" 'All that is ours.

" 'Why should we give it?

" 'For the sake of the crust.'

" 'The original has no date, but is in the spelling of the middle of the seventeenth century,' remarked Musgrave. 'I am afraid, however, that it can be of little help to you in solving this mystery.'

" 'At least,' said I, 'it gives us another mystery, and one which is even more interesting than the first. It may be that the solution of the one may prove to be the solution of the other. You will excuse me, Musgrave, if I say that your butler appears to me to have been a very clever man, and to have had a clearer insight than ten generations of his masters.'

" 'I hardly follow you,' said Musgrave. 'The paper seems to me of no practical importance.'

" 'But to me it seems immensely practical, and I fancy that Brunton took the same view. He had probably seen it before that night on which you caught him.'

" 'It is very possible. We took no pains to hide it.'

" 'He simply wished, I should imagine, to refresh his memory upon that last occasion. He had, as I understand, some sort of map or chart which he was comparing with the manuscript, and which he thrust into his pocket when you appeared?'

" 'That is true. But what could he have to do with this old family custom of ours, and what does this rigmarole mean?'

" 'I don't think that we should have much difficulty in determining that,' said I. 'With your permission we will take the first train down to Sussex and go a little more deeply into the matter upon the spot.'

"The same afternoon saw us both at Hurlstone. Possibly you have seen

pictures and read descriptions of the famous old building, so I will confine
my account of it to saying that it is built in the shape of an L, the long arm
being the more modern portion, and the shorter the ancient nucleus from
which the other has developed. Over the low, heavy-lintelled door, in the
centre of this old part, is chiselled the date 1607, but experts are agreed that
the beams and stone-work are really much older than this. The enormously
thick walls and tiny windows of this part had in the last century driven the
family into building the new wing, and the old one was used now as a
storehouse and a cellar when it was used at all. A splendid park, with fine
old timber, surrounded the house, and the lake, to which my client had
referred, lay close to the avenue, about two hundred yards from the building.

"I was already firmly convinced, Watson, that there were not three
separate mysteries here, but one only, and that if I could read the Musgrave
Ritual aright, I should hold in my hand the clue which would lead me to the
truth concerning both the butler Brunton, and the maid Howells. To that,
then, I turned all my energies. Why should this servant be so anxious to
master this old formula? Evidently because he saw something in it which
had escaped all those generations of country squires, and from which he
expected some personal advantage. What was it, then, and how had it affected his fate?

"It was perfectly obvious to me on reading the Ritual that the measurements must refer to some spot to which the rest of the document alluded,
and that if we could find that spot we should be in a fair way towards
knowing what the secret was which the old Musgraves had thought it necessary to embalm in so curious a fashion. There were two guides given us to
start with, an oak and an elm. As to the oak, there could be no question at
all. Right in front of the house, upon the left-hand side of the drive, there
stood a patriarch among oaks, one of the most magnificent trees that I have
ever seen.

" 'That was there when your Ritual was drawn up?' said I, as we drove
past it.

" 'It was there at the Norman Conquest, in all probability,' he answered. 'It has a girth of 23 ft.'

"Here was one of my fixed points secured.

" 'Have you any old elms?' I asked.

" 'There used to be a very old one over yonder, but it was struck by
lightning ten years ago, and we cut down the stump.'

" 'You can see where it used to be?'

" 'Oh, yes.'

" 'There are no other elms?'

" 'No old ones, but plenty of beeches.'

" 'I should like to see where it grew.'

"We had driven up in a dog-cart, and my client led me away at once, without our entering the house, to the scar on the lawn where the elm had stood. It was nearly midway between the oak and the house. My investigation seemed to be progressing.

" 'I suppose it is impossible to find out how high the elm was?' I asked.

" 'I can give you it at once. It was 64 ft.'

" 'How do you come to know it?' I asked in surprise.

" 'When my old tutor used to give me an exercise in trigonometry it always took the shape of measuring heights. When I was a lad I worked out every tree and building on the estate.'

"This was an unexpected piece of luck. My data were coming more quickly than I could have reasonably hoped.

" 'Tell me,' I asked, 'did your butler ever ask you such a question?'

"Reginald Musgrave looked at me in astonishment. 'Now that you call it to my mind,' he answered, 'Brunton *did* ask me about the height of the tree some months ago, in connection with some little argument with the groom.'

"This was excellent news, Watson, for it showed me that I was on the right road. I looked up at the sun. It was low in the heavens, and I calculated that in less than an hour it would lie just above the topmost branches of the old oak. One condition mentioned in the Ritual would then be fulfilled. And the shadow of the elm must mean the farther end of the shadow, otherwise the trunk would have been chosen as the guide. I had then to find where the far end of the shadow would fall when the sun was just clear of the oak."

"That must have been difficult, Holmes, when the elm was no longer there."

"Well, at least, I knew that if Brunton could do it, I could also. Besides, there was no real difficulty. I went with Musgrave to his study and whittled myself this peg, to which I tied this long string, with a knot at each yard. Then I took two lengths of a fishing-rod, which came to just six feet, and I went back with my client to where the elm had been. The sun was just grazing the top of the oak. I fastened the rod on end, marked out the direction of the shadow, and measured it. It was 9 ft. in length.

"Of course, the calculation was now a simple one. If a rod of 6 ft. threw a shadow of 9 ft., a tree of 64 ft. would throw one of 96 ft., and the line of one would of course be in the line of the other. I measured out the distance, which brought me almost to the wall of the house, and I thrust a peg into the spot. You can imagine my exultation, Watson, when within 2 in. of my peg I saw a conical depression in the ground, I knew that it was the mark made by Brunton in his measurements, and that I was still upon his trail.

"From this starting point I proceeded to step, having first taken the cardinal points by my pocket compass. Ten steps with each foot took me along parallel with the wall of the house, and again I marked my spot with a peg. Then I carefully paced off five to the east and two to the south. It brought me to the very threshold of the old door. Two steps to the west meant now that I was to go two paces down the stone-flagged passage, and this was the place indicated by the Ritual.

"Never have I felt such a cold chill of disappointment, Watson. For a moment it seemed to me that there must be some radical mistake in my calculations. The setting sun shone full upon the passage floor, and I could see that the old foot-worn grey stones, with which it was paved, were firmly cemented together, and had certainly not been moved for many a long year. Brunton had not been at work here. I tapped upon the floor, but it sounded the same all over, and there was no sign of any crack or crevice. But fortunately, Musgrave, who had begun to appreciate the meaning of my proceedings, and who was now as excited as myself, took out his manuscript to check my calculations.

"'And under,' he cried: 'you have omitted the "and under."'"

"I had thought that it meant that we were to dig, but now, of course, I saw at once that I was wrong. 'There is a cellar under this, then?' I cried.

"'Yes, and as old as the house. Down here, through this door.'

"We went down a winding stone stair, and my companion, striking a match, lit a large lantern which stood on a barrel in the corner. In an instant it was obvious that we had at last come upon the true place, and that we had not been the only people to visit the spot recently.

"It had been used for the storage of wood, but the billets, which had evidently been littered over the floor, were now piled at the sides so as to leave a clear space in the middle. In this space lay a large and heavy flag-stone, with a rusted iron ring in the centre, to which a thick shepherd's check muffler was attached.

"'By Jove!' cried my client, 'that's Brunton's muffler. I have seen it on him, and could swear to it. What has the villain been doing here?'

"At my suggestion a couple of the county police were summoned to be present, and I then endeavoured to raise the stone by pulling on the cravat. I could only move it slightly, and it was with the aid of one of the constables that I succeeded at last in carrying it to one side. A black hole yawned beneath, into which we all peered, while Musgrave, kneeling at the side, pushed down the lantern.

"A small chamber about 7 ft. deep and 4 ft. square lay open to us. At one side of this was a squat, brass-bound, wooden box, the lid of which was hinged upwards, with this curious, old-fashioned key projecting from the lock. It was furred outside by a thick layer of dust, and damp and worms had eaten through the wood so that a crop of living fungi was growing on the inside of it. Several discs of metal—old coins apparently—such as I hold here, were scattered over the bottom of the box, but it contained nothing else.

"At the moment, however, we had no thought for the old chest, for our eyes were riveted upon that which crouched beside it. It was the figure of a man, clad in a suit of black, who squatted down upon his hams with his forehead sunk upon the edge of the box and his two arms thrown out on each side of it. The attitude had drawn all the stagnant blood to his face, and no man could have recognised that distorted, liver-coloured countenance; but his height, his dress, and his hair were all sufficient to show my client, when we had drawn the body up, that it was indeed his missing butler. He had been dead some days, but there was no wound or bruise upon his person to show how he had met his dreadful end. When his body had been carried from the cellar we found ourselves still confronted with a problem which was almost as formidable as that with which we had started.

"I confess that so far, Watson, I had been disappointed in my investigation. I had reckoned upon solving the matter when once I had found the place referred to in the Ritual; but now I was there, and was apparently as far as ever from knowing what it was which the family had concealed with such elaborate precautions. It is true that I had thrown a light upon the fate of Brunton, but now I had to ascertain how that fate had come upon him, and what part had been played in the matter by the woman who had disappeared. I sat down upon a keg in the corner and thought the whole matter carefully over.

"You know my methods in such cases, Watson: I put myself in the man's place, and having first gauged his intelligence, I try to imagine how I should myself have proceeded under the same circumstances. In this case the matter was simplified by Brunton's intelligence being quite first rate, so that it was unnecessary to make any allowance for personal equation, so the astronomers have dubbed it. He knew that something valuable was concealed. He had spotted the place. He found that the stone which covered it was just too heavy for a man to move unaided. What would he do next? He could not get help from outside, even if he had someone whom he could trust, without the unbarring of doors, and considerable risk of detection. It was better, if he could, to have his helpmate inside the house. But whom could he ask? This girl had been devoted to him. A man always finds it hard to realize that he may have finally lost a woman's love, however badly he may have treated her. He would try by a few attentions to make his peace with the girl Howells, and then would engage her as his accomplice. Together they would come at night to the cellar, and their united force would suffice to raise the stone. So far I could follow their actions as if I had actually seen them.

"But for two of them, and one a woman, it must have been heavy work, the raising of that stone. A burly Sussex policeman and I had found it no light job. What would they do to assist them? Probably what I should have done myself. I rose and examined carefully the different billets of wood which were scattered round the floor. Almost at once I came upon what I expected. One piece, about 3 ft. in length, had a marked indentation at one end, while several were flattened at the sides as if they had been compressed by some considerable weight. Evidently as they had dragged the stone up they had thrust the chunks of wood into the chink, until at last, when the opening was large enough to crawl through, they would hold it open by a billet placed lengthwise, which might very well become indented at the lower end, since the whole weight of the stone would press it down on to the edge of the other slab. So far I was still on safe ground.

"And now, how was I to proceed to reconstruct this midnight drama? Clearly only one could get into the hole, and that one was Brunton. The girl must have waited above. Brunton then unlocked the box, handed up the contents, presumably—since they were not to be found—and then—and then what happened?

"What smouldering fire of vengeance had suddenly sprung into flame in this passionate Celtic woman's soul when she saw the man who had wronged her—wronged her perhaps far more than we suspected—in her power? Was it a chance that the wood had slipped and that the stone had shut Brunton into what had become his sepulchre? Had she only been guilty of silence as to his fate? Or had some sudden blow from her hand dashed the support away and sent the slab crashing down into its place. Be that as it might, I seemed to see that woman's figure, still clutching at her treasure-trove, and flying wildly up the winding stair with her ears ringing perhaps with the muffled screams from behind her, and with the drumming of frenzied hands against the slab of stone which was choking her faithless lover's life out.

"Here was the secret of her blanched face, her shaken nerves, her peals of hysterical laughter on the next morning. But what had been in the box? What had she done with that? Of course, it must have been the old metal and pebbles which my client had dragged from the mere. She had thrown them in there at the first opportunity, to remove the last trace of her crime.

"For twenty minutes I had sat motionless thinking the matter out. Musgrave still stood with a very pale face swinging his lantern and peering down into the hole.

" 'These are coins of Charles I,' said he, holding out the few which had been left in the box. 'You see we were right in fixing our date for the Ritual.'

" 'We may find something else of Charles I,' I cried, as the probable meaning of the first two questions of the Ritual broke suddenly upon me. 'Let me see the contents of the bag you fished from the mere.'

" 'We ascended to his study, and he laid the débris before me. I could understand his regarding it as of small importance when I looked at it, for the metal was almost black, and the stones lustreless and dull. I rubbed one of them on my sleeve, however, and it glowed afterwards like a spark, in the dark hollow of my hand. The metal-work was in the form of a double-ring, but it had been bent and twisted out of its original shape.

" 'You must bear in mind,' said I, 'that the Royal party made headway in England even after the death of the King, and that when they at last fled they probably left many of their most precious possessions buried behind them, with the intention of returning for them in more peaceful times.'

" 'My ancestor, Sir Ralph Musgrave, was a prominent Cavalier, and the right-hand man of Charles II in his wanderings,' said my friend.

" 'Ah, indeed!' I answered. 'Well, now, I think that really should give us the last link that we wanted. I must congratulate you on coming into possession, though in rather a tragic manner, of a relic which is of great intrinsic value, but even of greater importance as an historical curiosity.'

" 'What is it, then?' he gasped in astonishment.

" 'It is nothing less than the ancient crown of the Kings of England.'

" 'The crown!'

" 'Precisely. Consider what the Ritual says. How does it run? "Whose was it?" "His who is gone." That was after the execution of Charles. Then, "Who shall have it?" "He who will come." That was Charles II, whose advent was already foreseen. There can, I think, be no doubt that this battered and shapeless diadem once encircled the brows of the Royal Stuarts.'

" 'And how came it in the pond?'

" 'Ah, that is a question which will take some time to answer,' and with that I sketched out the whole long chain of surmise and of proof which I had constructed. The twilight had closed in and the moon was shining brightly in the sky before my narrative was finished.

" 'And how was it, then, that Charles did not get his crown when he returned?' asked Musgrave, pushing back the relic into its linen bag.

" 'Ah, there you lay your finger upon the one point which we shall probably never be able to clear up. It is likely that the Musgrave who held the secret died in the interval, and by some oversight left this guide to his descendant without explaining the meaning of it. From that day to this it has been handed down from father to son, until at last it came within reach of a man who tore its secret out of it and lost his life in the venture.'

"And that's the story of the Musgrave Ritual, Watson. They have the crown down at Hurlstone—though they had some legal bother, and a considerable sum to pay before they were allowed to retain it. I am sure that if you mentioned my name they would be happy to show it to you. Of the woman nothing was ever heard, and the probability is that she got away out of England, and carried herself, and the memory of her crime, to some land beyond the seas."

Rudyard Kipling (1865–1936) was born in Bombay, where his father was a university professor of architectural sculpture. As was customary, Kipling was sent back to England for schooling; he returned to Lahore (now Pakistan) and became an editor of the Civil and Military Gazette. *Through his fiction and poetry, Kipling introduced many readers in England to the Anglo-Indian "world." Early in his career, Kipling was a public figure, well known for his novels, tales, and poetry* (Barracks-Room Ballads); *he traveled widely, and for a period of time after his marriage to an American woman (1892) lived in Vermont. In 1907 Kipling was awarded the Nobel Prize for literature. For further reading:* Plain Tales from the Hills *(1888);* Life's Handicap *(1891);* Under the Deodars *(1899).*

RUDYARD KIPLING

At Twenty-Two

Narrow as the womb, deep as the Pit, and dark as the heart of a man.—Sonthal Miner's Proverb.

"*A* weaver went out to reap but stayed to unravel the corn-stalks. Ha! Ha! Ha! Is there any sense in a weaver?"

Janki Meah glared at Kundoo, but, as Janki Meah was blind, Kundoo was not impressed. He had come to argue with Janki Meah, and, if chance favored, to make love to the old man's pretty young wife.

This was Kundoo's grievance, and he spoke in the name of all the five men who, with Janki Meah, composed the gang in Number Seven gallery of Twenty-Two. Janki Meah had been blind for the thirty years during which he had served the Jimahari Collieries with pick and crowbar. All through those thirty years he had regularly, every morning before going down, drawn from the overseer his allowance of lamp-oil—just as if he had been an eyed miner. What Kundoo's gang resented, as hundreds of gangs had resented before, was Janki Meah's selfishness. He would not add the oil to the common stock of his gang, but would save and sell it.

"I knew these workings before you were born," Janki Meah used to reply: "I don't want the light to get my coal out by, and I am not going to help you. The oil is mine, and I intend to keep it."

A strange man in many ways was Janki Meah, the white-haired, hot tempered, sightless weaver who had turned pitman. All day long—except on Sundays and Mondays when he was usually drunk—he worked in the Twenty-Two shaft of the Jimahari Colliery as cleverly as a man with all the senses. At evening he went up in the great steam-hauled cage to the pit-bank, and there called for his pony—a rusty, coal-dusty beast, nearly as old as Janki Meah. The pony would come to his side, and Janki Meah would clamber on to its back and be taken at once to the plot of land which he, like the other miners, received from the Jimahari Company. The pony knew that place, and when, after six years, the Company changed all the allotments to prevent the miners from acquiring proprietary rights, Janki Meah represented, with tears in his eyes, that were his holdings shifted, he would never be able to find his way to the new one. "My horse only knows that place," pleaded Janki Meah and so he was allowed to keep his land.

On the strength of this concession and his accumulated oil-savings, Janki Meah took a second wife—a girl of the Jolaha main stock of the Meahs, and singularly beautiful. Janki Meah could not see her beauty; wherefore he took her on trust, and forbade her to go down the pit. He had not worked for thirty years in the dark without knowing that the pit was no place for pretty women. He loaded her with ornaments—not brass or pewter, but real silver ones—and she rewarded him by flirting outrageously with Kundoo of Number Seven gallery gang. Kundoo was really the gang-head, but Janki Meah insisted upon all the work being entered in his own name, and chose the men that he worked with. Custom—stronger even than the Jimahari Company—dicated that Janki, by right of his years, should manage these things, and should, also, work despite his blindness. In Indian mines where they cut into the solid coal with the pick and clear it out from floor to ceiling, he could come to no great harm. At Home, where they undercut the coal and bring it down in crashing avalanches from the roof, he would never have been allowed to set foot in a pit. He was not a popular man, because of his oil-savings; but all the gangs admitted that Janki knew all the *khads*, or workings, that had ever been sunk or worked since the Jimahari Company first started operations on the Tarachunda fields.

Pretty little Unda only knew that her old husband was a fool who could be managed. She took no interest in the collieries except in so far as they swallowed up Kundoo five days out of the seven, and covered him with coal-dust. Kundoo was a great workman, and did his best not to get drunk, because, when he had saved forty rupees, Unda was to steal everything that she could find in Janki's house and run with Kundoo to a land where there were no mines, and every one kept three fat bullocks and a mulch-buffalo. While this scheme ripened it was his custom to drop in upon

Janki and worry him about the oil savings. Unda sat in a corner and nod-ded approval. On the night when Kundoo had quoted that objectionable proverb about weavers, Janki grew angry.

"Listen, you pig," said he, "blind I am, and old I am, but, before ever you were born, I was grey among the coal. Even in the days when the Twenty-Two *khad* was unsunk and there were not two thousand men here, I was known to have all knowledge of the pits. What *khad* is there that I do not know, from the bottom of the shaft to the end of the last drive? Is it the Baromba *khad,* the oldest, or the Twenty-Two where Tibu's gallery runs up to Number Five?"

"Hear the old fool talk!" said Kundoo, nodding to Unda. "No gallery of Twenty-Two will cut into Five before the end of the Rains. We have a month's solid coal before us. The Babuji says so."

"Babuji! Pigji! Dogji! What do these fat slugs from Calcutta know? He draws and draws and draws, and talks and talks and talks, and his maps are all wrong. I, Janki, know that this is so. When a man has been shut up in the dark for thirty years, God gives him knowledge. The old gallery that Tibu's gang made is not six feet from Number Five."

"Without doubt God gives the blind knowledge," said Kundoo, with a look at Unda. "Let it be as you say. I, for my part, do not know where lies the gallery of Tibu's gang, but *I* am not a withered monkey who needs oil to grease his joints with."

Kundoo swung out of the hut laughing, and Unda giggled. Janki turned his sightless eyes toward his wife and swore. "I have land, and I have sold a great deal of lamp-oil," mused Janki; "but I was a fool to marry this child."

A week later the Rains set in with a vengeance, and the gangs paddled about in coal-slush at the pit-banks. Then the big mine-pumps were made ready, and the Manager of the Colliery ploughed through the wet toward the Tarachunda River swelling between its soppy banks. "Lord send that this beastly beck doesn't misbehave," said the Manager, piously, and he went to take counsel with his Assistant about the pumps.

But the Tatachunda misbehaved very much indeed. After a fall of three inches of rain in an hour it was obliged to do something. It topped its bank and joined the flood water that was hemmed between two low hills just where the embankment of the Colliery main line crossed. When a large part of a rain-fed river, and a few acres of flood-water, made a dead set for a nine-foot culvert, the culvert may spout its finest, but the water cannot *all* get out. The Manager pranced upon one leg with excitement, and his lan-guage was improper.

He had reason to swear, because he knew that one inch of water on land meant a pressure of one hundred tons to the acre; and here were about five feet of water forming, behind the railway embankmant, over the shallower workings of Twenty-Two. You must understand that, in a coal-mine, the coal nearest the surface is worked first from the central shaft. That is to say, the miners may clear out the stuff to within ten, twenty, or thirty feet of the surface, and, when all is worked out, leave only a skin of earth upheld by some few pillars of coal. In a deep mine where they know that they have any amount of material at hand, men prefer to get all their mineral out at one shaft, rather than make a number of little holes to tap the comparatively unimportant surface-coal.

And the Manager watched the flood.

The culvert spouted a nine-foot gush; but the water still formed, and the word was sent to clear the men out of Twenty-Two. The cages came up crammed and crammed again with the men nearest the pit-eye, as they call the place where you can see daylight from the bottom of the main shaft. All away and away up the long black galleries the flare-lamps were winking and dancing like so many fireflies, and the men and the women waited for the clanking, rattling, thundering cages to come down and fly up again. But the outworkings were very far off, and word could not be passed quickly, though the heads of the gangs and the Assistant shouted and swore and tramped and stumbled. The Manager kept one eye on the great troubled pool behind the embankment, and prayed that the culvert would give way and let the water through in time. With the other eye he watched the cages come up and saw the headmen counting the roll of the gangs. With all his heart and soul he swore at the winder who controlled the iron drum that wound up the wire rope on which hung the cages.

In a little time there was a down-draw in the water behind the embankment—a sucking whirl-pool, all yellow and yeasty. The water had smashed through the skin of the earth and was pouring into the old shallow workings of Twenty-Two.

Deep down below, a rush of black water caught the last gang waiting for the cage, and as they clambered in, the whirl was about their waists. The cage reached the pit-bank, and the Manager called the roll. The gangs were all safe except Gang Janki, Gang Mogul, and Gang Rahim, eighteen men, with perhaps ten basket-women who loaded the coal into the little iron carriages that ran on the tramways of the main galleries. These gangs were in the out-workings, three-quarters of a mile away, on the extreme fringe of the mine. Once more the cage went down, but with only two English men in it, and dropped into a swirling, roaring current that had almost touched the roof of some of the lower side-galleries. One of the wooden balks with which they propped the old workings shot past on the current, just missing the cage.

"If we don't want our ribs knocked out, we'd better go," said the Manager. "We can't even save the Company's props."

The cage drew out of the water with a splash, and a few minutes later, it was officially reported that there were at least ten feet of water in the pit's eye. Now ten feet of water there meant that all other places in the mine were flooded except such galleries as were more than ten feet above the level of the bottom of the shaft. The deep workings would be full, the main galleries would be full, but in the high workings reached by inclines from the main roads, there would be a certain amount of air cut off, so to speak, by the water and squeezed up by it. The little science-primers explain how water behaves when you pour it down test-tubes. The flooding of Twenty-Two was an illustration on a large scale.

"By the Holy Grove, what has happened to the air!" It was a Sonthal gangman of Gang Mogul in Number Nine gallery, and he was driving a six-foot way through the coal. Then there was a rush from the other galleries, and Gang Janki and Gang Rahim stumbled up with their basket-women.

"Water has come in the mine," they said, "and there is no way of getting out."

"I went down," said Janki—"down the slope of my gallery, and I felt the water."

"There has been no water in the cutting in our time," clamored the women. "Why cannot we go away?"

"Be silent!" said Janki. "Long ago, when my father was here, water came to Ten—no, Eleven—cutting, and there was great trouble. Let us get away to where the air is better."

The three gangs and the basket-women left Number Nine gallery and went further up Number Sixteen. At one turn of the road they could see the pitchy black water lapping on the coal. It had touched the roof of a gallery that they knew well—a gallery where they used to smoke their *huqas* and manage their flirtations. Seeing this, they called aloud upon their Gods, and the Mehas, who are thrice bastered Muhammadans, strove to recollect the name of the Prophet. They came to a great open square whence nearly all the coal had been extracted. It was the end of the out-workings, and the end of the mine.

Far away down the gallery a small pumping-engine, used for keeping dry a deep working and fed with steam from above, was throbbing faithfully. They heard it cease.

"They have cut off the steam," said Kundoo, hopefully. "They have given the order to use all the steam for the pit-bank pumps. They will clear out the water."

"If the water has reached the smoking-gallery," said Janki, "all the Company's pumps can do nothing for three days."

"It is very hot," moaned Jasoda, the Meah basket-woman. "There is a very bad air here because of the lamps."

"Put them out," said Janki; "why do you want lamps?" The lamps were put out and the company sat still in the utter dark. Somebody rose quietly and began walking ofer the coals. It was Janki, who was touching the walls with his hands. "Where is the ledge?" he murmured to himself.

"Sit, sit!" said Kundoo. "If we die, we die. The air is very bad."

But Janki still stumbled and crept and tapped with his pick upon the walls. The women rose to their feet.

"Stay all where you are. Without the lamps you cannot see, and I—I am always seeing," said Janki. Then he paused, and called out: "Oh, you who have been in the cutting more than ten years, what is the name of this open place? I an an old man and I have forgotten."

"Bullia's Room," answered the Sonthal, who had complained of the vileness of the air.

"Again," said Janki.

"Bullia's Room."

"Then I have found it," said Janki. "The name only had slipped my memory. Tibu's gang's gallery is here."

"A lie," said Kundoo. "There have been no galleries in this place since my day."

"Three paces was the depth of the ledge," muttered Janki, without heeding—"and—oh, my poor bones!—I have found it! It is here, up this ledge. Come all you, one by one, to the place of my voice, and I will count you."

There was a rush in the dark, and Janki felt the first man's face hit his knees as the Sonthal scrambled up the ledge.

"Who?" cried Janki.

"I, Sunua Manji."

"Sit you down," said Janki. "Who next?"

One by one the women and the men crawled up the ledge which ran along one side of "Bullia's Room." Degraded Muhammadan, pig-eating Mushar and wild Sonthal, Janki ran his hand over them all.

"Now follow after," said he, "catching hold of my heel, and the women catching the men's clothes." He did not ask whether the men had brought their picks with them. A miner, black or white, does not drop his pick. One by one, Janki leading, they crept into the old gallery—a six-foot way with a scant four feet from thill to roof.

"The air is better here," said Jasoda. They could hear her heart beating in thick, sick bumps.

"Slowly, slowly," said Janki. "I am an old man, and I forget many things. This is Tibu's gallery, but where are the four bricks where they used to put their *huqa* fire on when the Sahibs never saw? Slowly, slowly, O you people behind."

They heard his hands disturbing the small coal on the floor of the gallery and then a dull sound. "This is one unbaked brick, and this is another and another. Kundoo is a young man—let him come forward. Put a knee upon this brick and strike here. When Tibu's gang were at dinner on the last day before the good coal ended, they heard the men of Five on the other side, and Five worked *their* gallery two Sundays later—or it may have been one. Strike there, Kundoo, but give me room to go back."

Kundoo, doubting, drove the pick, but the first soft crush of the coal was a call to him. He was fighting for his life and for Unda—pretty little Unda with rings on all her toes—for Unda and the forty rupees. The women sang the Song of the Pick—the terrible, slow, swinging melody with the muttered chorus that repeats the sliding of the loosened coal, and, to each cadence, Kundoo smote in the black dark. When he could do no more, Sunua Manji took the pick, and struck for his life and his wife, and his village beyond the blue hills over the Tatachunda River. An hour the men worked, and then the women cleared away the coal.

"It is farther than I thought," said Janki.

"The air is very bad; but strike, Kundoo, strike hard."

For the fifth time Kundoo took up the pick as the Sonthal crawled back. The song had scarcely recommenced when it was broken by a yell from Kundoo that echoed down the gallery: *"Par hua! Par hua!* We are through, we are through!" The imprisoned air in the mine shot through the opening, and the women at the far end of the gallery heard the water rush through the pillars of "Bullia's Room" and roar against the ledge. Having fulfilled the law under which it worked, it rose no farther. The women screamed and pressed forward. "The water has come—we shall be killed! Let us go."

Kundoo crawled through the gap and found himself in a propped gallery by the simple process of hitting his head against a beam.

"Do I know the pits or do I not?" chuckled Janki. "This is the Number Five; go you out slowly, giving me your names. Ho! Rahim, count your gang! Now let us go forward, each catching hold of the other as before."

They formed a line in the darkness and Janki led them—for a pit-man in a strange pit is only one degree less liable to err than an ordinary mortal underground for the first time. At last they saw a flare-lamp, and Gangs Janki, Mogul, and Rahim of Twenty-Two stumbled dazed into the glare of the draught-furnace at the bottom of Five; Janki feeling his way and the rest behind.

"Water has come into Twenty-Two. God knows where are the others. I have brought these men from Tibu's gallery in our cutting; making connection through the north side of the gallery. Take us to the cage," said Janki Meah.

At the pit-bank of Twenty-Two, some thousand people clamored and wept and shouted. One hundred men—one thousand men—had been drowned in the cutting. They would all go to their homes to-morrow. Where were their men? Little Unda, her cloth drenched with the rain, stood at the pit-mouth calling down the shaft for Kundoo. They had swung the cages clear of the mouth, and her only answer was the murmur of the flood in the pit's eye two hundred and sixty feet below.

"Look after that woman! She'll chuck herself down the shaft in a minute," shouted the Manager.

But he need not have troubled; Unda was afraid of Death. She wanted Kundoo. The Assistant was watching the flood and seeing how far he could wade into it. There was a lull in the water, and the whirlpool had slackened. The mine was full, and the people at the pit-bank howled.

"My faith, we shall be lucky if we have five hundred hands on the place to-morrow!" said the Manager. "There's some chance yet of running a temporary dam across that water. Shove in anything—tubs and bullock-carts if you haven't enough bricks. Make them work *now* if they never worked before. Hi! you gangers, make them work."

Little by little the crowd was broken into detachments, and pushed toward the water with promises of overtime. The dam-making began, and when it was fairly under way, the Manager thought that the hour had come for the pumps. There was no fresh inrush into the mine. The tall, red, iron-clamped pump-beam rose and fell, and the pumps snored and guttered and shrieked as the first water poured out of the pipe.

"We must run her all to-night," said the Manager, wearily, "but there's no hope for the poor devils down below. Look here, Gur Sahai, if you are proud of your engines, show me what they can do now."

Gur Sahai grinned and nodded, with his right hand upon the lever and an oil-can in his left. He could do no more than he was doing, but he could keep that up till the dawn. Were the Company's pumps to be beaten by the vagaries of that troublesome Tarachunda River? Never, never! And the pumps sobbed and panted: "Never, never!" The Manager sat in the shelter of the pit-bank roofing, trying to dry himself by the pump-boiler fire, and, in the dreary dusk, he saw the crowds on the dam scatter and fly.

"That's the end," he groaned. " 'Twill take us six weeks to persuade 'em that we haven't tried to drown their mates on purpose. Oh, for a decent, rational Geordie!"

But the flight had no panic in it. Men had run over from Five with astounding news, and the foremen could not hold their gangs together. Presently, surrounded by a clamorous crew, Gangs Rahim, Mogul, and Janki, and ten basket-women, walked up to report themselves, and pretty little Unda stole away to Janki's hut to prepare his evening meal.

"Alone I found the way," explained Janki Meah, "and now will the Company give me pension?"

The simple pit-folk shouted and leaped and went back to the dam, reassured in their old belief that, whatever happened, so great was the power of the Company whose salt they ate, none of them could be killed. But Gur Sahai only bared his white teeth and kept his hand upon the lever and proved his pumps to the uttermost.

"I say," said the Assistant to the Manager, a week later, "do you recollect *Germinal?*"

"Yes. 'Queer thing. I thought of it in the cage when that balk went by. Why?"

"Oh, this business seems to be *Germinal* upside down. Janki was in my veranda all this morning, telling me that Kundoo had eloped with his wife—Unda or Anda, I think her name was."

"Hillo! And those were the cattle that you risked your life to clear out of Twenty-Two!"

"No—I was thinking of the Company's props, not the Company's men."

"Sounds better to say so *now;* but I don't believe you, old fellow."

H. G. WELLS

The Lord of the Dynamos

The chief attendant of the three dynamos that buzzed and rattled at Camberwell, and kept the electric railway going, came out of Yorkshire, and his name was James Holroyd. He was a practical electrician, but fond of whiskey, a heavy red-haired brute with irregular teeth. He doubted the existence of the deity, but accepted Carnot's cycle, and he had read Shakespeare and found him weak in chemistry. His helper came out of the mysterious East, and his name was Azuma-zi. But Holroyd called him Pooh-bah. Holroyd liked a nigger help because he could stand kicking—a habit with Holroyd—and did not pry into the machinery and try to learn the ways of it. Certain odd possibilities of the negro mind brought into abrupt contact with the crown of our civilisation Holroyd never fully realised, though just at the end he got some inkling of them.

To define Azuma-zi was beyond ethnology. He was, perhaps, more negroid than anything else, though his hair was curly rather than frizzy, and his nose had a bridge. Moreover, his skin was brown rather than black, and the whites of his eyes were yellow. His broad cheek-bones and narrow chin gave his face something of the viperine V. His head, too, was broad behind, and low and narrow at the forehead, as if his brain had been twisted round in the reverse way to a European's. He was short of stature and still shorter of English. In conversation he made numerous odd noises of no known marketable value, and his infrequent words were carved and wrought into heraldic grotesqueness. Holroyd tried to elucidate his religious beliefs, and—especially after whiskey—lectured to him against superstition and missionaries. Azuma-zi, however, shirked the discussion of his gods, even though he was kicked for it.

Azuma-zi had come, clad in white but insufficient raiment, out of the stoke-hole of the *Lord Clive,* from the Straits Settlements, and beyond, into London. He had heard even in his youth of the greatness and riches of London, where all the women are white and fair, and even the beggars in the streets are white; and he had arrived, with newly earned gold coins in his pocket, to worship at the shrine of civilisation. The day of his landing was a dismal one; the sky was dun, and a wind-worried drizzle filtered down to the greasy streets, but he plunged boldly into the delights of Shadwell, and was presently cast up, shattered in health, civilised in costume, penniless, and, except in matters of the direst necessity, practically a dumb animal, to toil for James Holroyd and to be bullied by him in the dynamo shed at Camberwell. And to James Holroyd bullying was a labour of love.

There were three dynamos with their engines at Camberwell. The two that have been there since the beginning are small machines; the larger one was new. The smaller machines made a reasonable noise; their straps hummed over the drums, every now and then the brushes buzzed and fizzled, and the air churned steadily, whoo! whoo! whoo! between their poles. One was loose in its foundations and kept the shed vibrating. But the big dynamo drowned these little noises altogether with the sustained drone of its iron core, which somehow set part of the iron-work humming. The place made the visitor's head reel with the throb, throb, throb of the engines, the rotation of the big wheels, the spinning ball valves, the occasional spittings of the steam, and over all the deep, unceasing, surging note of the big dynamo. This last noise was from an engineering point of view a defect; but Azuma-zi accounted it unto the monster for mightiness and pride.

If it were possible we would have the noises of that shed always about the reader as he reads, we would tell all our story to such an accompaniment. It was a steady stream of din, from which the ear picked out first one threat and then another; there was the intermittent snorting, panting, and seething of the steam-engines, the suck and thud of their pistons, the dull beat on the air as the spokes of the great driving-wheels came round, a note the leather straps made as they ran tighter and loose, and a fretful tumult from the dynamos; and, over all, sometimes inaudible, as the ear tired of it, and then creeping back upon the senses again, was this trombone note of the big machine. The floor never felt steady and quiet beneath one's feet, but quivered and jarred. It was a confusing, unsteady place, and enough to send any one's thoughts jerking into odd zigzags. And for three months, while the big strike of the engineers was in progress, Holroyd, who was a blackleg, and Azuma-zi, who was a mere black, were never out of the stir and eddy of it, but slept and fed in the little wooden shanty between the shed and the gates.

Holroyd delivered a theological lecture on the text of his big machine soon after Azuma-zi came. He had to shout to be heard in the din. "Look at that," said Holroyd; "where's your 'eathen idol to match 'im?" And Azuma-zi looked. For a moment Holroyd was inaudible, and then Azuma-zi heard: "Kill a hundred men. Twelve per cent on the ordinary shares," said Holroyd, "and that's something like a Gord!"

Holroyd was proud of his big dynamo, and expatiated upon its size and power to Azuma-zi until heaven knows what odd currents of thought that, and the incessant whirling and shindy, set up within the curly, black cranium. He would explain in the most graphic manner the dozen or so ways in which a man might be killed by it, and once he gave Azuma-zi a shock as a sample of its quality. After that, in the breathing-times of his labour—it was heavy labour, being not only his own but most of Holroyd's—Azuma-zi would sit and watch the big machine. Now and then the brushes would sparkle and spit blue flashes, at which Holroyd would swear, but all the rest was as smooth and rhythmic as breathing. The band ran shouting over the shaft, and ever behind one as one watched was the complacent thud of the piston. So it lived all day in this big airy shed, with him and Holroyd to wait upon it; not prisoned up and slaving to drive a ship as the other engines he knew—mere captive devils of the British Solomon—had been, but a machine enthroned. Those two smaller dynamos, Azuma-zi by force of contrast despised; the large one he privately christened the Lord of the Dynamos. They were fretful and irregular, but the big dynamo was steady. How great it was! How serene and easy in its working! Greater and calmer even than the Buddahs he had seen at Rangoon, and yet not motionless, but living! The great block coils spun, spun, spun, the rings ran round under the brushes, and the deep note of its coil steadied the whole. It affected Azuma-zi queerly.

Azuma-zi was not fond of labour. He would sit about and watch the Lord of the Dynamos while Holroyd went away to persuade the yard porter to get whiskey, although his proper place was not in the dynamo shed but behind the engines, and, moreover, if Holroyd caught him skulking he got hit for it with a rod of stout copper wire. He would go and stand close to the colossus and look up at the great leather band running overhead. There was a black patch on the band that came round, and it pleased him somehow among all the clatter to watch this return again and again. Odd thoughts spun with the whirl of it. Scientific people tell us that savages give souls to rocks and trees—and a machine is a thousand times more alive than a rock or a tree. And Azuma-zi was practically a savage still; the veneer of civilisation lay no deeper than his slop suit, his bruises and the coal grime on his face and hands. His father before him had worshipped a meteoric stone, kindred blood, it may be, had splashed the broad wheels of Juggernaut.

He took every opportunity Holroyd gave him of touching and handling the great dynamo that was fascinating him. He polished and cleaned it until the metal parts were blinding in the sun. He felt a mysterious sense of service in doing this. He would go up to it and touch its spinning coils gently. The gods he had worshipped were all far away. The people in London hid their gods.

At last his dim feelings grew more distinct, and took shape in thoughts and acts. When he came into the roaring shed one morning he salaamed to the Lord of the Dynamos; and then, when Holroyd was away, he went and whispered to the thundering machine that he was its servant, and prayed it to have pity on him and save him from Holroyd. As he did so a rare gleam of light came in through the open archway of the throbbing machine-shed, and the Lord of the Dynamos, as he whirled and roared, was radiant with pale gold. Then Azuma-zi knew that his service was acceptable to his Lord. After that he did not feel so lonely as he had done, and he had indeed been very much alone in London. And even when his work time was over, which was rare, he loitered about the shed.

Then, the next time Holroyd maltreated him, Azuma-zi went presently to the Lord of the Dynamos and whispered, "Thou seest, O my Lord!" and the angry whirr of the machinery seemed to answer him. Thereafter it appeared to him that whenever Holroyd came into the shed a different note came into the sounds of the great dynamo. "My Lord bides his time," said Azuma-zi to himself. "The inquity of the fool is not yet ripe." And he waited and watched for the day of reckoning. One day there was evidence of short circuiting, and Holroyd, making an unwary examination—it was in the afternoon—got a rather severe shock. Azuma-zi from behind the engine saw him jump off and curse at the peccant coil.

"He is warned," said Azuma-zi to himself. "Surely my Lord is very patient."

Holroyd had at first initiated his "nigger" into such elementary conceptions of the dynamo's working as would enable him to take temporary charge of the shed in his absence. But when he noticed the manner in which Azuma-zi hung about the monster, he became suspicious. He dimly perceived his assistant was "up to something," and connecting him with the anointing of the coils with oil that had rotted the varnish in one place, he issued an edict, shouted above the confusion of the machinery, "Don't 'ee go nigh that big dynamo any more, Pooh-bah, or a'll take thy skin off!" Besides, if it pleased Azuma-zi to be near the big machine, it was plain sense and decency to keep him away from it.

Azuma-zi obeyed at the time, but later he was caught bowing before the Lord of the Dynamos. At which Holroyd twisted his arm and kicked him as he turned to go away. As Azuma-zi presently stood behind the engine and glared at the back of the hated Holroyd, the noises of the machinery took a new rhythm, and sounded like four words in his native tongue.

It is hard to say exactly what madness is. I fancy Azuma-zi was mad. The incessant din and whirl of the dynamo shed may have churned up his little store of knowledge and big store of superstitious fancy, at last, into something akin to frenzy. At any rate, when the idea of making Holroyd a sacrifice to the Dynamo Fetich was thus suggested to him, it filled him with a strange tumult of exultant emotion.

That night the two men and their black shadows were alone in the shed together. The shed was lit with one big arc light that winked and flickered purple. The shadows lay black behind the dynamos, the ball governors of the engines whirled from light to darkness, and their pistons beat loud and steady. The world outside seen through the open end of the shed seemed incredibly dim and remote. It seem absolutely silent, too, since the riot of the machinery drowned every external sound. Far away was the black fence of the yard with grey, shadowy houses behind, and above was the deep blue sky and the pale little stars. Azuma-zi suddenly walked across the centre of the shed above which the leather bands were running, and went into the shadow by the big dynamo. Holroyd heard a click, and the spin of the armature changed.

"What are you dewin' with that switch?" he bawled in surprise. "Ha'n't I told you—"

Then he saw the set expression of Azuma-zi's eyes as the Asiatic came out of the shadow towards him.

In another moment the two men were grappling fiercely in front of the great dynamo.

"You coffee-headed fool!" gasped Holroyd, with a brown hand at his throat. "Keep off those contact rings." In another moment he was tripped and reeling back upon the Lord of the Dynamos. He instinctively loosened his grip upon his antagonist to save himself from the machine.

The messenger, sent in furious haste from the station to find out what had happened in the dynamo shed, met Azuma-zi at the porter's lodge by the gate. Azuma-zi tried to explain something, but the messenger could make nothing of the black's incoherent English, and hurried on to the shed. The machines were all noisily at work, and nothing seemed to be disarranged. There was, however, a queer smell of singed hair. Then he saw an odd-looking, crumpled mass clinging to the front of the big dynamo, and, approaching, recognised the distorted remains of Holroyd.

The man stared and hesitated a moment. Then he saw the face and shut his eyes convulsively. He turned on his heel before he opened them, so that he should not see Holroyd again, and went out of the shed to get advice and help.

When Azuma-zi saw Holroyd die in the grip of the Great Dynamo he had been a little scared about the consequences of his act. Yet he felt strangely elated, and knew that the favour of the Lord Dynamo was upon him. His plan was already settled when he met the man coming from the station, and the scientific manager who speedily arrived on the scene jumped at the obvious conclusion of suicide. This expert scarcely noticed Azuma-zi except to ask a few questions. Did he see Holroyd kill himself? Azuma-zi explained he had been out of sight at the engine furnace until he heard a difference in the noise from the dynamo. It was not a difficult examination, being untinctured by suspicion.

The distorted remains of Holroyd, which the electrician removed from the machine, were hastily covered by the porter with a coffee-stained table-cloth. Somebody, by a happy inspiration, fetched a medical man. The expert was chiefly anxious to get the machine at work again, for seven or eight trains had stopped midway in the stuffy tunnels of the electric railway. Azuma-zi, answering or misunderstanding the questions of the people who had by authority or impudence come into the shed, was presently sent back to the stoke-hole by the scientific manager. Of course a crowd collected outside the gates of the yard,—a crowd, for no known reason, always hovers for a day or two near the scene of a sudden death in London; two or three reporters percolated somehow into the engine-shed, and one even got to Azuma-zi; but the scientific expert cleared them out again, being himself an amateur journalist.

Presently the body was carried away, and public interest departed with it. Azuma-zi remained very quietly at his furnace, seeing over and over again in the coals a figure that wriggled violently and became still. An hour after the murder, to any one coming into the shed it would have looked exactly as if nothing remarkable had ever happened there. Peeping presently from his engine-room the black saw the Lord Dynamo spin and whirl beside his little brothers, the driving wheels were beating round, and the steam in the pistons went thud, thud, exactly as it had been earlier in the evening. After all, from the mechanical point of view, it had been a most insignificant incident—the mere temporary deflection of a current. But now the slender form and slender shadow of the scientific manager replaced the sturdy outline of Holroyd travelling up and down the lane of light upon the vibrating floor under straps between the engines and the dynamos.

"Have I not served my Lord?" said Azuma-zi, inaudibly, from his shadow, and the note of the great dynamo rang out full and clear. As he looked at the big, whirling mechanism the strange fascination of it that had been a little in abeyance since Holroyd's death resumed its sway.

Never had Azuma-zi seen a man killed so swiftly and pitilessly. The big, humming machine had slain its victim without wavering for a second from it steady beating. It was indeed a mighty god.

The unconscious scientific manager stood with his back to him, scribbling on a piece of paper. His shadow lay at the foot of the monster.

"Was the Lord Dynamo still hungry? His servant was ready."

Azuma-zi made a stealthy step forward, then stopped. The scientific manager suddenly stopped writing, and walked down the shed to the endmost of the dynamos, and began to examine the brushes.

Azumz-zi hesitated, and then slipped across noiselessly into the shadow by the switch. There he waited. Presently the manager's footsteps could be heard returning. He stopped in his old position, unconscious of the stoker crouching ten feet away from him. Then the big dynamo suddenly fizzled, and in another moment Aumza-zi had sprung out of the darkness upon him.

First, the scientific manager was gripped round the body and swung towards the big dynamo, then, kicking with his knee and forcing his antagonist's head down with his hands, he loosened the grip on his waist and swung round away from the machine. Then the black grasped him again, putting a curly head against his chest, and they swayed and panted as it seemed for an age or so. Then the scientific manager was impelled to catch a black ear in his teeth and bite furiously. The black yelled hideously.

They rolled over on the floor, and the black, who had apparently slipped from the vice of the teeth or parted with some ear—the scientific manager wondered which at the time—tried to throttle him. The scientific manager was making some ineffectual efforts to claw something with his hands and to kick, when the welcome sound of quick footsteps sounded on the floor. The next moment Azuma-zi had left him and darted towards the big dynamo. There was a splutter amid the roar.

The officer of the company, who had entered, stood staring as Azuma-zi caught the naked terminals in his hands, gave one horrible convulsion, and then hung motionless from the machine, his face violently distorted.

"I'm jolly glad you came in when you did," said the scientific manager, still sitting on the floor.

He looked at the still quivering figure. "It is not a nice death to die, apparently—but it is quick."

The official was still staring at the body. He was a man of slow apprehension.

There was a pause.

The scientific manager got up on his feet rather awkwardly. He ran his fingers along his collar thoughtfully, and moved his head to and fro several times.

"Poor Holroyd! I see now." Then almost mechanically he went towards the switch in the shadow and turned the current into the railway circuit again. As he did so the singed body loosened its grip upon the machine and fell forward on its face. The cone of the dynamo roared out loud and clear, and the armature beat the air.

So ended prematurely the Worship of the Dynamo Deity, perhaps the most short-lived of all religions. Yet withal it could boast a Martyrdom and a Human Sacrifice.

Nathaniel Hawthorne (1804–1864) was born in Salem, Massachusetts. After graduation from Bowdoin College, Hawthorne returned home and for a dozen years lived in seclusion while teaching himself to become a literary artist. After his marriage in 1842, he lived in Salem and of financial necessity became surveyor in the Custom House. Characteristically, his work blends realism, melodrama, and the Gothic conventions; his themes center on the mysteries of the human heart, the nature of sin, and the significance of "darkness." Publication of The Scarlet Letter *(1850) established Hawthorne as a major American writer of prose fiction. For further reading:* Twicetold Tales *(1837 and 1842);* Tales of Hawthorne, *edited by Carl Van Doren (1921).*

NATHANIEL HAWTHORNE

Dr. Heidegger's Experiment

That very singular man, old Dr. Heidegger, once invited four venerable friends to meet him in his study. There were three white-bearded gentlemen, Mr. Medbourne, Colonel Killigrew, and Mr. Gascoigne, and a withered gentlewoman, whose name was the Widow Wycherly. They were all melancholy old creatures, who had been unfortunate in life, and whose greatest misfortune it was that they were not long ago in their graves. Mr. Medbourne, in the vigor of his age, had been a prosperous merchant, but had lost his all by a frantic speculation, and was not little better than a mendicant. Colonel Killigrew had wasted his best years, and his health and substance, in the pursuit of sinful pleasures, which had given birth to a brood of pains, such as the gout, and divers other torments of soul and body. Mr. Gascoigne was a ruined politician, a man of evil fame, or at least had been so till time had buried him from the knowledge of the present generation, and made him obscure instead of infamous. As for the Widow Wycherly, tradition tells us that she was a great beauty in her day; but, for a long while past, she had lived in deep seclusion, on account of certain scandalous stories which had prejudiced the gentry of the town against her. It is a circumstance worth mentioning that each of these three old gentlemen, Mr. Medbourne, Colonel Killigrew, and Mr. Gascoigne, were early lovers of the Widow Wycherly, and had once been on the point of cutting each other's throats for her sake. And, before proceeding further, I will merely hint that Dr. Heidegger and all his four guests were sometimes thought to be a little beside themselves,—as is not unfrequently the case with old people, when worried either by present troubles or woful recollections.

"My dear old friends," said Dr. Heidegger, motioning them to be seated, "I am desirous of your assistance in one of those little experiments with which I amuse myself here in my study."

If all stories were true, Dr. Heidegger's study must have been a very curious place. It was a dim, old-fashioned chamber, festooned with cobwebs, and besprinkled with antique dust. Around the walls stood several oaken bookcases, the lower shelves of which were filled with rows of gigantic folios and black-letter quartos, and the upper with little parchment-covered duodecimos. Over the central bookcase was a bronze bust of Hippocrates, with which, according to some authorities, Dr. Heidegger was accustomed to hold consultations in all difficult cases of his practice. In the obscurest corner of the room stood a tall and narrow oaken closet, with its door ajar, within which doubtfully appeared a skeleton. Between two of the bookcases hung a looking-glass, presenting its high and dusty plate within a tarnished gilt frame. Among many wonderful stories related of this mirror, it was fabled that the spirits of all the doctor's deceased patients dwelt within its verge, and would stare him in the face whenever he looked titherward. The opposite side of the chamber was ornamented with the full-length portrait of a young lady, arrayed in the faded magnificence of silk, satin, and brocade, and with a visage as faded as her dress. Above half a century ago, Dr. Heidegger had been on the point of marriage with this young lady; but, being affected with some slight disorder, she had swallowed one of her lover's prescriptions, and died on the bridal evening. The greatest curiosity of the study remains to be mentioned; it was a ponderous folio volume, bound in black leather, with massive silver clasps. There were no letters on the back, and nobody could tell the title of the book. But it was well known to be a book of magic; and once, when a chambermaid had lifted it, merely to brush away the dust, the skeleton had rattled in its closet, the picture of the young lady had stepped one foot upon the floor, and several ghastly faces had peeped forth from the mirror; while the brazen head of Hippocrates frowned, and said,—"Forbear!"

Such was Dr. Heidegger's study. On the summer afternoon of our tale a small round table, as black as ebony, stood in the centre of the room, sustaining a cut-glass vase of beautiful form and elaborate workmanship. The sunshine came through the window between the heavy festoons of two faded damask curtains, and fell directly across this vase; so that a mild splendor was reflected from it on the ashen visages of the five old people who sat around. Four champagne glasses were also on the table.

"My dear old friends," repeated Dr. Heidegger, "may I reckon on your aid in performing an exceedingly curious experiment?"

Now Dr. Heidegger was a very strange old gentleman, whose eccentricity had become the nucleus for a thousand fantastic stories. Some of these fables, to my shame be it spoken, might possibly be traced back to my own veracious self; and if any passages of the present tale should startle the reader's faith, I must be content to bear the stigma of a fiction monger.

When the doctor's four guests heard him talk of his proposed experiment, they anticipated nothing more wonderful than the murder of a mouse in an air pump, or the examination of a cobweb by the microscope, or some similar nonsense, with which he was constantly in the habit of pestering his intimates. But without waiting for a reply, Dr. Heidegger hobbled across the chamber, and returned with the same ponderous folio, bound in black leather, which common report affirmed to be a book of magic. Undoing the silver clasps, he opened the volume, and took from among its black-letter pages a rose, or what was once rose, though now the green leaves and crimson petals had assumed one brownish hue, and the ancient flower seemed ready to crumble to dust in the doctor's hands.

"This rose," said Dr. Heidegger, with a sigh, "this same withered and crumbling flower, blossomed five and fifty years ago. It was given me by Sylvia Ward, whose portrait hangs yonder; and I meant to wear it in my bosom at our wedding. Five and fifty years it has been treasured between the leaves of this old volume. Now, would you deem it possible that this rose of half a century could ever bloom again?"

"Nonsense!" said the Widow Wycherly, with a peevish toss of her head. "You might as well ask whether an old woman's wrinkled face could ever bloom again."

"See!" answered Dr. Heidegger.

He uncovered the vase, and threw the faded rose into the water which it contained. At first, it lay lightly on the surface of the fluid, appearing to imbibe none of its moisture. Soon, however, a singular change began to be visible. The crushed and dried petals stirred, and assumed a deepening tinge of crimson, as if the flower were reviving from a deathlike slumber; the slender stalk and twigs of foliage became green; and there was the rose of half a century, looking as fresh as when Sylvia Ward had first given it to her lover. It was scarcely full blown; for some of its delicate red leaves curled modestly around its moist bosom, within which two or three dewdrops were sparkling.

"That is certainly a very pretty deception," said the doctor's friends; carelessly, however, for they had witnessed greater miracles at a conjurer's show; "pray how was it effected?"

"Did you never hear of the 'Fountain of Youth?' " asked Dr. Heidegger, "which Ponce De Leon, the Spanish adventurer, went in search of two or three centuries ago?"

"But did Ponce De Leon ever find it?" said the Widow Wycherly.

"No," answered Dr. Heidegger, "for he never sought in the right place. The famous Fountain of Youth, if I am rightly informed, is situated in the southern part of the Floridian peninsula, not far from Lake Macaco. Its source is overshadowed by several gigantic magnolias, which, though numberless centuries old, have been kept as fresh as violets by the virtues of this wonderful water. An acquaintance of mine, knowing my curiosity in such matters, has sent me what you see in the vase."

"Ahem!" said Colonel Killigrew, who believed not a word of the doctor's story; "and what may be the effect of this fluid on the human frame?"

"You shall judge for yourself, my dear colonel," replied Dr. Heidegger; "and all of you, my respected friends, are welcome to so much of this admirable fluid as may restore to you the bloom of youth. For my own part, having had much trouble in growing old, I am in no hurry to grow young again. With your permission, therefore, I will merely watch the progress of the experiment."

While he spoke, Dr. Heidegger had been filling the four champagne glasses with the water of the Fountain of Youth. It was apparently impregnated with an effervescent gas, for little bubbles were continually ascending from the depths of the glasses, and bursting in silvery spray at the surface. As the liquor diffused a pleasant perfume, the old people doubted not that it possessed cordial and comfortable properties; and though utter sceptics as to its rejuvenescent power, they were inclined to swallow it at once. But Dr. Heidegger besought them to stay a moment.

"Before you drink, my respectable old friends," said he, "it would be well that, with the experience of a lifetime to direct you, you should draw up a few general rules for your guidance, in passing a second time through the perils of youth. Think what a sin and shame it would be, if, with your peculiar advantages, you should not become patterns of virtue and wisdom to all the young people of the age!"

The doctor's four venerable friends made him no answer, except by a feeble and tremulous laugh; so very ridiculous was the idea that, knowing how closely repentance treads behind the steps of error, they should ever go astray again.

"Drink then," said the doctor, bowing: "I rejoice that I have so well selected the subjects of my experiment."

With palsied hands, they raised the glasses to their lips. The liquor, if it really possessed such virtues as Dr. Heidegger imputed to it, could not have been bestowed on four human beings who needed it more wofully. They looked as if they had never known what youth or pleasure was, but had been the offspring of Nature's dotage, and always the gray, decrepit, sapless, miserable creatures, who now sat stooping round the doctor's table, without life enough in their souls or bodies to be animated even by the prospect of growing young again. They drank off the water, and replaced their glasses on the table.

Assuredly there was an almost immediate improvement in the aspect of the party, not unlike what might have been produced by a glass of generous wine, together with a sudden glow of cheerful sunshine brightening over all their visages at once. There was a healthful suffusion on their cheeks, instead of the ashen hue that had made them look so corpse-like. They gazed at one another, and fancied that some magic power had really begun to smooth away the deep and sad inscriptions which Father Time had been so long engraving on their brows. The Widow Wycherly adjusted her cap, for she felt almost like a woman again.

"Give us more of this wonderous water!" cried they, eagerly. "We are younger—but we are still too old! Quick—give us more!"

"Patience, patience!" quoth Dr. Heidegger, who sat watching the experiment with philosophic coolness. "You have been a long time growing old. Surely, you might be content to grow young in half an hour! But the water is at your service."

Again he filled their glasses with the liquor of youth, enough of which still remained in the vase to turn half the old people in the city to the age of their own grandchildren. While the bubbles were yet sparkling on the brim, the doctor's four guests snatched their glasses from the table, and swallowed the contents at a single gulp. Was it delusion? even while the draught was passing down their throats, it seemed to have wrought a change on their whole systems. Their eyes grew clear and bright; a dark shade deepened among their silvery locks, they sat around the table, three gentlemen of middle age and a woman, hardly beyond her buxom prime.

"My dear widow, you are charming!" cried Colonel Killigrew, whose eyes had been fixed upon her face, while the shadows of age were flitting from it like darkness from the crimson daybreak.

The fair widow knew, of old, that Colonel Killigrew's compliments were not always measured by sober truth; so she started up and ran to the mirror, still dreading that the ugly visage of an old woman would meet her gaze. Meanwhile, the three gentlemen behaved in such a manner as proved that the water of the Fountain of Youth possessed some intoxicating qualities; unless, indeed, their exhilaration of spirits were merely a lightsome dizziness caused by the sudden removal of the weight of years. Mr.

Gascoigne's mind seemed to run on political topics, but whether relating to the past, present, or future, could not easily be determined, since the same ideas and phrases have been in vogue these fifty years. Now he rattled forth full-throated sentences about patriotism, national glory, and the people's right; now he muttered some perilous stuff or other, in a sly and doubtful whisper, so cautiously that even his own conscience could scarcely catch the secret; and now, again, he spoke in measured accents, and a deeply deferential tone, as if a royal ear were listening to his well-turned periods. Colonel Killigrew all this time had been trolling forth a jolly bottle song, and ringing his glass in symphony with the chorus, while his eyes wandered toward the buxom figure of the Widow Wycherly. On the other side of the table, Mr. Medbourne was involved in a calculation of dollars and cents, with which was strangely intermingled a project for supplying the East Indies with ice, by harnessing a team of whales to the polar icebergs.

As for the Widow Wycherly, she stood before the mirror courtesying and simpering to her own image, and greeting it as the friend whom she loved better than all the world beside. She thrust her face close to the glass, to see whether some long-remembered wrinkle or crow's foot had indeed vanished. She examined whether the snow had so entirely melted from her hair that the venerable cap could be safely thrown aside. At last, turning briskly away, she came with a sort of dancing step to the table.

"My dear old doctor," cried she, "pray favor me with another glass!"

"Certainly, my dear madam, certainly!" replied the complaisant doctor; "see! I have already filled the glasses."

There, in fact, stood the four glasses, brimful of this wonderful water, the delicate spray of which, as it effervesced from the surface, resembled the tremulous glitter of diamonds. It was now so nearly sunset that the chamber had grown duskier than ever; but a mild and moonlike splendor gleamed from within the vase, and rested alike on the four guests and on the doctor's venerable figure. He sat in a high-backed, elaborately-carved, oaken armchair, with a gray dignity of aspect that might have well befitted that very Father Time, whose power had never been disputed, save by this fortunate company. Even while quaffing the third draught of the Fountain of Youth, they were almost awed by the expression of his mysterious visage.

But, the next moment, the exhilarating gush of young life shot through their veins. They were now in the happy prime of youth. Age, with its miserable train of cares and sorrows and diseases, was remembered only as the trouble of a dream, from which they had joyously awoke. The fresh gloss of the soul, so early lost, and without which the world's successive scenes had been but a gallery of faded pictures, again threw its enchantment over all their prospects. They felt like new-created beings in a new-created universe.

"We are young! We are young!" they cried exultingly.

Youth, like the extremity of age, had effaced the strongly-marked characteristics of middle life, and mutually assimilated them all. They were a group of merry youngsters, almost maddened with the exuberant frolicsomeness of their years. The most singular effect of their gayety was an impulse to mock the infirmity and decrepitude of which they had so lately been the victims. They laughed loudly at their old-fashioned attire, the wide-skirted coats and flapped waistcoats of the young men, and the ancient cap and gown of the blooming girl. One limped across the floor like a gouty grandfather; one set a pair of spectacles astride his nose, and pretended to pore over the black-letter pages of the book of magic; a third seated himself in an arm-chair, and strove to imitate the venerable dignity of Dr. Heidegger. Then all shouted mirthfully, and leaped about the room. The Widow Wycherly—if so fresh a damsel could be called a widow—tripped up to the doctor's chair, with a mischievous merriment in her rosy face.

"Doctor, you dear old soul." cried she, "get up and dance with me!" And then the four young people laughed louder than ever, to think what a queer figure the poor old doctor would cut.

"Pray excuse me," answered the doctor quietly. "I am old and rheumatic, and my dancing days were over long ago. But either of these gay young gentlemen will be glad of so pretty a partner."

"Dance with me, Clara!" cried Colonel Killigrew.

"No, no, I will be her partner!" shouted Mr. Gascoigne.

"She promised me her hand, fifty years ago!" exclaimed Mr. Medbourne.

They all gathered round her. One caught both her hands in his passionate grasp—another threw his arm about her waist—the third buried his hand among the glossy curls that clustered beneath the widow's cap. Blushing, panting, struggling, chiding, laughing, her warm breath fanning each of their faces by turns, she strove to disengage herself, yet still remained in their triple embrace. Never was there a livelier picture of youthful rivalship, with bewitching beauty for the prize. Yet, by a strange deception, owing to the duskiness of the chamber, and the antique dresses which they still wore, the tall mirror is said to have reflected the figures of the three old, gray, withered grandsires, ridiculously contending for the skinny ugliness of a shrivelled grandam.

But they were young: their burning passions proved them so. Inflamed to madness by the coquetry of the girl-widow, who neither granted nor quite withheld her favors, the three rivals began to interchange threatening glances. Still keeping hold of the fair prize, they grappled fiercely at one another's throats. As they struggled to and fro, the table was overturned, and the vase dashed into a thousand fragments. The precious Water of

Youth flowed in a bright stream across the floor, moistening the wings of a butterfly, which, grown old in the decline of summer, had alighted there to die. The insect fluttered lightly through the chamber, and settled on the snowy head of Dr. Heidegger.

"Come, come, gentlemen!—come, Madam Wycherly," exclaimed the doctor, "I really must protest against this riot."

They stood still and shivered; for it seemed as if gray Time were calling them back from their sunny youth, far down into the chill and darksome vale of years. They looked at old Dr. Heidegger, who sat in his carved arm-chair, holding the rose of half a century, which he had rescued from among the fragments of the shattered vase. At the motion of his hand, the four rioters resumed their seats; the more readily, because their violent exertions had wearied them, youthful though they were.

"My poor Sylvia's rose!" ejaculated Dr. Heidegger, holding it in the light of the sunset clouds; "it appears to be fading again."

And so it was. Even while the party were looking at it, the flower continued to shrivel up, till it became as dry and fragile as when the doctor had first thrown it into the vase. He shook off the few drops of moisture which clung to its petals.

"I love it as well thus as in its dewy freshness," observed he, pressing the withered rose to his withered lips. While he spoke, the butterfly fluttered down from the doctor's snowy head, and fell upon the floor.

His guests shivered again. A strange chillness, whether of the body or spirit they could not tell, was creeping gradually over them all. They gazed at one another, and fancied that each fleeting moment snatched away a charm, and left a deepening furrow where none had been before. Was it an illusion? Had the changes of a lifetime been crowded into so brief a space, and were they now four aged people, sitting with their old friend, Dr. Heidegger?

"Are we grown old again, so soon?" cried they, dolefully.

In truth they had. The Water of Youth possessed merely a virtue more transient than that of wine. The delirium which it created had effervesced away. Yes! they were old again. With a shuddering impulse, that showed her a woman still, the widow clasped her skinny hands before her face, and wished that the coffin lid were over it, since it could be no longer beautiful.

NOTE.—In an English review, not long since, I have been accused of plagiarizing the idea of this story from a chapter in one of the novels of Alexandre Dumas. There has undoubtedly been a plagiarism on one side or the other; but as my story was written a good deal more than twenty years ago, and as the novel is of considerably more recent date, I take pleasure in thinking that M. Dumas has done me the honor to appropriate one of the fanciful conceptions of my earlier days. He is heartily welcome to it; nor is it the only instance, by many, in which

"Yes, friends, ye are old again," said Dr. Heidegger, "and lo! the Water of Youth is all lavished on the ground. Well—I bemoan it not; for if the fountain gushed at my very doorstep, I would not stoop to bathe my lips in it—no, though its delirium were for years instead of moments. Such is the lesson ye have taught me!"

But the doctor's four friends had taught no such lesson to themselves. They resolved forthwith to make a pilgrimage to Florida, and quaff at morning, noon, and night, from the Fountain of Youth.

the great French romancer has exercised the privilege of commanding genius by confiscating the intellectual property of less famous people to his own use and behoof.
    September, 1860.

Edgar Allan Poe (1809–1849) was the son of theatrical parents, both of whom died when he was a child; later Poe lived in the household of John Allan, a Richmond merchant. For one year (1826) Poe was a brilliant student and athlete at the University of Virginia, but Mr. Allan withdrew financial support, probably because of Poe's gambling debts. Poe enlisted in the Army; eventually he was appointed a cadet at the U.S. Military Academy (West Point). But he withdrew and, having been disowned entirely by Mr. Allan, became a writer-critic-editor, often in precarious circumstance, for the remainder of his life. Poe had an unfortunate intolerance for alcohol and died in Baltimore under mysterious circumstances, probably by violence. Poe is widely credited with "inventing" the detective story. For further reading: Poe's Short Stories, *edited by Killis Campbell (1927).*

EDGAR ALLAN POE

A Tale of the Ragged Mountains

During the fall of the year 1827, while residing near Charlottesville, Virginia, I casually made the acquaintance of Mr. Augustus Bedloe. This young gentleman was remarkable in every respect, and excited in me a profound interest and curiosity. I found it impossible to comprehend him either in his moral or his physical relations. Of his family I could obtain no satisfactory account. Whence he came, I never ascertained. Even about his age—although I call him a young gentleman—there was something which perplexed me in no little degree. He certainly *seemed* young—and he made a point of speaking about his youth—yet there were moments when I should have had little trouble in imagining him a hundred years of age. But in no regard was he more peculiar than in his personal appearance. He was singularly tall and thin. He stooped much. His limbs were exceedingly long and emaciated. His forehead was broad and low. His complexion was absolutely bloodless. His mouth was large and flexible, and his teeth were more

wildly uneven, although sound, than I had ever before seen teeth in a human head. The expression of his smile, however, was by no means unpleas-
ing, as might be supposed; but it had no variation whatever. It was one of
profound melancholy—of a phaseless and unceasing gloom. His eyes were
abnormally large, and round like those of a cat. The pupils, too, upon any
accession or diminution of light, underwent contraction or dilation, just
such as is observed in the feline tribe. In moments of excitement the orbs
grew bright to a degree almost inconceivable; seeming to emit luminous
rays, not of a reflected, but of an intrinsic lustre, as does a candle or the
sun; yet their ordinary condition was so totally vapid, filmy and dull, as to
convey the idea of the eyes of a long-interred corpse.

These peculiarities of person appeared to cause him much annoyance,
and he was continually alluding to them in a sort of half explanatory, half
apologetic strain, which, when I first heard it, impressed me very painfully.
I soon, however, grew accustomed to it, and my uneasiness wore off. It
seemed to be his design rather to insinuate than directly to assert that,
physically, he had not always been what he was—that a long series of
neuralgic attacks had reduced him from a condition of more than usual
personal beauty, to that which I saw. For many years past he had been
attended by a physician, named Templeton—an old gentleman, perhaps
seventy years of age—whom he had first encountered at Saratoga, and from
whose attention, while there, he either received, or fancied that he received,
great benefit. The result was that Bedloe, who was wealthy, had made an
arrangement with Doctor Templeton, by which the latter, in consideration
of a liberal annual allowance, had consented to devote his time and medical
experience exclusively to the care of the invalid.

Doctor Templeton had been a traveller in his younger days, and, at
Paris, had become a convert, in great measure, to the doctrines of Mesmer.
It was altogether by means of magnetic remedies that he had succeeded in
alleviating the acute pains of his patient; and this success had very naturally
inspired the latter with a certain degree of confidence in the opinions from
which the remedies had been educed. The doctor, however, like all enthusiasts, had struggled hard to make a thorough convert of his pupil, and finally
so far gained his point as to induce the sufferer to submit to numerous
experiments. By a frequent repetition of these a result had arisen, which of
late days has become so common as to attract little or no attention, but
which, at the period of which I write, had very rarely been known in America. I mean to say, that between Doctor Templeton and Bedloe there had
grown up, little by little, a very distinct and strongly marked *rapport,* or
magnetic relation. I am not prepared to assert, however, that this *rapport*
extended beyond the limits of the simple sleep-producing power; but this
power itself had attained great intensity. At the first attempt to induce the
magnetic somnolency, the mesmerist entirely failed. In the fifth or sixth he

succeeded very partially, and after long continued effort. Only at the twelfth was the triumph complete. After this the will of the patient succumbed rapidly to that of the physician, so that, when I first became acquainted with the two, sleep was brought about almost instantaneously, by the mere volition of the operator, even when the invalid was unaware of his presence. It is only now, in the year 1845, when similar miracles are witnessed daily by thousands, that I dare venture to record this apparent impossibility as a matter of serious fact.

The temperature of Bedloe was, in the highest degree, sensitive, excitable, enthusiastic. His imagination was singularly vigorous and creative; and no doubt it derived additional force from the habitual use of morphine, which he swallowed in great quantity, and without which he would have found it impossible to exist. It was his practice to take a very large dose of it immediately after breakfast, each morning—or rather immediately after a cup of strong coffee, for he ate nothing in the forenoon—and then set forth alone, or attended only by a dog, upon a long ramble among the chain of wild and dreary hills that lie westward and southward of Charlottesville, and are there dignified by the title of the Ragged Mountains.

Upon a dim, warm, misty day, towards the close of November, and during the strange *interregnum* of the seasons which in America is termed the Indian Summer, Mr. Bedloe departed as usual for the hills. The day passed, and still he did not return.

About eight o'clock at night, having become seriously alarmed at his protracted absence, we were about setting out in search of him, when he unexpectedly made his appearance, in health no worse than usual, and in rather more than ordinary spirits. The account which he gave of his expedition, and of the events which had detained him, was a singular one indeed.

"You will remember," said he, "that it was about nine in the morning when I left Charlottesville. I bent my steps immediately to the mountains, and about ten, entered a gorge which was entirely new to me. I followed the windings of this pass with much interest. The scenery which presented itself on all sides, although scarcely entitled to be called grand, had about it an indescribable, and to me, a delicious aspect of dreary desolation. The solitude seemed absolutely virgin. I could not help believing that the green sods and the gray rocks upon which I trod, had been trodden never before by the foot of a human being. So entirely secluded and in fact inaccessible, except through a series of accidents, is the entrance of the ravine, that it is by no means impossible that I was indeed the first adventurer—the very first and sole adventurer who had ever penetrated its recesses.

"The thick and peculiar mist, or smoke, which distinguishes the Indian Summer, and which now hung heavily over all objects, served, no doubt, to deepen the vague impressions which these objects created. So dense was this pleasant fog, that I could at no time see more than a dozen yards of the path before me. This path was excessively sinuous, and as the sun could not be seen, I soon lost all idea of the direction in which I journeyed. In the meantime the morphine had its customary effect—that of enduing all the external world with an intensity of interest. In the quivering of a leaf—in the hue of a blade of grass—in the shape of a trefoil—in the humming of a bee—in the gleaming of a dew-drop—in the breathing of the wind—in the faint odours that came from the forest—there came a whole universe of suggestion—a gay and motley train of rhapsodical and immethodical thought.

"Busied in this, I walked on for several hours, during which the mist deepened around me to so great an extent, that at length I was reduced to an absolute groping of the way. And now an indescribable uneasiness possessed me—a species of nervous hesitation and tremor. I feared to tread, lest I should be precipitated into some abyss. I remembered too, strange stories told about these Ragged Hills, and of the uncouth and fierce races of men who tenanted their groves and caverns. A thousand vague fancies oppressed and disconcerted me—fancies the more distressing because vague. Very suddenly my attention was arrested by the loud beating of a drum.

"My amazement, was, of course, extreme. A drum in these hills was a thing unknown. I could not have been more surprised at the sound of the trump of the Archangel. But a new and still more astounding source of interest and perplexity arose. There came a wild rattling or jingling sound, as if of a bunch of large keys—and upon the instant a dusky-visaged and half-naked man rushed past me with a shriek. He came so close to my person that I felt his hot breath upon my face. He bore in one hand an instrument composed of an assemblage of steel rings, and shook them vigorously as he ran. Scarcely had he disappeared in the mist, before, panting after him, with open mouth and glaring eyes there darted a huge beast. I could not be mistaken in its character. It was a hyena.

"The sight of this monster rather relieved than heightened my terrors—for I now made sure that I dreamed, and endeavoured to arouse myself to waking consciousness. I stepped boldly and briskly forward. I rubbed my eyes. I called aloud. I pinched my limbs. A small spring of water presented itself to my view, and here, stooping, I bathed my hands and my head and neck. This seemed to dissipate the equivocal sensations which had hitherto annoyed me. I arose, as I thought, a new man, and proceeded steadily and complacently on my unknown way.

"At length, quite overcome by exertion, and by a certain oppressive closeness of the atmosphere, I seated myself beneath a tree. Presently there came a feeble gleam of sunshine, and the shadow of the leaves of the tree fell faintly but definitely upon the grass. At this shadow I gazed wonderingly for many minutes. Its character stupified me with astonishment. I looked upward. The tree was a palm.

"I now arose hurriedly, and in a state of fearful agitation—for the fancy that I dreamed would serve me no longer. I saw—I felt that I had perfect command of my senses—and these senses now brought to my soul a world of novel and singular sensation. The heat became all at once intolerable. A strange odour loaded the breeze.—A low continuous murmur, like that arising from a full, but gently flowing river, came to my ears intermingled with the peculiar hum of multitudinous human voices.

"While I listened in an extremity of astonishment which I need not attempt to describe, a strong and brief gust of wind bore off the incumbent fog as if by the wand of an enchanter.

"I found myself at the foot of a high mountain, and looking down into a vast plain, through which wound a majestic river. On the margin of this river stood an Eastern-looking city, such as we read of in the Arabian Tales, but of a character even more singular than any there described. From my position, which was far above the level of the town, I could perceive its every nook and corner, as if delineated on a map. The streets seemed innumerable, and crossed each other irregularly in all directions, but were rather long winding alleys than streets, and absolutely swarmed with inhabitants. The houses were wildly picturesque. On every hand was a wilderness of balconies, of verandahs, of minarets, of shrines, and fantastically carved oriels. Bazaars abounded; and in these were displayed rich wares in infinite variety and profusion—silks, muslins, the most dazzling cutlery, the most magnificent jewels and gems. Besides these things, were seen, on all sides, banners and palanquins, litters with stately dames close veiled, elephants gorgeously caparisoned, idols grotesquely hewn, drums, banners and gongs, spears, silver and gilded maces. And amid the crowd and the clamour, and the general intricacy and confusion—amid the million of black and yellow men, turbaned and robed, and of flowing beard, there roamed a countless multitude of holy filleted bulls, while vast legions of the filthy but sacred ape clambered, chattering and shrieking, about the cornices of the mosques, or clung to the minarets and oriels. From the swarming streets to the banks of the river, there descended innumerable flights of steps leading to bathing places, while the river itself seemed to force a passage with difficulty through the vast fleets of deeply burdened ships that far and wide encountered its surface. Beyond the limits of the city arose, in frequent majestic groups, the palm and the cocoa, with other gigantic and weird trees of vast age; and here and there might be seen a field of rice, the thatched hut of a peasant, a tank, a stray temple, a gipsy camp, or a solitary graceful maiden taking her way, with a pitcher upon her head, to the banks of the magnificent river.

"You will say now, of course, that I dreamed, but not so. What I saw—what I heard—what I felt—what I thought—had about it nothing of the unmistakable idiosyncrasy of the dream. All was rigorously self-consistent. At first, doubting that I was really awake, I entered into a series of tests,

which soon convinced me that I really was. Now, when one dreams, and, in
the dream, suspects that he dreams, the suspicion *never fails to confirm itself,*
and the sleeper is almost immediately aroused. Thus Novalis errs not in
saying that 'we are near waking when we dream that we dream.' Had the
vision occurred to me as I describe it, without my suspecting it as a dream,
then a dream it might absolutely have been, but, occurring as it did, and
suspected and tested as it was, I am forced to class it among other phenomena."

"In this I am not sure that you are wrong," observed Dr. Templeton,
"but proceed. You arose and descended into the city."

"I arose," continued Bedloe, regarding the Doctor with an air of profound astonishment, "I arose, as you say, and descended into the city. On
my way, I fell in with an immense populace, crowding through every avenue, all in the same direction, and exhibiting in every action the wildest
excitement. Very suddenly, and by some inconceivable impulse, I became
intensely imbued with personal interest in what was going on. I seemed to
feel that I had an important part to play, without exactly understanding
what it was. Against the crowd which environed me, however, I experienced
a deep sentiment of animosity. I shrank from amid them, and, swiftly, by a
circuitous path, reached and entered the city. Here all was the wildest tu-
malt and contention. A small party of men, clad in garments half Indian,
half European, and officered by gentlemen in a uniform partly British, were
engaged, at great odds, with the swarming rabble of the alleys. I joined the
weaker party, arming myself with the weapons of a fallen officer, and fighting I knew not whom with the nervous ferocity of despair. We were soon
overpowered by numbers, and driven to seek refuge in a species of kiosk.
Here we barricaded ourselves, and, for the present, were secure. From a
loop-hole near the summit of the kiosk, I perceived a vast crowd, in furious
agitation, surrounding and assaulting a gay palace that overhung the river.
Presently, from an upper window of this palace, there descended an effemi-
nate-looking person, by means of a string made of the turbans of his attendants. A boat was at hand, in which he escaped to the opposite bank of the
river.

"And now a new object took possession of my soul. I spoke a few
hurried but energetic words to my companions, and, having succeeded in
gaining over a few of them to my purpose, made a frantic sally from the
kiosk. We rushed amid the crowd that surrounded it. They retreated, at
first, before us. They rallied, fought madly, and retreated again. In the
meantime we were borne far from the kiosk, and became bewildered and
entangled among the narrow streets of tall overhanging houses, into the
recesses of which the sun had never been able to shine. The rabble pressed
impetuously upon us, harassing us with their spears, and overwhelming us
with flights of arrows. These latter were very remarkable, and resembled in

some respects the writhing creese of the Malay. They were made to imitate the body of a creeping serpent, and were long and black, with a poisoned barb. One of them struck me upon the right temple. I reeled and fell. An instantaneous and dreadful sickness seized me. I struggled—I gasped—I died."

"You will hardly persist *now*," said I, smiling, "that the whole of your adventure was not a dream. You are not prepared to maintain that you are dead?"

When I said these words, I of course expected some lively sally from Bedloe in reply; but, to my astonishment, he hesitated, trembled, became fearfully pallid, and remained silent. I looked towards Templeton. He sat erect and rigid in his chair—his teeth chattered, and his eyes were starting from their sockets. "Proceed!" he at length said hoarsely to Bedloe.

"For many minutes," continued the latter, "my sole sentiment—my sole feeling—was that of darkness and nonentity, with the consciousness of death. At length, there seemed to pass a violent and sudden shock through my soul, as if of electricity. With it came the sense of elasticity and of light. This latter I felt—not saw. In an instant I seemed to rise from the ground. But I had no bodily, no visible, audible, or palpable presence. The crowd had departed. The tumult had ceased. The city was in comparative repose. Beneath me lay my corpse, with the arrow in my temple, the whole head greatly swollen and disfigured. But all these things I felt—not saw. I took interest in nothing. Even the corpse seemed a matter in which I had no concern. Volition I had none, but appeared to be impelled into motion, and flitted buoyantly out of the city, retracing the circuitous path by which I had entered it. When I had attained that point of the ravine in the mountains at which I had encountered the hyena, I again experienced a shock as of a galvanic battery; the sense of weight, of volition, of substance, returned. I became my original self, and bent my steps eagerly homewards—but the past had not lost the vividness of the real—and not now, even for an instant, can I compel my understanding to regard it as a dream."

"Nor was it," said Templeton, with an air of deep solemnity, "yet it would be difficult to say how otherwise it should be termed. Let us suppose only, that the soul of the man of to-day is upon the verge of some stupendous psychal discoveries. Let us content ourselves with this supposition. For the rest I have some explanation to make. Here is a water-colour drawing, which I should have shown you before, but which an unaccountable sentiment of horror has hitherto prevented me from showing."

We looked at the picture which he presented. I saw nothing in it of an extraordinary character; but its effect upon Bedloe was prodigious. He nearly fainted as he gazed. And yet it was but a miniature portrait—a miraculously accurate one, to be sure—of his own very remarkable features. At least this was my thought as I regarded it.

"You will perceive," said Templeton, "the date of this picture—it is here, scarcely visible, in this corner—1780. In this year was the portrait taken. It is the likeness of a dead friend—a Mr. Oldeb—to whom I became much attached at Calcutta, during the administration of Warren Hastings. I was then only twenty years old. When I first saw you, Mr. Bedloe, at Saratoga, it was the miraculous similarity which existed between yourself and the painting which induced me to accost you, to seek your friendship, and to bring about those arrangements which resulted in my becoming your constant companion. In accomplishing this point, I was urged partly, and perhaps principally, by a regretful memory of the deceased, but also, in part, by an uneasy, and not altogether horrorless curiosity respecting yourself.

"In your detail of the vision which presented itself to you amid the hills, you have described, with the minutest accuracy, the Indian city of Benares, upon the Holy River. The riots, the combats, the massacre, were the actual events of the insurrection of Cheyte Sing, which took place in 1780, when Hastings was put in imminent peril of his life. The man escaping by the string of turbans was Cheyte Sing himself. The party in the kiosk were sepoys and British officers, headed by Hastings. Of this party I was one, and did all I could to prevent the rash and fatal sally of the officer who fell, in the crowded alleys, by the poisoned arrow of a Bengalee. That officer was my dearest friend. It was Oldeb. You will perceive by these manuscripts," (here the speaker produced a note-book in which several pages appeared to have been freshly written) "that at the very period in which you fancied these things amid the hills, I was engaged in detailing them upon paper here at home."

In about a week after this conversation, the following paragraphs appeared in a Charlottesville paper:—

"We have the painful duty of announcing the death of Mr. AUGUSTUS BEDLO, a gentleman whose amiable manners and many virtues have long endeared him to the citizens of Charlottesville.

"Mr. B., for some years past, has been subject to neuralgia, which has often threatened to terminate fatally; but this can be regarded only as the mediate cause of his decease. The proximate cause was one of especial singularity. In an excursion to the Ragged Mountains, a few days since, a slight cold and fever were contracted, attended with great determination of blood to the head. To relieve this, Dr. Templeton resorted to topical bleeding. Leeches were applied to the temples. In a fearfully brief period the patient died, when it appeared that in the jar containing the leeches had been introduced, by accident, one of the venomous vermicular sangsues which are now and then found in the neighbouring ponds. This creature fastened itself upon a small artery in the right temple. Its close resemblance to the medicinal leech caused the mistake to be overlooked until too late.

"N.B. The poisonous sangsue of Charlottesville may always be distinguished from the medicinal leech by its blackness, and especially by its writhing or vermicular motions, which very nearly resemble those of a snake."

I was speaking with the editor of the paper in question, upon the topic of this remarkable accident, when it occurred to me to ask how it happened that the name of the deceased had been given as Bedlo.

"I presume," said I, "you have authority for this spelling, but I have always supposed the name to be written with an *e* at the end."

"Authority?—no," he replied. "It is a mere typographical error. The name is Bedloe with an *e* all the world over, and I never knew it to be spelt otherwise in my life."

"Then," said I, mutteringly, as I turned upon my heel; "then, indeed, has it come to pass that one truth is stranger than any fiction—for Bedlo without the *e*, what is it but Oldeb conversed? And this man tells me it is a typographical error."

*Mark Twain (Samuel Langhorne Clemens) (1835–
1910) grew up in the river town of Hannibal,
Missouri. At thirteen, he worked in a print shop and
was an itinerant reporter; later he became a professional steamboat pilot. When river traffic was disrupted by the Civil War, and after an extraordinarily
brief army experience, Clemens traveled overland to
the Western territories of the United States, where
eventually he became a celebrated lecturer, reporter,
and humorist. His most popular early work exploits
Western folk materials—the tall tale, the practical
joke. His best novel,* Huckleberry Finn *(1884), is a
classic of American prose fiction. For further reading:* The Celebrated Jumping Frog of Calaveras
County *(1867);* The Complete Short Stories of
Mark Twain, *edited by Charles Neider (1958).*

MARK TWAIN

The Californian's Tale

Thirty-five years ago I was out prospecting on the Stanislaus, tramping
all day long with pick and pan and horn, and washing a hatful of dirt here
and there, always expecting to make a rich strike, and never doing it. It was
a lovely region, woodsy, balmy, delicious, and had once been populous,
long years before, but now the people had vanished and the charming
paradise was a solitude. They went away when the surface diggings gave
out. In one place, where a busy little city with banks and newspapers and
fire companies and a mayor and aldermen had been, was nothing but a
wide expanse of emerald turf, with not even the faintest sign that human life
had ever been present there. This was down toward Tuttletown. In the
country neighborhood thereabouts, along the dusty roads, one found at
intervals the prettiest little cottage homes, snug and cozy, and so cobweb-
bed with vines snowed thick with roses that the doors and windows were
wholly hidden from sight—sign that these were deserted homes, forsaken
years ago by defeated and disappointed families who could neither sell
them nor give them away. Now and then, half an hour apart, one came

across solitary log cabins of the earliest mining days, built by the first gold-miners, the predecessors of the cottage-builders. In some few cases these cabins were still occupied; and when this was so, you could depend upon it that the occupant was the very pioneer who had built the cabin; and you could depend on another thing, too—that he was there because he had once had his opportunity to go home to the States rich, and had not done it; had rather lost his wealth, and had then in his humiliation resolved to sever all communication with his home, relatives and friends, and be to them thenceforth as one dead. Round about California in that day were scattered a host of these living dead men—pride-smitten poor fellows, grizzled and old at forty, whose secret thoughts were made all of regrets and longings—regrets for their wasted lives, and longings to be out of the struggle and done with it all.

It was a lonesome land! Not a sound in all those peaceful expanses of grass and woods but the drowsy hum of insects; no glimpse of man or beast; nothing to keep up your spirits and make you glad to be alive. And so, at last, in the early part of the afternoon, when I caught sight of a human creature, I felt a most grateful uplift. This person was a man about forty-five years old, and he was standing at the gate of one of those cozy little rose-clad cottages of the sort already referred to. However, this one hadn't a deserted look; it had the look of being lived in and petted and cared for and looked after; and so had its front yard, which was a garden of flowers, abundant, gay, and flourishing. I was invited in, of course, and required to make myself at home—it was the custom of the country.

It was delightful to be in such a place, after long weeks of daily and nightly familiarity with miners' cabins—with all which this implies of dirt floor, never-made beds, tin plates and cups, bacon and beans and black coffee, and nothing of ornament but war pictures from the Eastern illus-trated papers tacked to the log walls. That was all hard, cheerless, material-istic desolation, but here was a nest which had aspects to rest the tired eye and refresh that something in one's nature which, after long fasting, recog-nizes, when confronted by the belongings of art, howsoever cheap and modest they may be, that it has unconsciously been famishing and now has found nourishment. I could not have believed that a rag carpet could feast me so, and so content me; or that there could be such solace to the soul in wall-paper and framed lithographs, and bright-colored tidies and lamp-mats, and Windsor chairs, and varnished what-nots, with sea-shells and books and china vases on them, and the score of little unclassifiable tricks and touches that a woman's hand distributes about a home, which one sees without knowing he sees them, yet would miss in a moment if they were taken away. The delight that was in my heart showed in my face and the man saw it and was pleased; saw it so plainly that he answered it as if it had been spoken.

"All her work," he said, caressingly; "she did it all herself—every bit," and he took the room in with a glance which was full of affectionate worship. One of those soft Japanese fabrics with which women drape with careful negligence the upper part of a picture-frame was out of adjustment. He noticed it, and rearranged it with cautious pains, stepping back several times to gauge the effect before he got it to suit him. Then he gave it a light finishing pat or two with his hand, and said: "She always does that. You can't tell just what it lacks, but it does lack something until you've done that—you can see it yourself after it's done, but that is all you know; you can't find out the law of it. It's like the finishing pats a mother gives the child's hair after she's got it combed and brushed, I reckon. I've seen her fix all these things so much that I can do them all just her way, though I don't know the law of any of them. But she knows the law. She knows the why and the how both; but I don't know the why; I only know the how."

He took me into a bedroom so that I might wash my hands; such a bedroom as I had not seen for years: white counterpane, white pillows, carpeted floor, papered walls, pictures, dressing-table, with mirror and pin-cushion and dainty toilet things; and in the corner a wash-stand, with real china-ware bowl and pitcher, and with soap in a china dish, and on a rack more than a dozen towels—towels too clean and white for one out of practice to use without some vague sense of profanation. So my face spoke again, and he answered with gratified words:

"All her work; she did it all herself—every bit. Nothing here that hasn't felt the touch of her hand. Now you would think—But I mustn't talk so much."

By this time I was wiping my hands and glancing from detail to detail of the room's belongings, as one is apt to do when he is in a new place, where everything he sees is a comfort to his eye and his spirit; and I became conscious, in one of those unaccountable ways, you know, that there was something there somewhere that the man wanted me to discover for myself. I knew it perfectly, and I knew he was trying to help me by furtive indications with his eye, so I tried hard to get on the right track, being eager to gratify him. I failed several times, as I could see out of the corner of my eye without being told; but at last I knew I must be looking straight at the thing—knew it from the pleasure issuing in invisible waves from him. He broke into a happy laugh, and rubbed his hands together, and cried out:

"That's it! You've found it. I knew you would. It's her picture."

I went to the little black-walnut bracket on the farther wall, and did find there what I had not yet noticed—a daguerreotype-case. It contained the sweetest girlish face, and the most beautiful, as it seemed to me, that I had ever seen. The man drank the admiration from my face, and was fully satisfied.

"Nineteen her last birthday," he said, as he put the picture back; "and that was the day we were married. When you see her—ah, just wait till you see her!"

"Where is she? When will she be in?"

"Oh, she's away now. She's gone to see her people. They live forty or fifty miles from here. She's been gone two weeks to-day."

"When do you expect her back?"

"This is Wednesday. She'll be back Saturday, in the evening—about nine o'clock, likely."

I felt a sharp sense of disappointment.

"I'm sorry, because I'll be gone then," I said, regretfully.

"Gone? No—why should you go? Don't go. She'll be so disappointed."

She would be disappointed—that beautiful creature! If she had said the words herself they could hardly have blessed me more. I was feeling a deep, strong longing to see her—a longing so supplicating, so insistent, that it made me afraid. I said to myself: "I will go straight away from this place, for my peace of mind's sake."

"You see, she likes to have people come and stop with us—people who know things, and can talk—people like you. She delights in it; for she knows—oh, she knows nearly everything herself, and can talk, oh, like a bird—and the books she reads, why, you would be astonished. Don't go; it's only a little while, you know, and she'll be so disappointed."

I heard the words, but hardly noticed them, I was so deep in my thinkings and strugglings. He left me, but I didn't know. Presently he was back, with the picture-case in his hand, and he held it open before me and said:

"There, now, tell her to her face you could have stayed to see her, and you wouldn't."

That second glimpse broke down my good resolution. I would stay and take the risk. That night we smoked the tranquil pipe, and talked till late about various things, but mainly about her; and certainly I had had no such pleasant and restful time for many a day. The Thursday followed and slipped comfortably away. Toward twilight a big miner from three miles away came—one of the grizzled, stranded pioneers—and gave us warm salutation, clothed in grave and sober speech. Then he said:

"I only just dropped over to ask about the little madam, and when is she coming home. Any news from her?"

"Oh yes, a letter. Would you like to hear it, Tom?"

"Well, I should think I would, if you don't mind, Henry!"

Henry got the letter out of his wallet, and said he would skip some of the private phrases, if we were willing; then he went on and read the bulk of it—a loving, sedate, and altogether charming and gracious piece of handi-work, with a postscript full of affectionate regards and messages to Tom, and Joe, and Charley, and other close friends and neighbors.

As the reader finished, he glanced at Tom, and cried out:

"Oho, you're at it again! Take your hands away, and let me see your eyes. You always do that when I read a letter from her. I will write and tell her."

"Oh no, you mustn't, Henry. I'm getting old, you know, and any little disappointment makes me want to cry. I thought she'd be here herself, and now you've got only a letter."

"Well, now, what put that in your head? I thought everybody knew she wasn't coming till Saturday."

"Saturday! Why, come to think, I did know it. I wonder what's the matter with me lately? Certainly I knew it. Ain't we all getting ready for her? Well, I must be going now. But I'll be on hand when she comes, old man!"

Late Friday afternoon another gray veteran tramped over from his cabin a mile or so away, and said the boys wanted to have a little gaiety and a good time Saturday night, if Henry thought she wouldn't be too tired after her journey to be kept up.

"Tired? She tired! Oh, hear the man! Joe, *you* know she'd sit up six weeks to please any one of you!"

When Joe heard that there was a letter, he asked to have it read, and the loving messages in it for him broke the old fellow all up; but he said he was such an old wreck that *that* would happen to him if she only just mentioned his name. "Lord, we miss her so!" he said.

Saturday afternoon I found I was taking out my watch pretty often. Henry noticed it, and said, with a startled look:

"You don't think she ought to be here so soon, do you?"

I felt caught, and a little embarrassed; but I laughed, and said it was a habit of mine when I was in a state of expectancy. But he didn't seem quite satisfied; and from that time on he began to show uneasiness. Four times he walked me up the road to a point whence we could see a long distance; and there he would stand, shading his eyes with his hand, and looking. Several times he said:

"I'm getting worried, I'm getting right down worried. I know she's not due till about nine o'clock, and yet something seems to be trying to warn me that something's happened. You don't think anything has happened, do you?"

I began to get pretty thoroughly ashamed of him for his childishness; and at last, when he repeated that imploring question still another time, I lost my patience for the moment, and spoke pretty brutally to him. It seemed to shrivel him up and cow him; and he looked so wounded and so humble after that, that I detested myself for having done the cruel and unnecessary thing. And so I was glad when Charley, another veteran, arrived toward the edge of the evening, and nestled up to Henry to hear the letter read, and talked over the preparations for the welcome. Charley fetched out one hearty speech after another, and did his best to drive away his friend's bodings and apprehensions.

"Anything *happened* to her? Henry, that's pure nonsense. There isn't anything going to happen to her; just make your mind easy as to that. What did the letter say? Said she was well, didn't it? And said she'd be here by nine o'clock, didn't it? Did you ever know her to fail of her word? Why, you know you never did. Well, then, don't you fret; she'll *be* here, and that's absolutely certain, and as sure as you are born. Come, now, let's get to decorating—not much time left."

Pretty soon Tom and Joe arrived, and then all hands set about adorning the house with flowers. Toward nine the three miners said that as they had brought their instruments they might as well tune up, for the boys and girls would soon be arriving now, and hungry for a good, old-fashioned break-down. A fiddle, a banjo, and a clarinet—these were the instruments. The trio took their places side by side, and began to play some rattling dance-music, and beat time with their big boots.

It was getting very close to nine. Henry was standing in the door with his eyes directed up the road, his body swaying to the torture of his mental distress. He had been made to drink his wife's health and safety several times, and now Tom shouted:

"All hands stand by! One more drink, and she's here!"

Joe brought the glasses on a waiter, and served the party. I reached for one of the two remaining glasses, but Joe growled, under his breath:

"Drop that! Take the other."

Which I did. Henry was served last. He had hardly swallowed his drink when the clock began to strike. He listened till it finished, his face growing pale and paler; then he said:

"Boys, I'm sick with fear. Help me—I want to lie down!"

They helped him to the sofa. He began to nestle and drowse, but presently spoke like one talking in his sleep, and said: "Did I hear the horses' feet? Have they come?"

One of the veterans answered, close to his ear: "It was Jimmy Parrish come to say the party got delayed, but they're right up the road a piece, and coming along. Her horse is lame, but she'll be here in half an hour."

"Oh, I'm *so* thankful nothing has happened!"

He was asleep almost before the words were out of his mouth. In a moment those handy men had his clothes off, and had tucked him into his bed in the chamber where I had washed my hands. They closed the door and came back. Then they seemed preparing to leave; but I said: "Please don't go, gentlemen. She won't know me; I am a stranger."

They glanced at each other. Then Joe said:

"She? Poor thing, she's been dead nineteen years!"

"Dead?"

"That or worse. She went to see her folks half a year after she was married, and on her way back, on a Saturday evening, the Indians captured her within five miles of this place, and she's never been heard of since."

"And he lost his mind in consequence?"

"Never has been sane an hour since. But he only gets bad when that time of the year comes round. Then we begin to drop in here, three days before she's due, to encourage him up, and ask if he's heard from her, and Saturday we all come and fix up the house with flowers, and get everything ready for a dance. We've done it every year for nineteen years. The first Saturday there was twenty-seven of us, without counting the girls; there's only three of us now, and the girls are all gone. We drug him to sleep, or he would go wild; then he's all right for another year—thinks she's with him till the last three or four days come round; then he begins to look for her, and gets out his poor old letter, and we come and ask him to read it to us. Lord, she was a darling!"

Ambrose Bierce (1842–1914) was the youngest of nine children and grew up on a marginal Ohio farm. In 1861 he enlisted as a drummer boy in the Ninth Indiana Volunteers. He saw major Civil War action, usually as a staff officer, was twice wounded, and was eventually discharged as a brevet (temporary) major. Later, in San Francisco, he became an editor and journalist. His short fiction deals with the macabre, the supernatural, the malevolent; his heroes are lonely men, victims, and the doomed. Bierce was neither very happy nor generally well liked in San Francisco; eventually he journeyed to Mexico, where he was probably shot by one or another revolutionary faction. In any event, he disappeared and was never heard of again. For further reading: Tales of Soldiers and Civilians *(1891);* Can Such Things Be *(1893);* In the Midst of Life *(1898).*

AMBROSE BIERCE

One Kind of Officer

I OF THE USES OF CIVILITY

"Captain Ransome, it is not permitted to you to know *anything*. It is sufficient that you obey my order—which permit me to repeat. If you perceive any movement of troops in your front you are to open fire, and if attacked hold this position as long as you can. Do I make myself understood, sir?"

"Nothing could be plainer. Lieutenant Price,"—this to an officer of his own battery, who had ridden up in time to hear the order—"the general's meaning is clear, is it not?"

"Perfectly."

The lieutenant passed on to his post. For a moment General Cameron and the commander of the battery sat in their saddles, looking at each other in silence. There was no more to say; apparently too much had already been said. Then the superior officer nodded coldly and turned his horse to ride away. The artillerist saluted slowly, gravely, and with extreme formality. One acquainted with the niceties of military etiquette would have said that by his manner he attested a sense of the rebuke that he had incurred. It is one of the important uses of civility to signify resentment.

When the general had joined his staff and escort, awaiting him at a little distance, the whole cavalcade moved off toward the right of the guns and vanished in the fog. Captain Ransome was alone, silent, motionless as an equestrian statue. The gray fog, thickening every moment, closed in about him like a visible doom.

II   UNDER WHAT CIRCUMSTANCES MEN DO NOT WISH TO BE SHOT

The fighting of the day before had been desultory and indecisive. At the points of collision the smoke of battle had hung in blue sheets among the branches of the trees till beaten into nothing by the falling rain. In the softened earth the wheels of cannon and ammunition wagons cut deep, ragged furrows, and movements of infantry seemed impeded by the mud that clung to the soldiers' feet as, with soaken garments and rifles imperfectly protected by capes of overcoats they went dragging in sinuous lines hither and thither through dripping forest and flooded field. Mounted officers, their heads protruding from rubber ponchos that glittered like black armor, picked their way, singly and in loose groups, among the men, coming and going with apparent aimlessness and commanding attention from nobody but one another. Here and there a dead man, his clothing defiled with earth, his face covered with a blanket or showing yellow and claylike in the rain, added his dispiriting influence to that of the other dismal features of the scene and augmented the general discomfort with a particular dejection. Very repulsive these wrecks looked—not at all heroic, and nobody was accessible to the infection of their patriotic example. Dead upon the field of honor, yes; but the field of honor was so very wet! It makes a difference.

The general engagement that all expected did not occur, none of the small advantages accruing, now to this side and now to that, in isolated and accidental collisions being followed up. Half-hearted attacks provoked a sullen resistance which was satisfied with mere repulse. Orders were obeyed with mechanical fidelity; no one did any more than his duty.

"The army is cowardly to-day," said General Cameron, the commander of a Federal brigade, to his adjutant-general.

"The army is cold," replied the officer addressed, "and—yes, it doesn't wish to be like that."

He pointed to one of the dead bodies, lying in a thin pool of yellow water, its face and clothing bespattered with mud from hoof and wheel.

The army's weapons seemed to share its military delinquency. The rattle of rifles sounded flat and contemptible. It had no meaning and scarcely roused to attention and expectancy the unengaged parts of the line-of-battle and the waiting reserves. Heard at a little distance, the reports of cannon were feeble in volume and *timbre:* they lacked sting and resonance. The guns seemed to be fired with light charges, unshotted. And so the futile day wore on to its dreary close, and then to a night of discomfort succeeded a day of apprehension.

An army has a personality. Beneath the individual thoughts and emotions of its component parts it thinks and feels as a unit. And in this large, inclusive sense of things lies a wiser wisdom than the mere sum of all that it knows. On that dismal morning this great brute force, groping at the bottom of a white ocean of fog among trees that seemed as sea weeds, had a dumb consciousness that all was not well; that a day's manœuvring had resulted in a faulty disposition of its parts, a blind diffusion of its strength. The men felt insecure and talked among themselves of such tactical errors as with their meager military vocabulary they were able to name. Field and line officers gathered in groups and spoke more learnedly of what they apprehended with no greater clearness. Commanders of brigades and divisions looked anxiously to their connections on the right and on the left, sent staff officers on errands of inquiry and pushed skirmish lines silently and cautiously forward into the dubious region between the known and the unknown. At some points on the line the troops, apparently of their own volition, constructed such defenses as they could without the silent spade and the noisy ax.

One of these points was held by Captain Ransome's battery of six guns. Provided always with intrenching tools, his men had labored with diligence during the night, and now his guns thrust their black muzzles through the embrasures of a really formidable earthwork. It crowned a slight acclivity devoid of undergrowth and providing an unobstructed fire that would sweep the ground for an unknown distance in front. The position could hardly have been better chosen. It had this peculiarity, which Captain Ransome, who was greatly addicted to the use of the compass, had not failed to observe: it faced northward, whereas he knew that the general line of the army must face eastward. In fact, that part of the line was "refused"—that is to say, bent backward, away from the enemy. This implied that Captain Ransome's battery was somewhere near the left flank of the army; for an army in line of battle retires its flanks if the nature of the ground will permit, they being its vulnerable points. Actually, Captain Ransome appeared to hold the extreme left of the line, no troops being visible in that direction beyond his own. Immediately in rear of his guns occurred that conversation between him and his brigade commander, the concluding and more picturesque part of which is reported above.

III   HOW TO PLAY THE CANNON WITHOUT NOTES

Captain Ransome sat motionless and silent on horseback. A few yards away his men were standing at their guns. Somewhere—everywhere within a few miles—were a hundred thousand men, friends and enemies. Yet he was alone. The mist had isolated him as completely as if he had been in the heart of a desert. His world was a few square yards of wet and trampled earth about the feet of his horse. His comrades in that ghostly domain were invisible and inaudible. These were conditions favorable to thought, and he was thinking. Of the nature of his thoughts his clear-cut handsome features yielded no attesting sign. His face was as inscrutable as that of the sphinx. Why should it have made a record which there was none to observe? At the sound of a footstep he merely turned his eyes in the direction whence it came; one of his sergeants, looking a giant in stature in the false perspective of the fog, approached, and when clearly defined and reduced to his true dimensions by propinquity, saluted and stood at attention.

"Well, Morris," said the officer, returning his subordinate's salute.

"Lieutenant Price directed me to tell you, sir, that most of the infantry has been withdrawn. We have not sufficient support."

"Yes, I know."

"I am to say that some of our men have been out over the works a hundred yards and report that our front is not picketed."

"Yes."

"They were so far forward that they heard the enemy."

"Yes."

"They heard the rattle of the wheels of artillery and the commands of officers."

"Yes."

"The enemy is moving toward our works."

Captain Ransome, who had been facing to the rear of his line—toward the point where the brigade commander and his cavalcade had been swallowed up by the fog—reined his horse about and faced the other way. Then he sat motionless as before.

"Who are the men who made that statement?" he inquired, without looking at the sergeant; his eyes were directed straight into the fog over the head of his horse.

"Corporal Hassman and Gunner Manning."

Captain Ransome was a moment silent. A slight pallor came into his face, a slight compression affected the lines of his lips, but it would have required a closer observer than Sergeant Morris to note the change. There was none in the voice.

"Sergeant, present my compliments to Lieutenant Price and direct him to open fire with all the guns. Grape."

The sergeant saluted and vanished in the fog.

IV   TO INTRODUCE GENERAL MASTERSON

Searching for his division commander, General Cameron and his escort had followed the line of battle for nearly a mile to the right of Ransome's battery, and there learned that the division commander had gone in search of the corps commander. It seemed that everybody was looking for his immediate superior—an ominous circumstance. It meant that nobody was quite at ease. So General Cameron rode on for another half-mile, where by good luck he met General Masterson, the division commander, returning.

"Ah, Cameron," said the higher officer, reining up, and throwing his right leg cross the pommel of his saddle in a most unmilitary way—"anything up? Found a good position for your battery, I hope—if one place is better than another in a fog."

"Yes, general," said the other, with the greater dignity appropriate to his less exalted rank, "my battery is very well placed. I wish I could say that it is as well commanded."

"Eh, what's that? Ransome? I think him a fine fellow. In the army we should be proud of him."

It was customary for officers of the regular army to speak of it as "the army." As the greatest cities are most provincial, so the self-complacency of aristocracies is most frankly plebeian.

"He is too fond of his opinion. By the way, in order to occupy the hill that he holds I had to extend my line dangerously. The hill is on my left—that is to say the left flank of the army."

"Oh, no, Hart's brigade is beyond. It was ordered up from Drytown during the night and directed to hook on to you. Better go and—"

The sentence was unfinished: a lively cannonade had broken out on the left, and both officers, followed by their retinues of aides and orderlies making a great jingle and clank, rode rapidly toward the spot. But they were soon impeded, for they were compelled by the fog to keep within sight of the line-of-battle, behind which were swarms of men, all in motion across their way. Everywhere the line was assuming a sharper and harder definition, as the men sprang to arms and the officers, with drawn swords, "dressed" the ranks. Color-bearers unfurled the flags, buglers blew the "assembly," hospital attendants appeared with stretchers. Field officers mounted and sent their impedimenta to the rear in care of negro servants. Back in the ghostly spaces of the forest could be heard the rustle and murmur of the reserves, pulling themselves together.

Nor was all this preparation vain, for scarcely five minutes had passed since Captain Ransome's guns had broken the truce of doubt before the whole region was aroar: the enemy had attacked nearly everywhere.

V   HOW SOUNDS CAN FIGHT SHADOWS

Captain Ransome walked up and down behind his guns, which were firing rapidly but with steadiness. The gunners worked alertly, but without haste or apparent excitement. There was really no reason for excitement; it is not much to point a cannon into a fog and fire it. Anybody can do as much as that.

The men smiled at their noisy work, performing it with a lessening alacrity. They cast curious regards upon their captain, who had now mounted the banquette of the fortification and was looking across the parapet as if observing the effect of his fire. But the only visible effect was the substitution of wide, low-lying sheets of smoke for their bulk of fog. Suddenly out of the obscurity burst a great sound of cheering, which filled the intervals between the reports of the guns with startling distinctness! To the few with leisure and opportunity to observe, the sound was inexpressibly strange—so loud, so near, so menacing, yet nothing seen! The men who had smiled at their work smiled no more, but performed it with a serious and feverish activity.

From his station at the parapet Captain Ransome now saw a great multitude of dim gray figures taking shape in the mist below him and swarming up the slope. But the work of the guns was now fast and furious. They swept the populous declivity with gusts of grape and canister, the whirring of which could be heard through the thunder of the explosions. In this awful tempest of iron the assailants struggled forward foot by foot across their dead, firing into the embrasures, reloading, firing again, and at last falling in their turn, a little in advance of those who had fallen before. Soon the smoke was dense enough to cover all. It settled down upon the attack and, drifting back, involved the defense. The gunners could hardly see to serve their pieces, and when occasional figures of the enemy appeared upon the parapet—having had the good luck to get near enough to it, between two embrasures, to be protected from the guns—they looked so unsubstantial that it seemed hardly worth while for the few infantrymen to go to work upon them with the bayonet and tumble them back into the ditch.

As the commander of a battery in action can find something better to do than cracking individual skulls, Captain Ransome had retired from the parapet to his proper post in rear of his guns, where he stood with folded arms, his bugler beside him. Here, during the hottest of the fight, he was approached by Lieutenant Price, who had just sabred a daring assailant inside the work. A spirited colloquy ensued between the two officers—spirited, at least, on the part of the lieutenant, who gesticulated with energy and shouted again and again into his commander's ear in the attempt to make himself heard above the infernal din of the guns. His gestures, if coolly noted by an actor, would have been pronounced to be those of protestation: one would have said that he was opposed to the proceedings. Did he wish to surrender?

Captain Ransome listened without a change of countenance or attitude, and when the other man had finished his harangue, looked him coldly in the eyes and during a seasonable abatement of the uproar said:

"Lieutenant Price, it is not permitted to you to know *anything*. It is sufficient that you obey my orders."

The lieutenant went to his post, and the parapet being now apparently clear Captain Ransome returned to it to have a look over. As he mounted the banquette a man sprang upon the crest, waving a great brilliant flag. The captain drew a pistol from his belt and shot him dead. The body, pitching forward, hung over the inner edge of the embankment, the arms straight downward, both hands still grasping the flag. The man's few followers turned and fled down the slope. Looking over the parapet, the captain saw no living thing. He observed also that no bullets were coming into the work.

He made a sign to the bugler, who sounded the command to cease firing. At all other points the action had already ended with a repulse of the Confederate attack; with the cessation of this cannonade the silence was absolute.

VI   WHY, BEING AFFRONTED BY A, IT IS NOT BEST TO AFFRONT B

General Masterson rode into the redoubt. The men, gathered in groups, were talking loudly and gesticulating. They pointed at the dead, running from one body to another. They neglected their foul and heated guns and forgot to resume their outer clothing. They ran to the parapet and looked over, some of them leaping down into the ditch. A score were gathered about a flag rigidly held by a dead man.

"Well, my men," said the general cheerily, "you have had a pretty fight of it."

They stared; nobody replied; the presence of the great man seem to embarrass and alarm.

Getting no response to his pleasant condescension, the easy-mannered officer whistled a bar of two of a popular air, and riding forward to the parapet, looked over at the dead. In an instant he had whirled his horse about and was spurring along in rear of the guns, his eyes everywhere at once. An officer sat on the trail of one of the guns, smoking a cigar. As the general dashed up he rose and tranquilly saluted.

"Captain Ransome!"—the words fell sharp and harsh, like the clash of steel blades—"you have been fighting our own men—our own men, sir; do you hear? Hart's brigade!"

"General, I know that."

"You know it—you know that, and you sit here smoking? Oh, damn it, Hamilton, I'm losing my temper," this to his provost-marshal. "Sir—Captain Ransome, be good enough to say—to say why you fought our own men."

"That I am unable to say. In my orders that information was withheld."

Apparently the general did not comprehend.

"Who was the aggressor in this affair, you or General Hart?" he asked.

"I was."

"And could you not have known—could you not see, sir, that you were attacking our own men?"

The reply was astounding!

"I knew that, general. It appeared to be none of my business."

Then, breaking the dead silence that followed his answer, he said:

"I must refer you to General Cameron."

"General Cameron is dead, sir—as dead as he can be—as dead as any man in this army. He lies back yonder under a tree. Do you mean to say that he had anything to do with this horrible business?"

Captain Ransome did not reply. Observing the altercation his men had gathered about to watch the outcome. They were greatly excited. The fog, which had been partly dissipated by the firing, had again closed in so darkly about them that they drew more closely together till the judge on horseback and the accused standing calmly before him had but a narrow space free from intrusion. It was the most informal of courts-martial, but all felt that the formal one to follow would but affirm its judgment. It had no jurisdiction, but it had the significance of prophecy.

"Captain Ransome," the general cried impetuously, but with something in his voice that was almost entreaty, "if you can say anything to put a better light upon your incomprehensible conduct I beg you will do so."

Having recovered his temper this generous soldier sought for something to justify his naturally sympathetic attitude toward a brave man in the imminence of a dishonorable death.

"Where is Lieutenant Price?" the captain said.

The officer stood forward, his dark saturnine face looking somewhat forbidding under a bloody handkerchief bound about his brow. He understood the summons and needed no invitation to speak. He did not look at the captain, but addressed the general:

"During the engagement I discovered the state of affairs, and apprised the commander of the battery. I ventured to urge that the firing cease. I was insulted and ordered to my post."

"Do you know anything of the orders under which I was acting?" asked the captain.

"Of any orders under which the commander of the battery was acting," the lieutenant continued, still addressing the general, "I know nothing."

Captain Ransome felt his world sink away from his feet. In those cruel words he heard the murmur of the centuries breaking upon the shore of eternity. He heard the voice of doom; it said, in cold, mechanical, and measured tones: "Ready, aim, fire!" and he felt the bullets tear his heart to shreds. He heard the sound of the earth upon his coffin and (if the good God was so merciful) the song of a bird above his forgotten grave. Quietly detaching his sabre from its supports, he handed it up to the provost-marshal.

Henry James (1843–1916) was born in New York of a distinguished family. At nineteen he entered Harvard Law School, but soon became a professional writer. In 1876, James removed permanently to London; toward the end of his life he became a British citizen. As a novelist, short-story writer, and critic, James exerted profound influence on the development of twentieth-century fiction. In addition, he was one of the first great theoreticians of fictional method. Among other things, he developed the convention of a "central intelligence," a protagonist through whose consciousness the story flows; he refined the use of symbol to the end of richer meaning. In the matter of prose style, James is an acknowledged master. Characteristically, he presented, with a display of irony, dramatic situations which treated the subtle nuances of social situation, morality, and decency. His major novels include The Portrait of a Lady *(1881) and* The Ambassadors *(1903). For further reading:* The Complete Tales of Henry James, *edited by Leon Edel (12 vols., 1962–1965).*

HENRY JAMES

Europe

I

"*O*ur feeling is, you know, that Becky *should go.*" That earnest little remark comes back to me, even after long years, as the first note of something that began, for my observation, the day I went with my sister-in-law to take leave of her good friends. It is a memory of the American time, which revives so at present—under some touch that doesn't signify—that it rounds itself off as an anecdote. That walk to say good-bye was the beginning; and the end, so far as I was concerned with it, was not till long after; yet even the end also appears to me now as of the old days. I went, in those days, on occasion, to see my sister-in-law, in whose affairs, on my brother's death, I had had to take a helpful hand. I continued to go, indeed after these little matters were straightened out, for the pleasure, periodically, of the impression—the change to the almost pastoral sweetness of the good Boston suburb from the loud, longitudinal New York. It was another world, with other manners, a different tone, a different taste; a savour nowhere so mild, yet so distinct, as in the square white house—with the pair of elms, like gigantic wheat-sheaves in front, the rustic orchard not far behind, the old-fashioned doorlights, the big blue and white jars in the porch, the straight, bricked walk from the high-gate—that enshrined the extraordinary merit of Mrs. Rimmle and her three daughters.

These ladies were so much of the place and the place so much of themselves that, from the first of their being revealed to me, I felt that nothing else at Brookbridge much mattered. They were what, for me, at any rate, Brookbridge had most to give: I mean in the way of what it was naturally strongest in, the thing that we called in New York the New England expression, the air of Puritanism reclaimed and refined. The Rimmles had brought it down to a wonderful delicacy. They struck me even then—all four almost equally—as very ancient and very earnest, and I think theirs must have been the house, in all the world, in which "culture" first came to the aid of morning calls. The head of the family was the widow of a great public character—as public characters were understood at Brookbridge—whose speeches on anniversaries formed a part of the body of national eloquence spouted in the New England schools by little boys covetous of the most marked, though perhaps the easiest, distinction. He was reported to have been celebrated, and in such fine declamatory connections that he seemed to gesticulate even from the tomb. He was understood to have made, in his wife's company, the tour of Europe at a date not immensely removed from that of the battle of Waterloo. What was the age, then, of the bland, firm, antique Mrs. Rimmle at the period of her being first revealed to me? That is a point I am not in a position to determine—I remember mainly that I was young enough to regard her as having reached the limit. And yet the limit for Mrs. Rimmle must have been prodigiously extended; the scale of its extension is, in fact, the very moral of this reminiscence. She was old and her daughters were old, but I was destined to know them all as older. It was only by comparison and habit that—however much I recede—Rebecca, Maria, and Jane were the "young ladies."

I think it was felt that, though their mother's life, after thirty years of widowhood, had had a grand backward stretch, her blandness and firmness—and this in spite of her extreme physical frailty—would be proof against any surrender not overwhelmingly justified by time. It had appeared, years before, at a crisis of which the waves had not even yet quite subsided, a surrender not justified by anything, that she should go, with her daughters, to Europe for her health. Her health was supposed to require constant support; but when it had at that period tried conclusions with the idea of Europe, it was not the idea of Europe that had been insidious enough to prevail. She had not gone, and Becky, Maria, and Jane had not gone, and this was long ago. They still merely floated in the air of the visit achieved, with such introductions and such acclamations, in the early part of the century; they still, with fond glances at the sunny parlour-walls, only referred, in conversation, to divers pictoral and other reminders of it. The Miss Rimmles had quite been brought up on it, but Becky, as the most literary, had most mastered the subject. There were framed letters—tributes to their eminent father—suspended among the mementos, and of two or three of these, the most foreign and complimentary, Becky had executed translations that figured beside the text. She knew already, through this and other illumination, so much about Europe that it was hard to believe, for her, in that limit of adventure which consisted only of her having been twice to Philadelphia. The others had not been to Philadelphia, but there was a legend that Jane had been to Saratoga. Becky was a short, stout, fair person with round, serious eyes, a high forehead, the sweetest, neatest enunciation, and a miniature of her father—"done in Rome"—worn as a breastpin. She had written the life, she had edited the speeches, of the original of this ornament, and now at last, beyond the seas, she was really to tread in his footsteps.

Fine old Mrs. Rimmle, in the sunny parlour and with a certain austerity of cap and chair—though with a gay new "front" that looked like rusty brown plush—had had so unusually good a winter that the question of her sparing two members of her family for an absence had been threshed as fine, I could feel, as even under that Puritan roof any case of conscience had ever been threshed. They were to make their dash while the coast, as it were, was clear, and each of the daughters had tried—heroically, angelically, and for the sake of each of her sisters—not to be one of the two. What I encountered that first time was an opportunity to concur with enthusiasm in the general idea that Becky's wonderful preparation would be wasted if she were the one to stay with their mother. They talked of Becky's preparation—they had a sly, old-maidish humour that was as mild as milk—as if it were some mixture, for application somewhere, that she kept in a precious bottle. It had been settled, at all events, that, armed with this concoction and borne aloft by their introductions, she and Jane were to start. They were wonderful on their introductions, which proceeded naturally from their mother and were addressed to the charming families that, in vague generations, had so admired vague Mr. Rimmle. Jane, I found at Brookbridge, had to be described, for want of other description, as the pretty one, but it would not have served to identify her unless you had seen the others. *Her* preparation was only this figment of her prettiness—only, that is, unless one took into account something that, on the spot, I silently divined: the lifelong, secret, passionate ache of her little rebellious desire. They were all growing old in the yearning to go, but Jane's yearning was the sharpest. She struggled with it as people at Brookbridge mostly struggled with what they liked, but fate, by threatening to prevent what she *dis*liked, and what was therefore duty—which was to stay at home instead of Maria—had bewildered her, I judged, not a little. It was she who, in the words I have quoted, mentioned to me Becky's case and Becky's affinity as the clearest of all. Her mother, moreover, on the general subject, had still more to say.

"I positively desire, I really quite insist that they shall go," the old lady explained to us from her stiff chair. "We've talked about it so often, and they've had from me so clear an account—I've amused them again and again with it—of what is to be seen and enjoyed. If they've had hitherto too many duties to leave, the time seems to have come to recognize that there are also many duties to *seek*. Wherever we go we find them—I always remind the girls of that. There's a duty that calls them to those wonderful countries, just as it called, at the right time, their father and myself—if it be only that of laying up for the years to come the same store of remarkable impressions, the same wealth of knowledge and food for conversation as, since my return, I have found myself so happy to possess." Mrs. Rimmle spoke of her return as of something of the year before last, but the future of her daughters was, somehow, by a different law, to be on the scale of great vistas, of endless aftertastes. I think that, without my being quite ready to say it, even this first impression of her was somewhat upsetting; there was a large, placid perversity, a grim secrecy of intention in her estimate of the ages.

"Well, I'm so glad you don't delay it longer," I said to Miss Becky before we withdrew. "And whoever should go," I continued in the spirit of the sympathy with which the good sisters had already inspired me, "I quite feel, with your family, you know, that *you* should. But of course I hold that every one should." I suppose I wished to attenuate my solemnity; there was something in it, however, that I couldn't help. It must have been a faint foreknowledge.

"Have you been a great deal yourself?" Miss Jane, I remember, inquired.

"Not so much but that I hope to go a good deal more. So perhaps we shall meet," encouragingly suggested.

I recall something—something in the nature of susceptibility to encouragement—that this brought into the more expressive brown eyes to which Miss Jane mainly owed it that she was the pretty one. "Where, do you think?"

I tried to think. "Well, on the Italian lakes—Como, Bellagio, Lugano." I liked to say the names to them.

" 'Sublime, but neither bleak nor bare—nor misty are the mountains there!' " Miss Jane softly breathed, while her sister looked at her as if her familiarity with the poetry of the subject made her the most interesting feature of the scene she evoked.

But Miss Becky presently turned to me. "Do you know everything—?"

"Everything?"

"In Europe."

"Oh, yes," I laughed, "and one or two things even in America."

The sisters seemed to me furtively to look at each other. "Well, you'll have to be quick—to meet *us*," Miss Jane resumed.

"But surely when you're once there you'll stay on."

"Stay on?"—they murmured it simultaneously and with the oddest vibration of dread as well as of desire. It was as if they had been in the presence of a danger and yet wished me, who "knew everything," to torment them with still more of it.

Well, I did my best. "I mean it will never do to cut it short."

"No, that's just what I keep saying," said brilliant Jane. "It would be better, in that case, not to go."

"Oh, don't talk about not going—at this time!" It was none of my business, but I felt shocked and impatient.

"No, not at *this* time!" broke in Miss Maria, who, very red in the face, had joined us. Poor Miss Maria was known as the flushed one; but she was not flushed—she only had an unfortunate surface. The third day after this was to see them embark.

Miss Becky, however, desired as little as any one to be in any way extravagant. "It's only the thought of our mother," she explained.

I looked a moment at the old lady, with whom my sister-in-law was engaged. "Well—your mother's magnificent."

"*Isn't* she magnificent?"—they eagerly took it up.

She *was*—I could reiterate it with sincerity, though I perhaps mentally drew the line when Miss Maria again risked, as a fresh ejaculation: "I think she's better than Europe!"

"Maria!" they both, at this, exclaimed with a strange emphasis; it was as if they feared she had suddenly turned cynical over the deep domestic drama of their casting of lots. The innocent laugh with which she answered them gave the measure of her cynicism.

We separated at last, and my eyes met Mrs. Rimmle's as I held for an instant her aged hand. It was doubtless only my fancy that her calm, cold look quietly accused me of something. Of what *could* it accuse me? Only, I thought, of thinking.

II

I left Brookbridge the next day, and for some time after that had no occasion to hear from my kinswoman; but when she finally wrote there was a passage in her letter that affected me more than all the rest. "Do you know the poor Rimmles never, after all, 'went'? The old lady, at the eleventh hour, broke down; everything broke down, and all of *them* on top of it, so that the dear things are with us still. Mrs. Rimmle, the night after our call,

had, in the most unexpected manner, a turn for the worse—something in
the nature (though they're rather mysterious about it) of a seizure; Becky
and Jane felt it—dear, devoted, stupid angels that they are—heartless to
leave her at such a moment, and Europe's indefinitely postponed. However,
they think they're still going—or *think* they think it—when she's better.
They also think—or think they think—that she *will* be better. I certainly
pray she may." So did I—quite fervently. I was conscious of a real pang—
I didn't know how much they had made me care.

Late that winter my sister-in-law spent a week in New York; when
almost my first inquiry on meeting her was about the health of Mrs.
Rimmle.

"Oh, she's rather bad—she really is, you know. It's not surprising that
at her age she should be infirm."

"Then what the deuce *is* her age?"

"I can't tell you to a year—but she's immensely old."

"That of course I saw," I replied—"unless you literally mean so old
that the records have been lost."

My sister-in-law thought. "Well, I believe she wasn't positively young
when she married. She lost three or four children before these women were
born."

We surveyed together a little, on this, the "dark backward." "And they
were born, I gather, *after* the famous tour? Well, then, as the famous tour
was in a manner to celebrate—wasn't it?—the restoration of the Bour-
bons—" I considered, I gasped. "My dear child, what on earth do you make
her out?"

My relative, with her Brookbridge habit, transferred her share of the
question to the moral plane—turned it forth to wander, by implication at
least, in the sandy desert of responsibilities. "Well, you know, we all immensely admire her."

"You can't admire her more than I do. She's awful."

My interlocutress looked at me with a certain fear. "She's *really* ill."

"Too ill to get better?"

"Oh, no—we hope not. Because then they'll be able to go."

"And *will* they go, if she should?"

"Oh, the moment they should be quite satisfied. I mean *really*," she
added.

I'm afraid I laughed at her—the Brookbridge "really" was a thing so
by itself. "But if she shouldn't get better?" I went on.

"Oh, don't speak of it! They want so to go."

"It's a pity they're so infernally good," I mused.

"No—don't say that. It's what keeps them up."

"Yes, but isn't it what keeps *her* up too?"

My visitor looked grave. "Would you like them to kill her?"

I don't know that I was then prepared to say I should—though I believe I came very near it. But later on I burst all bounds, for the subject grew and grew. I went again before the good sisters ever did—I mean I went to Europe. I think I went twice, with a brief interval, before my fate again brought round for me a couple of days at Brookbridge. I had been there repeatedly, in the previous time, without making the acquaintance of the Rimmles; but now that I had had the revelation I couldn't have it too much, and the first request I preferred was to be taken again to see them. I remember well indeed the scruple I felt—the real delicacy—about betraying that *I* had, in the pride of my power, since our other meeting, stood, as their phrase went, among romantic scenes; but they were themselves the first to speak of it, and what, moreover, came home to me was that the coming and going of their friends in general—Brookbridge itself having even at that period one foot in Europe—was such as to place constantly before them the pleasure that was only postponed. They were thrown back, after all, on what the situation, under a final analysis, had most to give—the sense that, as every one kindly said to them and they kindly said to every one, Europe would keep. Every one felt for them so deeply that their own kindness in alleviating every one's feeling was really what came out most. Mrs. Rimmle was still in her stiff chair and in the sunny parlour, but if *she* made no scruple of introducing the Italian lakes my heart sank to observe that she dealt with them, as a topic, not in the least in the leavetaking manner in which Falstaff babbled of green fields.

I am not sure that, after this, my pretexts for a day or two with my sister-in-law were not apt to be a mere cover for another glimpse of these particulars: I at any rate never went to Brookbridge without an irrepressible eagerness for our customary call. A long time seems to me thus to have passed, with glimpses and lapses, considerable impatience and still more pity. Our visits indeed grew shorter, for, as my companion said, they were more and more of a strain. It finally struck me that the good sisters even shrank from me a little, as from one who penetrated their circumstances in spite of himself. It was as if they knew where I thought they ought to be, and were moved to deprecate at last, by a systematic silence on the subject of that hemisphere, the criminality I fain would fix on them. They were full instead—as with the instinct of throwing dust in my eyes—of little pathetic hypocrisies about Brookbridge interests and delights. I dare say that as time went on my deeper sense of their situation came practically to rest on my companion's report of it. I think I recollect, at all events, every word we ever exchanged about them, even if I have lost the thread of the special occasions. The impression they made on me after each interval always broke out with extravagance as I walked away with her.

"*She* may be as old as she likes—I don't care. It's the fearful age the 'girls' are reaching that constitutes the scandal. One shouldn't pry into such matters, I know; but the years and the chances are really going. They're all growing old together—it will presently be too late; and their mother meanwhile perches over them like a vulture—what shall I call it?—calculating. Is she waiting for them successively to drop off? She'll survive them each and all. There's something too remorseless in it."

"Yes; but what do you want her to do? If the poor thing *can't* die, she can't. Do you want her to take poison or to open a blood-vessel? I dare say she would prefer to go."

"I beg your pardon," I must have replied; "you daren't say anything of the sort. If she would prefer to go she *would* go. She would feel the propriety, the decency, the necessity of going. She just prefers *not* to go. She prefers to stay and keep up the tension, and her calling them 'girls' and talking of the good time they'll still have is the mere conscious mischief of a subtle old witch. They won't have *any* time—there isn't any time to have! I mean there's, on her own part, no real loss of measure or of perspective in it. She *knows* she's a hundred and ten, and takes a cruel pride in it."

My sister-in-law differed with me about this; she held that the old woman's attitude was an honest one and that her magnificent vitality, so great in spite of her infirmities, made it inevitable she should attribute youth to persons who had come into the world so much later. "Then suppose she should die?"—so my fellow-student of the case always put it to me.

"Do you mean while her daughters are away? There's not the least fear of that—not even if at the very moment of their departure she should be *in extremis.* They would find her all right on their return."

"But think how they would feel not to have been with her!"

"That's only, I repeat, on the unsound assumption. If they would only go to-morrow—literally make a good rush for it—they'll be with her when they come back. That will give them plenty of time." I'm afraid I even heartlessly added that if she *should,* against every probability, pass away in their absence, they wouldn't have to come back at all—which would be just the compensation proper to their long privation. And then Maria would come out to join the two others, and they would be—though but for the too scanty remnant of their career—as merry as the day is long.

I remained ready, somehow, pending the fulfilment of that vision, to sacrifice Maria; it was only over the urgency of the case for the others respectively that I found myself balancing. Sometimes it was for Becky I thought the tragedy deepest—sometimes, and in quite a different manner, I thought it most dire for Jane. It was Jane, after all, who had most sense of life. I seemed in fact dimly to descry in Jane a sense—as yet undescried by herself or by any one—of all sorts of queer things. Why didn't *she* go? I used desperately to ask; why didn't she make a bold personal dash for it, strike up a partnership with some one or other of the traveling spinsters in whom Brookbridge more and more abounded? Well, there came a flash for

me at a particular point of the grey middle desert: my correspondent was
able to let me know that poor Jane at last *had* sailed. She had gone of a
sudden—I like my sister-in-law's view of suddenness—with the kind Hathaways, who had made an irresistible grab at her and lifted her off her feet.
They were going for the summer and for Mr. Hathaway's health, so that the
opportunity was perfect, and it was impossible not to be glad that something very like physical force had finally prevailed. This was the general
feeling at Brookbridge, and I might imagine what Brookbridge had been
brought to from the fact that, at the very moment she was hustled off, the
doctor called to her mother at the peep of dawn, had considered that *he* at
least must stay. There had been real alarm—greater than ever before; it
actually did seem as if this time the end had come. But it was Becky,
strange to say, who, though fully recognising the nature of the crisis, had
kept the situation in hand and insisted upon action. This, I remember,
brought back to me a discomfort with which I had been familiar from the
first. One of the two had sailed, and I was sorry it was not the other. But if
it had been the other I should have been equally sorry.

I saw with my eyes, that very autumn, what a fool Jane would have
been if she had again backed out. Her mother had of course survived the
peril of which I had heard, profiting by it indeed as she had profited by
every other; she was sufficiently better again to have come down stairs. It
was there that, as usual, I found her, but with a difference of effect produced somehow by the absence of one of the girls. It was as if, for the
others, though they had not gone to Europe, Europe had come to them:
Jane's letters had been so frequent and so beyond even what could have
been hoped. It was the first time, however, that I perceived on the old
woman's part a certain failure of lucidity. Jane's flight was, clearly, the
great fact with her, but she spoke of it as if the fruit had now been plucked
and the parenthesis closed. I don't know what sinking sense of still further
physical duration I gathered, as a menace, from this first hint of her confusion of mind.

"My daughter has been; my daughter has been—" She kept saying it,
but didn't say where; that seemed unnecessary, and she only repeated the
words to her visitors with a face that was all puckers and yet now, save in
so far as it expressed an ineffaceable complacency, all blankness. I think
she wanted us a little to know that she had not stood in the way. It added
to something—I scarce knew what—that I found myself desiring to extract
privately from Becky. As our visit was to be of the shortest my opportunity—for one of the young ladies always came to the door with us—was at
hand. Mrs. Rimmle, as we took leave, again sounded her phrase, but she
added this time: "I'm so glad she's going to have always——"

I knew so well what she meant that, as she again dropped, looking at
me queerly and becoming momentarily dim, I could help her out. "Going to
have what *you* have?"

"Yes, yes—my privilege. Wonderful experience," she mumbled. She bowed to me a little as if I would understand. "She has things to tell."

I turned, slightly at a loss, to Becky. "She has then already arrived?"

Becky was at that moment looking a little strangely at her mother, who answered my questions. "She reached New York this morning—she comes on to-day."

"Oh, then——!" But I let the matter pass as I met Becky's eye—I saw there was a hitch somewhere. It was not she but Maria who came out with us; on which I cleared up the question of their sister's reappearance.

"Oh, no, not to-night," Maria smiled; "that's only the way mother puts it. We shall see her about the end of November—the Hathaways are so indulgent. They kindly extended their tour."

"For *her* sake? How sweet of them!" my sister-in-law exclaimed.

I can see our friend's plain, mild old face take on a deeper mildness, even though a higher colour, in the light of the open door. "Yes, it's for Jane they prolong it. And do you know what they write?" She gave us time, but it was too great a responsibility to guess. "Why, that it has brought her out."

"Oh, I knew it *would!*" my companion sympathetically sighed.

Maria put it more strongly still. "They say we wouldn't know her."

This sounded a little awful, but it was, after all, what I had expected.

III

My correspondent in Brookbridge came to me that Christmas, with my niece, to spend a week; and the arrangement had of course been prefaced by an exchange of letters, the first of which from my sister-in-law scarce took space for acceptance of my invitation before going on to say: "The Hathaways are back—but without Miss Jane!" She presented in a few words the situation thus created at Brookbridge, but was not yet, I gathered, fully in possession of the other one—the situation created in "Europe" by the presence there of that lady. The two together, at any rate, demanded, I quickly felt, all my attention, and perhaps my impatience to receive my relative was a little sharpened by my desire for the whole story. I had it at last, by the Christmas fire, and I may say without reserve that it gave me all I could have hoped for. I listened eagerly, after which I produced the comment: "Then she simply refused——"

"To budge from Florence? Simply. She had it out there with the poor Hathaways, who felt responsible for her safety, pledged to restore her to her mother's, to her sisters' hands, and showed herself in a light, they mention under their breath, that made their dear old hair stand on end. Do you know what, when they first got back, they said of her—at least it was *his* phrase—to two or three people?"

I thought a moment. "That she had 'tasted blood'?"

My visitor fairly admired me. "How clever of you to guess! It's exactly what he did say. She appeared—she continues to appear, it seems—in a new character."

I wondered a little. "But that's exactly—don't you remember?—what Miss Maria reported to us from them; that we 'wouldn't know her.' "

My sister-in-law perfectly remembered. "Oh, yes—she broke out from the first. But when they left her she was worse."

"Worse?"

"Well, different—different from anything she ever *had* been, or—for that matter—had had a chance to be." My interlocutress hung fire a moment, but presently faced me. "Rather strange and free and obstreperous."

"Obstreperous?" I wondered again.

"Peculiarly so, I inferred, on the question of not coming away. She wouldn't hear of it, and, when they spoke of her mother, said she had given her mother up. She had thought she should like Europe, but didn't know she should like it so much. They had been fools to bring her if they expected to take her away. She was going to see what she could—she hadn't yet seen half. The end of it was, at any rate, that they had to leave her alone."

I seemed to see it all—to see even the scared Hathaways. "So she is alone?"

"She told them, poor thing, it appears, and in a tone they'll never forget, that she was, at all events, quite old enough to be. She cried—she quite went on—over not having come sooner. That's why the only way for her." my companion mused, "*is,* I suppose, to stay. They wanted to put her with some people or other—to find some American family. But she says she's on her own feet."

"And she's still in Florence?"

"No—I believe she was to travel. She's bent on the East."

I burst out laughing. "Magnificent Jane! It's most interesting. Only I feel that I distinctly *should* 'know' her. To my sense, always, I must tell you, she had it in her."

My relative was silent a little. "So it now appears Becky always felt."

"And yet pushed her off? Magnificent Becky!"

My companion met my eyes a moment. "You don't know the queerest part. I mean the way it has *most* brought her out."

I turned it over; I felt I should like to know—to that degree indeed that, oddly enough, I jocosely disguised my eagerness. "You don't mean she has taken to drink!"

My visitor hesitated. "She has taken to flirting."

I expressed disappointment. "Oh, she took to *that* long ago. Yes," I declared at my kinswoman's stare, "she positively flirted—with *me!*"

"The stare perhaps sharpened. "Then you flirted with *her?*"

"How else could I have been as sure as I wanted to be? But has she means?"

"Means to flirt?"—my friend looked an instant as if she spoke literally. "I don't understand about the means—though of course they have something. But I have my impression," she went on. "I think that Becky——" It seemed almost too grave to say.

But *I* had no doubts. "That Becky's backing her?"

She brought it out. "Financing her."

"Stupendous Becky! So that morally then——"

"Becky's quite in sympathy. But isn't it too odd?" my sister-in-law asked.

"Not in the least. Didn't we know, as regards Jane, that Europe was to bring her out? Well, it has also brought out Rebecca."

"It has indeed!" my companion indulgently sighed. "So what would it do if she were there?"

"I should like immensely to see. And we *shall* see."

"Why, do you believe she'll still go?"

"Certainly. She *must*."

But my friend shook it off. "She won't."

"She shall!" I retorted with a laugh. But the next moment I said: "And what does the old woman say?"

"To Jane's behavior? Not a word—never speaks of it. She talks now much less than she used—only seems to wait. But it's my belief she thinks."

"And—do you mean—knows?"

"Yes, knows that she's abandoned. In her silence there she takes it in."

"It's her way of making Jane pay?" At this, somehow, I felt more serious. "Oh, dear, dear—she'll disinherit her!"

When, in the following June, I went on to return my sister-in-law's visit the first object that met my eyes in her little white parlour was a figure that, to my stupefaction, presented itself for the moment as that of Mrs. Rimmle. I had gone to my room after arriving, and, on dressing, had come down: the apparition I speak of had arisen in the interval. Its ambiguous character lasted, however, but a second or two—I had taken Becky for her mother because I knew no one but her mother of that extreme age. Becky's age was quite startling; it had made a great stride, though, strangely enough, irrecoverably seated as she now was in it, she had a wizened brightness that I had scarcely yet seen in her. I remember indulging on this occasion in two silent observations: one to the effect that I had not hitherto been conscious of her full resemblance to the old lady, and the other to the effect that, as I had said to my sister-in-law at Christmas, "Europe," even as reaching her only through Jane's sensibilities, had really at last brought her out. She was in fact "out" in a manner of which this encounter offered to my eyes a unique example: it was the single hour, often as I had been at Brookbridge, of my meeting her elsewhere than in her mother's drawing-room. I surmise that, besides being adjusted to her more marked time of life, the garments she wore abroad, and in particular her little plain bonnet, presented points of resemblance to the close sable sheath and the quaint old headgear that, in the white house behind the elms, I had from far back associated with the external image in the stiff chair. Of course I immediately spoke of Jane, showing an interest and asking for news; on which she answered me with a smile, but not at all as I had expected.

"*Those* are not really the things you want to know—where she is, whom she's with, how she manages and where she's going next—oh, no!" And the admirable woman gave a laugh that was somehow both light and sad—sad, in particular, with a strange, long weariness. "What you do want to know is when she's coming back."

I shook my head very kindly, but out of a wealth of experience that, I flattered myself, was equal to Miss Becky's. "I do know it. Never."

Miss Becky, at this, exchanged with me a long, deep look. "Never."

We had, in silence, a little luminous talk about it, in the course of which she seemed to tell me the most interesting things. "And how's your mother?" I then inquired.

She hesitated, but finally spoke with the same serenity. "My mother's all right. You see, she's not alive."

"Oh, Becky!" my sister-in-law pleadingly interjected.

But Becky only addressed herself to me. "Come and see if she is. *I* think she isn't—but Maria perhaps isn't so clear. Come, at all events, and judge and tell me."

It was a new note, and I was a little bewildered. "Ah, but I'm not a doctor!"

"No, thank God—you're not. That's why I ask you." And now she said good-bye.

I kept her hand a moment. "*You're* more alive than ever!"

"I'm very tired." She took it with the same smile, but for Becky it was much to say.

IV

"Not alive," the next day, was certainly what Mrs. Rimmle looked when, coming in according to my promise, I found her, with Miss Maria, in her usual place. Though shrunken and diminished she still occupied her high-backed chair with a visible theory of erectness, and her intensely aged face—combined with something dauntless that belonged to her very presence and that was effective even in this extremity—might have been that of some centenarian sovereign, of indistinguishable sex, brought forth to be shown to the people as a disproof of the rumor of extinction. Mummified and open-eyed she looked at me, but I had no impression that she made me out. I had come this time without my sister-in-law, who had frankly pleaded to me—which also, for a daughter of Brookbridge, was saying much—that the house had grown too painful. Poor Miss Maria excused Miss Becky on the score of her not being well—and that, it struck me, was saying most of all. The absence of the others gave the occasion a different note; but I talked with Miss Maria for five minutes and perceived that—save for her saying, of her own movement, anything about Jane—she now spoke as if her mother had lost hearing or sense, or both, alluding freely and distinctly, though indeed favourably, to her condition. "She has expected your visit and she much enjoys it," my interlocutress said, while the old woman, soundless and motionless, simply fixed me without expression. Of course there was little to keep me; but I became aware, as I rose to go, that there was more than I had supposed. On my approaching her to take leave Mrs. Rimmle gave signs of consciousness.

"Have you heard about Jane?"

I hesitated, feeling a responsibility, and appealed for direction to Maria's face. But Maria's face was troubled, was turned altogether to her mother's. "About her life in Europe?" I then rather helplessly asked.

The old woman fronted me, on this, in a manner that made me feel silly. "Her life?"—and her voice, with this second effort, came out stronger. "Her death, if you please."

"Her death?" I echoed, before I could stop myself, with the accent of deprecation.

Miss Maria uttered a vague sound of pain, and I felt her turn away, but the marvel of her mother's little unquenched spark still held me. "Jane's dead. We've heard," said Mrs. Rimmle. "We've heard from—where is it we've heard from?" She had quite revived—she appealed to her daughter.

The poor old girl, crimson, rallied to her duty. "From Europe."

Mrs. Rimmle made at us both a little grim inclination of the head. "From Europe." I responded, in silence, with a deflection from every rigour, and, still holding me, she went on. "And now Rebecca's going."

She had gathered by this time such emphasis to say it that again, before I could help myself, I vibrated in reply. "To Europe—now?" It was as if for an instant she had made me believe it.

She only stared at me, however, from her wizened mask; then her eyes followed my companion. "Has she gone?"

"Not yet, mother." Maria tried to treat it as a joke, but her smile was embarrassed and dim.

"Then where is she?"

"She's lying down."

The old woman kept up her hard, queer gaze, but directing it, after a minute, to me. "She's going."

"Oh, some day!" I foolishly laughed; and on this I got to the door, where I separated from my younger hostess, who came no further. Only, as I held the door open, she said to me under cover of it and very quietly:

"It's poor mother's idea."

I saw—it was her idea. Mine was—for some time after this, even after I had returned to New York and to my usual occupations—that I should never again see Becky. I had seen her for the last time, I believed, under my sister-in-law's roof, and in the autumn it was given to me to hear from that fellow-admirer that she had succumbed at last to the situation. The day of the call I have just described had been a date in the process of her slow shrinkage—it was literally the first time she had, as they said at Brookbridge, given up. She had been ill for years, but the other state of health in the contemplation of which she had spent so much of her life had left her, till too late, no margin for meeting it. The encounter, at last, came simply in the form of the discovery that it *was* too late; on which, naturally, she had given up more and more. I had heard indeed, all summer, by letter, how Brookbridge had watched her do so; whereby the end found me in a manner prepared. Yet in spite of my preparation there remained with me a soreness, and when I was next—it was some six months later—on the scene of her martyrdom I replied, I fear, with an almost rabid negative to the question put to me in due course by my kinswoman. "Call on them? Never again!"

I went, none the less, the very next day. Everything was the same in the sunny parlour—everything that most mattered, I mean: the immemorial mummy in the high chair and the tributes, in the little frames on the walls, to the celebrity of its late husband. Only Maria Rimmle was different: if Becky, on my last seeing her, had looked as old as her mother, Maria—save that she moved about—looked older. I remember that she moved about, but I scarce remember what she said; and indeed what was there to say? When I risked a question, however, she had a reply.

"But *now* at least—?" I tried to put it to her suggestively.

At first she was vague. " 'Now?' "

"Won't Miss Jane come back?"

Oh, the headshake she gave me! "Never." It positively pictured to me, for the instant, a well-preserved woman, a sort of rich, ripe *seconde jeunesse* by the Arno.

"Then that's only to make more sure of your finally joining her."

Maria Rimmle repeated her headshake. "Never."

We stood so, a moment, bleakly face to face; I could think of no attenuation that would be particularly happy. But while I tried I heard a hoarse gasp that, fortunately, relieved me—a signal strange and at first formless from the occupant of the high-backed chair. "Mother wants to speak to you," Maria then said.

So it appeared from the drop of the old woman's jaw, the expression of her mouth opened as if for the emission of sound. It was difficult to me, somehow, to seem to sympathise without hypocrisy, but, so far as a step nearer could do so, I invited communication. "Have you heard where Becky's gone?" the wonderful witch's white lips then extraordinarily asked.

It drew from Maria, as on my previous visit, an uncontrollable groan, and this, in turn, made me take time to consider. As I considered, however, I had an inspiration. "To Europe?"

I must have adorned it with a strange grimace, but my inspiration had been right. "To Europe," said Mrs. Rimmle.

O. Henry (William Sydney Porter) (1862–1910)
ceased his formal education at fifteen and went to
work in an uncle's drug store. Later, as a bank clerk
in Austin, Texas, a shortage in his accounts led to a
conviction for embezzlement. While serving his sen-
tence in an Ohio penitentiary (he was assigned to the
pharmacy), Porter supposedly picked up the name O.
Henry. After release from prison, he moved to New
York (1902). Nearly all of O. Henry's stories ap-
peared in Sunday newspapers and were closely plot-
ted with a sharp, unexpected twist at the end. For
further reading: The Complete Works of O. Henry
(2 vols. 1953).

O. HENRY

Jeff Peters: A Personal Magnet

*J*eff Peters has been engaged in as many schemes for making money as
there are recipes for cooking rice in Charleston, S.C.

Best of all I like to hear him tell of his earlier days when he sold
liniments and cough cures on street corners, living hand to mouth, heart to
heart with the people, throwing heads or tails with fortune for his last coin.

"I struck Fisher Hill, Arkansaw," said he, "in a buckskin suit, mocca-
sins, long hair and a thirty-carat diamond ring that I got from an actor in
Texarkana. I don't know what he ever did with the pocket knife I swapped
him for it.

"I was Dr. Waugh-hoo, the celebrated Indian medicine man. I carried
only one best bet just then, and that was Resurrection Bitters. It was made
of life-giving plants and herbs accidentally discovered by Ta-qua-la, the
beautiful wife of the Chief of the Choctaw Nation, while gathering truck to
garnish a platter of boiled dog for the annual corn dance.

"Business hadn't been good at the last town, so I only had five dollars.
I went to the Fisher Hill druggist and he credited me for half-a-gross of
eight-ounce bottles and corks. I had the labels and ingredients in my valise,
left over from the last town. Life began to look rosy again after I got to my
hotel room with the water running from the tap, and the Resurrection
Bitters lining up on the table by the dozen.

"Fake? No, sir. There was two dollars' worth of fluid extract of cinchona and a dime's worth of aniline in that half gross of bitters. I've gone through towns years afterwards and had folks ask for 'em again.

"I hired a wagon that night and commenced selling the bitters on Main Street. Fisher Hill was a low, malarial town; and a compound hypothetical pneumo-cardiac antiscorbutic tonic was just what I diagnosed the crowd as needing. The bitters started off like sweetbreads on toast at a vegetarian dinner. I had sold two dozen at fifty cents apiece when I felt somebody pull my coat tail. I knew what that meant; so I climbed down and sneaked a five-dollar bill into the hand of a man with a German silver star on his lapel.

" 'Constable,' says I, 'it's a fine night.'

" 'Have you got a city license,' he asks, 'to sell this illegitimate essence of spooju that you flatter by the name of medicine?'

" 'I have not,' says I. 'I didn't know you had a city. If I can find it to-morrow I'll take one out if it's necessary.'

" 'I'll have to close you up till you do,' says the constable.

"I quit selling and went back to the hotel. I was talking to the landlord about it.

" 'Oh, you won't stand no show in Fisher Hill,' says he. 'Dr. Hoskins, the only doctor here, is a brother-in-law of the Mayor, and they won't allow no fake doctor to practise in town.'

" 'I don't practise medicine,' says I. 'I've got a State peddler's license, and I take out a city one wherever they demand it.'

"I went to the Mayor's office the next morning and they told me he hadn't showed up yet. They didn't know when he'd be down. So Doc Waugh-hoo hunches down again in a hotel chair and lights a jimpson-weed regalia, and waits.

"By and by a young man in a blue necktie slips into the chair next to me and asks the time.

" 'Half-past ten,' says I, 'and you are Andy Tucker. I've seen you work. Wasn't it you that put up the Great Cupid Combination package on the Southern States? Let's see, it was a Chilean diamond engagement ring, a wedding ring, a potato masher, a bottle of soothing syrup and Dorothy Vernon—all for fifty cents.'

"Andy was pleased to hear that I remembered him. He was a good street man; and he was more than that—he respected his profession, and he was satisfied with 300 per cent profit. He had plenty of offers to go into the illegitimate drug and garden-seed business; but he was never to be tempted off of the straight path.

"I wanted a partner, so Andy and me agreed to go out together. I told him about the situation in Fisher Hill and how finances was low on account of the local mixture of politics and jalap. Andy had just got in on the train that morning. He was pretty low himself, and was going to canvass the town for a few dollars to build a new battleship by popular subscription at Eureka Springs. So we went out and sat on the porch and talked it over.

"The next morning at eleven o'clock when I was sitting there alone, an Uncle Tom shuffles into the hotel and asked for the doctor to come and see Judge Banks, who, it seems, was the Mayor and a mighty sick man.

" 'I'm no doctor,' says I, 'Why don't you go and get the doctor?'

" 'Boss,' says he, 'Doc Hoskins am done gone twenty miles in de country to see some sick persons. He's de only doctor in de town, and Massa Banks am powerful bad off. He sent me to ax you to please, suh, come.'

" 'As man to man,' says I, 'I'll go and look him over.' So I put a bottle of Resurrection Bitters in my pocket and goes up on the hill to the Mayor's mansion, the finest house in town, with a mansard roof and two cast-iron dogs on the lawn.

"This Mayor Banks was in bed all but his whiskers and feet. He was making internal noises that would have had everybody in San Francisco hiking for the parks. A young man was standing by the bed holding a cup of water.

" 'Doc,' says the Mayor, 'I'm awful sick. I'm about to die. Can't you do nothing for me?'

" 'Mr. Mayor,' says I, 'I'm not a regular preordained disciple of S. Q. Lapius. I never took a course in a medical college,' says I. 'I've just come as a fellow man to see if I could be of assistance.'

" 'I'm deeply obliged,' says he. 'Doc Waugh-hoo, this is my nephew, Mr. Biddle. He has tried to alleviate my distress, but without success. Oh, Lordy! Ow-ow-ow!!' he sings out.

"I nods at Mr. Biddle and sets down by the bed and feels the Mayor's pulse. 'Let me see your liver—your tongue, I mean,' says I. Then I turns up the lids of his eyes and looks close at the pupils of 'em.

" 'How long have you been sick?' I asked.

" 'I was taken down—ow-ouch—last night,' says the Mayor. 'Gimme something for it, Doc, won't you?'

" 'Mr. Fiddle,' says I, 'raise the window shade a bit, will you?'

" 'Biddle,' says the young man. 'Do you feel like you could eat some ham and eggs, Uncle James?'

" 'Mr. Mayor,' says I, after laying my ear to his right shoulder-blade and listening, 'you've got a bad attack of super-inflammation of the right clavicle of the harpsichord!'

" 'Good Lord!' says he, with a groan. 'Can't you rub something on it, or set it or anything?'

"I picks up my hat and starts for the door.

" 'You ain't going, Doc?' says the Mayor with a howl. 'You ain't going away and leave me to die with this—superfluity of the clapboards, are you?'

" 'Common humanity, Dr. Whoa-ha,' says Mr. Biddle, 'ought to prevent your deserting a fellow human in distress.'

" 'Dr. Waugh-hoo, when you get through ploughing,' says I. And then I walks back to the bed and throws back my long hair.

" 'Mr. Mayor,' says I, 'there is only one hope for you. Drugs will do you no good. But there is another power higher yet, although drugs are high enough,' says I.

" 'And what is that?' says he.

" 'Scientific demonstrations,' says I. 'The triumph of mind over sarsaparilla. The belief that there is no pain and sickness except what is produced when we ain't feeling well. Declare yourself in arrears. Demonstrate.'

" 'What is this paraphernalia you speak of, Doc?' asks the Mayor.

" 'I am speaking,' says I, 'of the great doctrine of psychic financiering—of the enlightened school of long-distance, subconscientious treatment of fallacies and meningitis—of that wonderful indoor sport known as personal magnetism.'

" 'Can you work it Doc?' asks the Mayor.

" 'I'm one of the Sole Sanhedrims and Ostensible Hooplas of the Inner Pulpit,' says I. 'The lame walk and the blind rubber whenever I make a pass at 'em. I am a medium, a coloratura hypnotist and a spirituous control. It was only through me at the recent séances at Ann Arbor that the late President of the Vinegar Bitters Company could revisit the earth to communicate with his sister Jane. You see me peddling medicine on the streets,' says I, 'to the poor. I don't practise personal magnetism on them. I do not drag it in the dust,' says I, 'because they haven't got the dust.'

" 'Will you treat my case?' asks the Mayor.

" 'Listen,' says I. 'I've had a good deal of trouble with medical societies everywhere I've been. I don't practise medicine. But, to save your life, I'll give you the psychic treatment if you'll agree as mayor not to push the licence question.'

" 'Of course I will,' says he. 'And now get to work, Doc, for the pains are coming on again.'

" 'My fee will be two hundred and fifty dollars, cure guaranteed in two treatments,' says I.

" 'All right,' says the Mayor. 'I'll pay it. I guess my life's worth that much.'

"I sat down by the bed and looked him straight in the eye.

" 'Now,' says I, 'get your mind off the disease. You ain't sick. You haven't got a heart or a clavicle or a funny bone or brains or anything. You haven't got any pain. Declare error. Now you feel the pain that you didn't have leaving, don't you?'

" 'I do feel some little better, Doc,' says the Mayor, 'darned if I don't. Now state a few lies about my not having this swelling in my left side, and I think I could be propped up and have some sausage and buck-wheat cakes.'

"I made a few passes with my hands.

" 'Now,' says I, 'the inflammation's gone. The right lobe of the perihe-
lion has subsided. You're getting sleepy. You can't hold your eyes open any
longer. For the present the disease is checked. Now, you are asleep.'

"The Mayor shut his eyes slowly and began to snore.

" 'You observe, Mr. Tiddle,' says I, 'the wonders of modern science.'

" 'Biddle,' says he. 'When will you give Uncle the rest of the treatment,
Dr. Pooh-pooh?''

" 'Waugh-hoo,' says I. 'I'll come back at eleven to-morrow. When he
wakes up give him eight drops of turpentine and three pounds of steak.
Good morning.'

"The next morning I went back on time. 'Well, Mr. Riddle,' says I,
when he opened the bedroom door, 'and how is Uncle this morning?''

" 'He seems much better,' says the young man.

"The Mayor's colour and pulse was fine. I gave him another treatment,
and he said the last of the pain left him.

" 'Now,' says I, 'you'd better stay in bed for a day or two, and you'll be
all right. It's a good thing I happened to be in Fisher Hill, Mr. Mayor,' says
I, 'for all the remedies in the cornucopia that the regular schools of
medicine use couldn't have saved you. And now that error has flew and
pain proved a perjurer, let's allude to a cheerfuller subject—say the fee of
two hundred and fifty dollars. No cheques, please, I hate to write my name
on the back of a cheque almost as bad as I do on the front.'

" 'I've got the cash here,' says the Mayor, pulling a pocketbook from
under his pillow.

"He counts out five fifty-dollar notes and holds 'em in his hand.

" 'Bring the receipt,' he says to Biddle.

"I signed the receipt and the Mayor handed me the money. I put it in
my inside pocket careful.

" 'Now do your duty, officer,' says the Mayor, grinning much unlike a
sick man.

"Mr. Biddle lays his hand on my arm.

" 'You're under arrest, Dr. Waugh-hoo, alias Peters,' says he, 'for practising medicine without authority under the State law.'

" 'Who are you?' I asks.

" 'I'll tell you who he is,' says Mr. Mayor, sitting up in bed. 'He's a
detective employed by the State Medical Society. He's been following you
over five counties. He came to me yesterday and we fixed up this scheme to
catch you. I guess you won't do any more doctoring around these parts, Mr.
Fakir. What was it you said I had, Doc,' the Mayor laughs, 'compound—
well it wasn't softening of the brain, I guess, anyway.'

" 'A detective,' says I.

" 'Correct,' says Biddle. 'I'll have to turn you over to the Sheriff.'

" 'Let's see you do it,' says I, and I grabs Biddle by the throat and half throws him out the window, but he pulls a gun and sticks it under my chin, and I stand still. Then he puts handcuffs on me, and takes the money out of my pocket.

" 'I witness,' says he, 'that they're the same bills that you and I marked, Judge Banks. I'll turn them over to the Sheriff when we get to his office, and he'll send you a receipt. They'll have to be used as evidence in the case.'

" 'All right, Mr. Biddle,' says the Mayor. 'And now, Doc Waugh-hoo,' he goes on, 'why don't you demonstrate? Can't you pull the cork out of your magnetism with your teeth and hocus-pocus them handcuffs off?'

" 'Come on, officer,' says I, dignified. 'I may as well make the best of it.' And then I turns to old Banks and rattles my chains.

" 'Mr. Mayor,' says I, 'the time will come soon when you'll believe that personal magnetism is a success. And you'll be sure that it succeeded in this case, too.'

"And I guess it did.

"When we got nearly to the gate, I says: 'We might meet somebody now, Andy. I reckon you better take 'em off, and——' Hey? Why, of course it was Andy Tucker. That was his scheme; and that's how we got the capital to go into business together."

HAMLIN GARLAND

The Return of a Private

The nearer the train drew toward La Crosse, the soberer the little group of "vets" became. On the long way from New Orleans they had beguiled tedium with jokes and friendly chaff; or with planning with elaborate detail what they were going to do now, after the war. A long journey, slowly, irregularly, yet persistently pushing northward. When they entered on Wisconsin territory they gave a cheer, and another when they reached Madison, but after that they sank into a dumb expectancy. Comrades dropped off at one or two points beyond, until there were only four or five left who were bound for La Crosse County.

Three of them were gaunt and brown, the fourth was gaunt and pale, with signs of fever and ague upon him. One had a great scar down his temple, one limped, and they all had unnaturally large, bright eyes, showing emaciation. There were no hands greeting them at the station, no banks of gayly dressed ladies waving handkerchiefs and shouting "Bravo!" as they came in on the caboose of a freight train into the towns that had cheered and blared at them on their way to war. As they looked out or stepped upon the platform for a moment, while the train stood at the station, the loafers looked at them indifferently. Their blue coats, dusty and grimy, were too familiar now to excite notice, much less a friendly word. They were the last of the army to return, and the loafers were surfeited with such sights.

The train jogged forward so slowly that it seemed likely to be midnight before they should reach La Crosse. The little squad grumbled and swore, but it was no use; the train would not hurry, and, as a matter of fact, it was nearly two o'clock when the engine whistled "down brakes."

All of the group were farmers, living in districts several miles out of the town, and all were poor.

"Now, boys," said Private Smith, he of the fever and ague, "we are landed in La Crosse in the night. We've got to stay somewhere till mornin'. Now I ain't got no two dollars to waste on a hotel. I've got a wife and children, so I'm goin' to roost on a bench and take the cost of a bed out of my hide."

"Same here," put in one of the other men. "Hide'll grow on again, dollars'll come hard. It's going to be mighty hot skirmishin' to find a dollar these days."

"Don't think they'll be a deptuation of citizens waitin' to 'scort us to a hotel eh?" said another. His sarcasm was too obvious to require an answer.

Smith went on, "Then at daybreak we'll start for home—at least, I will."

"Well, I'll be dummed if I'll take two dollars out o' *my* hide," one of the younger men said. "I'm goin' to a hotel, ef I don't never lay up a cent."

"That'll do f'r you," said Smith; "but if you had a wife an' three young uns dependin' on yeh—"

"Which I ain't, thank the Lord! and don't intend havin' while the court knows itself."

The station was deserted, chill, and dark, as they came into it at exactly a quarter to two in the morning. Lit by the oil lamps that flared a dull red light over the dingy benches, the waiting room was not an inviting place. The younger man went off to look up a hotel, while the rest remained and prepared to camp down on the floor and benches. Smith was attended to tenderly by the other men, who spread their blankets on the bench for him, and, by robbing themselves, made quite a comfortable bed, though the narrowness of the bench made his sleeping precarious.

It was chill, though August, and the two men, sitting with bowed heads, grew stiff with cold and weariness, and were forced to rise now and again and walk about to warm their stiffened limbs. It did not occur to them, probably, to contrast their coming home with their going forth, or with the coming home of the generals, colonels, or even captains—but to Private Smith, at any rate, there came a sickness at heart almost deadly as he lay there on his hard bed and went over his situation.

In the deep of the night, lying on a board in the town where he had enlisted three years ago, all elation and enthusiasm gone out of him, he faced the fact that with the joy of home-coming was already mingled the bitter juice of care. He saw himself sick, worn out, taking up the work on his half-cleared farm, the inevitable mortgage standing ready with open jaw to swallow half his earnings. He had given three years of his life for a mere pittance of pay, and now!—

Morning dawned at last, slowly, with a pale yellow dome of light rising silently above the bluffs, which stand like some huge storm-devastated castle, just east of the city. Out to the left the great river swept on its massive yet silent way to the south. Bluejays called across the water from hillside to hillside through the clear, beautiful air, and hawks began to skim the tops of the hills. The older men were astir early, but Private Smith had fallen at last into a sleep, and they went out without waking him. He lay on his knapsack, his gaunt face turned toward the ceiling, his hands clasped on his breast, with a curious pathetic effect of weakness and appeal.

An engine switching near woke him at last, and he slowly sat up and stared about. He looked out of the window and saw that the sun was lightening the hills across the river. He rose and brushed his hair as well as he could, folded his blankets up, and went out to find his companions. They stood gazing silently at the river and at the hills.

"Looks natcher'l, don't it?" they said, as he came out.

"That's what it does," he replied. "An' it looks good. D' yeh see that peak?" He pointed at a beautiful symmetrical peak, rising like a slightly truncated cone, so high that it seemed the very highest of them all. It was touched by the morning sun and it glowed like a beacon, and a light scarf of gray morning fog was rolling up its shadowed side.

"My farm's just beyond that. Now, if I can only ketch a ride, we'll be home by dinner-time."

"I'm talkin' about breakfast." said one of the others.

"I guess it's one more meal o' hardtack f'r me," said Smith.

They foraged around, and finally found a restaurant with a sleepy old German behind the counter, and procured some coffee, which they drank to wash down their hardtack.

"Time'll come," said Smith, holding up a piece by the corner, "when this'll be a curiosity."

"I hope to God it will! I bet I've chawed hardtack enough to shingle every house in the coolly. I've chawed it when my lampers was down, and when they wasn't. I've took it dry, soaked, and mashed. I've had it wormy, musty, sour, and blue-mouldy. I've had it in little bits and big bits; 'fore coffee an' after coffee. I'm ready f'r a change. I'd like t' get holt jest about now o' some of the hot biscuits my wife c'n make when she lays herself out f'r company."

"Well, if you set there gabblin', you'll never *see* yer wife."

"Come on," said Private Smith. "Wait a moment, boys; less take suthin'. It's on me." He led them to the rusty tin dipper which hung on a nail beside the wooden water-pail, and they grinned and drank. Then shouldering their blankets and muskets, which they were "takin' home to the boys," they struck out on their last march.

"They called that coffee Jayvy," grumbled one of them, "but it never went by the road where government Jayvy resides. I reckon I know coffee from peas."

They kept together on the road along the turnpike, and up the winding road by the river, which they followed for some miles. The river was very lovely, curving down along its sandy beds, pausing now and then under broad basswood trees, or running in dark, swift, silent currents under tangles of wild grapevines, and drooping alders, and haw trees. At one of these lovely spots the three vets sat down on the thick green sward to rest, "on Smith's account." The leaves of the trees were as fresh and green as in June, the jays called cheery greetings to them, and kingfishers darted to and fro with swooping, noiseless flight.

"I tell yeh, boys, this knocks the swamps of Loueesiana into kingdom come."

"You bet. All they c'n raise down there is snakes, niggers, and p'rticler hell."

"An' fighting men," put in the older man.

"An fightin' men. If I had a good hook an' line I'd sneak a pick'rel out o' that pond. Say, remember that time I shot that alligator——"

"I guess we'd better be crawlin' along," interrupted Smith, rising and shouldering his knapsack, with considerable effort, which he tried to hide.

"Say, Smith, lemme give you a lift on that."

"I guess I c'n manage," said Smith, grimly.

"Course. But, yo' see, I may not have a chance right off to pay yeh back for the times you've carried my gun and hull caboodle. Say, now gimme that gun, anyway."

"All right, if yeh feel like it, Jim," Smith replied, and they trudged along doggedly in the sun, which was getting higher and hotter each half-mile.

"Ain't it queer there ain't no teams comin' along," said Smith, after a long silence.

"Well, no, seein's it's Sunday."

"By jinks, that's a fact. It *is* Sunday. I'll get home in time f'r dinner sure!" he exulted. "She don't hev dinner usially till about *one* on Sundays." And he fell into a muse, in which he smiled.

"Well, I'll git home jest about six o'clock, jest about when the boys are milkin' the cows," said old Jim Cranby. "I'll step into the barn, an' then I'll say: *'Heah!* why ain't this milkin' done before this time o' day?' An' then won't they yell!" he added, slapping his thigh in great glee.

Smith went on. "I'll jest go up the path. Old Rover'll come down the road to meet me. He won't bark; he'll know me, an' he'll come down waggin' his tail an' showin' his teeth. That's his way of laughin'. An' so I'll walk up to the kitchen door, an' I'll say, *'Dinner* f'r a hungry man!' An' then she'll jump up, an'——"

He couldn't go on. His voice choked at the thought of it. Saunders, the third man, hardly uttered a word, but walked silently behind the others. He had lost his wife the first year he was in the army. She died of pneumonia, caught in the autumn rains while working in the fields in his place.

They plodded along till at last they came to a parting of the ways. To the right the road continued up the main valley; to the left it went over the big ridge.

"Well, boys," began Smith, as they grounded their muskets and looked away up the valley, "here's where we shake hands. We've marched together a good many miles, an' now I s'pose we're done."

"Yes, I don't think we'll do any more of it f'r a while. I don't want to, I know."

"I hope I'll see yeh once in a while, boys, to talk over old times."

"Of course," said Saunders, whose voice trembled a little, too. "It ain't *exactly* like dyin'." They all found it hard to look at each other.

"But we'd ought'r go home with you," said Cranby. "You'll never climb that ridge with all them things on yer back."

"Oh, I'm all right! Don't worry about me. Every step takes me nearer home, yeh see. Well, good-by, boys."

They shook hands. "Good-by. Good luck!"

"Same to you. Lemme know how you find things at home."

"Good-by."

"Good-by."

He turned once before they passed out of sight, and waved his cap, and they did the same, and all yelled. Then all marched away with their long, steady, loping, veteran step. The solitary climber in blue walked on for a time, with his mind filled with the kindness of his comrades, and musing upon the many wonderful days they had had together in camp and field.

He thought of his chum, Billy Tripp. Poor Billy! A "mine" ball fell into his breast one day, fell wailing like a cat, and tore a great ragged hole in his heart. He looked forward to a sad scene with Billy's mother and sweetheart. They would want to know all about it. He tried to recall all that Billy had said, and the particulars of it, but there was little to remember, just that wild wailing sound high in the air, a dull slap, a short, quick, expulsive groan, and the boy lay with his face in the dirt in the ploughed field they were marching across.

That was all. But all the scenes he had since been through had not dimmed the horror, the terror of that moment, when his boy comrade fell, with only a breath between a laugh and a death-groan. Poor handsome Billy! Worth millions of dollars was his young life.

These sombre recollections gave way at length to more cheerful feelings as he began to approach his home coolly. The fields and houses grew familiar, and in one or two he was greeted by people seated in the doorways. But he was in no mood to talk, and pushed on steadily, though he stopped and accepted a drink of milk once at the well-side of a neighbor.

The sun was burning hot on that slope, and his step grew slower, in spite of his iron resolution. He sat down several times to rest. Slowly he crawled up the rough, reddish-brown road, which wound along the hillside, under the great trees, through dense groves of jack oaks, with tree-tops far below him on his left hand, and the hills far above him on his right. He crawled along like some minute, wingless variety of fly.

He ate some hardtack, sauced with wild berries, when he reached the summit of the ridge, and sat there for some time, looking down into his home coolly.

Sombre, pathetic figure! His wide, round, gray eyes gazing down into the beautiful valley, seeing and not seeing, the splendid cloud-shadows sweeping over the western hills and across the green and yellow wheat far below. His head drooped forward on his palm, his shoulders took on a tired stoop, his cheek-bones showed painfully. An observer might have said, "He is looking down upon his own grave."

II

Sunday comes in a Western wheat harvest with such sweet and sudden relaxation to man and beast that it would be holy for that reason, if for no other, and Sundays are usually fair in harvest-time. As one goes out into the field in the hot morning sunshine, with no sound abroad save the crickets and the indescribably pleasant silken rustling of the ripened grain, the reaper and the very sheaves in the stubble seem to be resting, dreaming.

Around the house, in the shade of the trees, the men sit, smoking, dozing, or reading the papers, while the women, never resting, move about at the housework. The men eat on Sundays about the same as on other days, and breakfast is no sooner over and out of the way than dinner begins.

But at the Smith farm there were no men dozing or reading. Mrs. Smith was alone with her three children, Mary, nine, Tommy, six, and little Ted, just past four. Her farm, rented to a neighbor, lay at the head of a coolly or narrow gully, made at some far-off post-glacial period by the vast and angry flood of water which gullied these tremendous furrows in the level prairie—furrows so deep that undisturbed portions of the original level rose like hills on either side, rose to quite considerable mountains.

The chickens wakened her as usual that Sabbath morning from dreams of her absent husband, from whom she had not heard for weeks. The shadows drifted over the hills, down the slopes, across the wheat, and up the opposite wall in a leisurely way, as if, being Sunday, they could take it easy also. The fowls clustered about the housewife as she went out into the yard. Fuzzy little chickens swarmed out from the coops, where their clucking and perpetually disgruntled mothers tramped about, petulantly thrusting their heads through the spaces between the slats.

A cow called in a deep, musical bass, and a calf answered from a little pen near by, and a pig scurried guiltily out of the cabbages. Seeing all this, seeing the pig in the cabbages, the tangle of grass in the garden, the broken fence which she had mended again and again—the little woman, hardly more than a girl, sat down and cried. The bright Sabbath morning was only a mockery without him.

A few years ago they had bought this farm, paying part, mortgaging the rest in the usual way. Edward Smith was a man of terrible energy. He worked "nights and Sundays," as the saying goes, to clear the farm of its brush and of its insatiate mortgage! In the midst of his Herculean struggle came the call for volunteers, and with the grim and unselfish devotion to his country which made the Eagle Brigade able to "whip its weight in wildcats," he threw down his scythe and grub-axe, turned his cattle loose, and became a blue-coated cog in a vast machine for killing men, and not thistles. While the millionaire sent his money to England for safe-keeping, this man, with his girl-wife and three babies, left them on a mortgaged farm, and went away to fight for an idea. It was foolish, but it was sublime for all that.

That was three years before, and the young wife, sitting on the well-curb on this bright Sabbath harvest morning, was righteously rebellious. It seemed to her that she had borne her share of the country's sorrow. Two brothers had been killed, the renter in whose hands her husband had left the farm had proved a villain; one year the farm had been without crops, and now the overripe grain was waiting the tardy hand of the neighbor who had rented it, and who was cutting his own grain first.

About six weeks before, she had received a letter saying, "We'll be discharged in a little while." But no other word had come from him. She had seen by the papers that his army was being discharged, and from day to day other soldiers slowly percolated in blue streams back into the State and county, but still *her* hero did not return.

Each week she had told the children that he was coming, and she had watched the road so long that it had become unconscious; and as she stood by the well, or by the kitchen door, her eyes were fixed unthinkingly on the road that wound down the coolly.

Nothing wears on the human soul like waiting. If the stranded mariner, searching the sun-bright seas, could once give up hope of a ship, that horrible grinding on his brain would cease. It was this waiting, hoping, on the edge of despair, that gave Emma Smith no rest.

Neighbors said, with kind intentions: "He's sick, maybe, an' can't start north just yet. He'll come along one o' these days."

"Why don't he write?" was her question, which silenced them all. This Sunday morning it seemed to her as if she could not stand it longer. The house seemed intolerably lonely. So she dressed the little ones in their best calico dresses and home-made jackets, and, closing up the house, set off down the coolly to Mother Gray's.

"Old Widder Gray" lived at the "mouth of the coolly." She was a widow woman with a large family of stalwart boys and laughing girls. She was the visible incarnation of hospitality and optimistic poverty. With Western open-heartedness she fed every mouth that asked food of her, and worked herself to death as cheerfully as her girls danced in the neighborhood harvest dances.

She waddled down the path to meet Mrs. Smith with a broad smile on her face.

"Oh, you little dears! Come right to your granny. Gimme me a kiss! Come right in, Mis' Smith. How are yeh, anyway? Nice morning, ain't it? Come in an' set down. Everything's in a clutter, but that won't scare you any."

She led the way into the best room, a sunny, square room, carpeted with a faded and patched rag carpet, and papered with white-and-green wall-paper, where a few faded effigies of dead members of the family hung in variously sized oval walnut frames. The house resounded with singing, laughter, whistling, tramping of heavy boots, and riotous scufflings. Half-grown boys came to the door and crooked their fingers at the children, who ran out, and were soon heard in the midst of the fun.

"Don't s'pose you've heard from Ed?" Mrs. Smith shook her head. 'He'll turn up some day, when you ain't lookin' for 'm." The good old soul had said that so many times that poor Mrs. Smith derived no comfort from it any longer.

"Liz heard from Al the other day. He's comin' some day this week. Anyhow, they expect him."

"Did he say anything of——"

"No, he didn't," Mrs. Gray admitted, "But then it was only a short letter, anyhow. Al ain't much for writin', anyhow.—But come out and see my new cheese. I tell yeh, I don't believe I ever had better luck in my life. If Ed should come, I want you should take him up a piece of this cheese."

It was beyond human nature to resist the influence of that noisy, hearty, loving household, and in the midst of the singing and laughing the wife forgot her anxiety, for the time at least, and laughed and sang with the rest.

About eleven o'clock a wagon-load drove up to the door, and Bill Gray, the widow's oldest son, and his whole family, from Sand Lake Coolly, piled out amid a good-natured uproar. Every one talked at once, except Bill, who sat in the wagon with his wrists on his knees, a straw in his mouth, and an amused twinkle in his blue eyes.

"Ain't heard nothin' o' Ed, I s'pose?" he asked in a kind of bellow. Mrs. Smith shook her head. Bill, with a delicacy very striking in such a great giant, rolled his quid in his mouth, and said:

"Didn't know but you had. I hear two or three of the Sand Lake boys are comin'. Left New Orleans some time this week. Didn't write nothin' about Ed, but no news is good news in such cases, mother always says."

"Well, go put out yer team," said Mrs. Gray, "an' go'n bring me in some taters, an', Sim, you go see if you c'n find some corn. Sadie, you put on the water to bile. Come now, hustle yer boots, all o' yeh. If I feed this yer crowd, we've got to have some raw materials. If y' think I'm goin' to feed yeh on pie—you're just mightily mistaken."

The children went off into the field, the girls put dinner on to boil, and then went to change their dresses and fix their hair. "Somebody might come," they said.

"Land sakes, *I hope* not! I don't know where in time I'd set 'em, 'less they'd eat at the second table," Mrs. Gray laughed, in pretended dismay.

The two older boys, who had served their time in the army, lay out on the grass before the house, and whittled and talked desultorily about the war and the crops, and planned buying a threshing-machine. The older girls and Mrs. Smith helped enlarge the table and put on the dishes, talking all the time in that cheery, incoherent, and meaningful way a group of such women have,—a conversation to be taken for its spirit rather than for its letter, though Mrs. Gray at last got the ear of them all and dissertated at length on girls.

"Girls in love ain' no use in the whole blessed week," she said. "Sundays they're a-lookin' down the road, expectin' he'll *come.* Sunday afternoons they can't think o' nothin' else, 'cause he's *here.* Monday mornin's they're sleepy and kind o' dreamy and slimpsy, and good f'r nothin' on Tuesday and Wednesday. Thursday they git absent-minded, an' begin to look off toward Sunday agin, an' mope aroun' and let the dishwater git cold, right under their noses. Friday they break dishes, an' go off in the best room an' snivel, an' look out o' the winder. Saturdays they have queer spurts o' workin' like all p'ssessed, an' spurts o' frizzin' their hair. An' Sunday they begin it all over agin."

The girls giggled and blushed, all through this tirade from their mother, their broad faces and powerful frames anything but suggestive of lackadaisical sentiment. But Mrs. Smith said:

"Now, Mrs. Gray, I hadn't ought to stay to dinner. You've got——"

"Now you set right down! If any of them girls' beaus comes, they'll have to take what's left, that's all. They ain't s'posed to have much appetite, nohow. No, you're goin' to stay if they starve, an' they ain't no danger o' that."

At one o'clock the long table was piled with boiled potatoes, cords of boiled corn on the cob, squash and pumpkin pies, hot biscuit, sweet pickles, bread and butter, and honey. Then one of the girls took down a conch-shell from a nail, and going to the door, blew a long, fine, free blast, that showed there was no weakness of lungs in her ample chest.

Then the children came out of the forest of corn, out of the creek, out of the loft of the barn, and out of the garden.

"They come to their feed f'r all the world jest like the pigs when y' holler 'poo-ee!' See 'em scoot!" laughed Mrs. Gray, every wrinkle on her face shining with delight.

The men shut up their jack-knives, and surrounded the horse-trough to souse their faces in the cold, hard water, and in a few moments the table was filled with a merry crowd, and a row of wistful-eyed youngsters circled the kitchen wall, where they stood first on one leg and then on the other, in impatient hunger.

"Now pitch in, Mrs. Smith," said Mrs. Gray, presiding over the table. "You know these men critters. They'll eat every grain of it, if yeh give 'em a chance. I swan, they're made o' India-rubber, their stomachs is, I know it."

"Haf to eat to work," said Bill, gnawing a cob with a swift, circular motion that rivalled a corn-sheller in results.

"More like workin' to eat," put in one of the girls, with a giggle. "More eat 'n work with you."

"*You* needn't say anything, Net. Any one that'll eat seven ears——"

"I didn't, no such thing. You piled your cobs on my plate."

"That'll do to tell Ed Varney. It won't go down here where we know yeh."

"Good land! Eat all yeh want! They's plenty more in the fiel's, but I can't afford to give you young uns tea. The tea is for us women-folks, and 'specially f'r Mis' Smith an' Bill's wife. We're a-goin' to tell fortunes by it."

One by one the men filled up and shoved back, and one by one the children slipped into their places, and by two o'clock the women alone remained around the débris-covered table, sipping their tea and telling fortunes.

As they got well down to the grounds in the cup, they shook them with a circular motion in the hand, and then turned them bottom-side-up quickly in the saucer, then twirled them three or four times one way, and three or four times the other, during a breathless pause. Then Mrs. Gray lifted the cup, and, gazing into it with profound gravity, pronounced the impending fate.

It must be admitted that, to a critical observer, she had abundant preparation for hitting close to the mark, as when she told the girls that "somebody was comin'." "It's a man," she went on gravely. "He is cross-eyed——"

"Oh, you hush!" cried Nettie.

"He has red hair, and is death on b'iled corn and hot biscuit."

The others shrieked with delight.

"But he's goin' to get the mitten, that red-headed feller is, for I see another feller comin' up behind him."

"Oh, lemme see, lemme see!" cried Nettie.

"Keep off," said the priestess, with a lofty gesture. "His hair is black. He don't eat so much, and he works more."

The girls exploded with a shriek of laughter, and pounded their sister on the back.

At last came Mrs. Smith's turn, and she was trembling with excitement as Mrs. Gray again composed her jolly face to what she considered a proper solemnity of expression.

"Somebody is comin' to *you*," she said, after a long pause. "He's got a musket on his back. He's a soldier. He's almost here. See?"

She pointed at two little tea-stems, which really formed a faint suggestion of a man with a musket on his back. He had climbed nearly to the edge of the cup. Mrs. Smith grew pale with excitement. She trembled so she could hardly hold the cup in her hand as she gazed into it.

"It's Ed," cried the old woman. "He's on his way home. Heavens an' earth! There he is now!" She turned and waved her hand out toward the road. They rushed to the door to look where she pointed.

A man in a blue coat, with a musket on his back, was toiling slowly up the hill on the sun-bright, dusty road, toiling slowly, with bent head half hidden by a heavy knapsack. So tired it seemed that walking was indeed a process of falling. So eager to get home he would not stop, would not look aside, but plodded on, amid the cries of the locusts, the welcome of the crickets, and the rustle of the yellow wheat. Getting back to God's country, and his wife and babies!

Laughing, crying, trying to call him and the children at the same time, the little wife, almost hysterical, snatched her hat and ran out into the yard. But the soldier had disappeared over the hill into the hollow beyond, and, by the time she had found the children, he was too far away for her voice to reach him. And, besides, she was not sure it was her husband, for he had not turned his head at their shouts. This seemed so strange. Why didn't he stop to rest at his old neighbor's house? Tortured by hope and doubt, she hurried up the coolly as fast as she could push the baby wagon, the blue-coated figure just ahead pushing steadily, silently forward up the coolly.

When the excited, panting little group came in sight of the gate they saw the blue-coated figure standing, leaning upon the rough rail fence, his chin on his palms, gazing at the empty house. His knapsack, canteen, blankets, and musket lay upon the dusty grass at his feet.

He was like a man lost in a dream. His wide, hungry eyes devoured the scene. The rough lawn, the little unpainted house, the field of clear yellow wheat behind it, down across which streamed the sun, now almost ready to touch the high hill to the west, the crickets crying merrily, a cat on the fence near by, dreaming, unmindful of the stranger in blue——

How peaceful it all was. O God! How far removed from all camps, hospitals, battle lines. A little cabin in a Wisconsin coolly, but it was majestic in its peace. How did he ever leave it for those years of tramping, thirsting, killing?

Trembling, weak with emotion, her eyes on the silent figure, Mrs. Smith hurried up to the fence. Her feet made no noise in the dust and grass, and they were close upon him before he knew of them. The oldest boy ran a little ahead. He will never forget that figure, that face. It will always remain as something epic, that return of the private. He fixed his eyes on the pale face covered with a ragged beard.

"Who *are* you, sir?" asked the wife, or, rather, started to ask, for he turned, stood a moment, and then cried:

"Emma!"

"Edward!"

The children stood in a curious row to see their mother kiss this bearded, strange man, the elder girl sobbing sympathetically with her mother. Illness had left the soldier partly deaf, and this added to the strangeness of his manner.

But the youngest child stood away, even after the girl had recognized her father and kissed him. The man turned to the baby, and said in a curiously unpaternal tone:

"Come here, my little man; don't you know me?" But the baby backed away under the fence and stood peering at him critically.

"My little man!" What meaning in those words! This baby seemed like some other woman's child, and not the infant he had left in his wife's arms. The war had come between him and his baby—he was only a strange man to him, with big eyes; a soldier, with mother hanging to his arm, and talking in a loud voice.

"And this is Tom," the private said, drawing the oldest boy to him. "*He'll* come and see me. *He* knows his poor old pap when he comes home from the war."

The mother heard the pain and reproach in his voice and hastened to apologize.

"You've changed so, Ed. He can't know yeh. This is papa, Teddy;

come and kiss him—Tom and Mary do. Come, won't you?" But Teddy still peered through the fence with solemn eyes, well out of reach. He resembled a half-wild kitten that hesitates, studying the tones of one's voice.

"I'll fix him," said the soldier, and sat down to undo his knapsack, out of which he drew three enormous and very red apples. After giving one to each of the older children, he said:

"*Now* I guess he'll come. Eh, my little man? Now come see your pap."

Teddy crept slowly under the fence, assisted by the overzealous Tommy, and a moment later was kicking and squalling in his father's arms. Then they entered the house, into the sitting room, poor, bare, art-forsaken little room, too, with its rag carpet, its square clock, and its two or three chromos ánd pictures from *Harper's Weekly* pinned about.

"Emma, I'm all tired out," said Private Smith, as he flung himself down on the carpet as he used to do, while his wife brought a pillow to put under his head, and the children stood about munching their apples.

"Tommy, you run and get me a pan of chips, and Mary, you get the tea-kettle on, and I'll go and make some biscuit."

And the soldier talked. Question after question he poured forth about the crops, the cattle, the renter, the neighbors. He slipped his heavy government brogan shoes off his poor, tired, blistered feet, and lay out with utter, sweet relaxation. He was a free man again, no longer a soldier under a command. At supper he stopped once, listened and smiled. "That's old Spot. I know her voice. I s'pose that's her calf out there in the pen. I can't milk her to-night, though. I'm too tired. But I tell you, I'd like a drink of her milk. What's become of old Rove?"

"He died last winter. Poisoned, I guess." There was a moment of sadness for them all. It was some time before the husband spoke again, in a voice that trembled a little.

"Poor old feller! He'd 'a' known me half a mile away. I expected him to come down the hill to meet me. It 'ud 'a' been more like comin' home if I could 'a' seen him comin' down the road an' waggin' his tail, an' laughin' that way he has. I tell yeh, it kind o' took hold o' me to see the blinds down an' the house shut up."

"But, yeh see, we—we expected you'd write again 'fore you started. And then we thought we'd see you if you *did* come," she hastened to explain.

"Well, I ain't worth a cent on writin'. Besides, it's just as well yeh didn't know when I was comin'. I tell you, it sounds good to hear them chickens out there, an' turkeys, an' the crickets. Do you know they don't have just the same kind o' crickets down South? Who's Sam hired t' help cut yer grain?"

"The Ramsey boys."

"Looks like a good crop; but I'm afraid I won't do much gettin' it cut.

This cussed fever an' ague has got me down pretty low. I don't know when I'll get rid of it. I'll bet I've took twenty-five pounds of quinine if I've taken a bit. Gimme another biscuit. I tell yeh, they taste good, Emma. I ain't had anything like it——Say, if you'd 'a' hear'd me braggin' to th' boys about your butter 'n' biscuits I'll bet your ears 'ud 'a' burnt."

The private's wife colored with pleasure. "Oh, you're always a-braggin' about your things. Everybody makes good butter."

"Yes; old lady Snyder, for instance."

"Oh, well, she ain't to be mentioned. She's Dutch."

"Or old Mis' Snively. One more cup o' tea, Mary. That's my girl! I'm feeling better already. I just b'lieve the matter with me is, I'm *starved.*"

This was a delicious hour, one long to be remembered. They were like lovers again. But their tenderness, like that of a typical American family, found utterance in tones, rather than in words. He was praising her when praising her biscuit, and she knew it. They grew soberer when he showed where he had been struck, one ball burning the back of his hand, one cutting away a lock of hair from his temple, and one passing through the calf of his leg. The wife shuddered to think how near she had come to being a soldier's widow. Her waiting no longer seemed hard. This sweet, glorious hour effaced it all.

Then they rose, and all went out into the garden and down to the barn. He stood beside her while she milked old Spot. They began to plan fields and crops for next year.

His farm was weedy and encumbered, a rascally renter had run away with his machinery (departing between two days), his children needed clothing, the years were coming upon him, he was sick and emaciated, but his heroic soul did not quail. With the same courage with which he had faced his Southern march he entered upon a still more hazardous future.

Oh, what mystic hour! The pale man with big eyes standing there by the well, with his young wife by his side. The vast moon swinging above the eastern peaks, the cattle winding down the pasture slopes with jangling bells, the crickets singing, the stars blooming out sweet and far and serene; the katydids rhythmically calling, the little turkeys crying querulously, as they settled to roost in the poplar tree near the open gate. The voices at the well drop lower, the little ones nestle in their father's arms at last, and Teddy falls asleep there.

The common soldier of the American volunteer army had returned. His war with the South was over, and his fight, his daily running fight with nature and against the injustice of his fellow-men, was begun again.

EDITH WHARTON

The Line of Least Resistance

Millicent was late–as usual. Mr. Mindon, returning unexpectedly from
an uninterrupted yacht race, reached home with the legitimate hope of
finding her at luncheon; but she was still out. "Was she lunching out then?"
he asked the butler, who replied, with the air of making an uncalled-for
concession to his master's curiosity, that Mrs. Mindon had given no orders
about luncheon.

Mr. Mindon, on this negative information (it was the kind from which
his knowledge of his wife's movements was mainly drawn), sat down to the
grilled cutlet and glass of Vichy that represented his share in the fabulous
daily total of the chef's book. Mr. Mindon's annual food consumption
probably amounted to about half of one per cent on his cook's perquisites,
and of the other luxuries of his complicated establishment he enjoyed considerably less than this fraction. Of course, it was nobody's fault but his
own. As Millicent pointed out, she couldn't feed her friends on mutton
chops and Vichy because of his digestive difficulty, nor could she return

their hospitality by asking them to play croquet with the children because that happened to be Mr. Mindon's chosen pastime. If that was the kind of life he wanted to lead he should have married a dyspeptic governess, not a young confiding girl, who little dreamed what marriage meant when she passed from her father's roof into the clutches of a tyrant with imperfect gastric secretions.

It was his fault, of course, but then Millicent had faults too, as she had been known to concede when she perceived that the contemplation of her merits was beginning to pall; and it did seem unjust to Mr. Mindon that their life should be one long adaptation to Millicent's faults at the expense of his own. Millicent was unpunctual—but that gave a sense of her importance to the people she kept waiting; she had nervous attacks—but they served to excuse her from dull dinners and family visits; she was bad-tempered—but that merely made the servants insolent to Mr. Mindon; she was extravagant—but that simply necessitated Mr. Mindon's curtailing his summer holiday and giving a closer attention to business. If ever a woman had the qualities of her faults, that woman was Millicent. Like the legendary goose, they laid golden eggs for her, and she nurtured them tenderly in return. If Millicent had been a perfect wife and mother, she and Mr. Mindon would probably have spent their summer in the depressing promiscuity of hotel piazzas. Mr. Mindon was shrewd enough to see that he reaped the advantages of his wife's imperfect domesticity, and that if her faults were the making of her, she was the making of him. It was therefore unreasonable to be angry with Millicent, even if she were late for luncheon, and Mr. Mindon, who prided himself on being a reasonable man, usually found some other outlet for his wrath.

On this occasion it was the unpunctuality of the little girls. They came in with their governess some minutes after he was seated; two small Millicents, with all her arts in miniature. They arranged their frocks carefully before seating themselves and turned up their little Greek noses at the food. Already they showed signs of finding fault with as much ease and discrimination as Millicent; and Mr. Mindon knew that this was an accomplishment not to be undervalued. He himself, for example, though Millicent charged him with being a discontented man, had never acquired her proficiency in deprecation; indeed, he sometimes betrayed a mortifying indifference to trifles that afforded opportunity for the display of his wife's fastidiousness. Mr. Mindon, though no biologist, was vaguely impressed by the way in which that accomplished woman had managed to transmit an acquired characteristic to her children: it struck him with wonder that traits of which he had marked the incipience in Millicent should have become intuitions in her offspring. To rebuke such costly replicas of their mother seemed dangerously like scolding Millicent—and Mr. Mindon's hovering resentment prudently settled on the governess.

He pointed out to her that the children were late for luncheon.

The governess was sorry, but Gladys was always unpunctual. Perhaps her papa would speak to her.

Mr. Mindon changed the subject. "What's that at my feet? There's a dog in the room!"

He looked round furiously at the butler, who gazed impartially over his head. Mr. Mindon knew that it was proper for him to ignore his servants, but was not sure to what extent they ought to reciprocate his treatment.

The governess explained that it was Gwendolen's puppy.

"Gwendolen's puppy? Who gave Gwendolen a puppy?"

"Fwank Antwim," said Gwendolen through a mouthful of mushroom soufflé.

"Mr. Antrim," the governess suggested, in a tone that confessed the futility of the correction.

"*We* don't call him Mr. Antrim; we call him Frank; he likes us to," said Gladys icily.

"You'll do no such thing!" her father snapped.

A soft body came in contact with his toe. He kicked out viciously, and the room was full of yelping.

"Take the animal out instantly!" he stormed; dogs were animals to Mr. Mindon. The butler continued to gaze over his head, and the two footmen took their cue from the butler.

"I won't—I won't—I won't let my puppy go!" Gwendolen violently lamented.

But she should have another, her father assured her—a much handsomer and more expensive one; his darling should have a prize dog; he would telegraph to New York on the instant.

"I don't want a pwize dog; I want Fwank's puppy!"

Mr. Mindon laid down his fork and walked out of the room, while the governess, cutting up Gwendolen's nectarine, said, as though pointing out an error in syntax, "You've vexed your papa again."

"I don't mind vexing papa—nothing happens," said Gwendolen, hugging her puppy; while Gladys, disdaining the subject of dispute, contemptuously nibbled caramels. Gladys was two years older than Gwendolen and had outlived the first freshness of her enthusiasm for Frank Antrim, who, with the notorious indiscrimination of the grownup, always gave the nicest presents to Gwendolen.

Mr. Mindon, crossing his marble hall between goddesses whose dishabille was still slightly disconcerting to his traditions, stepped out on the terrace above the cliffs. The lawn looked as expensive as a velvet carpet woven in one piece; the flower borders contained only exotics; and the stretch of blue-satin Atlantic had the air of being furrowed only by the keels of pleasure boats. The scene, to Mr. Mindon's imagination, never lost the keen edge of its costliness; he had yet to learn Millicent's trick of regarding a Newport villa as a mere pied à terre; but he could not help reflecting that, after all, it was to him she owed her fine sense of relativity. There are certain things one must possess in order not to be awed by them, and it was he who had enabled Millicent to take a Newport villa for granted. And still she was not satisfied! She had reached the point where taking the exceptional as a matter of course becomes in itself a matter of course; and Millicent could not live without novelty. That was the worst of it: she discarded her successes as rapidly as her gowns; Mr. Mindon felt a certain breathlessness in retracing her successive manifestations. And yet he had always made allowances: literally and figuratively, he had gone on making larger and larger allowances, till his whole income, as well as his whole point of view, was practically at Millicent's disposal. But, after all, there was a principle of give and take—if only Millicent could have been brought to see it! One of Millicent's chief sources of strength lay in her magnificent obtuseness: there were certain obligations that simply didn't exist for her, because she couldn't be brought to see them, and the principle of give and take (a favorite principle of Mr. Mindon's) was one of them.

There was Frank Antrim, for instance. Mr. Mindon, who had a high sense of propriety, had schooled himself, not without difficulty, into thinking Antrim a charming fellow. No one was more alive than Mr. Mindon to the expediency of calling the Furies the Eumenides. He knew that as long as he chose to think Frank Antrim a charming fellow, everything was as it should be and his home a temple of the virtues. But why on earth did Millicent let the fellow give presents to the children? Mr. Mindon was dimly conscious that Millicent had been guilty of the kind of failure she would least have liked him to detect—a failure in taste—and a certain exultation tempered his resentment. To anyone who had suffered as Mr. Mindon had from Millicent's keenness in noting such lapses in others, it was not unpleasant to find that she could be "bad form." A sense of unwonted astuteness fortified Mr. Mindon's wrath. He felt that he had every reason to be angry with Millicent, and decided to go and scold the governess; then he remembered that it was bad for him to lose his temper after eating, and, drawing a small phial from his pocket, he took a pepsin tablet instead.

Having vented his wrath in action, he felt calmer, but scarcely more happy. A marble nymph smiled at him from the terrace; but he knew how much nymphs cost, and was not sure that they were worth the price. Beyond the shrubberies he caught a glimpse of domed glass. His greenhouses were the finest in Newport; but since he neither ate fruit nor wore orchids, they yielded at best an indirect satisfaction. At length he decided to go and play with the little girls; but on entering the nursery he found them dressing for a party, with the rapt gaze and fevered cheeks with which Millicent would presently perform the same rite. They took no notice of him, and he crept downstairs again.

His study table was heaped with bills, and as it was bad for his digestion to look over them after luncheon, he wandered on into the other rooms. He did not stay long in the drawing room; it evoked too vividly the evening hours when he delved for platitudes under the inattentive gaze of listeners who obviously resented his not being somebody else. Much of Mr. Mindon's intercourse with ladies was clouded by the sense of this resentment, and he sometimes avenged himself by wondering if they supposed he would talk to them if he could help it. The sight of the dining-room door increased his depression by recalling the long dinners where, with the pantry draft on his neck, he languished between the dullest women of the evening. He turned away; but the ballroom beyond roused even more disturbing associations: an orchestra playing all night (Mr. Mindon crept to bed at eleven), carriages shouted for under his windows, and a morrow like the day after an earthquake.

In the library he felt less irritated but not more cheerful. Mr. Mindon had never quite known what the library was for; it was like one of those mysterious ruins over which archaeology endlessly disputes. It could not have been intended for reading, since no one in the house ever read, except an under-housemaid charged with having set fire to her bed in her surreptitious zeal for fiction; and smoking was forbidden there, because the hangings held the odor of tobacco. Mr. Mindon felt a natural pride in being rich enough to permit himself a perfectly useless room; but not liking to take the bloom from its inutility by sitting in it, he passed on to Millicent's boudoir.

Here at least was a room of manifold purposes, the center of Millicent's complex social system. Mr. Mindon entered with the awe of the modest investor treading the inner precincts of finance. He was proud of Millicent's social activities and liked to read over her daily list of engagements and the record of the invitations she received in a season. The number was perpetually swelling, like a rising stock. Mr. Mindon had a vague sense that she would soon be declaring an extra dividend. After all, one must be lenient to a woman as hard-working as Millicent. All about him were the evidences of her toil: her writing table disappeared under an avalanche of notes and cards; the wastepaper basket overflowed with torn correspondence; and, glancing down, Mr. Mindon saw a crumpled letter at his feet. Being a man of neat habits, he was often tried by Millicent's genial disorder; and his customary rebuke was the act of restoring the strayed object to its place.

He stooped to gather the bit of paper from the floor. As he picked it up his eye caught the words; he smoothed the page and read on. . . .

II

He seemed to be cowering on the edge of a boiling flood, watching his small thinking faculty spin round out of reach on the tumult of his sensations.

Then a fresh wave of emotion swept the tiny object—the quivering imperceptible ego—back to shore, and it began to reach out drowned tentacles in a faint effort after thought.

He sat up and glanced about him. The room looked back at him, coldly, unfamiliarly, as he had seen Millicent look when he asked her to be reasonable. And who are you? the walls seemed to say. Who am I? Mr. Mindon heard himself retorting. I'll tell you, by God! I'm the man that paid for you—paid for every scrap of you: silk hangings, china rubbish, glasses, chandeliers—every Frenchified rag of you. Why, if it weren't for me and my money you'd be nothing but a brick-and-plaster shell, naked as the day you were built—no better than a garret or a coal hole. Why, you wouldn't *be* at all if I chose to tear you down. I could tear the whole house down, if I chose.

He paused, suddenly aware that his eyes were on a photograph of Millicent, and that it was his wife he was apostrophizing. Her lips seemed to shape a "hush"; when he said things she didn't like she always told him not to talk so loud. Had he been talking loud? Well, who was to prevent him? Wasn't the house his and everything in it? Who was Millicent, to bid him hush?

Mr. Mindon felt a sudden increase of stature. He strutted across the room. Why, of course, the room belonged to him, the house belonged to him, and he belonged to himself! That was the best of it! For years he had been the man that Millicent thought him, the mere projection of her disdain; and now he was himself.

It was odd how the expression of her photograph changed, melting, as her face did, from contempt to cajolery, in one of those transitions that hung him breathless on the skirts of her mood. She was looking at him gently now, sadly almost, with the little grieved smile that seemed always to anticipate and pardon his obtuseness. Ah, Millicent! The clock struck and Mr. Mindon stood still. Perhaps she was smiling so now—or the other way. He could have told the other fool where each of her smiles led. There was a fierce enjoyment in his sense of lucidity. He saw it all now. Millicent had kept him for years in bewildered subjection to exigencies as inscrutable as the decrees of Providence; but now his comprehension of her seemed a mere incident in his omniscience.

His sudden translation to the absolute gave him a curious sense of spectatorship; he seemed to be looking on at his own thoughts. His brain was like a brightly-lit factory, full of flying wheels and shuttles. All the machinery worked with the greatest rapidity and precision. He was planning, reasoning, arguing, with unimagined facility; words flew out like sparks from each revolving thought. But suddenly he felt himself caught in the wheels of his terrific logic, and swept round, red and shrieking, till he was flung off into space.

The acuter thrill of one sobbing nerve detached itself against his consciousness. What was it that hurt so? Someone was speaking; a voice
probed to the central pain—

"Any orders for the stable, sir?"

And Mr. Mindon found himself the mere mouthpiece of a roving impulse that replied—

"No; but you may telephone for a cab for me—at once."

III

He drove to one of the hotels. He was breathing more easily now, restored
to the safe level of conventional sensation. His late ascent to the rarefied
heights of the unexpected had left him weak and exhausted; but he gained
reassurance from the way in which his thoughts were slipping back of themselves into the old grooves. He was feeling, he was sure, just as gentleman
ought to feel; all the consecrated phrases—"outraged honor," "a father's
heart," "the sanctity of home"—were flocking glibly at his call. He had the
self-confidence that comes of knowing one has on the right clothes. He had
certainly done the proper thing in leaving the house at once; but, too weak
and tired to consider the next step, he yielded himself to one of those
soothing intervals of abeyance when life seems to wait submissively at the
door.

As his cab breasted the current of the afternoon drive he caught the
greeting of the lady with whom he and Millicent were to have dined. He
was troubled by the vision of that disrupted dinner. He had not yet reached
the point of detachment at which offending Mrs. Targe might become im-
material, and again he felt himself jerked out of his grooves. What ought he
to do? Millicent, now, could have told him—if only he might have consulted Millicent! He pulled himself together and tried to think of his wrongs.

At the hotel, the astonished clerk led him upstairs, unlocking the door
of a room that smelt of cheap soap. The window had been so long shut that
it opened with a jerk, sending a shower of dead flies to the carpet. Out along
the sea front, at that hour, the south wind was hurrying the waters, but the
hotel stood in one of the sheltered streets, where in midsummer there is
little life in the air. Mr. Mindon sat down in the provisional attitude of a
visitor who is kept waiting. Over the fireplace hung a print of the "Landing
of Columbus"; a fly-blown portrait of General Grant faced it from the
opposite wall. The smell of soap was insufferable, and hot noises came up
irritatingly from the street. He looked at his watch; it was just four o'clock.

He wondered if Millicent had come in yet, and if she had read his
letter. The occupation of picturing how she would feel when she read it
proved less exhilarating than he had expected, and he got up and wandered
about the room. He opened a drawer in the dressing table, and seeing in it

some burnt matches and a fuzz of hair, shut it with disgust; but just as he was ringing to rebuke the housemaid he remembered that he was not in his own house. He sat down again, wondering if the afternoon post were in, and what letters it had brought. It was annoying not to get his letters. What would be done about them? Would they be sent after him? Sent where? It suddenly occurred to him that he didn't in the least know where he was going. He must be going somewhere, of course; he hadn't left home to settle down in that stifling room. He supposed he should go to town, but with the heat at ninety the prospect was not alluring. He might decide on Lenox or Saratoga; but a doubt as to the propriety of such a course set him once more adrift on a chartless sea of perplexities. His head ached horribly and he threw himself on the bed.

When he sat up, worn out with his thought, the room was growing dark. Eight o'clock! Millicent must be dressing—but no; tonight at least, he grimly reflected, she was condemned to the hateful necessity of dining alone; unless, indeed, her audacity sent her to Mrs. Targe's in the always acceptable role of the pretty woman whose husband has been "called away." Perhaps Antrim would be asked to fill his place!

The thought flung him on his feet, but its impetus carried him no farther. He was borne down by the physical apathy of a traveler who has a week's journey in his bones. He sat down and thought of the little girls, who were just going to bed. They would have welcomed him at that hour: he was aware that they cherished him chiefly as a pretext, a sanctuary from bedtime and lessons. He had never in his life been more than an alternative to anyone.

A vague sense of physical apprehension resolved itself into hunger stripped of appetite, and he decided that he ought to urge himself to eat. He opened his door on a rising aroma of stale coffee and fry.

In the dining room, where a waiter offered him undefinable food in thick-lipped saucers, Mr. Mindon decided to go to New York. Retreating from the heavy assault of a wedge of pie, he pushed back his chair and went upstairs. He felt hot and grimy in the yachting clothes he had worn since that morning, and the Fall River boat would at least be cool. Then he remembered the playful throngs that held the deck, the midnight hilarity of the waltz tunes, the horror of the morning coffee. His stomach was still tremulous from its late adventure into the unknown, and he shrank from further risks. He had never before realized how much he loved his home.

He grew soft at the vision of his vacant chair. What were they doing and saying without him? His little ones were fatherless—and Millicent? Hitherto he had evaded the thought of Millicent, but now he took a doleful pleasure in picturing her in ruins at his feet. Involuntarily he found himself stooping to her despair; but he straightened himself and said aloud, "I'll take the night train, then." The sound of his voice surprised him, and he started up. Was that a footstep outside?—a message, a note? Had they found out where he was, and was his wretched wife mad enough to sue for mercy? His ironical smile gave the measure of her madness; but the step passed on, and he sat down rather blankly. The impressiveness of his attitude was being gradually sapped by the sense that no one knew where he was. He had reached the point where he could not be sure of remaining inflexible unless someone asked him to relent.

IV

At the sound of a knock he clutched his hat and bag.

"Mindon, I say!" a genial voice adjured him; and before he could take counsel with his newly-acquired dignity, which did not immediately respond to a first summons, the door opened on the reassuring presence of Laurence Meysy.

Mr. Mindon felt the relief of a sufferer at the approach of the eminent specialist. Laurence Meysy was the past tense of a dangerous man: though timeworn, still a favorite; a circulating library romance, dog-eared by many a lovely hand, and still perused with pleasure, though, alas! no longer on the sly. He was said to have wrought much havoc in his youth; and it being now his innocent pleasure to repair the damage done by others, he had become the consulting physician of injured husbands and imprudent wives.

Two gentlemen followed him: Mr. Mindon's uncle and senior partner, the eminent Ezra Brownrigg, and the Reverend Doctor Bonifant, rector of the New York church in which Mr. Mindon owned a pew that was almost as expensive as his opera box.

Mr. Brownrigg entered silently; to get at anything to say he had to sink an artesian well of meditation; but he always left people impressed by what he would have said if he had spoken. He greeted his nephew with the air of a distinguished mourner at a funeral—the mourner who consciously overshadows the corpse; and Doctor Bonifant did justice to the emotional side of the situation by fervently exclaiming, "Thank heaven, we are not too late!"

Mr. Mindon looked about him with pardonable pride. This scene suggested something between a vestry meeting and a conference of railway directors; and the knowledge that he himself was its central figure, that even his uncle was an accessory, an incident, a mere bit of still life brushed in by the artist Circumstance to throw Mr. Mindon into fuller prominence, gave that gentleman his first sense of equality with his wife. Equality? In another moment he towered above her, picturing her in an attitude of vaguely imagined penance at Doctor Bonifant's feet. Mr. Mindon had always felt about the clergy much as he did about his library: he had never quite known what they were for; but, with the pleased surprise of the pious naturalist, he now saw that they had their uses, like every other object in the economy of nature.

"My dear fellow," Meysy persuasively went on, "we've come to have a little chat with you."

Mr. Brownrigg and the Rector seated themselves. Mr. Mindon mechanically followed their example, and Meysy, asking the others if they minded his cigarette, cheerfully accommodated himself to the edge of the bed.

From the lifelong habit of taking the chair, Mr. Brownrigg coughed and looked at Doctor Bonifant. The Rector leaned forward, stroking his cheek with a hand on which a massive intaglio seemed to be rehearsing the part of the episcopal ring; then his deprecating glance transferred the burden of action to Laurence Meysy. Meysy seemed to be surveying the case through the mitigating medium of cigarette smoke. His view was that of the professional setting to rights the blunders of two amateurs. It was his theory that the art of carrying on a love affair was very nearly extinct; and he had a far greater contempt for Antrim than for Mr. Mindon.

"My dear fellow," he began, "I've seen Mrs. Mindon—she sent for me."

Mr. Brownrigg, peering between guarded lips, here interposed a "Very proper."

Of course Millicent had done the proper thing! Mr. Mindon could not repress a thrill of pride at her efficiency.

"Mrs. Mindon," Meysy continued, "showed me your letter." He paused. "She was perfectly frank—she throws herself on your mercy."

"That should be remembered in her favor," Doctor Bonifant murmured in a voice of absolution.

"It's a wretched business, Mindon—the poor woman's crushed—crushed. Your uncle here has seen her."

Mr. Brownrigg glanced suspiciously at Meysy, as though not certain whether he cared to corroborate an unauthorized assertion; then he said, "Mrs. Brownrigg has *not*."

Doctor Bonifant sighed; Mrs. Brownrigg was one of his most cherished parishioners.

"And the long and short of it is," Meysy summed up, "that we're here as your friends—and as your wife's friends—to ask you what you mean to do."

There was a pause. Mr. Mindon was disturbed by finding the initiative shifted to his shoulders. He had been talking to himself so volubly for the last six hours that he seemed to have nothing left to say.

"To do—to do?" he stammered. "Why, I mean to go away—leave her—"

"Divorce her?"

"Why—y-yes—yes—"

Doctor Bonifant sighed again, and Mr. Brownrigg's lips stirred like a door being cautiously unbarred.

Meysy knocked the ashes off his cigarette. "You've quite made up your mind, eh?"

Mr. Mindon faltered another assent. Then, annoyed at the uncertain sound of his voice, he repeated loudly, "I mean to divorce her."

The repetition fortified his resolve; and his declaration seemed to be sealed by the silence of his three listeners. He had no need to stiffen himself against entreaty; their mere presence was a pedestal for his wrongs. The words flocked of themselves, building up his conviction like a throng of masons buttressing a weak wall.

Mr. Brownrigg spoke upon his first pause. "There's the publicity—it's the kind of thing that's prejudicial to a man's business interests."

An hour earlier the words would have turned Mr. Mindon cold; now he brushed them aside. His business interests, forsooth! What good had his money ever done him? What chance had he ever had of enjoying it? All his toil hadn't made him a rich man—it had merely made Millicent a rich woman.

Doctor Bonifant murmered, "The children must be considered."

"They've never considered me!" Mr. Mindon retorted—and turned afresh upon his uncle. Mr. Brownrigg listened impassively. He was a very silent man, but his silence was not a receptacle for the speech of others—it was a hard convex surface on which argument found no footing. Mr. Mindon reverted to the Rector. Doctor Bonifant's attitude towards life was full of a benignant receptivity; as though, logically, a man who had accepted the Thirty-nine Articles was justified in accepting anything else that he chose. His attention had therefore an absorbent quality peculiarly encouraging to those who addressed him. He listened affirmatively, as it were.

Mr. Mindon's spirits rose. It was the first time that he had ever had an audience. He dragged his hearers over every stage of his wrongs, losing sight of the vital injury in the enumeration of incidental grievances. He had the excited sense that at last Millicent would know what he had always thought of her.

Mr. Brownrigg looked at his watch, and Doctor Bonifant bent his head as though under the weight of a pulpit peroration. Meysy, from the bed, watched the three men with the air of an expert who holds the solution of the problem.

He slipped to his feet as Mr. Mindon's speech flagged.

"I suppose you've considered, Mindon, that it rests with you to proclaim the fact that you're no longer—well, the chief object of your wife's affection?"

Mr. Mindon raised his head irritably; interrogation impeded the flow of his diatribe.

"That you—er,—in short, create the situation by making it known?" Meysy glanced at the Rector. "Am I right, Bonifant?"

The Rector took meditative counsel of his finger tips; then slowly, as though formulating a dogma, "Under certain conditions," he conceded, "what is unknown may be said to be nonexistent."

Mr. Mindon looked from one to the other.

"Damn it, man—before it's too late," Meysy followed up, "can't you see that *you're* the only person who can make you ridiculous?"

Mr. Brownrigg rose, and Mr. Mindon had the desperate sense that the situation was slipping out of his grasp.

"It rests with you," Doctor Bonifant murmured, "to save your children from even the shadow of obloquy."

"You can't stay here, at any rate," said Mr. Brownrigg heavily.

Mr. Mindon, who had risen, dropped weakly into his chair. His three counselors were now all on their feet, taking up their hats with the air of men who have touched the limit of duty. In another moment they would be gone, and with them Mr. Mindon's audience, his support, his confidence in the immutability of his resolve. He felt himself no more than an evocation of their presence; and, in dread of losing the identity they had created, he groped for a detaining word. "I shan't leave for New York till tomorrow."

"Tomorrow everything will be known," said Mr. Brownrigg, with his hand on the door.

Meysy glanced at his watch with a faint smile. "It's tomorrow now," he added.

He fell back, letting the older men pass out; but, turning as though to follow, he felt a drowning clutch upon his arm.

"It's for the children," Mr. Mindon stammered.

FRANK NORRIS

A Deal in Wheat

I THE BEAR—WHEAT AT SIXTY-TWO

*A*s Sam Lewiston backed the horse into the shafts of his buckboard and began hitching the tugs to the whiffletree, his wife came out from the kitchen door of the house and drew near, and stood for some time at the horse's head, her arms folded and her apron rolled around them. For a long moment neither spoke. They had talked over the situation so long and so comprehensively the night before that there seemed to be nothing more to say.

The time was late in the summer, the place a ranch in southwestern Kansas, and Lewiston and his wife were two of a vast population of farmers, wheat growers, who at that moment were passing through a crisis—a crisis that at any moment might culminate in tragedy. Wheat was down to sixty-six.

At length Emma Lewiston spoke.

"Well," she hazarded, looking vaguely out across the ranch toward the horizon, leagues distant; "well, Sam, there's always that offer of brother Joe's. We can quit—and go to Chicago—if the worst comes."

"And give up!" exclaimed Lewiston, running the lines through the torets. "Leave the ranch! Give up! After all these years!"

His wife made no reply for the moment. Lewiston climbed into the buckboard and gathered up the lines. "Well, here goes for the last try, Emmie," he said. "Good-by, girl. Maybe things will look better in town to-day."

"Maybe," she said gravely. She kissed her husband good-by and stood for some time looking after the buckboard traveling toward the town in a moving pillar of dust.

"I don't know," she murmured at length; "I don't know just how we're going to make out."

When he reached town, Lewiston tied the horse to the iron railing in front of the Odd Fellows' Hall, the ground floor of which was occupied by the post-office, and went across the street and up the stairway of a building of brick and granite—quite the most pretentious structure of the town—and knocked at a door upon the first landing. The door was furnished with a pane of frosted glass, on which, in gold letters, was inscribed, "Bridges & Co., Grain Dealers."

Bridges himself, a middle-aged man who wore a velvet skull-cap and who was smoking a Pittsburgh stogie, met the farmer at the counter and the two exchanged perfunctory greetings.

"Well," said Lewiston, tentatively, after awhile.

"Well, Lewiston," said the other, "I can't take that wheat of yours at any better than sixty-two."

"Sixty-*two.*"

"It's the Chicago price that does it, Lewiston. Truslow is bearing the stuff for all he's worth. It's Truslow and the bear clique that stick the knife into us. The price broke again this morning. We've just got a wire."

"Good heavens," murmured Lewiston, looking vaguely from side to side. "That—that ruins me. I *can't* carry my grain any longer—what with storage charges and—and—Bridges, I don't see just how I'm going to make out. Sixty-two cents a bushel! Why, man, what with this and with that it's cost me nearly a dollar a bushel to raise that wheat, and now Trus-low——"

He turned away abruptly with a quick gesture of infinite discouragement.

He went down the stairs, and making his way to where his buckboard was hitched, got in, and, with eyes vacant, the reins slipping and sliding in his limp, half-open hands, drove slowly back to the ranch. His wife had seen him coming, and met him as he drew up before the barn.

"Well?" she demanded.

"Emmie," he said as he got out of the buckboard, laying his arm across her shoulder, "Emmie, I guess we'll take up with Joe's offer. We'll go to Chicago. We're cleaned out!"

II   THE BULL—WHEAT AT A DOLLAR-TEN

. . . ——*and said Party of the Second Part further covenants and agrees to merchandise such wheat in foreign ports, it being understood and agreed between the Party of the First Part and the Party of the Second Part that the wheat hereinbefore mentioned is released and sold to the Party of the Second Part for export purposes only, and not for consumption or distribution within the boundaries of the United States of America or of Canada.*

"Now, Mr. Gates, if you will sign for Mr. Truslow I guess that'll be all," remarked Hornung when he had finished reading.

Hornung affixed his signature to the two documents and passed them over to Gates, who signed for his principal and client, Truslow—or, as he had been called ever since he had gone into the fight against Hornung's corner—the Great Bear. Hornung's secretary was called in and witnessed the signatures, and Gates thrust the contract into his Gladstone bag and stood up, smoothing his hat.

"You will deliver the warehouse receipts for the grain," began Gates.

"I'll send a messenger to Truslow's office before noon," interrupted Hornung. "You can pay by certified check through the Illinois Trust people."

When the other had taken himself off, Hornung sat for some moments gazing abstractedly toward his office windows, thinking over the whole matter. He had just agreed to release to Truslow, at the rate of one dollar and ten cents per bushel, one hundred thousand out of the two million and odd bushels of wheat that he, Hornung, controlled, or actually owned. And for the moment he was wondering if, after all, he had done wisely in not goring the Great Bear to actual financial death. He had made him pay one hundred thousand dollars. Truslow was good for this amount. Would it not have been better to have put a prohibitive figure on the grain and forced the Bear into bankruptcy? True, Hornung would then be without his enemy's money, but Truslow would have been eliminated from the situation, and that—so Hornung told himself—was always a consummation most devoutly, strenuously and diligently to be striven for. Truslow once dead was dead, but the Bear was never more dangerous than when desperate.

"But so long as he can't get *wheat*," muttered Hornung at the end of his reflections, "he can't hurt me. And he can't get it. That I *know*."

For Hornung controlled the situation. So far back as the February of that year an "unknown bull" had been making his presence felt on the floor of the Board of Trade. By the middle of March the commercial reports of the daily press had begun to speak of "the powerful bull clique"; a few weeks later that legendary condition of affairs implied and epitomized in the magic words "Dollar Wheat" had been attained, and by the first of April, when the price had been boosted to one dollar and ten cents a bushel, Hornung had disclosed his hand, and in place of mere rumours, the definite and authoritative news that May wheat had been cornered in the Chicago pit went flashing around the world from Liverpool to Odessa and from Duluth to Buenos Ayres.

It was—so the veteran operators were persuaded—Truslow himself who had made Hornung's corner possible. The Great Bear had for once overreached himself, and, believing himself all-powerful, had hammered the price just the fatal fraction too far down. Wheat had gone to sixty-two—for the time, and under the circumstances, an abnormal price. When the reaction came it was tremendous. Hornung saw his chance, seized it, and in a few months had turned the tables, had cornered the product, and virtually driven the bear clique out of the pit.

On the same day that the delivery of the hundred thousand bushels was made to Truslow, Hornung met his broker at his lunch club.

"Well," said the latter, "I see you let go that line of stuff to Truslow."

Hornung nodded; but the broker added:

"Remember, I was against it from the very beginning. I know we've cleared up over a hundred thou'. I would have fifty times preferred to have lost twice that and *smashed Truslow dead.* Bet you what you like he makes us pay for it somehow."

"Huh!" grunted his principal. "How about insurance, and warehouse charges, and carrying expenses on that lot? Guess we'd have had to pay those, too, if we'd held on."

But the other put up his chin, unwilling to be persuaded. "I won't sleep easy," he declared, "till Truslow is busted."

III   THE PIT

Just as Going mounted the steps on the edge of the pit the great gong struck, a roar of a hundred voices developed with the swiftness of successive explosions, the rush of a hundred men surging downward to the centre of the pit filled the air with the stamp and grind of feet, a hundred hands in eager strenuous gestures tossed upward from out of the brown of the crowd, the official reporter in his cage on the margin of the pit leaned far forward with straining ear to catch the opening bid, and another day of battle was begun.

Since the sale of the hundred thousand bushels of wheat to Truslow the

"Hornung crowd" had steadily shouldered the price higher until on this particular morning it stood at one dollar and a half. That was Hornung's price. No one else had any grain to sell.

But not ten minutes after the opening, Going was surprised out of all countenance to hear shouted from the other side of the pit these words:

"Sell May at one-fifty."

Going was for the moment touching elbows with Kimbark on one side and with Merriam on the other, all three belonging to the "Hornung crowd." Their answering challenge of *"Sold"* was as the voice of one man. They did not pause to reflect upon the strangeness of the circumstance. (That was for afterward.) Their response to the offer was as unconscious as reflex action and almost as rapid, and before the pit was well aware of what had happened the transaction of one thousand bushels was down upon Going's trading-card and fifteen hundred dollars had changed hands. But here was a marvel—the whole available supply of wheat cornered, Hornung master of the situation, invincible, unassailable; yet behold a man willing to sell, a Bear bold enough to raise his head.

"That was Kennedy, wasn't it, who made that offer?" asked Kimbark, as Going noted down the trade—"Kennedy, that new man?"

"Yes; who do you suppose he's selling for; who's willing to go short at this stage of the game?"

"Maybe he ain't short."

"Short! Great heavens, man; where'd he get the stuff?"

"Blamed if I know. We can account for every handful of May. Steady! Oh, there he goes again."

"Sell a thousand May at one-fifty," vociferated the bear-broker, throwing out his hand, one finger raised to indicate the number of "contracts" offered. This time it was evident that he was attacking the Hornung crowd deliberately, for, ignoring the jam of traders that swept toward him, he looked across the pit to where Going and Kimbark were shouting *"Sold! Sold!"* and nodded his head.

A second time Going made memoranda of the trade, and either the Hornung holdings were increased by two thousand bushels of May wheat or the Hornung bank account swelled by at least three thousand dollars of some unknown short's money.

Of late—so sure was the bull crowd of its position—no one had even thought of glancing at the inspection sheet on the bulletin board. But now one of Going's messengers hurried up to him with the announcement that this sheet showed receipts at Chicago for that morning of twenty-five thousand bushels, and not credited to Hornung. Some one had got hold of a line of wheat overlooked by the "clique" and was dumping it upon them.

"Wire the Chief," said Going over his shoulder to Merriam. This one struggled out of the crowd, and on a telegraph blank scribbled:

"Strong bear movement—New man—Kennedy—Selling in lots of five contracts—Chicago receipts twenty-five thousand."

The message was despatched, and in a few moments the answer came back, laconic, of military terseness:

"Support the market."

And Going obeyed, Merriam and Kimbark following, the new broker fairly throwing the wheat at them in thousand-bushel lots.

"Sell May at 'fifty; sell May; sell May." A moment's indecision, an instant's hesitation, the first faint suggestion of weakness, and the market would have broken under them. But for the better part of four hours they stood their ground, taking all that was offered, in constant communication with the Chief, and from time to time stimulated and steadied by his brief, unvarying command:

"Support the market."

At the close of the session they had bought in the twenty-five thousand bushels of May. Hornung's position was as stable as a rock, and the price closed even with the opening figure—one dollar and a half.

But the morning's work was the talk of all La Salle Street. Who was back of the raid? What was the meaning of this unexpected selling? For weeks the pit trading had been merely nominal. Truslow, the Great Bear, from whom the most serious attack might have been expected, had gone to his country seat at Geneva Lake, in Wisconsin, declaring himself to be out of the market entirely. He went bass-fishing every day.

IV   THE BELT LINE

On a certain day toward the middle of the month, at a time when the mysterious Bear had unloaded some eighty thousand bushels upon Hornung, a conference was held in the library of Hornung's home. His broker attended it, and also a clean-faced, bright-eyed individual whose name of Cyrus Ryder might have been found upon the pay-roll of a rather well-known detective agency. For upward of half an hour after the conference began the detective spoke, the other two listening attentively, gravely.

"Then, last of all," concluded Ryder, "I made out I was a hobo, and began stealing rides on the Belt Line Railroad. Know the road? It just circles Chicago. Truslow owns it. Yes? Well, then I began to catch on. I noticed that cars of certain numbers—thirty-one nought thirty-four, thirty-two one ninety—well, the numbers don't matter, but anyhow, these cars were always switched onto the sidings by Mr. Truslow's main elevator D soon as they came in. The wheat was shunted in, and they were pulled out again. Well, I spotted one car and stole a ride on her. Say, look here, *that car went right around the city on the Belt, and came back to D again, and the same wheat in her all the time.* The grain was reinspected—it was raw, I tell you—and the warehouse receipts made out just as though the stuff had come in from Kansas or Iowa."

"The same wheat all the time!" interrupted Hornung.

"The same wheat—your wheat, that you sold to Truslow."

"Great snakes!" ejaculated Hornung's broker. "Truslow never took it abroad at all."

"Took it abroad! Say, he's just been running it around Chicago, like the supers in 'Shenandoah,' round an' round, so you'd think it was a new lot, an' selling it back to you again."

No wonder we couldn't account for so much wheat."

"Bought it from us at one-ten, and made us buy it back—our own wheat—at one-fifty."

Hornung and his broker looked at each other in silence for a moment. Then all at once Hornung struck the arm of his chair with his fist and exploded in a roar of laughter. The broker stared for one bewildered moment, then followed his example.

"Sold! Sold!" shouted Hornung almost gleefully. "upon my soul it's as good as a Gilbert and Sullivan show. And we—— Oh, Lord! Billy, shake on it, and hats off to my distinguished friend, Truslow. He'll be President some day. Hey! What? Prosecute him? Not I."

"He's done us out of a neat hatful of dollars for all that," observed the broker, suddenly grave.

"Billy, it's worth the price."

"We've got to make it up somehow."

"Well, tell you what. We were going to boost the price to one seventy-five next week, and make that our settlement figure."

"Can't do it now. Can't afford it."

"No. Here; we'll let out a big link; we'll put wheat at two dollars, and let it go at that."

"Two it is, then," said the broker.

V   THE BREAD LINE

The street was very dark and absolutely deserted. It was a district on the "South Side," not far from the Chicago River, given up largely to wholesale stores, and after nightfall was empty of all life. The echoes slept but lightly hereabouts, and the slightest footfall, the faintest noise, woke them upon the instant and sent them clamouring up and down the length of the pavement between the iron shuttered fronts. The only light visible came from the side door of a certain "Vienna" bakery, where at one o'clock in the morning loaves of bread were given away to any who should ask. Every evening about nine o'clock the outcasts began to gather about the side door. The stragglers came in rapidly, and the line—the "bread line," as it was called—began to form. By midnight it was usually some hundred yards in length, stretching almost the entire length of the block.

Toward ten in the evening, his coat collar turned up against the fine drizzle that pervaded the air, his hands in his pockets, his elbows gripping his sides, Sam Lewiston came up and silently took his place at the end of the line.

Unable to conduct his farm upon a paying basis at the time when Truslow, the "Great Bear," had sent the price of grain down to sixty-two cents a bushel, Lewiston had turned over his entire property to his creditors, and, leaving Kansas for good, had abandoned farming, and had left his wife at her sister's boarding-house in Topeka with the understanding that she was to join him in Chicago so soon as he had found a steady job. Then he had come to Chicago and had turned workman. His brother Joe conducted a small hat factory on Archer Avenue, and for a time he found there a meager employment. But difficulties had occurred, times were bad, the hat factory was involved in debts, the repealing of a certain import duty on manufactured felt overcrowded the home market with cheap Belgian and French products, and in the end his brother had assigned and gone to Milwaukee.

Thrown out of work, Lewiston drifted aimlessly about Chicago, from pillar to post, working a little, earning here a dollar, there a dime, but always sinking, sinking, till at last the ooze of the lowest bottom dragged at his feet and the rush of the great ebb went over him and engulfed him and shut him out from the light, and a park bench became his home and the "bread line" his chief makeshift of subsistence.

He stood now in the enfolding drizzle, sodden, stupefied with fatigue. Before and behind stretched the line. There was no talking. There was no sound. The street was empty. It was so still that the passing of a cable-car in the adjoining thoroughfare grated like prolonged rolling explosions, beginning and ending at immeasurable distances. The drizzle descended incessantly. After a long time midnight struck.

There was something ominous and gravely impressive in this interminable line of dark figures, close-pressed, soundless; a crowd, yet absolutely still; a close-packed, silent file, waiting, waiting in the vast deserted night-ridden street; waiting without a word, without a movement, there under the night and under the slow-moving mists of rain.

Few in the crowd were professional beggars. Most of them were workmen, long since out of work, forced into idleness by long-continued "hard times," by ill luck, by sickness. To them the "bread line" was a godsend. At least they could not starve. Between jobs here in the end was something to hold them up—a small platform, as it were, above the sweep of black water, where for a moment they might pause and take breath before the plunge.

The period of waiting on this night of rain seemed endless to those silent, hungry men; but at length there was a stir. The line moved. The side door opened. Ah, at last! They were going to hand out the bread.

But instead of the usual white-aproned undercook with his crowded hampers there now appeared in the doorway a new man—a young fellow who looked like a bookkeeper's assistant. He bore in his hand a placard, which he tacked to the outside of the door. Then he disappeared within the bakery, locking the door after him.

A shudder of poignant despair, an unformed, inarticulate sense of calamity, seemed to run from end to end of the line. What had happened? Those in the rear, unable to read the placard, surged forward, a sense of bitter disappointment clutching at their hearts.

The line broke up, disintegrated into a shapeless throng—a throng that crowded forward and collected in front of the shut door whereon the placard was affixed. Lewiston, with the others pushed forward. On the placard he read these words:

"Owing to the fact that the price of grain has been increased to two dollars a bushel, there will be no distribution of bread from this bakery until further notice."

Lewiston turned away, dumb, bewildered. Till morning he walked the streets, going on without purpose, without direction. But now at last his luck had turned. Overnight the wheel of his fortunes had creaked and swung upon its axis, and before noon he had found a job in the street-cleaning brigade. In the course of time he rose to be first shift-boss, then deputy inspector, then inspector, promoted to the dignity of driving in a red wagon with rubber tires and drawing a salary instead of mere wages. The wife was sent for and a new start made.

But Lewiston never forgot. Dimly he began to see the significance of things. Caught once in the cogs and wheels of a great and terrible engine, he had seen—none better—its workings. Of all the men who had vainly stood in the "bread line" on that rainy night in early summer, he, perhaps, had been the only one who had struggled up to the surface again. How many others had gone down in the great ebb? Grim question; he dared not think how many.

He had seen the two ends of a great wheat operation—a battle between Bear and Bull. The stories (subsequently published in the city's press) of Truslow's countermove in selling Hornung his own wheat, supplied the unseen section. The farmer—he who raised the wheat—was ruined upon one hand; the working-man—he who consumed it—was ruined upon the other. But between the two, the great operators, who never saw the wheat they traded in, bought and sold the world's food, gambled in the nourishment of entire nations, practised their tricks, their chicanery and oblique shifty "deals," were reconciled in their differences, and went on through their appointed way, jovial, contented, enthroned, and unassailable.

STEPHEN CRANE

The Bride Comes to Yellow Sky

I

The great Pullman was whirling onward with such dignity of motion that
a glance from the window seemed simply to prove that the plains of Texas
were pouring eastward. Vast flats of green grass, dull-hued spaces of mesquit and cactus, little groups of frame houses, woods of light and tender
trees, all were sweeping into the east, sweeping over the horizon, a precipice.

A newly married pair had boarded this coach at San Antonio. The
man's face was reddened from many days in the wind and sun, and a direct
result of his new black clothes was that his brick-colored hands were constantly performing in a most conscious fashion. From time to time he
looked down respectfully at his attire. He sat with a hand on each knee, like
a man waiting in a barber's shop. The glances he devoted to other passengers were furtive and shy.

The bride was not pretty, nor was she very young. She wore a dress of blue cashmere, with small reservations of velvet here and there, and with steel buttons abounding. She continually twisted her head to regard her puff sleeves, very stiff, straight, and high. They embarrassed her. It was quite apparent that she had cooked, and that she expected to cook, dutifully. The blushes caused by the careless scrutiny of some passengers as she had entered the car were strange to see upon this plain, underclass countenance, which was drawn in placid, almost emotionless lines.

They were evidently very happy. "Ever been in a parlor-car before?" he asked, smiling with delight.

"No," she answered; "I never was. It's fine, ain't it?"

"Great! and then after a while we'll go forward to the diner, and get a big lay-out. Finest meal in the world. Charge a dollar."

"Oh, do they?" cried the bride. "Charge a dollar? Why, that's too much—for us—ain't it, Jack?"

"Not this trip, anyhow," he answered bravely. "We're going to go the whole thing."

Later he explained to her about the trains. "You see, it's a thousand miles from one end of Texas to the other; and this train runs right across it, and never stops but four times." He had the pride of an owner. He pointed out to her the dazzling fittings of the coach; and in truth her eyes opened wider as she contemplated the sea-green figured velvet, the shining brass, silver, and glass, the wood that gleamed as darkly brilliant as the surface of a pool of oil. At one end a bronze figure sturdily held a support for a separated chamber, and at convenient places on the ceiling were frescos in olive and silver.

To the minds of the pair, their surroundings reflected the glory of their marriage that morning in San Antonio; this was the environment of their new estate; and the man's face in particular beamed with an elation that made him appear ridiculous to the negro porter. The individual at times surveyed them from afar with an amused and superior grin. On other occasions he bullied them with skill in ways that did not make it exactly plain to them that they were being bullied. He subtly used all the manners of the most unconquerable kind of snobbery. He oppressed them; but of this oppression they had small knowledge, and they speedily forgot that infrequently a number of travelers covered them with stares of derisive enjoyment. Historically there was supposed to be something infinitely humorous in their situation.

"We are due in Yellow Sky at 3:42," he said, looking tenderly into her eyes.

"Oh, are we?" she said, as if she had not been aware of it. To evince surprise at her husband's statement was part of her wifely amiability. She took from a pocket a little silver watch; and as she held it before her, and stared at it with a frown of attention, the new husband's face shone.

"I bought it in San Anton' from a friend of mine," he told her gleefully.

"It's seventeen minutes past twelve," she said, looking up at him with a kind of shy and clumsy coquetry. A passenger, noting this play, grew excessively sardonic, and winked at himself in one of the numerous mirrors.

At last they went to the dining-car. Two rows of negro waiters, in glowing white suits, surveyed their entrance with the interest, and also the equanimity, of men who had been forewarned. The pair fell to the lot of a waiter who happened to feel pleasure in steering them through their meal. He viewed them with the manner of a fatherly pilot, his countenance radiant with benevolence. The patronage, entwined with the ordinary deference, was not plain to them. And yet, as they returned to their coach, they showed in their faces a sense of escape.

To the left, miles down a long purple slope, was a little ribbon of mist where moved the keening Rio Grande. The train was approaching it at an angle, and the apex was Yellow Sky. Presently it was apparent that, as the distance from Yellow Sky grew shorter, the husband became commensurately restless. His brick-red hands were more insistent in their prominence. Occasionally he was even rather absent-minded and far-away when the bride leaned forward and addressed him.

As a matter of truth, Jack Potter was beginning to find the shadow of a deed weigh upon him like a leaden slab. He, the town marshal of Yellow Sky, a man known, liked, and feared in his corner, a prominent person, had gone to San Antonio to meet a girl he believed he loved, and there, after the usual prayers, had actually induced her to marry him, without consulting Yellow Sky for any part of the transaction. He was now bringing his bride before an innocent and unsuspecting community.

Of course people in Yellow Sky married as it pleased them, in accordance with a general custom; but such was Potter's thought of his duty to his friends, or of their idea of his duty, or of an unspoken form which does not control men in these matters, that he felt he was heinous. He had committed an extraordinary crime. Face to face with this girl in San Antonio, and spurred by his sharp impulse, he had gone headlong over all the social hedges. At San Antonio he was like a man hidden in the dark. A knife to sever any friendly duty, any form, was easy to his hand in that remote city. But the hour of Yellow Sky—the hour of daylight—was approaching.

He knew full well that his marriage was an important thing to his town. It could only be exceeded by the burning of the new hotel. His friends could not forgive him. Frequently he had reflected on the advisability of telling them by telegraph, but a new cowardice had been upon him. He feared to do it. And now the train was hurrying him toward a scene of amazement, glee, and reproach. He glanced out of the window at the line of haze swingingly slowly toward the train.

Yellow Sky had a kind of brass band, which played painfully, to the delight of the populace. He laughed without heart as he thought of it. If the citizens could dream of his prospective arrival with his bride, they would parade the band at the station and excort them, amid cheers and laughing congratulations, to his adobe home.

He resolved that he would use all the devices of speed and plains-craft in making the journey from the station to his house. Once within the safe citadel, he could issue some sort of a vocal bulletin, and then not go among the citizens until they had time to wear off a little of their enthusiasm.

The bride look anxiously at him. "What's worrying you, Jack?"

He laughed again. "I'm not worrying, girl; I'm only thinking of Yellow Sky."

She flushed in comprehension.

A sense of mutual guilt invaded their minds and developed a finer tenderness. They looked at each other with eyes softly aglow. But Potter often laughed the same nervous laugh; the flush upon the bride's face seemed quite permanent.

The traitor to the feelings of Yellow Sky narrowly watched the speeding landscape. "We're nearly there," he said.

Presently the porter came and announced the proximity of Potter's home. He held a brush in his hand, and, with all his airy superiority gone, he brushed Potter's new clothes as the latter slowly turned this way and way. Potter fumbled out a coin and gave it to the porter, as he had seen others do. It was a heavy and muscle-bound business, as that of a man shoeing his first horse.

The porter took their bag, and as the train began to slow they moved forward to the hooded platform of the car. Presently the two engines and their long string of coaches rushed into the station of Yellow Sky.

"They have to take water here," said Potter, from a constricted throat and in mournful cadence, as one announcing death. Before the train stopped his eye had swept the length of the platform, and he was glad and astonished to see there was none upon it but the station-agent, who, with a slightly hurried and anxious air, was walking toward the watertanks. When the train had halted, the porter alighted first, and placed in position a little temporary step.

"Come on, girl," said Potter, hoarsely. As he helped her down they each laughed on a false note. He took the bag from the negro, and bade his wife cling to his arm. As they slunk rapidly away, his hang-dog glance perceived that they were unloading the two trunks, and also that the station-agent, far ahead near the baggage-car, had turned and was running toward him, making gestures. He laughed, and groaned as he laughed, when he noted the first effect of his marital bliss upon Yellow Sky. He gripped his wife's arm firmly to his side, and they fled. Behind them the porter stood, chuckling fatuously.

II

The California express on the Southern Railway was due at Yellow Sky in twenty-one minutes. There were six men at the bar of the Weary Gentleman Saloon. One was a drummer, who talked a great deal and rapidly; three were Texans, who did not care to talk at that time; and two were Mexican sheep-herders, who did not talk as a general practice in the Weary Gentleman Saloon. The barkeeper's dog lay on the board walk that crossed in front of the door. His head was on his paws, and he glanced drowsily here and there with the constant vigilance of a dog that is kicked on occasion. Across the sandy street were some vivid green grass-plots, so wonderful in appearance, amid the sands that burned near them in a blazing sun, that they caused a doubt in the mind. They exactly resembled the grass mats used to represent lawns on the stage. At the cooler end of the railway station, a man without a coat sat in a tilted chair and smoked his pipe. The fresh-cut bank of the Rio Grande circled near the town, and there could be seen beyond it a great plum-colored plain of mesquit.

Save for the busy drummer and his companions in the saloon, Yellow Sky was dozing. The new-comer leaned gracefully upon the bar, and recited many tales with the confidence of a bard who has come upon a new field.

"—and at the moment that the old man fell down-stairs with the bureau in his arms, the old woman was coming up with two scuttles of coal, and of course—"

The drummer's tale was interrupted by a young man who suddenly appeared in the open door. He cried: "Scratchy Wilson's drunk, and has turned loose with both hands." The two Mexicans at once set down their glasses and faded out of the rear entrance of the saloon.

The drummer, innocent and jocular, answered: "All right, old man. S'pose he has? Come in and have a drink, anyhow."

But the information had made such an obvious cleft in every skull in the room that the drummer was obliged to see its importance. All had become instantly solemn. "Say," said he, mystified, "what is this?" His three companions made the introductory gesture of eloquent speech; but the young man at the door forestalled them.

"It means, my friend," he answered, as he came into the saloon, "that for the next two hours this town won't be a health resort."

The barkeeper went to the door, and locked and barred it; reaching out of the window, he pulled in heavy wooden shutters, and barred them. Immediately a solemn, chapel-like gloom was upon the place. The drummer was looking from one to another.

"But say," he cried, "what is this, anyhow? You don't mean there is going to be a gun-fight?"

"Don't know whether there'll be a fight or not," answered one man, grimly; "but there'll be some shootin'—some good shootin'."

The young man who had warned them waved his hand. "Oh, there'll be a fight fast enough, if any one wants it. Anybody can get a fight out there in the street. There's a fight just waiting."

The drummer seemed to be swayed between the interest of a foreigner and a perception of personal danger.

"What did you say his name was?" he asked.

"Scratchy Wilson," they answered in chorus.

"And will he kill anybody? What are you going to do? Does this happen often? Does he rampage around like this once a week or so? Can he break in that door?"

"No; he can't break down that door," replied the barkeeper. "He's tried it three times. But when he comes you'd better lay down on the floor, stranger. He's dead sure to shoot at it, and a bullet may come through."

Thereafter the drummer kept a strict eye upon the door. The time had not yet been called for him to hug the floor, but, as a minor precaution, he sidled near to the wall. "Will he kill anybody?" he said again.

The men laughed low and scornfully at the question.

"He's out to shoot, and he's out for trouble. Don't see any good in experimentin' with him."

"But what do you do in a case like this? What do you do?"

A man responded: "Why, he and Jack Potter—"

"But," in chorus the other men interrupted, "Jack Potter's in San Anton'."

"Well, who is he? What's he got to do with it?"

"Oh, he's the town marshal. He goes out and fights Scratchy when he gets in one of these tears."

"Wow!" said the drummer, mopping his brow. "Nice job he's got."

The voices had toned away to mere whisperings. The drummer wished to ask further questions, which were born of an increasing anxiety and bewilderment; but when he attempted them, the men merely looked at him in irritation and motioned him to remain silent. A tense waiting hush was upon them. In the deep shadows of the room their eyes shone as they listened for sounds from the street. One man made three gestures at the barkeeper; and the latter, moving like a ghost, handed him a glass and a bottle. The man poured a full glass of whisky, and set down the bottle noiselessly. He gulped the whisky in a swallow, and turned again toward the door in immovable silence. The drummer saw that the barkeeper, without a sound, had taken a Winchester from beneath the bar. Later he saw this individual beckoning to him, so he tiptoed across the room.

"You better come with me back of the bar."

"No, thanks," said the drummer, perspiring; "I'd rather be where I can make a break for the back door."

Whereupon the man of bottles made a kindly but peremptory gesture. The drummer obeyed it, and, finding himself seated on a box with his head below the level of the bar, balm was laid upon his soul at sight of various zinc and copper fittings that bore a resemblance to armor-plate. The bar-keeper took a seat comfortably upon an adjacent box.

"You see," he whispered, "this here Scratchy Wilson is a wonder with a gun—a perfect wonder; and when he goes on the war-trail, we hunt our holes—naturally. He's about the last one of the old gang that used to hang out along the river here. He's a terror when he's drunk. When he's sober he's all right—kind of simple—wouldn't hurt a fly—nicest fellow in town. But when he's drunk—whoo!"

There were periods of stillness. "I wish Jack Potter was back from San Anton'." said the barkeeper. "He shot Wilson up once,—in the leg,—and he would sail in and pull out the kinks in this thing."

Presently they heard from a distance the sound of a shot, followed by three wild yowls. It instantly removed a bond from the men in the darkened saloon. There was a shuffling of feet. They looked at each other. "Here he comes," they said.

III

A man in a maroon-colored flannel shirt, which had been purchased for purposes of decoration, and made principally by some Jewish women on the East Side of New York, rounded a corner and walked into the middle of the main street of Yellow Sky. In either hand the man held a long, heavy, blue-black revolver. Often he yelled, and these cries rang through a sem-blance of a deserted village, shrilly flying over the roofs in a volume that seemed to have no relation to the ordinary vocal strength of a man. It was as if the surrounding stillness formed the arch of a tomb over him. These cries of ferocious challenge rang against walls of silence. And his boots had red tops with gilded imprints, of the kind beloved in winter by little sledding boys on the hillsides of New England.

The man's face flamed in a rage begot of whisky. His eyes, rolling, and yet keen for ambush, hunted the still doorways and windows. He walked with the creeping movement of the midnight cat. As it occurred to him, he roared menacing information. The long revolvers in his hands were as easy as straws; they were moved with an electric swiftness. The little fingers of each hand played sometimes in a musician's way. Plain from the low collar of the shirt, the cords of his neck straightened and sank, straightened and sank, as passion moved him. The only sounds were his terrible invitations. The calm adobes preserved their demeanor at the passing of this small thing in the middle of the street.

There was no offer of fight—no offer of fight. The man called to the sky. There were no attractions. He bellowed and fumed and swayed his revolver here and everywhere.

The dog of the barkeeper of the Weary Gentleman Saloon had not appreciated the advance of events. He yet lay dozing in front of his master's door. At sight of the dog, the man paused and raised his revolver humorously. At sight of the man, the dog sprang up and walked diagonally away, with a sullen head, and growling. The man yelled, and the dog broke into a gallop. As it was about to enter an alley, there was a loud noise, a whistling, and something spat the ground directly before it. The dog screamed, and, wheeling in terror, galloped head-long in a new direction. Again there was a noise, a whistling, and sand was kicked viciously before it. Fear-stricken, the dog turned and flurried like an animal in a pen. The man stood laughing, his weapons at his hips.

Ultimately the man was attracted by the closed door of the Weary Gentleman Saloon. He went to it, and, hammering with a revolver, demanded drink.

The door remaining imperturbable, he picked a bit of paper from the walk, and nailed it to the framework with a knife. He then turned his back contemptuously upon this popular resort, and, walking to the opposite side of the street, and spinning there on his heel quickly and lithely, fired at the bit of paper. He missed it by a half-inch. He swore at himself, and went away. Later he comfortably fusilladed the windows of his most intimate friend. The man was playing with this town; it was a toy for him.

But still there was no offer of fight. The name of Jack Potter, his ancient antagonist, entered his mind, and he concluded that it would be a glad thing if he should go to Potter's house, and by bombardment induce him to come out and fight. He moved in the direction of his desire, chanting Apache scalp-music.

When he arrived at it, Potter's house presented the same still front as had the other adobes. Taking up a strategic position, the man howled a challenge. But this house regarded him as might a great stone god. It gave no sign. After a decent wait, the man howled further challenges, mingling with them wonderful epithets.

Presently there came the spectacle of a man churning himself into deepest rage over the immobility of a house. He fumed at it as the winter wind attacks a prairie cabin in the North. To the distance there should have gone the sound of a tumult like the fighting of two hundred Mexicans. As necessity bade him, he paused for breath or to reload his revolvers.

IV

Potter and his bride walked sheepishly and with speed. Sometimes they laughed together shamefacedly and low.

"Next corner, dear," he said finally.

They put forth the efforts of a pair walking bowed against a strong wind. Potter was about to raise a finger to point the first appearance of the new home when, as they circled the corner, they came face to face with a man in a maroon-colored shirt, who was feverishly pushing cartridges into a large revolver. Upon the instant the man dropped his revolver to the ground, and, like lightning, whipped another from its holster. The second weapon was aimed at the bridegroom's chest.

There was a silence. Potter's mouth seemed to be merely a grave for his tongue. He exhibited an instinct to at once loosen his arm from the woman's grip, and he dropped the bag to the sand. As for the bride, her face had gone as yellow as old cloth. She was a slave to hideous rites, gazing at the apparitional snake.

The two men faced each other at a distance of three paces. He of the revolver smiled with a new and quiet ferocity.

"Tried to sneak up on me," he said. "Tried to sneak up on me!" His eyes grew more baleful. As Potter made a slight movement, the man thrust his revolver venomously forward. "No; don't you do it, Jack Potter. Don't you move a finger toward a gun just yet. Don't you move an eyelash. The time has come for me to settle with you, and I'm goin' to do it my own way, and loaf along with no interferin'. So if you don't want a gun bent on you, just mind what I tell you."

Potter looked at his enemy. "I ain't got a gun on me, Scratchy," he said. "Honest, I ain't." He was stiffening and steadying, but yet somewhere at the back of his mind a vision of the Pullman floated: the sea-green figured velvet, the shining brass, silver, and glass, the wood that gleamed as darkly brilliant as the surface of a pool of oil—all the glory of the marriage, the environment of the new estate. "You know I fight when it comes to fighting, Scratchy Wilson; but I ain't got a gun on me. You'll have to do all the shootin' yourself."

His enemy's face went livid. He stepped forward, and lashed his weapon to and fro before Potter's chest. "Don't you tell me you ain't got no gun on you, you whelp. Don't tell me no lie like that. There ain't a man in Texas ever seen you without no gun. Don't take me for no kid." His eyes blazed with light, and his throat worked like a pump.

"I ain't takin' you for no kid," answered Potter. His heels had not moved an inch backward. "I'm takin' you for a——fool. I tell you I ain't got a gun, and I ain't. If you're goin' to shoot me up, you better begin now; you'll never get a chance like this again."

So much enforced reasoning had told on Wilson's rage; he was calmer. "If you ain't got a gun, why ain't you got a gun?" he sneered. "Been to Sunday-school?"

"I ain't got a gun because I've just come from San Anton' with my wife. I'm married," said Potter. "And if I'd thought there was going to be any galoots like you prowling around when I brought my wife home, I'd had a gun, and don't you forget it."

"Married!" said Scratchy, not at all comprehending.

"Yes, married. I'm married," said Potter, distinctly.

"Married?" said Scratchy. Seemingly for the first time, he saw the drooping, drowning woman at the other man's side. "No!" he said. He was like a creature allowed a glimpse of another world. He moved a pace backward, and his arm, with the revolver, dropped to his side. "Is this the lady?" he asked.

"Yes; this is the lady," answered Potter.

There was another period of silence.

"Well, said Wilson at last, slowly, "I s'pose it's all off now."

"It's all off if you say so, Scratchy. You know I didn't make the trouble." Potter lifted his valise.

Well, I 'low it's off, Jack," said Wilson. He was looking at the ground. "Married!" He was not a student of chivalry; it was merely that in the presence of this foreign condition he was a simple child of the earlier plains. He picked up his starboard revolver, and, placing both weapons in their holsters, he went away. His feet made funnel-shaped tracks in the heavy sand.

LUIGI PIRANDELLO

MODERN MASTERS

LUIGI PIRANDELLO

The Tortoise

Strange as it may seem, even in America there are people who believe
that tortoises are lucky. Nobody has the faintest idea how such a belief
came into existence. What's quite certain, however, is that they—the tortoises, I mean—show no sign of having the slightest suspicion that they
enjoy this power.

Mr. Myshkow has a friend who's a firm believer in this quality of
theirs. He speculates on the Stock Exchange and every morning, before he
goes off to do a hard day's gambling, he puts his tortoise down in front of
a little flight of steps. If the tortoise makes it obvious that he wants to climb
up them, he's quite convinced that the stocks he's thinking of gambling on
will rise in value. If it tucks its head and paws in, then they'll remain steady.
If it turns away and starts moving off, then he unhesitatingly acts on the
assumption that they're going to slump. And he's never once been wrong.

Having said which, he goes into a shop where they sell tortoises, buys one, and places it in Mr. Myshkow's hand. "Now make your fortune," he says.

Mr. Myshkow's a very sensitive plant. As he carries the tortoise home, he shudders, "Ugh! Ugh!" His sturdy, full-blooded springy little body is trembling all over. Maybe it's pleasure he's shuddering with; maybe there's a touch of the horrors too. It's not that he's worried in the least about the way passers-by are turning and looking at him, carrying that tortoise in his hand. No, he's trembling at the thought that what looks like a cold inert stone, *isn't* a stone at all. No, it's inhabited on the inside by a mysterious little animal that's quite capable at any moment of popping out its little wrinkled old nun's head and plonking its four rough skew-whiff paws on to his hand. Let's hope it won't do anything of the sort. Heaven knows what might happen! Why, shuddering from head to foot, Mr. Myshkow might throw it on the ground!

When he gets home. . . . Well, you wouldn't exactly say his two children, Helen and John, went into raptures over the tortoise the instant they caught sight of it—when, that is, he put it down on the carpet in the drawing-room, looking for all the world like an overgrown pebble.

It's quite incredible how *old* the eyes of these two children of Mr. Myshkow look, compared with *his* eyes, which are so extraordinarily childlike.

The two children let the unbearable weight of the four leaden eyes fall on that tortoise, placed there like an overgrown pebble on the carpet. Then they look at their father, with so great a conviction that he won't be able to give them a plausible explanation of why he's done this unheard of thing—putting a tortoise on the drawing-room carpet, indeed!—that poor Mr. Myshkow suddenly feels himself shrivelling up. He spreads out his hands in an appealing gesture. He opens his mouth in an empty smile and says that, well, after all, it's only a harmless little tortoise. And you can even—if you want to, that is—you can even *play* with it.

And like the good-hearted fellow that he is—he's always been a bit of an overgrown schoolboy—he's determined to prove it to them. He throws himself down on his hands and knees on the carpet and cautiously, and with the utmost consideration, he prods the tortoise in the rear in an attempt to persuade it to pop its paws and head out and to get moving. Good gracious, yes, little tortoise, you must—if only so that you can see what a lovely cheerful house I've brought you into—all glass and mirrors. He's quite unprepared for what John does. Suddenly and unceremoniously the boy hits upon a much more immediately successful expedient for getting the tortoise to emerge from that stone-like state in which it's so stubbornly determined to remain. With the toe of his shoe he turns it over onto its shell, and immediately we see the little creature lash out with its little paws and painfully thrust about with its head in an attempt to get itself back into its natural position.

Helen watches all this happen and then, without her eyes becoming any the less old-looking, sniggers. It's like the noise a rusty pully makes as the bucket hurtles madly down into the depths of a well.

As you'll have observed, there's no respect on the part of the children for the good luck that tortoises are supposed to bring you. On the contrary, they have made it blindingly clear to us that both of them tolerate its presence only on condition that it allows itself to be considered by them as an extremely stupid toy to be treated thus—that's to say, kicked about with the toe of your shoe. Mr. Myshkow finds this very saddening. He looks at the tortoise, which he's immediately put right way up again, and which has now resumed its stone-like state. He looks into the eyes of his children, and is suddenly made aware of a mysterious relationship between the agedness of those eyes and the centuries old stone-like inertia of the animal on the carpet, and he's profoundly disturbed. He's utterly dismayed because he is so incurably youthful in a world which gives such obvious proof of its decrepitude by embracing such far-fetched and unexpected relationships. It dismays him that, without realizing what's happening, he may perhaps be left to await something which may never again happen, since children, now, here on earth, are born centenarians like tortoises.

Once more his mouth opens in an empty smile—it's feebler than ever this time—and he hasn't got the courage to admit why his friend made him a present of that tortoise.

Mr. Myshkow enjoys a pretty rare ignorance of life. As far as he's concerned, life's never really been very clear-cut; nor is he greatly burdened with any real weight of knowledge. Why, it can quite well happen to him too. Yes, one fine morning—just as he's got one leg raised preparatory to getting into the bath—he'll suddenly catch sight of his naked body. There he'll stand, just like that, strangely affected by the sight of his own body, for all the world as if, in the forty-two years he's lived through, he's never set eyes on it before, and is now discovering it for the first time. Good grief, it's not a very presentable body, is it? All naked like that! I mean, you feel thoroughly ashamed about the whole thing, even when it's you yourself that's looking at it. He prefers to know nothing at all about himself. He makes a considerable song and dance about this fact, however: that he's done all this thinking with this particular body, even if it does look the way it does in one or two places that nobody usually gets a peep at—the bits that have remained hidden under his suit and his socks for the forty-two years he's been a member of this world. It seems quite incredible to him that he's lived all his life in that body of his. No! No! Well then, where have you been living? Go on, where have you been living, without being the slightest bit aware of where you were? Perhaps he's been flying about overhead all the time flitting from body to body, choosing them from among the many shapes that have fallen to his lot since he was a child, because—Oh no, his body certainly hasn't always been this one! But Heaven only knows what it's been at other times! It really does dishearten him. Yes, it hurts him not to be able to explain to himself why his own body has necessarily to be the one that it is, and not another quite different one. Best not to think about it. And in the bath he starts smiling again that empty smile of his, quite unmindful of the fact that he's been in the bath some considerable time now. Ah, those muslin curtains across the panes of the big window! Look how they seem to catch and reflect the light! Over the top of the brass curtain rods he glimpses the graceful, slight waving-to-and-fro of the tops of the trees in the park as the spring air catches them. Now he's drying that ugly body of his. Oh, it really *is*! Nonetheless, however, he's forced to agree that life is very beautiful, and wholly to be enjoyed, even in that hideous body of his which has, in the period since those childhood days—Heaven only knows how!—contrived to enter into the most secret intimacy with a woman as impenetrable as Mrs. Myshkow his wife.

For the whole nine years that he's been married, it's as if he's been wrapped up—somehow suspended—in the mysterious world of that highly improbable union with Mrs. Myshkow.

He's never dared to take one single step without being left in an agony of doubt, after he's taken it, as to whether he might dare to take another. So he's always experienced a kind of apprehensive wriggling throughout his whole body, and a kind of dismay in his soul, at suddenly finding himself so far from his starting-point, as a result of those halting steps she's allowed him to take. Should he or should he not infer that he was entitled, therefore, to take them?

So it was, one fine day, that he found himself the husband of Mrs. Myshkow, almost without being quite sure that he was.

She, even after nine years, is still so detached and isolated from everything, in her own porcelain statue beauty, so enclosed, so enamelled, as you might say, in a mode of life so impenetrably her own, that it seems absolutely impossible that she's found a way of uniting herself in marriage with a man so carnal and fullblooded as he is. On the other hand, it's only too comprehensible how, from their union, those two withered children have been born. Perhaps, if Mr. Myshkow had been able to carry them in *his* womb, instead of relying on his wife's, they wouldn't have been born like that. But she had to carry them in her womb, nine months for each of them, and so, conceived, in all probability, in their entirety right from the very beginning, they'd been compelled to remain shut up there for the proper length of time in that majolica belly, like sugared almonds in a box. Well, that's the reason why they'd become so tremendously ancient, even before they were born.

Naturally, for the whole nine years that they've been married, he's lived in constant terror lest Mrs. Myshkow should seize upon some thoughtlessly uttered word of his, some unforseen gesture, and use it as a pretext for demanding a divorce. The first day of their marriage was the most terrible of all for him because, as you can easily imagine, he'd got as far as that without being at all sure that Mrs. Myshkow knew what he had to do before he could effectively call himself her husband. Luckily, she did know. Afterwards, however, she'd never given him the slightest hint that she remembered the consideration and tenderness he'd put into his wooing and taking her that night. It was just as if he hadn't contributed anything at all to making it possible for him to take her; as if there were no tender memories for her to recall. Still, a first child, Helen, had been born. Then a second, John. And never a flicker of tender remembrance from her. Without the remotest sign of emotion on either occasion, she'd gone away both times to the maternity home, and then, a month and a half later, she'd come back home, the first time with a little girl, the second time with a little boy—this second baby even older than the first. It was enough to make you throw up your hands in despair. She'd absolutely forbidden him both times to go and visit her in the maternity home. As a result, having failed completely, both the first and the second time, to observe that she was pregnant, and not knowing anything afterwards about either the labour pains or the pains attending the birth itself, he'd found himself in the house with two small children who were rather like puppies you'd bought on a trip. There wasn't any real certainty that they'd been born of her body and that they really belonged to him.

But Mr. Myshkow hasn't the slightest doubt that they are his. In fact he sees in those two children one of the most ancient and time-honoured of proofs—confirmed twice over, what's more!—that Mrs. Myshkow finds in living with him adequate recompense for the agony that bringing those two children into the world must have cost her.

That's why he's completely bowled over when his wife acts in the way she does. She's just come back in from visiting her mother, who's arrived in New York and who's staying for a day or two at an hotel, prior to leaving for England. Finding him still down on his knees on the drawing-room carpet, amidst the cold, coarse derision of those two children of his, she doesn't say a word. Or, to put it more precisely, by simply turning her back on him without a word, and returning immediately to the hotel where her mother's staying, she says everything. About an hour later she sends him round a note. Peremptorily she tells him that either the tortoise gets out of the house, or she's leaving him. She'll be leaving, three days from now, for England, with her mother.

As soon as he's gathered his wits sufficiently to be able to think straight again, Mr. Myshkow realizes that the tortoise can really be nothing but a pretext. And so trivial a pretext, too. Good grief! It's so easily dealt with! And yet, you know, just because it is so easily dealt with it may, perhaps, be much more difficult to get round it than if his wife had made it a condition of their remaining together that he should change his body, or, if he couldn't manage that, to remove that nose from his face and replace it with another that better pleased her taste.

He has no desire, however, that the marriage should fail because of him. In his reply to his wife he tells her that it's quite safe for her to return home. He'll go and dump the tortoise somewhere. He doesn't care in the slghtest whether it remains in the house. He only accepted it because they told him that tortoises were lucky. But—well, when you think how comfortably off he is, with a wife like her, and children like theirs, what need has he got of lucky mascots and things like that? What greater good fortune could he possibly desire?

He goes out, tortoise in hand once again, to dump it in some place more appropriate to the cross-grained little creater than his house. It's evening now, and he's only just become aware of the fact. He's lost in amazement. Accustomed though he is to the phantasmagoric sight of that enormous city in which he lives, he still sees it with fresh eyes every time he looks at it. He's still astounded (and made a little melancholy, too) when he thinks of all those prodigious buildings, and of how they're refused the right to impose themselves on the world as enduring monuments, and are forced just to stand there, like colossal and provisional appearances of reality in some immense Fair, with their multi-coloured, flashing advertising signs reaching into the distance and conjuring up a world of infinite sadness. He's sad, too, as he thinks of so many other things which are equally precarious and mutable.

As he walks along he forgets that he's got the tortoise in his hand. Then he remembers it and reflects that he'd have done better to have left it in the park near his home. Instead, he's set off in the direction of the shop where it was bought. At the bottom of 49th Street, if he remembers correctly.

He continues on his way, although quite convinced in his own mind that, at that time of night, he'll find the shop shut. It's as if, in some odd way, not only his sadness but his tiredness, too, makes him feel a positive need to go and bang his head against that closed door.

When he reaches the shop he stands looking at the door. Yes, the shop's well and truly shut. Then he looks at the tortoise in his hand. What's he to do with it? Leave it there on the doorstep? He hears a taxi coming along the street and gets into it. After it's gone a little way, he'll get out, leaving the tortoise inside.

What a pity the little creature, still lurking away inside its shell like that, shows no sign of having a highly-developed imagination. It would be pleasant to think of a tortoise travelling all round the streets of New York by night.

No. No. Mr. Msyhkow repents his intention, as if it were something cruel he'd thought of. He gets out of the taxi. He's near Park Avenue by this time, with its interminable chain of flower-beds down the middle, and its low, hooped railings. He thinks he'll leave the tortoise in one of those flower-beds, but he's hardly put the creature down before a policeman pounces on him—the one who's on traffic duty at the intersection with 50th Street, under the gigantic tower of the Waldorf-Astoria. The policeman wants to know what he's put in the flower-bed. A bomb? Well, no. Not exactly a bomb. And Mr. Myshkow gives him a reassuring smile, just to prove to him how incapable he'd be of doing such a thing. Only a tortoise. The policeman orders him to retrieve it immediately. "Animals may not be introduced into the flower-beds. By Order!" But surely that doesn't apply to this animal? Mr. Myshkow tries to coax him into agreeing that it's more of a stone than an animal. Surely he doesn't really think it could cause any trouble! What's more—*for serious family reasons*—he simply must get rid of it. The policeman thinks he's trying to take the mickey out of him and turns nasty. Whereupon Mr. Myshkow immediately retrieves the tortoise from the flower-bed. It hasn't budged an inch.

"They tell me they're lucky," he adds with a smile. "Wouldn't *you* like to take it? Here you are—it's all yours!"

The policeman shakes himself furiously and imperiously gestures to him to get the hell out of here.

So here once again is Mr. Myshkow, with the tortoise in his hand and in a state of considerable embarrassment. Oh dear, if only he could leave it *somewhere*, even in the middle of the road, just so long as it was out of sight of that policeman who'd looked on him with so unfavourable an eye— obviously because he hadn't believed in those serious family reasons. Suddenly an idea flashes into his mind. Yes, this business about the tortoise is unquestionably a pretext on his wife's part, and, if he gets past her this time, she'll immediately find some other excuse. It'll be difficult, however, to find one more ridiculous than this one, and for it still to provide her with sufficient cause for complaint in the eyes of the judge and of the whole world and his wife. It would be foolish, therefore, to let this opportunity slip. There and then he decides to go back home with the tortoise.

He finds his wife in the drawing-room. Without saying a word to her he bends down and puts the tortoise on the carpet in front of her. It looks just like an overgrown pebble.

His wife leaps to her feet, rushes into the bedroom, and reappears with her hat on.

"I shall tell the judge that you prefer the company of that tortoise to that of your wife!"

And out she sweeps.

It's just as if that little creature down there on the carpet had understood every word she'd said. It suddenly unsheathes its four little paws, its tail and its head, and, swaying from side to side—you'd almost swear it was dancing—moves about the drawing-room.

Mr. Myshkow can scarcely refrain from rejoicing—but only rather half-heartedly. He applauds very quietly. He gets the feeling, as he looks at the tortoise, that it's telling him something. Only he's . . . well, he's not really convinced that . . .

"I'm in luck! I'm in luck!"

The son of a prosperous grain merchant and senator, Thomas Mann (1875–1955) of Lübeck, Germany, became one of the foremost fiction writers of his artistically gifted generation. He came to early attention with the novel Buddenbrooks *(1900); thereafter, for fifty-five years he wrote stories, essays, and long novels which have philosophical implications. Mann was an early critic of Nazi ideology and practice; in turn, the Nazis revoked his German citizenship and burned his books. Mann lived in California from 1942 to 1952, and eventually became an American citizen. Upon his return to Europe, he lived in Zurich, Switzerland, until his death. He received the Nobel Prize for literature in 1929. A recurring note in all his work is a grotesqueness, with implications of the sadistic; his stories concerning the nature of the artist and the artist's life are particularly incisive. One of his best-known novels is* The Magic Mountain *(1901); one of the most amusing is* Confessions of Felix Krull, Confidence Man *(1954). For further reading:* Stories of Three Decades *(1936).*

THOMAS MANN

At the Prophet's

*T*here are strange places, strange minds, strange regions of the spirit, lofty and poverty-stricken. Along the peripheries of the big cities, where the street-lights grow scarcer and the policemen walk in couples, you must climb the stairs in the houses until you cannot go any higher, climb into the attics under slanting roofs, where pale young geniuses, criminals of dreams, sit brooding with folded arms; climb into cheap and imposingly decorated studios, where lonely, rebel artists, consumed from within, hungry yet proud, contend with their latest and wildest ideals in clouds of cigarette smoke. Here is the end of things, here is ice, purity, and nothingness. Here no contract is valid, no concession, no consideration, no measure, and no value. Here the air has grown so thin, so chaste, that the miasmata of life

213

can no longer thrive. Here stubbornness reigns, the uttermost logical conclusion, the ego upon its desperate throne, freedom, madness, and death.

It was Good Friday, eight o'clock in the evening. Several of the people
whom Daniel had invited came at the same time. They had received invitations on quarto sheets, upon which there was an eagle which bore a naked
rapier in its claws through the air, and which contained in a singular hand-
writing a request to participate in a kind of convention on Good Friday
evening, when Daniel's proclamations were to be read, And so now they
met at the appointed hour in the desolate and half-dark suburban street in
front of the banal block of flats which contained the physical home of the
prophet.

A few were acquainted with one another and exchanged greetings.
These were a Polish artist and the thin girl who lived with him; a lyric poet,
a tall, black-bearded Semite, with his heavy-limbed, pallid wife, who wore
clothes like draperies; an individual who looked at once sickly and martial,
being a spiritualist who was also a retired cavalry captain; and a young
philosopher with the appearance of a kangaroo. Only the short-story writer,
a gentlemen with a stiff hat and a cultivated moustache, knew no one. He
came from another sphere and had come here only accidentally. He had a
certain relationship to life and a book of his was much read in middle-class
circles. He was determined to behave in a strictly modest fashion, to be
appreciative, and on the whole to act like one who is merely tolerated. He
followed the others into the house at a short distance.

They mounted the stairs, one after the other, supporting themselves on
the cast-iron railing. They were silent, for they were people who knew the
value of words and were not accustomed to talk needlessly. In the dim light
of the little oil-lamps which stood upon the window-sills at every turn of the
stairs, they read the names upon the door-plates of the flats as they went
past. They mounted past the care-haunted abodes of an insurance official,
a midwife, a laundress, an "agent," a chiropodist—quietly, without contempt, but estranged. They climbed up this narrow staircase hall as up some
half-lighted shaft, full of confidence and without pausing, for from above,
far up where one could go no higher, a faint glow greeted them, a soft and
fugitive and errant glow from the highest altitudes.

Finally they stood at the goal, under the roof, in the light of six candles, which were burning in different candlesticks upon a little table covered by a faded little altar-cloth at the head of the stairs. On the door,
which looked like the entrance to a store-room, there was a grey oblong of
cardboard, on which was to be read the name "Daniel" in Roman letters,
done with black chalk. They rang.

A boy with a large head and a friendly expression opened the door. He
wore a new suit of blue cloth and polished top-boots, and carried a candle
in his hand. He lighted them obliquely across the small, dark corridor into

an unpapered garret-like room, which was quite empty save for a wooden clothes-rack. Without a word, but with a gesture which was accompanied by a stammering guttural sound, the boy indicated that the guests should take off their wraps, and when the short-story writer, out of a sense of general friendliness, asked him a question, it became evident that the child was dumb. Holding his light, he led the guests once more across the corridor to another door and let them enter. The short-story writer brought up the rear. He wore a cut-away and gloves and was determined to act as though in church.

The room they entered was moderately large and was filled by an awesome shimmering, swaying brightness, engendered by twenty or twenty-five lighted candles. A young girl, with a white turned-over collar and cuffs relieving her simple dress, stood close beside the door and gave her hand to all who entered. This was Maria Josefa, Daniel's sister, with her innocent but foolish face. The short-story writer knew her. He had met her at a library tea. She had sat there upright, with her cup in her hand, and had spoken of her brother with a clear voice full of devotion. She worshipped Daniel.

The short-story writer's eyes wandered about the room in search of him.

"He is not here," said Maria Josefa. "He is absent, I don't know where. But he will be here among us in spirit and follow the proclamations, word for word, when they are read."

"Who is going to read them?" asked the short-story writer, in a low, reverent voice. He was really in earnest about it. He was a well-meaning and modest person, venerating all the phenomena of life, and quite willing to learn and to revere what was worthy of being revered.

"A disciple of my brother's," answered Maria Josefa, "whom we are expecting from Switzerland. He is not here yet. He will be on hand at the right moment."

Opposite the door a large chalk drawing was visible in the candlelight. It stood upon the table, its upper edge leaning against the slanting ceiling. The drawing, which was done in a bold, violent manner, represented Napoleon, standing in a clumsy and despotic attitude in front of a fireplace warming his jack-booted feet. At the right of the entrance rose an altar-like shrine, upon which, between candles burning in silver candelabra, stood a painted holy figure, with outspread hands, and eyes turned upward. A *priedieu* stood in front of this, and on approaching it one observed, leaning upright against one of the feet of the holy figure, a small amateur photograph. This showed a young man of about thirty years with a tremendously high, pale, retreating forehead and a smooth-shaven, bony face, like that of a bird of prey, full of concentrated spirituality.

The writer of short stories paused for a while before this picture of

Daniel; then he ventured cautiously farther into the room. Behind a large, round table, into whose polished yellow surface, surrounded by a wreath of laurel, the same sword-bearing eagle which had been seen on the invitations was burned, towered a severe, narrow chair of a spiry Gothic design like a throne and supreme seat among a number of low wooden stools. A long bench of rude carpentry, covered with some cheap stuff, extended along the roomy niche formed by wall and roof, and in this niche there was a low window. Presumably because the squat tiled stove had proved to be over-heated, the window was open, and presented a view of a segment of blue night, in the depths and distance of which the irregularly spaced gas-lamps lost themselves as yellow, glowing dots in ever greater intervals.

Opposite the window the room narrowed down to a kind of alcove-like chamber, which was lighted more brightly than the other part of this attic, and appeared to be used partly as study, partly as chapel. At the back of this room there was a couch, covered by a thinnish, washed-out stuff. To the right, one could see a curtained book-rack, on top of which burned candles in candelabra and oil-lamps of antique shape. To the left was set a white-covered table, upon which stood a crucifix, a seven-branched can-dlestick, a goblet filled with red wine, and a piece of plum-cake upon a plate.

In the foreground of this alcove there stood upon a low platform a column of gilded plaster, surmounted by an iron candelabrum; the capital of the column was covered by an altar-cloth of blood-red silk. And upon this rested a pile of manuscript sheets of folio size: Daniel's proclamations. A light-coloured wall-paper bedecked with little Empire wreaths covered the walls and the slanting part of the ceiling. Death-masks, rose wreaths, a large, rusty sword, hung upon the walls, and besides the large picture of Napoleon, there were portraits, of various sorts, of Luther, Nietzsche, Molt-ke, Alexander the Sixth, Robespierre, and Savonarola distributed about the room.

"All this has been lived!" said Maria Josefa, peering into the re-spectfully restrained visage of the short-story writer to see what effect these furnishings had produced. But in the mean time other guests had come, quietly and solemnly, and people began to seat themselves on benches and chairs, in hushed expectancy. In addition to those who had arrived first, there now sat there a fantastic draughtsman, with senile, infantile face, a limping lady, who was accustomed to introduce herself as one devoted to "erotics," and an unmarried young mother of noble birth, who had been cast out by her family. She was without any intellectual interests whatever, and had found hospitality in these circles solely upon the ground of her motherhood. There was also an elderly authoress and a deformed musi-cian—all in all some twelve persons. The short-story writer had withdrawn into the window niche, and Maria Josefa sat on a chair close to the door, her hands lying upon her knees, side by side. And thus they waited for the disciple from Switzerland, who would be on hand at the right moment.

Suddenly another guest arrived—the rich lady who loved to visit such affairs as a kind of hobby. She had come from the fashionable part of the city in her silken coupé, out of her splendid mansion with the Gobelins and the door-casings of *giallo antico,* had climbed up all the stairs, and now came through the door, beautiful, fragrant, luxurious, in a dress of blue cloth with yellow embroidery, a Parisian hat upon her reddish brown hair, and a smile in her Titian eyes. She came out of curiosity, out of ennui, out of joy in contrarieties, out of sheer goodwill towards all that was a little out of the common, out of a kindly extravagance of feelings. She greeted Daniel's sister and the short-story writer, who was frequently a guest at her house, and then seated herself on the bench in front of the window niche between the erotic lady and the philosopher who had the appearance of a kangaroo, as though that was all quite in order.

"I've almost come too late," said she softly with her beautiful, mobile mouth to the short-story writer, who sat behind her. "I had people to tea, and so things dragged along."

The short-story writer was much affected and thanked Heaven that he was in a presentable dress. "How beautiful she is!" thought he. "She is worthy of being the mother of that daughter of hers."

"And Fräulein Sonia?" he asked her across her shoulder. "Didn't you bring Fräulein Sonia with you?"

Sonia was the daughter of the rich lady, and in the eyes of the short-story writer she was an unbelievable example of a perfect creature, a marvel of versatile education, an attained ideal of culture. He spoke her name twice, for it gave him an inexpressible pleasure to pronounce it.

"Sonia is ill," said the rich lady. "Yes—would you believe it?—she has a bad foot. Oh, it is nothing, a swelling, a kind of little inflammation or congestion. It has been cut. It might not have been necessary, perhaps, but she insisted upon it herself."

"She insisted upon it herself!" repeated the short-story writer in an enthusiastic whisper. "That is like her! But how in the world can one express one's sympathy?"

"Well, I'll take her your greetings!" said the rich woman, And as he was silent, she added: "Doesn't that satisfy you?"

"No, it does not," said he very softly, and as she prized his books, she answered with a smile:

"Well, then, send her a flower or two."

"Thanks!" said he. "Thanks! I'll do so!" And he thought to himself: "A flower or two? A nosegay! A big bouquet! I'll drive tomorrow to the florist's before breakfast!" And he felt he had a certain relation to life.

A slight noise was heard without, the door opened and closed quickly and with a jerk, and a short and stocky young man in a dark lounge-suit stood before the guests in the candlelight: the disciple from Switzerland. He cast a swift and threatening look over the room, strode with heavy steps towards the plaster column in front of the alcove, established himself behind this on the low platform with a firmness as though he wished to take root there, seized the uppermost sheet of manuscript, and instantly began to read.

He was about twenty-eight years of age, short-necked, and ugly. His cropped hair grew in the form of an acute point unusually far down on his forehead, which besides was low and furrowed. His face, beardless, sullen, and heavy, revealed a doglike nose, coarse cheek-bones, a pair of sunken cheeks, and coarse, protuberant lips, which seemed to shape the words they spoke only by a great effort, reluctantly, and with a kind of limp anger. His face was brutal and yet pale. He read with a wild and overloud voice, which, however, at the same time trembled inwardly, shook, and suffered from scantiness of breath. The hand that held the written sheet was broad and red, and yet it trembled. He embodied an eerie mixture of brutality and weakness, and the things he read coincided in a strange way with his looks.

They were sermons, comparisons, theses, laws, visions, prophecies, and appeals in the manner of orders of the day, and these followed one another in a variegated and endless string, in a mixture of styles, in tones borrowed from the Psalms and from Revelation, intermingled with military-strategic as well as philosophical-critical "trade" expressions. A feverish ego, terribly excited, thrust itself upward in solitary megalomania and threatened the world with a torrent of convulsive words. *Christus Imperator maximus* was his name and he recruited death-devoted troops for the subjugation of the terrestrial globe, issued messages, set up his implacable conditions, longed for poverty and chastity, and in a spirit of boundless revolt kept on reiterating with a kind of unnatural lust the imperative of unconditional obedience. Buddha, Alexander, Napoleon, and Jesus were all designated as his humble predecessors, not worthy of unloosing the shoe-latchets of this spiritual emperor.

The disciple read for an hour; then, trembling, he took a gulp from the goblet of red wine and reached for new proclamations. Sweat stood in pearls on his low forehead, his thick lips quivered, and between the words he kept on blowing his breath with a short, snorting sound through his nose, like a bellowing exhaust. The solitary ego sang, raved, and commanded. It lost itself in mad metaphors, went down in a whirl of illogic, and suddenly popped up again horribly and quite unexpectedly in another place. Blasphemies and hosannas, incense and fumes of blood, were intermingled. The world was conquered in thunderous battles and then redeemed.

It would have been difficult to establish the effect of Daniel's proclamations upon the auditors. Some of them, with heads thrown back, looked with lack-lustre eyes at the ceiling; others, bent over their knees, held their faces buried in their hands. The eyes of the lady devoted to "erotics" grew dim in a peculiar manner every time the word "chastity" was spoken, and the philosopher with the appearance of a kangaroo now and again described something vague in the air with his long and crooked index finger. The short-story writer had for a long time been seeking in vain some adequate support for his aching back. At ten o'clock he was visited by the vision of a ham sandwich, but he shied this off manfully.

About half past ten one saw that the disciple held the last folio sheet in his red and trembling right hand. He had finished. "Soldiers!" he wound up, with the last ounce of his strength, with a failing voice of thunder, "I deliver unto you to be plundered—the world!" He then stepped down from the platform, regarded everybody with a threatening look, and vanished as violently as he had come, through the door.

The audience remained for a moment immovably in the position which they had last assumed. Then, as with a common resolve, they stood up and went away immediately, after each, with a soft word or two, had pressed the hand of Maria Josefa, who, innocent and calm, again stood in her white collar close beside the door.

The dumb lad was on hand outside. He lighted the guests to the cloak-room, helped them to put on their wraps, and led them through the narrow hall with the staircase, upon which, from the supreme height of Daniel's realm, the moving light of the candles fell, down to the house door, which he unlocked. The guests, one after the other, stepped out upon the desolate suburban street.

The coupé of the rich lady had halted in front of the house. One saw how the coachman on the box between the two brilliant lanterns touched his hat with his whip-hand. The short-story writer accompanied the rich lady to the carriage door.

"How did you stand it?" he asked.

"I don't like to express an opinion upon such things," she replied. "Perhaps he is really a genius, or something similar."

"Yes, what is genius?" he asked thoughtfully. "All requirements are present in this Daniel—loneliness, freedom, intellectual passion, magnificent visual capacity, belief in himself, even the proximity of crime and madness. What is lacking? Possibly the human? A little feeling, longing, love? But that is an entirely improvised hypothesis.

"Give Sonia my greetings," he said as she reached him her hand in farewell after seating herself, and he studied her face intently to see how she would take his speaking simply of "Sonia," not of "Fräulein Sonia," or of "your daughter."

She prized his books, and so she suffered it with a smile.

"I'll do so."

"Thanks!" said he, and a whirl of hope bewildered him. "And now I'll eat supper like a wolf!"

He had a certain relationship to life.

Hermann Hesse (1877–1962) was born in Calw, Wüttemberg, the son of a linguist specializing in the languages of the Far East. A person of chronically unresolved intention, Hesse drifted through a series of occupations before his first two novels, most notably Unser Rad *(1905), brought him both recognition and the profession of author. Previously little known in the United States, Hesse's wide acceptance in America came after he was awarded the Nobel Prize for literature (1946); one of his central themes of considerable current appeal concerns the individual's quest for peace and inner harmony in a world of modernity. Representative works are* Steppenwolf *(1927) and his last, great novel,* Magister Ludi *(1943). For further reading:* Strange News from Another Planet *(translated by Denver Lindley, 1972).*

HERMANN HESSE

The Poet

*T*he story is told of the Chinese poet Han Fook that from early youth he was animated by an intense desire to learn all about the poet's art and to perfect himself in everything connected with it. In those days he was still living in his home city on the Yellow River and had become engaged—at his own wish and with the aid of his parents, who loved him tenderly—to a girl of good family; the wedding was to be announced shortly for a chosen day of good omen. Han Fook at this time was about twenty years old and a handsome young man, modest and of agreeable manners, instructed in the sciences and, despite his youth, already known among the literary folk of his district for a number of remarkable poems. Without being exactly rich, he had the expectation of comfortable means, which would be increased by the dowry of his bride, and since this bride was also very beautiful and virtuous, nothing whatever seemed lacking to the youth's happiness. Nevertheless, he was not entirely content, for his heart was filled with the ambition to become a perfect poet.

Then one evening when a lantern festival was being celebrated on the river, it happened that Han Fook was wandering alone on the opposite bank. He leaned against the trunk of a tree that hung out over the water, and mirrored in the river he saw a thousand lights floating and trembling, he saw men and women and young girls on the boats and barges, greeting each other and glowing like beautiful flowers in their festive robes, he heard the girl singers, the hum of the zither and the sweet tones of the flute players, and over all this he saw the bluish night arched like the dome of a temple. The youth's heart beat high as he took in all this beauty, a lonely observer in pursuit of his whim. But much as he longed to go across the river and take part in the feast and be in the company of his bride-to-be and his friends, much deeper was his longing to absorb it all as a perceptive observer and to reproduce it in a wholly perfect poem: the blue of the night and the play of light on the water and the joy of the guests and the yearning of the silent onlooker leaning against the tree trunk on the bank. He realized that at all festivals and with all joys of this earth he would never feel wholly comfortable and serene at heart; even in the midst of life he would remain solitary and be, to a certain extent, a watcher, an alien, and he felt that his soul, unlike most others, was so formed that he must be alone to experience both the beauty of the earth and the secret longings of a stranger. Thereupon he grew sad, and pondered this matter, and the conclusion of his thoughts was this, that true happiness and deep satisfaction could only be his if on occasion he succeeded in mirroring the world so perfectly in his poems that in these mirror images he would possess the essence of the world, purified and made eternal.

Han Fook hardly knew whether he was still awake or had fallen asleep when he heard a slight rustling and saw a stranger standing beside the trunk of the tree, an old man of reverend aspect, wearing a violet robe. Han Fook roused himself and greeted the stranger with the salutation appropriate to the aged and distinguished; the stranger, however, smiled and spoke a few verses in which everything the young man had just felt was expressed so completely and beautifully and so exactly in accord with the rules of the great poets that the youth's heart stood still with amazement.

"Oh, who are you?" he cried, bowing deeply. "You who can see into my soul and who recite more beautiful verses than I ever heard from any of my teachers!"

The stranger smiled once more with the smile of one made perfect, and said: "If you wish to be a poet, come to me. You will find my hut beside the source of the Great River in the northwestern mountains. I am called Master of the Perfect Word."

Thereupon the aged man stepped into the narrow shadow of the tree and instantly disappeared, and Han Fook, searching for him in vain and finding no trace of him, finally decided that it had all been a dream caused by his fatigue. He hastened across to the boats and joined in the festival, but amid the conversation and the music of the flutes he continued to hear the mysterious voice of the stranger, and his soul seemed to have gone away with the old man, for he sat remote and with dreaming eyes among the merry folk, who teased him for being in love.

A few days later Han Fook's father prepared to summon his friend and relations to decide upon the day of the wedding. The bridegroom demurred and said: "Forgive me if I seem to offend against the duty a son owes his father. But you know how great my longing is to distinguish myself in the art of poetry, and even though some of my friends praise my poems, nevertheless I know very well that I am still a beginner and still on the first stage of the journey. Therefore, I beg you to let me go my way in loneliness for a while and devote myself to my studies, for it seems to me that having a wife and a house to govern will keep me from these things. But now I am still young and without other duties, and I would like to live for a time for my poetry, from which I hope to gain joy and fame."

This speech filled his father with great surprise and he said: "This art must indeed be dearer to you than anything, since you wish to postpone your wedding on account of it. Or has something arisen between you and your bride? If so, tell me so that I can help to reconcile you, or select another girl."

The son swore, however, that his bride-to-be was no less dear to him than she had been yesterday and always, and that no shadow of discord had fallen between them. Then he told his father that on the day of the lantern festival a Master had become known to him in a dream, and that he desired to be his pupil more ardently than all the happiness in the world.

"Very well," his father said, "I will grant you a year. In this time you may pursue your dream, which perhaps was sent to you by a god."

"It may even take two years," Han Fook said hesitantly. "Who can tell?"

So his father let him go, and was troubled; the youth, however, wrote a letter to his bride, said farewell, and departed.

When he had wandered for a very long time, he reached the source of the river, and in complete isolation he found a bamboo hut, and in front of the hut on a woven mat sat the aged man whom he had seen beside the tree on the river bank. He sat playing a lute, and when he saw his guest approach with reverence he did not rise or greet him but simply smiled and let his delicate fingers run over the strings, and a magical music flowed like a silver cloud through the valley, so that the youth stood amazed and in his sweet astonishment forgot everything, until the Master of the Perfect Word laid aside his little lute and stepped into the hut. Then Han Fook followed him reverently and stayed with him as his servant and pupil.

With the passing of a month he had learned to despise all the poems he had hitherto composed, and he blotted them out of his memory. And after more months he blotted out all the songs that he had learned from his teachers at home. The Master rarely spoke to him; in silence he taught him the art of lute playing until the pupil's being was entirely saturated with music. Once Han Fook made a little poem which described the flight of two birds in the autumn sky, and he was pleased with it. He dared not show it to the Master, but one evening he sang it outside the hut, and the Master listened attentively. However, he said no word. He simply played softly on his lute and at once the air grew cool and twilight fell suddenly, a sharp wind arose although it was midsummer, and through the sky which had grown gray flew two herons in majestic migration, and everything was so much more beautiful and perfect than in the pupil's verses that the latter became sad and was silent and felt that he was worthless. And this is what the ancient did each time, and when a year had passed, Han Fook had almost completely mastered the playing of the lute, but the art of poetry seemed to him ever more difficult and sublime.

When two years had passed, the youth felt a devouring homesickness for his family, his native city, and his bride, and he besought the Master to let him leave.

The Master smiled and nodded. "You are free, he said, "and may go where you like. You may return, you may stay away, just as it suits you."

Then the pupil set out on his journey and traveled uninterruptedly until one morning in the half light of dawn he stood on the bank of his native river and looked across the arched bridge to his home city. He stole secretly into his father's garden and listened through the window of the bedchamber to his father's breathing as he slept, and he slipped into the orchard beside his bride's house and climbed a pear tree, and from there he saw his bride standing in her room combing her hair. And while he compared all these things which he was seeing with his eyes to the mental pictures he had painted of them in his homesickness, it became clear to him that he was, after all, destined to be a poet, and he saw that in poets' dreams reside a beauty and enchantment that one seeks in vain in the things of the real world. And he climbed down from the tree and fled out of the garden and over the bridge, away from his native city, and returned to the high mountain valley. There, as before, sat the old Master in front of his hut on his modest mat, striking the lute with his fingers, and instead of a greeting he recited two verses about the blessings of art, and at their depth and harmony the young man's eyes filled with tears.

Once more Han Fook stayed with the Master of the Perfect Word, who, now that his pupil had mastered the lute, instructed him in the zither, and the months melted away like snow before the west wind. Twice more it happened that he was overcome by homesickness. On the one occasion he ran away secretly at night, but before he had reached the last bend in the valley the night wind blew across the zither hanging at the door of the hut, and the notes flew after him and called him back so that he could not resist them. But the next time he dreamed he was planting a young tree in his garden, and his wife and children were assembled there and his children were watering the tree with wine and milk. When he awoke, the moon was shining into his room and he got up, disturbed in mind, and saw in the next room the Master lying asleep with his gray beard trembling gently; then he was overcome by a bitter hatred for this man who, it seemed to him, destroyed his life and cheated him of his future. He was about to throw himself upon the Master and murder him when the ancient opened his eyes and began to smile with a sad sweetness and gentleness that disarmed his pupil.

"Remember, Han Fook," the aged man said softly, "you are free to do what you like. You may go to your home and plant trees, you may hate me and kill me, it makes very little difference."

"Oh, how could I hate you?" the poet cried, deeply moved. "That would be like hating heaven itself."

And he stayed and learned to play the zither, and after that the flute, and later he began under his Master's guidance to make poems, and he slowly learned the secret art of apparently saying only simple and homely things but thereby stirring the hearer's soul like wind on the surface of the water. He described the coming of the sun, how it hesitates on the mountain's rim, and the noiseless darting of the fishes when they flee like shadows under the water, and the swaying of a young birch tree in the spring wind, and when people listened it was not only the sun and the play of the fish and the whispering of the birch tree, but it seemed as though heaven and earth each time chimed together for an instant in perfect harmony, and each hearer was impelled to think with joy or pain about what he loved or hated, the boy about sport, the youth about his beloved, and the old man about death.

Han Fook no longer knew how many years he had spent with the Master beside the source of the Great River; often it seemed to him as though he had entered this valley only the evening before and been received by the ancient playing on his stringed instrument; often, too, it seemed as though all the ages and epochs of man had vanished behind him and become unreal.

And then one morning he awoke alone in the house, and though he searched everywhere and called, the Master had disappeared. Overnight it seemed suddenly to have become autumn, a raw wind tugged at the old hut, and over the ridge of the mountain great flights of migratory birds were moving, though it was not yet the season for that.

Then Han Fook took the little lute with him and descended to his native province, and when he came among men they greeted him with the salutation appropriate to the aged and distinguished, and when he came to his home city he found that his father and his bride and his relations had died and other people were living in their houses. In the evening, however, the festival of the lanterns was celebrated on the river and the poet Han Fook stood on the far side on the darker bank, leaning against the trunk of an ancient tree. And when he played on the little lute, the women began to sigh and looked into the night, enchanted and overwhelmed, and the young men called for the lute player, whom they could not find anywhere, and they exclaimed that none of them had ever heard such tones from a lute. But Han Fook only smiled. He looked into the river where floated the mirrored images of the thousand lamps; and just as he could no longer distinguish between the reflections and reality, so he found in his soul no difference between this festival and that first one he saw when he had stood there as a youth and heard the words of the strange Master.

Zsigmond Móricz (1879–1942), one of Hungary's best-known prose writers, came from a family of small peasants. After he studied theology, philosophy, and law without receiving a degree, he became a school teacher and journalist. He came to prominence through his contributions of short stories to Nyugat (West), *a pioneering journal of modern Hungarian literature. In this period, Móricz' style derived from French naturalism and Art Nouveau. Under the shadow of strengthening Hungarian Fascism, Móricz's political views became increasingly more radical, a development which was reflected in later works such as* Little Orphan *(1941) and* Sándor Róza *(1940–1942). For further reading:* Hungarian Short Stories, *edited by A. Alvarez (1967).*

ZSIGMOND MÓRICZ

Everything Is Good at the End of the World

*T*he farm was at the centre of the world, the house was at the centre of the farm, mother dear was at the centre of the house and around her were her ten children.

But four-year-old little Rozi was only a state-supported orphan. She wasn't in the house, nor was she on the farm, she wasn't even in the world, she was just nowhere at all. She wormed her way in amongst the other children, but they knew she didn't belong among them.

Of course, little Rozi did not know what the words state-supported child meant. She had the same mother as the others and she even said "mother dear" to the big and stocky dark-haired woman who was now ordering her numerous children to undress.

It was bath time and everyone had to be clean for the day after tomorrow, which was Easter.

They were all swarming about like bees in a hive, chirping away like birds in a nest, and bickering like old wives at the market. Every one of them was a girl. Ten girls in all. That was why they had taken in a state-

227

supported child. If they had to provide for ten girls, there might as well be one more who paid.

Father dear was not at home just then and they were all glad of it. Uncle Tülkös was so dreadfully angry that his wife tricked him every year by coming up with daughter after daughter that he had taken to drink, and when he came home, he came with a whip and beat every last one of his clan.

Rozi could also have been getting undressed, but she just stood there pouting and watching how mother dear paid no attention to her whatever. Nobody paid any attention to her, for getting undressed caused so much commotion that every child was all taken up with herself. The oldest girl was fourteen and the youngest was still in the cradle. There were two other four-year-olds like Rozi, the twins. Who could ever have learned all their names? Even their mother got them mixed up all the time, never knowing which was Mari, Juli, Sári, Klári, or Cica-Maca (those were the twins). The three small ones did not even have names. Anyway, what would have been the use of calling to a six-month-old baby?

But there was one most unusual thing, and that was how inexpressibly grand Rozi felt among her sisters—much, much better than they felt among themselves. This little child even had a past of her own. It was not the first time she had got acquainted with a family, for this was the third place she had come to in her short life to bask in parental love. And it was just for this reason that she was the sole person hurt by the fact that nobody was paying the slightest attention to her—neither mother dear nor the children, neither Mari nor Juli, neither Sári nor Klári. She just stood to one side, moping and wondering what was to be done with her.

Mother dear emptied the hot water out of the cauldron into a large tub which was brought in from outside, and the girls piled in one after the other. The tub looked like a butt during the wine harvest, filled with bunches of grapes.

But Rozi was still standing there all by herself, not knowing what was to become of her. She stuck her thumb in her mouth and stood watching and watching.

The noise in the raftered room was shattering and nearly burst it apart, and all the time mother dear kept shouting:

"Stop that racket, you're driving me crazy!"

And this made them yell all the more, they just giggled in the tub and yelled.

So many naked girls. Mari already had thighs as big as bread loaves. Little Rozi was sulking, but dared not say a word. This was the way it was at mealtime also, it was the way of the world, and she had become quite used to it. She only got bread last, after everyone else had got it, provided there was any left. If there was none, then she got none. And she did not cry or yell or make demands. There was really something very mysterious about how a state-supported child learned that she was not supposed to cry or yell or ask, but only to wait. . . . And Rozi really would wait like a little beggar before the door for someone to give her alms. There was a fully developed sense of a have-not's rights in that tiny four-year-old girl. She had the right to stand there and wait until all ten children had bathed. She recalled that she had bathed with them during the winter and mother dear had even had to smack her hand to make her wait her turn. This was no longer necessary. It was very long ago, but she had not forgotten that her mission was to wait. So she waited. But watching was allowed.

"Go and have some milk!" mother dear cried out to her. "There's milk."

Yes, but for some incredible reason Rozi did not like milk. She didn't want any.

"No," she said stubbornly.

Mother dear always forgot which child liked what. There was always somebody who ate her portion before she even noticed.

"You don't want any milk?"

"No. Drink it yourself."

"The devil take your belly!" mother dear snapped at Rozi, and she began scrubbing the neck of one of her daughters with a rag and then with sand, for it was as black as the heifer's.

"Get out!" she yelled at Rozi.

The child had to be punished. The child always had to be punished or she would become unruly.

Rozi did not budge. She was so incorrigible, that state-supported child, that it was useless to order her about.

"Are you going to get out of here this minute?" And she gave her such a push that the little girl hurried out through the open door into the cool kitchen without knowing where she would stop.

Now she was standing out on the porch. The door was closed. She could have reached the door handle but she was so well trained that she just stared at it. For a long time she just stood there and stared and stared, but did not touch it. At the thought of the milk, however, she became hungry.

Without further ado she started out that very minute, leaving the door of the room and entering the pantry. It had a string for a handle, which she pulled, and this funny trick of simply pulling at a string made the door open. Rozi went in, and there was the bread right in front of her nose, half a loaf. She went to it, grabbed hold of it with her two dirty little hands, and broke off the tip. There was the bread in her hand. She turned around with a little skip and toddled along unconcerned. She passed the door of the room, heard the row, the giggling and yelling in there, and just kept on going, going, towards home. She headed for the hay, where they had slept the night before. . . .

Uncle Tülkös had come home reeking last night, so drunk he could barely walk. He kept taking big steps and banging his head against the wall, which little Rozi thought the most natural thing in the world. And Uncle Tülkös fished out a funny-looking thing that they had used to thresh the wheat at the end of summer—a thing with a small stick hanging from the end of a big one—and with that long thing he began to beat and thwack mother dear. And then the children who were now giggling so much began screaming. The ten girls shrieked like ten trumpets. Only little Rozi did not scream. Little Rozi did not have the right to scream.

She was asleep by then anyway, but mother dear snatched Rozi from her nook and ran into the yard with her even though it was really cold, and they all ran barefoot into the barn at the end of the yard and hid in the straw and hay. Oh, such big houses there were made of hay in that yard, even bigger than the one they lived in. And then the girls all made nests in the stack and hid one another inside, and it was dark and Uncle Tülkös did not go there after all and did not find them, and she was there, too, hidden in a hole with Sári. She was lucky she had fallen asleep without having undressed, and even her little shoes were still on, so she just slept and nothing else happened to her. Thus she was not even so very cold, and now she ran and ran, to her home in the straw house, trying to find the nest they had hidden in yesterday. She could not find it, but she did not search, for she felt protected by now and began to eat the bread she had brought, the heel of the loaf.

And the little state-supported orphan, like a dog when it steals or a little mouse when it finds something to nibble at, just stood there with her head stuck into the hay and munched away. She always loved bread and was very happy that she had some and ate it as if it were hers. She was smart in her own little clever way even though she was very young. She knew how the bread was baked and she knew how to get a piece off for herself even when she had no knife. And if she had had one, she would not have cut the bread anyway, for she did not know how. . . .

Her snack lasted until loud noises began coming from the direction of the house. This did not happen for quite a while. The baths were over and somehow mother dear thought of little Rozi. She yelled out for her to come in from the porch, but no answer came from there. She had to go out herself, and immediately she saw that the door to the pantry was ajar, because the little girl was not yet smart enough to hide her tracks. Of course, mother dear also saw that something sinful had happened to the bread and from this she knew right away where to look for little Rozi. And in less than one minute she was at the haystack, where she grabbed the little girl by the neck, lifting her up like a frog, shaking her, and giving the state-supported child powerful slaps wherever she could.

"You won't have a bath, you thieving pig!" she cried. "Now you can just stink at Easter and drop dead!"

But Rozi, the little ward of the state, had become used to this. Nor could it be any other way. How could she not get beaten? Why, she was always being beaten. And it didn't hurt so much that she had to scream. It hurt, but she was used to it; she was prepared to suffer a beating for every bite of food she got, so if they beat her she just kept silent. Why bother to cry? Nobody would comfort her, nobody would save her from the beating, and there was nobody to dry her tears. A state-supported child gets beaten and that's all. She knew nothing yet about her being a state-supported child, she only knew that this was the procedure with these things. If she was beaten, she did not cry. If she found food, she ate it. If they hit her, she kept silent.

But this time a miracle happened.

The state appeared on the scene.

The Lady came, the superintendent Lady who was in charge of seeing to the care this foundling received after she was placed. And now she came out to the farmstead to see how little Rozi was doing and what Easter would bring, and she just happened to catch mother dear whipping the state-supported child.

Something very strange happened because of this. The gentle and quiet Lady began to yell, and stocky, dark-haired mother dear became very quiet.

"You think there's nobody else I can give this child to?" the Lady said. "You'll see that there certainly is. . . . Look at this little girl. Where are her clothes? Where are your clothes?"

With the inspiration of the innocent, Rozi said:

"Mother dear always gives them to Cica and Maca."

"What? You dress your cats in the child's clothes?"

And mother dear said ne'er a word.

The little wonder child understood that something was very wrong here. The Lady was stupid and thought her sisters were cats.

"Not cats, girls."

"Is that so?!" the Lady understood at last. "You dress your own children in the state's clothes? It's a good thing I found this out. Gather all of her clothes together immediately, I'm taking her away from here. I have just the place for her in the village."

There was no choice. Mother dear had to gather her clothes together and the Lady put the little girl up on the wagon and took her away just like that. And little Rozi did not utter a sound but prudently stuck to her policy of saying nothing when they dealt with her.

At last the wagon reached the village and came to a halt in front of a lovely house, out of which came a plump and pleasant lady with red cheeks who took Rozi in her arms and thanked the Lady very profusely for bringing her such a pretty Easter present.

Once again little Rozi felt as if she were not in the world, and she just kept quiet and stared sullenly out of her tiny dark eyes.

"I want to go to mother dear," she said, and wiped the kisses off her face.

But the plump woman just laughed and took her into the room, where she showed her a big doll and said:

"Look around. Everything you see will be yours if you stay here."

But Rozi just grew more and more suspicious, and she wouldn't have even believed Jesus himself if he had told her that her mother dear was not her mother dear. In vain did they tell her the woman hadn't given birth to her and she had no mother.

And she became more frightened and angry than ever that these strangers wanted to steal away her mother dear.

The Lady had already gone, saying reassuringly to the fat woman as she left:

"Just treat her well and you'll see that little Rozi will soon love you."

Little Rozi was on the verge of tears. Everything that had happened today, the baths, the beating, the Lady, the wagon, it was all too much for one Good Friday.

"I'm going to put you to bed, my little one. I have so very much work to do," said the plump woman, and she laid little Rozi down on the big couch just as she was and covered her with warm shawls.

Little Rozi just let her, for she thought slyly to herself in her cunning little head:

"Just you go out of here."

The very minute the plump woman left she jumped up and without any hesitation ran right out of the lovely room, past the big doll with long hair, out into the yard and on to the street. And she was so very lucky that nobody even noticed her. Everybody in the whole village was busy getting ready for Easter. There was nobody on the street and little Rozi could go wherever her feet would carry her.

She ran down the street on to the dusty highway and went wherever the road led her until she reached the end of the village. Then she kept on going and just walked and walked and walked, and she saw how the sky touched the earth, and thought to herself in her wee little head that that was the end of the world and everything would be good there.

And soon she even thought that she might grasp the end of the world with her little hand, but then a tree would suddenly appear on the road, and then a well, and the end of the world just did not want to come. She kept on going until she finally reached a village she had never seen before.

But she just continued walking and walking, although she was so very tired that she kept stopping and shivering with cold. Her lips were purple and her whole body was covered with gooseflesh, but she didn't know what that meant. She didn't even know that two and two made four.

All of a sudden a woman called out to her:

"Where are you going, little girl?"

There were big shaggy dogs all around and little Rozi was scared to death and just stared at the woman.

Suddenly, however, the woman clapped her hands together in recognition.

"I know this child, she's one of Mrs. Tülkös' daughters. However did you get here?"

Only now did Rozi come to her crafty little senses. She did not dare say that she had run away, so she said:

"I came with my mother dear to the market and mother dear lost me. I want to go to mother dear."

And for the first time that day she burst into tears. This time she felt that only crying would help her, for if she cried she would not have to talk, and if she cried they would feel sorry for her and do whatever she asked. And if she cried everything would be all right because everybody was afraid of tears, that is, of course, only strangers, for at home nobody was afraid if she cried, it was not worth the bother to cry at home.

And the crying did help her, after all. The woman took her hand, and when she felt how cold little Rozi's tiny hand was, she took her in her arms, covered her with her apron and brought her into the house. There they put her to bed and asked her all sorts of questions and felt sorry for her.

And sly little Rozi accepted all their sympathy and would only tell them:

"Everything is good at the end of the world."

Nobody understood her. She slept there that night, and the next morning, the morning of Easter Saturday, the man of the house harnassed the horses to his wagon—because these people were rich and had horses and a wagon and a big house—and took her home to mother dear.

Oh, what an uproar there was as the children ran to her, and even mother dear winked at her, laughing in the strangest way!

"Well, you no-good dog, are you going to break off the heel of the bread again? You know," she explained to the woman, "she gets as much as she can eat, and still the little pig ran away from her bath into the haystack to eat bread. . . . The best thing to do would be to stamp out the insides of a state-supported brat like her!"

With that she bent down to little Rozi and wiped her face. But she could not resist giving her a resounding slap on the behind.

Little Rozi looked up and in the distance past the gate she saw the bottom of the sky. She felt very surprised that the end of the world was here, too. She had never noticed it before. . . .

"Well, is it good here at home, you brat?"

"There," she pointed far away with her tiny finger.

"What's there?"

"There . . . there. . . ."

She did not dare say that it is better there, at the end of the world. . . . It would be good there.

Arcadii Timotheich Averchenko (1881–1925) wrote short fiction, drama, and humorous skits. He was a principal contributor to the St. Petersburg literary journal, Satyricon (1906–1919), and a central figure in a coterie of writers at that time. Often fantastic in vision, his skits were regular features at such theatre-cabarets as the "Crooked Mirror." As did many other artists at the time of the Revolution (1917), Averchenko left Russia; a few years later he died in Constantinople. Little is known about the final period of his life; only a few of his stories are available in English.

ARCADII AVERCHENKO

The Young Man Who Flew Past

This sad and tragic occurrence began thus:

*T*hree persons, in three different poses, were carrying on an animated conversation on the sixth floor of a large apartment building.

The woman, with plump beautiful arms, was clutching a bed sheet to her breast, forgetting that a bed sheet could not do double duty and cover her shapely bare knees at the same time. The woman was crying, and in the intervals between sobs she was saying:

"Oh, John! I swear to you I'm not guilty! He set my head in a whirl, he seduced me—and, I assure you, all against my will, I resisted—"

One of the men, still in his hat and overcoat, was gesticulating wildly and upbraiding the third person in the room:

"Scoundrel! I'm going to show you right now that you will perish like a cur and the law will be on my side! You shall pay for this meek victim! You reptile! You base seducer!"

The third in this room was a young man who, although not dressed with the greatest meticulousness at the present moment, bore himself, nevertheless, with great dignity.

"I? Why, I haven't done anything! I——" he protested, gazing sadly into an empty corner of the room.

"You haven't? Take this, then, you scoundrel!"

The powerful man in the overcoat flung open the window giving out upon the street, gathered the young man who was none too meticulously dressed in his arms, and heaved him out.

Finding himself flying through the air the young man bashfully buttoned his vest, and whispered to himself in consolation:

"Never mind! Our failures merely serve to harden us!"

And he kept on flying downward.

He had not yet had time to reach the next floor (the fifth) in his flight, when a deep sigh issued from his breast.

A recollection of the woman whom he had just left poisoned with its bitterness all the delight in the sensation of flying.

"My God!" thought the young man. "Why, I loved her! And she could not find the courage even to confess everything to her husband! God be with her! Now I can feel that she is distant, and indifferent to me."

With this last thought he had already reached the fifth floor and, as he flew past a window he peeked in, prompted by curiosity.

A young student was sitting reading a book at a lopsided table, his head propped up in his hands.

Seeing him, the young man who was flying past recalled his life; recalled that heretofore he had passed all his days in worldly distractions, forgetful of learning and books; and he felt drawn to the light of knowledge, to the discovery of nature's mysteries with a searching mind, drawn to admiration before the genius of the great masters of words.

"Dear, beloved student!" he wanted to cry out to the man reading, "you have awakened within me all my dormant aspirations and cured me of the empty infatuation with the vanities of life, which have led me to such grievous disenchantment on the sixth floor—"

But, not wishing to distract the student from his studies, the young man refrained from calling out, flying down to the fourth floor instead, and here his thoughts took a different turn.

His heart contracted with a strange sweet pain, while his head grew dizzy—from delight and admiration.

A young woman was sitting at the window of the fourth floor and, with a sewing machine before her, was at work upon something.

But her beautiful white hands had forgotten about work at that moment, and her eyes—blue as cornflowers—were looking into the distance, pensive and dreamy.

The young man could not take his eyes off this vision, and some new feeling, great and mighty, spread and grew within his heart.

And he understood that all his former encounters with women had been no more than empty infatuations, and that only now he understood that strange mysterious word—Love.

And he was attracted to the quiet domestic life; to the endearments of a being beloved beyond words; to a smiling existence, joyous and peaceful.

The next story, past which he was flying just then, confirmed him still more in his inclination.

In the window of the third floor he saw a mother who, singing a soft lullaby and laughing, was bouncing a plump smiling baby; love, and a kind maternal pride were sparkling in her eyes.

"I, too, want to marry the girl on the fourth floor, and have just such rosy plump children as the one on the third floor," mused the young man, "and I would devote myself entirely to my family and find my happiness in this self-sacrifice."

But the second floor was now approaching. And the picture which the young man saw in a window of this floor forced his heart to contract again.

A man with disheveled hair and wandering gaze was seated at a luxurious writing table. He was gazing at a framed photograph before him; at the same time he was writing with his right hand and, holding a revolver in his left, was pressing its muzzle to his temple.

"Stop, madman!" the young man wanted to call out. "Life is so beautiful!" But some instinctive feeling restrained him.

The luxurious appointments of the room, its richness and comfort, led the young man to reflect that there was something else in life which could disrupt even all this comfort and contentment, as well as a whole family; something of the utmost force—mighty, terrific. . . .

"What can it be?" he wondered with a heavy heart. And, as if on purpose, Life gave him a harsh unceremonious answer in a window of the first floor, which he had reached by now.

Nearly concealed by the draperies, a young man was sitting at the window, sans coat and vest; a half-dressed woman was sitting on his knees, lovingly entwining the head of her beloved with her round rosy arms and passionately hugging him to her magnificent bosom. . . .

The young man who was flying past recalled that he had seen this woman (well-dressed) out walking with her husband—but this man was decidedly not her husband. Her husband was older, with curly black hair, half-gray, while this man had beautiful fair hair.

And the young man recalled his former plans: of studying, after the student's example; of marrying the girl on the fourth floor; of a peaceful domestic life, à la the third—and once more his heart was heavily oppressed.

He perceived all the ephemerality, all the uncertainty of the happiness of which he had dreamed; beheld, in the near future, a whole procession of young men with beautiful fair hair about his wife and himself; remembered the torments of the man on the second floor and the measures which that man was taking to free himself from these torments—and he understood.

"After all I have witnessed living is not worth while! It is both foolish and tormenting," thought the young man, with a sickly, sardonic smile; and, contracting his eyebrows, he determinedly finished his flight to the very sidewalk.

Nor did his heart tremble when he touched the flagstones of the pavement with his hands and, breaking those now useless members, he dashed out his brains against the hard indifferent stone.

And, when the curious gathered around his motionless body, it never occurred to any of them what a complex drama the young man had lived through just a few moments before.

Franz Kafka (1883–1924) was born in Prague (Czechoslovakia), the son of an authoritarian, unapproachable father. Kafka studied law at the German University (1906) and went to work in the offices of the workman's compensation section of the Austrian government. After a considerable period of irresolution in his personal life, Kafka became engaged almost at the same time that he contracted tuberculosis and died. Much of his work survives because his literary executor, Max Brod, declined to carry out Kafka's expressed wish that upon his death all his manuscripts be destroyed. Kafka's novels and short fiction present a dream-like world where realistic detail and situation suggest the anxieties, the contradictions, and the lack of resolution in a complex world. For further reading: The Penal Colony *(translated by Willa Muir and Edwin Muir, 1948).*

FRANZ KAFKA

Jackals and Arabs

We were camping in the oasis. My companions were asleep. The tall, white figure of an Arab passed by; he had been seeing to the camels and was on his way to his own sleeping place.

I threw myself on my back in the grass; I tried to fall asleep; I could not; a jackal howled in the distance; I sat up again. And what had been so far away was all at once quite near. Jackals were swarming round me, eyes gleaming dull gold and vanishing again, lithe bodies moving nimbly and rhythmically, as if at the crack of a whip.

One jackal came from behind me, nudging right under my arm, pressing against me, as if he needed my warmth, and then stood before me and spoke to me almost eye to eye.

"I am the oldest jackal far and wide. I am delighted to have met you here at last. I had almost given up hope, since we have been waiting endless years for you; my mother waited for you, and her mother, and all our foremothers right back to the first mother of all the jackals. It is true, believe me!"

"That is surprising," said I, forgetting to kindle the pile of firewood which lay ready to smoke away jackals, "that is very surprising for me to hear. It is by pure chance that I have come here from the far North, and I am making only a short tour of your country. What do you jackals want, then?"

As if emboldened by this perhaps too friendly inquiry the ring of jackals closed in on me; all were panting and openmouthed.

"We know," began the eldest, "that you have come from the North; that is just what we base our hopes on. You Northerners have the kind of intelligence that is not to be found among Arabs. Not a spark of intelligence, let me tell you, can be struck from their cold arrogance. They kill animals for food, and carrion they despise."

"Not so loud," said I, "there are Arabs sleeping near by."

"You are indeed a stranger here," said the jackal, "or you would know that never in the history of the world has any jackal been afraid of an Arab. Why should we fear them? Is it not misfortune enough for us to be exiled among such creatures?"

"Maybe, maybe," said I, "matters so far outside my province I am not competent to judge; it seems to me a very old quarrel; I suppose it's in the blood, and perhaps will only end with it."

"You are very clever," said the old jackal; and they all began to pant more quickly; the air pumped out of their lungs although they were standing still; a rank smell which at times I had to set my teeth to endure streamed from their open jaws, "you are very clever; what you have just said agrees with our old tradition. So we shall draw blood from them and the quarrel will be over."

"Oh!" said I, more vehemently than I intended, "they'll defend themselves; they'll shoot you down in dozens with their muskets."

"You misunderstand us," said he, "a human failing which persists apparently even in the far North. We're not proposing to kill them. All the water in the Nile couldn't cleanse us of that. Why, the mere sight of their living flesh makes us turn tail and flee into cleaner air, into the desert, which for that very reason is our home."

And all the jackals around, including many new-comers from farther away, dropped their muzzles between their forelegs and wiped them with their paws; it was as if they were trying to conceal a disgust so overpowering that I felt like leaping over their heads to get away.

"Then what are you proposing to do?" I asked, trying to rise to my feet; but I could not get up; two young beasts behind me had locked their teeth through my coat and shirt; I had to go on sitting. "These are your trainbearers," explained the old jackal, quite seriously, "a mark of honor." "They must let go!" I cried, turning now to the old jackal, now to the youngsters. "They will, of course," said the old one, "if that is your wish.

But it will take a little time, for they have got their teeth well in, as is our custom, and must first loosen their jaws bit by bit. Meanwhile, give ear to our petition." "Your conduct hasn't exactly inclined me to grant it," said I. "Don't hold it against us that we are clumsy," said he, and now for the first time had recourse to the natural plaintiveness of his voice, "we are poor creatures, we have nothing but our teeth; whatever we want to do, good or bad, we can tackle it only with our teeth." "Well, what do you want?" I asked, not much mollified.

"Sir," he cried, and all the jackals howled together; very remotely it seemed to resemble a melody. "Sir, we want you to end this quarrel that divides the world. You are exactly the man whom our ancestors foretold as born to do it. We want to be troubled no more by Arabs; room to breathe; a skyline cleansed of them; no more bleating of sheep knifed by an Arab; every beast to die a natural death; no interference till we have drained the carcass empty and picked its bones clean. Cleanliness, nothing but cleanliness is what we want"—and now they were all lamenting and sobbing— "how can you bear to live in such a world, O noble heart and kindly bowels? Filth is their white; filth is their black; their beards are a horror; the very sight of their eye sockets makes one want to spit; and when they lift an arm, the murk of hell yawns in the armpit. And so, sir, and so, dear sir, by means of your all-powerful hands slit their throats through with these scissors!" And in answer to a jerk of his head a jackal came trotting up with a small pair of sewing scissors, covered with ancient rust, dangling from an eyetooth.

"Well, here's the scissors at last, and high time to stop!" cried the Arab leader of our caravan who had crept upwind towards us and now cracked his great whip.

The jackals fled in haste, but at some distance rallied in a close huddle, all the brutes so tightly packed and rigid that they looked as if penned in a small fold girt by flickering will-o'-the-wisps.

"So you've been treated to their entertainment too, sir," said the Arab, laughing as gaily as the reserve of his race permitted. "You know, then, what the brutes are after?" I asked. "Of course," said he, "it's common knowledge; so long as Arabs exist, that pair of scissors goes wandering through the desert and will wander with us to the end of our days. Every European is offered it for the great work; every European is just the man that Fate has chosen for them. They have the most lunatic hopes, these beasts; they're just fools, utter fools. That's why we like them; they are our dogs; finer dogs than any of yours. Watch this, now, a camel died last night and I have had it brought here."

Four men came up with the heavy carcass and threw it down before us. It had hardly touched the ground before the jackals lifted up their voices. As if irresistibly drawn by cords each of them began to waver forward, crawling on his belly. They had forgotten the Arabs, forgotten their hatred, the all-obliterating immediate presence of the stinking carrion bewitched them. One was already at the camel's throat, sinking his teeth straight into an artery. Like a vehement small pump endeavoring with as much determination as hopefulness to extinguish some raging fire, every muscle in his body twitched and labored at the task. In a trice they were all on top of the carcass, laboring in common, piled mountain-high.

And now the caravan leader lashed his cutting whip crisscross over their backs. They lifted their heads, half swooning in ecstasy; saw the Arabs standing before them; felt the sting of the whip on their muzzles; leaped and ran backwards a stretch. But the camel's blood was already lying in pools, reeking to heaven, the carcass was torn wide open in many places. They could not resist it; they were back again; once more the leader lifted his whip; I stayed his arm.

"You are right, sir," said he, "we'll leave them to their business; besides, it's time to break camp. Well, you've seen them. Marvelous creatures, aren't they? And how they hate us!"

KAREL ČAPEK

The Last Judgment

*T*he notorious multiple-killer Kugler, pursued by several warrants and a whole army of policemen and detectives, swore that he'd never be taken. He wasn't either—at least not alive. The last of his nine murderous deeds was shooting a policeman who tried to arrest him. The policeman indeed died, but not before putting a total of seven bullets into Kugler. Of these seven, three were fatal. Kugler's death came so quickly that he felt no pain. And so it seemed Kugler had escaped earthly justice.

When his soul left his body, it should have been surprised at the sight of the next world—a world beyond space, grey, and infinitely desolate—but it wasn't. A man who has been jailed on two continents looks upon the next life merely as new surroundings. Kugler expected to struggle through, equipped only with a bit of courage, as he had in the last world.

At length the inevitable Last Judgment got around to Kugler.

Heaven being eternally in a state of emergency, Kugler was brought before a special court of three judges and not, as his previous conduct would ordinarily merit, before a jury. The courtroom was furnished simply, almost like courtrooms on earth, with this one exception: there was no provision for swearing in witnesses. In time, however, the reason for this will become apparent.

243

The judges were old and worthy councillors with austere, bored faces. Kugler complied with the usual tedious formalities: Ferdinand Kugler, unemployed, born on such and such a date, died . . . at this point it was shown Kugler didn't know the date of his own death. Immediately he realized this was a damaging omission in the eyes of the judges; his spirit of helpfulness faded.

"Do you plead guilty or not guilty?" asked the presiding judge.

"Not guilty," said Kugler obdurately.

"Bring in the first witness," the judge sighed.

Opposite Kugler appeared an extraordinary gentleman, stately, bearded, and clothed in a blue robe strewn with golden stars.

At his entrance the judges arose. Even Kugler stood up, reluctant but fascinated. Only when the old gentleman took a seat did the judges again sit down.

"Witness," began the presiding judge, "Omniscient God, this court has summoned You in order to hear Your testimony in the case against Kugler, Ferdinand. As You are the Supreme Truth, You need not take the oath. In the interest of the proceedings, however, we ask You to keep to the subject at hand rather than branch out into particulars—unless they have a bearing on this case.

"And you, Kugler, don't interrupt the Witness. He knows everything, so there's no use denying anything.

"And now, Witness, if You would please begin."

That said, the presiding judge took off his spectacles and leaned comfortably on the bench before him, evidently in preparation for a long speech by the Witness. The oldest of the three judges nestled down in sleep. The recording angel opened the Book of Life.

God, the Witness, coughed lightly and began:

"Yes. Kugler, Ferdinand. Ferdinand Kugler, son of a factory worker, was a bad, unmanageable child from his earliest days. He loved his mother dearly, but was unable to show it; this made him unruly and defiant. Young man, you irked everyone! Do you remember how you bit your father on the thumb when he tried to spank you? You had stolen a rose from the notary's garden."

"The rose was for Irma, the tax collector's daughter," Kugler said.

"I know," said God. "Irma was seven years old at that time. Did you ever hear what happened to her?"

"No, I didn't."

"She married Oscar, the son of the factory owner. But she contracted a venereal disease from him and died of a miscarriage. You remember Rudy Zaruba?"

"What happened to him?"

"Why, he joined the navy and died accidentally in Bombay. You two were the worst boys in the whole town. Kugler, Ferdinand, was a thief before his tenth year and an inveterate liar. He kept bad company, too: old Gribble, for instance, a drunkard and an idler, living on handouts. Nevertheless, Kugler shared many of his own meals with Gribble."

The presiding judge motioned with his hand, as if much of this was perhaps unnecessary, but Kugler himself asked hesitantly, "And . . . what happened to his daughter?"

"Mary?" asked God. "She lowered herself considerably. In her fourteenth year she married. In her twentieth year she died, remembering you in the agony of her death. By your fourteenth year you were nearly a drunkard yourself, and you often ran away from home. Your father's death came about from grief and worry; your mother's eyes faded from crying. You brought dishonor to your home, and your sister, your pretty sister Martha, never married. No young man would come calling at the home of a thief. She's still living alone and in poverty, sewing until late each night. Scrimping has exhausted her, and patronizing customers hurt her pride."

"What's she doing right now?"

"This very minute she's buying thread at Wolfe's. Do you remember that shop? Once, when you were six years old, you bought a colored glass marble there. On that very same day you lost it and never, never found it. Do you remember how you cried with rage?"

"Whatever happened to it?" Kugler asked eagerly.

"Well, it rolled into the drain and under the gutterspout. As a matter of fact, it's still there, after thirty years. Right now it's raining on earth and your marble is shivering in the gush of cold water."

Kugler bent his head, overcome by this revelation.

But the presiding judge fitted his spectacles back on his nose and said mildly, "Witness, we are obliged to get on with the case. Has the accused committed murder?"

Here the Witness nodded his head.

"He murdered nine people. The first one he killed in a brawl, and it was during his prison term for this crime that he became completely corrupted. The second victim was his unfaithful sweetheart. For that he was sentenced to death, but he escaped. The third was an old man whom he robbed. The fourth was a night watchman."

"Then he died?" Kugler asked.

"He died after three days in terrible pain," God said. "And he left six children behind him. The fifth and sixth victims were an old married couple. He killed them with an axe and found only sixteen dollars, although they had twenty thousand hidden away."

Kugler jumped up.

"Where?"

"In the straw mattress," God said. "In a linen sack inside the mattress.

That's where they hid all the money they acquired from greed and penny-pinching. The seventh man he killed in America; a countryman of his, a bewildered, friendless immigrant."

"So it was in the mattress," whispered Kugler in amazement.

"Yes," continued God. "The eighth man was merely a passerby who happened to be in Kugler's way when Kugler was trying to outrun the police. At that time Kugler had periostitis and was delirious from the pain. Young man, you were suffering terribly. The ninth and last was the policeman who killed Kugler exactly when Kugler shot him."

"And why did the accused commit murder?" asked the presiding judge.

"For the same reasons others have," answered God. "Out of anger or desire for money; both deliberately and accidentally—some with pleasure, others from necessity. However, he was generous and often helpful. He was kind to women, gentle with animals, and he kept his word. Am I to mention his good deeds?"

"Thank You," said the presiding judge, "but it isn't necessary. Does the accused have anything to say in his own defense?"

"No," Kugler replied with honest indifference.

"The judges of this court will now take this matter under advisement," declared the presiding judge, and the three of them withdrew.

Only God and Kugler remained in the courtroom.

"Who are they?" asked Kugler, indicating with his head the men who had just left.

"People like you," answered God. "They were judges on earth, so they're judges here as well."

Kugler nibbled his fingertips. "I expected . . . I mean, I never really thought about it. But I figured You would judge, since—"

"Since I'm God," finished the Stately Gentleman. "But that's just it, don't you see? Because I know everything, I can't possibly judge. That wouldn't do at all. By the way, do you know who turned you in this time?"

"No, I don't," said Kugler, surprised.

"Lucky, the waitress. She did it out of jealousy."

"Excuse me," Kugler ventured, "but You forgot about that good-for-nothing Teddy I shot in Chicago."

"Not at all," God said. "He recovered and is alive this very minute. I know he's an informer, but otherwise he's a very good man and terribly fond of children. You shouldn't think of any person as being completely worthless."

"But I still don't understand why You aren't the judge," Kugler said thoughtfully.

"Because my knowledge is infinite. If judges knew everything, absolutely everything, then they would also understand everything. Their hearts would ache. They couldn't sit in judgment—and neither can I. As it is, they know only about your crimes. I know all about you. The entire Kugler. And that's why I cannot judge."

"But why are they judging . . . the same people who were judges on earth?"

"Because man belongs to man. As you see, I'm only the witness. But the verdict is determined by man, even in heaven. Believe me, Kugler, this is the way it should be. Man isn't worthy of divine judgment. He deserves to be judged only by other men."

At that moment the three returned from their deliberation.

In heavy tones the presiding judge announced, "For repeated crimes of first degree murder, manslaughter, robbery, disrespect for the law, illegally carrying weapons, and for the theft of a rose: Kugler, Ferdinand, is sentenced to lifelong punishment in hell. The sentence is to begin immediately.

"Next case, please: Torrance, Frank."

"Is the accused present in court?"

*Strates Myriveles (Strates Stamatopoulos) (1892–
), one of Greece's foremost men of letters, was
born on the island of Lesbos. After studying literature and law at the University of Athens, he was for
many years a journalist. He was director of the
Greek Parliament Library and also was general program director of the Greek National Broadcasting
Institute from 1936–1959. In 1958, Myriveles was
elected to the Greek National Academy; he served
four times as president of the Greek National Writers Society. His realistic novels and short stories,
which have had great influence on modern Greek literature, are characterized by lyrical expression and
sharp delineation of character. Outside of Greece, he
is best known for* Life in the Tomb *(1932).*

STRATES MYRIVELES

The Chronicle of an Old Rose-Tree

I want to write the story of a rose-tree. We lived together for sixteen long years, sixteen of the most significant years of my life, replete with harrowing events. I loved that rose-tree, for she was an old rose-tree with many branches and many roses. I feel she was fond of me, too. Such a feeling can blossom between a man and a tree.

I know a true, strange story, told to me at Mytilini, a long time ago by some old convicts who were serving life-sentences at Castro. One of them had committed an appalling murder. He set fire to his house and burned up his wife and children—thinking the children weren't his. He was the one who told me what happened, his eyes scalding in tears. Such a mystery is man.

During his long years behind bars, he was once acquainted with another convict, a lad who had come to prison fresh as a daisy, and had left as a man with gray hair. In the prison yard, the lad planted a walnut; it sprouted. All his thoughts and cares from that time on were for tending this plant. For fear that it might get hurt before it became strong he surrounded it with wire; he watered it with his ration of drinking water. Years passed, and the lad became a man; the walnut tree grew up, sturdy and joyful.

One day the warden called the man into his office. He had been granted a pardon, and he could get his stuff and go. The prisoner stood speechless, amazed.

"And the walnut tree?" he stammered.

"What do you mean, the walnut tree?"

"I have no one in the world but that walnut tree," said the stunned prisoner.

The warden laughed.

"Well, what can we do? The walnut tree has to stay in its place."

The prisoner lowered his head; he could speak no more. He made a bundle of his rags. He sat on the horse-block facing the tree, and looked at it and shed bitter tears. Then a miracle happened, witnessed by all the prisoners who still tell of it. In the spring time of its life, all green with fresh, cool foliage, the tree began to wither. The leaves turned ragged and yellow; they crumpled completely, and fell. The trunk too, dried down to its roots.

The old man's eyes were big with burning tears while he told me this story.

But my rose-tree did not commit suicide because of grief. A knife cut off her life.

But let me tell her story from the beginning.

When the Germans entered Athens, I received a telegram from my uncle who owned a house there. He was stranded on Lesbos, where he died a year later, at eighty-five. His telegram told me to move my wife and children immediately into his vacant home—before the Germans requisitioned it.

It was an old Athenian mansion, two stories, with eight large rooms, and a small garden in front. A beautiful trellis overarched the garden gate; each spring the fragrance of leaves and flowers filled all of Eresso Street. In the middle of the yard, in the middle of a white and gray marble patio, there stood the rose-tree: a grand rose-tree. How old was she? I seem to remember her from my student years when I went sometimes to visit my uncle. Three trunks grew upward for more than six feet, each trunk big as my arm. Higher, a multitude of branches were always loaded with roses, and gave off a strong scent, winter and summer, for the blossoms appeared the year round. Around the courtyard was an iron fence, and the rose-tree hung over the spiked top, enticing the passers-by with her roses.

My uncle, the owner, was a strange old bachelor who spent most of his life in this house. As a student he came from the island, and he had rented one of its rooms from the first owner, an old French countess. Finally he bought the house and let her stay until she died of old age. She was a childless woman, alone, without anyone in the world. Alone, she idled her time reading old Parisian magazines, or she sometimes hummed Parisian songs of times past. She hummed them softly and heard them all alone. My uncle was like a parched reed; he lived alone there during and after his student years, an engineer by profession. He was slender, tall, austere, and always an elegant, meticulous dresser. He wore a fuzzed gray top hat, dangled a slim cane, and wrote in an impeccable *katharevousa*. He lived all alone beneath the gilded ceilings in those eight large rooms.

My uncle, it seemed, was also in love with the rose-tree; and she must have been the one and only love in his life, a life never adorned by a woman's grace. I say he must have been in love, for when the rose-tree grew tall above the iron spikes, the street urchins climbed the fence to gather the flowers. One day my uncle seized his pistol and chased them away—like a jealous lover. That day he called in workers to double the height of the iron fence so that no young rival could molest his tree.

In the sixteen years I lived there the rose-tree grew taller and taller, and put new branches over the second iron spikes.

My study was on the ground floor. It looked out a large window and into the yard. There the flowers of the rose-tree were abundant and rich in fragrance, for they were mayroses. To be sure the tree bloomed best in spring, but miraculously there were also blossoms in winter, in the fall, and all the year round. Even when Athens was covered with snow, she kept giving roses. If I opened my window, she spilled her branches into my room, soothing the bitter years of the occupation and the Communist reign of terror. She gave me great comfort. She was a symbol of hope. We were cold and hungry. We listened to the bullets ricochetting off the iron fence, but the rose-tree moved her blooming branches near us. No matter, we used to say. The sun will rise again, the grapes and peaches will bear fruit again, and love will come again to men who have become wild beasts, driven by a stupid, incomprehensible hate.

The streets had become deserted; no one dared show his face. One day a young woman passed by Exarcheia, hugging the walls. She held a bottle of milk. A rascal, on a rooftop, saw her, took aim and fired, killing her. Two or three neighbors rushed out to the rescue. Holding the bottle tight to her chest, she lived long enough to say:

"Give the milk to my child, neighbors. . . ."

Then she died.

I cut a rose, put it in a vase on my desk, in memory of the unknown mother. Later, peace gradually came and Greek ceased to fear Greek. Spring came, and our rose-tree reddened from top to bottom. It was so old, and yet so brimming with youth. Passers-by walked outside and stopped on the sidewalk to look at it, as one looks at a beautiful woman. They smiled at her and inhaled her strong fragrance. Couples in love stopped and asked for a rose. My jealous uncle was no longer alive, and those of us in the courtyard offered the blossoms. When we were not at home, a young gallant clambered up the fence, and holding to an iron spike, reached out to steal a rose for his young, fair Juliana.

Once I watched him from my desk, scampering down, jumping back red of face, redder than his rose, looking all round for fear that he might have been seen. The man behind the window saw him and smiled, for he too had stolen roses and even now, on occasion, cannot leave them alone. But the lad was not aware of that. The young man was of heroic countenance, as if he had plucked an edelweiss from the steepest peak of the Alps. For that, the man inside smiles at the rose-tree whose pillaged branch is still moving. The two exchange an understanding glance, so intended.

Then the good old days returned. Holy week came, churches opened their doors, and the Athenians swallowed their tears and waited for Easter. Then the maidens of the neighborhood came—and Neapolis has many lovely maidens—knocked at our door and asked that the rose-tree contribute to the decoration of the Epitaph. The young myrrh-bearers left with their baskets full.

All this, and much more, belongs to the Annals of the Rose-tree. I wonder how much more interesting the old rose-tree's diary would be, starting with the time when the hands of the young French aristocrat first planted and watered the bush every evening from the well of the yard. Those hands which aged year by year within the eight empty rooms, withered, disfigured, died, and disintegrated many years ago.

And so did that young islander, the student of the Polytechnic, for forty years the only occupant of the house, who lived, grew, and grayed near the rose-tree. That jealous lover of hers who once when he saw a flock of urchins plundering its roses, chased them, waving his pistol. At that time he was a high state official, with a white mustache and a thin cane with a silver handle. He remained faithful to our rose-tree till he died.

Our old rose-tree also had its heroic and tragic days. Every March 25 of our four-year occupation by the Germans, every October 28 of our cruel occupation, my children and all young school children, cut all the roses to take to the tomb of the Unknown Soldier. Schoolboys and girls marched in procession with bouquets held high, and with the National Anthem on their lips. All around, bullets from the machine guns hissed; the armored car tracks chewed Athen's asphalt. But our children advanced in formation, still singing. They looked hungry and gaunt, their legs emaciated, the bloom of youth gone from their faces.

But high in their hands, above their heads, the roses shone red. The conquerors grabbed the flowers, trampled them furiously. The children returned dusty, dirty, ragged, bruised, beaten by rifle butts. But their great eyes shone with the Greek flame that burned inside them day and night.

Then came the blackest December that ever hovered over Athens. For forty days mortars boomed and burst, shattering the branches of the rose-tree. Neapolis was stunned, silent in fear and horror. One day the old rose-tree stooped: below her branches the sidewalk by our gate was red. It was not the red paint with which the maniacs splashed walls with their slogans of fratricide. It was blood. Real, warm, oozing blood gushing from large wounds from a street that had known only the joyful shouts of children. Now the street echoed the moans of murdered men, six or seven innocent persons dying there.

After their homes had been blown up by the maniacs, these men had started from a corner of Athens, roving the streets, seeking shelter. A little bell hung from the top of our yard gate. My wife heard the bell ringing, ringing furiously. Germans, she thought, and was afraid to open the gate. When the row ceased, she found in front of our gate a heap of wretched, bloody corpses. These men had been ringing the little bell, seeking refuge.

But our old rose-tree was still there. Her roses spread and heartened us. Roses are everywhere, she said to us. It is enough to push aside the leaves and thorns, she kept telling us. Always there is a cool spring, delicate and pure, waiting, its hands filled with flowers. Even in the heartaches of men there is green in the heart of winter. Heave open your soul's windows, and they will find a way of placing their bouquets inside. Deep inside.

When I first occupied the house, the rose-tree filled the whole square of the yard, in the plot of ground at the center of the flagstone patio. Then two significant events occurred in that space. First, a new little plant sprung from the soil; no one knew what it was. Partaking of the water we gave the rose-tree, it kept growing under the rose's shade. When the new plant was about knee-high, a friend who knew about trees told us that by its leaves it looked like a plum-tree. Each year it grew fast, taking its water and nourishment from the same soil that fed the thick roots of the rose-tree. With the years, its slender trunk made its way through the branches that shaded it and popped out in full view of the sun it had been reaching for. It had become a grown tree, a strong, powerful tree that selfishly overwhelmed our rose-tree.

One spring, for the first time, its foliage filled with white blossoms, and then its branches bowed with red plums. It was bedecked with fruit like a Christmas tree. It covered the rose-tree, spread its branches triumphantly above the yard, and hung its plums invitingly over the iron fence. The street urchins no longer climbed the fence for roses. Suspended from the fence, they reached the tips of the plum branches and filled their pockets with unripe plums. The shady branches of the plum had shrouded the rose-tree which had accorded it hospitality for so many years, and the rose-tree began to wither. The other was a new life, rampant, straining for light and juices; under the earth its roots swelled strong and avid, clutched the roots of the rose-tree, hugging them, twining around them, and sucking their soil. I watched this drama day after day. Now the plum tree soared in full beauty and untrammeled youth, spread its branches everywhere, conquered air, and light, and also conquered the soil.

Our rose-tree began to wither. Most of the trunks began to rot, and I cut them to rid the space of dried up branches. Each spring a few new shoots sprang from the roots, but they made little progress. They were sickly and feeble. They grew a little, then they wilted and withered. The remaining stalk produced only a few flowers. There was no longer the abundance of past years. But the rose-tree persisted in giving forth some flowers, in revealing her presence even in this desperate battle. Finally she made the great decision. She imitated her adversary. From a large, thick bush, she became a climbing rose. She gathered all her remaining forces into upward growth and began to climb the plum tree, in two twining tresses, like two green snakes that twirled upward in search of the sun. To succeed in this, she used as support the very stout trunk of the plum tree. She clung to it and began to climb among its limbs. It was a relentless struggle to the end. Each time the two stalks gained growth, they stopped to rest at that step, on some node of the tree, and then sprang upward again.

We saw this metamorphosis and thought that that was the end, that we would no longer see roses. Then we stopped paying attention to what was happening. By now the rose was so entwined with the plum tree that we could no longer tell them apart.

Meanwhile, the plum tree grew taller, as high as our two-story house. On the second floor, above my study, was my son's study. I rarely went up there because I did not want to intrude while he worked. But one day, when he was away in the country, I entered the room and stood at the window. When I opened the outside shutters, suddenly a branch whisked in and a fragrance caressed my face. It was a large cluster of roses. They had bloomed in the crown of the plum tree, in the splendid sun, a trophy, and a shout of victory.

It was something thrilling.

From then on, high up in the branches of the plum tree, we saw more roses. The last roses kept blooming.

The plum tree was the first, most significant event in the life of the old rose-tree. The second event was something more modest, but quite pleasing.

In the enclosed square where the two trees stood, from the year that we moved into the house, there grew two night-blooming plants. They sprang up each year, on opposite sides of the square, one to the left, one to the right. Who knows where the seeds came from? Each year the two stems emerged. They were fragile, succulent, full of sap and vigor. When fall came, they put out red buds which opened at dusk and gave forth a strong aroma all through the night. It was a sweet aroma that one could almost taste. In bloom they stood on each side of the rose and the plum tree like two large lighted candlesticks. They withered with winter, and we raked them away with the leaves. In time the soil was trampled on, and the earth became hard as concrete. The plants poked up again, nevertheless, each late spring, all freshness anew, growing within a few days and becoming loaded with buds. We had these annuals all sixteen years that we had the house.

Now the old mansion has been torn down in order to raise a new building. Down came the double iron fence that protected the rose-tree from her passing lovers. And down came the plum tree, chopped down, falling with the rose-tree in its embrace. So were the two luminous night-blooming plants extinguished forever. And with them died the romantic memory of the old French countess, whose spirit till then only the flowers of the rose-tree evoked. And so remembrance of the tall, slender old bachelor died, too, he who guarded the roses with his loaded revolver.

In this short story I wanted to save some vestiges from the life of sixteen years, a life filled with fears and griefs, and with the joys and anguish of children and trees.

Isaac (Emmanuilovich) Babel (1894–1941) was born in Odessa, the son of a Jewish shopkeeper; at fifteen he graduated from the Nicholas I Commercial School and began to write stories in French. His friendship with Maxim Gorky was an important factor in his literary development. Following Gorky's advice, Babel sought a life of "adventure" and during the civil war was assigned to Budyonny's cavalry as a correspondent for ROSTA (later TASS); service in Poland became the basis of his most famous collection of stories, Red Cavalry *(1926). A recurring theme in the Cossack tales is the manner in which a protagonist—often an intellectual, a Jew—comes to terms with violence or the value judgment that a man's true worth is in his ability to fight. Babel was arrested in 1939; his death certificate is dated two years later. After fourteen years, ironically, his death sentence was "revoked." For further reading:* Odessa Stories *(1923);* The Collected Stories *1955).*

ISAAC BABEL

The Awakening

*A*ll the people in our circle—small-time middlemen, shop-keepers, clerks in banks and steamship offices—were teaching their children music. Our fathers, seeing no way out for themselves, had struck on the notion of a lottery. This lottery they founded on the bones of the little ones. Odessa was possessed by this madness more than other towns were and, true enough, for several decades running our town supplied the Wunderkinder for the concert platforms of the world. Mischa Elman, Zimbalist, Gabrilovitch—they all came from Odessa! Jascha Heifetz got his start among us.

When a boy turned four or five his mother would lead the tiny and puny creature to Mr. Zagursky. Zagursky ran a factory of Wunderkinder, a factory that turned out Jewish dwarfs in little lace collars and little pumps of patent leather. He sought them out in the lairs of Moldavanka, in the malodorous courtyards of the Old Market. Zagursky gave them the first

255

impetus; later on the children were sent off to Professor Auer in St. Petersburg. Mighty harmony dwelt within the souls of these starvelings with their
bloated livid heads. They became celebrated virtuosi. And so my father
decided to catch up with them, even though I was overage for a Wunder-
kind—I was going on fourteen; in height and puniness, however, I might
have passed for an eight-year-old. Which constituted the last hope.

I was led off to Zagursky. Because of his high regard for my grandfather he consented to take only one rouble for each lesson—a cheap enough
rate. My grandfather, Leivi Itzok, was the laughingstock of the town and, at
the same time, its ornament. He walked about the streets in an opera hat
and foot clouts and resolved points of doubt in the most obscure matters.
They would ask him what a Gobelin was, why the Jacobins had betrayed
Robespierre, how synthetic silk was prepared, what the Caesarian section
was. My grandfather was able to answer all these questions. So, out of high
regard for his learning and madness Zagursky took only one rouble a lesson
from us. And it was also because he was afraid of Grandfather that he went
to a lot of bother with me, since there was really nothing to bother with.
The sounds slithered off my violin like metal shavings. These sounds grated
on my own heart, yet my father would not give up. The talk at home was
about nothing but Mischa Elman, who had been exempted from military
service by the Czar himself. Zimbalist, according to information gathered
by my father, had been presented to the King of England and had played at
Buckingham Palace; the parents of Gabrilovitch had bought two mansions
in St. Petersburg. These Wunderkinder had brought riches to their parents.
My father might have reconciled himself to poverty, but fame was something he had to have.

"It is impossible," people who dined at his expense used to murmur in
his ear, "it is impossible that the grandson of such a grandfather should
fail—" However, my mind was on other things. During my violin exercises
I would put the books of Turgenev or Dumas on the music stand and, as I
scraped away, kept devouring page after page. In the daytime I told all sorts
of cock-and-bull stories to the little boys in the neighborhood; at night I
transferred these stories to paper. Writing was a hereditary compulsion in
the family. Leivi Itzok, who had become touched in his old age, had been
writing a novel all his life under the title of *The Man Without a Head*. I took
after him.

Three times a week, loaded down with violin case and music, I used to
plod to Witte Street (at one time called Gentry Street), to Zagursky's studio.
There, lined along the wall awaiting their turns, hysterically fervent Jewish
women sat hugging against their weak knees violins the dimensions of
which exceeded those of the beings who were slated to play them in Buckingham Palace.

The door to the sanctum would open. Big-headed, freckled children with necks as slender as flower stalks and a hectic flush on their cheeks would come staggering out of Zagursky's study. The door would slam to after swallowing up the next dwarf. On the other side of the wall the teacher, sporting a Windsor tie, and curly red hair and legs more fluid than solid, was straining himself, chanting the notes and conducting. The director of this monstrous lottery was populating Moldavanka and the stygian dead ends of the Old Market with the specters of pizzicato and cantilena. Later on Professor Auer brought this sing-song to a diabolical brilliance.

I had no business among these sectarians. Much the same sort of dwarf as all of them, I nevertheless discerned a different admonition in the voice of my ancestors.

The first step came hard to me. One day I left the house laden like a beast of burden with violin case, violin, notes and twelve roubles—payment for a month's tuition. I was walking along Nezhinskaya Street and should have turned into Gentry Street to get to Zagursky's house; instead I went up Tiraspolskaya and found myself in the port. The hours supposed to be spent in learning the violin flew by in Practical Harbor. Thus did my liberation begin. Zagursky's reception room never saw me again. Matters of greater importance took up all my thoughts. Together with Nemanov, a classmate of mine, I took to haunting the steamer *Kensington,* visiting a certain old sailor by the name of Mr. Trottybairn. Nemanov was a year younger than I, but from the age of eight he had been carrying on the most intricate trading in the world. He was a genius in business and carried out whatever he promised to do. He is now a millionaire in New York, a director of the General Motors company, a firm which is just as tremendous as Ford. Nemanov dragged me along everywhere because I submitted to him in all things without offering a word of objection. He used to buy tobacco pipes from Mr. Trottybairn which were smuggled in. These pipes were turned out at Lincoln by a brother of the old sailor.

"Gentlemen," Mr. Trottybairn used to say to us, "mark my word: children must be made with one's own hands. Smoking a factory-made pipe is the same as putting an enema tube into your mouth. Do you know who Benvenuto Cellini was? There was a master! My brother in Lincoln could tell you about him. My brother doesn't stand in anybody's way. He is simply convinced that children must be made with one's own hands and not the hands of others. We cannot do otherwise than agree with him, gentlemen."

Nemanov sold Trottybairn's pipes to bank directors, foreign consuls, wealthy Greeks. He made 100 percent profit on them.

The pipes of the Lincoln master breathed poesy. A thought, a drop of eternity had been set within each one of them. A small yellow eye glinted in the mouthpiece of each; their cases were lined with satin. I tried to picture to myself how Matthew Trottybairn, the last of the master pipe makers, was living in old England as he resisted the course of things.

"We cannot do otherwise than agree, gentlemen, that children must be made with one's own hands."

The heavy waves near the sea wall removed me further and further from our house, permeated with the smell of onions and Jewish destiny. From Practical Harbor I migrated to the other side of the breakwater, where a small patch of sandy shoal was inhabited by urchins from Seafront Street. They did not bother putting on their pants from morning till night, diving under the wherries, stealing coconuts for their dinner, and biding their time till the watermelon-laden barges would come trailing one another from Kherson and Kamenka and they would have a chance to split some of these watermelons against the stanchions in the port.

To be able to swim became a dream of mine. It was shameful to confess to these bronzed urchins that I, who had been born in Odessa, had not seen the sea until I was ten and that at fourteen I still did not know how to swim.

How late it befell me to learn the things one had to know! In my childhood, nailed down to the Gemara, I had led the life of a sage; when I grew up I took to climbing trees.

The ability to swim proved beyond me. The hydrophobia of all my ancestors—Spanish rabbis and Frankford money-changers—kept dragging me to the bottom. The water would not bear me up. Covered with welts, bloated with briny water, I would return to shore, to my violin and notes. I was bound to the instruments of my crime and was dragging them with me. The struggle of the rabbis against the sea continued until such time as the water god of those places—Ephim Nikitich Smolich, a proofreader on the Odessa *News*—took pity on me. Pity for little Jewish boys dwelt within the athletic bosom of this man. He was supreme ruler over hordes of rachitic starvelings. Nikitich used to collect them from the bedbug-ridden hovels of Moldavanka, lead them to the sea, bury them in the sand, do gymnastics with them, dive with them, teach them songs and, as he broiled himself under the direct rays of the sun, would tell them stories about fishermen and animals. To grownups Nikitich explained that he was a natural philosopher. The Jewish children laughed so hard at Nikitich's stories that they rolled on the ground; they fawned and squealed like puppies. The sun spattered them with crawling freckles that were the color of lizards.

This old man watched my monomachy against the sea as a silent by-stander. Perceiving that the fight was hopeless and that I would never learn how to swim, he included me among the number of the lodgers in his heart. All of it was here with us, that gay heart of his; it never put on airs, it was not tainted with greed and was not disquieted. With his coppery shoulders, the head of an aged gladiator and bronzed legs that were just the least bit bandy, he would lie in our midst beyond the breakwater as if he were the sovereign of those waters abounding in watermelon rinds and reeking of kerosene. I came to love this man as only a boy afflicted with hysteria and headaches can come to love an athlete. I would not leave his side and tried to be of service to him.

"Don't go at it so hard," he told me. "Strengthen your nerves. Swimming will come of itself. How can it be that the water won't bear you up— why shouldn't it?"

Noticing how I was drawn to him, Nikitich made an exception of me among all his disciples, inviting me to visit him in his clean, roomy garret carpeted with matting, showed me his dogs, his hedgehog, turtle and pigeons. In exchange for his largess I brought him a tragedy I had written recently.

"I just knew that you wrote a bit," said Nikitich. "You even have that look about you. More and more often your eyes don't watch anything in particular—"

He read my writings, shrugged, passed his hand over his short gray curls, paced about his garret a little.

"I would guess," he pronounced drawlingly, pausing after each word, "that the divine spark is in you—"

We went out into the street. The old man stopped, tapped his stick hard against the sidewalk and fixed me with his eyes.

"What do you lack? The fact that you're young is no calamity—that will pass with the years. . . . What you lack is a feeling for nature."

With his stick he pointed out a tree to me; it had a brownish trunk and a low crown.

"What tree is that?"

I did not know.

"What's growing on that bush?"

I did not know that either. We were walking through a small square on the Alexandrovsky Prospect. The old man kept pointing his stick at all the trees; he clutched my shoulder whenever birds happened to fly past and compelled me to listen to the individual voice of each.

"What bird is singing now?"

I could not tell him anything in answer. The names of trees and birds, their division into genera, where the birds were flying to, what direction the sun rose in, when the dew was heaviest—all these things were beyond my ken.

"And you have the audacity to write? A man who does not live in the midst of nature the way a stone or an animal lives won't write two worthwhile lines in his whole lifetime. Your landscapes resemble descriptions of stage sets. What were your parents thinking about for fourteen years, may the Devil take me?"

What had my parents been thinking about? About protested promissory notes, about Mischa Elman's mansions. I did not say anything about this to Nikitich; I kept my mouth shut.

At home, during dinner, I did not touch my food. It stuck in my throat.

"A feeling for nature!" I kept thinking. "My God, why had no conception of that ever entered my head? Where can I find a man who will explain everything to me about the ways of birds and the names of trees? What do I know about them? I might be able to recognize lilacs—and even then only when they're in bloom. Lilacs—and acacias. De Ribas and Greek streets are lined with acacias—"

At dinner Father told a new story about Jascha Heifetz. Just before reaching Robinat's, Father had run into Mendelson, Jascha's uncle. The boy, it turned out, was getting eight hundred roubles for each appearance. Count that up—see how much that comes to if one gives fifteen concerts a month!

I did count it up: the result was twelve thousand a month. As I was doing the multiplication and carrying four, I happened to look out the window. In a gently billowing cape, with his tightly coiled, rusty-colored curls struggling out from under his soft hat, leaning upon a cane, Mr. Zagursky, my music teacher, was making stately progress through our small, concrete-paved courtyard. One could hardly say that he had been very prompt in discovering my truancy. By now more than three months had passed since my violin had foundered on the sands near the breakwater.

Zagursky was approaching our front door. I made a dash for the back entrance—and remembered it had been nailed up the evening before to keep burglars out. Whereupon I locked myself in the washroom. Within half an hour the whole family had gathered around my door. The women were weeping. One of my grandmothers was rubbing her fat shoulder against the door and going off into hysterical peals of sobbing. My father was silent. When he did break into speech he was quieter and more articulate than he had ever been in his whole life.

"I am an officer in the army," said my father. "I have an estate. I go hunting. The mouzhiks pay me rent. I have placed my son in the Cadet Corps. There is no need for me to worry about my son—"

He fell silent. The women were breathing hard. Then a terrific blow crashed against the washroom door. My father was pounding against it with his whole body; he persisted in running full tilt against it.

"I am an officer in the army!" he was screaming. "I go hunting! I'll kill him—this is the end!"

The hook flew off the door; there was a bolt on the door—it was still holding by a single nail. The women were rolling on the floor, they were catching my father's legs; out of his mind by now, he was struggling to get free. An old woman—my father's mother—came hurrying to find out what the hubbub was about.

"My child," she said to her son in Yiddish, "great is our grief. It has no bounds. The only thing lacking in our house is bloodshed. I do not want to see bloodshed in our house—"

My father broke into moans. I heard his steps receding. The bolt was hanging by its single nail.

I sat in my fortress till nightfall. When everybody had gone to bed my Aunt Bobka led me off to my grandmother's. The way there was a long one. The moonlight lay in a catalepsy upon unknown bushes, upon trees for which there were no names. . . . Some unseen bird in the distance emitted a whistle and became extinguished: it may have gone to sleep. . . . What bird was it? What did they call it? Is there any dewfall of evenings? Where is the constellation of Ursa Major located? Where does the sun rise? . . .

We were walking along Post Office Street. Aunt Bobka had a firm hold of my hand, so that I would not run away. She was right. Flight was what I had in mind.

JEAN-PAUL SARTRE

The Wall

*T*hey pushed us into a big white room and I began to blink because the light hurt my eyes. Then I saw a table and four men behind the table, civilians, looking over the papers. They had bunched another group of prisoners in the back and we had to cross the whole room to join them. There were several I knew and some others who must have been foreigners. The two in front of me were blond with round skulls; they looked alike. I suppose they were French. The smaller one kept hitching up his pants; nerves.

It lasted about three hours; I was dizzy and my head was empty; but the room was well heated and I found that pleasant enough: for the past 24 hours we hadn't stopped shivering. The guards brought the prisoners up to the table, one after the other. The four men asked each one his name and occupation. Most of the time they didn't go any further—or they would simply ask a question here and there: "Did you have anything to do with the sabotage of munitions?" Or "Where were you the morning of the 9th and what were you doing?" They didn't listen to the answers or at least didn't seem to. They were quiet for a moment and then looking straight in front of them began to write. They asked Tom if it were true he was in the International Brigade; Tom couldn't tell them otherwise because of the papers they found in his coat. They didn't ask Juan anything but they wrote for a long time after he told them his name.

"My brother José is the anarchist," Juan said, "you know he isn't here any more. I don't belong to any party, I never had anything to do with politics."

They didn't answer. Juan went on, "I haven't done anything. I don't want to pay for somebody else."

His lips trembled. A guard shut him up and took him away. It was my turn.

"Your name is Pablo Ibbieta?"

"Yes."

The man looked at the papers and asked me, "Where's Ramon Gris?"

"I don't know."

"You hid him in your house from the 6th to the 19th."

"No."

They wrote for a minute and then the guards took me out. In the corridor Tom and Juan were waiting between two guards. We started walking. Tom asked one of the guards, "So?"

"So what?" the guard said.

"Was that the cross-examination or the sentence?"

"Sentence," the guard said.

"What are they going to do with us?"

The guard answered dryly, "Sentence will be read in your cell."

As a matter of fact, our cell was one of the hospital cellars. It was terrifically cold there because of the drafts. We shivered all night and it wasn't much better during the day. I had spent the previous five days in a cell in a monastery, a sort of hole in the wall that must have dated from the middle ages: since there were a lot of prisoners and not much room, they locked us up anywhere. I didn't miss my cell; I hadn't suffered too much from the cold but I was alone; after a long time it gets irritating. In the cellar I had company. Juan hardly ever spoke: he was afraid and he was too young to have anything to say. But Tom was a good talker and he knew Spanish well.

There was a bench in the cellar and four mats. When they took us back we sat and waited in silence. After a long moment, Tom said, "We're screwed."

"I think so too," I said, "but I don't think they'll do anything to the kid."

"They don't have a thing against him," said Tom. "He's the brother of a militiaman and that's all."

I looked at Juan: he didn't seem to hear. Tom went on, "You know what they do in Saragossa? They lay the men down on the road and run over them with trucks. A Moroccan deserter told us that. They said it was to save ammunition."

"It doesn't save gas," I said.

I was annoyed at Tom: he shouldn't have said that.

"Then there's officers walking along the road," he went on, "supervising it all. They stick their hands in their pockets and smoke cigarettes. You think they finish off the guys? Hell no. They let them scream. Sometimes for an hour. The Moroccan said he damned near puked the first time."

"I don't believe they'll do that here," I said. "Unless they're really short on ammunition."

Day was coming in through four airholes and a round opening they had made in the ceiling on the left, and you could see the sky through it. Through this hole, usually closed by a trap, they unloaded coal into the cellar. Just below the hole there was a big pile of coal dust; it had been used to heat the hospital but since the beginning of the war the patients were evacuated and the coal stayed there, unused; sometimes it even got rained on because they had forgotten to close the trap.

Tom began to shiver. "Good Jesus Christ I'm cold," he said. "Here it goes again."

He got up and began to do exercises. At each movement his shirt opened on his chest, white and hairy. He lay on his back, raised his legs in the air and bicycled. I saw his great rump trembling. Tom was husky but he had too much fat. I thought how rifle bullets or the sharp points of bayonets would soon be sunk into this mass of tender flesh as in a lump of butter. It wouldn't have made me feel like that if he'd been thin.

I wasn't exactly cold, but I couldn't feel my arms and shoulders any more. Sometimes I had the impression I was missing something and began to look around for my coat and then suddenly remembered they hadn't given me a coat. It was rather uncomfortable. They took our clothes and gave them to their soldiers, leaving us only our shirts—and those canvas pants that hospital patients wear in the middle of summer. After a while Tom got up and sat next to me, breathing heavily.

"Warmer?"

"Good Christ, no. But I'm out of wind."

Around eight o'clock in the evening a major came in with two *falangistas*. He had a sheet of paper in his hand. He asked the guard, "What are the names of those three?"

"Steinbock, Ibbieta and Mirbal," the guard said.

The major put on his eyeglasses and scanned the list: "Steinbock . . . Steinbock . . . Oh yes . . . You are sentenced to death. You will be shot tomorrow morning." He went on looking. "The other two as well."

"That's not possible," Juan said. "Not me."

The major looked at him amazed. "What's your name?"

"Juan Mirbal," he said.

"Well, your name is there," said the major. "You're sentenced."

"I didn't do anything," Juan said.

The major shrugged his shoulders and turned to Tom and me.

"You're Basque?"

"Nobody is Basque."

He looked annoyed. "They told me there were three Basques. I'm not going to waste my time running after them. Then naturally you don't want a priest?"

We didn't even answer.

He said, "A Belgian doctor is coming shortly. He is authorized to spend the night with you." He made a military salute and left.

"What did I tell you," Tom said. "We get it."

"Yes," I said, "it's a rotten deal for the kid."

I said that to be decent but I didn't like the kid. His face was too thin and fear and suffering had disfigured it, twisting all his features. Three days before he was a smart sort of kid, not too bad; but now he looked like an old fairy and I thought how he'd never be young again, even if they were to let him go. It wouldn't have been too hard to have a little pity for him but pity disgusts me, or rather it horrifies me. He hadn't said anything more but he had turned grey; his face and hands were both grey. He sat down again and looked at the ground with round eyes. Tom was good hearted, he wanted to take his arm, but the kid tore himself away violently and made a face.

"Let him alone," I said in a low voice, "you can see he's going to blubber."

Tom obeyed regretfully; he would have liked to comfort the kid, it would have passed his time and he wouldn't have been tempted to think about himself. But it annoyed me: I'd never thought about death because I never had any reason to, but now the reason was here and there was nothing to do but think about it.

Tom began to talk. "So you think you've knocked guys off, do you?" he asked me. I didn't answer. He began explaining to me that he had knocked off six since the beginning of August; he didn't realize the situation and I could tell he didn't *want* to realize it. I hadn't quite realized it myself, I wondered if it hurt much, I thought of bullets, I imagined their burning hail through my body. All that was beside the real question; but I was calm: we had all night to understand. After a while Tom stopped talking and I watched him out of the corner of my eye; I saw he too had turned grey and he looked rotten; I told myself "Now it starts." It was almost dark, a dim glow filtered through the airholes and the pile of coal and made a big stain beneath the spot of sky; I could already see a star through the hole in the ceiling: the night would be pure and icy.

The door opened and two guards came in, followed by a blonde man in a tan uniform. He saluted us. "I am the doctor," he said. "I have authorization to help you in these trying hours."

He had an agreeable and distinguished voice. I said, "What do you want here?"

"I am at your disposal. I shall do all I can to make your last moments less difficult."

"What did you come here for? There are others, the hospital's full of them."

"I was sent here," he answered with a vague look. "Ah! Would you like to smoke?" he asked hurriedly, "I have cigarettes and even cigars."

He offered us English cigarettes and *puros,* but we refused. I looked him in the eyes and he seemed irritated. I said to him, "You aren't here on an errand of mercy. Beside, I know you. I saw you with the fascists in the barracks yard the day I was arrested."

I was going to continue, but something surprising suddenly happened to me; the presence of this doctor no longer interested me. Generally when I'm on somebody I don't let go. But the desire to talk left me completely; I shrugged and turned my eyes away. A little later I raised my head; he was watching me curiously. The guards were sitting on a mat. Pedro, the tall thin one, was twiddling his thumbs, the other shook his head from time to time to keep from falling asleep.

"Do you want a light?" Pedro suddenly asked the doctor. The other nodded "Yes": I think he was about as smart as a log, but he surely wasn't bad. Looking in his cold blue eyes it seemed to me that his only sin was lack of imagination. Pedro went out and came back with an oil lamp which he set on the corner of the bench. It gave a bad light but it was better than nothing: they had left us in the dark the night before. For a long time I watched the circle of light the lamp made on the ceiling. I was fascinated. Then suddenly I woke up, the circle of light disappeared and I felt myself crushed under an enormous weight. It was not the thought of death or fear; it was nameless. My cheeks burned and my head ached.

I shook myself and looked at my two friends. Tom had hidden his face in his hands. I could only see the fat white nape of his neck. Little Juan was the worst; his mouth was open and his nostrils trembled. The doctor went to him and put his hand on his shoulder to comfort him, but his eyes stayed cold. Then I saw the Belgian's hand drop stealthily along Juan's arm, down to the wrist. Juan paid no attention. The Belgian took his wrist between three fingers, distractedly, the same time drawing back a little and turning his back to me. But I leaned backward and saw him take a watch from his pocket and look at it for a moment, never letting go of the wrist. After a minute he let the hand fall inert and went and leaned his back against the wall, then, as if he suddenly remembered something very important which had to be jotted down on the spot, he took a notebook from his pocket and wrote a few lines. "Bastard," I thought angrily, "let him come and take my pulse. I'll shove my fist in his rotten face."

He didn't come but I felt him watching me. I raised my head and returned his look. Impersonally, he said to me, "Doesn't it seem cold to you here?" He looked cold, he was blue.

"I'm not cold," I told him.

He never took his hard eyes off me. Suddenly I understood and my hands went to my face: I was drenched in sweat. In this cellar, in the midst of winter, in the midst of drafts, I was sweating. I ran my hands through my hair, gummed together with perspiration; at the same time I saw my shirt was damp and sticking to my skin: I had been dripping for an hour and hadn't felt it. But that swine of a Belgian hadn't missed a thing; he had seen the drops rolling down my cheeks and thought: this is the manifestation of an almost pathological state of terror; and he had felt normal and proud of being alive because he was cold. I wanted to stand up and smash his face but no sooner had I made the slightest gesture than my rage and shame were wiped out; I fell back on the bench with indifference.

I satisfied myself by rubbing my neck with my handkerchief because now I felt the sweat dropping from my hair onto my neck and it was unpleasant. I soon gave up rubbing, it was useless; my handkerchief was already soaked and I was still sweating. My buttocks were sweating too and my damp trousers were glued to the bench.

Suddenly Juan spoke. "You're a doctor?"

"Yes," the Belgian said.

"Does it hurt . . . very long?"

"Huh? When . . . ? Oh, no," the Belgian said paternally. "Not at all. It's over quickly." He acted as though he were calming a cash customer.

"But I . . . they told me . . . sometimes they have to fire twice."

"Sometimes," the Belgian said, nodding. "It may happen that the first volley reaches no vital organs."

"Then they have to reload their rifles and aim all over again?" He thought for a moment and then added hoarsely, "That takes time!"

He had a terrible fear of suffering, it was all he thought about: it was his age. I never thought much about it and it wasn't fear of suffering that made me sweat.

I got up and walked to the pile of coal dust. Tom jumped up and threw me a hateful look: I had annoyed him because my shoes squeaked. I wondered if my face looked as frightened as his: I saw he was sweating too. The sky was superb, no light filtered into the dark corner and I had only to raise my head to see the Big Dipper. But it wasn't like it had been: the night before I could see a great piece of sky from my monastery cell and each hour of the day brought me a different memory. Morning, when the sky was a hard, light blue, I thought of beaches on the Atlantic; at noon I saw the sun and I remembered a bar in Seville where I drank *manzanilla* and ate olives and anchovies; afternoons I was in the shade and I thought of the deep shadow which spreads over half a bull-ring leaving the other half shimmering in sunlight; it was really hard to see the whole world reflected in the sky like that. But now I could watch the sky as much as I pleased, it no longer evoked anything in me. I liked that better. I came back and sat near Tom. A long moment passed.

Tom began speaking in a low voice. He had to talk, without that he wouldn't have been able to recognize himself in his own mind. I thought he was talking to me but he wasn't looking at me. He was undoubtedly afraid to see me as I was, grey and sweating: we were alike and worse than mirrors of each other. He watched the Belgian, the living.

"Do you understand?" he said. "I don't understand."

I began to speak in a low voice too. I watched the Belgian.

"Why? What's the matter?"

"Something is going to happen to us that I can't understand."

There was a strange smell about Tom. It seemed to me I was more sensitive than usual to odors. I grinned. "You'll understand in a while."

"It isn't clear," he said obstinately. "I want to be brave but first I have to know . . . Listen, they're going to take us into the courtyard. Good. They're going to stand up in front of us. How many?"

"I don't know. Five or eight. Not more."

"All right. There'll be eight. Someone'll holler 'aim!' and I'll see eight rifles looking at me. I'll think how I'd like to get inside the wall, I'll push against it with my back . . . with every ounce of strength I have, but the wall will stay, like in a nightmare. I can imagine all that. If you only knew how well I can imagine it."

"All right, all right!" I said, "I can imagine it too."

"It must hurt like hell. You know, they aim at the eyes and the mouth to disfigure you," he added mechanically. "I can feel the wounds already; I've had pains in my head and in my neck for the past hour. Not real pains. Worse. This is what I'm going to feel tomorrow morning. And then what?"

I well understood what he meant but I didn't want to act as if I did. I had pains too, pains in my body like a crowd of tiny scars. I couldn't get used to it. But I was like him, I attached no importance to it. "After," I said, "you'll be pushing up daisies."

He began to talk to himself: he never stopped watching the Belgian. The Belgian didn't seem to be listening. I knew what he had come to do; he wasn't interested in what we thought; he came to watch our bodies, bodies dying in agony while yet alive.

"It's like a nightmare," Tom was saying. "You want to think of something, you always have the impression that it's all right, that you're going to understand and then it slips, it escapes you and fades away. I tell myself there will be nothing afterwards. But I don't understand what it means. Sometimes I almost can . . . and then it fades away and I start thinking about the pains again, bullets, explosions. I'm a materialist, I swear it to you; I'm not going crazy. But something's the matter. I see my corpse; that's not hard but *I'm* the one who sees it, with *my* eyes. I've got to think . . . think that I won't see anything anymore and the world will go on for the others. We aren't made to think that, Pablo. Believe me: I've already stayed up a whole night waiting for something. But this isn't the same: this will creep up behind us, Pablo, and we won't be able to prepare for it."

"Shut up," I said, "Do you want me to call a priest?"

He didn't answer. I had already noticed he had the tendency to act like a prophet and call me Pablo, speaking in a toneless voice. I didn't like that: but it seems all the Irish are that way. I had the vague impression he smelled of urine. Fundamentally, I hadn't much sympathy for Tom and I didn't see why, under the pretext of dying together, I should have any more. It would have been different with some others. With Ramon Gris, for example. But I felt alone between Tom and Juan. I liked that better, anyhow with Ramon I might have been more deeply moved. But I was terribly hard just then and I wanted to stay hard.

He kept on chewing his words, with something like distraction. He certainly talked to keep himself from thinking. He smelled of urine like an old prostate case. Naturally, I agreed with him, I could have said everything he said: it isn't *natural* to die. And since I was going to die, nothing seemed natural to me, not this pile of coal dust, or the bench, or Pedro's ugly face. Only it didn't please me to think the same things as Tom. And I knew that, all through the night, every five minutes, we would keep on thinking things at the same time. I looked at him sideways and for the first time he seemed strange to me: he wore death on his face. My pride was wounded: for the past twenty-four hours I had lived next to Tom, I had listened to him, I had spoken to him and I knew we had nothing in common. And now we looked as much alike as twin brothers, simply because we were going to die together. Tom took my hand without looking at me.

"Pablo, I wonder . . . I wonder if it's really true that everything ends."

I took my hand away and said, "Look between your feet, you pig."

There was a big puddle between his feet and drops fell from his pants-leg.

"What is it?" he asked frightened.

"You're pissing in your pants," I told him.

"It isn't true," he said furiously. "I'm not pissing. I don't feel anything."

The Belgian approached us. He asked with false solicitude, "Do you feel ill?"

Tom did not answer. The Belgian looked at the puddle and said nothing.

"I don't know what it is," Tom said ferociously. "But I'm not afraid. I swear I'm not afraid."

The Belgian did not answer. Tom got up and went to piss in a corner.

He came back buttoning his fly, and sat down without a word. The Belgian was taking notes.

All three of us watched him because he was alive. He had the motions of a living human being, the cares of a living human being; he shivered in the cellar the way the living are supposed to shiver; he had an obedient, well-fed body. The rest of us hardly felt ours—not in the same way anyhow. I wanted to feel my pants between my legs but I didn't dare; I watched the Belgian, balancing on his legs, master of his muscles, someone who could think about tomorrow. There we were, three bloodless shadows; we watched him and we sucked his life like vampires.

Finally he went over to little Juan. Did he want to feel his neck for some professional motive or was he obeying an impulse of charity? If he was acting by charity it was the only time during the whole night. He caressed Juan's head and neck. The kid let himself be handled, his eyes never leaving him, then suddenly, he seized the hand and looked at it strangely. He held the Belgian's hand between his own two hands and there was nothing pleasant about them, two grey pincers gripping his fat and reddish hand. I suspected what was going to happen and Tom must have suspected it too: but the Belgian didn't see a thing, he smiled paternally. After a moment the kid brought the fat red hand to his mouth and tried to bite it. The Belgian pulled away quickly and stumbled back against the wall. For a second he looked at us with horror, he must have suddenly understood that we were not men like him. I began to laugh and one of the guards jumped up. The other was asleep, his wide open eyes were blank.

I felt relaxed and over-excited at the same time. I didn't want to think any more about what would happen at dawn, at death. It made no sense. I only found words or emptiness. But as soon as I tried to think of anything else I saw rifle barrels pointing at me. Perhaps I lived through my execution twenty times; once I even thought it was for good: I must have slept a minute. They were dragging me to the wall and I was struggling; I was asking for mercy. I woke up with a start and looked at the Belgian: I was afraid I might have cried out in my sleep. But he was stroking his moustache, he hadn't noticed anything. If I had wanted to, I think I could have slept a while; I had been awake for forty-eight hours. I was at the end of my rope. But I didn't want to lose two hours of life: they would come to wake me up at dawn, I would follow them, stupefied with sleep and I would have croaked without so much as an "Oof!"; I didn't want that, I didn't want to die like an animal, I wanted to understand. Then I was afraid of having nightmares. I got up, walked back and forth, and, to change my ideas, I began to think about my past life. A crowd of memories came back to me pellmell. There were good and bad ones—or at least I called them that *before*. There were faces and incidents. I saw the face of a little *novillero* who was gored in Valencia during the *Feria*, the face of one of my uncles, the face of Ramon Gris. I remembered my whole life: how I was out of work for three months in 1926, how I almost starved to death. I remembered a night I spent on a bench in Granada: I hadn't eaten for three days. I was angry, I didn't want to die. That made me smile. How madly I ran after happiness, after women, after liberty. Why? I wanted to free Spain, I admired Pi y Margall, I joined the anarchist movement, I spoke in public meetings: I took everything as seriously as if I were immortal.

At that moment I felt that I had my whole life in front of me, and I thought, "It's a damned lie." It was worth nothing because it was finished. I wondered how I'd been able to walk, to laugh with the girls: I wouldn't have moved so much as my little finger if I had only imagined I would die like this. My life was in front of me, shut, closed, like a bag and yet everything inside of it was unfinished. For an instant I tried to judge it. I wanted to tell myself, this is a beautiful life. But I couldn't pass judgment on it; it was only a sketch; I had spent my time counterfeiting eternity, I had understood nothing. I missed nothing: there were so many things I could have missed, the taste of *manzanilla* or the baths I took in summer in a little creek near Cadiz; but death had disenchanted everything.

The Belgian suddenly had a bright idea. "My friends," he told us, "I will undertake—if the military administration will allow it—to send a message for you, a souvenir to those who love you . . ."

Tom mumbled, "I don't have anybody."

I said nothing. Tom waited an instant then looked at me with curiosity. "You don't have anything to say to Concha?"

"No."

I hated this tender complicity: it was my own fault, I had talked about Concha the night before, I should have controlled myself. I was with her for a year. Last night I would have given an arm to see her again for five minutes. That was why I talked about her, it was stronger than I was. Now I had no more desire to see her, I had nothing more to say to her. I would not even have wanted to hold her in my arms: my body filled me with horror because it was grey and sweating—and I wasn't sure that her body didn't fill me with horror. Concha would cry when she found out I was dead, she would have no taste for life for months afterwards. But I was still the one who was going to die. I thought of her soft, beautiful eyes. When she looked at me something passed from her to me. But I knew it was over: if she looked at me *now* the look would stay in her eyes, it wouldn't reach me. I was alone.

Tom was alone too but not in the same way. Sitting cross-legged, he had begun to stare at the bench with a sort of smile, he looked amazed. He put out his hand and touched the wood cautiously as if he were afraid of breaking something, then drew back his hand quickly and shuddered. If I had been Tom I wouldn't have amused myself by touching the bench; this was some more Irish nonsense, but I too found that objects had a funny look: they were more obliterated, less dense than usual. It was enough for me to look at the bench, the lamp, the pile of coal dust, to feel that I was going to die. Naturally I couldn't think clearly about my death but I saw it everywhere, on things, in the way things fell back and kept their distance, discreetly, as people who speak quietly at the bedside of a dying man. It was *his* death which Tom had just touched on the bench.

In the state I was in, if someone had come and told me I could go home quietly, that they would leave me my life whole, it would have left me cold: several hours or several years of waiting is all the same when you have lost the illusion of being eternal. I clung to nothing, in a way I was calm. But it was a horrible calm—because of my body; my body, I saw with its eyes, I heard with its ears, but it was no longer me; it sweated and trembled by itself and I didn't recognize it any more. I had to touch it and look at it to find out what was happening, as if it were the body of someone else. At times I could still feel it, I felt sinkings, and fallings, as when you're in a plane taking a nosedive, or I felt my heart beating. But that didn't reassure me. Everything that came from my body was all cock-eyed. Most of the time it was quiet and I felt no more than a sort of weight, a filthy presence against me; I had the impression of being tied to an enormous vermin. Once I felt my pants and I felt they were damp; I didn't know whether it was sweat or urine, but I went to piss on the coal pile as a precaution.

The Belgian took out his watch, looked at it. He said, "It's three-thirty."

Bastard! He must have done it on purpose. Tom jumped; we hadn't noticed time was running out; night surrounded us like a shapeless, somber mass, I couldn't even remember that it had begun.

Little Juan began to cry. He wrung his hands, pleaded, "I don't want to die. I don't want to die."

He ran across the whole cellar waving his arms in the air, then fell sobbing on one of the mats. Tom watched him with mournful eyes, without the slightest desire to console him. Because it wasn't worth the trouble: the kid made more noise than we did, but he was less touched: he was like a sick man who defends himself against his illness by fever. It's much more serious when there isn't any fever.

He wept: I could clearly see he was pitying himself; he wasn't thinking about death. For one second, one single second, I wanted to weep myself, to weep with pity for myself. But the opposite happened: I glanced at the kid, I saw his thin sobbing shoulders and I felt inhuman: I could pity neither the others nor myself. I said to myself, "I want to die cleanly."

Tom had gotten up, he placed himself just under the round opening and began to watch for daylight. I was determined to die cleanly and I only thought of that. But ever since the doctor told us the time, I felt time flying, flowing away drop by drop.

It was still dark when I heard Tom's voice: "Do you hear them?"

Men were marching in the courtyard.

"Yes."

"What the hell are they doing? They can't shoot in the dark."

After a while we heard no more. I said to Tom, "It's day."

Pedro got up, yawning, and came to blow out the lamp. He said to his buddy, "Cold as hell."

The cellar was all grey. We heard shots in the distance.

"It's starting," I told Tom. "They must do it in the court in the rear."

Tom asked the doctor for a cigarette. I didn't want one; I didn't want cigarettes or alcohol. From that moment on they didn't stop firing.

"Do you realize what's happening?" Tom said.

He wanted to add something but kept quiet, watching the door. The door opened and a lieutenant came in with four soldiers. Tom dropped his cigarette.

"Steinbock?"

Tom didn't answer. Pedro pointed him out.

"Juan Mirbal?"

"On the mat."

"Get up," the lieutenant said.

Juan did not move. Two soldiers took him under the arms and set him on his feet. But he fell as soon as they released him.

The soldiers hesitated.

"He's not the first sick one," said the lieutenant. "You two carry him; they'll fix it up down there."

He turned to Tom. "Let's go."

Tom went out between two soldiers. Two others followed, carrying the kid by the armpits. He hadn't fainted; his eyes were wide open and tears ran down his cheeks. When I wanted to go out the lieutenant stopped me.

"You Ibbieta?"

"Yes."

"You wait here; they'll come for you later."

They left. The Belgian and the two jailers left too, I was alone. I did not understand what was happening to me but I would have liked it better if they had gotten it over with right away. I heard shots at almost regular intervals; I shook with each one of them. I wanted to scream and tear out my hair. But I gritted my teeth and pushed my hands in my pockets because I wanted to stay clean.

After an hour they came to get me and led me to the first floor, to a small room that smelt of cigars and where the heat was stifling. There were two officers sitting smoking in the armchairs, papers on their knees.

"You're Ibbieta?"

"Yes."

"Where is Ramon Gris?"

"I don't know."

The one questioning me was short and fat. His eyes were hard behind his glasses. He said to me, "Come here."

I went to him. He got up and took my arms, staring at me with a look that should have pushed me into the earth. At the same time he pinched my biceps with all his might. It wasn't to hurt me, it was only a game: he wanted to dominate me. He also thought he had to blow his stinking breath square in my face. We stayed for a moment like that, and I almost felt like laughing. It takes a lot to intimidate a man who is going to die; it didn't work. He pushed me back violently and sat down again. He said, "It's his life against yours. You can have yours if you tell us where he is."

These men dolled up with their riding crops and boots were still going to die. A little later than I, but not too much. They busied themselves looking for names in their crumpled papers, they ran after other men to imprison or suppress them; they had opinions on the future of Spain and on other subjects. Their little activities seemed shocking and burlesqued to me; I couldn't put myself in their place, I thought they were insane. The little man was still looking at me, whipping his boots with the riding crop. All his gestures were calculated to give him the look of a live and ferocious beast.

"So? You understand?"

"I don't know where Gris is," I answered. "I thought he was in Madrid."

The other officer raised his pale hand indolently. This indolence was also calculated. I saw through all their little schemes and I was stupefied to find there were men who amused themselves that way.

"You have a quarter of an hour to think it over," he said slowly. "Take him to the laundry, bring him back in fifteen minutes. If he still refuses he will be executed on the spot."

They knew what they were doing: I had passed the night in waiting; then they had made me wait an hour in the cellar while they shot Tom and Juan and now they were locking me up in the laundry; they must have prepared their game the night before. They told themselves that nerves eventually wear out and they hoped to get me that way.

They were badly mistaken. In the laundry I sat on a stool because I felt very weak and I began to think. But not about their proposition. Of course I knew where Gris was; he was hiding with his cousins, four kilometers from the city. I also knew that I would not reveal his hiding place unless they tortured me (but they didn't seem to be thinking about that). All that was perfectly regulated, definite and in no way interested me. Only I would have liked to understand the reasons for my conduct. I would rather die than give up Gris. Why? I didn't like Ramon Gris any more. My friendship for him had died a little while before dawn at the same time as my love for Concha, at the same time as my desire to live. Undoubtedly I thought highly of him: he was tough. But it was not for this reason that I consented to die in his place; his life had no more value than mine; no life had value. They were going to slap a man up against a wall and shoot at him until he died, whether it was I or Gris or somebody else made no difference. I knew he was more useful than I to the cause of Spain but I thought to hell with Spain and anarchy; nothing was important. Yet I was there, I could save my skin and give up Gris and I refused to do it. I found that somehow comic; it was obstinacy. I thought, "I must be stubborn!" And a droll sort of gaiety spread over me.

They came for me and brought me back to the two officers. A rat ran out from under my feet and that amused me. I turned to one of the *falangistas* and said, "Did you see the rat?"

He didn't answer. He was very sober, he took himself seriously. I wanted to laugh but I held myself back because I was afraid that once I got started I wouldn't be able to stop. The *falangista* had a moustache. I said to him again, "You ought to shave off your moustache, idiot." I thought it funny that he would let the hairs of his living being invade his face. He kicked me without great conviction and I kept quiet.

"Well," said the fat officer, "have you thought about it?"

I looked at them with curiosity, as insects of a very rare species. I told them, "I know where he is. He is hidden in the cemetery. In a vault or in the gravediggers' shack."

It was a farce. I wanted to see them stand up, buckle their belts and give orders busily.

They jumped to their feet. "Let's go. Molés, go get fifteen men from Lieutenant Lopez. You," the fat man said, "I'll let you off if you're telling the truth, but it'll cost you plenty if you're making monkeys out of us."

They left in a great clatter and I waited peacefully under the guard of *falangistas*. From time to time I smiled, thinking about the spectacle they would make. I felt stunned and malicious. I imagined them lifting up tombstones, opening the doors of the vaults one by one. I represented this situation to myself as if I had been someone else: this prisoner obstinately playing the hero, these grim *falangistas* with their moustaches and their men in uniform running among the graves; it was irresistibly funny. After half an hour the little fat man came back alone. I thought he had come to give the orders to execute me. The others must have stayed in the cemetery.

The officer looked at me. He didn't look at all sheepish. "Take him into the big courtyard with the others," he said. "After the military operations a regular court will decide what happens to him."

"Then they're not . . . not going to shoot me? . . ."

"Not now, anyway. What happens afterwards is none of my business."

I still didn't understand. I asked, "But why?"

He shrugged his shoulders without answering and the soldiers took me away. In the big courtyard there were about a hundred prisoners, women, children and a few old men. I began walking around the central grass-plot, I was stupefied. At noon they let us eat in the mess hall. Two or three people questioned me. I must have known them, but I didn't answer: I didn't even know where I was.

Around evening they pushed about ten new prisoners into the court. I recognized Garcia, the baker. He said, "What damned luck you have! I didn't think I'd see you alive."

"They sentenced me to death," I said, "and then they changed their minds, I don't know why."

"They arrested me at two o'clock," Garcia said.

"Why?" Garcia had nothing to do with politics.

"I don't know," he said. "They arrest everybody who doesn't think the way they do." He lowered his voice. "They got Gris."

I began to tremble. "When?"

"This morning. He messed it up. He left his cousin's on Tuesday because they had an argument. There were plenty of people to hide him but he didn't want to owe anything to anybody. He said, 'I'd go hide in Ibbieta's place, but they got him, so I'll go hide in the cemetery.'"

"In the cemetery?"

"Yes. What a fool. Of course they went by there this morning, that was sure to happen. They found him in the gravediggers' shack. He shot at them and they got him."

"In the cemetery!"

Everything began to spin and I found myself sitting on the ground: I laughed so hard I cried.

Alberto Moravia (Alberto Pincherle) (1907–   ) is of a well-to-do family of Rome. Because of a lengthy illness, Moravia spent his early years in bed reading; thus, he is a self-educated writer whose first work was done from his bed in a sanitarium. In the past fifteen years Moravia has emerged steadily as the leading Italian novelist and short-story writer of his generation. Typically, his work treats the themes of alienation, sexual relationships, and the condition of modern man; these protagonists of the Roman middle class are often shown in isolation or as personally corrupt, made so by the social system in which they were formed. The first novel, Time of Indifference *(1929), utilizes much of his subsequent thematic materials;* The Woman of Rome *(1947) was acclaimed internationally. Moravia has written several hundred short stories, almost all for Italian newspapers. For further reading:* Roman Tales *(1957).*

ALBERTO MORAVIA

The Automaton

*A*fter he had finished dressing, Guido went and looked at himself in the wardrobe mirror and had, as usual, a feeling of dissatisfaction. He was, in fact, wearing clothes that were entirely new and of the best quality—a new jacket of herringbone cloth, new grey flannel trousers, a new tie with bright-coloured stripes, new red woolen socks, and new wash-leather shoes; and yet he failed to achieve elegance, he looked like a lay figure in the window of a multiple store.

Guido left the bedroom, the untidiness of which irritated him, and went into the living-room. Here all was clean and tidy and gleaming; he felt calm again, in spite of the fact that, ever since he had woken up that morning, he had been tormented by a suspicion of having forgotten something: an appointment? a telephone call? a bill to pay? a festive anniversary? Finally he shook his head and went over to the record-player in the corner beside the fireplace. The record-player, of American make, was automatic; that is, when you pressed an external knob, the arm with the stylus rose by itself, moved across, lowered itself and came to rest at the edge of the disc. Guido took a disc of light music at random from the holder, inserted it and pressed the knob. Then an unexpected thing happened: the arm raised itself, moved across, but did not lower itself; instead, it went on moving across in what seemed a thoughtful sort of manner, and finally, instead of at the edge, came to rest at the centre of the disc. There was a crackling, scraping sound, the arm darted back across the disc, lifted itself up again and with a loud click went back to its original position.

Guido took off the disc and examined it in the light by the window: it was ruined; deep scratches could be seen in several places. For once the automatic device had failed to work. Guido, considerably disconcerted, put on another record, but the arm raised and lowered itself without any further errors. As he listened to the music, he wondered what could have been the reason for the record-player's strange behaviour, but he was aware that the probable technical explanation did not satisfy him. At that moment his wife came in.

She was leading by the hand their two children, Piero and Lucia, both of them under five years old, both of them with fine, sensitive faces, particularly Piero who strongly resembled a photograph of Guido at the same age. She said to the two children: "Run and give Papa a kiss," and she herself remained in the middle of the room while they, obedient and affectionate, ran over and climbed on their father's knee. Guido, in turn, embraced them; and as he did so, he looked over their curly heads at his wife and noticed, as though he were seeing her for the first time, that she was tall, thin and flat, dried up and drained of feminine charm. He noticed also that she wore glasses and that her nose was slightly red; that she was wearing a blue, full skirt and a sweater of a darker blue. It seemed to him all at once that all these details must have a significance of their own, rather like the details of picture-puzzles that can be explained by one single word; but his wife did not give him time to find it. "Come along, let's go," she said; "it's getting late already, and if we wait any longer there's a danger of our finding the roads crammed with cars." "Let's go," repeated Guido; and he followed his wife, who had again taken the children by the hand.

The flat was on the ground floor of a new building in the Parioli district; its entrance door opened on to a minute garden with cement paths, beds of tulips and little trees cut to the shape of globes and cones. The family crossed this garden and came out into a narrow street flanked with new buildings and encumbered with rows of cars along the pavements. Guido was now again asking himself what he had forgotten that morning, and, still with this thought in mind, helped his wife and children into the car, put it into gear and started off. They went quickly down on to the Via Flaminia, crossed the bridge and turned along the Lungotevere. The goal of their expedition was the Lake of Albano. It was Sunday and a beautiful day, as his wife observed, sitting at the back with the little girl; it was a pity, it was really a pity that they could not have a picnic, but it had rained recently and the ground was still damp. To this, Guido made no answer. His wife went on talking volubly and sensibly, addressing herself now to her husband and now to the two children. Guido, for his part, concentrated his whole attention on the road which, crowded as it was, and with people on Sunday outings into the bargain, demanded more prudence and skill than usual.

After a long stretch of the Via Appia Antica, Guido turned into the Via Appia Pignatelli and thence into the Via Appia Nuova. He kept up a regular speed, not driving very fast even when the road in front of him was clear. His eyes, meanwhile, took note of a quantity of things which seemed interesting but whose significance escaped him—the glitter on the chromium plating of a big black car in front of them, the immaculate whiteness, speckled with points of light, of a cylindrical petrol-tank half hidden amongst the budding trees of spring, the lime-washed brilliancy of houses, the silvery gleam of an aeroplane as it came down diagonally across the sky to land at the Ciampino airport, a sudden flash from a window struck by a ray of sunshine, the chalky tinge of the warning lines painted on the trunks of the plane-trees along the road. All these white, gleaming, flashing things contrasted stridently with a big black cloud which had spread over the sky and threatened to spoil the fine day; the landscape, too, of a bright, tender, almost milky green, was out of harmony against the dark, stormy background. Once again Guido wondered what could be the significance of this contrast, but he could find no solution: and yet he was sure that there was one. His wife, behind him, was talking to the little girl; the little boy, who was sitting beside him, had knelt up on the seat with his hands on the back of it and was taking part in the conversation between his mother and sister. The fresh, shrill voices of the children asking questions, the calm voice of the mother answering them, also concealed some meaning or other, he was sure; but Guido, as with all the other things that he noticed one by one, failed to discover it, although he was convinced that it was there.

Then the children stopped talking and in the silence that followed Guido's wife seemed to become conscious of his silence and asked him: "What's the matter? Are you in a bad humour?"

"No, I'm not in a bad humour."

"You're not in a good humour either, are you?"

"I'm in a middling humour, my usual sort of humour."

"That's just what I value most in you, your middling humour, as you call it; but I had the impression that you were in a bad humour."

"Why d'you like my middling humour?"

"I don't know, it gives me a feeling of security. The feeling of being with a man in whom one can have complete confidence."

"And that man is *me?*"

"Yes, you"; his wife spoke quietly, objectively, as if about a third person. "I have confidence in you because I know that you're a good husband and a good father. I know that with you there can't be any surprises; that you always do the right thing. This confidence makes me happy."

"You're happy with me?"

"Well, yes"; his wife appeared to reflect for a moment, scrupulously; "yes, I am happy, I can say without any doubt that I'm happy. You've given me everything I wanted, a home, children, a comfortable, secure life. Are you glad I'm happy with you?" She leant forward and gave him a light, affectionate caress on the back of the neck. Guido replied: "Yes, I'm glad."

They had left the Via Appia Nuova now for the Via dei Laghi and were moving between green fields in which could be seen, here and there, the little quivering white and pink clouds of fruit-trees in blossom. Then there was a yellow mimosa beside a blue house; and then some Judas trees whose branches were thick with wine-red flowers. "I wasn't in a bad humour," said Guido; "I was merely thinking about something that happened a short time ago."

"What was that?"

He told her about the record and about the failure of the mechanism of the record-player, and concluded: "The record's ruined now. But above all I can't find any explanation of why in the world the record-player failed to work."

His wife said jokingly: "Obviously machines sometimes get fed up with being machines and want to prove that they're not."

"Yes indeed, it may be that."

The little boy, who was still kneeling on the seat beside Guido, suddenly asked his mother whether they were going to have strawberries to eat that day. His mother explained that there were no strawberries at that time of the year; strawberries were fruit and spring was the season of flowers, as he could see for himself if he looked at the countryside. Guido listened for a few moments to his wife's discourse and then made a last, feebler attempt to remember what he was convinced he had forgotten that morning, but he could find no solution. A business appointment, possibly, for the next day, which was Monday: in any case, at his office everything was written down in the appointments book and it would be easy to make certain of it.

By now they had come on to the road that runs round the Lake of Albano which, nevertheless, was not yet visible, being hidden by the gardens of the numerous villas. Then, at a bend in the road, the lake began gradually to appear: first the precipitous slopes, covered in dark, thick furry green, then, far below, as though at the bottom of a funnel, the motionless, sombre lake in which the high banks and the cloudy sky were reflected with uneven shadows. Guido cast a hasty glance at the lake and again had the feeling of a significance concealed behind numerous, scattered details. The road, now, was uphill, and he changed gear from fourth to third. At the top of the hill could be seen a belvedere outlined against the sky, beyond which, supposedly, there would be a sheer drop of several hundreds of feet.

Suddenly Guido felt as if he were coming out of a long tunnel into the open, emerging from a close, stagnant atmosphere into the clear, light air. And in company with this sensation there came to him a precise thought— to drive the car at full speed into the void beyond the top of the hill, to hurl himself, together with his wife and children, into the lake. The car would take a leap of eight or nine hundred feet and fall straight into the lake; death would be instantaneous. Guido wondered whether this thought was inspired by some kind of hatred for his family and realized that this was not so. On the contrary, it seemed to him that he had never loved them so much as at this moment when he desired to destroy them. But was it then truly a thought, or was it a temptation? It was a temptation, an almost irresistible temptation, of a deathly, tenacious, consuming sweetness, such as might inspire the kind of compassion that is unwilling to remain impotent.

The car swerved to the right until it grazed the verge of the road as it went rapidly up the hill towards the belvedere. But as it passed the highest point, Guido found himself faced by a small meadow that he had not foreseen; the precipice had been left behind and now the moment had passed: to plunge into the void would have been a natural thing, to go back in order to do so would be a crime. He stopped the car, put on the hand-brake and sat still. He had no particular feeling; merely it seemed to him that he had left the clear, light air and gone back into an atmosphere of closeness and stagnation. His wife, as she got out of the car, said: "Well done, it was a good idea to stop; we'll go and have a look at the lake."

When they were standing, all four of them, at the edge of the belvedere and leaning forward, hand in hand, to gaze at the lake, Guido remembered, all of a sudden, what it was that he had forgotten: that this Sunday was the anniversary of their wedding-day; they had spoken of it the evening before, after the children had been put to bed; and the expedition had been, in fact, planned to celebrate the occasion.

Samuel Beckett (1906–   ) was born in Dublin but as a lecteur d'anglais *moved in the late twenties to the continent. He usually lived outside of Paris, where he led a life of austerity and comparative isolation. Beckett's work is associated with that of Joyce (whom he knew personally over the years); as with Joyce, Beckett retains a fascination with the artistic possibilities of language. Beckett's protagonists typically are from the seamy "under" side of society; they include bums, tramps, untutored philosophers, and characters mad or nearly so. Although his chief characters may be marginal to society, they usually display dignity and a certain admirable "style." His most celebrated play is* Waiting for Godot *(1952). In 1969 Beckett received the Nobel Prize for literature. For further reading:* Novels and Texts for Nothing *(1955).*

SAMUEL BECKETT

Stories and Texts for Nothing, III

Leave, I was going to say leave all that. What matter who's speaking, someone said what matter who's speaking. There's going to be a departure, I'll be there, it won't be me, I'll be here, I'll say I'm far, it won't be me, I won't say anything, there's going to be a story, someone's going to try and tell a story. Yes, enough denials, all is false, there's no one, it's agreed, there's nothing, enough phrases, let's be dupes, dupes of time, all time, until it's over, all over, and the voices are stilled, they're only voices, only lies. Here, leave here and go elsewhere, or stay here, but coming and going. Move first, there must be a body, as of old, I don't say no, I won't say no any more, I'll say I have a body, a body that moves, forward, backward, up and down, as required. With a clutter of limbs and organs, all that's needed to live once again, to hold out, a short spell, I'll call that living, I'll say it's me, I'll stand up, I'll think no more, I'll be too taken up, standing up, keeping standing up, moving about, holding out, getting to the next day, the next week, that will be enough, a week will be enough, a week in spring, that will be bracing. It's enough to will, I'm going to will, will myself a body, will myself a head, a little strength, a little courage, I'm going to start, a week is soon over, then back here, this inextricable place, far from the days, the days are far, it's not going to be easy. And why, after all, no no, leave it, don't start that again, don't listen to everything, don't say everything, all is old, all one, that's settled. There you are up, I give you my word, I swear it's mine, work your hands, palp your skull, seat of the understanding, without it nothing doing, then the rest, the lower parts, can't do without them, and say what you are, what kind of man, have a guess, there must be a man, or a woman, feel between your legs, no need of beauty, or strength, a week is soon over, no one's going to love you, don't worry. No, not like that, too sudden, I gave myself a fright. And to start with stop panting, no one's going to kill you, oh no, no one's going to love you and no one's going to kill you. You may emerge in the high depression of Gobi, there you'll feel at home. I'll wait for you here, my mind at rest, at rest for you, no, I'm alone, I alone am, it's I must go, this time it's I. I know what I'll do, I'll be a man, I must, a kind of man, a kind of old infant, I'll have a nurse, she'll be fond of me, she'll give me her hand, to cross over, she'll let me loose in gardens, I'll be good, I'll sit in a corner and comb my beard, smooth it down, to be nicer looking, a little nicer, if it could be like that. She'll say to me, Come, lamb, it's time for home. I won't have any responsibility, she'll have all the responsibility, her name will be Nanny, I'll call her Nanny, if it could only be like that. Come, pet, it's time for bottle. Who taught me all I know, I alone, when I was still a wanderer, I deduced it all, from nature, with the aid of an all-in-one, I know it's not true, but it's too late now, too late to deny it, the knowledge is there, items of knowledge, gleaming in turn, far and near, flickering over the abyss, allies. Leave it and go, I must go, I must say so anyway, the moment is come, one doesn't know why. What does it matter where you say you are, here or elsewhere, fixed or movable, shape-less or oblong like man, without light or in the light of heaven, I don't know, it seems to matter, it's not going to be easy. If I went back to where all went out and then on from there, no, that wouldn't lead anywhere, that never led anywhere, the memory of it has gone out too, a great flame and then blackness, a great spasm and then no more bulk or traversable space, I don't know. I tried to have me fall, off the cliff, in the street in the midst of mortals, that led nowhere, I gave up. Travel the road again that cast me up here, before going back the way I came, or on, wise advice. That's so that I'll never stir again, dribble on here till time is done, murmuring every ten centuries, it's not me, it's not true, it's not me, I'm far. No no, I'll speak now of the future, I'll speak in the future, as in the days when I said to myself, in the night, Tomorrow I'll put on my blue tie, the one with the stars, and put it on, when the night was past. Quick quick before I weep. I'll have a friend, my own age, my own bog, an old warrior, we'll fight our

battles over again and compare our scratches. Quick quick. He had served
in the navy, perhaps under Jellicoe, while I was potting at the invader from
behind a barrel of Guinness, with my arquebus. We have not long, that's
right, in the present, not long to live, it's our last winter of all, halleluiah.
We wonder what will carry us off finally. He's gone in the wind, I in the
bladder rather. We envy each other, he envies me, I envy him, on and off.
I catheterize myself unaided, with trembling hand, standing in the public
pisshouse, bent double, under cover of my cape, people take me for a dirty
old man. Meanwhile he waits for me on a bench, coughing up his guts,
spitting into a snuff-box which no sooner overflows than he empties it into
the canal, out of public-spiritedness. We have deserved well of our mother-
land, she'll get us into hospital before we die. We spend our life, it's ours,
trying to unite in the same instant a ray of sunshine and a free bench, in an
oasis of public greenery, we have taken to a love of nature, in our sere and
yellow, it belongs to one and all, in places. He reads to me in choking
murmur from the paper of the day before, he had better been the blind one.
Our passion is horse-racing, dog-racing too, we have no political opinions,
just limply republican. But we also have a warm spot for the Windsors, the
Hanoverians, I forget, the Hohenzollerns is it. Nothing human is foreign to
us, once we have digested the dogs and horses. No, alone, I'd be better off
alone, it would be quicker. He'd feed me, he had a friend, a pork-butcher,
he'd ram my soul back down my gullet with black pudding. With his conso-
lations, allusions to cancer, recollections of imperishable raptures, he'd prevent discouragement from sapping my foundations. And I, instead of con-
centrating on my own horizons, which might have enabled me to throw
them under a lorry, would have my mind distracted by his. I'd say to him,
Come on, son, leave all that, think no more about it, and it's I would think
no more about it, besotted with brotherliness. And the obligations, I have in
mind particularly the appointments at ten o'clock in the morning, rain, hail
or shine, in front of Duggan's, thronging already with sporting men in a
hurry to get their bets out of harm's way before the bars opened. We were,
there we are past and gone again, so much the better, so much the better,
most punctual, I must say. To see the remains of Vincent arriving in sheets
of rain, with the brave involuntary swagger of the old tar, his head swathed
in a bloody clout and a gleam in his eye, was for the acute observer an
example of what man is capable of, in his thirst for enjoyment. With one
hand he sustained his sternum, with the heel of the other his spinal column,
no, that's all memories, last shifts more ancient than the flood. To see
what's happening here, where there's no one, where nothing happens, to get
something to happen here, someone to be here, then put an end to it, make
silence, enter silence, or another noise, a noise of other voices than those of
life and death, of lives and deaths that never will be mine, enter my story,
in order to leave it, no, that's all fiddle-faddle. Is it possible I'll sprout a

head in the end, all my own, in which to brew some poisons worthy of me, and legs to kick my heels, I'd be there at last, I could go, it's all I ask, no, I can't ask anything. Nothing but the head and the two legs, or just one, in the middle, I'd go hopping. Or nothing but the head, nice and round, nice and smooth, no need of features, I'd roll, downhill, almost a pure spirit, no, that wouldn't work, all's uphill from here, there'd have to be a leg, or the equivalent, an annular joint or so, contractile, with them you go a long way. To set forth from Duggan's door, on a spring morning of rain and shine, not knowing if you'll ever come to evening, what's wrong there? It would be so easy. To be buried in that flesh or in another, in that arm held by a friendly hand, and in that hand, without arms, without hands, and without soul in those trembling souls, through the crowd, the hoops, the toy balloons, what's wrong there? I don't know, I'm here, that's all I know, and that it's still not me, that's what you have to make the best of. There's no flesh anywhere, nor any means of dying, leave all that, to want to leave all that, without knowing what that means, all that, it's soon said, soon done, in vain, nothing has stirred, no one spoken. Here nothing will happen, there will be no one here, for many a long day. Departures, stories, they're not for tomorrow. And the voices, wherever they come from, are stone dead.

Tommaso Landolfi (1908–   ) was born in Pico, Italy, and among other things, studied Russian at the University of Lorience. Long considered one of Italy's most avant garde, experimental writers of novels and short fiction, Landolfi has also translated major works of Russian literature into the Italian. Although he has been called the Italian Kafka, Landolfi's own work is clearly influenced by Russian writers, especially Gogol and Dostoevsky; on the other hand, Landolfi's art is singularly his own and is unusual in the present age for its broad, often boisterous humor. Two collections of short stories are now in English for further reading: Gogol's Wife and Other Stories *(1963);* The Cancerqueen and Other Stories *(1971).*

TOMMASO LANDOLFI

Wedding Night

*A*t the end of the wedding banquet the chimney sweep was announced. The father, out of joviality, and because it seemed proper to him that a ceremony such as the cleaning of the chimney should be celebrated on just that day, gave the order to let him come in. But the man did not appear; he preferred to remain in the kitchen, where the great hearth was. Not all the toasts had yet been given, and this was why some of the guests, in their heart of hearts, criticized the interruption; nonetheless, due to the uproar made by the children, everyone rose from the table.

The bride had never seen a chimney sweep: she had been in boarding school when he used to come. Going into the kitchen she saw a tall, rather corpulent man, with a serious gray beard and bent shoulders; he was dressed in a corduroy suit the color of linseed oil. His stoop was counterbalanced by the weight of two huge mountain boots which seemed to hold his entire body erect. Although he had just washed very carefully, the skin of his face was deeply tinted with black, as though many black-heads of varying dimensions had taken root there; a black deposit, gathered between the lines of his forehead and cheeks, conferred a quality of meditative wisdom on that physiognomy. But this impression quickly dissolved, and the man's great timidity became quite obvious, especially when his features broke into a sort of smile.

He nearly frightened the young bride, because he was standing behind the door, though he acted frightened himself; and, as if he had been caught doing something reprehensible and had to justify his presence in that place, he began to repeat, speaking directly to the young bride, some sentences which she did not hear or did not understand. He stammered insistently and behaved as if he thought that what he said concerned her greatly and, all the while, he looked at her with the eyes of a beaten dog and yet significantly. From the very first moment the young bride was aware of his caterpillar nature.

He took off his jacket and began to unbutton his vest. She slipped out through the other door, but continued to follow what was going on in the kitchen; she had the feeling that something improper was about to happen and that her presence might make him uneasy in the performance of his rites. Somehow she almost felt ashamed for him. But there was no noise to feed her imagination and so she went back in again. The children had been sent away and he was alone. At that moment he was climbing a ladder set up inside the hood of the fireplace; his feet were bare and he was in his shirtsleeves, a brown shirt. Across his chest, fastened with leather straps, he had a tool which resembled the scraper for a kneading trough but whose use remained forever unknown to the young bride. And he had a kind of black gag, tied up behind his ears, which fitted over his mouth and nose. But she did not see him enter the flue of the chimney, because she ran away again.

When she came back the second time, the kitchen was empty and a strange smell, a terrible smell, had spread through it. Looking around her, the young bride connected it first with the man's large shoes set in a corner next to a bundle of clothes; it was, however, the death smell of the soot which was piling up on the hearthstone, falling in intermittent showers to the rhythm of a dull scraping which gnawed at the marrow of the house and which she felt echoing in her own entrails. In the intervals, a muffled rubbing revealed the man's laborious ascent.

An instant of absolute silence fell, an instant of lacerating suspense for the young bride. She continued to stare at the mouth of the flue, there under the hood at the end of the fireplace's black funnel; this mouth was not square but narrow, a dark slit.

Then a very high, guttural, inhuman cry sounded from some mysterious place, from the well, from the stones of the house, from the soul of the kitchen's pots and pans, from the very breast of the young bride, who was shaken by it through and through. That bestial howl of agony soon proved to be a kind of joyous call: the man had burst through onto the roof. The muffled rubbings resumed more rapidly now; finally a black foot came down out of the slit searching for support—the foot of a hanged man. The foot found the first rung of the ladder and the young bride ran away.

In the courtyard, as the bride sat on a millstone, the old housekeeper, one of those women for whom everything is new, assumed the task of keeping her informed; she walked back and forth bringing her the news with a mysterious air. "Now he is doing his cleaning under the hood," and the young bride pictured him as he shook off the soot, standing upright on the pile like a gravedigger on a mound of earth. "But what does he put on his feet to claw into the wall?" And then she ran after him to ask him: "My good man, what do you put on your feet to claw into the wall?" A gay reply followed which could not be heard clearly. "Now he is eating breakfast," and the housekeeper remained inside. Then she reappeared with a few small edelweiss; she said that the man had taken them out of a very clean little box and had offered them for the young bride.

After some time he himself came out, dressed again and with a pack on his back. He crossed the courtyard to leave, but the father stopped him and began to question him benevolently about his life. The young bride approached, too. Here the man, in the weak sun of winter, his face darker, his beard flecked with black and his eyes puckered by the light, looked like a big moth, a nocturnal bird surprised by the day. Or rather he looked like a spider or crab louse; the fact is that the hood of the hearth, when seen from below and if there is enough light outside, is not completely black but leaks a gray and slimy sheen.

He said that for thirty-five years he had been traveling through those towns cleaning the chimneys, that next year he would take his young son along to teach him the trade, that picking edelweiss was now forbidden and he had been able to gather those few flowers on the sly, and other such inconsequential things. Yet, whether astute or halting, it was quite clear that he only wished to hide himself behind those words, that he let the curtain of words fall in the same way that the cuttlefish beclouds the water.

He knew about all the deaths in the family, yet none of them had ever seen him!

By now the young bride felt that she was no longer ashamed for him, but was actually ashamed of herself.

After the chimney sweep had gone, she placed the few edelweiss beneath the portraits of the dead.

A Catholic born in Cologne, Heinrich Böll (1917–
) grew up in Germany during the emergence of
the Nazi regime, and during World War II was a
combat infantryman for six years, usually on the
Russian fronts. As a prominent postwar German
writer, he is credited with a major role in the so-
called renewal of German literature during the occupation and after; his work includes essays, radio
plays, novels, and short stories. To the postwar German social scene Böll brings an ironic vision of alienation and despair as well as a mordant comic vein.
His first novel concerns life in the Wehrmacht: The
Train Was on Time (1949); a typical later novel is
Billiards at Half-Past Nine (1959). Böll was awarded a Nobel Prize for literature in 1972. For further
reading: 18 Stories (translated by Leila Vennewitz,
1966).

HEINRICH BÖLL

My Melancholy Face

As I stood by the harbor to watch the gulls, my melancholy face attracted a policeman who walked the beat in this quarter. I was completely
absorbed in the sight of the floating birds, who shot up and plunged down,
looking in vain for something edible: the harbor was desolate, the water
greenish, thick with dirty oil, and in its crusted skin floated all kinds of
discarded rubbish. Not a ship was to be seen, the cranes were rusty, the
warehouses decayed; it seemed that not even rats populated the black de-
bris on the quai; it was quiet. For many years all connections with the
outside had been cut off.

I had fixed my eyes on one particular gull whose flight I was watching.
It hovered near the surface of the water, nervous as a swallow that senses
the approach of a thunderstorm; only once in a while did it dare the
screeching leap upward to unite its course with that of its companions. If I
could have made one wish, I would have chosen bread to feed it to the gulls,
to break crumbs and fix a white point for the purposeless wings, to set a

goal toward which they would fly; to tighten this shrieking web of chaotic trails by a toss of a bread crumb, grasping into them as into a pile of strings that one gathers up. But like them, I too was hungry; tired too, yet happy in spite of my melancholy because it was good to stand there, hands in my pockets, and watch the gulls and drink sadness.

But suddenly an official hand was laid on my shoulder, and a voice said: "Come along!" With this, the hand tried to jerk me around by the shoulder. I stood where I was, shook it off, and said calmly: "You're crazy." "Comrade," the still invisible person said to me, "I'm warning you."

"My dear sir," I replied.

"There are no 'sirs'," he cried angrily. "We're all comrades!" And now he stepped up beside me, looked at me from the side, and I was forced to pull back my happily roaming gaze and sink it into his good eyes: he was serious as a buffalo who has eaten nothing but duty for decades.

"What grounds . . . ," I tried to begin.

"Grounds enough," he said, "your melancholy face."

I laughed.

"Don't laugh!" His anger was genuine. At first I had thought he was bored, because there were no unregistered whores, no staggering sailors, no thieves or absconders to arrest, but now I saw that it was serious: he wanted to arrest me.

"Come along . . . !"

"And why?" I asked calmly.

Before I became aware of it, my left wrist was enclosed in a thin chain, and at this moment I realized that I was lost again. One last time I turned to the roving gulls, glanced into the beautiful gray sky, and tried, with a sudden twist, to throw myself into the water, for it seemed better to me, after all, to drown alone in this filthy water than to be strangled in some backyard by the myrmidons or be locked up again. But the policeman, with a jerk, drew me so close that escape was no longer possible.

"And why?" I asked again.

"There's a law that you have to be happy."

"I am happy," I cried.

"Your melancholy face . . . ," he shook his head.

"But this law is new," I said.

"It's thirty-six hours old, and you know very well that every new law goes into effect twenty-four hours after its proclamation."

"But I don't know it."

"That's no excuse. It was announced day before yesterday, over all the loudspeakers, in all the papers, and it was published in handbills to those," here he looked at me scornfully, "those who have no access to the blessings of the press or the radio; they were scattered over every street in the area. So we'll see where you've spent the last thirty-six hours, comrade."

He dragged me on. Only now did I feel that it was cold and I had no coat, only now did my hunger assert itself and growl before the gates of my stomach, only now did I realize that I was also dirty, unshaven, ragged, and that there were laws that said every comrade was obliged to be clean, shaved, happy, and well-fed. He shoved me in front of him like a scarecrow who, convicted of stealing, had to leave the home of its dreams on the edge of the field. The streets were empty, the way to the precinct not long, and although I had known they would find some reason to arrest me again, still my heart grew heavy, because he led me through the places of my youth, which I had wanted to visit after viewing the harbor: gardens that had been full of shrubs, lovely in their disorder, overgrown paths—all this was now planned, ordered, neat, laid out in squares for the patriotic leagues which had to carry out their exercises here Mondays, Wednesdays, and Saturdays. Only the sky had its former shape and the air was like in those days when my heart had been full of dreams.

Here and there in passing I saw that already in many of the love barracks the state sign had been hung out for those whose turn to participate in the hygienic pleasure was on Wednesday; also many bars seemed authorized to display the sign of drinking, a beer glass stamped out of lead with stripes of the patriotic colors of the area: light-brown, dark-brown, light-brown. No doubt joy reigned already in the hearts of those who had been entered in the hearts of those who had been entered in the state lists of Wednesday drinkers, and could partake of a Wednesday beer.

The unmistakable sign of zeal adhered to everyone who met us, the thin aura of industry surrounded them, probably all the more when they caught sight of the policeman; they all walked faster, showed a perfectly dutiful face, and the women who came out of the stores tried to give their faces an expression of that joy which was expected from them, for they were commanded to show joy, vigorous cheerfulness about the duties of the housewife, who was encouraged to refresh the public worker with a good meal in the evening.

But all these people avoided us skillfully, so that no one had to cross our path directly; wherever signs of life were evident on the street, they disappeared twenty steps ahead of us. Everyone tried to step quickly into a store or turn a corner, and many may have entered an unfamiliar house and waited uneasily behind the door until our steps had faded away.

Only once, just as we were passing a crossing, an older man met us; briefly, I recognized the badge of the schoolteacher on him; it was too late for him to dodge us, and he now tried, after he had first greeted the policeman according to the prescribed regulations (that is, he hit himself three times on the head with a flat hand as a sign of absolute humility), then he tried to fulfill his duty, which demanded that he spit in my face three times and call me the obligatory name: "Traitorous swine." He aimed well, but the day had been hot, his throat must have been dry, because only a few meager, rather unsubstantial drops hit me—which I—against regulations—automatically tried to wipe off with my sleeve; whereupon the policeman kicked me in the behind and hit me with his fist in the middle of my backbone, adding in a calm voice: "Stage 1," which meant the first, mildest form of punishment every policeman could use.

The schoolteacher hurried away quickly. Otherwise everyone succeeded in avoiding us; only one woman, a pale, puffy blonde, taking her prescribed airing beside a love barrack before the evening pleasure, quickly threw me a kiss and I smiled gratefully, while the policeman tried to act as though he hadn't noticed anything. They are urged to allow these women freedoms that would immediately bring any other comrade a heavy punishment. Since they contribute substantially to the improvement of general working morale, they are thought of as standing outside the law, a concession whose significance the state philosopher Dr. Dr. Dr. Bleigoeth branded in the obligatory Journal of (State) Philosophy as a sign of beginning liberalization. I had read it the day before on my way to the capital, when I found a few pages of the magazine in the outhouse of a farm. A student—probably the farmer's son—had glossed it with astute comments.

Luckily we were about to reach the police station, when the sirens started to sound, which meant that the streets would overflow with thousands of people whose faces bore an expression of mild joy (for it was "recommended" not to show too great a joy after work since it would indicate that work was a burden; jubilation, however, was to reign at the beginning of work, jubilation and song)—all these thousands of people would have had to spit at me. Actually the sirens indicated that it was ten minutes before closing, for everyone was expected to indulge in a thorough washing for ten minutes, in accordance with the slogan of the present Chief of State: Happiness and Soap.

At the door to the precinct of this quarter, a plain concrete structure, two guards were posted who bestowed upon me in passing the usual "physical measures": they hit me violently on the temples with their bayonets and cracked the barrels of their pistols against my collarbone, following the preamble to State Law No. 1: "every policeman except the arresting officer is to prove himself before every apprehended (they mean arrested) as an individual power; to the arresting officer falls the good fortune of executing all necessary bodily measures during the interrogation." The State Law No. 1 itself has the following wording: "Every policeman *may* punish anyone; he *must* punish everyone who has been found guilty of a transgression. There is, for all comrades, no exemption from punishment, but a possibility of exemption from punishment."

We now walked through a long, bare corridor, with many large windows; then a door opened automatically, because in the meantime the guards had announced our arrival, since in those days when everyone was happy, good, orderly, and everyone exerted himself to consume the prescribed pound of soap a day, in those days the arrival of an apprehended (an arrested) was indeed an event.

We entered an almost empty room, which contained only a desk with a telephone and two chairs; I was to place myself in the middle of the room; the policeman took off his helmet and sat down.

At first it was silent and nothing happened; they always do it that way; that's the worst part; I felt how my face sagged more and more, I was hungry and tired, and even the last trace of that joy of melancholy had vanished, for I knew that I was lost.

After a few seconds a tall, pale man entered in the brownish uniform of the pre-examiner; he sat down without saying a word and looked at me.

"Occupation?"

"Simple Comrade."

"Born?"

"1.1 one," I said.

"Last employment?"

"Prisoner."

The two looked at each other.

"When and where released?"

"Yesterday, house 12, cell 13."

"Released to where?"

"To the capital."

"Papers."

I took my release paper out of my pocket and handed it over. He fastened it to the green card on which he had started to write my statements.

"Former offense?"

"Happy face."

The two looked at each other.

"Explain," said the pre-examiner.

"At that time," I said, "my happy face attracted a policeman on a day when general mourning was ordered. It was the anniversary of the death of the chief."

"Length of punishment?"

"Five."

"Conduct?"

"Bad."

"Reason?"

"Lack of initiative."

"That's all."

Then the pre-examiner stood up, walked up to me and knocked out exactly three front middle teeth: a sign that I should be branded as a backslider, a measure I had not reckoned with. Then the pre-examiner left the room and a heavy fellow in a dark brown uniform stepped in: the Interrogator.

They all beat me: the Interrogator, the Senior Interrogator, the Head Interrogator, the Preliminary and Final Judge, and also the policeman carried out all the physical measures, as the law commanded; and they sentenced me to ten years because of my melancholy face, just as five years ago they had sentenced me to five years because of my happy face.

But I must try to have no face at all any more, if I succeed in enduring the next ten years with happiness and soap.

James Joyce (1882–1941) was born, reared, and educated in Dublin, Ireland; the city and its inhabitants became central material for virtually all his subsequent literary works, including the novelistic masterpiece, Ulysses *(1922). Nevertheless, Joyce's attitudes towards Dublin and the Irish in general remained ambivalent; somewhat abruptly he elected a now-famous self-imposed exile from his native city. Thus, for years, Joyce and his family lived in Trieste, Paris, or Zurich, where, while writing, he made a living as a teacher of languages for the Berlitz Schools. Partially blind and impoverished, with his work banned by censors and pirated by publishers, Joyce nevertheless forged one of the greatest literary careers of the twentieth century. The short stories came early in his development as a literary artist and are notable for their exploitation of symbol, key, and poetic moments, and for their uncompromising, often scathing view of his native city and its inhabitants. Although Joyce was early recognized as a literary genius by a few fellow writers and critics, his great reputation came about in the years following his death. For further reading:* Dubliners *(1914).*

JAMES JOYCE

A Little Cloud

*E*ight years before he had seen his friend off at the North Wall and wished him godspeed. Gallaher had got on. You could tell that at once by his travelled air, his well-cut tweed suit, and fearless accent. Few fellows had talents like his and fewer still could remain unspoiled by such success. Gallaher's heart was in the right place and he had deserved to win. It was something to have a friend like that.

Little Chandler's thoughts ever since lunchtime had been of his meeting with Gallaher, of Gallaher's invitation and of the great city London where Gallaher lived. He was called Little Chandler because, though he was but slightly under the average stature, he gave one the idea of being a little man. His hands were white and small, his frame was fragile, his voice was quiet and his manners were refined. He took the greatest care of his fair silken hair and moustache and used perfume discreetly on his handkerchief. The half-moons of his nails were perfect and when he smiled you caught a glimpse of a row of childish white teeth.

As he sat at his desk in the King's Inns he thought what changes those eight years had brought. The friend whom he had known under a shabby and necessitous guise had become a brilliant figure on the London Press. He turned often from his tiresome writing to gaze out of the office window. The glow of a late autumn sunset covered the grass plots and walks. It cast a shower of kindly golden dust on the untidy nurses and decrepit old men who drowsed on the benches; it flickered upon all the moving figures—on the children who ran screaming along the gravel paths and on everyone who passed through the gardens. He watched the scene and thought of life; and (as always happened when he thought of life) he became sad. A gentle melancholy took possession of him. He felt how useless it was to struggle against fortune, this being the burden of wisdom which the ages had bequeathed to him.

He remembered the books of poetry upon his shelves at home. He had bought them in his bachelor days and many an evening, as he sat in the little room off the hall, he had been tempted to take one down from the bookshelf and read out something to his wife. But shyness had always held him back; and so the books had remained on their shelves. At times he repeated lines to himself and this consoled him.

When his hour had struck he stood up and took leave of his desk and of his fellow-clerks punctiliously. He emerged from under the feudal arch of the King's Inns, a neat modest figure, and walked swiftly down Henrietta Street. The golden sunset was waning and the air had grown sharp. A horde of grimy children populated the street. They stood or ran in the roadway or crawled up the steps before the gaping doors or squatted like mice upon the thresholds. Little Chandler gave them no thought. He picked his way deftly through all that minute vermin-like life and under the shadow of the gaunt spectral mansions in which the old nobility of Dublin had roystered. No memory of the past touched him, for his mind was full of a present joy.

He had never been in Corless's but he knew the value of the name. He knew that people went there after the theatre to eat oysters and drink liqueurs; and he had heard that the waiters there spoke French and German. Walking swiftly by at night he had seen cabs drawn up before the door and richly dressed ladies, escorted by cavaliers, alight and enter quickly. They wore noisy dresses and many wraps. Their faces were powdered and they caught up their dresses when they touched earth, like alarmed Atalantas. He had always passed without turning his head to look. It was his habit to walk swiftly in the street even by day and whenever he found himself in the city late at night he hurried on his way apprehensively and excitedly. Sometimes, however, he courted the causes of his fear. He chose the darkest and narrowest streets and, as he walked boldly forward, the silence that was spread about his footsteps troubled him, the wandering, silent figures troubled him; and at times a sound of low fugitive laughter made him tremble like a leaf.

He turned to the right towards Capel Street. Ignatius Gallaher on the London Press! Who would have thought it possible eight years before? Still, now that he reviewed the past, Little Chandler could remember many signs of future greatness in his friend. People used to say that Ignatius Gallaher was wild. Of course, he did mix with a rakish set of fellows at that time, drank freely and borrowed money on all sides. In the end he had got mixed up in some shady affair, some money transaction: at least, that was one version of his flight. But nobody denied him talent. There was always a certain . . . something in Ignatius Gallaher that impressed you in spite of yourself. Even when he was out at elbows and at his wits' end for money he kept up a bold face. Little Chandler remembered (and the remembrance brought a slight flush of pride to his cheek) one of Ignatius Gallaher's sayings when he was in a tight corner:

"Half time now, boys," he used to say lightheartedly. "Where's my considering cap?"

That was Ignatius Gallaher all out; and, damn it, you couldn't but admire him for it.

Little Chandler quickened his pace. For the first time in his life he felt himself superior to the people he passed. For the first time his soul revolted against the dull inelegance of Capel Street. There was no doubt about it: if you wanted to succeed you had to go away. You could do nothing in Dublin. As he crossed Grattan Bridge he looked down the river towards the lower quays and pitied the poor stunted houses. They seemed to him a band of tramps, huddled together along the river-banks, their old coats covered with dust and soot, stupefied by the panorama of sunset and waiting for the first chill of night to bid them arise, shake themselves and begone. He wondered whether he could write a poem to express his idea. Perhaps Gallaher might be able to get it into some London paper for him. Could he write something original? He was not sure what idea he wished to express but the thought that a poetic moment had touched him took life within him like an infant hope. He stepped onward bravely.

Every step brought him nearer to London, farther from his own sober inartistic life. A light began to tremble on the horizon of his mind. He was not so old—thirty-two. His temperament might be said to be just at the point of maturity. There were so many different moods and impressions that he wished to express in verse. He felt them within him. He tried to weigh his soul to see if it was a poet's soul. Melancholy was the dominant note of his temperament, he thought, but it was a melancholy tempered by recurrences of faith and resignation and simple joy. If he could give expression to it in a book of poems perhaps men would listen. He would never be popular: he saw that. He could not sway the crowd but he might appeal to a little circle of kindred minds. The English critics, perhaps, would recognise him as one of the Celtic school by reason of the melancholy tone of his poems; besides that, he would put in allusions. He began to invent sentences and phrases from the notice which his book would get. *"Mr. Chandler has the gift of easy and graceful verse.".* . . *"A wistful sadness pervades these poems.".* . . *"The Celtic note."* It was a pity his name was not more Irish-looking. Perhaps it would be better to insert his mother's name before the surname: Thomas Malone Chandler, or better still: T. Malone Chandler. He would speak to Gallaher about it.

He pursued his revery so ardently that he passed his street and had to turn back. As he came near Corless's his former agitation began to overmaster him and he halted before the door in indecision. Finally he opened the door and entered.

The light and noise of the bar held him at the doorways for a few moments. He looked about him, but his sight was confused by the shining of many red and green wine-glasses. The bar seemed to him to be full of people and he felt that the people were observing him curiously. He glanced quickly to right and left (frowning slightly to make his errand appear serious), but when his sight cleared a little he saw that nobody had turned to look at him: and there, sure enough, was Ignatius Gallaher leaning with his back against the counter and his feet planted far apart.

"Hallo, Tommy, old hero, here you are! What is it to be? What will you have? I'm taking whisky: better stuff than we get across the water. Soda? Lithia? No mineral? I'm the same. Spoils the flavour. . . .Here, *garçon,* bring us two halves of malt whisky, like a good fellow. . . .Well, and how have you been pulling along since I saw you last? Dear God, how old we're getting! Do you see any signs of aging in me—eh, what? A little grey and thin on the top—what?"

Ignatius Gallaher took off his hat and displayed a large closely cropped head. His face was heavy, pale and clean-shaven. His eyes, which were of bluish slate-colour, relieved his unhealthy pallor and shone out plainly above the vivid orange tie he wore. Between these rival features the lips appeared very long and shapeless and colourless. He bent his head and felt with two sympathetic fingers the thin hair at the crown. Little Chandler shook his head as a denial. Ignatius Gallaher put on his hat again.

"It pulls you down," he said, "Press life. Always hurry and scurry, looking for copy and sometimes not finding it: and then, always to have something new in your stuff. Damn proofs and printers, I say, for a few days. I'm deuced glad, I can tell you, to get back to the old country. Does a fellow good, a bit of a holiday. I feel a ton better since I landed again in dear dirty Dublin. . . . Here you are, Tommy. Water? Say when."

Little Chandler allowed his whisky to be very much diluted.

"You don't know what's good for you, my boy," said Ignatius Gallaher. "I drink mine neat."

"I drink very little as a rule," said Little Chandler modestly. "An odd half-one or so when I meet any of the old crowd: that's all."

"Ah, well," said Ignatius Gallaher, cheerfully, "here's to us and to old times and old acquaintance."

They clinked glasses and drank the toast.

"I met some of the old gang to-day," said Ignatius Gallaher. "O'Hara seems to be in a bad way. What's he doing?"

"Nothing," said Little Chandler. "He's gone to the dogs."

"But Hogan has a good sit, hasn't he?"

"Yes; he's in the Land Commission."

"I met him one night in London and he seemed to be very flush. . . .Poor O'Hara! Boose, I suppose?"

"Other things, too," said Little Chandler shortly.

Ignatius Gallaher laughed.

"Tommy," he said, "I see you haven't changed an atom. You're the very same serious person that used to lecture me on Sunday mornings when I had a sore head and a fur on my tongue. You'd want to knock about a bit in the world. Have you never been anywhere even for a trip?"

"I've been to the Isle of Man," said Little Chandler.

Ignatius Gallaher laughed.

"The Isle of Man!" he said. "Go to London or Paris: Paris, for choice. That'd do you good."

"Have you seen Paris?"

"I should think I have! I've knocked about there a little."

"And is it really so beautiful as they say?" asked Little Chandler.

He sipped a little of his drink while Ignatius Gallaher finished his boldly.

"Beautiful?" said Ignatius Gallaher, pausing on the word and on the flavour of his drink. "It's not so beautiful, you know. Of course, it is beautiful. . . . But it's the life of Paris; that's the thing. Ah, there's no city like Paris for gaiety, movement, excitement. . . ."

Little Chandler finished his whisky and, after some trouble, succeeded in catching the barman's eye. He ordered the same again.

"I've been to the Moulin Rouge," Ignatius Gallaher continued when the barman had removed their glasses, "and I've been to all the Bohemian cafés. Hot stuff! Not for a pious chap like you, Tommy."

Little Chandler said nothing until the barman returned with two glasses: then he touched his friend's glass lightly and reciprocated the former toast. He was beginning to feel somewhat disillusioned. Gallaher's accent and way of expressing himself did not please him. There was something vulgar in his friend which he had not observed before. But perhaps it was only the result of living in London amid the bustle and competition of the Press. The old personal charm was still there under this new gaudy manner. And, after all, Gallaher had lived, he had seen the world. Little Chandler looked at his friend enviously.

"Everything in Paris is gay," said Ignatius Gallaher. "They believe in enjoying life—and don't you think they're right? If you want to enjoy yourself properly you must go to Paris. And, mind you, they've a great feeling for the Irish there. When they heard I was from Ireland they were ready to eat me, man."

Little Chandler took four or five sips from his glass.

"Tell me," he said, "is it true that Paris is so . . . immoral as they say?"

Ignatius Gallaher made a catholic gesture with his right arm.

"Every place is immoral," he said. "Of course you do find spicy bits in Paris. Go to one of the students' balls, for instance. That's lively, if you like, when the *cocottes* begin to let themselves loose. You know what they are, I suppose?"

"I've heard of them," said Little Chandler.

Ignatius Gallaher drank off his whisky and shook his head.

"Ah," he said, "you may say what you like. There's no woman like the Parisienne—for style, for go."

"Then it is an immoral city," said Little Chandler, with timid insistence—"I mean, compared with London or Dublin?"

"London!" said Ignatius Gallaher. "It's six of one and half-a-dozen of the other. You ask Hogan, my boy. I showed him a bit about London when he was over there. He'd open your eye. . . . I say, Tommy, don't make punch of that whisky: liquor up."

"No, really. . . ."

"O, come on, another one won't do you any harm. What is it? The same again, I suppose?"

"Well . . . all right."

"*François*, the same again. . . .Will you smoke, Tommy?"

Ignatius Gallaher produced his cigar-case. The two friends lit their cigars and puffed at them in silence until their drinks were served.

"I'll tell you my opinion," said Ignatius Gallaher, emerging after some time from the clouds of smoke in which he had taken refuge, "it's a rum world. Talk of immorality! I've heard of cases—what am I saying?—I've known them: cases of . . . immorality. . . ."

Ignatius Gallaher puffed thoughtfully at his cigar and then, in a calm historian's tone, he proceeded to sketch for his friend some pictures of the corruption which was rife abroad. He summarised the vices of many capitals and seemed inclined to award the palm to Berlin. Some things he could not vouch for (his friends had told him), but of others he had had personal experience. He spared neither rank nor caste. He revealed many of the secrets of religious houses on the Continent and described some of the practices which were fashionable in high society and ended by telling, with details, a story about an English duchess—a story which he knew to be true. Little Chandler was astonished.

"Ah, well," said Ignatius Gallaher, "here we are in old jog-along Dublin where nothing is known of such things."

"How dull you must find it," said Little Chandler, "after all the other places you've seen!"

"Well," said Ignatius Gallaher, "it's a relaxation to come over here, you know. And, after all, it's the old country, as they say, isn't it? You can't help having a certain feeling for it. That's human nature. . . . But tell me something about yourself. Hogan told me you had . . . tasted the joys of connubial bliss. Two years ago, wasn't it?"

Little Chandler blushed and smiled.

"Yes," he said. "I was married last May twelve months."

"I hope it's not too late in the day to offer my best wishes," said Ignatius Gallaher. "I didn't know your address or I'd have done so at the time."

He extended his hand, which Little Chandler took.

"Well, Tommy," he said, "I wish you and yours every joy in life, old chap, and tons of money, and may you never die till I shoot you. And that's the wish of a sincere friend, an old friend. You know that?"

"I know that," said Little Chandler.

"Any youngsters?" said Ignatius Gallaher.

Little Chandler blushed again.

"We have one child," he said.

"Son or daughter?"

"A little boy."

Ignatius Gallaher slapped his friend sonorously on the back.

"Bravo," he said, "I wouldn't doubt you, Tommy."

Little Chandler smiled, looked confusedly at his glass and bit his lower lip with three childishly white front teeth.

"I hope you'll spend an evening with us," he said, "before you go back. My wife will be delighted to meet you. We can have a little music and—"

"Thanks awfully, old chap," said Ignatius Gallaher, "I'm sorry we didn't meet earlier. But I must leave to-morrow night."

"To-night, perhaps . . . ?"

"I'm awfully sorry, old man. You see I'm over here with another fellow, clever young chap he is too, and we arranged to go to a little card party. Only for that . . ."

"O, in that case. . . ."

"But who knows?" said Ignatius Gallaher considerately. "Next year I may take a little skip over here now that I've broken the ice. It's only a pleasure deferred."

"Very well," said Little Chandler, "the next time you come we must have an evening together. That's agreed now, isn't it?"

"Yes, that's agreed," said Ignatius Gallaher. "Next year if I come, *parole d'honneur.*"

"And to clinch the bargain," said Little Chandler, "we'll just have one more now."

Ignatius Gallaher took out a large gold watch and looked at it.

"Is it to be the last?" he said. "Because you know, I have an a.p."

"O, yes, positively," said Little Chandler.

"Very well, then," said Ignatius Gallaher, "let us have another one as a *deoc an doruis*—that's good vernacular for a small whisky, I believe."

Little Chandler ordered the drinks. The blush which had risen to his face a few moments before was establishing itself. A trifle made him blush at any time: and now he felt warm and excited. Three small whiskies had gone to his head and Gallaher's strong cigar had confused his mind, for he was a delicate and abstinent person. The adventure of meeting Gallaher after eight years, of finding himself with Gallaher in Corless's surrounded by lights and noise, of listening to Gallaher's stories and of sharing for a brief space Gallaher's vagrant and triumphant life, upset the equipoise of his sensitive nature. He felt acutely the contrast between his own life and his friend's, and it seemed to him unjust. Gallaher was his inferior in birth and education. He was sure that he could do something better than his friend had ever done, or could ever do, something higher than mere tawdry journalism if he only got the chance. What was it that stood in his way? His unfortunate timidity! He wished to vindicate himself in some way, to assert his manhood. He saw behind Gallaher's refusal of his invitation. Gallaher was only patronising him by his friendliness just as he was patronising Ireland by his visit.

The barman brought their drinks. Little Chandler pushed one glass towards his friend and took up the other boldly.

"Who knows?" he said, as they lifted their glasses. "When you come next year I may have the pleasure of wishing long life and happiness to Mr. and Mrs. Ignatius Gallaher."

Ignatius Gallaher in the act of drinking closed one eye expressively over the rim of his glass. When he had drunk he smacked his lips decisively, set down his glass and said:

"No blooming fear of that, my boy. I'm going to have my fling first and see a bit of life and the world before I put my head in the sack—if I ever do."

"Some day you will," said Little Chandler calmly.

Ignatius Gallaher turned his orange tie and slate-blue eyes full upon his friend.

"You think so?" he said.

"You'll put your head in the sack," repeated Little Chandler stoutly, "like everyone else if you can find the girl."

He had slightly emphasised his tone and he was aware that he had betrayed himself; but, though the colour had heightened in his cheek, he did not flinch from his friend's gaze. Ignatius Gallaher watched him for a few moments and then said:

"If ever it occurs, you may bet your bottom dollar there'll be no mooning and spooning about it. I mean to marry money. She'll have a good fat account at the bank or she won't do for me."

Little Chandler shook his head.

"Why, man alive," said Ignatius Gallaher, vehemently, "do you know what it is? I've only to say the word and to-morrow I can have the woman and the cash. You don't believe it? Well, I know it. There are hundreds— what am I saying?—thousands of rich Germans and Jews, rotten with money, that'd only be too glad. . . . You wait a while, my boy. See if I don't play my cards properly. When I go about a thing I mean business, I tell you. You just wait."

He tossed his glass to his mouth, finished his drink and laughed loudly. Then he looked thoughtfully before him and said in a calmer tone:

"But I'm in no hurry. They can wait. I don't fancy tying myself up to one woman, you know."

He imitated with his mouth the act of tasting and made a wry face.

"Must get a bit stale, I should think," he said.

Little Chandler sat in the room off the hall, holding a child in his arms. To save money they kept no servant but Annie's young sister Monica came for an hour or so in the morning and an hour or so in the evening to help. But Monica had gone home long ago. It was a quarter to nine. Little Chandler had come home late for tea and, moreover, he had forgotten to bring Annie home the parcel of coffee from Bewley's. Of course she was in a bad humour and gave him short answers. She said she would do without any tea but when it came near the time at which the shop at the corner closed she decided to go out herself for a quarter of a pound of tea and two pounds of sugar. She put the sleeping child deftly in his arms and said:

"Here. Don't waken him."

A little lamp with a white china shade stood upon the table and its light fell over a photograph which was enclosed in a frame of crumpled horn. It was Annie's photograph. Little Chandler looked at it, pausing at the thin tight lips. She wore the pale blue summer blouse which he had brought her home as a present one Saturday. It had cost him ten and elevenpence; but what an agony of nervousness it had cost him! How he had suffered that day, waiting at the shop door until the shop was empty, standing at the counter and trying to appear at his ease while the girl piled ladies' blouses before him, paying at the desk and forgetting to take up the odd penny of his change, being called back by the cashier, and finally, striving to hide his blushes as he left the shop by examining the parcel to see if it was securely tied. When he brought the blouse home Annie kissed him and said it was very pretty and stylish; but when she heard the price she threw the blouse on the table and said it was a regular swindle to charge ten and elevenpence for it. At first she wanted to take it back but when she tried it on she was delighted with it, especially with the make of the sleeves, and kissed him and said he was very good to think of her.

Hm! . . .

He looked coldly into the eyes of the photograph and they answered coldly. Certainly they were pretty and the face itself was pretty. But he found something mean in it. Why was it so unconscious and ladylike? The composure of the eyes irritated him. They repelled him and defied him: there was no passion in them, no rapture. He thought of what Gallaher had said about rich Jewesses. Those dark Oriental eyes, he thought, how full they are of passion, of voluptuous longing! . . .Why had he married the eyes in the photograph?

He caught himself up at the question and glanced nervously round the room. He found something mean in the pretty furniture which he had brought for his house on the hire system. Annie had chosen it herself and it reminded him of her. It too was prim and pretty. A dull resentment against his life awoke within him. Could he not escape from his little house? Was it too late for him to try to live bravely like Gallaher? Could he go to London? There was the furniture still to be paid for. If he could only write a book and get it published, that might open the way for him.

A volume of Byron's poems lay before him on the table. He opened it cautiously with his left hand lest he should waken the child and began to read the first poem in the book:

"Hushed are the winds and still the evening gloom,
*   Not e'en a Zephyr wanders through the grove,*
* Whilst I return to view my Margaret's tomb*
*   And scatter flowers on the dust I love."*

He paused. He felt the rhythm of the verse about him in the room. How melancholy it was! Could he, too, write like that, express the melancholy of his soul in verse? There were so many things he wanted to describe: his sensation of a few hours before on Grattan Bridge, for example. If he could get back again into that mood. . . .

The child awoke and began to cry. He turned from the page and tried to hush it: but it would not be hushed. He began to rock it to and fro in his arms but its wailing cry grew keener. He rocked it faster while his eyes began to read the second stanza:

"Within this narrow cell reclines her clay,
  That clay where once . . ."

It was useless. He couldn't read. He couldn't do anything. The wailing of the child pierced the drum of his ear. It was useless, useless! He was a prisoner for life. His arms trembled with anger and suddenly bending to the child's face he shouted:

"Stop!"

The child stopped for an instant, had a spasm of fright and began to scream. He jumped up from his chair and walked hastily up and down the room with the child in his arms. It began to sob piteously, losing its breath for four or five seconds, and then bursting out anew. The thin walls of the room echoed the sound. He tried to soothe it but it sobbed more convulsively. He looked at the contracted and quivering face of the child and began to be alarmed. He counted seven sobs without a break between them and caught the child to his breast in fright. If it died! . . .

The door was burst open and a young woman ran in, panting.

"What is it? What is it?" she cried.

The child, hearing its mother's voice, broke out into a paroxysm of sobbing.

"It's nothing, Annie . . . it's nothing. . . . He began to cry . . ."

She flung her parcels on the floor and snatched the child from him.

"What have you done to him?" she cried, glaring into his face.

Little Chandler sustained for one moment the gaze of her eyes and his heart closed together as he met the hatred in them. He began to stammer:

"It's nothing. . . . He . . . he began to cry. . . . I couldn't . . . I didn't do anything. . . . What?"

Giving no heed to him she began to walk up and down the room, clasping the child tightly in her arms and murmuring:

"My little man! My little mannie! Was 'ou frightened, love? . . . There now, love! There now! . . . Lambabaun! Mamma's little lamb of the world! . . . There now!"

Little Chandler felt his cheeks suffused with shame and he stood back out of the lamplight. He listened while the paroxysm of the child's sobbing grew less and less; and tears of remorse started to his eyes.

VIRGINIA WOOLF

The Duchess and the Jeweller

Oliver Bacon lived at the top of a house overlooking the Green Park. He had a flat; chairs jutted out at the right angles—chairs covered in hide. Sofas filled the bays of the windows—sofas covered in tapestry. The windows, the three long windows, had the proper allowance of discreet net and figured satin. The mahogany sideboard bulged discreetly with the right brandies, whiskeys, and liqueurs. And from the middle window he looked down upon the glossy roofs of fashionable cars packed in the narrow straits of Piccadilly. A more central position could not be imagined. And at eight in the morning he would have his breakfast brought in on a tray by a man-servant: the man-servant would unfold his crimson dressing-gown; he would rip his letters open with his long pointed nails and would extract thick white cards of invitation upon which the engraving stood up roughly from duchesses, countesses, viscountesses, and Honourable Ladies. Then he would wash; then he would eat his toast; then he would read his paper by the bright burning fire of electric coals.

"Behold Oliver," he would say, addressing himself. "You who began life in a filthy little alley, you who . . ." and he would look down at his legs, so shapely in their perfect trousers; at his boots; at his spats. They were all shapely, shining; cut from the best cloth by the best scissors in Savile Row. But he dismantled himself often and became again a little boy in a dark alley. He had once thought *that* the height of his ambition—selling stolen dogs to fashionable women in Whitechapel. And once he had been done. "Oh, Oliver," his mother had wailed. "Oh, Oliver! When will you have sense, my son?" . . .Then he had gone behind a counter; had sold cheap watches; then he had taken a wallet to Amsterdam. . . .At that memory he would chuckle—the old Oliver remembering the young. Yes, he had done well with the three diamonds; also there was the commission on the emerald. After that he went into the private room behind the shop in Hatton Garden; the room with the scales, the safe, the thick magnifying glasses. And then . . . and then. . . . He chuckled. When he passed through the knots of jewellers in the hot evening who were discussing prices, gold mines, diamonds, reports from South Africa, one of them would lay a finger to the side of his nose and murmur, "Hum-m-m," as he passed. It was no more than a murmur; no more than a nudge on the shoulder, a finger on the nose, a buzz that ran through the cluster of jewellers in Hatton Garden on a hot afternoon—oh, many years ago now! But still Oliver felt it purring down his spine, the nudge, the murmur that meant, "Look at him—young Oliver, the young jeweller—there he goes." Young he was then. And he dressed better and better; and had, first a hansom cab; then a car; and first he went up to the dress circle, then down into the stalls. And he had a villa at Richmond, overlooking the river, with trellises of red roses; and Mademoiselle used to pick one every morning and stick it in his button-hole.

"So," said Oliver Bacon, rising and stretching his legs. "So. . . ."

And he stood beneath the picture of an old lady on the mantelpiece and raised his hands. "I have kept my word," he said, laying his hands together, palm to palm, as if he were doing homage to her. "I have won my bet." That was so; he was the richest jeweller in England; but his nose, which was long and flexible, like an elephant's trunk, seemed to say by its curious quiver at the nostrils (but it seemed as if the whole nose quivered, not only the nostrils) that he was not satisfied yet; still smelt something under the ground a little further off. Imagine a giant hog in a pasture rich with truffles; after unearthing this truffle and that, still it smells a bigger, a blacker truffle under the ground further off. So Oliver snuffed always in the rich earth of Mayfair another truffle, a blacker, a bigger further off.

Now then he straightened the pearl in his tie, cased himself in his smart blue overcoat; took his yellow gloves and his cane; and swayed as he descended the stairs and half snuffed, half sighed through his long sharp nose as he passed out into Piccadilly. For was he not still a sad man, a dissatisfied man, a man who seeks something that is hidden, though he had won his bet?

He swayed slightly as he walked, as the camel at the zoo sways from side to side when it walks along the asphalt paths laden with grocers and their wives eating from paper bags and throwing little bits of silver paper crumpled up on to the path. The camel despises the grocers; the camel is dissatisfied with its lot; the camel sees the blue lake and the fringe of palm trees in front of it. So the great jeweller, the greatest jeweller in the whole world, swung down Piccadilly, perfectly dressed, with his gloves, with his cane; but dissatisfied still, till he reached the dark little shop, that was famous in France, in Germany, in Austria, in Italy, and all over America—the dark little shop in the street off Bond Street.

As usual, he strode through the shop without speaking, though the four men, the two old men, Marshall and Spencer, and the two young men, Hammond and Wicks, stood straight and looked at him, envying him. It was only with one finger of the amber-coloured glove, waggling, that he acknowledged their presence. And he went in and shut the door of his private room behind him.

Then he unlocked the grating that barred the window. The cries of Bond Street came in; the purr of the distant traffic. The light from reflectors at the back of the shop struck upwards. One tree waved six green leaves, for it was June. But Mademoiselle had married Mr. Pedder of the local brewery—no one stuck roses in his buttonhole now.

"So," he half sighed, half snorted, "so—"

Then he touched a spring in the wall and slowly the panelling slid open, and behind it were the steel safes, five, no, six of them, all of burnished steel. He twisted a key; unlocked one; then another. Each was lined with a pad of deep crimson velvet; in each lay jewels—bracelets, necklaces, rings, tiaras, ducal coronets; loose stones in glass shells; rubies, emeralds, pearls, diamonds. All safe, shining, cool, yet burning, eternally, with their own compressed light.

"Tears!" said Oliver, looking at the pearls.

"Heart's blood!" he said, looking at the rubies.

"Gunpowder!" he continued, rattling the diamonds so that they flashed and blazed.

"Gunpowder enough to blow Mayfair—sky high, high, high!" He threw his head back and made a sound like a horse neighing as he said it.

The telephone buzzed obsequiously in a low muted voice on his table. He shut the safe.

"In ten minutes," he said. "Not before." And he sat down at his desk and looked at the heads of the Roman emperors that were graved on his sleeve links. And again he dismantled himself and became once more the little boy playing marbles in the alley where they sell stolen dogs on Sunday. He became that wily astute little boy, with lips like wet cherries. He dabbled his fingers in ropes of tripe; he dipped them in pans of frying fish; he dodged in and out among the crowds. He was slim, lissome, with eyes like licked stones. And now—now—the hands of the clock ticked on, one, two, three, four. . . . The Duchess of Lambourne waited his pleasure; the Duchess of Lambourne, daughter of a hundred Earls. She would wait for ten minutes on a chair at the counter. She would wait his pleasure. She would wait till he was ready to see her. He watched the clock in its shagreen case. The hand moved on. With each tick the clock handed him—so it seemed—pâté de foie gras, a glass of champagne, another of fine brandy, a cigar costing one guinea. The clock laid them on the table beside him as the ten minutes passed. Then he heard soft slow footsteps approaching; a rustle in the corridor. The door opened. Mr. Hammond flattened himself against the wall.

"Her Grace!" he announced.

And he waited there, flattened against the wall.

And Oliver, rising, could hear the rustle of the dress of the Duchess as she came down the passage. Then she loomed up, filling the door, filling the room with the aroma, the prestige, the arrogance, the pomp, the pride of all the Dukes and Duchesses swollen in one wave. And as a wave breaks, she broke, as she sat down, spreading and splashing and falling over Oliver Bacon, the great jeweller, covering him with sparkling bright colours, green, rose, violet; and odours; and iridescences; and rays shooting from fingers, nodding from plumes, flashing from silk; for she was very large, very fat, tightly girt in pink taffeta, and past her prime. As a parasol with many flounces, as a peacock with many feathers, shuts its flounces, folds its feathers, so she subsided and shut herself as she sank down in the leather armchair.

"Good morning, Mr. Bacon," said the Duchess. And she held out her hand which came through the slit of her white glove. And Oliver bent low as he shook it. And as their hands touched the link was forged between them once more. They were friends, yet enemies; he was master, she was mistress; each cheated the other, each needed the other, each feared the other, each felt this and knew this every time they touched hands thus in the little back room with the white light outside, and the tree with its six leaves, and the sound of the street in the distance and behind them the safes.

"And today, Duchess—what can I do for you today?" said Oliver, very softly.

The Duchess opened her heart, her private heart, gaped wide. And with a sign but no word she took from her bag a long wash-leather pouch—

it looked like a lean yellow ferret. And from a slit in the ferret's belly she dropped pearls—ten pearls. They rolled from the slit in the ferret's belly—one, two, three, four—like the eggs of some heavenly bird.

"All that's left me, dear Mr. Bacon," she moaned. Five, six, seven—down they rolled, down the slopes of the vast mountain sides that fell between her knees into one narrow valley—the eighth, the ninth, and the tenth. There they lay in the glow of the peach-blossom taffeta. Ten pearls.

"From the Appleby cincture," she mourned. "The last . . . the last of them all."

Oliver stretched out and took one of the pearls between finger and thumb. It was round, it was lustrous. But real was it, or false? Was she lying again? Did she dare?

She laid her plump padded finger across her lips. "If the Duke knew . . ." she whispered. "Dear Mr. Bacon, a bit of bad luck. . . ."

Been gambling again, had she?

"That villain! That sharper!" she hissed.

The man with the chipped cheek bone? A bad 'un. And the Duke was straight as a poker; with side whiskers; would cut her off, shut her up down there if he knew—what I know, thought Oliver, and glanced at the safe.

"Araminta, Daphne, Diana," she moaned. "It's for *them.*"

The ladies Araminta, Daphne, Diana—her daughters. He knew them; adored them. But it was Diana he loved.

"You have all my secrets," she leered. Tears slid; tears fell; tears, like diamonds, collecting powder in the ruts of her cherry blossom cheeks.

"Old friend," she murmured, "old friend."

"Old friend," he repeated, "old friend," as if he licked the words.

"How much?" he queried.

She covered the pearls with her hand.

"Twenty thousand," she whispered.

But was it real or false, the one he held in his hand? The Appleby cincture—hadn't she sold it already? He would ring for Spencer or Hammond. "Take it and test it," he would say. He stretched to the bell.

"You will come down tomorrow?" she urged, she interrupted. "The Prime Minister—His Royal Highness. . . ." She stopped. "And Diana . . ." she added.

Oliver took his hand off the bell.

He looked past her, at the backs of the houses in Bond Street. But he saw, not the houses in Bond Street, but a dimpling river; and trout rising and salmon; and the Prime Minister; and himself too, in white waistcoat; and then, Diana. He looked down at the pearl in his hand. But how could he test it, in the light of the river, in the light of the eyes of Diana? But the eyes of the Duchess were on him.

"Twenty thousand," she moaned. "My honour!"

The honour of the mother of Diana! He drew his cheque book towards him; he took out his pen.

"Twenty—" he wrote. Then he stopped writing. The eyes of the old woman in the picture were on him—of the old woman his mother.

"Oliver!" she warned him. "Have sense! Don't be a fool!"

"Oliver!" the Duchess entreated—it was "Oliver" now, not "Mr. Bacon." "You'll come for a long week-end?"

Alone in the woods with Diana! Riding alone in the woods with Diana!

"Thousand," he wrote, and signed it.

"Here you are," he said.

And there opened all the flounces of the parasol, all the plumes of the peacock, the radiance of the wave, the swords and spears of Agincourt, as she rose from her chair. And the two old men and the two young men, Spencer and Marshall, Wicks and Hammond, flattened themselves behind the counter envying him as he led her through the shop to the door. And he waggled his yellow glove in their faces, and she held her honour—a cheque for twenty thousand pounds with his signature—quite firmly in her hands.

"Are they false or are they real?" asked Oliver, shutting his private door. There they were, ten pearls on the blotting-paper on the table. He took them to the window. He held them under his lens to the light. . . . This, then, was the truffle he had routed out of the earth! Rotten at the centre—rotten at the core!

"Forgive me, oh, my mother!" he sighed, raising his hand as if he asked pardon of the old woman in the picture. And again he was a little boy in the alley where they sold dogs on Sunday.

"For," he murmured, laying the palms of his hands together, "it is to be a long week-end."

D. H. (David Henry) Lawrence (1885–1930), short-story writer, critic, poet, and novelist of genius, was the son of a coal miner in Nottinghamshire. A scholarship student at college, he subsequently taught school (the sciences) until his literary success made possible the less secure but more flexible life of the professional writer. The major themes of his best-known novels, Sons and Lovers *(1913) and* Women In Love *(1920), encompass the anxieties of human life, the difficulty or impossibility of rewarding sexual relationships, and the distinctions between individuals on the basis of class origin. His style is often poetic, and everywhere his works present psychological insights of great perception. Among other things Lawrence is a stimulating cultural critic, and a travel writer of high quality:* Twilight in Italy *(1916),* Etruscan Places *(1932). During his brief lifetime Lawrence wandered and lived in a great many places, including Mexico, Australia, and the United States; after residence in Taos, New Mexico, he died of tuberculosis at Vence, in the south of France. For further reading:* The Complete Stories of D. H. Lawrence *(1961).*

D. H. LAWRENCE

Tickets, Please

*T*here is in the Midlands a single-line tramway system which boldly leaves the county town and plunges off into the black, industrial countryside, up hill and down dale, through the long ugly villages of workmen's houses, over canals and railways, past churches perched high and nobly over the smoke and shadows, through stark, grimy cold little market-places, tilting away in a rush past cinemas and shops down to the hollow where the collieries are, then up again, past a little rural church, under the ash trees, on in a rush to the terminus, the last little ugly place of industry, the cold little town that shivers on the edge of the wild, gloomy country beyond. There the green and creamy coloured tram-car seems to pause and purr with curious satisfaction. But in a few minutes—the clock on the turret of the Co-operative Wholesale Society's shops gives the time—away it starts once more on the adventure. Again there are the reckless swoops downhill, bouncing the loops: again the chilly wait in the hill-top market-place: again the breathless slithering round the precipitous drop under the church: again the patient halts at the loops, waiting for the outcoming car: so on and on, for two long hours, till at last the city looms beyond the fat gas-works, the narrow factories draw near, we are in the sordid streets of the great town, once more we sidle to a standstill at our terminus, abashed by the great crimson and cream-coloured city cars, but still perky, jaunty, somewhat dare-devil, green as a jaunty sprig of parsley out of a black colliery garden.

To ride on these cars is always an adventure. Since we are in war-time, the drivers are men unfit for active service: cripples and hunchbacks. So they have the spirit of the devil in them. The ride becomes a steeplechase. Hurray! we have leapt in a clear jump over the canal bridges—now for the four-lane corner. With a shriek and a trail of sparks we are clear again. To be sure, a tram often leaps the rails—but what matter! It sits in a ditch till other trams come to haul it out. It is quite common for a car, packed with one solid mass of living people, to come to a dead halt in the midst of unbroken blackness, the heart of nowhere on a dark night, and for the driver and the girl conductor to call, "All get off—car's on fire!" Instead, however, of rushing out in a panic, the passengers stolidly reply: "Get on—get on! We're not coming out. We're stopping where we are. Push on, George." So till flames actually appear.

The reason for this reluctance to dismount is that the nights are howlingly cold, black, and windswept, and a car is a haven of refuge. From village to village the miners travel, for a change of cinema, of girl, of pub. The trams are desperately packed. Who is going to risk himself in the black gulf outside, to wait perhaps an hour for another tram, then to see the forlorn notice "Depot Only," because there is something wrong! Or to greet a unit of three bright cars all so tight with people that they sail past with a howl of derision. Trams that pass in the night.

This, the most dangerous tram-service in England, as the authorities declare, with pride, is entirely conducted by girls, and driven by rash young men, a little crippled, or by delicate young men, who creep forward in terror. The girls are fearless young hussies. In their ugly blue uniform, skirts up to their knees, shapeless old peaked caps on their heads, they have all the sang-froid of an old non-commissioned officer. With a tram packed with howling colliers, roaring hymns downstairs and a sort of antiphony of obscenities upstairs, the lasses are perfectly at their ease. They pounce on the youths who try to evade their ticket-machine. They push off the men at the end of their distance. They are not going to be done in the eye—not they. They fear nobody—and everybody fears them.

"Hello, Annie!"

"Hello, Ted!"

"Oh, mind my corn, Miss Stone. It's my belief you've got a heart of stone, for you've trod on it again."

"You should keep it in your pocket," replies Miss Stone, and she goes sturdily upstairs in her high boots.

"Tickets, please."

She is peremptory, suspicious, and ready to hit first. She can hold her own against ten thousand. The step of that tram-car is her Thermopylae.

Therefore, there is a certain wild romance aboard these cars—and in the sturdy bosom of Annie herself. The time for soft romance is in the morning, between ten o'clock and one, when things are rather slack: that is, except market-day and Saturday. Thus Annie has time to look about her. Then she often hops off her car and into a shop where she has spied something, while the driver chats in the main road. There is very good feeling between the girls and the drivers. Are they not companions in peril, shipments aboard this careering vessel of a tram-car, for ever rocking on the waves of a stormy land.

Then, also, during the easy hours, the inspectors are most in evidence. For some reason, everybody employed in this tram-service is young: there are no grey heads. It would not do. Therefore the inspectors are of the right age, and one, the chief, is also goodlooking. See him stand on a wet, gloomy morning, in his long oilskin, his peaked cap well down over his eyes, waiting to board a car. His face is ruddy, his small brown moustache is weathered, he has a faint impudent smile. Fairly tall and agile, even in his waterproof, he springs aboard a car and greets Annie.

"Hello, Annie! Keeping the wet out?"

"Trying to."

There are only two people in the car. Inspecting is soon over. Then for a long and impudent chat on the foot-board, a good, easy, twelve-mile chat.

The inspector's name is John Thomas Raynor—always called John Thomas, except sometimes, in malice, Coddy. His face sets in fury when he is addressed, from a distance, with this abbreviation. There is considerable scandal about John Thomas in half a dozen villages. He flirts with the girl conductors in the morning, and walks out with them in the dark night, when they leave their tramcar at the depôt. Of course, the girls quit the service frequently. Then he flirts and walks out with the new-comer: always providing she is sufficiently attractive, and that she will consent to walk. It is remarkable, however, that most of the girls are quite comely, they are all young, and this roving life aboard the car gives them a sailor's dash and recklessness. What matter how they behave when the ship is in port? Tomorrow they will be aboard again.

Annie, however, was something of a Tartar, and her sharp tongue had kept John Thomas at arm's length for many months. Perhaps, therefore, she liked him all the more: for he always came up smiling, with impudence. She watched him vanquish one girl, then another. She could tell by the movement of his mouth and eyes, when he flirted with her in the morning, that he had been walking out with this lass, or the other, the night before. A fine cock-of-the-walk he was. She could sum him up pretty well.

In this subtle antagonism they knew each other like old friends, they were as shrewd with one another almost as man and wife. But Annie had always kept him sufficiently at arm's length. Besides, she had a boy of her own.

The Statutes fair, however, came in November, at Bestwood. It happened that Annie had the Monday night off. It was a drizzling ugly night, yet she dressed herself up and went to the fair ground. She was alone, but she expected soon to find a pal of some sort.

The roundabouts were veering round and grinding out their music, the side-shows were making as much commotion as possible. In the coco-nut shies there were no coco-nuts, but artificial wartime substitutes, which the lads declared were fastened into the irons. There was a sad decline in brilliance and luxury. None the less, the ground was muddy as ever, there was the same crush, the press of faces lighted up by the flares and the electric lights, the same smell of naphtha and a few fried potatoes, and of electricity.

Who should be the first to greet Miss Annie on the show-ground but John Thomas. He had a black overcoat buttoned up to his chin, and a tweed cap pulled down over his brows, his face between was ruddy and smiling and handy as ever. She knew so well the way his mouth moved.

She was very glad to have a "boy." To be at the Statutes without a fellow was no fun. Instantly, like the gallant he was, he took her on the Dragons, grim-toothed, roundabout switchbacks. It was not nearly so exciting as a tram-car actually. But, then, to be seated in a shaking, green dragon, uplifted above the sea of bubble faces, careering in a rickety fashion in the lower heavens, whilst John Thomas leaned over her, his cigarette in his mouth, was after all the right style. She was a plump, quick, alive little creature. So she was quite excited and happy.

John Thomas made her stay on for the next round. And therefore she could hardly for shame repulse him when he put his arm round her and drew her a little nearer to him, in a very warm and cuddly manner. Besides, he was fairly discreet, he kept his movement as hidden as possible. She looked down, and saw that his red, clean hand was out of sight of the crowd. And they knew each other so well. So they warmed up to the fair.

After the dragons they went on the horses. John Thomas paid each time, so she could but be complaisant. He, of course, sat astride on the outer horse—named "Black Bess"—and she sat sideways, towards him, on the inner horse—named "Wildfire." But of course John Thomas was not going to sit discreetly on "Black Bess," holding the brass bar. Round they spun and heaved, in the light. And round he swung on his wooden steed, flinging one leg across her mount, and perilously tipping up and down, across the space, half lying back, laughing at her. He was perfectly happy; she was afraid her hat was on one side, but she was excited.

He threw quoits on a table, and won for her two large, pale blue hat-pins. And then, hearing the noise of the cinemas, announcing another performance, they climbed the boards and went in.

Of course, during these performances pitch darkness falls from time to time, when the machine goes wrong. Then there is a wild whooping, and a loud smacking of simulated kisses. In these moments John Thomas drew Annie towards him. After all, he had a wonderfully warm, cosy way of holding a girl with his arm, he seemed to make such a nice fit. And, after all, it was pleasant to be so held: so very comforting and cosy and nice. He leaned over her and she felt his breath on her hair; she knew he wanted to kiss her on the lips. And, after all, he was so warm and she fitted in to him so softly. After all, she wanted him to touch her lips.

But the light sprang up; she also started electrically, and put her hat straight. He left his arm lying nonchalantly behind her. Well, it was fun, it was exciting to be at the Statutes with John Thomas.

When the cinema was over they went for a walk across the dark, damp fields. He had all the arts of love-making. He was especially good at holding a girl, when he sat with her on a stile in the black, drizzling darkness. He seemed to be holding her in space, against his own warmth and gratification. And his kisses were soft and slow and searching.

So Annie walked out with John Thomas, though she kept her own boy dangling in the distance. Some of the tram-girls chose to be huffy. But there, you must take things as you find them, in this life.

There was no mistake about it, Annie liked John Thomas a good deal. She felt so rich and warm in herself whenever he was near. And John Thomas really liked Annie, more than usual. The soft, melting way in which she could flow into a fellow, as if she melted into his very bones, was something rare and good. He fully appreciated this.

But with a developing acquaintance there began a developing intimacy. Annie wanted to consider him a person, a man: she wanted to take an intelligent interest in him, and to have an intelligent response. She did not want a mere nocturnal presence, which was what he was so far. And she prided herself that he could not leave her.

Here she made a mistake. John Thomas intended to remain a nocturnal presence; he had no idea of becoming an all-round individual to her. When she started to take an intelligent interest in him and his life and his character, he sheered off. He hated intelligent interest. And he knew that the only way to stop it was to avoid it. The possessive female was aroused in Annie. So he left her.

It is no use saying she was not surprised. She was at first startled, thrown out of her count. For she had been so *very* sure of holding him. For a while she was staggered, and everything became uncertain to her. Then she wept with fury, indignation, desolation, and misery. Then she had a spasm of despair. And then, when he came, still impudently, on to her car, still familiar, but letting her see by the movement of his head that he had gone away to somebody else for the time being, and was enjoying pastures new, then she determined to have her own back.

She had a very shrewd idea what girls John Thomas had taken out. She went to Nora Purdy. Nora was a tall, rather pale, but well-built girl, with beautiful yellow hair. She was rather secretive.

"Hey!" said Annie, accosting her; then softly, "Who's John Thomas on with now?"

"I don't know," said Nora.

"Why, tha does," said Annie, ironically lapsing into dialect. "Tha knows as well as I do."

"Well, I do, then," said Nora. "It isn't me, so don't bother."

"It's Cissy Meakin, isn't it?"

"It is, for all I know."

"Hasn't he got a face on him!" said Annie. "I don't half like his cheek. I could knock him off the footboard when he comes round at me."

"He'll get dropped on one of these days," said Nora.

"Ay, he will, when somebody makes up their mind to drop it on him. I should like to see him taken down a peg or two, shouldn't you?"

"I shouldn't mind," said Nora.

"You've got quite as much cause to as I have," said Annie. "But we'll drop on him one of these days, my girl. What? Don't you want to?"

"I don't mind," said Nora.

But as a matter of fact, Nora was much more vindictive than Annie.

One by one Annie went the round of the old flames. It so happened that Cissy Meakin left the tramway service in quite a short time. Her mother made her leave. Then John Thomas was on the qui vive. He cast his eyes over his old flock. And his eyes lighted on Annie. He thought she would be safe now. Besides, he liked her.

She arranged to walk home with him on Sunday night. It so happened that her car would be in the depôt at half-past nine: the last car would come in at 10:15. So John Thomas was to wait for her there.

At the depôt the girls had a little waiting-room of their own. It was quite rough, but cosy, with a fire and an oven and a mirror, and table and wooden chairs. The half-dozen girls who knew John Thomas only too well had arranged to take service this Sunday afternoon. So, as the cars began to

come in, early, the girls dropped into the waiting-room. And instead of
hurrying off home, they sat around the fire and had a cup of tea. Outside
was the darkness and lawlessness of war-time.

John Thomas came on the car after Annie, at about a quarter to ten.
He poked his head easily into the girls' waiting-room.

"Prayer-meeting?" he asked.

"Ay," said Laura Sharp. "Ladies only."

"That's me!" said John Thomas. It was one of his favourite exclamations.

"Shut the door, boy," said Muriel Baggaley.

"Oh which side of me?" said John Thomas.

"Which tha likes," said Polly Birkin.

He had come in and closed the door behind him. The girls moved in
their circle, to make a place for him near the fire. He took off his great-coat
and pushed back his hat.

"Who handles the teapot?" he said.

Nora Purdy silently poured him out a cup of tea.

"Want a bit o' my bread and drippin'? said Muriel Baggaley to him.

"Ay, give us a bit."

And he began to eat his piece of bread.

"There's no place like home, girls," he said.

They all looked at him as he uttered this piece of impudence. He
seemed to be sunning himself in the presence of so many damsels.

"Especially if you're not afraid to go home in the dark," said Laura
Sharp.

"Me! By myself I am."

They sat till they heard the last tram come in. In a few minutes Emma
Houselay entered.

"Come on, my old duck!" cried Polly Birkin.

"It *is* perishing," said Emma, holding her fingers to the fire.

"But—I'm afraid to, go home in, the dark," sang Laura Sharp, the tune
having got into her mind.

"Who're you going with to-night, John Thomas?" asked Muriel Baggaley, coolly.

"To-night?" said John Thomas. "Oh, I'm going home by myself to-
night—all on my lonely-o."

"That's me!" said Nora Purdy, using his own ejaculation.

The girls laughed shrilly.

"Me as well, Nora," said John Thomas.

"Don't know what you mean," said Laura.

"Yes, I'm toddling," said he, rising and reaching for his overcoat.

"Nay," said Polly. "We're all here waiting for you."

"We've got to be up in good time in the morning," he said, in the
benevolent official manner.

They all laughed.

"Nay," said Muriel. "Don't leave us all lonely, John Thomas. Take one!"

"I'll take the lot, if you like," he responded gallantly.

"That you won't, either," said Muriel. "Two's company; seven's too much of a good thing."

"Nay—take one," said Laura. "Fair and square, all above board and say which."

"Ay," cried Annie, speaking for the first time. "Pick, John Thomas; let's hear thee."

"Nay," he said. "I'm going home quiet to-night. Feeling good, for once."

"Wherabouts?" said Annie. "Take a good 'un, then. But tha's got to take one of us!"

"Nay, how can I take one," he said, laughing uneasily. "I don't want to make enemies."

"You'd only make *one*," said Annie.

"The chosen *one*," added Laura.

"Oh, my! Who said girls!" exclaimed John Thomas, again turning, as if to escape. "Well—good-night."

"Nay, you've got to make your pick," said Muriel. "Turn your face to the wall, and say which one touches you. Go on—we shall only just touch your back—one of us. Go on—turn your face to the wall, and don't look, and say which one touches you."

He was uneasy, mistrusting them. Yet he had not the courage to break away. They pushed him to a wall and stood him there with his face to it. Behind his back they all grimaced, tittering. He looked so comical. He looked around uneasily.

"Go on!" he cried.

"You're looking—you're looking!" they shouted.

He turned his head away. And suddenly, with a movement like a swift cat, Annie went forward and fetched him a box on the side of the head that sent his cap flying and himself staggering. He started round.

But at Annie's signal they all flew at him, slapping him, pinching him, pulling his hair, though more in fun than in spite or anger. He, however, saw red. His blue eyes flamed with strange fear as well as fury, and he butted through the girls to the door. It was locked. He wrenched at it. Roused, alert, the girls stood round and looked at him. He faced them, at bay. At that moment they were rather horrifying to him, as they stood in their short uniforms. He was distinctly afraid.

"Come on, John Thomas! Come on! Choose!" said Annie.

"What are you after? Open the door," he said.

"We shan't—not till you've chosen!" said Muriel.

"Chosen what?" he said.

"Chosen the one you're going to marry," she replied.

He hesitated a moment.

"Open the blasted door," he said, "and get back to your senses." He spoke with official authority.

"You've got to choose!" cried the girls.

"Come on!" cried Annie, looking him in the eye. "Come on! Come on!"

He went forward, rather vaguely. She had taken off her belt, and swinging it, she fetched him a sharp blow over the head with the buckle end. He sprang and seized her. But immediately the other girls rushed upon him, pulling and tearing and beating him. Their blood was now thoroughly up. He was their sport now. They were going to have their their own back, out of him. Strange, wild creatures, they hung on him and rushed at him to bear him down. His tunic was torn right up the back, Nora had hold at the back of his collar, and was actually strangling him. Luckily the button burst. He struggled in a wild frenzy of fury and terror, almost mad terror. His tunic was simply torn off his back, his shirt-sleeves were torn away, his arms were naked. The girls rushed at him, clenched their hands on him and pulled at him: or they rushed at him and pushed him, butted him with all their might: or they struck him wild blows. He ducked and cringed and struck sideways. They became more intense.

At last he was down. They rushed on him, kneeling on him. He had neither breath nor strength to move. His face was bleeding with a long scratch, his brow was bruised.

Annie knelt on him, the other girls knelt and hung on to him. Their faces were flushed, their hair wild, their eyes were all glittering strangely. He lay at last quite still, with face averted, as an animal lies when it is defeated and at the mercy of the captor. Sometimes his eye glanced back at the wild faces of the girls. His breast rose heavily, his wrists were torn.

"Now, then, my fellow!" gasped Annie at length. "Now then— now—"

At the sound of her terrifying, cold triumph, he suddenly started to struggle as an animal might, but the girls threw themselves upon him with unnatural strength and power, forcing him down.

"Yes—now, then!" gasped Annie at length.

And there was a dead silence, in which the thud of heart-beating was to be heard. It was a suspense of pure silence in every soul.

"Now you know where you are," said Annie.

The sight of his white, bare arm maddened the girls. He lay in a kind of trance of fear and antagonism. They felt themselves filled with supernatural strength.

Suddenly Polly started to laugh—to giggle wildly—helplessly—and

Emma and Muriel joined in. But Annie and Nora and Laura remained the same, tense, watchful, with gleaming eyes. He winced away from these eyes.

"Yes," said Annie, in a curious low tone, secret and deadly. "Yes! You've got it now. You know what you've done, don't you? You know what you've done."

He made no sound nor sign, but lay with bright, averted eyes, and averted, bleeding face.

"You ought to be *killed,* that's what you ought," said Annie, tensely. "You ought to be *killed.*" And there was a terrifying lust in her voice.

Polly was ceasing to laugh, and giving long-drawn Oh-h-hs and sighs as she came to herself.

"He's got to choose," she said vaguely.

"Oh, yes, he has," said Laura, with vindictive decision.

"Do you hear—do you hear?" said Annie. And with a sharp movement, that made him wince, she turned his face to her.

"Do you hear?" she repeated, shaking him.

But he was quite dumb. She fetched him a sharp slap on the face. He started, and his eyes widened. Then his face darkened with defiance, after all.

"Do you hear?" she repeated.

He only looked at her with hostile eyes.

"Speak!" she said, putting her face devilishly near his.

"What?" he said, almost overcome.

"You've got to *choose!*" she cried, as if it were some terrible menace, and as if it hurt her that she could not exact more.

"What?" he said, in fear.

"Choose your girl, Coddy. You've got to choose her now. And you'll get your neck broken if you play any more of your tricks, my boy. You're settled now."

There was a pause. Again he averted his face. He was cunning in his overthrow. He did not give in to them really—no, not if they tore him to bits.

"All right, then," he said, "I choose Annie." His voice was strange and full of malice. Annie let go of him as if he had been a hot coal.

"He's chosen Annie!" said the girls in chorus.

"Me!" cried Annie. She was still kneeling, but away from him. He was still lying prostrate, with averted face. The girls grouped uneasily around.

"Me!" repeated Annie, with a terrible bitter accent.

Then she got up, drawing away from him with strange disgust and bitterness.

"I wouldn't touch him," she said.

But her face quivered with a kind of agony, she seemed as if she would fall. The other girls turned aside. He remained lying on the floor, with his torn clothes and bleeding, averted face.

"Oh, if he's chosen—" said Polly.

"I don't want him—he can choose again," said Annie, with the same rather bitter hopelessness.

"Get up," said Polly, lifting his shoulder. "Get up."

He rose slowly, a strange, ragged, dazed creature. The girls eyed him from a distance, curiously, furtively, dangerously.

"Who wants him?" cried Laura, roughly.

"Nobody," they answered, with contempt. Yet each one of them waited for him to look at her, hoped he would look at her. All except Annie, and something was broken in her.

He, however, kept his face closed and averted from them all. There was a silence of the end. He picked up the torn pieces of his tunic, without knowing what to do with them. The girls stood about uneasily, flushed, panting, tidying their hair and their dress unconsciously, and watching him. He looked at none of them. He espied his cap in a corner and went and picked it up. He put it on his head, and one of the girls burst into a shrill, hysteric laugh at the sight he presented. He, however, took no heed but went straight to where his overcoat hung on a peg. The girls moved away from contact with him as if he had been an electric wire. He put on his coat and buttoned it down. Then he rolled his tunic-rags into a bundle, and stood before the locked door, dumbly.

"Open the door, somebody," said Laura.

"Annie's got the key," said one.

Annie silently offered the key to the girls. Nora unlocked the door.

"Tit for tat, old man," she said. "Show yourself a man, and don't bear a grudge."

But without a word or sign he had opened the door and gone, his face closed, his head dropped.

"That'll learn him," said Laura.

"Coddy!" said Nora.

"Shut up, for God's sake!" cried Annie fiercely, as if in torture.

"Well, I'm about ready to go, Polly. Look sharp!" said Muriel.

The girls were all anxious to be off. They were tidying themselves hurriedly, with mute stupefied faces.

AGATHA CHRISTIE

The Double Clue

"*B*ut above everything—no publicity," said Mr. Marcus Hardman for
perhaps the fourteenth time.

The word *publicity* occurred throughout his conversation with the regu-
larity of a leitmotif. Mr. Hardman was a small man, delicately plump, with
exquisitely manicured hands and a plaintive tenor voice. In his way, he was
somewhat of a celebrity and the fashionable life was his profession. He was
rich, but not remarkably so, and he spent his money zealously in the pursuit
of social pleasure. His hobby was collecting. He had the collector's soul.
Old lace, old fans, antique jewelry—nothing crude or modern for Marcus
Hardman.

Poirot and I, obeying an urgent summons, had arrived to find the little man writhing in an agony of indecision. Under the circumstances, to call in the police was abhorrent to him. On the other hand, not to call them in was to acquiesce in the loss of some of the gems of his collection. He hit upon Poirot as a compromise.

"My rubies, M. Poirot, and the emerald necklace—said to have belonged to Catherine de Medici. Oh, the emerald necklace!"

"If you will recount to me the circumstances of their disappearance?" suggested Poirot gently.

"I am endeavoring to do so. Yesterday afternoon I had a little tea party—quite an informal affair, some half a dozen people or so. I have given one or two of them during the season, and though perhaps I should not say so, they have been quite a success. Some good music—Nacora, the pianist, and Katherine Bird, the Australian contralto—in the big studio. Well, early in the afternoon, I was showing my guests my collection of medieval jewels. I keep them in the small wall safe over there. It is arranged like a cabinet inside, with colored velvet background, to display the stones. Afterward we inspected the fans—in that case on the wall. Then we all went to the studio for music. It was not until after everyone had gone that I discovered the safe rifled! I must have failed to shut it properly, and someone had seized the opportunity to denude it of its contents. The rubies, M. Poirot, the emerald necklace—the collection of a lifetime! What would I not give to recover them! But there must be no publicity! You fully understand that, do you not, M. Poirot? My own guests, my personal friends! It would be a horrible scandal!"

"Who was the last person to leave this room when you went to the studio?"

"Mr. Johnston. You may know him? The South African millionaire. He has just rented the Abbotburys' house in Park Lane. He lingered behind a few moments, I remember. But surely, oh, surely it could not be he!"

"Did any of your guests return to this room during the afternoon on any pretext?"

"I was prepared for that question, M. Poirot. Three of them did so. Countess Vera Rossakoff, Mr. Bernard Parker, and Lady Runcorn."

"Let us hear about them."

"The Countess Rossakoff is a very charming Russian lady, a member of the old régime. She has recently come to this country. She had bade me goodbye, and I was therefore somewhat surprised to find her in this room apparently gazing in rapture at my cabinet of fans. You know, M. Poirot, the more I think of it, the more suspicious it seems to me. Don't you agree?"

"Extremely suspicious; but let us hear about the others."

"Well, Parker simply came here to fetch a case of miniatures that I was anxious to show to Lady Runcorn."

"And Lady Runcorn herself?"

"As I daresay you know, Lady Runcorn is a middle-aged woman of considerable force of character who devotes most of her time to various charitable committees. She simply returned to fetch a handbag she had laid down somewhere."

"*Bien, monsieur.* So we have four possible suspects. The Russian countess, the English *grande dame,* the South African millionaire, and Mr. Bernard Parker. Who *is* Mr. Parker, by the way?"

The question appeared to embarrass Mr. Hardman considerably.

"He is—er—he is a young fellow. Well, in fact, a young fellow I know."

"I had already deduced as much," replied Poirot gravely. "What does he do, this M. Parker?"

"He is a young man about town—not, perhaps, quite in the swim, if I may so express myself."

"How did he come to be a friend of yours, may I ask?"

"Well—er—on one or two occasions he has—performed certain little commissions for me."

"Continue, monsieur," said Poirot.

Hardman looked piteously at him. Evidently the last thing he wanted to do was to continue. But as Poirot maintained an inexorable silence, he capitulated.

"You see, M. Poirot—it is well known that I am interested in antique jewels. Sometimes there is a family heirloom to be disposed of—which, mind you, would never be sold in the open market or to a dealer. But a private sale to me is a very different matter. Parker arranges the details of such things, he is in touch with both sides, and thus any little embarrassment is avoided. He brings anything of that kind to my notice. For instance, the Countess Rossakoff has brought some family jewels with her from Russia. She is anxious to sell them. Bernard Parker was to have arranged the transaction."

"I see," said Poirot thoughtfully. "And you trust him implicitly?"

"I have had no reason to do otherwise."

"M. Hardman, of these four people, which do you yourself suspect?"

"Oh, M. Poirot, what a question! They are my friends, as I told you. I suspect none of them—or all of them, whichever way you like to put it."

"I do not agree. You suspect one of those four. It is not Countess Rossakoff. It is not Mr. Parker. Is it Lady Runcorn or Mr. Johnston?"

"You drive me into a corner, M. Poirot, you do indeed. I am most anxious to have no scandal. Lady Runcorn belongs to one of the oldest families in England; but it is true, it is most unfortunately true, that her aunt, Lady Caroline, suffered from a most melancholy affliction. It was understood, of course, by all her friends, and her maid returned the teaspoons, or whatever it was, as promptly as possible. You see my predicament!"

"So Lady Runcorn had an aunt who was a kleptomaniac? Very interesting. You permit that I examine the safe?"

Mr. Hardman assenting, Poirot pushed back the door of the safe and examined the interior. The empty velvet-lined shelves gaped at us.

"Even now the door does not shut properly," murmured Poirot, as he swung it to and fro. "I wonder why? Ah, what have we here? A glove, caught in the hinge. A man's glove."

He held it out to Mr. Hardman.

"That's not one of my gloves," the latter declared.

"Aha! Something more!" Poirot bent deftly and picked up a small object from the floor of the safe. It was a flat cigarette case made of black moiré.

"My cigarette case!" cried Mr. Hardman.

"Yours? Surely not, monsieur. Those are not your initials."

He pointed to an entwined monogram of two letters executed in platinum.

Hardman took it in his hand.

"You are right," he declared. "It is very like mine, but the initials are different. A 'P' and a 'B.' Good heavens—Bernard Parker!"

"It would seem so," said Poirot. "A somewhat careless young man—especially if the glove is his also. That would be a double clue, would it not?"

"Bernard Parker!" murmured Hardman. "What a relief! Well, M. Poirot, I leave it to you to recover the jewels. Place the matter in the hands of the police if you think fit—that is, if you are quite sure that it is he who is guilty."

"See you, my friend," said Poirot to me, as we left the house together, "he has one law for the titled, and another law for the plain, this Mr. Hardman. Me, I have not yet been ennobled, so I am on the side of the plain. I have sympathy for this young man. The whole thing was a little curious, was it not? There was Hardman suspecting Lady Runcorn; there was I, suspecting the Countess and Johnston; and all the time, the obscure Mr. Parker was our man."

"Why did you suspect the other two?"

"*Parbleu!* It is such a simple thing to be a Russian refugee or a South African millionaire! Any woman can call herself a Russian countess; anyone can buy a house in Park Lane and call himself a South African millionaire. Who is going to contradict them? But I observe that we are passing through Bury Street. Our careless young friend lives here. Let us, as you say, strike while the iron is in the fire."

Mr. Bernard Parker was at home. We found him reclining on some cushions, clad in an amazing dressing gown of purple and orange. I have seldom taken a greater dislike to anyone than I did to this particular young man with his white, effeminate face and affected lisping speech.

"Good morning, monsieur," said Poirot briskly. "I come from M. Hardman. Yesterday, at the party, somebody has stolen all his jewels. Permit me to ask you, monsieur—is this your glove?"

Mr. Parker's mental processes did not seem very rapid. He stared at the glove, as though gathering his wits together.

"Where did you find it?" he asked at last.

"Is it your glove, monsieur?"

Mr. Parker appeared to make up his mind.

"No, it isn't," he declared.

"And this cigarette case, is that yours?"

"Certainly not. I always carry a silver one."

"Very well, monsieur. I go to put matters in the hands of the police."

"Oh, I say, I wouldn't do that, if I were you," cried Mr. Parker in some concern. "Beastly unsympathetic people, the police. Wait a bit. I'll go round and see old Hardman. Look here—oh, stop a minute."

But Poirot beat a determined retreat.

"We have given him something to think about, have we not?" he chuckled. "Tomorrow we will observe what has occurred."

But we were destined to have a reminder of the Hardman case that afternoon. Without the least warning the door flew open, and a whirlwind in human form invaded our privacy, bringing with her a swirl of sables (it was as cold as only an English June day can be) and a hat rampant with slaughtered ospreys. Countess Vera Rossakoff was a somewhat disturbing personality.

"You are M. Poirot? What is this that you have done? You accuse that poor boy! It is infamous. It is scandalous. I know him. He is a chicken, a lamb—never would he steal. He has done everything for me. Will I stand by and see him martyred and butchered?"

"Tell me, madame, is this his cigarette case?" Poirot held out the black moiré case.

The Countess paused for a moment while she inspected it.

"Yes, it is his. I know it well. What of it? Did you find it in the room? We were all there; he dropped it then, I suppose. Ah, you policemen, you are worse than the Red Guards—"

"And is this his glove?"

"How should I know? One glove is like another. Do not try to stop me—he must be set free. His character must be cleared. You shall do it. I will sell my jewels and give you much money."

"Madame—"

"It is agreed, then? No, no, do not argue. The poor boy! He came to me, the tears in his eyes. 'I will save you,' I said. 'I will go to this man—this ogre, this monster! Leave it to Vera.' Now it is settled, I go."

With as little ceremony as she had come, she swept from the room, leaving an overpowering perfume of an exotic nature behind her.

"What a woman!" I exclaimed. "And what furs!"

"Ah, yes, they were genuine enough! Could a spurious countess have real furs? My little joke, Hastings. . . . No, she is truly Russian, I fancy. Well, well, so Master Bernard went bleating to her."

"The cigarette case is his. I wonder if the glove is also—"

With a smile Poirot drew from his pocket a second glove and placed it by the first. There was no doubt of their being a pair.

"Where did you get the second one, Poirot?"

"It was thrown down with a stick on the table in the hall in Bury Street. Truly, a very careless young man, Monsieur Parker. Well, well, *mon ami*— we must be thorough. Just for the form of the thing, I will make a little visit to Park Lane."

Needless to say, I accompanied my friend. Johnston was out, but we saw his private secretary. It transpired that Johnston had only recently arrived from South Africa. He had never been in England before.

"He is interested in precious stones, is he not?" hazarded Poirot.

"Gold mining is nearer the mark," laughed the secretary.

Poirot came away from the interview thoughtful. Late that evening, to my utter surprise, I found him earnestly studing a Russian grammar.

"Good heavens, Poirot!" I cried. "Are you learning Russian in order to converse with the Countess in her own language?"

"She certainly would not listen to my English, my friend!"

"But surely, Poirot, well-born Russians invariably speak French?"

"You are a mine of information, Hastings! I will cease puzzling over the intricacies of the Russian alphabet."

He threw the book from him with a dramatic gesture. I was not entirely satisfied. There was a twinkle in his eye which I knew of old. It was an invariable sign that Hercule Poirot was pleased with himself.

"Perhaps," I said sapiently, "you doubt her being really a Russian. You are going to test her?"

"Ah, no, no, she is Russian all right."

"Well, then—"

"If you really want to distinguish yourself over this case, Hastings, I recommend 'First Steps in Russian' as an invaluable aid."

Then he laughed and would say no more. I picked up the book from the floor and dipped into it curiously, but could make neither head nor tail of Poirot's remarks.

The following morning brought us no news of any kind, but that did not seem to worry my little friend. At breakfast, he announced his intention of calling upon Mr. Hardman early in the day. We found the elderly society butterfly at home, and seemingly a little calmer than on the previous day.

"Well, M. Poirot, any news?" he demanded eagerly.

Poirot handed him a slip of paper.

"That is the person who took the jewels, monsieur. Shall I put matters in the hands of the police? Or would you prefer me to recover the jewels without bringing the police into the matter?"

Mr. Hardman was staring at the paper. At last he found his voice.

"Most astonishing. I should infinitely prefer to have no scandal in the matter. I give you *carte blanche,* M. Poirot. I am sure you will be discreet."

Our next procedure was to hail a taxi, which Poirot ordered to drive to the Carlton. There he inquired for Countess Rossakoff. In a few minutes we were ushered up into the lady's suite. She came to meet us with outstretched hands, arrayed in a marvelous negligee of barbaric design.

"M. Poirot!" she cried. "You have succeeded? You have cleared that poor infant?"

"Madame la Comtesse, your friend M. Parker is perfectly safe from arrest."

"Ah, but you are the clever little man! Superb! And so quickly too."

"On the other hand, I have promised Mr. Hardman that the jewels shall be returned to him today."

"So?"

"Therefore, madame, I should be extremely obliged if you would place them in my hands without delay. I am sorry to hurry you, but I am keeping a taxi—in case it should be necessary for me to go on to Scotland Yard; and we Belgians, madame, we practice the thrift."

The Countess had lighted a cigarette. For some seconds she sat perfectly still, blowing smoke rings, and gazing steadily at Poirot. Then she burst into a laugh, and rose. She went across to the bureau, opened a drawer, and took out a black silk handbag. She tossed it lightly to Poirot. Her tone, when she spoke, was perfectly light and unmoved.

"We Russians, on the contrary, practice prodigality," she said. "And to do that, unfortunately, one must have money. You need not look inside. They are all there."

Poirot rose.

"I congratulate you, madame, on your quick intelligence and your promptitude."

"Ah! But since you were keeping your taxi waiting, what else could I do?"

"You are too amiable, madame. You are remaining long in London?"

"I am afraid not—owing to you."

"Accept my apologies."

"We shall meet again elsewhere, perhaps."

"I hope so."

"And I—do not!" exclaimed the Countess with a laugh. "It is a great compliment that I pay you there—there are very few men in the world whom I fear. Goodbye, M. Poirot."

"Goodbye, Madame la Comtesse. Ah—pardon me, I forgot! Allow me to return you your cigarette case."

And with a bow he handed to her the little black moiré case we had found in the safe. She accepted it without any change of expression—just a lifted eyebrow and a murmured: "I see!"

"What a woman!" cried Poirot enthusiastically as we descended the stairs. "*Mon Dieu, quelle femme!* Not a word of argument—of protestation, of bluff! One quick glance, and she had sized up the position correctly. I tell you, Hastings, a woman who can accept defeat like that—with a careless smile—will go far! She is dangerous; she has the nerves of steel; she—" He tripped heavily.

"If you can manage to moderate your transports and look where you're going, it might be as well," I suggested. "When did you first suspect the Countess?"

"*Mon ami,* it was the glove and the cigarette case—the double clue, shall we say?—that worried me. Bernard Parker might easily have dropped one or the other—but hardly both. Ah, no, that would have been *too* careless! In the same way, if someone else had placed them there to incriminate Parker, one would have been sufficient—the cigarette case or the glove— again not both. So I was forced to the conclusion that one of the two things did *not* belong to Parker. I imagined at first that the case was his, and that the glove was not. But when I discovered the fellow to the glove, I saw that it was the other way about. Whose, then, was the cigarette case? Clearly, it could not belong to Lady Runcorn. The initials were wrong. Mr. Johnston? Only if he were here under a false name. I interviewed his secretary, and it was apparent at once that everything was clear and above-board. There was no reticence about Mr. Johnston's past. The Countess, then? She was supposed to have brought jewels with her from Russia; she had only to take the stones from their settings, and it was extremely doubtful if they could ever be identified. What could be easier for her than to pick up one of Parker's gloves from the hall that day and thrust it into the safe? But, *bien sûr,* she did not intend to drop her own cigarette case."

"But if the case was hers, why did it have 'B. P.' on it? The Countess' initials are *V. R.*"

Poirot smiled gently upon me.

"Exactly, *mon ami;* but in the Russian alphabet, *B* is *V* and *P* is *R.*"

"Well, you couldn't expect me to guess that. I don't know Russian."

"Neither do I, Hastings. That is why I bought my little book—and urged it on your attention."

He sighed.

"A remarkable woman. I have a feeling, my friend—a very decided feeling—I shall meet her again. Where, I wonder?"

Elizabeth Bowen (1899–1973) was born in Ireland (Dublin) and was educated in England, including a period at the London Council of Art. A prolific writer, she published at least six collections of stories, nine novels, and several collections of essays, including literary criticism. Primarily a novelist of manners, Elizabeth Bowen is an extraordinary stylist; her novels and short stories present engaging descriptions of landscapes and settings in which her protagonists live, the details of which emerge as symbolically important in the rich context of her work. Two of her best novels are The Death of the Heart *(1939) and* The Heat of the Day *(1949). For further reading:* Stories by Elizabeth Bowen *(1959).*

ELIZABETH BOWEN

Her Table Spread

*A*lban had few opinions on the subject of marriage; his attitude to women was negative, but in particular he was not attracted to Miss Cuffe. Coming down early for dinner, red satin dress cut low, she attacked the silence with loud laughter before he had spoken. He recollected having heard that she was abnormal—at twenty-five, of statuesque development, still detained in childhood. The two other ladies, in beaded satins, made entrances of a surprising formality. It occurred to him, his presence must constitute an occasion: they certainly sparkled. Old Mr. Rossiter, uncle to Mrs. Treye, came last, more sourly. They sat for some time without the addition of lamplight. Dinner was not announced; the ladies, by remaining on guard, seemed to deprecate any question of its appearance. No sound came from other parts of the Castle.

Miss Cuffe was an heiress to whom the Castle belonged and whose guests they all were. But she carefully followed the movements of her aunt, Mrs. Treye; her ox-eyes moved from face to face in happy submission rather than expectancy. She was continually preoccupied with attempts at gravity, as though holding down her skirts in a high wind. Mrs. Treye and Miss Carbin combined to cover her excitement; still, their looks frequently stole from the company to the windows, of which there were too many. He received a strong impression someone outside was waiting to come in. At last, with a sigh, they got up: dinner had been announced.

The Castle was built on high ground, commanding the estuary; a steep hill, with trees, continued above it. On fine days the view was remarkable, of almost Italian brilliance, with that constant reflection up from the water that even now prolonged the too-long day. Now, in continuous evening rain, the winding wooded line of the further shore could be seen and, nearer the windows, a smothered island with the stump of a watch-tower. Where the Castle stood, a higher tower had answered the island's. Later a keep, then wings, had been added; now the fine peaceful residence had French windows opening on to the terrace. Invasions from the water would henceforth be social, perhaps amorous. On the slope down from the terrace, trees began again; almost, but not quite concealing the destroyer. Alban, who knew nothing, had not yet looked down.

It was Mr. Rossiter who first spoke of the destroyer—Alban meanwhile glancing along the table; the preparations had been stupendous. The destroyer had come to-day. The ladies all turned to Alban: the beads on their bosoms sparkled. So this was what they had here, under their trees. Engulfed by their pleasure, from now on he disappeared personally. Mr. Rossiter, rising a note, continued. The estuary, it appeared, was deep, with a channel buoyed up it. By a term of the Treaty, English ships were permitted to anchor in these waters.

"But they've been afraid of the rain!" chimed in Valeria Cuffe.

"Hush," said her aunt, "That's silly. Sailors would be accustomed to getting wet."

But, Miss Carbin reported, that spring there *had* been one destroyer. Two of the officers had been seen dancing at the hotel at the head of the estuary.

"So," said Alban, "you are quite in the world." He adjusted his glasses in her direction.

Miss Carbin—blonde, not forty, and an attachment of Mrs. Treye's— shook her head despondently. "We were all away at Easter. Wasn't it curious they should have come then? The sailors walked in the demesne but never touched the daffodils."

"As though I should have cared!" exclaimed Valeria passionately.

"Morale too good," stated Mr. Rossiter.

"But next evening," continued Miss Carbin, "the officers did not go to the hotel. They climbed up here through the trees to the terrace—you see, they had no idea. Friends of ours were staying here at the Castle, and they apologised. Our friends invited them in to supper. . . ."

"Did they accept?"

The three ladies said in a breath: "Yes, they came."

Valeria added urgently, "So don't you *think*—?"

"So to-night we have a destroyer to greet you," Mrs. Treye said quickly to Alban. "It is quite an event; the country people are coming down from the mountains. These waters are very lonely; the steamers have given up since the bad times; there is hardly a pleasure-boat. The weather this year has driven visitors right away."

"You are beautifully remote."

"Yes," agreed Miss Carbin. "Do you know much about the Navy? Do you think, for instance, that this is likely to be the same destroyer?"

"*Will they remember?*" Valeria's bust was almost on the table. But with a rustle Mrs. Treye pressed Valeria's toe. For the dining-room also looked out across the estuary, and the great girl had not once taken her eyes from the window. Perhaps it was unfortunate that Mr. Alban should have coincided with the destroyer. Perhaps it was unfortunate for Mr. Alban too.

For he saw now he was less than half the feast; unappeased, the party sat looking through him, all grouped at the end of the table—to the other, chairs had been pulled up. Dinner was being served very slowly. Candles— possible to see from the water—were lit now; some wet peonies glistened. Outside, day still lingered hopefully. The bushes over the edge of the terrace were like heads—you could have sworn sometimes you saw them mounting, swaying in manly talk. Once, wound up in the rain, a bird whistled, seeming hardly a bird.

"Perhaps since then they have been to Greece, or Malta?"

"That would be the Mediterranean fleet," said Mr. Rossiter.

They were sorry to think of anything out in the rain to-night.

"The decks must be streaming," said Miss Carbin.

Then Valeria, exclaiming, "Please excuse me!" pushed her chair in and ran from the room.

"She is impulsive," explained Mrs. Treye. "Have *you* been to Malta, Mr. Alban?"

In the drawing-room, empty of Valeria, the standard lamps had been lit. Through their ballet-skirt shades, rose and lemon, they gave out a deep, welcoming light. Alban, at the ladies' invitation, undraped the piano. He played, but they could see he was not pleased. It was obvious he had always been a civilian, and when he had taken his place on the piano-stool—which he twirled round three times, rather fussily—his dinner-jacket wrinkled across the shoulders. It was sad they should feel so indifferent, for he came from London. Mendelssohn was exasperating to them—they opened all four windows to let the music downhill. They preferred not to draw the curtains; the air, though damp, being pleasant tonight, they said.

The piano was damp, but Alban played almost all his heart out. He played out the indignation of years his mild manner concealed. He had failed to love; nobody did anything about this; partners at dinner gave him less than half their attention. He knew some spring had dried up at the root of the world. He was fixed in the dark rain, by an indifferent shore. He played badly, but they were unmusical. Old Mr. Rossiter, who was not what he seemed, went back to the dining-room to talk to the parlourmaid.

Valeria, glittering vastly, appeared in a window.

"Come *in*!" her aunt cried in indignation. She would die of a chill, childless, in fact unwedded; the Castle would have to be sold and where would they all be?

But—"Lights down there!" Valeria shouted above the music.

They had to run out for a moment, laughing and holding cushions over their bare shoulders. Alban left the piano: they looked boldly down from the terrace. Indeed, there they were: two lights like arc-lamps, blurred by rain and drawn down deep in reflection into the steady water. There were, too, ever so many portholes, all lit up.

"Perhaps they are playing bridge," said Miss Carbin.

"Now I wonder if Uncle Robert ought to have called," said Mrs. Treye. "Perhaps we have seemed remiss—one calls on a regiment."

"Patrick could row him out to-morrow."

"He hates the water." She sighed. "Perhaps they will be gone."

"Let's go for a row now—let's go for a row with a lantern," besought Valeria, jumping and pulling her aunt's elbow. They produced such indignation she disappeared again—wet satin skirts and all—into the bushes. The ladies could do no more: Alban suggested the rain might spot their dresses.

"They must lose a great deal, playing cards throughout an evening for high stakes," Miss Carbin said with concern as they all sat down again.

"Yes, if you come to think of it, somebody must win."

But the naval officers who so joyfully supped at Easter had been, Miss Carbin knew, a Mr. Graves and a Mr. Garrett: *they* would certainly lose. "At all events, it is better than dancing at the hotel; there would be nobody of their type."

"There is nobody there at all."

"I expect they are best where they are. . . . Mr. Alban, a Viennese Waltz?"

He played while the ladies whispered, waving the waltz time a little distractedly. Mr. Rossiter, coming back, momentously stood: they turned in hope: even the waltz halted. But he brought no news. "You should call Valeria in. You can't tell who may be round the place. She's not fit to be out to-night."

"Perhaps she's not out."

"She is," said Mr. Rossiter crossly. "I just saw her racing past the window with a lantern."

Valeria's mind was made up: she was a princess. Not for nothing had she had the dining-room silver polished and all set out. She would pace around in red satin that swished behind, while Mr. Alban kept on playing a loud waltz. They would be dazed at all she had to offer—also her two new statues and the leopard-skin from the auction.

When he and she were married (she inclined a little to Mr. Garrett) they would invite all the Navy up the estuary and give them tea. Her estuary would be filled up, like a regatta, with loud excited battleships tooting to one another and flags flying. The terrace would be covered with grateful sailors, leaving room for the band. She would keep the peacocks her aunt did not allow. His friends would be surprised to notice that Mr. Garrett had meanwhile become an admiral, all gold. He would lead the other admirals into the castle and say, while they wiped their feet respectfully: "These are my wife's statues; she has given them to me. One is Mars, one is Mercury. We have a Venus, but she is not dressed. And wait till I show you our silver and gold plates . . ."The Navy would be unable to tear itself away.

She had been excited for some weeks at the idea of marrying Mr. Alban, but now the lovely appearance of the destroyer put him out of her mind. He would not have done; he was not handsome. But she could keep him to play the piano on quiet afternoons.

Her friends had told her Mr. Garrett was quite a Viking. She was so very familiar with his appearance that she felt sometimes they had already been married for years—though still, sometimes, he could not realise his good luck. She still had to remind him the island was hers too. . . . To-night, Aunt and darling Miss Carbin had so fallen in with her plans, putting on their satins and decorating the drawing-room, that the dinner became a betrothal feast. There was some little hitch about the arrival of Mr. Garrett—she had heard that gentlemen sometimes could not tie their ties. And now he was late and would be discouraged. So she must now go half-way down to the water and wave a lantern.

But she put her two hands over the lantern, then smothered it in her dress. She had a panic. Supposing she should prefer Mr. Graves?

She had heard Mr. Graves was stocky, but very merry; when he came to supper at Easter he slid in the gallery. He would teach her to dance, and take her to Naples and Paris. . . . Oh, dear, oh, dear, then they must fight for her; that was all there was to it. . . . She let the lantern out of her skirts and waved. Her fine arm with bangles went up and down, up and down, with the staggering light; the trees one by one jumped up from the dark, like savages.

Inconceivably the destroyer took no notice.

Undisturbed by oars, the rain stood up from the waters; not a light rose to peer, and the gramophone, though it remained very faint, did not cease or alter.

In mackintoshes, Mr. Rossiter and Alban meanwhile made their way to the boat-house, Alban did not know why. "If that goes on," said Mr.

Rossiter, nodding towards Valeria's lantern, "they'll fire one of their guns at us."

"Oh, no. Why?" said Alban. He buttoned up, however, the collar of his mackintosh.

"Nervous as cats. It's high time that girl was married. She's a nice girl in many ways, too."

"Couldn't we get the lantern away from her?" They stepped on a paved causeway and heard the water nibble the rocks.

"She'd scream the place down. She's of age now, you see."
"But if—"

"Oh, she won't do that; I was having a bit of fun with you." Chuckling equably, Mrs. Treye's uncle unlocked and pulled open the boat-house door. A bat whistled out.

"Why are we here?"

"She might come for the boat; she's a fine oar," said Mr. Rossiter wisely. The place was familiar to him; he lit an oil-lamp and, sitting down on a trestle with a staunch air of having done what he could, reached a bottle of whisky out of the boat. He motioned the bottle to Alban. "It's a wild night," he said. "Ah, well, we don't have these destroyers every day."

"That seems fortunate."

"Well, it is and it isn't." Restoring the bottle to the vertical, Mr. Rossiter continued: "It's a pity you don't want a wife. You'd be the better for a wife, d'you see, a young fellow like you. She's got a nice character; she's a girl you could shape. She's got a nice income." The bat returned from the rain and knocked round the lamp. Lowering the bottle frequently, Mr. Rossiter talked to Alban (whose attitude remained negative) of women in general and the parlourmaid in particular. . . .

"*Bat!*" Alban squealed irrepressibly, and with his hand to his ear—where he still felt it—fled from the boat-house. Mr. Rossiter's conversation continued. Alban's pumps squelched as he ran; he skidded along the causeway and baulked at the upward steps. His soul squelched equally: he had been warned; he had been warned. He had heard they were all mad; he had erred out of headiness and curiosity. A degree of terror was agreeable to his vanity: by express wish he had occupied haunted rooms. Now he had no other pumps in this country, no idea where to buy them, and a ducal visit ahead. Also, wandering as it were among the apples and amphoras of an art school, he had blundered into the life room: woman revolved gravely.

"Hell," he said to the steps, mounting, his mind blank to the outcome.

He was nerved for the jumping lantern, but half-way up to the Castle darkness was once more absolute. Her lantern had gone out; he could orientate himself—in spite of himself—by her sobbing. Absolute desperation. He pulled up so short that, for balance, he had to cling to a creaking tree.

"Hi!" she croaked. Then: "You *are* there! I hear you!"

"Miss Cuffe—"

"How too bad you are! I never heard you rowing. I thought you were never coming—"

"Quietly, my dear girl."

"Come up quickly. I haven't even seen you. Come up to the windows—"

"Miss Cuffe—"

"Don't you remember the way?" As sure but not so noiseless as a cat in the dark, Valeria hurried to him.

"Mr. Garrett—" she panted. "I'm Miss Cuffe. Where have you been? I've destroyed my beautiful red dress and they've eaten up your dinner. But we're still waiting. Don't be afraid; you'll soon be there now. I'm Miss Cuffe; this is my Castle—"

"Listen, it's I, Mr. Alban—"

"Ssh, ssh, Mr. Alban: *Mr. Garrett has landed.*"

Her cry, his voice, some breath of the joyful intelligence, brought the others on to the terrace, blind with lamplight.

"Valeria?"

"Mr. Garrett has landed!"

Mrs. Treye said to Miss Carbin under her breath, "Mr. Garrett has come."

Miss Carbin, half weeping with agitation, replied, "We must go in." But uncertain who was to speak next, or how to speak, they remained leaning over the darkness. Behind, through the windows, lamps spread great skirts of light, and Mars and Mercury, unable to contain themselves, stooped from their pedestals. The dumb keyboard shone like a ballroom floor.

Alban, looking up, saw their arms and shoulders under the bright rain. Close by, Valeria's fingers creaked on her warm wet satin. She laughed like a princess, magnificently justified. Their unseen faces were all three lovely, and, in the silence after the laughter, such a strong tenderness reached him that, standing there in full manhood, he was for a moment not exiled. For the moment, without moving or speaking, he stood in the dark, in a flame, as though all three said: "My darling. . . ."

Perhaps it was best for them all that early, when next day first lightened the rain, the destroyer steamed out—below the extinguished Castle where Valeria lay with her arms wide, past the boat-house, where Mr. Rossiter lay insensible and the bat hung masked in its wings—down the estuary into the open sea.

SEAN O'FAOLAIN

The Trout

*O*ne of the first places Julia always ran to when they arrived in G—— was The Dark Walk. It is a laurel walk, very old; almost gone wild, a lofty midnight tunnel of smooth, sinewy branches. Underfoot the tough brown leaves are never dry enough to crackle: there is always a suggestion of damp and cool trickle.

She raced right into it. For the first few yards she always had the memory of the sun behind her, then she felt the dusk closing swiftly down on her so that she screamed with pleasure and raced on to reach the light at the far end; and it was always just a little too long in coming so that she emerged gasping, clasping her hands, laughing, drinking in the sun. When she was filled with the heat and glare she would turn and consider the ordeal again.

This year she had the extra joy of showing it to her small brother, and of terrifying him as well as herself. And for him the fear lasted longer because his legs were so short and she had gone out at the far end while he was still screaming and racing.

When they had done this many times they came back to the house to tell everybody that they had done it. He boasted. She mocked. They squab-bled.

"Cry babby!"

"You were afraid yourself, so there!"

"I won't take you any more."

"You're a big pig."

"I hate you."

Tears were threatening so somebody said, "Did you see the well?" She opened her eyes at that and held up her long lovely neck suspiciously and decided to be incredulous. She was twelve and at that age little girls are beginning to suspect most stories: they have already found out too many, from Santa Claus to the Stork. How could there be a well! In The Dark Walk? That she had visited year after year? Haughtily she said, "Non-sense."

But she went back, pretending to be going somewhere else, and she found a hole scooped in the rock at the side of the walk, choked with damp leaves, so shrouded by ferns that she only uncovered it after much search-ing. At the back of this little cavern there was about a quart of water. In the water she suddenly perceived a panting trout. She rushed for Stephen and dragged him to see, and they were both so excited that they were no longer afraid of the darkness as they hunched down and peered in at the fish panting in his tiny prison, his silver stomach going up and down like an engine.

Nobody knew how the trout got there. Even old Martin in the kitchen-garden laughed and refused to believe that it was there, or pretended not to believe, until she forced him to come down and see. Kneeling and pushing back his tattered old cap he peered in.

"Be cripes, you're right. How the divil in hell did that fella get there?"

She stared at him suspiciously.

"You knew?" she accused; but he said, "The divil a know"; and reached down to lift it out. Convinced she hauled him back. If she had found it then it was her trout.

Her mother suggested that a bird had carried the spawn. Her father thought that in the winter a small streamlet might have carried it down there as a baby, and it had been safe until the summer came and the water began to dry up. She said, "I see," and went back to look again and consid-er the matter in private. Her brother remained behind, wanting to hear the whole story of the trout, not really interested in the actual trout but much interested in the story which his mummy began to make up for him on the lines of, "So one day Daddy Trout and Mammy Trout. . . ."When he retailed it to her she said, "Pooh."

It troubled her that the trout was always in the same position; he had no room to turn; all the time the silver belly went up and down; otherwise he was motionless. She wondered what he ate and in between visits to Joey Pony, and the boat and a bathe to get cool, she thought of his hunger. She brought him down bits of dough; once she brought him a worm. He ignored the food. He just went on panting. Hunched over him she thought how, all the winter, while she was at school he had been in there. All the winter, in The Dark Walk, all day, all night, floating around alone. She drew the leaf of her hat down around her ears and chin and stared. She was still thinking of it as she lay in bed.

It was late June, the longest days of the year. The sun had sat still for a week, burning up the world. Although it was after ten o'clock it was still bright and still hot. She lay on her back under a single sheet, with her long legs spread, trying to keep cool. She could see the D of the moon through the fir-tree—they slept on the ground floor. Before they went to bed her mummy had told Stephen the story of the trout again, and she, in her bed, had resolutely presented her back to them and read her book. But she kept one ear cocked.

"And so, in the end, this naughty fish who would not stay at home got bigger and bigger and bigger, and the water got smaller and smaller. . . ."

Passionately she had whirled and cried, "Mummy, don't make it a horrible old moral story!" Her mummy had brought in a Fairy Godmother, then, who sent lots of rain, and filled the well, and a stream poured out and the trout floated away down to the river below. Staring at the moon she knew that there are no such things as Fairy Godmothers and that the trout, down in The Dark Walk, was panting like an engine. She heard somebody unwind a fishing-reel. Would the *beasts* fish him out!

She sat up. Stephen was a hot lump of sleep, lazy thing. The Dark Walk would be full of little scraps of moon. She leaped up and looked out the window, and somehow it was not so lightsome now that she saw the dim mountains far away and the black firs against the breathing land and heard a dog say, bark-bark. Quietly she lifted the ewer of water, and climbed out the window and scuttled along the cool but cruel gravel down to the maw of the tunnel. Her pyjamas were very short so that when she splashed water it wet her ankles. She peered into the tunnel. Something alive rustled inside there. She raced in, and up and down she raced, and flurried, and cried aloud, "Oh, Gosh, I can't find it," and then at last she did. Kneeling down in the damp she put her hand into the slimy hole. When the body lashed they were both mad with fright. But she gripped him and shoved him into the ewer and raced, with her teeth ground, out to the other end of the tunnel and down the steep paths to the river's edge.

All the time she could feel him lashing his tail against the side of the ewer. She was afraid he would jump right out. The gravel cut into her soles until she came to the cool ooze of the river's bank where the moon-mice on the water crept into her feet. She poured out watching until he plopped. For a second he was visible in the water. She hoped he was not dizzy. Then all she saw was the glimmer of the moon in the silent-flowing river, the dark firs, the dim mountains, and the radiant pointed face laughing down at her out of the empty sky.

She scuttled up the hill, in the window, plonked down the ewer and flew through the air like a bird into bed. The dog said bark-bark. She heard the fishing-reel whirring. She hugged herself and giggled. Like a river of joy her holiday spread before her.

In the morning Stephen rushed to her, shouting that "he" was gone, and asking "where" and "how." Lifting her nose in the air she said superciliously, "Fairy Godmother, I suppose?" and strolled away patting the palms of her hands.

V. S. Pritchett (1900–   ) was born in Ipswich, Suffolk, and after attending Alleyn's School (London), worked in the leather trade, and then the glue, shellac, and photographic trades (Paris) in the early twenties. He became a free-lance correspondent and critic for various London publications, most notably the New Statesman *(since 1946). In addition to the novels, Pritchett is known for a distinguished series of collected short stories beginning with* The Spanish Virgin and Other Stories *(1930); an inveterate traveller, he has written a number of nonfiction books and—among others—an excellent biography of Balzac. For further reading:* Collected Stories *(1956).*

V. S. PRITCHETT

Many are Disappointed

*H*eads down to the wind from the hidden sea, the four men were cycling up a deserted road in the country. Bert, who was the youngest, dreamed:

"You get to the pub, and there's a girl at the pub, a dark girl with bare arms and bare legs in a white frock, the daughter of the house, or an orphan—may be it's better she should be an orphan—and you say something to her, or better still, you don't say anything to her—she just comes and puts her arms round you, and you can feel her skin through her frock and she brings you some beer and the other chaps aren't there and the people don't say anything except laugh and go away, because its all natural and she doesn't have a baby. Same at the next place, same anywhere, different place, different girl, or same girl—same girl aways turning up, always waiting. Dunno how she got there. Just slips along without you knowing it and waiting like all those songs . . ."

And there the pub was. It stood on the crown of the long hill, straight ahead of them, a small red brick house with out-buildings and a single chimney trailing out smoke against the strong white light which seemed to be thrown up by great reflectors from the hidden sea.

"There's our beer, Mr. Blake," shouted Sid on his pink racing tyres, who was the first to see it, the first to see everything. The four men glanced up.

Yes, there's our beer, they said. Our ruddy beer. They had been think-ing about it for miles. A pub at the cross-roads, a pub where the old Roman road crossed this road that went on to the land's end, a funny place for a pub but a pub all right, the only pub for ten miles at Harry's ruddy Roman road, marked on the map which stuck out of the backside pocket of Harry's breeches. Yes, that was the pub, and Ted, the oldest and the married one, slacked on the long hill and said all he hoped was that the Romans had left a drop in the bottom of the barrel for posterity.

When they had left in the morning there had been little wind. The skylarks were over the fields and the sun itself was like one of their steel wheels flashing in the sky. Sid was the first, but Harry with the stubborn red neck and the close dull fair curls was the leader. In the week he sat in the office making the plan. He had this mania for Roman roads. "Ask our Mr. Newton," they said, "the man with the big head and the brain." They had passed through the cream-walled villages and out again to pick up once more the singing of the larks; and then cloud had covered the sun like a grey hand, west of Handleyford the country had emptied and it was aston-ishing to hear a bird. Reeds were in the small meadows. Hedges crawled uncut and there had been no villages, only long table-lands of common and bald wiry grass for sheep and the isolated farm with no ivy on the brick.

Well, they were there at last. They piled their bicycles against the wall of the house. They were shy before these country places. They waited for Ted. He was walking the last thirty yards. They looked at the four windows with their lace curtains and the varnished door. There was a chicken in the road and no sound but the whimper of the telegraph wire on the hill. In an open barn was a cart tipped down, its shaft white with the winter's mud, and last year's swallow nests, now empty, were under the eaves. Then Ted came and when he had piled his bicycle, they read the black sign over the door. "Tavern," it said. A funny old-fashioned word, Ted said, that you didn't often see.

"Well," Sid said, "a couple of pints all round?"

They looked to Harry. He always opened doors, but this door was so emphatically closed that he took off his fur gauntlet first and knocked before he opened it. The four men were surprised to see a woman standing behind the door, waiting there as if she had been listening to them. She was a frail, drab woman, not much past thirty, in a white blouse that drooped low over her chest.

"Good morning," said Sid. "This the bar?"

"The bar?" said the woman timidly. She spoke in a flat wondering voice and not in the sing song of this part of the country.

"Yes, the bar," Ted said, "It says 'Tavern,'" he said, nodding up at the notice.

"Oh yes," she said, hesitating. "Come in. Come in here."

She showed them not into the bar but into a sitting-room. There was a bowl of tomatoes in the window and a notice said "Teas."

The four men were tall and large beside her in the little room and she gazed up at them as if she feared they would burst its walls. And yet she was pleased. She was trying to smile.

"This is on me," Sid said. "Mild and bitter four times."

"O.K., Mr. Blake," Ted said. "Bring me my beer."

"But let's get into the bar," said Bert.

Seeing an armchair Ted sank into it and now the woman was reassured. She succeeded in smiling but she did not go out of the room. Sid looked at her and her smile was vacant and faint like the smile fading on an old photograph. Her hair was short, an impure yellow and the pale skin of her face and her neck and her breast seemed to be moist as if she had just got out of bed. The high strong light of this place drank all colour from her.

"There isn't a bar," she said. "This isn't a public-house. They call it the Tavern, but it isn't a tavern by rights."

Very anxiously she raised her hands to her blouse.

'What!" they exclaimed. "Not a pub! Here, Harry, it's marked on your map." They were dumbfounded and angry.

"What you mean, don't sell beer," they said.

Their voices were very loud.

"Yes," said Harry. "Here it is. See? Inn."

He put the map before her face accusingly.

"You don't sell beer?" said Bert. He looked at the pale-blue-veined chest of the woman.

"No," she said. She hesitated. "Many are disappointed," she said, and she spoke like a child reciting a piece without knowing its meaning. He lowered his eyes.

"You bet they ruddy well are," said Ted from the chair.

"Where is the pub?" said Sid.

She put out her hand and a little girl came into the room and clung close to her mother. Now she felt happier.

"My little girl," she said.

She was a tiny, frail child with yellow hair and pale blue eyes like her mother's. The four men smiled and spoke more quietly because of the resemblance between the woman and her child.

"Which way did you come?" she asked, and her hand moving over the child's hair got courage from the child. "Handleyford?" she said. "That's it. It's ten miles. The Queen's Arms, Handleyford, the way you came. That's the nearest pub."

"My God!" said Bert. "What a country!"

"The Queen's Arms," said Ted stupefied.

He remembered it. They were passing through Handleyford. He was the oldest, a flat wide man in loose clothes, loose in the chin too, with watery rings under his eyes and a small golden sun of baldness at the back of his head. "Queen's Arms" he had called. "Here, what's the ruddy game?" But the others had grinned back at him. When you drop back to number four on the hills it comes back to you: they're single, nothing to worry about, you're married and you're forty. What's the hurry? Ease up, take what you can get. "Queeen's Arms"—he remembered looking back. The best things are in the past.

"Well, that's that!" said Sid.

"Queen's Arms, Harry," Ted said.

And Bert looked at the woman. "Let's go on," he said fiercely. She was not the woman he had expected. Then he blushed and turned away from the woman.

She was afraid they were going and in a placating voice she said "I do teas."

Sid was sitting on the arm of a chair and the child was gazing at a gold ring he wore on his little finger. He saw the child was gazing and he smiled.

"What's wrong with tea?" Sid said.

"Ask the man with the brain," said Ted. "Ask the man with the map."

Harry said, "If you can't have beer, you'd better take what you can get, Mr. Richards."

"Tea," nodded Sid to the woman. "Make it strong."

The woman looked at Sid as if he had performed a miracle.

"I'll get you tea," she said eagerly. "I always do teas for people." She spoke with delight as if a bell had suddenly tinkled inside her. Her eyes shone. She would get them tea, she said, and bread and butter, but no eggs, because the man had not been that morning, and no ham. It was too early, she said, for ham. "But there are tomatoes," she said. And then, like a child, "I put them in the window so as people can see."

"O.K.," Sid said. "Four teas."

She did not move at once but still, like a shy child, stood watching them, waiting for them to be settled and fearful that they would not stay. But at last she put out her hand to the child and hurried out to the kitchen.

"Well, Mr. Blake," said Ted, "there's a ruddy sell."

"Have a gasper, Mr. Richards," said Sid.

"Try my lighter," said Ted.

He clicked the lighter but no flame came.

"Wrong number," said Ted. "Dial O and try again." A steak, said Sid, had been his idea. A couple of pints just to ease the passage and then some real drinking, Ted said. But Bert was drumming on a biscuit tin and was looking inside. There was nothing in it. "Many," said Bert, "are disappointed."

They looked at the room. There were two new treacle-coloured armchairs. There was a sofa with a pattern of black ferns on it. The new plush was damp and sticky to the hands from the air of the hidden sea. There was a gun-metal fender and there was crinkled, green paper in the fireplace. A cupboard with a glass door was empty except for the lowest shelf. On that was a thick book called *The Marvels of Science.*

The room was cold. They thought in the winter it must be damn' cold. They thought of the ten drizzling miles to Handleyford.

They listened to the cold clatter of the plates in the kitchen and the sound of the woman's excited voice and the child's. There was the bare linoleum on the floor and the chill glass of the window. Outside was the road with blown sand at the edges and, beyond a wall, there were rows of cabbages, then a bit of field and the expressionless sky. There was no sound on the road. They—it occurred to them—had been the only sound on that road for hours.

The woman came in with a cup and then with a plate. The child brought a plate and the woman came in with another cup. She looked in a dazed way at the men, amazed that they were still there. It seemed to Ted, who was married, that she didn't know how to lay a table. "And now I've forgotten the sugar," she laughed. Every time she came into the room she glanced at Bert timidly and yet pityingly, because he was the youngest and had been the most angry. He lowered his eyes and avoided her look. But to Ted she said, "That's right, you make yourselves comfortable," and at Sid she smiled because he had been the kindest. At Harry she did not look at all.

She was very startled then when he stood at the door and said "Where's this Roman road?"

She was in the kitchen. She told him the road by the white gate and showed him from the doorway of the house.

"There he goes," said Sid at the window. "He's looking over the gate."

They waited. The milk was put on the table. The woman came in at last with the bread and butter and the tea.

"He'll miss his tea next," Ted said.

"Well," Ted said, when Harry came back. "See any Romans?"

"It's just grass," Harry said. "Nothing on it." He stared in his baffled, bull-necked way.

"No beer and no Romans," Ted said.

The woman, who was standing there, smiled. In a faltering voice, wishing to make them happy, she said:

"We don't often get no Romans here."

"Oh God!" Bert laughed very loudly and Ted shook with laughter too. Harry stared.

"Don't take any notice of them, missus," Sid said. And then to them: "She means gypsies."

"That come with brooms," she said, bewildered by their laughter, wondering what she had done.

When she had gone and had closed the door, Bert and Ted touched their heads with their fingers and said she was dippy, but Sid told them to speak quietly.

Noisily they had drawn up their chairs and were eating and drinking. Ted cut up tomatoes, salted them, and put them on his bread. They were good for the blood, he told them, and Harry said they reckoned at home his grandad got the cancer he died of from eating tomatoes day after day. Bert, with his mouth full, said he'd read somewhere that tea was the most dangerous drink on earth. Then the child came in with a paper and said her mother had sent it. Sid looked at the door when it closed again.

"Funny thing," he said. "I think I've seen that woman before."

That, they said was Sid's trouble. He'd seen too many girls before.

He was a lanky man with a high forehead and a Hitler moustache and his lips lay over his mouth as if they were kissing the air or whispering to it. He was a dark, harsh-looking, cocksure man, but with a gentle voice and it was hard to see his eyes under his strong glasses. His lashes were long and his lids often half lowered which gave him an air of seriousness and shyness. But he stuck his thumbs in his waistcoat and stuck out his legs to show his loud check stockings and he had that ring on his finger. "Move that up a couple and he'd be spliced," they said. "Not me," he said, "Look at Ted." A man with no ideals, Bert thought, a man whose life was hidden behind the syrup-thick lens of his glasses. Flash Sid. See the typists draw themselves up, tilt back their heads and get their hands ready to keep him off. Not a man with ideals. See them watch his arms and his hands, see them start tapping hard on the typewriter keys and pretending to be busy when he leant over to tell them a story. And then, when he was gone, see them peep through the Enquiry window to watch where he went, quarrel about him and dawdle in the street when the office closed, hoping to see him.

"Well," said Harry when they had cleared the table and got out the map. Sid said:

"You gen'lemen settle it. I'll go and fix her up."

Sid's off, they said. First on the road, always leading, getting the first of the air, licking the cream off everything.

He found her in the kitchen and he had to lower his head because of the ceiling. She was sitting drably at the table which was covered with unwashed plates and the remains of a meal. There were unwashed clothes on the backs of the chairs and there was a man's waistcoat. The child was reading a comic paper at the table and singing in a high small voice.

A delicate stalk of neck, he thought, and eyes like the pale wild scabious you see in the ditches.

Four shillings, she said, would that be too much?

She put her hand nervously to her breast.

"That's all right," Sid said and put the money in her hand. It was coarsened by work. "We cleared up everything," he said.

"Don't get many people, I expect," he said.

"Not this time of year."

"A bit lonely," he said.

"Some think it is," she said.

"How long have you been here?" he said.

"Only three years. It seems," she said with her continual wonder, "longer."

"I thought it wasn't long," Sid said. "I thought I seen you somewhere. You weren't in . . . in Horsham, were you?"

"I come from Ashford," she said.

"Ashford," he said. "I knew you weren't from these parts."

She brightened and she was fascinated because he took of his glasses and she saw the deep serious shadows of his eyes and the pale drooping of the naked lids. The eyes looked tired and as if they had seen many things and she was tired too.

"I bin ill," she said. Her story came irresistibly to her lips. "The doctor told us to come here. My husband gave up his job and everything. Things are different here. The money's not so good . . ." Her voice quickened, "But I try to make it up with the teas."

She paused, trying to read from his face if she should say any more. She seemed to be standing on the edge of another country. The pale blue eyes seemed to be the pale sky of a far away place where she had been living.

"I nearly died," she said. She was a little amazed by this fact.

"You're O.K. now," Sid said.

"I'm better," she said. "But it seems I get lonely now I'm better."

"You want your health but you want a bit of company," Sid said.

"My husband says, 'You got your health what you want company for?'"

She put this to Sid in case her husband was not right but she picked up her husband's waistcoat from the chair and looked over its buttons because she felt, timorously, she had been disloyal to her husband.

"A woman wants company," said Sid.

He looked shy now to her, like Bert, the young one; but she was most astonished that someone should agree with her and not her husband.

Then she flushed and put out her hand to the little girl who came to her mother's side, pressing against her. The woman felt safer and raised her eyes and looked more boldly at him.

"You and your friends going far?"

He told her. She nodded, counting the miles as if she were coming along with them. And then Sid felt a hand touch his.

It was the child's hand touching the ring on his finger.

'Ha!" laughed Sid. "You saw that before." He was quick. The child was delighted with his quickness. The woman put the waistcoat down at once. He took off the ring and put it in the palm of his hand and bent down so that his head nearly brushed the woman's arm. "That's lucky," he said. "Here," he said. He slipped the ring on the child's little finger. "See," he said. "Keeps me out of mischief. Keep a ring on your little finger and you'll be lucky."

The child looked at him without belief.

"Here y'are," he said, taking back the ring. "Your mother wants it," he said, winking at the woman. "She's got her's on the wrong finger. Little one luck, big one trouble."

She laughed and she blushed and her eyes shone. He moved to the door and her pale lips pouted a little. Then, taking the child by the hand she hurried over to him as if both of them would cling to him. Excitedly, avidly, they followed him to the other room.

"Come on, Mr. Blake," said Ted. The three others rose to their feet.

The child clung to her mother's hand and danced up and down. She was in the midst of them. They zipped up their jackets, stubbed their cigarettes, folded up the map. Harry put on his gauntlets. He stared at the child and then slowly took off his glove and pulled out a sixpence. "No," murmured Ted, the married man, but the child was too quick.

They went out of the room and stood in the road. They stretched themselves in the open air. The sun was shining now on the fields. The woman came to the door to see them. They took their bicycles from the wall, looked up and down the road and then swung on. To the sea, the coast road and then perhaps a girl, some girl. But the others were shouting.

"Good-bye," they called. "Good-bye."

And Bert, the last, remembered then to wave good-bye too, and glanced up at the misleading notice. When they were all together, heads down to the wind, they turned again. "Good God," they said. The woman and the child had come out into the middle of the road hand in hand and their arms were still raised and their hands were fluttering under the strong light of that high place. It was long time before they went back into the house.

And now for a pub, a real pub, the three men called to Harry. Sid was ahead on his slim pink tyres getting the first of the new wind, with the ring shining on his finger.

GRAHAM GREENE

Brother

*T*he Communists were the first to appear. They walked quickly, a group of about a dozen, up the boulevard which runs from Combat to Ménilmontant; a young man and a girl lagged a little way behind because the man's leg was hurt and the girl was helping him along. They looked impatient, harassed, hopeless, as if they were trying to catch a train which they knew already in their hearts they were too late to catch.

The proprietor of the café saw them coming when they were still a long way off; the lamps at that time were still alight (it was later that the bullets broke the bulbs and dropped darkness all over that quarter of Paris), and the group showed up plainly in the wide barren boulevard. Since sunset only one customer had entered the café, and very soon after sunset firing could be heard from the direction of Combat; the Métro station had closed hours ago. And yet something obstinate and undefeatable in the proprietor's character prevented him from putting up the shutters; it might have been avarice; he could not himself have told what it was as he pressed his broad yellow forehead against the glass and stared this way and that, up the boulevard and down the boulevard.

But when he saw the group and their air of hurry he began immediately to close his café. First he went and warned his only customer, who was practising billiard shots, walking round and round the table, frowning and stroking a thin moustache between shots, a little green in the face under the low diffused lights.

"The Reds are coming," the proprietor said, "you'd better be off. I'm putting up the shutters."

"Don't interrupt. They won't harm me," the customer said. "This is a tricky shot. Red's in baulk. Off the cushion. Screw on spot." He shot his ball straight into a pocket.

"I knew you couldn't do anything with that," the proprietor said, nodding his bald head. "You might just as well go home. Give me a hand with the shutters first. I've sent my wife away." The customer turned on him maliciously, rattling the cue between his fingers. "It was your talking that spoilt the shot. You've cause to be frightened, I dare say. But I'm a poor man. I'm safe. I'm not going to stir." He went across to his coat and took out a dry cigar. "Bring me a bock." He walked round the table on his toes and the balls clicked and the proprietor padded back into the bar, elderly and irritated. He did not fetch the beer but began to close the shutters; every move he made was slow and clumsy. Long before he had finished the group of Communists was outside.

He stopped what he was doing and watched them with furtive dislike. He was afraid that the rattle of the shutters would attract their attention. If I am very quiet and still, he thought, they may go on, and he remembered with malicious pleasure the police barricade across the Place de la République. That will finish them. In the meanwhile I must be very quiet, very still, and he felt a kind of warm satisfaction at the idea that worldly wisdom dictated the very attitude most suited to his nature. So he stared through the edge of a shutter, yellow, plump, cautious, hearing the billiard balls crackle in the other room, seeing the young man come limping up the pavement on the girl's arm, watching them stand and stare with dubious faces up the boulevard towards Combat.

But when they came into the café he was already behind the bar, smiling and bowing and missing nothing, noticing how they had divided forces, how six of them had begun to run back the way they had come.

The young man sat down in a dark corner above the cellar stairs and the others stood round the door waiting for something to happen. It gave the proprietor an odd feeling that they should stand there in his café not asking for a drink, knowing what to expect, when he, the owner, knew nothing, understood nothing. At last the girl said "Cognac," leaving the others and coming to the bar, but when he had poured it out for her, very careful to give a fair and not a generous measure, she simply took it to the man sitting in the dark and held it to his mouth.

"Three francs," the proprietor said. She took the glass and sipped a little and turned it so that the man's lips might touch the same spot. Then she knelt down and rested her forehead against the man's forehead and so they stayed.

"Three francs," the proprietor said, but he could not make his voice bold. The man was no longer visible in his corner, only the girl's back, thin and shabby in a black cotton frock, as she knelt, leaning forward to find the man's face. The proprietor was daunted by the four men at the door, by the knowledge that they were Reds who had no respect for private property, who would drink his wine and go away without paying, who would rape his women (but there was only his wife, and she was not there), who would rob his bank, who would murder him as soon as look at him. So with fear in his heart he gave up the three francs as lost rather than attract any more attention.

Then the worst that he contemplated happened.

One of the men at the door came up to the bar and told him to pour out four glasses of cognac. "Yes, yes," the proprietor said, fumbling with the cork, praying secretly to the Virgin to send an angel, to send the police, to send the Gardes Mobiles, now, immediately, before the cork came out, "that will be twelve francs."

"Oh, no," the man said, "we are all comrades here. Share and share alike. Listen," he said, with earnest mockery, leaning across the bar, "all we have is yours just as much as it's ours, comrade," and stepping back a pace he presented himself to the proprietor, so that he might take his choice of stringy tie, of threadbare trousers, of starved features. "And it follows from that, comrade, that all you have is ours. So four cognacs. Share and share alike."

"Of course," the proprietor said, "I was only joking." Then he stood with bottle poised, and the four glasses tingled upon the counter. "A machine-gun," he said, "up by Combat," and smiled to see how for the moment the men forgot their brandy as they fidgeted near the door. Very soon now, he thought, and I shall be quit of them.

"A machine-gun," the Red said incredulously, "They're using machine-guns?"

"Well," the proprietor said, encouraged by this sign that the Gardes Mobiles were not very far away, "you can't pretend that you aren't armed yourselves." He leant across the bar in a way that was almost paternal. "After all, you know, your ideas—they wouldn't do in France. Free love."

"Who's talking of free love?" the Red said.

The proprietor shrugged and smiled and nodded at the corner. The girl knelt with her head on the man's shoulder, her back to the room. They were quite silent and the glass of brandy stood on the floor beside them. The girl's beret was pushed back on her head and one stocking was laddered and darned from the knee to ankle.

"What, those two? They aren't lovers."

"I," the proprietor said, "with my bourgeois notions would have thought. . . ."

"He's her brother," the Red said.

The men came clustering round the bar and laughed at him, but softly as if a sleeper or a sick person were in the house. All the time they were listening for something. Between their shoulders the proprietor could look out across the boulevard; he could see the corner of the Faubourg du Temple.

"What are you waiting for?"

"For friends," the Red said. He made a gesture with open palm as if to say, You see, we share and share alike. We have no secrets.

Something moved at the corner of the Faubourg du Temple.

"Four more cognacs," the Red said.

"What about those two?" the proprietor asked.

"Leave them alone. They'll look after themselves. They're tired."

How tired they were. No walk up the boulevard from Ménilmontant could explain the tiredness. They seemed to have come farther and fared a great deal worse than their companions. They were more starved; they were infinitely more hopeless, sitting in their dark corner away from the friendly gossip, the amicable desperate voices which now confused the proprietor's brain, until for a moment he believed himself to be a host entertaining friends.

He laughed and made a broad joke directed at the two of them; but they made no sign of understanding. Perhaps they were to be pitied, cut off from the camaraderie round the counter; perhaps they were to be envied for their deeper comradeship. The proprietor thought for no reason at all of the bare grey trees of the Tuileries like a series of exclamation marks drawn against the winter sky. Puzzled, disintegrated, with all his bearings, lost, he stared out through the door towards the Faubourg.

It was as if they had not seen each other for a long while and would soon again be saying good-bye. Hardly aware of what he was doing he filled the four glasses with brandy. They stretched out worn blunted fingers for them.

"Wait," he said. "I've got something better than this"; then paused, conscious of what was happening across the boulevard. The lamplight splashed down on blue steel helmets; the Gardes Mobiles were lining out across the entrance to the Faubourg, and a machine-gun pointed directly at the café windows.

So, the proprietor thought, my prayers are answered. Now I must do my part not look, not warn them, save myself. Have they covered the side door? I will get the other bottle. Real Napoleon brandy. Share and share alike.

He felt a curious lack of triumph as he opened the trap of the bar and came out. He tried not to walk quickly back towards the billiard room. Nothing that he did must warn these men; he tried to spur himself with the thought that every slow casual step he took was a blow for France, for his café, for his savings. He had to step over the girl's feet to pass her; she was asleep. He noted the sharp shoulder blades thrusting through the cotton, and raised his eyes and met her brother's, filled with pain and despair.

He stopped. He found he could not pass without a word. It was as if he needed to explain something, as if he belonged to the wrong party. With false bonhomie he waved the corkscrew he carried in the other's face. "Another cognac, eh?"

"It's no good talking to them," the Red said. "They're German. They don't understand a word."

"German?"

"That's what's wrong with his leg. A concentration camp."

The proprietor told himself that he must be quick, that he must put a door between him and them, that the end was very close, but he was bewildered by the hopelessness in the man's gaze. "What's he doing here?" Nobody answered him. It was as if his question were too foolish to need a reply. With his head sunk upon his breast the proprietor went past, and the girl slept on. He was like a stranger leaving a room where all the rest are friends. A German. They don't understand a word; and up, up through the heavy darkness of his mind, through the avarice and the dubious triumph, a few German words remembered from very old days climbed like spies into the light: a line from the *Lorelei* learnt at school, *Kamerad* with its war-time suggestion of fear and surrender, and oddly from nowhere the phrase *mein Bruder*. He opened the door of the billiard room and closed it behind him and softly turned the key.

"Spot in baulk," the customer explained and leant across the great green table, but while he took aim, wrinkling his narrow peevish eyes, the firing started. It came in two bursts with a rip of glass between. The girl cried out something, but it was not one of the words he knew. Then feet ran across the floor, the trap of the bar slammed. The proprietor sat back against the table and listened and listened for any further sound; but silence came in under the door and silence through the keyhole.

"The cloth. My God, the cloth," the customer said, and the proprietor looked down at his own hand which was working the corkscrew into the table.

"Will this absurdity never end?" the customer said. "I shall go home."

"Wait," the proprietor said. "Wait." He was listening to voices and footsteps in the other room. These were voices he did not recognize. Then a car drove up and presently drove away again. Somebody rattled the handle of the door.

"Who is it?" the proprietor called.

"Who are you? Open that door."

"Ah," the customer said with relief, "the police. Where was I now? Spot in baulk." He began to chalk his cue. The proprietor opened the door. Yes, the Gardes Mobiles had arrived; he was safe again, though his windows were smashed. The Reds had vanished as if they had never been. He looked at the raised trap, at the smashed electric bulbs, at the broken bottle which dripped behind the bar. The café was full of men, and he remembered with odd relief that he had not had time to lock the side door.

"Are you the owner?" the officer asked. "A bock for each of these men and a cognac for myself. Be quick about it."

The proprietor calculated: "Nine francs fifty," and watched closely with bent head the coins rattle down upon the counter.

"You see," the officer said with significance, "we pay." He nodded towards the side door. "Those others: did they pay?"

No, the proprietor admitted, they had not paid, but as he counted the coins and slipped them into the till, he caught himself silently repeating the officer's order—"A bock for each of these men." Those others, he thought, one's got to say that for them, they weren't mean about the drink. It was four cognacs with them. But, of course, they did not pay. "And my windows," he complained aloud with sudden asperity, "what about my windows?"

"Never you mind," the officer said, "the government will pay. You have only to send in your bill. Hurry up now with my cognac. I have no time for gossip."

"You can see for yourself" the proprietor said, "how the bottles have been broken. Who will pay for that?"

"Everything will be paid for," the officer said.

"And now I must go to the cellar to fetch more."

He was angry at the reiteration of the word pay. They enter my café, he thought, they smash my windows, they order me about and think that all is well if they pay, pay, pay. It occurred to him that these men were intruders.

"Step to it," the officer said and turned and rebuked one of the men who had leant his rifle against the bar.

At the top of the cellar stairs the proprietor stopped. They were in darkness, but by the light from the bar he could just make out a body half-way down. He began to tremble violently, and it was some seconds before he could strike a match. The young German lay head downwards, and the blood from his head had dropped on to the step below. His eyes

were open and stared back at the proprietor with the old despairing expression of life. The proprietor would not believe that he was dead. "Kamerad,"
he said bending down, while the match singed his fingers and went out,
trying to recall some phrase in German, but he could only remember, as he
bent lower still, "mein Bruder." Then suddenly he turned and ran up the
steps, waved the match-box in the officer's face, and called out in a low
hysterical voice to him and his men and to the customer stooping under the
low green shade, "Cochons. Cochons."

"What was that? What was that?" the officer exclaimed. "Did you say
that he was your brother? It's impossible," and he frowned incredulously at
the proprietor and rattled the coins in his pocket.

Frank O'Connor (1903–1966) is a pseudonym of Michael O'Donovan, a largely self-educated Irish writer who, after service in the Irish Republican Army (against the British), became a librarian, a director of the celebrated Abbey Theatre (Dublin), and a member of the Irish Academy of Letters. O'Connor is remembered primarily for approximately twenty-five volumes of short stories. Although he felt his gifts were primarily lyrical, he was a rewriter of great tenacity, and some of his stories went through fifty revisions. In his later years, O'Connor came, on occasion, to the United States and lectured at American universities. For further reading: The Stories of Frank O'Connor (1952); More Stories by Frank O'Connor (1954).

FRANK O'CONNOR

Christmas Morning

I never really liked my brother, Sonny. From the time he was a baby he was always the mother's pet and always chasing her to tell her what mischief I was up to. Mind you, I was usually up to something. Until I was nine or ten I was never much good at school, and I really believe it was to spite me that he was so smart at his books. He seemed to know by instinct that this was what Mother had set her heart on, and you might almost say he spelt himself into her favour.

"Mummy," he'd say, "will I call Larry in to his t-e-a?" or: "Mummy, the k-e-t-e-l is boiling," and, of course, when he was wrong she'd correct him, and next time he'd have it right and there would be no standing him. "Mummy," he'd say, "aren't I a good speller?" Cripes, we could all be good spellers if we went on like that!

Mind you, it wasn't that I was stupid. Far from it. I was just restless and not able to fix my mind for long on any one thing. I'd do the lessons for the year before, or the lessons for the year after: what I couldn't stand were the lessons we were supposed to be doing at the time. In the evenings I used to go out and play with the Doherty gang. Not, again, that I was rough, but

I liked the excitement, and for the life of me I couldn't see what attracted Mother about education.

"Can't you do your lessons first and play after?" she'd say, getting white with indignation. "You ought to be ashamed of yourself that your baby brother can read better than you."

She didn't seem to understand that I wasn't, because there didn't seem to me to be anything particularly praiseworthy about reading, and it struck me as an occupation better suited to a sissy kid like Sonny.

"The dear knows what will become of you," she'd say. "If only you'd stick to your books you might be something good like a clerk or an engineer."

"I'll be a clerk, Mummy," Sonny would say smugly.

"Who wants to be an old clerk?" I'd say, just to annoy him. "I'm going to be a soldier."

"The dear knows, I'm afraid that's all you'll ever be fit for," she would add with a sigh.

I couldn't help feeling at times that she wasn't all there. As if there was anything better a fellow could be!

Coming on to Christmas, with the days getting shorter and the shopping crowds bigger, I began to think of all the things I might get from Santa Claus. The Dohertys said there was no Santa Claus, only what your father and mother gave you, but the Dohertys were a rough class of children you wouldn't expect Santa to come to anyway. I was rooting round for whatever information I could pick up about him, but there didn't seem to be much. I was no hand with a pen, but if a letter would do any good I was ready to chance writing to him. I had plenty of initiative and was always writing off for free samples and prospectuses.

"Ah, I don't know will he come at all this year," Mother said with a worried air. "He has enough to do looking after steady boys who mind their lessons without bothering about the rest."

"He only comes to good spellers, Mummy," said Sonny. "Isn't that right?"

"He comes to any little boy who does his best, whether he's a good speller or not," Mother said firmly.

Well, I did my best. God knows I did! It wasn't my fault if, four days before the holidays, Flogger Dawley gave us sums we couldn't do, and Peter Doherty and myself had to go on the lang. It wasn't for love of it, for, take it from me, December is no month for mitching, and we spent most of our time sheltering from the rain in a store on the quays. The only mistake we made was imagining we could keep it up till the holidays without being spotted. That showed real lack of foresight.

Of course, Flogger Dawley noticed and sent home word to know what was keeping me. When I came in on the third day the mother gave me a look I'll never forget, and said: "Your dinner is there." She was too full to talk. When I tried to explain to her about Flogger Dawley and the sums she brushed it aside and said: "You have no word." I saw then it wasn't the langing she minded but the lies, though I still didn't see how you could lang without lying. She didn't speak to me for days. And even then I couldn't make out what she saw in education, or why she wouldn't let me grow up naturally like anyone else.

To make things worse, it stuffed Sonny up more than ever. He had the air of one saying: "I don't know what they'd do without me in this blooming house." He stood at the front door, leaning against the jamb with his hands in his trouser pockets, trying to make himself look like Father, and shouted to the other kids so that he could be heard all over the road.

"Larry isn't left go out. He went on the lang with Peter Doherty and me mother isn't talking to him."

And at night, when we were in bed, he kept it up.

"Santa Claus won't bring you anything this year, aha!"

"Of course he will," I said.

"How do you know?"

"Why wouldn't he?"

"Because you went on the lang with Doherty. I wouldn't play with them Doherty fellows."

"You wouldn't be left."

"I wouldn't play with them. They're no class. They had the bobbies up to the house."

"And how would Santa know I was on the lang with Peter Doherty?" I growled, losing patience with the little prig.

"Of course he'd know. Mummy would tell him."

"And how could Mummy tell him and he up at the North Pole? Poor Ireland, she's rearing them yet! 'Tis easy seen you're only an old baby."

"I'm not a baby, and I can spell better than you, and Santa won't bring you anything."

"We'll see whether he will or not," I said sarcastically, doing the old man on him.

But, to tell the God's truth, the old man was only bluff. You could never tell what powers these superhuman chaps would have of knowing what you were up to. And I had a bad conscience about the langing because I'd never before seen the mother like that.

That was the night I decided that the only sensible thing to do was to see Santa myself and explain to him. Being a man, he'd probably understand. In those days I was a good-looking kid and had a way with me when I liked. I had only to smile nicely at one old gent on the North Mall to get a penny from him, and I felt if only I could get Santa by himself I could do the same with him and maybe get something worth while from him. I wanted a model railway: I was sick of Ludo and Snakes-and-Ladders.

I started to practise lying awake, counting five hundred and then a thousand, and trying to hear first eleven, then midnight, from Shandon. I felt sure Santa would be round by midnight, seeing that he'd be coming from the north, and would have the whole of the South Side to do afterwards. In some ways I was very farsighted. The only trouble was the things I was farsighted about.

I was so wrapped up in my own calculations that I had little attention to spare for Mother's difficulties. Sonny and I used to go to town with her, and while she was shopping we stood outside a toyship in the North Main Street, arguing about what we'd like for Christmas.

On Christmas Eve when Father came home from work and gave her the housekeeping money, she stood looking at it doubtfully while her face grew white.

"Well?" he snapped, getting angry. "What's wrong with that?"

"What's wrong with it?" she muttered. "On Christmas Eve!"

"Well," he asked truculently, sticking his hands in his trouser pockets as though to guard what was left, "do you think I get more because it's Christmas?"

"Lord God," she muttered distractedly. "And not a bit of cake in the house, nor a candle, nor anything."

"All right," he shouted, beginning to stamp. "How much will the candle be?"

"Ah, for pity's sake," she cried, "will you give me the money and not argue like that before the children? Do you think I'll leave them with nothing on the one day of the year?"

"Bad luck to you and your children!" he snarled. "Am I to be slaving from one year's end to another for you to be throwing it away on toys? Here," he added, tossing two half-crowns on the table, "that's all you're going to get, so make the most of it."

"I suppose the publicans will get the rest," she said bitterly.

Later she went into town, but did not bring us with her, and returned with a lot of parcels, including the Christmas candle. We waited for Father to come home to his tea, but he didn't so we had our own tea and a slice of Christmas cake each, and then Mother put Sonny on a chair with the holy-water stoup to sprinkle the candle, and when he lit it she said: "The light of heaven to our souls." I could see she was upset because Father wasn't in— it should be the oldest and youngest. When we hung up our stockings at bedtime he was still out.

Then began the hardest couple of hours I ever put in. I was mad with sleep but afraid of losing the model railway, so I lay for a while, making up things to say to Santa when he came. They varied in tone from frivolous to grave, for some old gents like kids to be modest and well-spoken, while others prefer them with spirit. When I had rehearsed them all I tried to wake Sonny to keep me company, but that kid slept like the dead.

Eleven struck from Shandon, and soon after I heard the latch, but it was only Father coming home.

"Hello, little girl," he said, letting on to be surprised at finding Mother waiting up for him, and then broke into a self-conscious giggle. "What have you up so late?"

"Do you want your supper?" she asked shortly.

"Ah, no, no," he replied. "I had a bit of pig's cheek at Daneen's on my way up (Daneen was my uncle). I'm very fond of a bit of pig's cheek. . . . My goodness, is it that late?" he exclaimed, letting on to be astonished. "If I knew that I'd have gone to the North Chapel for midnight Mass. I'd like to hear the *Adeste* again. That's a hymn I'm very fond of—a most touching hymn."

Then he began to hum it falsetto.

> Adeste fideles
> Solus domus dagus.

Father was very fond of Latin hymns, particularly when he had a drop in, but as he had no notion of the words he made them up as he went along, and this always drove Mother mad.

"Ah, you disgust me!" she said in a scalded voice, and closed the room door behind her. Father laughed as if he thought it a great joke; and he struck a match to light his pipe and for a while puffed at it noisily. The light under the door dimmed and went out but he continued to sing emotionally.

> Dixie medearo
> Tutum tonum tantum
> Venite adoremus.

He had it all wrong but the effect was the same on me. To save my life I couldn't keep awake.

Coming on to dawn, I woke with the feeling that something dreadful had happened. The whole house was quiet, and the little bedroom that looked out on the foot and a half of back yard was pitch-dark. It was only when I glanced at the window that I saw how all the silver had drained out of the sky. I jumped out of bed to feel my stocking, well knowing that the worst had happened. Santa had come while I was asleep, and gone away with an entirely false impression of me, because all he had left me was some sort of book, folded up, a pen and pencil, and a tuppenny bag of sweets. Not even Snakes-and-Ladders! For a while I was too stunned even to think. A fellow who was able to drive over rooftops and climb down chimneys without getting stuck—God, wouldn't you think he'd know better?

Then I began to wonder what that foxy boy, Sonny, had. I went to his side of the bed and felt his stocking. For all his spelling and sucking-up he hadn't done so much better, because, apart from a bag of sweets like mine, all Santa had left him was a popgun, one that fired a cork on a piece of string and which you could get in any huckster's shop for sixpence.

All the same, the fact remained that it was a gun, and a gun was better than a book any day of the week. The Dohertys had a gang, and the gang fought the Strawberry Lane kids who tried to play football on our road. That gun would be very useful to me in many ways, while it would be lost on Sonny who wouldn't be let play with the gang, even if he wanted to.

Then I got the inspiration, as it seemed to me, direct from heaven. Suppose I took the gun and gave Sonny the book! Sonny would never be any good in the gang: he was fond of spelling and a studious child like him could learn a lot of spellings from a book like mine. As he hadn't seen Santa any more than I had, what he hadn't seen wouldn't grieve him. I was doing no harm to anyone; in fact, if Sonny only knew, I was doing him a good turn which he might have cause to thank me for later. That was one thing I was always keen on; doing good turns. Perhaps this was Santa's intention the whole time and he had merely become confused between us. It was a mistake that might happen to anyone. So I put the book, the pencil, and the pen into Sonny's stocking and the popgun into my own, and returned to bed and slept again. As I say, in those days I had plenty of initiative.

It was Sonny who woke me, shaking me to tell me that Santa had come and left me a gun. I let on to be surprised and rather disappointed in the gun, and to divert his mind from it made him show me his picture book, and cracked it up to the skies.

As I knew, that kid was prepared to believe anything, and nothing would do him then but to take the presents in to show Father and Mother. This was a bad moment for me. After the way she had behaved about the langing, I distrusted Mother, though I had the consolation of believing that the only person who could contradict me was now somewhere up by the North Pole. That gave me a certain confidence, so Sonny and I burst in with our presents, shouting: "Look what Santa Claus brought!"

Father and Mother woke, and Mother smiled, but only for an instant. As she looked at me her face changed. I knew that look; I knew it only too well. It was the same she had worn the day I came home from langing, when she said I had no word.

"Larry," she said in low voice, "where did you get that gun?"

"Santa left it in my stocking, Mummy," I said, trying to put on an injured air, though it baffled me how she guessed that he hadn't. "He did, honest."

"You stole it from that poor child's stocking while he was asleep," she said, her voice quivering with indignation. "Larry, Larry, how could you be so mean?"

"Now, now, now," Father said deprecatingly, "'tis Christmas morning."

"Ah," she said with real passion, "it's easy it comes to you. Do you think I want my son to grow up a liar and a thief?"

"Ah, what thief, woman?" he said testily. "Have sense, can't you?" He was as cross if you interrupted him in his benevolent moods as if they were of the other sort, and this one was probably exacerbated by a feeling of guilt for his behaviour of the night before. "Here, Larry," he said, reaching out for the money on the bedside table, "here's sixpence for you and one for Sonny. Mind you don't lose it now!"

But I looked at Mother and saw what was in her eyes. I burst out crying, threw the popgun on the floor, and ran bawling out of the house before anyone on the road was awake. I rushed up the lane behind the house and threw myself on the wet grass.

I understood it all, and it was almost more than I could bear; that there was no Santa Claus, as the Dohertys said, only Mother trying to scrape together a few coppers from the housekeeping; that Father was mean and common and a drunkard, and that she had been relying on me to raise her out of the misery of the life she was leading. And I knew that the look in her eyes was the fear that, like my father, I should turn out to be mean and common and a drunkard.

DORIS LESSING

A Sunrise on the Veld

*E*very night that winter he said aloud into the dark of the pillow: Half-past four! Half-past four! till he felt his brain had gripped the words and held them fast. Then he fell asleep at once, as if a shutter had fallen; and lay with his face turned to the clock so that he could see it first thing when he woke.

It was half-past four to the minute, every morning. Triumphantly pressing down the alarm-knob of the clock, which the dark half of his mind had outwitted, remaining vigilant all night and counting the hours as he lay relaxed in sleep, he huddled down for a last warm moment under the clothes, playing with the idea of lying abed for this once only. But he played with it for the fun of knowing that it was a weakness he could defeat without effort; just as he set the alarm each night for the delight of the moment when he woke and stretched his limbs, feeling the muscles tighten, and thought: Even my brain—even that! I can control every part of myself.

Luxury of warm rested body, with the arms and legs and fingers waiting like soldiers for a word of command! Joy of knowing that the precious hours were given to sleep voluntarily!—for he had once stayed awake three nights running, to prove that he could, and then worked all day, refusing even to admit that he was tired; and now sleep seemed to him a servant to be commanded and refused.

The boy stretched his frame full-length, touching the wall at his head with his hands, and the bedfoot with his toes; then he sprung out, like a fish leaping from water. And it was cold, cold.

He always dressed rapidly, so as to try and conserve his night-warmth till the sun rose two hours later; but by the time he had on his clothes his hands were numbed and he could scarcely hold his shoes. These he could not put on for fear of waking his parents, who never came to know how early he rose.

As soon as he stepped over the lintel, the flesh of his soles contracted on the chilled earth, and his legs began to ache with cold. It was night: the stars were glittering, the trees standing black and still. He looked for signs of day, for the greying of the edge of a stone, or a lightening in the sky where the sun would rise, but there was nothing yet. Alert as an animal he crept past the dangerous window, standing poised with his hand on the sill for one proudly fastidious moment, looking in at the stuffy blackness of the room where his parents lay.

Feeling for the grass-edge of the path with his toes, he reached inside another window further along the wall, where his gun had been set in readiness the night before. The steel was icy, and numbed fingers slipped along it, so that he had to hold it in the crook of his arm for safety. Then he tiptoed to the room where the dogs slept, and was fearful that they might have been tempted to go before him; but they were waiting, their haunches crouched in reluctance at the cold, but ears and swinging tails greeting the gun ecstatically. His warning undertone kept them secret and silent till the house was a hundred yards back: then they bolted off into the bush, yelping excitedly. The boy imagined his parents turning in their beds and muttering: Those dogs again! before they were dragged back in sleep; and he smiled scornfully. He always looked back over his shoulder at the house before he passed a wall of trees that shut it from sight. It looked so low and small, crouching there under a tall and brilliant sky. Then he turned his back on it, and on the frowsting sleepers, and forgot them.

He would have to hurry. Before the light grew strong he must be four miles away; and already a tint of green stood in the hollow of a leaf, and the air smelled of morning and the stars were dimming.

He slung the shoes over his shoulder, *veld skoen* that were crinkled and hard with the dews of a hundred mornings. They would be necessary when the ground became too hot to bear. Now he felt the chilled dust push up between his toes, and he let the muscles of his feet spread and settle into the shapes of the earth; and he thought: I could walk a hundred miles on feet like these! I could walk all day, and never tire!

He was walking swiftly through the dark tunnel of foliage that in daytime was a road. The dogs were invisibly ranging the lower travelways of the bush, and he heard them panting. Sometimes he felt a cold muzzle on his leg before they were off again, scouting for a trail to follow. They were not trained, but free-running companions of the hunt, who often tired of the long stalk before the final shots, and went off on their own pleasure. Soon he could see them, small and wild-looking in a wild strange light, now that the bush stood trembling on the verge of colour, waiting for the sun to paint earth and grass afresh.

The grass stood to his shoulders; and the trees were showering a faint silvery rain. He was soaked; his whole body was clenched in a steady shiver.

Once he bent to the road that was newly scored with animal trails, and regretfully straightened, reminding himself that the pleasure of tracking must wait till another day.

He began to run along the edge of a field, noting jerkily how it was filmed over with fresh spiderweb, so that the long reaches of great black clods seemed netted in glistening grey. He was using the steady lope he had learned by watching the natives, the run that is a dropping of the weight of the body from one foot to the next in a slow balancing movement that never tires, nor shortens the breath; and he felt the blood pulsing down his legs and along his arms, and the exultation and pride of body mounted in him till he was shutting his teeth hard against a violent desire to shout his triumph.

Soon he had left the cultivated part of the farm. Behind him the bush was low and black. In front was a long *vlei,* acres of long pale grass that sent back a hollowing gleam of light to a satiny sky. Near him thick swathes of grass were bent with the weight of water, and diamond drops sparkled on each frond.

The first bird woke at his feet and at once a flock of them sprang into the air calling shrilly that day had come; and suddenly, behind him, the bush woke into song, and he could hear the guinea-fowl calling far ahead of him. That meant they would now be sailing down from their trees into thick grass, and it was for them he had come: he was too late. But he did not mind. He forgot he had come to shoot. He set his legs wide, and balanced from foot to foot, and swung his gun up and down in both hands hori-

zontally, in a kind of improvised exercise, and let his head sink back till it
was pillowed in his neck muscles, and watched how above him small rosy
clouds floated in a lake of gold.

Suddenly it all rose in him: it was unbearable. He leapt up into the air,
shouting and yelling wild, unrecognizable noises. Then he began to run, not
carefully, as he had before, but madly, like a wild thing. He was clean crazy,
yelling mad with the joy of living and a superfluity of youth. He rushed
down the *vlei* under a tumult of crimson and gold, while all the birds of the
world sang about him. He ran in great leaping strides, and shouted as he
ran, feeling his body rise into the crisp rushing air and fall back surely on to
sure feet; and thought briefly, not believing that such a thing could happen
to him, that he could break his ankle any moment, in this thick tangled
grass. He cleared bushes like a *duiker,* leaped over rocks; and finally came
to a dead stop at a place where the ground fell abruptly away below him to
the river. It had been a two-mile-long dash through waist-high growth, and
he was breathing hoarsely and could no longer sing. But he poised on a
rock and looked down at stretches of water that gleamed through stooping
trees, and thought suddenly, I am fifteen! Fifteen! The words came new to
him; so that he kept repeating them wonderingly, with swelling excitement;
and he felt the years of his life with his hands, as if he were counting
marbles, each one hard and separate and compact, each one a wonderful
shining thing. That was what he was: fifteen years of this rich soil, and this
slow-moving water, and air that smelt like a challenge whether it was warm
and sultry at noon, or as brisk as cold water, like it was now.

There was nothing he couldn't do, nothing! A vision came to him, as
he stood there, like when a child hears the word "eternity" and tries to
understand it, and time takes possession of the mind. He felt his life ahead
of him as a great and wonderful thing, something that was his; and he said
aloud, with the blood rising to his head: all the great men of the world have
been as I am now, and there is nothing I can't become, nothing I can't do;
there is no country in the world I cannot make part of myself, if I choose.
I contain the world. I can make of it what I want. If I choose, I can change
everything that is going to happen: it depends on me, and what I decide
now.

The urgency, and the truth and the courage of what his voice was
saying exulted him so that he began to sing again, at the top of his voice,
and the sound went echoing down the river gorge. He stopped for the echo,
and sang again: stopped and shouted. That was what he was!—he sang, if
he chose; and the world had to answer him.

And for minutes he stood there, shouting and singing and waiting for
the lovely eddying sound of the echo; so that his own new strong thoughts
came back and washed round his head, as if someone were answering him
and encouraging him; till the gorge was full of soft voices clashing back and

forth from rock to rock over the river. And then it seemed as if there was a new voice. He listened, puzzled, for it was not his own. Soon he was leaning forward, all his nerves alert, quite still: somewhere close to him there was a noise that was no joyful bird, nor tinkle of falling water, nor ponderous movement of cattle.

There it was again. In the deep morning hush that held his future and his past, was a sound of pain, and repeated over and over: it was a kind of shortened scream, as if someone, something, had no breath to scream. He came to himself, looked about him, and called for the dogs. They did not appear: they had gone off on their own business, and he was alone. Now he was clean sober, all the madness gone. His heart beating fast, because of that frightened screaming, he stepped carefully off the rock and went towards a belt of trees. He was moving cautiously, for not so long ago he had seen a leopard in just this spot.

At the edge of the trees he stopped and peered, holding his gun ready; he advanced, looking steadily about him, his eyes narrowed. Then, all at once, in the middle of a step, he faltered, and his face was puzzled. He shook his head impatiently, as if he doubted his own sight.

There, between two trees, against a background of gaunt black rocks, was a figure from a dream, a strange beast that was horned and drunken-legged, but like something he had never even imagined. It seemed to be ragged. It looked like a small buck that had black ragged tufts of fur standing up irregularly all over it, with patches of raw flesh beneath . . . but the patches of rawness were disappearing under moving black and came again elsewhere; and all the time the creature screamed, in small gasping screams, and leaped drunkenly from side to side, as if it were blind.

Then the boy understood: it *was* a buck. He ran closer, and again stood still, stopped by a new fear. Around him the grass was whispering and alive. He looked wildly about, and then down. The ground was black with ants, great energetic ants that took no notice of him, but hurried and scurried towards the fighting shape, like glistening black water flowing through the grass.

And, as he drew in his breath and pity and terror seized him, the beast fell and the screaming stopped. Now he could hear nothing but one bird singing, and the sound of the rustling, whispering ants.

He peered over at the writhing blackness that jerked convulsively with the jerking nerves. It grew quieter. There were small twitches from the mass that still looked vaguely like the shape of a small animal.

It came into his mind that he should shoot it and end its pain; and he raised the gun. Then he lowered it again. The buck could no longer feel; its fighting was a mechanical protest of the nerves. But it was not that which made him put down the gun. It was a swelling feeling of rage and misery and protest that expressed itself in the thought: if I had not come it would have died like this: so why should I interfere? All over the bush things like this happen; they happen all the time; this is how life goes on, by living things dying in anguish. He gripped the gun between his knees and felt in his own limbs the myriad swarming pain of the twitching animal that could no longer feel, and set his teeth, and said over and over again under his breath: I can't stop it. I can't stop it. There is nothing I can do.

He was glad that the buck was unconscious and had gone past suffering so that he did not have to make a decision to kill it even when he was feeling with his whole body: this is what happens, this is how things work.

It was right—that was what he was feeling. *It was right and nothing could alter it.*

The knowledge of fatality, of what has to be, had gripped him and for the first time in his life; and he was left unable to make any movement of brain or body, except to say: "Yes, yes. That is what living is." It had entered his flesh and his bones and grown in to the furthest corners of his brain and would never leave him. And at that moment he could not have performed the smallest action of mercy, knowing as he did, having lived on it all his life, the vast unalterable, cruel *veld*, where at any moment one might stumble over a skull or crush the skeleton of some small creature.

Suffering, sick, and angry, but also grimly satisfied with his new stoicism, he stood there leaning on his rifle, and watched the seething black mound grow smaller. At his feet, now, were ants trickling back with pink fragments in their mouths, and there was a fresh acid smell in his nostrils. He sternly controlled the uselessly convulsing muscles of his empty stomach, and reminded himself: the ants must eat too! At the same time he found that the tears were streaming down his face, and his clothes were soaked with the sweat of that other creature's pain.

The shape had grown small. Now it looked like nothing recognizable. He did not know how long it was before he saw the blackness thin, and bits of white showed through, shining in the sun—yes, there was the sun, just up, glowing over the rocks. Why, the whole thing could not have taken longer than a few minutes.

He began to swear, as if the shortness of the time was in itself unbearable, using the words he had heard his father say. He strode forward, crushing ants with each step, and brushing them off his clothes, till he stood above the skeleton, which lay sprawled under a small bush. It was clean-picked. It might have been lying there years, save that on the white bone were pink fragments of gristle. About the bones ants were ebbing away, their pincers full of meat.

The boy looked at them, big black ugly insects. A few were standing and gazing up at him with small glittering eyes.

"Go away!" he said to the ants, very coldly. "I am not for you—not just yet, at any rate. Go away." And he fancied that the ants turned and went away.

He bent over the bones and touched the sockets in the skull; that was where the eyes were, he thought incredulously, remembering the liquid dark eyes of a buck. And then he bent the slim foreleg bone, swinging it horizontally in his palm.

That morning, perhaps an hour ago, this small creature had been stepping proud and free through the bush, feeling the chill on its hide even as he himself had done, exhilarated by it. Proudly stepping the earth, tossing its horns, frisking a pretty white tail, it had sniffed the cold morning air. Walking like kings and conquerors it had moved through this free-held bush, where each blade of grass grew for it alone, and where the river ran pure sparkling water for its slaking.

And then—what had happened? Such a swift surefooted thing could surely not be trapped by a swarm of ants?

The boy bent curiously to the skeleton. Then he saw that the back leg that lay uppermost and strained out in the tension of death, was snapped midway in the thigh, so that broken bones jutted over each other uselessly. So that was it! Limping into the ant-masses it could not escape, once it had sensed the danger. Yes, but how had the leg been broken? Had it fallen, perhaps? Impossible, a buck was too light and graceful. Had some jealous rival horned it?

What could possibly have happened? Perhaps some Africans had thrown stones at it, as they do, trying to kill it for meat, and had broken its leg. Yes, that must be it.

Even as he imagined the crowd of running shouting natives, and the flying stones, and the leaping buck, another picture came into his mind. He saw himself, on any one of these bright ringing mornings, drunk with excitement, taking a snap shot at some half-seen buck. He saw himself, with the gun lowered, wondering whether he had missed or not; and thinking at last that it was late, and he wanted his breakfast, and it was not worth while to track miles after an animal that would very likely get away from him in any case.

For a moment he would not face it. He was a small boy again, kicking sulkily at the skeleton, hanging his head, refusing to accept the responsibility.

Then he straightened up, and looked down at the bones with an odd expression of dismay, all the anger gone out of him. His mind went quite empty: all around him he could see trickles of ants disappearing into the grass. The whispering noise was faint and dry, like the rustling of a cast snakeskin.

At last he picked up his gun and walked homewards. He was telling himself half defiantly that he wanted his breakfast. He was telling himself that it was getting very hot, much too hot to be out roaming the bush.

Really, he was tired. He walked heavily, not looking where he put his feet. When he came within sight of his home he stopped, knitting his brows.

There was something he had to think out. The death of that small animal was a thing that concerned him, and he was by no means finished with it. It lay at the back of his mind uncomfortably.

Soon, the very next morning, he would get clear of everybody and go to the bush and think about it.

ELIZABETH BOWEN

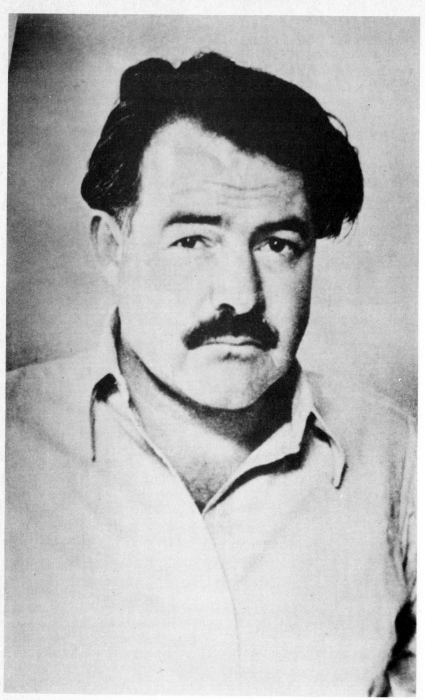

ERNEST HEMINGWAY

SHERWOOD ANDERSON

The Egg

*M*y father was, I am sure, intended by nature to be a cheerful, kindly man. Until he was thirty-four years old he worked as a farm-hand for a man named Thomas Butterworth whose place lay near the town of Bidwell, Ohio. He had then a horse of his own and on Saturday evenings drove into town to spend a few hours in social intercourse with other farm-hands. In town he drank several glasses of beer and stood about in Ben Head's saloon—crowded on Saturday evenings with visiting farm-hands. Songs were sung and glasses thumped on the bar. At ten o'clock father drove home along a lonely country road, made his horse comfortable for the night and himself went to bed, quite happy in his position in life. He had at that time no notion of trying to rise in the world.

It was in the spring of his thirty-fifth year that father married my mother, then a country school-teacher, and in the following spring I came wriggling and crying into the world. Something happened to the two people. They became ambitious. The American passion for getting up in the world took possession of them.

It may have been that mother was responsible. Being a school-teacher she had no doubt read books and magazines. She had, I presume, read of how Garfield, Lincoln, and other Americans rose from poverty to fame and greatness and as I lay beside her—in the days of lying-in—she may have dreamed that I would some day rule men and cities. At any rate she induced father to give up his place as a farm-hand, sell his horse and embark on an independent enterprise of his own. She was a tall silent woman with a long nose and troubled grey eyes. For herself she wanted nothing. For father and myself she was incurably ambitious.

The first venture into which the two people went turned out badly. They rented ten acres of poor stony land on Griggs's Road, eight miles from Bidwell, and launched into chicken raising. I grew into boyhood on the place and got my first impressions of life there. From the beginning they were impressions of disaster and if, in my turn, I am a gloomy man inclined to see the darker side of life, I attribute it to the fact that what should have been for me the happy joyous days of childhood were spent on a chicken farm.

One unversed in such matters can have no notion of the many and tragic things that can happen to a chicken. It is born out of an egg, lives for a few weeks as a tiny fluffy thing such as you will see pictured on Easter cards, then becomes hideously naked, eats quantities of corn and meal bought by the sweat of you father's brow, gets diseases called pip, cholera, and other names, stands looking with stupid eyes at the sun, becomes sick and dies. A few hens and now and then a rooster, intended to serve God's mysterious ends, struggle through to maturity. The hens lay eggs out of which come other chickens and the dreadful cycle is thus made complete. It is all unbelievably complex. Most philosophers must have been raised on chicken farms. One hopes for so much from a chicken and is so dreadfully disillusioned. Small chickens, just setting out on the journey of life, look so bright and alert and they are in fact so dreadfully stupid. They are so much like people they mix one up in one's judgments of life. If disease does not kill them they wait until your expectations are thoroughly aroused and then walk under the wheels of a wagon—to go squashed and dead back to their maker. Vermin infest their youth, and fortunes must be spent for curative powders. In later life I have seen how a literature has been built up on the subject of fortunes to be made out of the raising of chickens. It is intended to be read by the gods who have just eaten of the tree of the knowledge of good and evil. It is a hopeful literature and declares that much may be done by simple ambitious people who own a few hens. Do not be led astray by it.

It was not written for you. Go hunt for gold on the frozen hills of Alaska, put your faith in the honesty of a politician, believe if you will that the world is daily growing better and that good will triumph over evil, but do not read and believe the literature that is written concerning the hen. It was not written for you.

I, however, digress. My tale does not primarily concern itself with the hen. If correctly told it will centre on the egg. For ten years my father and mother struggled to make our chicken farm pay and then they gave up that struggle and began another. They moved into the town of Bidwell, Ohio, and embarked in the restaurant business. After ten years of worry with incubators that did not hatch, and with tiny—and in their own way love-ly—balls of fluff that passed on into semi-naked pullethood and from that into dead henhood, we threw all aside and packing our belongings on a wagon drove down Griggs's Road toward Bidwell, a tiny caravan of hope looking for a new place from which to start on our upward journey through life.

We must have been a sad looking lot, not, I fancy, unlike refugees fleeing from a battlefield. Mother and I walked in the road. The wagon that contained our goods had been borrowed for the day from Mr. Albert Griggs, a neighbor. Out of its sides stuck the legs of cheap chairs and at the back of the pile of beds, tables, and boxes filled with kitchen utensils was a crate of live chickens, and on top of that the baby carriage in which I had been wheeled about in my infancy. Why we stuck to the baby carriage I don't know. It was unlikely other children would be born and the wheels were broken. People who have few possessions cling tightly to those they have. That is one of the facts that make life so discouraging.

Father rode on top of the wagon. He was then a bald-headed man of forty-five, a little fat and from long association with mother and the chick-ens he had become habitually silent and discouraged. All during our ten years on the chicken farm he had worked as a laborer on neighboring farms and most of the money he had earned had been spent for remedies to cure chicken diseases, on Wilmer's White Wonder Cholera Cure or Professor Bidlow's Egg Producer or some other preparations that mother found ad-vertised in the poultry papers. There were two little patches of hair on father's head just above his ears. I remember that as a child I used to sit looking at him when he had gone to sleep in a chair before the stove on Sunday afternoons in the winter. I had at that time already begun to read books and have notions of my own and the bald path that led over the top of his head was, I fancied, something like a broad road, such a road as Caesar might have made on which to lead his legions out of Rome and into the wonders of an unknown world. The tufts of hair that grew above father's ears were, I thought, like forests. I fell into a half-sleeping, half-waking state and dreamed I was a tiny thing going along the road into a far beautiful place where there were no chicken farms and where life was a happy eggless affair.

One might write a book concerning our flight from the chicken farm into town. Mother and I walked the entire eight miles—she to be sure that nothing fell from the wagon and I to see the wonder of the world. On the seat of the wagon beside father was his greatest treasure. I will tell you of that.

On a chicken farm where hundreds and even thousands of chickens come out of eggs surprising things sometimes happen. Grotesques are born out of eggs as out of people. The accident does not often occur—perhaps once in a thousand births. A chicken is, you see, born that has four legs, two pairs of wings, two heads or what not. The things do not live. They go quickly back to the hand of their maker that has for a moment trembled. The fact that the poor little things could not live was one of the tragedies of life to father. He had some sort of notion that if he could but bring into henhood or roosterhood a five-legged hen or a two-headed rooster his fortune would be made. He dreamed of taking the wonder about to county fairs and of growing rich by exhibiting it to other farm-hands.

At any rate he saved all the little monstrous things that had been born on our chicken farm. They were preserved in alcohol and put each in its own glass bottle. These he had carefully put into a box and on our journey into town it was carried on the wagon seat beside him. He drove the horses with one hand and with the other clung to the box. When we got to our destination the box was taken down at once and the bottles removed. All during our days as keepers of a restaurant in the town of Bidwell, Ohio, the grotesques in their little glass bottles sat on a shelf back of the counter. Mother sometimes protested but father was a rock on the subject of his treasure. The grotesques were, he declared, valuable. People, he said, liked to look at strange and wonderful things.

Did I say that we embarked in the restaurant business in the town of Bidwell, Ohio? I exaggerated a little. The town itself lay at the foot of a low hill and on the shore of a small river. The railroad did not run through the town and the station was a mile away to the north at a place called Pickleville. There had been a cider mill and pickle factory at the station, but before the time of our coming they had both gone out of business. In the morning and in the evening busses came down to the station along a road called Turner's Pike from the hotel on the main street of Bidwell. Our going to the out of the way place to embark in the restaurant business was mother's idea. She talked of it for a year and then one day went off and rented an empty store building opposite the railroad station. It was her idea that the restaurant would be profitable. Travelling men, she said, would be always waiting around to take trains out of town and town people would come to the station to await incoming trains. They would come to the restaurant to buy pieces of pie and drink coffee. Now that I am older I know that she had another motive in going. She was ambitious for me. She wanted me to rise in the world, to get into a town school and become a man of the towns.

At Pickleville father and mother worked hard as they always had done. At first there was the necessity of putting our place into shape to be a restaurant. That took a month. Father built a shelf on which he put tins of vegetables. He painted a sign on which he put his name in large red letters. Below his name was the sharp command—"EAT HERE"—that was so seldom obeyed. A show case was bought and filled with cigars and tobacco. Mother scrubbed the floor and the walls of the room. I went to school in the town and was glad to be away from the farm and from the presence of the discouraged, sad-looking chickens. Still I was not very joyous. In the evening I walked home from school along Turner's Pike and remembered the children I had seen playing in the town school yard. A troop of little girls had gone hopping about and singing. I tried that. Down along the frozen road I went hopping solemnly on one leg. "Hippity Hop To The Barber Shop," I sang shrilly. Then I stopped and looked doubtfully about. I was afraid of being seen in my gay mood. It must have seemed to me that I was doing a thing that should not be done by one who, like myself, had been raised on a chicken farm where death was a daily visitor.

Mother decided that our restaurant should remain open at night. At ten in the evening a passenger train went north past our door followed by a local freight. The freight crew had switching to do in Pickleville and when the work was done they came to our restaurant for hot coffee and food. Sometimes one of them ordered a fried egg. In the morning at four they returned north-bound and again visited us. A little trade began to grow up. Mother slept at night and during the day tended the restaurant and fed our boarders while father slept. He slept in the same bed mother had occupied during the night and I went off to the town of Bidwell and to school. During the long nights, while mother and I slept, father cooked meats that were to go into sandwiches for the lunch baskets of our boarders. Then an idea in regard to getting up in the world came into his head. The American spirit took hold of him. He also became ambitious.

In the long nights when there was little to do father had time to think. That was his undoing. He decided that he had in the past been an unsuccessful man because he had not been cheerful enough and that in the future he would adopt a cheerful outlook on life. In the early morning he came upstairs and got into bed with mother. She woke and the two talked. From my bed in the corner I listened.

It was father's idea that both he and mother should try to entertain the people who came to eat at our restaurant. I cannot now remember his words, but he gave the impression of one about to become in some obscure way a kind of public entertainer. When people, particularly young people from the town of Bidwell, came into our place, as on very rare occasions they did, bright entertaining conversation was to be made. From Father's words I gathered that something of the jolly inn-keeper effect was to be sought. Mother must have been doubtful from the first, but she said nothing discouraging. It was father's notion that a passion for the company of himself and mother would spring up in the breasts of the younger people of the town of Bidwell. In the evening bright happy groups would come singing down Turner's Pike. They would troop shouting with joy and laughter into our place. There would be song and festivity. I do not mean to give the impression that father spoke so elaborately of the matter. He was as I have said an uncommunicative man. "They want some place to go. I tell you they want some place to go," he said over and over. That was as far as he got. My own imagination has filled in the blanks.

For two or three weeks this notion of father's invaded our house. We did not talk much, but in our daily lives tried earnestly to make smiles take the place of glum looks. Mother smiled at the boarders and I, catching the infection, smiled at our cat. Father became a little feverish in his anxiety to please. There was no doubt, lurking somewhere in him, a touch of the spirit of the showman. He did not waste much of his ammunition on the railroad men he served at night but seemed to be waiting for a young man or woman from Bidwell to come in to show what he could do. On the counter in the restaurant there was a wire basket kept always filled with eggs, and it must have been before his eyes when the idea of being entertaining was born in his brain. There was something pre-natal about the way eggs kept themselves connected with the development of his idea. At any rate an egg ruined his new impulse in life. Late one night I was awakened by a roar of anger coming from father's throat. Both mother and I sat upright in our beds. With trembling hands she lighted a lamp that stood on a table by her head. Downstairs the front door of our restaurant went shut with a bang and in a few minutes father tramped up the stairs. He held an egg in his hand and his hand trembled as though he were having a chill. There was a half insane light in his eyes. As he stood glaring at us I was sure he intended throwing the egg at either mother or me. Then he laid it gently on the table beside the lamp and dropped on his knees beside mother's bed. He began to cry like a boy and I, carried away by his grief, cried with him. The two of us filled the little upstairs room with our wailing voices. It is ridiculous, but of the picture we made I can remember only the fact that mother's hand continually stroked the bald path that ran across the top of his head. I have forgotten what mother said to him and how she induced him to tell her of what had happened downstairs. His explanation also has gone out of my mind. I remember only my own grief and fright and the shiny path over father's head glowing in the lamp light as he knelt by the bed.

As to what happened downstairs. For some unexplainable reason I know the story as well as though I had been a witness to my father's discomfiture. One in time gets to know many unexplainable things. On that evening young Joe Kane, son of a merchant of Bidwell, came to Pickleville to meet his father, who was expected on the ten o'clock evening train from the South. The train was three hours late and Joe came into our place to loaf about and to wait for its arrival. The local freight train came in and the freight crew were fed. Joe was left alone in the restaurant with father.

From the moment he came into our place the Bidwell young man must have been puzzled by my father's actions. It was his notion that father was angry at him for hanging around. He noticed that the restaurant keeper was apparently disturbed by his presence and he thought of going out. However, it began to rain and he did not fancy the long walk to town and back. He bought a five-cent cigar and ordered a cup of coffee. He had a newspaper in his pocket and took it out and began to read. "I'm waiting for the evening train. It's late," he said apologetically.

For a long time father, whom Joe Kane had never seen before, remained silently gazing at his visitor. He was no doubt suffering from an attack of stage fright. As so often happens in life he had thought so much and so often of the situation that now confronted him that he was somewhat nervous in its presence.

For one thing, he did not know what to do with his hands. He thrust one of them nervously over the counter and shook hands with Joe Kane. "How-de-do," he said. Joe Kane put his newspaper down and stared at him. Father's eye lighted on the basket of eggs that sat on the counter and he began to talk. "Well," he began hesitatingly, "well, you have heard of Christopher Columbus, eh?" He seemed to be angry. "That Christopher Columbus was a cheat," he declared emphatically. "He talked of making an egg stand on its end. He talked, he did, and then he went and broke the end of the egg."

My father seemed to his visitor to be beside himself at the duplicity of Christopher Columbus. He muttered and swore. He declared it was wrong to teach children that Christopher Columbus was a great man when, after all, he cheated at the critical moment. He had declared he would make an egg stand on end and then when his bluff had been called he had done a trick. Still grumbling at Columbus, father took an egg from the basket on the counter and began to walk up and down. He rolled the egg between the palms of his hands. He smiled genially. He began to mumble words regarding the effect to be produced on an egg by the electricity that comes out of the human body. He declared that without breaking its shell and by virtue of rolling it back and forth in his hands he could stand the egg on its end. He explained that the warmth of his hands and the gentle rolling movement he gave the egg created a new centre of gravity, and Joe Kane was mildly interested. "I have handled thousands of eggs," father said. "No one knows more about eggs than I do."

He stood the egg on the counter and it fell on its side. He tried the trick again and again, each time rolling the egg between the palms of his hands and saying the words regarding the wonders of electricity and the laws of gravity. When after a half hour's effort he did succeed in making the egg stand for a moment he looked up to find that his visitor was no longer watching. By the time he had succeeded in calling Joe Kane's attention to the success of his effort the egg had again rolled over and lay on its side.

Afire with the showman's passion and at the same time a good deal disconcerted by the failure of his first effort, father now took the bottles containing the poultry monstrosities down from their place on the shelf and began to show them to his visitor. "How would you like to have seven legs and two heads like this fellow?" he asked, exhibiting the most remarkable of his treasures. A cheerful smile played over his face. He reached over the counter and tried to slap Joe Kane on the shoulder as he had seen men do in Ben Head's saloon when he was a young farmhand and drove to town on Saturday evenings. His visitor was made a little ill by the sight of the body of the terribly deformed bird floating in the alcohol in the bottle and got up to go. Coming from behind the counter father took hold of the young man's arm and led him back to his seat. He grew a little angry and for a moment had to turn his face away and force himself to smile. Then he put the bottles back on the shelf. In an outburst of generosity he fairly compelled Joe Kane to have a fresh cup of coffee and another cigar at his expense. Then he took a pan and filling it with vinegar, taken from a jug that sat beneath the counter, he declared himself about to do a new trick. "I will heat this egg in this pan of vinegar," he said. "Then I will put it through the neck of a bottle without breaking the shell. When the egg is inside the bottle it will resume its normal shape and the shell will become hard again. Then I will give the bottle with the egg in it to you. You can take it about with you wherever you go. People will want to know how you got the egg in the bottle. Don't tell them. Keep them guessing. That is the way to have fun with this trick."

Father grinned and winked at his visitor. Joe Kane decided that the man who confronted him was mildly insane but harmless. He drank the cup of coffee that had been given him and began to read his paper again. When the egg had been heated in vinegar father carried it on a spoon to the counter and going into a back room got an empty bottle. He was angry because his visitor did not watch him as he began to do his trick, but nevertheless went cheerfully to work. For a long time he struggled, trying to get the egg to go through the neck of the bottle. He put the pan of vinegar back on the stove, intending to reheat the egg, then picked it up and burned his fingers. After a second bath in the hot vinegar the shell of the egg had been softened a little but not enough for his purpose. He worked and worked and a spirit of desperate determination took possession of him. When he thought that at last the trick was about to be consummated the delayed train came in at the station and Joe Kane started to go nonchalantly out at the door. Father made a last desperate effort to conquer the egg and make it do the things that would establish his reputation as one who knew how to entertain guests who came into his restaurant. He worried the egg. He attempted to be somewhat rough with it. He swore and the sweat stood out on his forehead. The egg broke under his hand. When the contents spurted over his clothes, Joe Kane, who had stopped at the door, turned and laughed.

A roar of anger rose from my father's throat. He danced and shouted a string of inarticulate words. Grabbing another egg from the basket on the counter, he threw it, just missing the head of the young man as he dodged through the door and escaped.

Father came upstairs to mother and me with an egg in his hand. I do not know what he intended to do. I imagine he had some idea of destroying it, of destroying all eggs, and that he intended to let mother and me see him begin. When, however, he got into the presence of mother something happened to him. He laid the egg gently on the table and dropped on his knees by the bed as I have already explained. He later decided to close the restaurant for the night and to come upstairs and get into bed. When he did so he blew out the light and after much muttered conversation both he and mother went to sleep. I suppose I went to sleep also, but my sleep was troubled. I awoke at dawn and for a long time looked at the egg that lay on the table. I wondered why eggs had to be and why from the egg came the hen who again laid the egg. The question got into my blood. It has stayed there, I imagine, because I am the son of my father. At any rate, the problem remains unsolved in my mind. And that, I conclude, is but another evidence of the complete and final triumph of the egg—at least as far as my family is concerned.

Katherine Anne Porter (1894–   ) was born in In-
dian Creek, Texas, and was educated in private
schools and the Ursuline Convent; she has traveled in
Europe, Bermuda, and Mexico, and has lived in
many parts of the United States. Primarily a writer
of short fiction, she has also published essays, trans-
lations, and nonfiction; a single novel, Ship of Fools
(1962), was many years in the making and was wide-
ly acclaimed. Her considerable reputation rests on
relatively few short stories, which are compactly writ-
ten and which display a controlled style and technical
resources of a high order. In 1966 she won both the
Pulitzer Prize and the National Book Award. For
further reading: The Collected Stories of Katherine
Anne Porter *(1965).*

KATHERINE ANNE PORTER

Rope

On the third day after they moved to the country he came walking back from the village carrying a basket of groceries and a twenty-four-yard coil of rope. She came out to meet him, wiping her hands on her green smock. Her hair was tumbled, her nose was scarlet with sunburn; he told her that already she looked like a born country woman. His gray flannel shirt stuck to him, his heavy shoes were dusty. She assured him he looked like a rural character in a play.

Had he brought the coffee? She had been waiting all day long for coffee. They had forgot it when they ordered at the store the first day.

Gosh, no, he hadn't. Lord, now he'd have to go back. Yes, he would if it killed him. He thought, though, he had everything else. She reminded him it was only because he didn't drink coffee himself. If he did he would remember it quick enough. Suppose they ran out of cigarettes? Then she saw the rope. What was that for? Well, he thought it might do to hang clothes on, or something. Naturally she asked him if he thought they were going to run a laundry? They already had a fifty-foot line hanging right before his eyes. Why, hadn't he noticed it, really? It was a blot on the landscape to her.

He thought there were a lot of things a rope might come in handy for. She wanted to know what, for instance. He thought a few seconds, but nothing occurred. They could wait and see, couldn't they? You need all sorts of strange odds and ends around a place in the country. She said, yes, that was so; but she thought just at that time when every penny counted, it seemed funny to buy more rope. That was all. She hadn't meant anything else. She hadn't just seen, not at first, why he felt it was necessary.

Well, thunder, he had bought it because he wanted to, and that was all there was to it. She thought that was reason enough, and couldn't understand why he hadn't said so, at first. Undoubtedly it would be useful, twenty-four yards of rope, there were hundreds of things, she couldn't think of any at the moment, but it would come in. Of course. As he had said, things always did in the country.

But she was a little disappointed about the coffee, and oh, look, look, look at the eggs! Oh, my, they're all running! What had he put on top of them? Hadn't he known eggs mustn't be squeezed? Squeezed, who had squeezed them, he wanted to know. What a silly thing to say. He had simply brought them along in the basket with the other things. If they got broke it was the grocer's fault. He should know better than to put heavy things on top of eggs.

She believed it was the rope. That was the heaviest thing in the pack, she saw him plainly when he came in from the road, the rope was a big package on top of everything. He desired the whole wide world to witness that this was not a fact. He had carried the rope in one hand and the basket in the other, and what was the use of her having eyes if that was the best they could do for her?

Well, anyhow, she could see one thing plain: no eggs for breakfast. They'd have to scramble them now, for supper. It was too damned bad. She had planned to have steak for supper. No ice, meat wouldn't keep. He wanted to know why she couldn't finish breaking the eggs in a bowl and set them in a cool place.

Cool place! If he could find one for her, she'd be glad to set them there. Well, then, it seemed to him they might very well cook the meat at the same time they cooked the eggs and then warm up the meat for tomorrow. The idea simply choked her. Warmed-over meat, when they might as well have had it fresh. Second best and scraps and makeshifts, even to the meat! He rubbed her shoulder a little. It doesn't really matter so much, does it, darling? Sometimes when they were playful, he would rub her shoulder and she would arch and purr. This time she hissed and almost clawed. He was getting ready to say that they could surely manage somehow when she turned on him and said, if he told her they could manage somehow she would certainly slap his face.

He swallowed the words red hot, his face burned. He picked up the rope and started to put it on the top shelf. She would not have it on the top shelf, the jars and tins belonged there; positively she would not have the top shelf cluttered up with a lot of rope. She had borne all the clutter she meant to bear in the flat in town, there was space here at least and she meant to keep things in order.

Well, in that case, he wanted to know what the hammer and nails were doing up there? And why had she put them there when she knew very well he needed that hammer and those nails upstairs to fix the window sashes? She simply slowed down everything and made double work on the place with her insane habit of changing things around and hiding them.

She was sure she begged his pardon, and if she had had any reason to believe he was going to fix the sashes this summer she would have left the hammer and nails right where he put them; in the middle of the bedroom floor where they could step on them in the dark. And now if he didn't clear the whole mess out of there she would throw them down the well.

Oh, all right, all right—could he put them in the closet? Naturally not, there were brooms and mops and dustpans in the closet, and why couldn't he find a place for his rope outside her kitchen? Had he stopped to consider there were seven God-forsaken rooms in the house, and only one kitchen?

He wanted to know what of it? And did she realize she was making a complete fool of herself? And what did she take him for, a three-year old idiot? The whole trouble with her was she needed something weaker than she was to heckle and tyrannize over. He wished to God now they had a couple of children she could take it out on. Maybe he'd get some rest.

Her face changed at this, she reminded him he had forgot the coffee and had bought a worthless piece of rope. And when she thought of all the things they actually needed to make the place even decently fit to live in, well, she could cry, that was all. She looked so forlorn, so lost and despairing he couldn't believe it was only a piece of rope that was causing all the racket. What *was* the matter, for God's sake?

Oh, would he please hush and go away, and *stay* away, if he could, for five minutes? By all means, yes, he would. He'd stay away indefinitely if she wished. Lord, yes, there was nothing he'd like better than to clear out and never come back. She couldn't for the life of her see what was holding him, then. It was a swell time. Here she was, stuck, miles from a railroad, with a half-empty house on her hands, and not a penny in her pocket, and everything on earth to do; it seemed the God-sent moment for him to get out from under. She was surprised he hadn't stayed in town as it was until she had come out and done the work and got things straightened out. It was his usual trick.

It appeared to him that this was going a little far. Just a touch out of bounds, if she didn't mind his saying so. Why the hell had he stayed in town the summer before? To do a half-dozen extra jobs to get the money he had sent her. That was it. She knew perfectly well they couldn't have done it otherwise. She had agreed with him at the time. And that was the only time so help him he had ever left her to do anything by herself.

Oh, he could tell that to his great-grandmother. She had her notion of what had kept him in town. Considerably more than a notion, if he wanted to know. So, she was going to bring all that up again, was she? Well, she could just think what she pleased. He was tired of explaining. It may have looked funny but he had simply got hooked in, and what could he do? It was impossible to believe that she was going to take it seriously. Yes, yes, she knew how it was with a man: if he was left by himself a minute, some woman was certain to kidnap him. And naturally he couldn't hurt her feelings by refusing!

Well, what was she raving about? Did she forget she had told him those two weeks alone in the country were the happiest she had known for four years? And how long had they been married when she said that? All right, shut up! If she thought that hadn't stuck in his craw.

She hadn't meant she was happy because she was away from him. She meant she was happy getting the devilish house nice and ready for him. That was what she had meant, and now look! Bringing up something she had said a year ago simply to justify himself for forgetting her coffee and breaking the eggs and buying a wretched piece of rope they couldn't afford. She really thought it was time to drop the subject, and now she wanted only two things in the world. She wanted him to get that rope from underfoot, and go back to the village and get her coffee, and if he could remember it, he might bring a metal mitt for the skillets, and two more curtain rods, and if there were any rubber gloves in the village, her hands were simply raw, and a bottle of milk of magnesia from the drugstore.

He looked out at the dark blue afternoon sweltering on the slopes, and mopped his forehead and sighed heavily and said, if only she could wait a minute for *anything*, he was going back. He had said so, hadn't he, the very instant they found he had overlooked it?

Oh, yes, well . . . run along. She was going to wash windows. The country was so beautiful! She doubted they'd have a moment to enjoy it. He meant to go, but he could not until he had said that if she wasn't such a hopeless melancholiac she might see that this was only for a few days. Couldn't she remember anything pleasant about the other summers? Hadn't they ever had any fun? She hadn't time to talk about it, and now would he please not leave that rope lying around for her to trip on? He picked it up, somehow it had toppled off the table, and walked out with it under his arm.

Was he going this minute? He certainly was. She thought so. Sometimes it seemed to her he had second sight about the precisely perfect moment to leave her ditched. She had meant to put the mattresses out to sun, if they put them out this minute they would get at least three hours, he must have heard her say that morning she meant to put them out. So of course he would walk off and leave her to it. She supposed he thought the exercise would do her good.

Well, he was merely going to get her coffee. A four-mile walk for two pounds of coffee was ridiculous, but he was perfectly willing to do it. The habit was making a wreck of her, but if she wanted to wreck herself there was nothing he could do about it. If he thought it was coffee that was making a wreck of her, she congratulated him: he must have a damned easy conscience.

Conscience or no conscience, he didn't see why the mattresses couldn't very well wait until tomorrow. And anyhow, for God's sake, were they living *in* the house, or were they going to let the house ride them to death? She paled at this, her face grew livid about the mouth, she looked quite dangerous, and reminded him that housekeeping was no more her work than it was his: she had other work to do as well, and when did he think she was going to find time to do it at this rate?

Was she going to start on that again? She knew as well as he did that his work brought in the regular money, hers was only occasional, if they depended on what *she* made—and she might as well get straight on this question once for all!

That was positively not the point. The question was, when both of them were working on their own time, was there going to be a division of the housework, or wasn't there? She merely wanted to know, she had to make her plans. Why, he thought that was all arranged. It was understood that he was to help. Hadn't he always, in summers?

Hadn't he, though? Oh, just hadn't he? And when, and where, and doing what? Lord, what an uproarious joke!

It was such a very uproarious joke that her face turned slightly purple, and she screamed with laughter. She laughed so hard she had to sit down, and finally a rush of tears spurted from her eyes and poured down into the lifted corners of her mouth. He dashed towards her and dragged her up to her feet and tried to pour water on her head. The dipper hung by a string on a nail and he broke it loose. Then he tried to pump water with one hand while she struggled in the other. So he gave it up and shook her instead.

She wrenched away, crying out for him to take his rope and go to hell, she had simply given him up: and ran. He heard her high-heeled bedroom slippers clattering and stumbling on the stairs.

He went out around the house and into the lane; he suddenly realized he had a blister on his heel and his shirt felt as if it were on fire. Things broke so suddenly you didn't know where you were. She could work herself into a fury about simply nothing. She was terrible, damn it: not an ounce of reason. You might as well talk to a sieve as that woman when she got going. Damned if he'd spend his life humoring her. Well, what to do now? He would take back the rope and exchange it for something else. Things accumulated, things were mountainous, you couldn't move them or sort them out or get rid of them. They just lay and rotted around. He'd take it back. Hell, why should he? He wanted it. What was it anyhow? A piece of rope. Imagine anybody caring more about a piece of rope than about a man's feelings. What earthly right had she to say a word about it? He remembered all the useless, meaningless things she bought for herself: Why? because I wanted it, that's why! He stopped and selected a large stone by the road. He would put the rope behind it. He would put it in the tool-box when he got back. He'd heard enough about it to last him a life-time.

When he came back she was leaning against the post box beside the road waiting. It was pretty late, the smell of broiled steak floated nose high in the cooling air. Her face was young and smooth and freshlooking. Her unmanageable funny black hair was all on end. She waved to him from a distance, and he speeded up. She called out that supper was ready and waiting, was he starved?

You bet he was starved. Here was the coffee. He waved it at her. She looked at his other hand. What was that he had there?

Well, it was the rope again. He stopped short. He had meant to exchange it but forgot. She wanted to know why he should exchange it, if it was something he really wanted. Wasn't the air sweet now, and wasn't it fine to be here?

She walked beside him with one hand hooked into his leather belt. She pulled and jostled him a little as he walked, and leaned against him. He put his arm clear around her and patted her stomach. They exchanged wary smiles. Coffee, coffee for the Ootsum-Wootsums! He felt as if he were bringing her a beautiful present.

He was a love, she firmly believed, and if she had had her coffee in the morning, she wouldn't have behaved so funny. . . . There was a whippoorwill still coming back, imagine, clear out of season, sitting in the crab-apple tree calling all by himself. Maybe his girl stood him up. Maybe she did. She hoped to hear him once more, she loved whippoorwills. . . . He knew how she was, didn't he?

Sure, he knew how she was.

F. Scott Fitzgerald (1896–1940) was born of Roman Catholic parents in Minneapolis and was educated at the Newman School before entering Princeton (Class of 1917). Fitzgerald left Princeton to accept a commission as an infantry lieutenant and was assigned to a training camp in Alabama; there he met Zelda Sayre, whom he married in 1920, after the success of his first novel, This Side of Paradise. *The young couple moved in "café society" through New York and Europe; their life-style and Fitzgerald's works became synonymous with the Jazz Age (1920–1929).* The Great Gatsby *(1925) climaxed this stage of his career;* Tender Is the Night *(1934), his most complex artistic statement, reflects the personal and economic tensions of the later years. For further reading:* Tales of the Jazz Age *(1926) and* Taps at Reveille *(1935).*

F. SCOTT FITZGERALD

The Long Way Out

We were talking about some of the older castles in Touraine and we touched upon the iron cage in which Louis XI imprisoned Cardinal Balue for six years, then upon oubliettes and such horrors. I had seen several of the latter, simply dry wells thirty or forty feet deep where a man was thrown to wait for nothing; since I have such a tendency to claustrophobia that a Pullman berth is a certain nightmare, they had made a lasting impression. So it was rather a relief when a doctor told this story—that is, it was a relief when he began it, for it seemed to have nothing to do with the tortures long ago.

There was a young woman named Mrs. King who was very happy with her husband. They were well-to-do and deeply in love, but at the birth of her second child she went into a long coma and emerged with a clear case of schizophrenia or "split personality." Her delusion, which had something to do with the Declaration of Independence, had little bearing on the case and as she regained her health it began to disappear. At the end of ten months she was a convalescent patient scarcely marked by what had happened to her and very eager to go back into the world.

She was only twenty-one, rather girlish in an appealing way and a favorite with the staff of the sanitarium. When she became well enough so that she could take an experimental trip with her husband there was a general interest in the venture. One nurse had gone into Philadelphia with her to get a dress, another knew the story of her rather romantic courtship in Mexico and everyone had seen her two babies on visits to the hospital. The trip was to Virginia Beach for five days.

It was a joy to watch her make ready, dressing and packing meticulously and living in the gay trivialities of hair waves and such things. She was ready half an hour before the time of departure and she paid some visits on the floor in her powder-blue gown and her hat that looked like one minute after an April shower. Her frail lovely face, with just that touch of startled sadness that often lingers after an illness, was alight with anticipation.

"We'll just do nothing," she said. "That's my ambition. To get up when I want to for three straight mornings and stay up late for three straight nights. To buy a bathing suit by myself and order a meal."

When the time approached Mrs. King decided to wait downstairs instead of in her room and as she passed along the corridors with an orderly carrying her suitcase she waved to the other patients, sorry that they too were not going on a gorgeous holiday. The superintendent wished her well, two nurses found excuse to linger and share her infectious joy.

"What a beautiful tan you'll get, Mrs King."

"Be sure and send a postcard."

About the time she left her room her husband's car was hit by a truck on his way from the city—he was hurt internally and not expected to live more than a few hours. The information was received at the hospital in a glassed-in office adjoining the hall where Mrs. King waited. The operator, seeing Mrs. King and knowing that the glass was not sound proof, asked the head nurse to come immediately. The head nurse hurried aghast to a doctor and he decided what to do. So long as the husband was still alive it was best to tell her nothing, but of course she must know that he was not coming today.

Mrs. King was greatly disappointed.

"I suppose it's silly to feel that way," she said. "After all these months what's one more day? He said he'd come tomorrow, didn't he?"

The nurse was having a difficult time but she managed to pass it off until the patient was back in her room. Then they assigned a very experienced and phlegmatic nurse to keep Mrs. King away from other patients and from newspapers. By the next day the matter would be decided one way or another.

But her husband lingered on and they continued to prevaricate. A little before noon next day one of the nurses was passing along the corridor when she met Mrs. King, dressed as she had been the day before but this time carrying her own suitcase.

"I'm going to meet my husband," she explained. "He couldn't come yesterday but he's coming today at the same time."

The nurse walked along with her. Mrs. King had the freedom of the building and it was difficult to simply steer her back to her room, and the nurse did not want to tell a story that would contradict what the authorities were telling her. When they reached the front hall she signaled to the operator who fortunately understood. Mrs. King gave herself a last inspection in the mirror and said:

"I'd like to have a dozen hats just like this to remind me to be this happy always."

When the head nurse came in frowning a minute later she demanded: "Don't tell me George is delayed?"

"I'm afraid he is. There is nothing much to do but be patient."

Mrs. King laughed ruefully. "I wanted him to see my costume when it was absolutely new."

"Why, there isn't a wrinkle in it."

"I guess it'll last till tomorrow. I oughtn't to be blue about waiting one more day when I'm so utterly happy."

"Certainly not."

That night her husband died and at a conference of doctors next morning there was some discussion about what to do—it was a risk to tell her and a risk to keep it from her. It was decided finally to say that Mr. King had been called away and thus destroy her hope of an immediate meeting; when she was reconciled to this they could tell her the truth.

As the doctors came out of the conference one of them stopped and pointed. Down the corridor toward the outer hall walked Mrs. King carrying her suitcase.

Dr. Pirie, who had been in special charge of Mrs. King caught his breath.

"This is awful," he said. "I think perhaps I'd better tell her now. There's no use saying he's away when she usually hears from him twice a week, and if we say he's sick she'll want to go to him. Anybody else like the job?"

II

One of the doctors in the conference went on a fortnight's vacation that afternoon. On the day of his return in the same corridor at the same hour, he stopped at the sight of a little procession coming toward him—an orderly carrying a suitcase, a nurse and Mrs. King dressed in the powder blue colored suit and wearing the spring hat.

"Good morning, Doctor," she said. "I'm going to meet my husband and we're going to Virginia Beach. I'm going to the hall because I don't want to keep him waiting."

He looked into her face, clear and happy as a child's. The nurse signaled to him that it was as ordered, so he merely bowed and spoke of the pleasant weather.

"It's a beautiful day," said Mrs. King, "but of course even if it was raining it would be a beautiful day for me."

The doctor looked after her, puzzled and annoyed—why are they letting this go on, he thought. What possible good can it do?

Meeting Dr. Pirie, he put the question to him.

"We tried to tell her," Dr. Pirie said. "She laughed and said we were trying to see whether she's still sick. You could use the word unthinkable in an exact sense here—his death is unthinkable to her."

"But you can't just go on like this."

"Theoretically no," said Dr. Pirie. "A few days ago when she packed up as usual the nurse tried to keep her from going. From out in the hall I could see her face, see her begin to go to pieces—for the first time, mind you. Her muscles were tense and her eyes glazed and her voice was thick and shrill when she very politely called the nurse a liar. It was touch and go there for a minute whether we had a tractable patient or a restraint case— and I stepped in and told the nurse to take her down to the reception room."

He broke off as the procession that had just passed appeared again, headed back to the ward. Mrs. King stopped and spoke to Dr. Pirie.

"My husband's been delayed," she said. "Of course I'm disappointed but they tell me he's coming tomorrow and after waiting so long one more day doesn't seem to matter. Don't you agree with me, Doctor?"

"I certainly do, Mrs. King."

She took off her hat.

"I've got to put aside these clothes—I want them to be as fresh tomorrow as they are today." She looked closely at the hat. "There's a speck of dust on it, but I think I can get it off. Perhaps he won't notice."

"I'm sure he won't."

"Really I don't mind waiting another day. It'll be this time tomorrow before I know it, won't it?"

When she had gone along the younger doctor said:

"There are still the two children."

"I don't think the children are going to matter. When she 'went under,' she tied up this trip with the idea of getting well. If we took it away she'd have to go to the bottom and start over."

"Could she?"

"There's no prognosis," said Dr. Pirie. "I was simply explaining why she was allowed to go to the hall this morning."

"But there's tomorrow morning and the next morning."

"There's always the chance," said Dr. Pirie, "that some day he will be there."

The doctor ended his story here, rather abruptly. When we pressed him to tell what happened he protested that the rest was anticlimax—that all sympathy eventually wears out and that finally the staff at the sanitarium had simply accepted the fact.

"But does she still go to meet her husband?"

"Oh yes, it's always the same—but the other patients, except new ones, hardly look up when she passes along the hall. The nurses manage to substitute a new hat every year or so but she still wears the same suit. She's always a little disappointed but she makes the best of it, very sweetly too. It's not an unhappy life as far as we know, and in some funny way it seems to set an example of tranquillity to the other patients. For God's sake let's talk about something else—let's go back to oubliettes."

*William Faulkner (1897–1962) was born in Missis-
sippi and except for brief periods in Canada as an
aviation cadet in World War I, in New Orleans, and
in Hollywood, he lived and worked virtually all his
life in Oxford, Mississippi. Although his immediate
family was connected with the university and although his great-grandfather was a sometimes novelist, Faulkner, himself, resisted formal education.
Nevertheless he was a wide reader, and wished early
to become a literary artist; his first publication was a
book of poems. With* Satoris *(1929) and* The Sound
and the Fury *(1929), Faulkner began to dramatize
his Yoknapatawpha County, a mythical terrain
which is the setting for many of his major short stories and novels. Through his highly imaginative,
complex use of Southern, regional materials, Faulkner gave an international readership a kind of univer-
sal moral vision. In 1950 he was awarded the Nobel
Prize for literature. Suggestion for further reading:*
Collected Stories *(1950).*

WILLIAM FAULKNER

Mule in the Yard

*I*t was a gray day in late January, though not cold because of the fog.
Old Het, just walked in from the poorhouse, ran down the hall toward the
kitchen, shouting in a strong, bright, happy voice. She was about seventy
probably, though by her own counting, calculated from the ages of various
housewives in the town from brides to grandmothers whom she claimed to
have nursed in infancy, she would have to be around a hundred and at least
triplets. Tall, lean, fog-beaded, in tennis shoes and a long rat-colored cloak
trimmed with what forty or fifty years ago had been fur, a modish though
not new purple toque set upon her headrag and carrying (time was when
she made her weekly rounds from kitchen to kitchen carrying a brocaded
carpetbag though since the advent of the ten-cent stores the carpetbag became an endless succession of the convenient paper receptacles with which
they supply their customers for a few cents) the shopping-bag, she ran into

the kitchen and shouted with strong and childlike pleasure: "Miss Mannie! Mule in de yard!"

Mrs. Hait, stooping to the stove, in the act of drawing from it a scuttle of live ashes, jerked upright; clutching the scuttle, she glared at old Het, then she too spoke at once, strong too, immediate. "Them sons of bitches," she said. She left the kitchen, not running exactly, yet with a kind of out-raged celerity, carrying the scuttle—a compact woman of forty-odd, with an air of indomitable yet relieved bereavement, as though that which had relicted her had been a woman and not a particularly valuable one at that. She wore a calico wrapper and a sweater coat, and a man's felt hat which they in the town knew had belonged to her ten years' dead husband. But the man's shoes had not belonged to him. They were high shoes which but-toned, with toes like small tulip bulbs, and in the town they knew that she had bought them new for herself. She and old Het ran down the kitchen steps and into the fog. That's why it was not cold: as though there lay supine and prisoned between earth and mist the long winter night's suspira-tion of the sleeping town in dark, close rooms—the slumber and the rous-ing; the stale waking thermostatic, by re-heating heat-engendered: it lay like a scum of cold grease upon the steps and the wooden entrance to the basement and upon the narrow plank walk which led to a shed building in the corner of the yard: upon these planks, running and still carrying the scuttle of live ashes, Mrs. Hait skated viciously.

"Watch out!" old Het, footed securely by her rubber soles, cried happi-ly. "Dey in de front!" Mrs. Hait did not fall. She did not even pause. She took in the immediate scene with one cold glare and was running again when there appeared at the corner of the house and apparently having been born before their eyes of the fog itself, a mule. It looked taller than a giraffe. Longheaded, with a flying halter about its scissorlike ears, it rushed down upon them with violent and apparitionlike suddenness.

"Dar hit!" old Het cried, waving the shopping-bag. "Hoo!" Mrs. Hait whirled. Again she skidded savagely on the greasy planks as she and the mule rushed parallel with one another toward the shed building, from whose open doorway there now projected the static and astonished face of a cow. To the cow the fog-born mule doubtless looked taller and more incredibly sudden than a giraffe even, and apparently bent upon charging right through the shed as though it were made of straw or were purely and simply mirage. The cow's head likewise had a quality transient and abrupt and unmundane. It vanished, sucked into invisibility like a match flame, though the mind knew and the reason insisted that she had withdrawn into the shed, from which, as proof's burden, there came an indescribable sound of shock and alarm by shed and beast engendered, analogous to a single note from a profoundly struck lyre or harp. Toward this sound Mrs. Hait sprang, immediately, as if by pure reflex, as though in invulnerable compact of female with female against a world of mule and man. She and the mule converged upon the shed at top speed, the heavy scuttle poised lightly in her hand to hurl. Of course it did not take this long, and likewise it was the mule which refused the gambit. Old Het was still shouting "Dar hit! Dar hit!" when it swerved and rushed at her where she stood tall as a stove pipe, holding the shopping-bag which she swung at the beast as it rushed past her and vanished beyond the other corner of the house as though sucked back into the fog which had produced it, profound and instantaneous and without any sound.

With that unhasteful celerity Mrs. Hait turned and set the scuttle down on the brick coping of the cellar entrance and she and old Het turned the corner of the house in time to see the now wraithlike mule at the moment when its course converged with that of a choleric-looking rooster and eight Rhode Island Red hens emerging from beneath the house. Then for an instant its progress assumed the appearance and trappings of an apotheosis: hell-born and hell-returning, in the act of dissolving completely into the fog, it seemed to rise vanishing into a sunless and dimensionless medium borne upon and enclosed by small winged goblins.

"Dey's mo in de front!" old Het cried.

"Them sons of bitches," Mrs. Hait said, again in that grim, prescient voice without rancor or heat. It was not the mules to which she referred; it was not even the owner of them. It was her whole town-dwelling history as dated from that April dawn ten years ago when what was left of Hait had been gathered from the mangled remains of five mules and several feet of new Manila rope on a blind curve of the railroad just out of town; the geographical hap of her very home; the very components of her bereavement—the mules, the defunct husband, and the owner of them. His name was Snopes; in the town they knew about him too—how he bought his stock at the Memphis market and brought it to Jefferson and sold it to farmers and widows and orphans black and white, for whatever he could contrive—down to a certain figure; and about how (usually in the dead season of winter) teams and even small droves of his stock would escape from the fenced pasture where he kept them and, tied one to another with sometimes quite new hemp rope (and which item Snopes included in the subsequent claim), would be annihilated by freight trains on the same blind curve which was to be the scene of Hait's exit from this world; once a town wag sent him through the mail a printed train schedule for the division. A squat, pasty man perennially tieless and with a strained, harried expression, at stated intervals he passed athwart the peaceful and somnolent life of the town in dust and uproar, his advent heralded by shouts and cries, his passing marked by a yellow cloud filled with tossing jug-shaped heads and clattering hooves and the same forlorn and earnest cries of the drovers; and last of all and well back out of the dust, Snopes himself moving at a harried and panting trot, since it was said in the town that he was deathly afraid of the very beasts in which he cleverly dealt.

The path which he must follow from the railroad station to his pasture crossed the edge of town near Hait's home; Hait and Mrs. Hait had not been in the house a week before they waked one morning to find it surrounded by galloping mules and the air filled with the shouts and cries of the drovers. But it was not until that April dawn some years later, when those who reached the scene first found what might be termed foreign matter among the mangled mules and the savage fragments of new rope, that the town suspected that Hait stood in any closer relationship to Snopes and the mules than that of helping at periodical intervals to drive them out of his front yard. After that they believed that they knew; in a three days' recess of interest, surprise, and curiosity they watched to see if Snopes would try to collect on Hait also.

But they learned only that the adjuster appeared and called upon Mrs. Hait and that a few days later she cashed a check for eight thousand five hundred dollars, since this was back in the old halcyon days when even the companies considered their southern branches and divisions the legitimate prey of all who dwelt beside them. She took the cash: she stood in her sweater coat and the hat which Hait had been wearing on the fatal morning a week ago and listened in cold, grim silence while the teller counted the money and the president and the cashier tried to explain to her the virtues of a bond, then of a savings account, then of a checking account, and departed with the money in a salt sack under her apron; after a time she painted her house: that serviceable and time-defying color which the railroad station was painted, as though out of sentiment or (as some said) gratitude.

The adjuster also summoned Snopes into conference, from which he emerged not only more harried-looking than ever, but with his face stamped with a bewildered dismay which it was to wear from then on, and that was the last time his pasture fence was ever to give inexplicably away at dead of night upon mules coupled in threes and fours by adequate rope even though not always new. And then it seemed as though the mules themselves knew this, as if, even while haltered at the Memphis block at his bid, they sensed it somehow as they sensed that he was afraid of them. Now, three of four times a year and as though by fiendish concord and as soon as they were freed of the box car, the entire uproar—the dust cloud filled with shouts earnest, harried, and dismayed, with plunging demoniac shapes—would become translated in a single burst of perverse and uncontrollable violence, without any intervening contact with time, space, or earth, across the peaceful and astonished town and into Mrs. Hait's yard, where, in a certain hapless despair which abrogated for the moment even

physical fear, Snopes ducked and dodged among the thundering shapes
about the house (for whose very impervious paint the town believed that he
felt he had paid and whose inmate lived within it a life of idle and queenlike
ease on money which he considered at least partly his own) while gradually
that section and neighborhood gathered to look on from behind adjacent
window curtains and porches screened and not, and from the sidewalks and
even from halted wagons and cars in the street—housewives in the wrap-
pers and boudoir caps of morning, children on the way to school, casual
Negroes and casual whites in static and entertained repose.

They were all there when, followed by old Het and carrying the stub of
a worn-out broom, Mrs. Hait ran around the next corner and onto the
handkerchief-sized plot of earth which she called her front yard. It was
small; any creature with a running stride of three feet could have spanned
it in two paces, yet at the moment, due perhaps to the myopic and distortive
quality of the fog, it seemed to be as incredibly full of mad life as a drop of
water beneath the microscope. Yet again she did not falter. With the broom
clutched in her hand and apparently with a kind of sublime faith in her own
invulnerability, she rushed on after the haltered mule which was still in that
arrested and wraithlike process of vanishing furiously into the fog, its wake
indicated by the tossing and dispersing shapes of the nine chickens like so
many jagged scraps of paper in the dying air blast of an automobile, and
the madly dodging figure of a man. The man was Snopes; beaded too with
moisture, his wild face gaped with hoarse shouting and the two heavy lines
of shaven beard descending from the corners of it as though in alluvial
retrospect of years of tobacco, he screamed at her: "Fore God, Miz Hait! I
done everything I could!" She didn't even look at him

"Ketch that big un with the bridle on," she said in her cold, panting
voice. "Git that big un outen here."

"Sho!" Snopes shrieked. "Jest let um take their time. Jest don't git um
excited now."

"Watch out!" old Het shouted. "He headin fer de back again!"

"Git the rope," Mrs. Hait said, running again. Snopes glared back at
old Het.

"Fore God, where is ere rope?" he shouted.

"In de cellar fo God!" old Het shouted, also without pausing. "Go
roun de udder way en head um." Again she and Mrs. Hait turned the
corner in time to see again the still-vanishing mule with the halter once
more in the act of floating lightly onward in its cloud of chickens with
which, they being able to pass under the house and so on the chord of a
circle while it had to go around on the arc, it had once more coincided.
When they turned the next corner they were in the back yard again.

"Fo God!" old Het cried. "He fixin to misuse de cow!" For they had gained on the mule now, since it had stopped. In fact, they came around the corner on a tableau. The cow now stood in the centre of the yard. She and the mule faced one another a few feet apart. Motionless, with lowered heads and braced forelegs, they looked like two book ends from two distinct pairs of a general pattern which some one of amateurly bucolic leanings might have purchased, and which some child had salvaged, brought into idle juxtaposition and then forgotten; and, his head and shoulders projecting above the back-flung slant of the cellar entrance where the scuttle still sat, Snopes standing as though buried to the armpits for a Spanish-Indian-American suttee. Only again it did not take this long. It was less than tableau; it was one of those things which later even memory cannot quite affirm. Now and in turn, man and cow and mule vanished beyond the next corner, Snopes now in the lead, carrying the rope, the cow next with her tail rigid and raked slightly like the stern staff of a boat. Mrs. Hait and old Het ran on, passing the open cellar gaping upon its accumulation of human necessities and widowed womanyears—boxes for kindling wood, old papers and magazines, the broken and outworn furniture and utensils which no woman ever throws away; a pile of coal and another of pitch pine for priming fires—and ran on and turned the next corner to see man and cow and mule all vanishing now in the wild cloud of ubiquitous chickens which had once more crossed beneath the house and emerged. They ran on, Mrs. Hait in grim and unflagging silence, old Het with the eager and happy amazement of a child. But when they gained the front again they saw only Snopes. He lay flat on his stomach, his head and shoulders upreared by his outstretched arms, his coat tail swept forward by its own arrested momentum about his head so that from beneath it his slack-jawed face mused in wild repose like that of a burlesqued nun.

"Whar'd dey go?" old Het shouted at him. He didn't answer.

"Dey tightenin' on de curves!" she cried. "Dey already in de back again!" That's where they were. The cow made a feint at running into her shed, but deciding perhaps that her speed was too great, she whirled in a final desperation of despair-like valor. But they did not see this, nor see the mule, swerving to pass her, crash and blunder for an instant at the open cellar door before going on. When they arrived, the mule was gone. The scuttle was gone too, but they did not notice it; they saw only the cow standing in the centre of the yard as before, panting, rigid, with braced forelegs and lowered head facing nothing, as if the child had returned and removed one of the book ends for some newer purpose or game. They ran on. Mrs. Hait ran heavily now, her mouth too open, her face putty-colored and one hand pressed to her side. So slow was their progress that the mule in its third circuit of the house overtook them from behind and soared past with undiminished speed, with brief demon thunder and a keen ammonia-

sweet reek of sweat sudden and sharp as a jeering cry, and was gone. Yet
they ran doggedly on around the next corner in time to see it succeed at last
in vanishing into the fog; they heard its hoofs, brief, staccato, and derisive,
on the paved street, dying away.

"Well!" old Het said, stopping. She panted, happily. "Gentlemen,
hush! Ain't we had—" Then she became stone still; slowly her head turned,
high-nosed, her nostrils pulsing; perhaps for the instant she saw the open
cellar door as they had last passed it, with no scuttle beside it. "Fo God I
smells smoke!" she said. "Chile, run git yo money."

That was still early, not yet ten o'clock. By noon the house had burned
to the ground. There was a farmers' supply store where Snopes could be
usually found; more than one had made a point of finding him there by
that time. They told him about how when the fire engine and the crowd
reached the scene, Mrs. Hait, followed by old Het carrying her shopping-
bag in one hand and a framed portrait of Mr. Hait in the other, emerged
with an umbrella and wearing a new, dun-colored, mail-order coat, in one
pocket of which lay a fruit jar filled with smoothly rolled banknotes and in
the other a heavy, nickel-plated pistol, and crossed the street to the house
opposite, where with old Het beside her in another rocker, she had been
sitting ever since on the veranda, grim, inscrutable, the two of them rocking
steadily, while hoarse and tireless men hurled her dishes and furniture and
bedding up and down the street.

"What are you telling me for?" Snopes said. "Hit warn't me that set
that ere scuttle of live fire where the first thing that passed would knock hit
into the cellar."

"It was you that opened the cellar door, though."

"Sho. And for what? To git that rope, her own rope, where she told me
to git it."

"To catch your mule with, that was trespassing on her property. You
can't get out of it this time, I. O. There ain't a jury in the county that won't
find for her."

"Yes, I reckon not. And just because she is a woman. That's why.
Because she is a durn woman. All right. Let her go to her durn jury with
hit. I can talk too; I reckon hit's a few things I could tell a jury myself
about—" He ceased. They were watching him.

"What? Tell a jury about what?"

"Nothing. Because hit ain't going to no jury. A jury between her and
me? Me and Mannie Hait? You boys don't know her if you think she's
going to make trouble over a pure accident couldn't nobody help. Why,
there ain't a fairer, finer woman in the county than Miz Mannie Hait. I just
wisht I had a opportunity to tell her so." The opportunity came at once. Old
Het was behind her, carrying the shopping-bag. Mrs. Hait looked once,

quietly, about at the faces, making no response to the murmur of curious salutation, then not again. She didn't look at Snopes long either, nor talk to him long.

"I come to buy that mule," she said.

"What mule?" They looked at one another. "You'd like to own that mule?" She looked at him. "Hit'll cost you a hundred and fifty, Miz Mannie."

"You mean dollars?"

"I don't mean dimes nor nickels neither, Miz Mannie."

"Dollars," she said. "That's more than mules was in Hait's time."

"Lots of things is different since Hait's time. Including you and me."

"I reckon so," she said. Then she went away. She turned without a word, old Het following.

"Maybe one of them others you looked at this morning would suit you," Snopes said. She didn't answer. Then they were gone.

"I don't know as I would have said that last to her", one said.

"What for?" Snopes said. "If she was aiming to law something outen me about that fire, you reckon she would have come and offered to pay me money for hit?" That was about one o'clock. About four o'clock he was shouldering his way through a throng of Negroes before a cheap grocery store when one called his name. It was old Het, the now bulging shopping-bag on her arm, eating bananas from a paper sack.

"Fo God I wuz jest dis minute huntin fer you," she said. She handed the banana to a woman beside her and delved and fumbled in the shopping-bag and extended a greenback. "Miz Mannie gimme dis to give you; I wuz jest on de way to de sto whar you stay at. Here." He took the bill.

"What's this? From Miz Hait?"

"Fer de mule." The bill was for ten dollars. "You don't need to gimme no receipt. I kin be de witness I give hit to you."

"Ten dollars? For that mule? I told her a hundred and fifty dollars."

"You'll have to fix dat up wid her yo'self. She jest gimme dis to give ter you when she sot out to fetch de mule."

"Set out to fetch—She went out there herself and taken my mule outen my pasture?"

"Lawd, chile," old Het said, "Miz Mannie ain't skeered of no mule. Ain't you done foun dat out?"

And then it became late, what with the yet short winter days; when she came in sight of the two gaunt chimneys against the sunset, evening was already finding itself. But she could smell the ham cooking before she came in sight of the cow shed even, though she could not see it until she came around in front where the fire burned beneath an iron skillet set on bricks and where nearby Mrs. Hait was milking the cow. "Well," old Het said, "you is settled down, ain't you?" She looked into the shed, neated and raked and swept even, and floored now with fresh hay. A clean new lantern burned on a box, beside it a pallet bed was spread neatly on the straw and turned neatly back for the night. "Why, you is fixed up," she said with pleased astonishment. Within the door was a kitchen chair. She drew it out and sat down beside the skillet and laid the bulging shopping-bag beside her.

"I'll tend dis meat whilst you milks. I'd offer to strip dat cow fer you ef I wuzn't so wo out wid all dis excitement we been had." She looked around her. "I don't believe I sees yo new mule, dough." Mrs. Hait grunted, her head against the cow's flank. After a moment she said,

"Did you give him that money?"

"I give um ter him. He ack surprise at first, lak maybe he think you didn't aim to trade dat quick. I tole him to settle de details wid you later. He taken de money, dough. So I reckin dat's offen his mine en yo'n bofe." Again Mrs. Hait grunted. Old Het turned the ham in the skillet. Beside it the coffee pot bubbled and steamed. "Cawfee smell good too," she said. "I ain't had no appetite in years now. A bird couldn't live on de vittles I eats. But jest lemme git a whiff er cawfee en seem lak hit always whets me a little. Now, ef you jest had nudder little piece o dis ham, now—Fo God, you got company aready." But Mrs. Hait did not even look up until she had finished. Then she turned without rising from the box on which she sat.

"I reckon you and me better have a little talk," Snopes said. "I reckon I got something that belongs to you and I hear you got something that belongs to me." He looked about, quickly, ceaselessly, while old Het watched him. He turned to her. "You go away, aunty. I don't reckon you want to set here and listen to us."

"Lawd, honey," old Het said. "Don't you mind me. I done already had so much troubles myself dat I kin set en listen to udder folks' widout hit worryin me a-tall. You gawn talk whut you came ter talk; I jest set here en tend de ham." Snopes looked at Mrs. Hait.

"Ain't you going to make her go away?" he said.

"What for?" Mrs. Hait said. "I reckon she ain't the first critter that ever come on this yard when hit wanted and went or stayed when hit liked." Snopes made a gesture, brief, fretted, restrained.

"Well," he said. "All right. So you taken the mule."

"I paid you for it. She give you the money."

"Ten dollars. For a hundred-and-fifty-dollar mule. Ten dollars."

"I don't know anything about hundred-and-fifty-dollar mules. All I know is what the railroad paid." Now Snopes looked at her for a full moment.

"What do you mean?"

"Them sixty dollars a head the railroad used to pay you for mules back when you and Hait—"

"Hush," Snopes said; he looked about again, quick, ceaseless. "All right. Even call it sixty dollars. But you just sent me ten."

"Yes, I sent you the difference." He looked at her, perfectly still. "Between that mule and what you owed Hait."

"What I owed—"

"For getting them five mules onto the tr—"

"Hush!" he cried. "Hush!" Her voice went on, cold, grim, level.

"For helping you. You paid him fifty dollars each time, and the railroad paid you sixty dollars a head for the mules. Ain't that right?" He watched her. "The last time you never paid him. So I taken that mule instead. And I sent you the ten dollars difference."

"Yes," he said in a tone of quiet, swift, profound bemusement; then he cried: "But look! Here's where I got you. Hit was our agreement that I wouldn't never owe him nothing until after the mules was—"

"I reckon you better hush yourself," Mrs. Hait said.

"—until hit was over. And this time, when over had come, I never owed nobody no money because the man hit would have been owed to wasn't nobody," he cried triumphantly. "You see?" Sitting on the box, motionless, downlooking, Mrs. Hait seemed to muse. "So you just take your ten dollars back and tell me where my mule is and we'll just go back good friends to where we started at. Fore God, I'm as sorry as ere a living man about that fire—"

"Fo God!" old Het said, "hit was a blaze, wuzn't it?"

"—but likely with all that ere railroad money you still got, you just been wanting a chance to build new, all along. So here. Take hit." He put the money into her hand. "Where's my mule?" But Mrs. Hait didn't move at once.

"You want to give it back to me?" she said.

"Sho. We been friends all the time; now we'll just go back to where we left off being. I don't hold no hard feelings and don't you hold none. Where you got the mule hid?"

"Up at the end of that ravine ditch behind Spilmer's." she said.

"Sho. I know. A good, sheltered place, since you ain't got nere barn. Only if you'd a just left hit in the pasture, hit would a saved us both trouble. But hit ain't no hard feelings though. And so I'll bid you goodnight. You're all fixed up, I see. I reckon you could save some more money by not building no house a-tall."

"I reckon I could," Mrs. Hait said. But he was gone.

"Whut did you leave de mule dar fer?" old Het said.

"I reckon that's far enough," Mrs. Hait said.

"Fer enough?" But Mrs. Hait came and looked into the skillet, and old Het said, "Wuz hit me er you dat mentioned something erbout er nudder piece o dis ham?" So they were both eating when in the not-quite-yet accomplished twilight Snopes returned. He came up quietly and stood, holding his hands to the blaze as if he were quite cold. He did not look at any one now.

"I reckon I'll take that ere ten dollars," he said.

"What ten dollars?" Mrs. Hait said. He seemed to muse upon the fire. Mrs. Hait and old Het chewed quietly, old Het alone watching him.

"You ain't going to give hit back to me?" he said.

"You was the one that said to let's go back to where we started," Mrs. Hait said.

"Fo God you wuz, en dat's de fack," old Het said. Snopes mused upon the fire; he spoke in a tone of musing and amazed despair:

"I go to the worry and the risk and the agoment for years and years and I get sixty dollars. And you, one time, without no trouble and no risk, without even knowing you are going to git it, git eighty-five hundred dollars. I never begrudged hit to you; can't nere a man say I did, even if hit did seem a little strange that you should git it all when he wasn't working for you and you never even knowed where he was at and what doing; that all you done to git it was to be married to him. And now, after all these ten years of not begruding you hit, you taken the best mule I had and you ain't even going to pay me ten dollars for hit. Hit ain't right. Hit ain't justice."

"You got de mule back, en you ain't satisfried yit," old Het said. "Whut does you want?" Now Snopes looked at Mrs. Hait.

"For the last time I ask hit," he said. "Will you or won't you give hit back?"

"Give what back?" Mrs. Hait said. Snopes turned. He stumbled over something—it was old Het's shopping-bag—and recovered and went on. They could see him in silhouette, as though framed by the two blackened chimneys against the dying west; they saw him fling up both clenched hands in a gesture almost Gallic, of resignation and impotent despair. Then he was gone. Old Het was watching Mrs. Hait.

"Honey," she said, "Whut did you do wid de mule?" Mrs. Hait leaned forward to the fire. On her plate lay a stale biscuit. She lifted the skillet and poured over the biscuit the grease in which the ham had cooked.

"I shot it," she said.

"You which?" old Het said. Mrs. Hait began to eat the biscuit. "Well," old Het said, happily, "de mule burnt de house en you shot de mule. Dat's whut I calls justice." It was getting dark fast now, and before her was still the three-mile walk to the poorhouse. But the dark would last a long time in January, and the poorhouse too would not move at once. She sighed with weary and happy relaxation. "Gentlemen, hush! Ain't we had a day!"

DASHIELL HAMMETT

The Gatewood Caper

*H*arvey Gatewood had issued orders that I was to be admitted as soon as I arrived, so it took me only a little less than fifteen minutes to thread my way past the doorkeepers, office boys, and secretaries who filled up most of the space between the Gatewood Lumber Corporation's front door and the president's private office. His office was large, all mahogany and bronze and green plush, with a mahogany desk as big as a bed in the center of the floor.

Gatewood, leaning across the desk, began to bark at me as soon as the obsequious clerk who had bowed me in bowed himself out.

"My daughter was kidnaped last night! I want the gang that did it if it takes every cent I got!"

"Tell me about it," I suggested.

But he wanted results, it seemed, and not questions, and so I wasted nearly an hour getting information that he could have given me in fifteen minutes.

He was a big bruiser of a man, something over 200 pounds of hard red flesh, and a czar from the top of his bullet head to the toes of his shoes that would have been at least number twelves if they hadn't been made to measure.

He had made his several millions by sandbagging everybody that stood in his way, and the rage he was burning up with now didn't make him any easier to deal with.

His wicked jaw was sticking out like a knob of granite and his eyes were filmed with blood—he was in a lovely frame of mind. For a while it looked as if the Continental Detective Agency was going to lose a client, because I'd made up my mind that he was going to tell me all I wanted to know, or I'd chuck the job.

But finally I got the story out of him.

His daughter Audrey had left their house on Clay Street at about 7 o'clock the preceding evening, telling her maid that she was going for a walk. She had not returned that night—though Gatewood had not known that until after he had read the letter that came this morning.

The letter had been from someone who said that she had been kidnaped. It demanded $50,000 for her release, and instructed Gatewood to get the money ready in hundred-dollar bills—so that there would be no delay when he was told the manner in which the money was to be paid over to his daughter's captors. As proof that the demand was not a hoax, a lock of the girl's hair, a ring she always wore, and a brief note from her, asking her father to comply with the demands, had been enclosed.

Gatewood had received the letter at his office and had telephoned to his house immediately. He had been told that the girl's bed had not been slept in the previous night and that none of the servants had seen her since she started out for her walk. He had then notified the police, turning the letter over to them, and a few minutes later he had decided to employ private detectives also.

"Now," he burst out, after I had wormed these things out of him, and he had told me that he knew nothing of his daughter's accociates or habits, "go ahead and do something! I'm not paying you to sit around and talk about it!"

"What are you going to do?" I asked.

"Me? I'm going to put those——behind bars if it takes every cent I've got in the world!"

"Sure! But first you get that $50,000 ready, so you can give it to them when they ask for it."

He clicked his jaw shut and thrust his face into mine.

"I've never been clubbed into doing anything in my life! And I'm too old to start now!" he said. "I'm going to call these people's bluff!"

"That's going to make it lovely for your daughter. But, aside from what it'll do to her, it's the wrong play. Fifty thousand isn't a whole lot to you, and paying it over will give us two chances that we haven't got now. One when the payment is made—a chance either to nab whoever comes for it or get a line on them. And the other when your daughter is returned. No matter how careful they are, it's a cinch she'll be able to tell us something that will help us grab them."

He shook his head angrily, and I was tired of arguing with him. So I left, hoping he'd see the wisdom of the course I had advised before it was too late.

At the Gatewood residence I found butlers, second men, chauffeurs, cooks, maids, upstairs girls, downstairs girls, and a raft of miscellaneous flunkies—he had enough servants to run a hotel.

What they told me amounted to this: the girl had not received a phone call, note by messenger or telegram—the time-honored devices for luring a victim out to a murder or abduction—before she left the house. She had told her maid that she would be back within an hour or two; but the maid had not been alarmed when her mistress failed to return all that night.

Audrey was the only child, and since her mother's death she had come and gone to suit herself. She and her father didn't hit it off very well together—their natures were too much alike, I gathered—and he never knew where she was. There was nothing unusual about her remaining away all night. She seldom bothered to leave word when she was going to stay overnight with friends.

She was nineteen years old, but looked several years older, about five feet five inches tall, and slender. She had blue eyes, brown hair—very thick and long—was pale and very nervous. Her photographs, of which I took a handful, showed that her eyes were large, her nose small and regular and her chin pointed.

She was not beautiful, but in the one photograph where a smile had wiped off the sullenness of her mouth, she was at least pretty.

When she left the house she was wearing a light tweed skirt and jacket with a London tailor's label in them, a buff silk shirtwaist with stripes a shade darker, brown wool stockings, low-heeled brown oxfords, and an untrimmed gray felt hat.

I went up to her rooms—she had three on the third floor—and looked through all her stuff. I found nearly a bushel of photographs of men, boys, and girls; and a great stack of letters of varying degrees of intimacy, signed with a wide assortment of names and nicknames. I made notes of all the addresses I found.

Nothing in her rooms seemed to have any bearing on her abduction, but there was a chance that one of the names and addresses might be of someone who had served as a decoy. Also, some of her friends might be able to tell us something of value.

I dropped in at the Agency and distributed the names and addresses among the three operatives who were idle, sending them out to see what they could dig up.

Then I reached the police detectives who were working on the case—O'Gar and Thode—by telephone, and went down to the Hall of Justice to meet them. Lusk, a post office inspector, was also there. We turned the job around and around, looking at it from every angle, but not getting very far. We were all agreed, however, that we couldn't take a chance on any publicity, or work in the open, until the girl was safe.

They had had a worse time with Gatewood than I—he had wanted to put the whole thing in the newspapers, with the offer of a reward, photographs and all. Of course, Gatewood was right in claiming that this was the most effective way of catching the kidnapers—but it would have been tough on his daughter if her captors happened to be persons of sufficiently hardened character. And kidnapers as a rule aren't lambs.

I looked at the letter they had sent. It was printed with pencil on ruled paper of the kind that is sold in pads by every stationery dealer in the world. The envelope was just as common, also addressed in pencil, and postmarked *San Francisco, September 20,* 9 P.M. That was the night she had been seized.

The letter read:

> Sir:
> We have your charming daughter and place a value of $50,000 upon her. You will get the money ready in $100 bills at once so there will be no delay when we tell you how it is to be paid over to us.
> We beg to assure you that things will go badly with your daughter should you not do as you are told, or should you bring the police into this matter, or should you do anything foolish.
> $50,000 is only a small fraction of what you stole while we were living in mud and blood in France for you, and we mean to get that much or else.
> Three

A peculiar note in several ways. They are usually written with a great pretense of partial illiterateness. Almost always there's an attempt to lead suspicion astray. Perhaps the ex-service stuff was there for that purpose—or perhaps not.

Then there was a postscript:

> We know someone who will buy her even after we are through with her—in case you won't listen to reason.

The letter from the girl was written jerkily on the same kind of paper, apparently with the same pencil.

Daddy—

    Please do as they ask! I am so afraid—

Audrey

A door at the other end of the room opened, and a head came through. "O'Gar! Thode! Gatewood just called up. Get up to his office right away!"

The four of us tumbled out of the Hall of Justice and into a police car.

Gatewood was pacing his office like a maniac when we pushed aside enough hirelings to get to him. His face was hot with blood and his eyes had an insane glare in them.

"She just phoned me!" he cried thickly, when he saw us.

It took a minute or two to get him calm enough to tell us about it.

"She called me on the phone. Said, 'Oh, Daddy! Do something! I can't stand this—they're killing me!' I asked her if she knew where she was, and she said, 'No, but I can see Twin Peaks from here. There's three men and a woman, and—' And then I heard a man curse, and a sound as if he had struck her, and the phone went dead. I tried to get central to give me the number, but she couldn't! It's a damned outrage the way the telephone system is run. We pay enough for service, God Knows and we . . ."

O'Gar scratched his head and turned away from Gatewood. "In sight of Twin Peaks! There are hundreds of houses that are!"

Gatewood meanwhile had finished denouncing the telephone company and was pounding on his desk with a paperweight to attract our attention.

"Have you people done anything at all?" he demanded.

I answered him with another question: "Have you got the money ready?"

"No," he said, "I won't be held up ay anybody!"

But he said it mechanically, without his usual conviction—the talk with his daughter had shaken him out of some of his stubborness. He was thinking of her safety a little now instead of only his own fighting spirit.

We went at him hammer and tongs for a few minutes, and after a while he sent a clerk out for the money.

We split up the field then. Thode was to take some men from headquarters and see what he could find in the Twin Peaks end of town; but we weren't very optimistic over the prospects there—the territory was too large.

Lusk and O'Gar were to carefully mark the bills that the clerk brought from the bank, and then stick as close to Gatewood as they could without attracting attention. I was to go out to Gatewood's house and stay there.

The abductors had plainly instructed Gatewood to get the money ready immediately so that they could arrange to get it on short notice—not giving him time to communicate with anyone or make plans.

Gatewood was to get hold of the newspapers, give them the whole story, with the $10,000 reward he was offering for the abductor's capture, to be published as soon as the girl was safe—so we would get the help of publicity at the earliest possible moment without jeopardizing the girl.

The police in all the neighboring towns had already been notified—that had been done before the girl's phone message had assured us that she was held in San Franciso.

Nothing happened at the Gatewood residence all that evening. Harvey Gatewood came home early; and after dinner he paced his library floor and drank whiskey until bedtime, demanding every few minutes that we, the detectives in the case, do something besides sit around like a lot of damned mummies. O'Gar, Lusk, and Thode were out in the street, keeping an eye on the house and neighborhood.

At midnight Harvey Gatewood went to bed. I declined a bed in favor of the library couch, which I dragged over beside the telephone, an extension of which was in Gatewood's bedroom

At 2:30 the telephone bell rang. I listened in while Gatewood talked from his bed.

A man's voice, crisp and curt: "Gatewood?"

"Yes."

"Got the dough?"

"Yes."

Gatewood's voice was thick and blurred—I could imagine the boiling that was going on inside him.

"Good!" came the brisk voice. "Put a piece of paper around it and leave the house with it, right away! Walk down Clay Street, keeping on the same side as your house. Don't walk too fast and keep walking. If everything's all right, and there's no elbows tagging along, somebody'll come up to you between your house and the waterfront. They'll have a handkerchief up to their face for a second, and then they'll let it fall to the ground.

"When you see that, you'll lay the money on the pavement, turn around, and walk back to your house. If the money isn't marked, and you don't try any fancy tricks, you'll get your daughter back in an hour or two. If you try to pull anything—remember what we wrote you! Got it straight?"

Gatewood sputtered something that was meant for an affirmative, and the telephone clicked silent.

I didn't waste any of my precious time tracing the call—it would be from a public telephone, I knew—but yelled up the stairs to Gatewood, "You do as you were told, and don't try any foolishness!"

Then I ran out into the early morning air to find the police detectives and the post office inspector.

They had been joined by two plainclothesmen, and had two automobiles waiting. I told them what the situation was, and we laid hurried plans.

O'Gar was to drive in one of the cars down Sacramento Street, and Thode, in the other, down Washington Street. These streets parallel Clay, one on each side. They were to drive slowly, keeping pace with Gatewood, and stopping at each cross street to see that he passed.

When he failed to cross within a reasonable time they were to turn up to Clay Street—and their actions from then on would have to be guided by chance and their own wits.

Lusk was to wander along a block or two ahead of Gatewood, on the opposite side of the street, pretending to be mildly intoxicated.

I was to shadow Gatewood down the street, with one of the plain-clothesmen behind me. The other plainclothesman was to turn in a call at headquarters for every available man to be sent to City Street. They would arrive too late, of course, and as likely as not it would take them some time to find us; but we had no way of knowing what was going to turn up before the night was over.

Our plan was sketchy enough, but it was the best we could do—we were afraid to grab whoever got the money from Gatewood. The girl's talk with her father that afternoon had sounded too much as if her captors were desperate for us to take any chances on going after them roughshod until she was out of their hands.

We had hardly finished our plans when Gatewood, wearing a heavy overcoat, left his house and turned down the street.

Farther down, Lusk, weaving along, talking to himself, was almost invisible in the shadows. There was no one else in sight. That meant that I had to give Gatewood at least two blocks' lead, so that the man who came for the money wouldn't tumble to me. One of the plainclothesmen was half a block behind me, on the other side of the street.

We walked two blocks down, and then a chunky man in a derby hat came into sight. He passed Gatewood, passed me, went on.

Three blocks more.

A touring car, large, black, powerfully engined and with lowered curtains, came from the rear, passed us, went on. Possibly a scout. I scrawled its license number down on my pad without taking my hand out of my overcoat pocket.

Another three blocks.

A policeman passed, strolling in ignorance of the game being played under his nose; and then a taxicab with a single male passenger. I wrote down its license number

Four blocks with no one in sight of me but Gatewood—I couldn't see Lusk any more.

Just ahead of Gatewood a man stepped out of a black doorway, turned around, called up to a window for someone to come down and open the door for him.

We went on.

Coming from nowhere, a woman stood on the sidewalk fifty feet ahead of Gatewood, a handkerchief to her face. It fluttered to the pavement.

Gatewood stopped, standing stiff-legged. I could see his right hand come up, lifting the side of the overcoat in which it was pocketed—and I knew his hand was gripped around a pistol.

For perhaps half a minute he stood like a statue. Then his left hand came out of his pocket, and the bundle of money fell to the sidewalk in front of him, where it made a bright blur in the darkness. Gatewood turned abruptly, and began to retrace his steps homeward.

The woman had recovered her handkerchief. Now she ran to the bundle, picked it up, and scuttled to the black mouth of an alley a few feet distant—a rather tall woman, bent, and in dark clothes from head to feet.

In the black mouth of the alley she vanished.

I had been compelled to slow up while Gatewood and the woman stood facing each other, and I was more than a block away now. As soon as the woman disappeared, I took a chance and started pounding my rubber soles against the pavement.

The alley was empty when I reached it.

It ran all the way through to the next street, but I knew that the woman couldn't have reached the other end before I got to this one. I carry a lot of weight these days, but I can still step a block or two in good time. Along both sides of the alley were the rears of apartment buildings, each with its back door looking blankly, secretively, at me.

The plainclothesman who had been trailing behind me came up, then O'Gar and Thode in their cars, and soon, Lusk. O'Gar and Thode rode off immediately to wind through the neighboring streets, hunting for the woman. Lusk and the plainclothesman each planted himself on a corner from which two of the streets enclosing the block could be watched.

I went through the alley, hunting vainly for an unlocked door, an open window, a fire escape that would show recent use—any of the signs that a hurried departure from the alley might leave.

Nothing!

O'Gar came back shortly with some reinforcements from headquarters that he had picked up, and Gatewood.

Gatewood was burning.

"Bungled the damn thing again! I won't pay your agency a nickel, and I'll see that some of these so-called detectives get put back in a uniform and set to walking beats!"

"What'd the woman look like?" I asked him.

"I don't know! I thought you were hanging around to take care of her! She was old and bent, kind of, I guess, but I couldn't see her face for her veil. I don't know! What the hell were you men doing? It's a damned outrage the way . . ."

I finally got him quieted down and took him home, leaving the city men to keep the neighborhood under surveillance. There were fourteen or fifteen of them on the job now, and every shadow held at least one.

The girl would head for home as soon as she was released and I wanted to be there to pump her. There was an excellent chance of catching her abductors before they got very far, if she could tell us anything at all about them.

Home, Gatewood went up against the whiskey bottle again, while I kept one ear cocked at the telephone and the other at the front door. O'Gar or Thode phoned every half-hour or so to ask if we'd heard from the girl.

They had still found nothing.

At 9 o'clock they, with Lusk, arrived at the house. The woman in black had turned out to be a man and got away.

In the rear of one of the apartment buildings that touched the alley— just a foot or so within the back door—they found a woman's skirt, long coat, hat and veil—all black. Investigating the occupants of the house, they had learned that an apartment had been rented to a young man named Leighton three days before.

Leighton was not home, when they went up to his apartment. His rooms held a lot of cold cigarette butts, an empty bottle, and nothing else that had not been there when he rented it.

The inference was clear; he had rented the apartment so that he might have access to the building. Wearing women's clothes over his own, he had gone out of the back door—leaving it unlatched behind him—to meet Gatewood. Then he had run back into the building, discarded his disguise and hurried through the building, out the front door, and away before we had our feeble net around the block—perhaps dodging into dark doorways here and there to avoid O'Gar and Thode in their cars.

Leighton, it seemed, was a man of about thirty, slender, about five feet eight or nine inches tall, with dark hair and eyes; rather good-looking, and well-dressed on the two occasions when people living in the building had seen him, in a brown suit and a light brown felt hat.

There was no possibility, according to both of the detectives and the post office inspector, that the girl might have been held, even temporarily, in Leighton's apartment.

Ten o'clock came, and no word from the girl.

Gatewood had lost his domineering bullheadedness by now and was breaking up. The suspense was getting him, and the liquor he had put away wasn't helping him. I didn't like him either personally or by reputation, but this morning I felt sorry for him.

I talked to the Agency over the phone and got the reports of the operatives who had been looking up Audrey's friends. The last person to see her had been an Agnes Dangerfield, who had seen her walking down Market Street near Sixth, alone, on the night of her abduction—some time between

8:15 and 8:45. Audrey had been too far away from the Dangerfield girl to speak to her.

For the rest, the boys had learned nothing except that Audrey was a wild, spoiled youngster who hadn't shown any great care in selecting her friends—just the sort of girl who could easily fall into the hands of a mob of high-binders.

Noon struck. No sign of the girl. We told the newspapers to turn loose the story, with the added developments of the past few hours.

Gatewood was broken; he sat with his head in his hands, looking at nothing. Just before I left to follow a hunch I had, he looked up at me, and I'd never have recognized him if I hadn't seen the change take place.

"What do you think is keeping her away?" he asked.

I didn't have the heart to tell him what I had every reason to suspect, now that the money had been paid and she had failed to show up. So I stalled with some vague assurances and left.

I caught a cab and dropped off in the shopping district. I visited the five largest department stores, going to all the women's wear departments from shoes to hats, and trying to learn if a man—perhaps one answering Leighton's description—had been buying clothes in the past couple days that would fit Audrey Gatewood.

Failing to get any results, I turned the rest of the local stores over to one of the boys from the Agency, and went across the bay to canvass the Oakland stores.

At the first one I got action. A man who might easily have been Leighton had been in the day before, buying clothes of Audrey's size. He had bought lots of them, everything from lingerie to a coat, and—my luck was hitting on all cylinders—had had his purchases delivered to T. Offord, at an address on Fourteenth Street.

At the Fourteenth Street address, an apartment house, I found Mr. and Mrs. Theodore Offord's names in the vestibule for Apartment 202.

I had just found the apartment number when the front door opened and a stout, middle-aged woman in a gingham housedress came out. She looked at me a bit curiously, so I asked, "Do you know where I can find the superintendent?"

"I'm the superintendent," she said.

I handed her a card and stepped indoors with her. "I'm from the bonding department of the North American Casualty Company"—a repetition of the lie that was printed on the card I had given her—"and a bond for Mr. Offord has been applied for. Is he all right so far as you know?" With the slightly apologetic air of one going through with a necessary but not too important formality.

"A bond? That's funny! He is going away tomorrow."

"Well, I can't say what the bond is for," I said lightly. "We investigators just get the names and addresses. It may be for his present employer, or perhaps the man he is going to work for has applied for it. Or some firms have us look up prospective employees before they hire them, just to be safe."

"Mr. Offord, so far as I know, is a very nice young man," she said, "but he has been here only a week."

"Not staying long, then?"

"No. They came here from Denver, intending to stay, but the low altitude doesn't agree with Mrs. Offord, so they are going back."

"Are you sure they came from Denver?"

"Well," she said, "they told me they did."

"How many of them are there?"

"Only the two of them; they're young people."

"Well, how do they impress you?" I asked, trying to get over the impression that I thought her a woman of shrewd judgement.

"They seem to be a very nice young couple. You'd hardly know they were in their apartment most of the time, they're so quiet. I'm sorry they can't stay."

"Do they go out much?"

"I really don't know. They have their keys, and unless I should happen to pass them going in or out I'd never see them."

"Then, as a matter of fact you couldn't say whether they stayed away all night some nights or not. Could you?"

She eyed me doubtfully—I was stepping way over my pretext now, but I didn't think it mattered—and shook her head. "No, I couldn't say."

"They have many visitors?"

"I don't know. Mr. Offord is not—"

She broke off as a man came in quietly from the street, brushed past me, and started to mount the steps to the second floor.

"Oh, dear!" she whispered. "I hope he didn't hear me talking about him. That's Mr. Offord."

A slender man in brown, with a light brown hat—Leighton, perhaps.

I hadn't seen anything of him except his back, nor he anything except mine. I watched him as he climbed the stairs. If he had heard the woman mention his name he would use the turn at the head of the stairs to sneak a look at me.

He did.

I kept my face stolid, but I knew him.

He was "Penny" Quayle, a con man who had been active in the east four or five years before.

His face was as expressionless as mine. But he knew me.

A door on the second floor shut. I left the woman and started for the stairs.

"I think I'll go up and talk to him," I told her.

Coming silently to the door of Apartment 202, I listened. Not a sound. This was no time for hesitation. I pressed the bell-button.

As close together as the tapping of three keys under the fingers of an expert typist, but a thousand times more vicious, came three pistol shots. And waist-high in the door of Apartment 202 were three bullet holes.

The three bullets would have been in my fat carcass if I hadn't learned years ago to stand to one side of strange doors when making uninvited calls.

Inside the apartment sounded a man's voice, sharp, commanding. "Cut it, kid! For God's sake, not that!"

A woman's voice, shrill, spiteful, screaming blasphemies.

Two more bullets came through the door.

"Stop! No! No!" The man's voice had a note of fear in it now.

The woman's voice, cursing hotly. A scuffle. A shot that didn't hit the door.

I hurled my foot against the door, near the knob, and the lock broke away.

On the floor of the room, a man—Quayle—and a woman were tussling. He was bending over her, holding her wrists, trying to keep her down. A smoking pistol was in one of her hands. I got to it in a jump and tore it loose.

"That's enough!" I called to them when I was planted. "Get up and receive company."

Quayle released his antagonist's wrists, whereupon she struck at his eyes with curved, sharp-nailed fingers, tearing his cheek open. He scrambled away from her on hands and knees, and both of them got to their feet.

He sat down on a chair immediately, panting and wiping his bleeding cheek with a handkerchief.

She stood, hands on hips, in the center of the room, glaring at me. "I suppose," she spat, "you think you've raised hell!"

I laughed—I could afford to.

"If your father is in his right mind," I told her, "he'll do it with a razor strap when he gets you home again. A fine joke you picked out to play on him!"

"If *you'd* been tied to him as long as I have and had been bullied and held down as much, I guess *you'd* do most anything to get enough money so that you could go away and live your own life."

I didn't say anything to that. Remembering some of the business methods Harvey Gatewood had used—particularly some of his war contracts that the Department of Justice was still investigating—I suppose the worst that could be said about Audrey was that she was her father's own daughter.

"How'd you rap to it?" Quayle asked me, politely.

"Several ways," I said. "First, one of Audrey's friends saw her on Market Street between 8:15 and 8:45 the night she disappeared, and your letter to Gatewood was postmarked 9 P.M. Pretty fast work. You should have waited a while before mailing it. I suppose she dropped it in the post office on her way over here?"

Quayle nodded.

"Then second," I went on, "there was that phone call of hers. She knew it took anywhere from ten to fifteen minutes to get her father on the wire at the office. If she had gotten to a phone while imprisoned, time would have been so valuable that she'd have told her story to the first person she got hold of—the switchboard operator, most likely. So that made it look as if, besides wanting to throw out that Twin Peaks line, she wanted to stir the old man out of his bullheadedness.

"When she failed to show up after the money was paid, I figured it was a sure bet that she had kidnaped herself. I knew that if she came back home after faking this thing, we'd find out before we'd talked to her very long— and I figured she knew that too and would stay away.

"The rest was easy—I got some good breaks. We knew a man was working with her after we found the woman's clothes you left behind, and I took a chance on there being no one else in it. Then I figured she'd need clothes—she couldn't have taken any from home without tipping her mitt— and there was an even chance that she hadn't laid in a stock beforehand. She's got too many girl friends of the sort that do a lot of shopping to make it safe for her to have risked showing herself in stores. Maybe, then, the man would buy what she needed. And it turned out that he did, and that he was too lazy to carry away his purchases, or perhaps there were too many of them, and so he had them sent out. That's the story."

Quayle nodded again.

"I was damned careless," he said, and then, jerking a contemptuous thumb toward the girl, "But what can you expect? She's had a skinful of hop ever since we started. Took all my time and attention keeping her from running wild and gumming the works. Just now was a sample—I told her you were coming up and she goes crazy and tries to add your corpse to the wreckage!"

The Gatewood reunion took place in the office of the captain of inspectors on the second floor of the Oakland City Hall, and it was a merry little party.

For over an hour it was a tossup whether Harvey Gatewood would die of apoplexy, strangle his daughter or send her off to the state reformatory until she was of age. But Audrey licked him. Besides being a chip off the old block, she was young enough to be careless of consequences, while her father, for all his bullheadedness, had had some caution hammered into him.

The card she beat him with was a threat of spilling everything she knew about him to the newspapers, and at least one of the San Francisco papers had been trying to get his scalp for years.

I don't know what she had on him, and I don't think he was any too sure himself; but with his war contracts still being investigated by the Department of Justice, he couldn't afford to take a chance. There was no doubt at all that she would have done as she threatened.

And so, together, they left for home, sweating hate for each other from every pore.

We took Quayle upstairs and put him in a cell, but he was too experienced to let that worry him. He knew that if the girl was to be spared, he himself couldn't very easily be convicted of anything.

I was glad it was over. It had been a tough caper.

The son of a physician and a musician, Ernest Hemingway (1898–1961) was born and grew up in Oak Park, an affluent suburb of Chicago. When young, he excelled at music (the cello), boxing, and football. After high school, Hemingway worked briefly as a reporter in Kansas City; when the United States entered World War I, he volunteered for the ambulance service. He was wounded (while passing out chocolate) at the Italian Front. After the war, as a foreign correspondent he lived in Paris as a member of the expatriate community while learning to write fiction. A master stylist, a short-story writer of great distinction and influence, and a major novelist, Hemingway achieved international recognition with the publication of The Sun Also Rises *(1926) and* A Farewell to Arms *(1929). As an artist-correspondent he was aware of the major political developments of his time;* For Whom the Bell Tolls *(1940) reflects his involvement on the Republican (anti-Fascist) side of the Civil War in Spain. He was awarded the Nobel Prize for literature in 1955. For further reading:* The Fifth Column *and the* First Forty-nine Stories *(1938).*

ERNEST HEMINGWAY

In Another Country

*I*n the fall the war was always there, but we did not go to it any more. It was cold in the fall in Milan and the dark came very early. Then the electric lights came on, and it was pleasant along the streets looking in the windows. There was much game hanging outside the shops, and the snow powdered in the fur of the foxes and the wind blew their tails. The deer hung stiff and heavy and empty, and small birds blew in the wind and the wind turned their feathers. It was a cold fall and the wind came down from the mountains.

We were all at the hospital every afternoon, and there were different ways of walking across the town through the dusk to the hospital. Two of the ways were alongside canals, but they were long. Always, though, you crossed a bridge across a canal to enter the hospital. There was a choice of three bridges. On one of them a woman sold roasted chestnuts. It was warm, standing in front of her charcoal fire, and the chestnuts were warm afterward in your pocket. The hospital was very old and very beautiful, and you entered through a gate and walked across a courtyard and out a gate on the other side. There were usually funerals starting from the courtyard. Beyond the old hospital were the new brick pavilions, and there we met every afternoon and were all very polite and interested in what was the matter, and sat in the machines that were to make so much difference.

The doctor came up to the machine where I was sitting and said: "What did you like best to do before the war? Did you practise a sport?"

I said: "Yes, football."

"Good," he said. "You will be able to play football again better than ever."

My knee did not bend and the leg dropped straight from the knee to the ankle without a calf, and the machine was to bend the knee and make it move as in riding a tricycle. But it did not bend yet, and instead the machine lurched when it came to the bending part. The doctor said: "That will all pass. You are a fortunate young man. You will play football again like a champion."

In the next machine was a major who had a little hand like a baby's. He winked at me when the doctor examined his hand, which was between two leather straps that bounced up and down and flapped the stiff fingers, and said: "And will I too play football, captain-doctor?" He had been a very great fencer, and before the war the greatest fencer in Italy.

The doctor went to his office in a back room and brought a photograph which showed a hand that had been withered almost as small as the major's, before it had taken a machine course, and after was a little larger. The major held the photograph with his good hand and looked at it very carefully. "A wound?" he asked.

"An industrial accident," the doctor said.

"Very interesting, very interesting," the major said, and handed it back to the doctor.

"You have confidence?"

"No," said the major.

There were three boys who came each day who were about the same age I was. They were all three from Milan, and one of them was to be a lawyer, and one was to be a painter, and one had intended to be a soldier, and after we were finished with the machines, sometimes we walked back together to the Café Cova, which was next door to the Scala. We walked the short way through the communist quarter because we were four together. The people hated us because we were officers, and from a wine-shop some one called out, "A basso gli ufficiali!" as we passed. Another boy who walked with us sometimes and made us five wore a black silk handkerchief across his face because he had no nose and his face was to be rebuilt. He had gone out to the front from the military academy and been wounded within an hour after he had gone into the front line for the first time. They rebuilt his face, but he came from a very old family and they could never get the nose exactly right. He went to South America and worked in a bank. But this was a long time ago, and then we did not any of us know how it was going to be afterward. We only knew then that there was always the war, but that we were not going to it any more.

We all had the same medals, except the boy with the black silk bandage across his face, and he had not been at the front long enough to get any medals. The tall boy with a very pale face who was to be a lawyer had been a lieutenant of Arditi and had three medals of the sort we each had only one of. He had lived a very long time with death and was a little detached. We were all a little detached, and there was nothing that held us together except that we met every afternoon at the hospital. Although, as we walked to the Cova through the tough part of town, walking in the dark, with light and singing coming out of the wine-shops, and sometimes having to walk into the street when the men and women would crowd together on the sidewalk so that we would have had to jostle them to get by, we felt held together by there being something that had happened that they, the people who disliked us, did not understand.

We ourselves all understood the Cova, where it was rich and warm and not too brightly lighted, and noisy and smoky at certain hours, and there were always girls at the tables and the illustrated papers on a rack on the wall. The girls at the Cova were very patriotic, and I found that the most patriotic people in Italy were the café girls—and I believe they are still patriotic.

The boys at first were very polite about my medals and asked me what I had done to get them. I showed them the papers, which were written in very beautiful language and full of *fratellanza* and *abnegozione,* but which really said, with the adjectives removed, that I had been given the medals because I was an American. After that their manner changed a little toward me, although I was their friend against outsiders. I was a friend, but I was never really one of them after they had read the citations, because it had been different with them and they had done very different things to get their medals. I had been wounded, it was true; but we all knew that being wounded, after all, was really an accident. I was never ashamed of the ribbons, though, and sometimes, after the cocktail hour, I would imagine myself having done all the things they had done to get their medals; but walking home at night through the empty streets with the cold wind and all the shops closed, trying to keep near the street lights, I knew that I would never have done such things, and I was very much afraid to die, and often lay in bed at night by myself, afraid to die and wondering how I would be when I went back to the front again.

The three with the medals were like hunting hawks; and I was not a hawk, although I might seem a hawk to those who had never hunted; they, the three, knew better and so we drifted apart. But I stayed good friends with the boy who had been wounded his first day at the front, because he would never know now how he would have turned out; so he could never be accepted either, and I liked him because I thought perhaps he would not have turned out to be a hawk either.

The major, who had been the great fencer, did not believe in bravery, and spent much time while we sat in the machines correcting my grammar. He had complimented me on how I spoke Italian, and we talked together very easily. One day I had said that Italian seemed such an easy language to me that I could not take a great interest in it; everything was so easy to say. "Ah, yes," the major said, "Why, then, do you not take up the use of grammar?" So we took up the use of grammar, and soon Italian was such a difficult language that I was afraid to talk to him until I had the grammar straight in my mind.

The major came very regularly to the hospital. I do not think he ever missed a day, although I am sure he did not believe in the machines. There was a time when none of us believed in the machines, and one day the major said it was all nonsense. The machines were new then and it was we who were to prove them. It was an idiotic idea, he said, "a theory, like another." I had not learned my grammar, and he said I was a stupid impossible disgrace, and he was a fool to have bothered with me. He was a small man and he sat straight up in his chair with his right hand thrust into the machine and looked straight ahead at the wall while the straps thumped up and down with his fingers in them.

"What will you do when the war is over if it is over?" he asked me. "Speak grammatically!"

"I will go to the States."

"Are you married?"

"No, but I hope to be."

"The more of a fool you are," he said. He seemed very angry. "A man must not marry."

"Why, Signor Maggiore?"

Don't call me 'Signor Maggiore.' "

"Why must not a man marry?"

"He cannot marry. He cannot marry," he said angrily. "If he is to lose everything, he should not place himself in a position to lose that. He should not place himself in a position to lose. He should find things he cannot lose."

He spoke very angrily and bitterly, and looked straight ahead while he talked.

"But why should he necessarily lose it?"

"He'll lose it," the major said. He was looking at the wall. Then he looked down at the machine and jerked his little hand out from between the straps and slapped it hard against his thigh. "He'll lose it," he almost shouted. "Don't argue with me!" Then he called to the attendant who ran the machines. "Come and turn this damned thing off."

He went back into the other room for the light treatment and the massage. Then I heard him ask the doctor if he might use his telephone and he shut the door. When he came back into the room, I was sitting in another machine. He was wearing his cape and had his cap on, and he came directly toward my machine and put his arm on my shoulder.

"I am so sorry," he said, and patted me on the shoulder with his good hand. "I would not be rude. My wife has just died. You must forgive me."

"Oh—" I said, feeling sick for him. "I am so sorry."

He stood there biting his lower lip. "It is very difficult," he said "I cannot resign myself."

He looked straight past me and out through the window. Then he began to cry. "I am utterly unable to resign myself," he said and choked. And then crying, his head up looking at nothing, carrying himself straight and soldierly, with tears on both his cheeks and biting his lips, he walked past the machines and out the door.

The doctor told me that the major's wife, who was very young and whom he had not married until he was definitely invalided out of the war, died of pneumonia. She had been sick only a few days. No one had expected her to die. The major did not come to the hospital for three days. Then he came at the usual hour, wearing a black band on the sleeve of his uniform. When he came back, there were large framed photographs around the wall, of all sorts of wounds before and after they had been cured by the machines. In front of the machine the major used were three photographs of hands like his that were completely restored. I do not know where the doctor got them. I always understood we were the first to use the machines. The photographs did not make much difference to the major because he only looked out of the window.

Langston Hughes (1902–1967) was born in Joplin, Missouri. Embittered by American racial discrimination, his father left the family and went to live in Mexico; his mother, therefore, was forced to move from city to city in search of suitable work. The summer after graduation from high school, Hughes wrote "The Negro Speaks of Rivers," a poem later to become a classic. He traveled widely as a merchant seaman, and won prizes for his verse. While working as a busboy in a Washington hotel, Hughes placed some poems beside the plate of the poet, Vachel Lindsay; the following day Hughes found himself "discovered"—and received a scholarship to Lincoln University, where he graduated in 1929. He produced poetry, prose, drama, essays, and significant anthologies. A representative book of poems is Weary Blues *(1926); a typical novel,* Not Without Laughter *(1930). Hughes also wrote a series of humorous essays collected as* The Best of Simple *(1961). For further reading:* Laughing to Keep from Crying *(1952).*

LANGSTON HUGHES

Who's Passing for Who?

*O*ne of the great difficulties about being a member of a minority race is that so many kindhearted, well-meaning bores gather around to help. Usually, to tell the truth, they have nothing to help with, except their company—which is often appallingly dull.

Some members of the Negro race seem very well able to put up with it, though, in these uplifting years. Such was Caleb Johnson, colored social worker, who was always dragging around with him some nondescript white person or two, inviting them to dinner, showing them Harlem, ending up at the Savoy—much to the displeasure of whatever friends of his might be out that evening for fun, not sociology.

Friends are friends and, unfortunately, overearnest uplifters are uplifters—no matter what color they may be. If it were the white race that was ground down instead of Negroes, Caleb Johnson would be one of the first to offer Nordics the sympathy of his utterly inane society, under the impression that somehow he would be doing them a great deal of good.

You see, Caleb, and his white friends, too, were all bores. Or so we, who lived in Harlem's literary bohemia during the "Negro Renaissance" thought. We literary ones considered ourselves too broad-minded to be bothered with questions of color. We liked people of any race who smoked incessantly, drank liberally, wore complexion and morality as loose garments, and made fun of anyone who didn't do likewise. We snubbed and high-hatted any Negro or white luckless enough not to understand Gertrude Stein, Ulysses, Man Ray, the theremin, Jean Toomer, or George Antheil. By the end of the 1920's Caleb was just catching up to Dos Passos. He thought H. G. Wells good.

We met Caleb one night in Small's. He had three assorted white folks in tow. We would have passed him by with but a nod had he not hailed us enthusiastically, risen, and introduced us with great acclaim to his friends who turned out to be schoolteachers from Iowa, a woman and two men. They appeared amazed and delighted to meet all at once two Negro writers and a black painter in the flesh. They invited us to have a drink with them. Money being scarce with us, we deigned to sit down at their table.

The white lady said, "I've never met a Negro writer before."

The two men added, "Neither have we."

"Why, we know any number of *white* writers," we three dark bohemians declared with bored nonchalance.

"But Negro writers are much more rare," said the lady.

"There are plenty in Harlem," we said.

"But not in Iowa," said one of the men, shaking his mop of red hair.

"There are no good *white* writers in Iowa either, are there?" we asked superciliously.

"Oh, yes, Ruth Suckow came from there."

Whereupon we proceeded to light in upon Ruth Suckow as old hat and to annihilate her in favor of Kay Boyle. The way we flung names around seemed to impress both Caleb and his white guests. This, of course, delighted us, though we were too young and too proud to admit it.

The drinks came and everything was going well, all of us drinking, and we three showing off in a high-brow manner, when suddenly at the table just behind us a man got up and knocked down a woman. He was a brownskin man. The woman was blonde. As she rose he knocked her down again. Then the red-haired man from Iowa got up and knocked the colored man down.

He said, "Keep your hands off that white woman."

The man got up and said, "She's not a white woman. She's my wife."

One of the waiters added, "She's not white, sir, she's colored."

Whereupon the man from Iowa looked puzzled, dropped his fists, and said, "I'm sorry."

The colored man said, "What are you doing up here in Harlem anyway, interfering with my family affairs?"

The white man said, "I thought she was a white woman."

The woman who had been on the floor rose and said, "Well, I'm not a white woman, I'm colored, and you leave my husband alone."

Then they both lit in on the gentleman from Iowa. It took all of us and several waiters, too, to separate them. When it was over the manager requested us to kindly pay our bill and get out. He said we were disturbing the peace. So we all left. We went to a fish restaurant down the street. Caleb was terribly apologetic to his white friends. We artists were both mad and amused.

"Why did you say you were sorry," said the colored painter to the visitor from Iowa, "after you'd hit that man—and then found out it wasn't a white woman you were defending, but merely a light colored woman who looked white?"

"Well," answered the red-haired Iowan, "I didn't mean to be butting in if they were all the same race."

"Don't you think a woman needs defending from a brute, no matter what race she may be?" asked the painter.

"Yes, but I think it's up to you to defend your own women."

"Oh, so you'd divide up a brawl according to races, no matter who was right?"

"Well, I wouldn't say that."

"You mean you wouldn't defend a colored woman whose husband was knocking her down?" asked the poet.

Before the visitor had time to answer, the painter said, "No! You just got mad because you thought a black man was hitting a *white* woman."

"But she *looked* like a white woman," countered the man.

"Maybe she was just passing for colored," I said.

"Like some Negroes pass for white," Caleb interposed.

"Anyhow, I don't like it," said the colored painter, "the way you stopped defending her when you found out she wasn't white."

"No, we don't like it," we all agreed except Caleb.

Caleb said in extenuation, "But Mr. Stubblefield is new to Harlem."

The red-haired white man said, "Yes, it's my first time here."

"Maybe Mr. Stubblefield ought to stay out of Harlem," we observed.

"I agree," Mr. Stubblefield said. "Good night."

He got up then and there and left the café. He stalked as he walked. His red head disappeared into the night.

"Oh, that's too bad," said the white couple who remained. "Stubby's temper just got the best of him. But explain to us, are many colored folks really as fair as that woman?"

"Sure, lots of them have more white blood than colored, and pass for white."

"Do they?" said the lady and gentleman from Iowa.

"You never read Nella Larsen?" we asked.

"She writes novels," Caleb explained. "She's part white herself."

"Read her," we advised. "Also read the *Autobiography of an Ex-colored Man*." Not that we had read it ourselves—because we paid but little attention to the older colored writers—but we know it was about passing for white.

We all ordered fish and settled down comfortably to shocking our white friends with tales about how many Negroes there were passing for white all over America. We were determined to *épater le bourgeois* real good via this white couple we had cornered, when the woman leaned over the table in the midst of our dissertations and said, "Listen, gentlemen, you needn't spread the word, but me and my husband aren't white either. We've just been *passing* for white for the last fifteen years."

"What?"

"We're colored, too, just like you," said the husband. "But it's better passing for white because we make more money."

Well, that took the wind out of us. It took the wind out of Caleb, too. He thought all the time he was showing some fine white folks Harlem—and they were as colored as he was!

Caleb almost never cursed. But this time he said, "I'll be damned!"

Then everybody laughed. And laughed! We almost had hysterics. All at once we dropped our professionally self-conscious "Negro" manners, became natural, ate fish, and talked and kidded freely like colored folks do when there are no white folks around. We really had fun then, joking about that red-haired guy who mistook a fair colored woman for white. After the fish we went to two or three more night spots and drank until five o'clock in the morning.

Finally we put the light-colored people in a taxi heading downtown. They turned to shout a last good-by. The cab was just about to move off, when the woman called to the driver to stop.

She leaned out the window and said with a grin, "Listen, boys! I hate to confuse you again. But, to tell you the truth, my husband and I aren't colored at all. We're white. We just thought we'd kid you by passing for colored a little while—just as you said Negroes sometimes pass for white."

She laughed as they sped off toward Central Park, waving, "Good-by!"

We didn't say a thing. We just stood there on the corner in Harlem dumbfounded—not knowing now *which* way we'd been fooled. Were they really white—passing for colored? or colored—passing for white?

Whatever race they were, they had had too much fun at our expense—even if they did pay for the drinks.

John Steinbeck (1902–1968) resembles Sherwood Anderson, Faulkner, and Thomas Wolfe in that he wrote vividly about the region of his place of birth: Salinas, and Monterey County, California. Today the region is called the "Steinbeck Country"; he has immortalized the place of his origins. Steinbeck developed slowly as an artist and seemed to gain very little from his sporadic attendance at Stanford University. He was unsuccessful in New York as a reporter; back in California he lived an irregular life as a fruit picker, surveyor, and painter. When he turned to local materials in Tortilla Flat *(1935) and in* Of Mice and Men *(1937), his fictional powers developed rapidly. He was recognized as a richly lyrical, often irregular storyteller; his primitivistic sympathies are apparent in nearly all his work. The* Grapes of Wrath *(1940) won the Pulitzer Prize. He received the Nobel Prize for literature in 1962. For further reading:* The Long Valley *(1937).*

JOHN STEINBECK

The Chrysanthemums

The high grey-flannel fog of winter closed off the Salinas Valley from the sky and from all the rest of the world. On every side it sat like a lid on the mountains and made of the great valley a closed pot. On the broad, level land floor the gang plows bit deep and left the black earth shining like metal where the shares had cut. On the foothill ranches across the Salinas River, the yellow stubble fields seemed to be bathed in pale cold sunshine, but there was no sunshine in the valley now in December. The thick willow scrub along the river flamed with sharp and positive yellow leaves.

It was a time of quiet and of waiting. The air was cold and tender. A light wind blew up from the southwest so that the farmers were mildly hopeful of a good rain before long; but fog and rain do not go together.

Across the river, on Henry Allen's foothill ranch there was little work to be done, for the hay was cut and stored and the orchards were plowed up to receive the rain deeply when it should come. The cattle on the higher slopes were becoming shaggy and rough-coated.

Elisa Allen, working in her flower garden, looked down across the yard and saw Henry, her husband, talking to two men in business suits. The three of them stood by the tractor shed, each man with one foot on the side of the little Fordson. They smoked cigarettes and studied the machine as they talked.

Elisa watched them for a moment and then went back to her work. She was thirty-five. Her face was lean and strong and her eyes were as clear as water. Her figure looked blocked and heavy in her gardening costume, a man's black hat pulled low down over her eyes, clodhopper shoes, a figured print dress almost completely covered by a big corduroy apron with four big pockets to hold the snips, the trowel and scratcher, the seeds and the knife she worked with. She wore heavy leather gloves to protect her hands while she worked.

She was cutting down the old year's chrysanthemum stalks with a pair of short and powerful scissors. She looked down toward the men by the tractor shed now and then. Her face was eager and mature and handsome; even her work with the scissors was over-eager, over-powerful. The chrysanthemum stems seemed too small and easy for her energy.

She brushed a cloud of hair out of her eyes with the back of her glove, and left a smudge of earth on her cheek in doing it. Behind her stood the neat white farm house with red geraniums close-banked around it as high as the windows. It was a hard-swept looking little house, with hard-polished windows, and a clean mud-mat on the front steps.

Elisa cast another glance toward the tractor shed. The strangers were getting into their Ford coupe. She took off a glove and put her strong fingers down into the forest of new green chrysanthemum sprouts that were growing around the old roots. She spread the leaves and looked down among the close-growing stems. No aphids were there, no sowbugs or snails or cutworms. Her terrier fingers destroyed such pests before they could get started.

Elisa started at the sound of her husband's voice. He had come near quietly, and he leaned over the wire fence that protected her flower garden from cattle and dogs and chickens.

"At it again," he said. "You've got a strong new crop coming."

Elisa straightened her back and pulled on the gardening glove again. "Yes. They'll be strong this coming year." In her tone and on her face there was a little smugness.

"You've got a gift with things," Henry observed. "Some of those yellow chrysanthemums you had this year were ten inches across. I wish you'd work out in the orchard and raise some apples that big."

Her eyes sharpened. "Maybe I could do it, too. I've a gift with things, all right. My mother had it. She could stick anything in the ground and make it grow. She said it was having planters' hands that knew how to do it."

"Well, it sure works with flowers," he said.

"Henry, who were those men you were talking to?"

"Why, sure, that's what I came to tell you. They were from the Western Meat Company. I sold those thirty head of three-year-old steers. Got nearly my own price, too."

"Good," she said. "Good for you."

"And I thought," he continued, "I thought how it's Saturday afternoon, and we might go into Salinas for dinner at a restaurant, and then to a picture show—to celebrate, you see."

"Good," she repeated. "Oh, yes. That will be good."

Henry put on his joking tone. "There's fights tonight. How'd you like to go to the fights?"

"Oh, no," she said breathlessly. "No, I wouldn't like fights."

"Just fooling, Elisa. We'll go to a movie. Let's see. It's two now. I'm going to take Scotty and bring down those steers from the hill. It'll take us maybe two hours. We'll go in town about five and have dinner at the Cominos Hotel. Like that?"

"Of course I'll like it. It's good to eat away from home."

"All right, then, I'll go get up a couple of horses."

She said, "I'll have plenty of time to transplant some of these sets, I guess."

She heard her husband calling Scotty down by the barn. And a little later she saw the two men ride up the pale yellow hillside in search of the steers.

There was a little square sandy bed kept for rooting the chrysanthemums. With her trowel she turned the soil over and over, and smoothed it and patted it firm. Then she dug ten parallel trenches to receive the sets. Back at the chrysanthemum bed she pulled out the little crisp shoots, trimmed off the leaves of each one with her scissors and laid it on a small orderly pile.

A squeak of wheels and plod of hoofs came from the road. Elisa looked up. The country road ran along the dense bank of willows and cottonwoods that bordered the river, and up this road came a curious vehicle, curiously drawn. It was an old spring-wagon, with a round canvas top on it like the cover of a prairie schooner. It was drawn by an old bay horse and a little grey-and-white burro. A big stubble-bearded man sat between the cover flaps and drove the crawling team. Underneath the wagon, between the hind wheels, a lean and rangy mongrel dog walked sedately. Words were painted on the canvas, in clumsy, crooked letters. "Pots, pans, knives, sisors, lawn mores, Fixed." Two rows of articles, and the triumphantly definite "Fixed" below. The black paint had run down in little sharp points beneath each letter.

Elisa, squatting on the ground, watched to see the crazy, loose-jointed wagon pass by. But it didn't pass. It turned into the farm road in front of her house, crooked old wheels skirling and squeaking. The rangy dog darted from between the wheels and ran ahead. Instantly the two ranch shepherds flew out at him. Then all three stopped, and with stiff and quivering tails, with taut straight legs, with ambassadorial dignity, they slowly circled, sniffing daintily. The caravan pulled up to Elisa's wire fence and stopped. Now the newcomer dog, feeling out-numbered, lowered his tail and retired under the wagon with raised hackles and bared teeth.

The man on the wagon seat called out, "That's a bad dog in a fight when he gets started."

Elisa laughed. "I see he is. How soon does he generally get started?"

The man caught up her laughter and echoed it heartily. "Sometimes not for weeks and weeks," he said. He climbed stiffly down, over the wheel. The horse and the donkey drooped like unwatered flowers.

Elisa saw that he was a very big man. Although his hair and beard were greying, he did not look old. His worn black suit was wrinkled and spotted with grease. The laughter had disappeared from his face and eyes the moment his laughing voice ceased. His eyes were dark, and they were full of the brooding that gets in the eyes of teamsters and of sailors. The calloused hands he rested on the wire fence were cracked, and every crack was a black line. He took off his battered hat.

"I'm off my general road, ma'am," he said. "Does this dirt road cut over across the river to the Los Angeles highway?"

Elisa stood up and shoved the thick scissors in her apron pocket. "Well, yes, it does, but it winds around and then fords the river. I don't think your team could pull through the sand."

He replied with some asperity, "It might surprise you what them beasts can pull through."

"When they get started?" she asked.

He smiled for a second. "Yes. When they get started."

"Well," said Elisa, "I think you'll save time if you go back to the Salinas road and pick up the highway there."

He drew a big finger down the chicken wire and made it sing. "I ain't in any hurry, ma'am. I go from Seattle to San Diego and back every year. Takes all my time. About six months each way. I aim to follow nice weather."

Elisa took off her gloves and stuffed them in the apron pocket with the scissors. She touched the under edge of her man's hat, searching for fugitive hairs. "That sounds like a nice kind of a way to live," she said.

He leaned confidentially over the fence. "Maybe you noticed the writing on my wagon. I mend pots and sharpen knives and scissors. You got any of them things to do?"

"Oh, no," she said quickly. "Nothing like that." Her eyes hardened with resistance.

"Scissors is the worst thing," he explained. "Most people just ruin scissors trying to sharpen 'em, but I know how. I got a special tool. It's a little bobbit kind of thing, and patented. But it sure does the trick."

"No. My scissors are all sharp."

"All right, then. Take a pot," he continued earnestly, "a bent pot, or a pot with a hole. I can make it like new so you don't have to buy no new ones. That's a saving for you."

"No," she said shortly. "I tell you I have nothing like that for you to do."

His face fell to an exaggerated sadness. His voice took on a whining undertone. "I ain't had a thing to do today. Maybe I won't have no supper tonight. You see I'm off my regular road. I know folks on the highway clear from Seattle to San Diego. They save their things for me to sharpen up because they know I do it so good and save them money."

"I'm sorry," Elisa said irritably. "I haven't anything for you to do."

His eyes left her face and fell to searching the ground. They roamed about until they came to the chrysanthemum bed where she had been working. "What's them plants, ma'am?"

The irritation and resistance melted from Elisa's face. "Oh, those are chrysanthemums, giant whites and yellows. I raise them every year, bigger than anybody around here."

"Kind of a long-stemmed flower? Looks like a quick puff of colored smoke?" he asked.

"That's it. What a nice way to describe them."

"They smell kind of nasty till you get used to them," he said.

"It's a good bitter smell," she retorted, "not nasty at all."

He changed his tone quickly. "I like the smell myself."

"I had ten-inch blooms this year," she said.

The man leaned farther over the fence. "Look, I know a lady down the road a piece, has got the nicest garden you ever seen. Got nearly every kind of flower but no chrysantheums. Last time I was mending a copper-bottom washtub for her (that's a hard job but I do it good), she said to me, 'If you ever run acrost some nice chrysantheums I wish you'd try to get me a few seeds.' That's what she told me."

Elisa's eyes grew alert and eager. "She couldn't have known much about chrysanthemums. You *can* raise them from seed, but it's much easier to root the little sprouts you see there."

"Oh," he said. "I s'pose I can't take none to her, then."

"Why yes you can," Elisa cried. "I can put some in damp sand, and you can carry them right along with you. They'll take root in the pot if you keep them damp. And then she can transplant them."

"She'd sure like to have some, ma'am. You say they're nice ones?"

"Beautiful," she said. "Oh, beautiful." Her eyes shone. She tore off the battered hat and shook out her dark pretty hair. "I'll put them in a flower pot, and you can take them right with you. Come into the yard."

While the man came through the picket gate Elisa ran excitedly along the geranium-bordered path to the back of the house. And she returned carrying a big red flower pot. The gloves were forgotten now. She kneeled on the ground by the starting bed and dug up the sandy soil with her fingers and scooped it into the bright new flower pot. Then she picked up the little pile of shoots she had prepared. With her strong fingers she pressed them into the sand and tamped around them with her knuckles. The man stood over her. "I'll tell you what to do," she said. "You remember so you can tell the lady."

"Yes, I'll try to remember."

"Well, look. These will take root in about a month. Then she must set them out, about a foot apart in good rich earth like this, see?" She lifted a handful of dark soil for him to look at. "They'll grow fast and tall. Now remember this: In July tell her to cut them down, about eight inches from the ground."

"Before they bloom?" he asked.

"Yes, before they bloom." Her face was tight with eagerness. "They'll grow right up again. About the last of September the buds will start."

She stopped and seemed perplexed. "It's the budding that takes the most care," she said hesitantly. "I don't know how to tell you." She looked deep into his eyes, searchingly. Her mouth opened a little, and she seemed to be listening. "I'll try to tell you," she said. "Did you ever hear of planting hands?"

"Can't say I have, ma'am."

"Well, I can only tell you what it feels like. It's when you're picking off the buds you don't want. Everything goes right down into your fingertips. You watch your fingers work. They do it themselves. You can feel how it is. They pick and pick the buds. They never make a mistake. They're with the plant. Do you see? Your fingers and the plant. You can feel that, right up your arm. They know. They never make a mistake. You can feel it. When you're like that you can't do anything wrong. Do you see that? Can you understand that?"

She was kneeling on the ground looking up at him. Her breast swelled passionately.

The man's eyes narrowed. He looked away self-consciously. "Maybe I know," he said. "Sometimes in the night in the wagon there——"

Elisa's voice grew husky. She broke in on him, "I've never lived as you do, but I know what you mean. When the night is dark—why, the stars are sharp-pointed, and there's quiet. Why, you rise up and up! Every pointed star gets driven into your body. It's like that. Hot and sharp and—lovely."

Kneeling there, her hand went out toward his legs in the greasy black trousers. Her hesitant fingers almost touched the cloth. Then her hand dropped to the ground. She crouched low like a fawning dog.

He said, "It's nice, just like you say. Only when you don't have no dinner, it ain't."

She stood up then, very straight, and her face was ashamed. She held the flower pot out to him and placed it gently in his arms. "Here. Put it in your wagon, on the seat, where you can watch it. Maybe I can find something for you to do."

At the back of the house she dug in the can pile and found two old and battered aluminum saucepans. She carried them back and gave them to him. "Here, maybe you can fix these."

His manner changed. He became professional. "Good as new I can fix them." At the back of his wagon he set a little anvil, and out of an oily tool box dug a small machine hammer. Elisa came through the gate to watch him while he pounded out the dents in the kettles. His mouth grew sure and knowing. At a difficult part of the work he sucked his under-lip.

"You sleep right in the wagon?" Elisa asked.

"Right in the wagon, ma'am. Rain or shine I'm dry as a cow in there."

"It must be nice," she said. "It must be very nice. I wish women could do such things."

"It ain't the right kind of a life for a woman."

Her upper lip raised a little, showing her teeth. "How do you know? How can you tell?" she said.

"I don't know, ma'am," he protested. "Of course I don't know. Now here's your kettles, done. You don't have to buy no new ones."

"How much?"

"Oh, fifty cents'll do. I keep my prices down and my work good. That's why I have all them satisfied customers up and down the highway."

Elisa brought him a fifty-cent piece from the house and dropped it in his hand. "You might be surprised to have a rival some time. I can sharpen scissors, too. And I can beat the dents out of little pots. I could show you what a woman might do."

He put his hammer back in the oily box and shoved the little anvil out of sight. "It would be a lonely life for a woman, ma'am, and a scarey life, too, with animals creeping under the wagon all night." He climbed over the singletree, steadying himself with a hand on the burro's white rump. He settled himself in the seat, picked up the lines. "Thank you kindly, ma'am," he said. "I'll do like you told me; I'll go back and catch the Salinas road."

"Mind," she called, "if you're long in getting there, keep the sand damp."

"Sand, ma'am? . . . Sand? Oh, sure. You mean around the chrysanthemums. Sure I will." He clucked his tongue. The beasts leaned luxuriously into their collars. The mongrel dog took his place between the back wheels. The wagon turned and crawled out the entrance road and back the way it had come, along the river.

Elisa stood in front of her wire fence watching the slow progress of the caravan. Her shoulders were straight, her head thrown back, her eyes half-closed, so that the scene came vaguely into them. Her lips moved silently, forming the words "Good-bye—good-bye." Then she whispered, "That's a bright direction. There's a glowing there." The sound of her whisper startled her. She shook herself free and looked about to see whether anyone had been listening. Only the dogs had heard. They lifted their heads toward her from their sleeping in the dust, and then stretched out their chins and settled asleep again. Elisa turned and ran hurriedly into the house.

In the kitchen she reached behind the stove and felt the water tank. It was full of hot water from the noonday cooking. In the bathroom she tore off her soiled clothes and flung them into the corner. And then she scrubbed herself with a little block of pumice, legs and thighs, loins and chest and arms, until her skin was scratched and red. When she had dried herself she stood in front of a mirror in her bedroom and looked at her body. She tightened her stomach and threw out her chest. She turned and looked over her shoulder at her back.

After a while she began to dress, slowly. She put on her newest underclothing and her nicest stockings and the dress which was the symbol of her prettiness. She worked carefully on her hair, penciled her eyebrows and rouged her lips.

Before she was finished she heard the little thunder of hoofs and the shouts of Henry and his helper as they drove the red steers into the corral. She heard the gate bang shut and set herself for Henry's arrival.

His step sounded on the porch. He entered the house calling, "Elisa, where are you?"

"In my room, dressing. I'm not ready. There's hot water for your bath. Hurry up. It's getting late."

When she heard him splashing in the tub, Elisa laid his dark suit on the bed, and shirt and socks and tie beside it. She stood his polished shoes on the floor beside the bed. Then she went to the porch and sat primly and stiffly down. She looked toward the river road where the willow-line was still yellow with frosted leaves so that under the high grey fog they seemed a thin band of sunshine. This was the only color in the grey afternoon. She sat unmoving for a long time. Her eyes blinked rarely.

Henry came banging out of the door, shoving his tie inside his vest as he came. Elisa stiffened and her face grew tight. Henry stopped short and looked at her. "Why—why, Elisa. You look so nice!"

"Nice? You think I look nice? What do you mean by 'nice'?"

Henry blundered on. "I don't know. I mean you look different, strong and happy."

"I am strong? Yes, strong. What do you mean 'strong'?"

He looked bewildered. "You're playing some kind of a game," he said helplessly. "It's a kind of a play. You look strong enough to break a calf over your knee, happy enough to eat it like a watermelon."

For a second she lost her rigidity. "Henry! Don't talk like that. You didn't know what you said." She grew complete again. "I'm strong," she boasted. "I never knew before how strong."

Henry looked down toward the tractor shed, and when he brought his eyes back to her, they were his own again. "I'll get out the car. You can put on your coat while I'm starting."

Elisa went into the house. She heard him drive to the gate and idle down his motor, and then she took a long time to put on her hat. She pulled it here and pressed it there. When Henry turned the motor off she slipped into her coat and went out.

The little roadster bounced along on the dirt road by the river, raising the birds and driving the rabbits into the brush. Two cranes flapped heavily over the willow-line and dropped into the river-bed.

Far ahead on the road Elisa saw a dark speck. She knew.

She tried not to look as they passed it, but her eyes would not obey. She whispered to herself sadly, "He might have thrown them off the road. That wouldn't have been much trouble, not very much. But he kept the pot," she explained. "He had to keep the pot. That's why he couldn't get them off the road."

The roadster turned a bend and she saw the caravan ahead. She swung full around toward her husband so she could not see the little covered wagon and the mismatched team as the car passed them.

In a moment it was over. The thing was done. She did not look back.

She said loudly, to be heard above the motor, "It will be good, tonight, a good dinner."

"Now you've changed again," Henry complained. He took one hand from the wheel and patted her knee. "I ought to take you in to dinner oftener. It would be good for both of us. We get so heavy out on the ranch."

"Henry," she asked, "could we have wine at dinner?"

"Sure we could. Say! That will be fine."

She was silent for a while; then she said, "Henry, at those prize fights, do the men hurt each other very much?"

"Sometimes a little, not often. Why?"

"Well, I've read how they break noses, and blood runs down their chests. I've read how the fighting gloves get heavy and soggy with blood."

He looked around at her. "What's the matter, Elisa? I didn't know you read things like that." He brought the car to a stop, then turned to the right over the Salinas River bridge.

"Do any women ever go to the fights?" she asked.

"Oh, sure, some. What's the matter, Elisa? Do you want to go? I don't think you'd like it, but I'll take you if you really want to go."

She relaxed limply in the seat. "Oh, no. No. I don't want to go. I'm sure I don't." Her face was turned away from him. "It will be enough if we can have wine. It will be plenty." She turned up her coat collar so he could not see that she was crying weakly—like an old woman.

*Except for a few years at the University of Wisconsin and the Columbia University School of Advertising, Eudora Welty (1909–   ) has lived in and written about the history and contemporary culture of her home town of Jackson, Mississippi. A novelist of the highest order (*Delta Wedding, *1946;* Losing Battles, *1970), her greatest talent is for the short story. A strong regionalist, her work has a characteristic element of fantasy and a multiplicity of vision. An accomplished photographer, Ms. Welty also has a strong theoretical interest in the craft of writing, as in "How I Write" (*Three Papers on Fiction, *1962). For further reading see the short-story collections:* A Curtain of Green *(1941);* The Golden Apples *(1949);* Thirteen Stories *(1965).*

EUDORA WELTY

Livvie

Solomon carried Livvie twenty-one miles away from her home when he married her. He carried her away up on the Old Natchez Trace into the deep country to live in his house. She was sixteen—an only girl, then. Once people said he thought nobody would ever come along there. He told her himself that it had been a long time, and a day she did not know about, since that road was a traveled road with *people* coming and going. He was good to her, but he kept her in the house. She had not thought that she could not get back. Where she came from, people said an old man did not want anybody in the world to ever find his wife, for fear they would steal her back from him. Solomon asked her before he took her, "Would she be happy?"—very dignified, for he was a colored man that owned his land and had it written down in the courthouse; and she said, "Yes, sir," since he was an old man and she was young and just listened and answered. He asked her, if she was choosing winter, would she pine for spring, and she said, "No indeed." Whatever she said, always, was because he was an old man . . . while nine years went by. All the time, he got old, and he got so old he gave out. At last he slept the whole day in bed, and she was young still.

It was a nice house, inside and outside both. In the first place, it had three rooms. The front room was papered in holly paper, with green palmet-

tos from the swamp spaced at careful intervals over the walls. There was
fresh newspaper cut with fancy borders on the mantel-shelf, on which were
propped photographs of old or very young men printed in faint yellow—
Solomon's people. Solomon had a houseful of furniture. There was a double
settee, a tall scrolled rocker and an organ in the front room, all around a
three-legged table with a pink marble top, on which was set a lamp with
three gold feet, besides a jelly glass with pretty hen feathers in it. Behind the
front room, the other room had the bright iron bed with the polished knobs
like a throne, in which Solomon slept all day. There were snow-white curtains of wiry lace at the window, and a lace bed-spread belonged on the
bed. But what old Solomon slept so sound under was a big feather-stitched
piece-quilt in the pattern "Trip Around the World," which had twenty-one
different colors, four hundred and forty pieces, and a thousand yards of
thread, and that was what Solomon's mother made in her life and old age.
There was a table holding the Bible, and a trunk with a key. On the wall
were two calendars, and a diploma from somewhere in Solomon's family,
and under that Livvie's one possession was nailed, a picture of the little
white baby of the family she worked for, back in Natchez before she was
married. Going through that room and on to the kitchen, there was a big
wood stove and a big round table always with a wet top and with the knives
and forks in one jelly glass and the spoons in another, and a cut-glass
vinegar bottle between, and going out from those, many shallow dishes of
pickled peaches, fig preserves, watermelon pickles and blackberry jam always sitting there. The churn sat in the sun, the doors of the safe were
always both shut, and there were four baited mouse-traps in the kitchen,
one in every corner.

The outside of Solomon's house looked nice. It was not painted, but
across the porch was an even balance. On each side there was one easy
chair with high springs, looking out, and a fern basket hanging over it from
the ceiling, and a dishpan of zinnia seedlings growing at its foot on the
floor. By the door was a plow-wheel, just a pretty iron circle, nailed up on
one wall and a square mirror on the other, a turquoise-blue comb stuck up
in the frame, with the wash stand beneath it. On the door was a wooden
knob with a pearl in the end, and Solomon's black hat hung on that, if he
was in the house.

Out front was a clean dirt yard with every vestige of grass patiently
uprooted and the ground scarred in deep whorls from the strike of Livvie's
broom. Rose bushes with tiny blood-red roses blooming every month grew
in threes on either side of the steps. On one side was a peach tree, on the
other a pomegranate. Then coming around up the path from the deep cut of
the Natchez Trace below was a line of bare crape-myrtle trees with every
branch of them ending in a colored bottle, green or blue. There was no
word that fell from Solomon's lips to say what they were for, but Livvie
knew that there could be a spell put in trees, and she was familiar from the

time she was born with the way bottle trees kept evil spirits from coming
into the house—by luring them inside the colored bottles, where they cannot get out again. Solomon had made the bottle trees with his own hands
over the nine years, in labor amounting to about a tree a year, and without
a sign that he had any uneasiness in his heart, for he took as much pride in
his precautions against spirits coming in the house as he took in the house,
and sometimes in the sun the bottle trees looked prettier than the house did.

It was a nice house. It was in a place where the days would go by and
surprise anyone that they were over. The lamplight and the firelight would
shine out the door after dark, over the still and breathing country, lighting
the roses and the bottle tress, and all was quiet there.

But there was nobody, nobody at all, not even a white person. And if
there had been anybody, Solomon would not have let Livvie look at them,
just as he would not let her look at a field hand, or a field hand look at her.
There was no house near, except for the cabins of the tenants that were
forbidden to her, and there was no house as far as she had been, stealing
away down the still, deep Trace. She felt as if she waded a river when she
went, for the dead leaves on the ground reached as high as her knees, and
when she was all scratched and bleeding she said it was not like a road that
went anywhere. One day, climbing up the high bank, she had found a
graveyard without a church, with ribbon-grass growing about the foot of an
angel (she had climbed up because she thought she saw angel wings), and in
the sun, trees shining like burning flames through the great caterpillar nets
which enclosed them. Scarey thistles stood looking like the prophets in the
Bible in Solomon's house. Indian paint brushes grew over her head, and the
mourning dove made the only sound in the world. Oh for a stirring of the
leaves, and a breaking of the nets! But not by a ghost, prayed Livvie,
jumping down the bank. After Solomon took to his bed, she never went out,
except one more time.

Livvie knew she made a nice girl to wait on anybody. She fixed things
to eat on a tray like a surprise. She could keep from singing when she
ironed, and to sit by a bed and fan away the flies, she could be so still she
could not hear herself breathe. She could clean up the house and never drop
a thing, and wash the dishes without a sound, and she would step outside to
churn, for churning sounded too sad to her, like sobbing, and if it made her
home-sick and not Solomon, she did not think of that.

But Solomon scarcely opened his eyes to see her, and scarcely tasted
his food. He was not sick or paralyzed or in any pain that he mentioned,
but he was surely wearing out in the body, and no matter what nice hot
thing Livvie would bring him to taste, he would only look at it now, as if he
were past seeing how he could add anything more to himself. Before she
could beg him, he would go fast asleep. She could not surprise him any
more, if he would not taste, and she was afraid that he was never in the

world going to taste another thing she brought him—and so how could he last?

But one morning it was breakfast time and she cooked his eggs and grits, carried them in on a tray, and called his name. He was sound asleep. He lay in a dignified way with his watch beside him, on his back in the middle of the bed. One hand drew the quilt up high, though it was the first day of spring. Through the white lace curtains a little puffy wind was blowing as if it came from round cheeks. All night the frogs had sung out in the swamp, like a commotion in the room, and he had not stirred, though she lay wide awake and saying "Shh, frogs!" for fear he would mind them.

He looked as if he would like to sleep a little longer, and so she put back the tray and waited a little. When she tiptoed and stayed so quiet, she surrounded herself with a little reverie, and sometimes it seemed to her when she was so stealthy that the quiet she kept was for a sleeping baby, and that she had a baby and was its mother. When she stood at Solomon's bed and looked down at him, she would be thinking, "He sleeps so well," and she would hate to wake him up. And in some other way, too, she was afraid to wake him up because even in his sleep he seemed to be such a strict man.

Of course, nailed to the wall over the bed—only she would forget who it was—there was a picture of him when he was young. Then he had a fan of hair over his forehead like a king's crown. Now his hair lay down on his head, the spring had gone out of it. Solomon had a lightish face, with eyebrows scattered but rugged, the way privet grows, strong eyes, with second sight, a strict mouth, and a little gold smile. This was the way he looked in his clothes, but in bed in the daytime he looked like a different and smaller man, even when he was wide awake, and holding the Bible. He looked like somebody kin to himself. And then sometimes when he lay in sleep and she stood fanning the flies away, and the light came in, his face was like new, so smooth and clear that it was like a glass of jelly held to the window, and she could almost look through his forehead and see what he thought.

She fanned him and at length he opened his eyes and spoke her name, but he would not taste the nice eggs she had kept warm under a pan.

Back in the kitchen she ate heartily, his breakfast and hers, and looked out the open door at what went on. The whole day, and the whole night before, she had felt the stir of spring close to her. It was as present in the house as a young man would be. The moon was in the last quarter and outside they were turning the sod and planting peas and beans. Up and down the red fields, over which smoke from the brush-burning hung showing like a little skirt of sky, a white horse and a white mule pulled the plow. At intervals hoarse shouts came through the air and roused her as if she dozed neglectfully in the shade, and they were telling her, "Jump up!" She

could see how over each ribbon of field were moving men and girls, on foot
and mounted on mules, with hats set on their heads and bright with tall
hoes and forks as if they carried streamers on them and were going to some
place on a journey—and how as if at a signal now and then they would all
start at once shouting, hollering, cajoling, calling and answering back, running, being leaped on and breaking away, flinging to earth with a shout and
lying motionless in the trance of twelve o'clock. The old women came out
of the cabins and brought them the food they had ready for them, and then
all worked together, spread evenly out. The little children came too, like a
bouncing stream overflowing the fields, and set upon the men, the women,
the dogs, the rushing birds, and the wave-like rows of earth, their little
voices almost too high to be heard. In the middle distance like some white
and gold towers were the haystacks, with black cows coming around to eat
their edges. High above everything, the wheel of fields, house, and cabins,
and the deep road surrounding like a moat to keep them in, was the turning
sky, blue with long, far-flung white mare's-tail clouds, serene and still as
high flames. And sound asleep while all this went around him that was his,
Solomon was like a little still spot in the middle.

Even in the house the earth was sweet to breathe. Solomon had never
let Livvie go any farther than the chicken house and the well. But what if
she would walk now into the heart of the fields and take a hoe and work
until she fell stretched out and drenched with her efforts, like other girls,
and laid her cheek against the laid-open earth, and shamed the old man
with her humbleness and delight? To shame him! A cruel wish could come
in uninvited and so fast while she looked out the back door. She washed the
dishes and scrubbed the table. She could hear the cries of the little lambs.
Her mother, that she had not seen since her wedding day, had said one
time, "I rather a man be anything, than a woman be mean."

So all morning she kept tasting the chicken broth on the stove, and
when it was right she poured off a nice cup-ful. She carried it in to Solomon, and there he lay having a dream. Now what did he dream about? For
she saw him sigh gently as if not to disturb some whole thing he held round
in his mind, like a fresh egg. So even an old man dreamed about something
pretty. Did he dream of her, while his eyes were shut and sunken, and his
small hand with the wedding ring curled close in sleep around the quilt? He
might be dreaming of what time it was, for even through his sleep he kept
track of it like a clock, and knew how much of it went by, and waked up
knowing where the hands were even before he consulted the silver watch
that he never let go. He would sleep with the watch in his palm, and even
holding it to his cheek like a child that loves a plaything. Or he might dream
of journeys and travels on a steamboat to Natchez. Yet she thought he
dreamed of her; but even while she scrutinized him, the rods of the foot of
the bed seemed to rise up like a rail fence between them, and she could see

that people never could be sure of anything as long as one of them was asleep and the other awake. To look at him dreaming of her when he might be going to die frightened her a little, as if he might carry her with him that way, and she wanted to run out of the room. She took hold of the bed and held on, and Solomon opened his eyes and called her name, but he did not want anything. He would not taste the good broth.

Just a little after that, as she was taking up the ashes in the front room for the last time in the year, she heard a sound. It was somebody coming. She pulled the curtains together and looked through the slit.

Coming up the path under the bottle trees was a white lady. At first she looked young, but then she looked old. Marvelous to see, a little car stood steaming like a kettle out in the field-track—it had come without a road.

Livvie stood listening to the long, repeated knockings at the door, and after a while she opened it just a little. The lady came in through the crack, though she was more than middle-sized and wore a big hat.

"My name is Miss Baby Marie," she said.

Livvie gazed respectfully at the lady and at the little suitcase she was holding close to her by the handle until the proper moment. The lady's eyes were running over the room, from palmetto to palmetto, but she was saying, "I live at home . . . out from Natchez . . . and get out and show these pretty cosmetic things to the white people and the colored people both . . . all around . . . years and years. . . . Both shades of powder and rouge . . . It's the kind of work a girl can do and not go clear 'way from home . . ." And the harder she looked, the more she talked. Suddenly she turned up her nose and said, "It is not Christian or sanitary to put feathers in a vase," and then she took a gold key out of the front of her dress and began unlocking the locks on her suitcase. Her face drew the light, the way it was covered with intense white and red, with a little patty-cake of white between the wrinkles by her upper lip. Little red tassels of hair bobbed under the rusty wires of her picture-hat, as with an air of triumph and secrecy she now drew open her little suitcase and brought out bottle after bottle and jar after jar, which she put down on the table, the mantel-piece, the settee, and the organ.

"Did you ever see so many cosmetics in your life?" cried Miss Baby Marie.

"No'm," Livvie tried to say, but the cat had her tongue.

"Have you ever applied cosmetics?" asked Miss Baby Marie next.

"No'm," Livvie tried to say.

"Then look!" she said, and pulling out the last thing of all, "Try this!" she said. And in her hand was unclenched a golden lipstick which popped open like magic. A fragrance came out of it like incense, and Livvie cried out suddenly, "Chinaberry flowers!"

Her hand took the lipstick, and in an instant she was carried away in the air through the spring, and looking down with a half-drowsy smile from a purple cloud she saw from above a chinaberry tree, dark and smooth and neatly leaved, neat as a guinea hen in the dooryard, and there was her home that she had left. On one side of the tree was her mama holding up her heavy apron, and she could see it was loaded with ripe figs, and on the other side was her papa holding a fish-pole over the pond, and she could see it transparently, the little clear fishes swimming up to the brim.

"Oh, no, not chinaberry flowers—secret ingredients," said Miss Baby Marie. "My cosmetics have secret ingredients—not chinaberry flowers."

"It's purple," Livvie breathed, and Miss Baby Marie said, "Use it freely. Rub it on."

Livvie tiptoed out to the wash stand on the front porch and before the mirror put the paint on her mouth. In the wavery surface her face danced before her like a flame. Miss Baby Marie followed her out, took a look at what she had done, and said, "That's it."

Livvie tried to say "Thank you" without moving her parted lips where the paint lay so new.

By now Miss Baby Marie stood behind Livvie and looked in the mirror over her shoulder, twisting up the tassels of her hair. "The lipstick I can let you have for only two dollars," she said, close to her neck.

"Lady, but I don't have no money, never did have," said Livvie.

"Oh, but you don't pay the first time. I make another trip, that's the way I do. I come back again—later."

"Oh," said Livvie, pretending she understood everything so as to please the lady.

"But if you don't take it now, this may be the last time I'll call at your house," said Miss Baby Marie sharply. "It's far away from anywhere, I'll tell you that. You don't live close to anywhere."

"Yes'm. My husband, he keep the *money*," said Livvie, trembling. "He is strict as he can be. He don't know *you* walk in here—Miss Baby Marie!"

"Where is he?"

"Right now, he in yonder sound asleep, an old man. I wouldn't ever ask him for anything."

Miss Baby Marie took back the lipstick and packed it up. She gathered up the jars for both black and white and got them all inside the suitcase, with the same little fuss of triumph with which she had brought them out. She started away.

"Goodbye," she said, making herself look grand from the back, but at the last minute she turned around in the door. Her old hat wobbled as she whispered, "Let me see your husband."

Livvie obediently went on tiptoe and opened the door to the other room. Miss Baby Marie came behind her and rose on her toes and looked in.

"My, what a little tiny old, old man!" she whispered, clasping her hands and shaking her head over them. "What a beautiful quilt! What a tiny old, old man!"

"He can sleep like that all day," whispered Livvie proudly.

They looked at him awhile so fast asleep, and then all at once they looked at each other. Somehow that was as if they had a secret, for he had never stirred. Livvie then politely, but all at once, closed the door.

"Well! I'd certainly like to leave you with a lipstick!" said Miss Baby Marie vivaciously. She smiled in the door.

"Lady, but I told you I don't have no money, and never did have."

"And never will?" In the air and all around, like a bright halo around the white lady's nodding head, it was a true spring day.

"Would you take eggs, lady?" asked Livvie softly.

"No, I have plenty of eggs—plenty," said Miss Baby Marie.

"I still don't have no money," said Livvie, and Miss Baby Marie took her suitcase and went on somewhere else.

Livvie stood watching her go, and all the time she felt her heart beating in her left side. She touched the place with her hand. It seemed as if her heart beat and her whole face flamed from the pulsing color of her lips. She went to sit by Solomon and when he opened his eyes he could not see a change in her. "He's fixin' to die," she said inside. That was the secret. That was when she went out of the house for a little breath of air.

She went down the path and down the Natchez Trace a way, and she did not know how far she had gone, but it was not far, when she saw a sight. It was a man, looking like a vision—she standing on one side of the Old Natchez Trace and he standing on the other.

As soon as this man caught sight of her, he began to look himself over. Starting at the bottom with his pointed shoes, he began to look up, lifting his peg-top pants the higher to see fully his bright socks. His coat long and wide and leafgreen he opened like doors to see his high-up tawny pants and his pants he smoothed downward from the points of his collar, and he wore a luminous baby-pink satin shirt. At the end, he reached gently above his wide platter-shaped round hat, the color of a plum, and one finger touched at the feather, emerald green, blowing in the spring winds.

No matter how she looked, she could never look so fine as he did, and she was not sorry for that, she was pleased.

He took three jumps, one down and two up, and was by her side.

"My name is Cash," he said.

He had a guinea pig in his pocket. They began to walk along. She stared on and on at him, as if he were doing some daring spectacular thing, instead of just walking beside her. It was not simply the city way he was dressed that made her look at him and see hope in its insolence looking back. It was not only the way he moved along kicking the flowers as if he could break through everything in the way and destroy anything in the world, that made her eyes grow bright. It might be, if he had not appeared the way he did appear that day she would never have looked so closely at him, but the time people come makes a difference.

They walked through the still leaves of the Natchez Trace, the light and the shade falling through trees about them, the white irises shining like candles on the banks and the new ferns shining like green stars up in the oak branches. They came out at Solomon's house, bottle trees and all. Livvie stopped and hung her head.

Cash began whistling a little tune. She did not know what it was, but she had heard it before from a distance, and she had a revelation. Cash was a field hand. He was a transformed field hand. Cash belonged to Solomon. But he had stepped out of his overalls into this. There in front of Solomon's house he laughed. He had a round head, a round face, all of him was young, and he flung his head up, rolled it against the mare's-tail sky in his round hat, and he could laugh just to see Solomon's house sitting there. Livvie looked at it, and there was Solomon's black hat hanging on the peg on the front door, the blackest thing in the world.

"I been to Natchez," Cash said, wagging his head around against the sky. "*I* taken a trip, *I* ready for Easter!"

How was it possible to look so fine before the harvest? Cash must have stolen the money, stolen it from Solomon. He stood in the path and lifted his spread hand high and brought it down again and again in his laughter. He kicked up his heels. A little chill went through her. It was as if Cash was bringing that strong hand down to beat a drum or to rain blows upon a man, such an abandon and menace were in his laugh. Frowning, she went closer to him and his swinging arm drew her in at once and the fright was crushed from her body, as a little match-flame might be smothered out by what it lighted. She gathered the folds of his coat behind him and fastened her red lips to his mouth, and she was dazzled by herself then, the way he had been dazzled at himself to begin with.

In that instant she felt something that could not be told—that Solomon's death was at hand, that he was the same to her as if he were dead now. She cried out, and uttering little cries turned and ran for the house.

At once Cash was coming, following after, he was running behind her. He came close, and halfway up the path he laughed and passed her. He even picked up a stone and sailed it into the bottle trees. She put her hands over her head, and sounds clattered through the bottle trees like cries of outrage. Cash stamped and plunged zigzag up the front steps and in at the door.

When she got there, he had stuck his hands in his pockets and was turning slowing about in the front room. The little guinea pig peeped out. Around Cash, the pinned-up palmettos looked as if a lazy green monkey had walked up and down and around the walls leaving green prints of his hands and feet.

She got through the room and his hands were still in his pockets, and

she fell upon the closed door to the other room and pushed it open. She ran
to Solomon's bed, calling, "Solomon! Solomon!" The little shape of the old
man never moved at all, wrapped under the quilt as if it were winter still.

"Solomon!" She pulled the quilt away, but there was another one under that, and she fell on her knees beside him. He made no sound except a
sigh, and then she could hear in the silence the light springy steps of Cash
walking and walking in the front room, and the ticking of Solomon's silver
watch, which came from the bed. Old Solomon was far away in his sleep,
his face looked small, relentless, and devout, as if he were walking somewhere where she could imagine the snow falling.

Then there was a noise like a hoof pawing the floor, and the door gave
a creak, and Cash appeared beside her. When she looked up, Cash's face
was so black it was bright, and so bright and bare of pity that it looked
sweet to her. She stood up and held up her head. Cash was so powerful that
his presence gave her strength even when she did not need any.

Under their eyes Solomon slept. People's faces tell of things and places
not known to the one who looks at them while they sleep, and while Solomon slept under the eyes of Livvie and Cash his face told them like a
mythical story that all his life he had built, little scrap by little scrap, respect. A beetle could not have been more laborious or more ingenious in
the task of its destiny. When Solomon was young, as he was in his picture
overhead, it was the infinite thing with him, and he could see no end to the
respect he would contrive and keep in a house. He had built a lonely house,
the way he would make a cage, but it grew to be the same with him as a
great monumental pyramid and sometimes in his absorption of getting it
erected he was like the builder-slaves of Egypt who forgot or never knew
the origin and meaning of the thing to which they gave all the strength of
their bodies and used up all their days. Livvie and Cash could see that as a
man might rest from a life-labor he lay in his bed, and they could hear how,
wrapped in his quilt, he sighed to himself comfortably in sleep, while in his
dreams he might have been an ant, a beetle, a bird, an Egyptian, assembling
and carrying on his back and building with his hands, or he might have
been an old man of India or a swaddled baby, about to smile and brush all
away.

Then without warning old Solomon's eyes flew wide open under the
hedge-like brows. He was wide awake.

And instantly Cash raised his quick arm. A radiant sweat stood on his
temples. But he did not bring his arm down—it stayed in the air, as if
something might have taken hold.

It was not Livvie—she did not move. As if something said "Wait," she
stood waiting. Even while her eyes burned under motionless lids, her lips
parted in a stiff grimace, and with her arms stiff at her sides she stood above
the prone old man and the panting young one, erect and apart.

Movement when it came came in Solomon's face. It was an old and

strict face, a frail face, but behind it, like a covered light, came an anima-
tion that could play hide and seek, that would dart and escape, had always
escaped. The mystery flickered in him, and invited from his eyes. It was
that very mystery that Cash with his quick arm would have to strike, and
that Livvie could not weep for. But Cash only stood holding his arm in the
air, when the gentlest flick of his great strength, almost a puff of his breath,
would have been enough, if he had known how to give it, to send the old
man over the obstruction that kept him away from death.

If it could not be that the tiny illumination in the fragile and ancient
face caused a crisis, a mystery in the room that would not permit a blow to
fall, at least it was certain that Cash, throbbing in his Easter clothes, felt a
pang of shame that the vigor of a man would come to such an end that he
could not be struck without warning. He took down his hand and stepped
back behind Livvie, like a round-eyed schoolboy on whose unsuspecting
head the dunce cap has been set.

"Young ones can't wait," said Solomon.

Livvie shuddered violently, and then in a gush of tears she stooped for
a glass of water and handed it to him, but he did not see her.

"So here come the young man Livvie wait for. Was no prevention. No
prevention. Now I lay eyes on young man and it come to be somebody I
know all the time, and been knowing since he were born in a cotton patch,
and watched grow up year to year, Cash McCord, growed to size, growed
up to come in my house in the end—ragged and barefoot."

Solomon gave a cough of distaste. Then he shut his eyes vigorously,
and his lips began to move like a chanter's.

"When Livvie married, her husband were already somebody. He had
paid great cost for his land. He spread sycamore leaves over the ground
from wagon to door, day he brought her home, so her foot would not have
to touch ground. He carried her through his door. Then he growed old and
could not lift her, and she were still young."

Livvie's sobs followed his words like a soft melody repeating each
thing as he stated it. His lips moved for a little without sound, or she cried
too fervently, and unheard he might have been telling his whole life, and
then he said, "God forgive Solomon for sins great and small. God forgive
Solomon for carrying away too young girl for wife and keeping her away
from her people and from all the young people would clamor for her back."

Then he lifted up his right hand toward Livvie where she stood by the
bed and offered her his silver watch. He dangled it before her eyes, and she
hushed crying; her tears stopped. For a moment the watch could be heard
ticking as it always did, precisely in his proud hand. She lifted it away. Then
he took hold of the quilt; then he was dead.

Livvie left Solomon dead and went out of the room. Stealthily, nearly without noise, Cash went beside her. He was like a shadow, but his shiny shoes moved over the floor in spangles, and the green downy feather shone like a light in his hat. As they reached the front room, he seized her deftly as a long black cat and dragged her hanging by the waist round and round him, while he turned in a circle, his face bent down to hers. The first moment, she kept one arm and its hand stiff and still, the one that held Solomon's watch. Then the fingers softly let go, all of her was limp, and the watch fell somewhere on the floor. It ticked away in the still room, and all at once there began outside the full song of a bird.

They moved around and around the room and into the brightness of the open door, then he stopped and shook her once. She rested in silence in his trembling arms, unprotesting as a bird on a nest. Outside the redbirds were flying and crisscrossing, the sun was in all the bottles on the prisoned trees, and the young peach was shining in the middle of them with the bursting light of spring.

*Walter Van Tilburg Clark (1909–1971) was the son
of a university president; concomitant with his first
years as a writer, Clark taught in high schools. He
was the dramatics teacher and basketball coach at
Cazenovia, New York; an avid interest in sports remained a lifelong hobby. Although possibly not the
first written, his first published novel,* The Ox-Bow
Incident *(1940), remains his best longer work and in
an incisive, exciting way treats the consequences of
mob violence in the American West in the days of
law by the gun; many readers also saw in the novel—
which became a notable film—a parable of the rise
of the tyrants in Europe in the thirties. Suggestion
for further reading:* The Watchful Gods and Other
Stories *(1950).*

WALTER VAN TILBURG CLARK

The Rapids

Where the unpaved road curved over the top of the hill and descended
to the river, a man appeared, walking by himself. He was thin, and wore
spectacles, and his legs, when they showed through the flapping wings of his
red and blue dressing gown, were very white. He carried a towel in one
hand. Walking carefully, for his slippers were thin, he came down between
the fir trees, then between the alders and the willows, and stood at the edge
of the river.

Four terraces of red rock lay diagonally across the river at this point,
but they were tilted away from him, so that the heavy water gushed all on
the farther side, and narrowed until, from the lowest ledge, it jetted forth in
a single head, making a big, back-bellying bubble rimmed with foam in the
pool below. Closer to him, eddies from the main stream came over the
terraces at intervals, making thin, transparent falls a foot or two high.
Swarms of midget flies danced against these falls, keeping just free of the
almost invisible mist which blew from them.

Climbing cautiously from the bank to the rocks, the man walked out
onto the second terrace, which was the broadest, and had a gentle incline.
He bent over and felt of the rock. It was warm with sun. He took off his

450

dressing gown and sat down. Then he fished in the pocket of the gown, drew out a piece of soap, and put it beside the towel. Finally he pulled off his slippers and placed them on the edge of the towel, to hold it down if the wind blew. After this preparation, he sat with his arms around his knees and stared at the running water.

The sun felt good on his back. He wondered if he dared to remove his shorts, but the bridge from his road lay across the river close above him, so he decided not to. Also there was a building on the opposite bank at the point where the river jumped out into the pool. There were only two and a half walls of the building standing, and the windows had been out of those for a long time. Vines grew over the gray-tan stones and into the windows, and nothing was left of the roof. Still, it was a building, four stories high. So he kept on his shorts and sat in the sun and looked at the building, remembering the bit of its history he had heard. It had been a mill, way back toward the days of the Revolution. Since then this part of the country had failed. There were only small, poor farms in it now, and the remnants of villages. It gave him a queer feeling to look through the empty windows and see trees growing inside, and the steep, green bank behind them. The ruin was old for America. He was used to seeing empty mills that weren't ten years old. This one went a long way back.

After a time the draft in the river canyon felt chilly in spite of the sun. The man removed his spectacles with both hands, placed them on his dressing gown, picked up the cake of soap, and approached the nearest of the little falls. Standing beside it, with his feet in the shallow basin of turning water, he shivered before the breath of the river. Timidly he began to wash, laving his forearms and the back of his neck, determinedly splashing a palmful of water over his white chest and belly. Encouraged, he wet himself all over and rubbed on the soap vigorously, ducking his head into the fall and then working up a great lather on it, like a shining white wig. When he was well soaped, he couldn't open his eyes. Feeling for the rim of the fall, he moved gingerly, for the basin was slimy. Having come close enough, he squatted under the fall and let it drive the soap down from him until he could open his eyes and see the iridescent trail of the soap, like an oil mark, draining away from him down the gutter of rock. All of this time he moved his arms as much as he dared, because the water was cold.

Back out in the sun, he realized that he would have to do more. He had been too cramped in the basin, and much of his body was still greasy with soap. He walked carefully down the terrace toward the pool, gripping the stone with his toes, for his wet feet were uncertain. They left a trail of increasingly perfect tracks from the small puddle where he had stood beside his dressing gown to the last print at the edge of the terrace, which showed each toe faintly but distinctly, and the ball, the arch, and the heel—clearly a man's foot.

After hesitating, he let himself down over the edge until the cool water was about his shins. Then he stood on slimy stone like that in the basin. On all fours, he moved slowly, crabwise, along this submerged ledge, and slid off into deeper water. This was at the center of the pool, and the water was quiet, moved only by a side flow circling the pool from the falls, and occasionally by a light wind-ripple along the surface. Awkwardly, and with some splashing, he rubbed himself under water until the last slickness of soap was gone and his hands adhered to his thighs. Then he paddled aimlessly in the pool for a few minutes, treading water and observing himself below. His arms and legs appeared dwarfed and misshapen, his hands and feet immense and square. All of him that was under water looked yellow, and was hairy with particles of the slime he had stirred getting in. Altogether, he was a much more powerful and formidable man, seen through the glass of the pool. He began to feel adventurous.

He noticed that the green darkness of the pool paled on the side across from the ledges. A sub-aqueous, changeable gold was visible there under the black surface reflection of the forest on the hill. He paddled toward it, keeping his head above water and feeling before him with his hands. When he came to rest, balanced on his hands, he was on a sunken sand-bar—the dam which made the pool. The sand was coarse and white, and felt clean to his touch after the scum in the basin and on the ledge. Letting his feet down, he planted them firmly and walked up the incline of the sand-bar, feeling himself emerge into gusty air. At last he was on top, the water ankle-deep. Looking down from this eminence, he saw a boat farther along the ridge of the bar. It lay bottom up, and was so water-logged that it had ground into the sand until no part of it but the very center of the bottom was above water. Now and then a wind-ripple passed over even that.

The man was excited by the discovery. He waded to the boat and attempted to turn it right side up. The vacuum under it, or simply its weight, held it solidly. He was angered, and put forth all his thin might in repeated efforts, standing upright between tries, to breathe deeply and let the blood subside from his head. To the best of his efforts the boat rocked, and straining, he raised the gunwale as far as his knee. This encouraged him, but when he lifted again, the boat came no higher, and then remained passively immovable. He had to let it fall back into the water, where it rolled lightly, splashing around its shape like a stubborn live thing, run aground, but insisting upon its element. The man's feet had been driven down into the sand until he could not lift well from his position. Freeing himself, he climbed onto the crest of the bar again and stood with his legs apart, glaring at the boat. He considered leaving it and relinquishing himself to placid floating in the pool, whence he could eye the useless boat disdainfully. But when the blood in his temples ceased pounding, he had a cunning thought. Moving down into the water until he was on the outer side of the boat, he slid it backwards off the bar. Once it floated free, he could get his shoulder under it. This strategem succeeded. The boat rolled bulkily over, sending out a wave which broke on the sand-bar.

"That fixes you," the man said aloud.

However, the water in the boat was level with the water in the pool. Only a portion of the prow and of the square stern protruded. The man found that tilting the boat let in as much water as it let out. He laid hold of a chain at the prow and drew the boat onto the crest of the bar. It followed him with lumbering unwillingness. On the bar, a great deal more of it stood above water, and by teetering it fore and aft, he drove several belches of water out over the stern. Still the boat would not rise. The man climbed into it and began to scoop with both hands. The water flew in silver sheets, spread into silver drops, and splattered on the pool, but more of it fell through his hands than went overboard. He stood up and looked around. On a flat rock at the west edge of the pool, there sat a shining two-quart tin can. He clambered out of the boat, went down into the water, paddled industriously across, hoisted himself up the irregular rock steps, and procured the can.

Shortly he had all but an inch or two of water out of the boat. That persisted because of three little leaks, through which he could see minute streams gliding steadily in. He pushed the boat, with the can in it, off the sand-bar, and kicking noisily, propelled it to shore. Here he pulled grass and made small wads of it, with the heads standing up in tufts. These plugged the leaks quite effectively, and the man began to hum to himself while he bailed out the last water.

The boat, clumsy and flat-bottomed, with two bowed planks forming each side, had been battered down-stream in the flood of the spring rains. Much of the orange paint had been beaten from it, and the single thwart had been torn out, leaving four rusty nails projecting from each scar. The man searched out a squarish stone and hammered the nails down, humming more loudly. He was formulating a daring plan. He would work the boat around in front of the falls, where the big bubble bellied, and see how far he could go down the stony rapids below the pool. A man taking a risk like that couldn't have nails sticking out where they'd rake his legs if he had to move quickly.

At last he drifted on the pool, keeping the can with him. "Quite a boat," he maintained in a clear voice, and then, argumentatively, but with satisfaction, "I say it's quite a boat."

The boat, dull with the water it had soaked up, rode low and heavily. It refused to be coerced by hand paddling, and cruised, half sidewards, out into the middle of the pool, where it spun slowly three times in the circular current and then headed—or rather tailed—for the stagnant backwash between the shore boulders and the terrace of red rock. The man ceased humming and paddled frantically with his hands, first on one side and then on the other, for the boat was too wide for him to reach water on both sides at once. The boat turned completely around once more, and continued to back toward the extremely green scum in the crevice. The man abandoned himself, held onto the sides, and rode in backwards, muttering. The boat bumped gently, grated along the stone, stirred sinuously, and succeeded in wedging itself. The man sat and observed the pond scum with aversion.

Then he saw a long bamboo pole caught under a ledge. His spirits rose. The pole was within reach, and by bruising his knees a little, slithering on the wet mossiness of the boat, he grasped it. It was heavy, and rotten from enduring the river and from its long hiding in the pool, but having it, he felt confident again. "You'll do," he told the pole. He stood erect, and brandished it in both hands, like a cudgel. "Swell pole." He pressed it firmly against the holding rock, and leaned on it. The boat gave way and swam sluggishly out through the scum. The man, still standing, was immensely elated. "And now, Mr. Boat," he cried.

Maintaining his heroic erectness, he jabbed at rocks along the side and bottom, and brought the boat circuituously toward the back-rolling bubble. As he poled, he hummed grandly, even venturing some open-mouthed tra-las. Approaching the bubble more closely, he became quiet and knelt, preparatory to sitting. In this position, he watched the waterfall steadily. Coming very close, he was suddenly alarmed by the rapid streaming-away of the foam towards the rocks where the water jumped at a hundred points and turned white, like a miniature surf in a crossrip. He made a spasmodic thrust with the pole. The boat swung sedately around, slid its stern directly under the fall, lifted its snout, and sank backwards. The man clung amazed until the water was under his chin, and then, with a shout, let go and struck out wildly to avoid the rise of the boat.

He continued to swim, growing calmer, until he bumped on the sand-bar and could stand up in the water. Thence he saw his boat lodged against a rock below the bar, the waters protesting around it. The sight enraged him. He remained angry until he had secured the boat, bailed it out, recovered his pole, and returned round the edge of the pool to the fall. Then he swore at the fall to keep his temper up, and this time managed to enter the current just below the bubble. He sat down quickly, nervous because of the speed he expected, believing all at once that his pole was useless. But the boat was too water-logged. Slow and stately it turned upon the stream, let the anxious waters divide about it, coasted past the sand-bar, knocked gently from one rock to another at the head of the shallow rapids, and came to rest between two of them. The man relaxed and took his hands from the sides. "Well," he said, "Well, well."

Thereafter he became pink over his whole body from the exertion of dragging his boat back to the pool. He scraped his feet among the stones of the river bed and never noticed. He took three more rides, going a little farther each time, as he became acquainted with the most prominent rocks. He was so confident on the fifth ride that during the burdensome start he sat with his pole in his hands and regarded the world before him.

In the canyon below the rapids, where the rocky shores grew into cliffs with dense cedar and spruce forests above them, was a splendid curve which hid the lower river. Over the cliff and the forest, a great rounded thunderhead swelled voluminously out of the west and darkened the trees. It appeared to fill the sky, and its upper bosses were bright with sun. The man felt this cloud to be a recognition of the dimension of his undertaking, and gazed at it with stern exultation.

In the late afternoon a woman came over the hill on the road. When she first appeared, irritation was in her walk. The clouds had spread far east and were no longer gilded. The wind kept blowing her hair.

Part way down, she stopped, and stood with her hands on her hips. "For goodness sake," she exclaimed. "For goodness sake, what does that man think he's doing?" She stared. "And yelling his head off like a lunatic," she exclaimed.

The man was just launching out from the jade-colored, white-streaked, back-bellying bubble. He was standing upright in the orange boat, the bamboo pole held aloft like a spear. As he gravitated toward the rapids, his mouth could be seen to open tremendously and repeatedly. He waved his left arm in accompaniment. Faintly, even over the wind and the rush of the falls, the woman could hear the words. "Sailing, sailing," roared the man in the boat. He shook his spear. "Sailing, sailing," he roared, until the boat stumbled and knocked him to his knees. Even then his mouth opened and closed in the same way. Only when the boat stalled, with a white fan of water behind it, did he close his mouth. Then he scrambled out, grabbed the chain on the prow, and dragged, tugged and jerked the boat up the slope of rock and froth.

When the boat was in the pool again, he commenced at once to climb into it and to work his mouth. "Sailing, sailing," he bellowed.

The woman said, "Gracious heavens, he's absolutely crazy," and recovered herself. She advanced to the edge of the rock and yelled at the man. He was then half-way over the stern and kicking valiantly. The woman yelled, "John!" She leaned forward and stuck her chin out when she yelled. The man lay perfectly still for an instant, half-way over the stern. Then he slid back into the water and held onto the stern with one hand. He looked across at the woman. "Yes?" he asked.

The woman could see his mouth move. She looked angry but relieved, and eased her voice a little. "D. L. called you," she cried. "He wants you back in town."

"Bother D. L.," the man said to himself.

"What's that you said?" cried the woman.

"I said all right," the man yelled suddenly.

The woman put one hand on her hip. "He called hours ago. He'll be wild."

The man let go of the boat reluctantly and paddled across to the terrace. The woman stood where she was, waiting. The man drew himself out of the water slowly, with great care for his battered toes. Crabwise he ascended the slimy, submerged rock and crawled up onto the red rock in the wind. Cautiously he walked across the red rock to the spot where he had left his things. His tracks grew more distinct as he went.

"For goodness sake, get a move on," the woman called up at him.

His thin, unmuscular body was turning blue in the wind. Bending stiffly, he removed his slippers from the towel, straightened up, and began to wipe himself. He sat down to wipe his feet, and was tender of his toes. He put his spectacles on, using both hands. Then he stood up and donned the red and blue dressing gown and the leather slippers. He wobbled on one leg at a time while putting on his slippers, and screwed his face up while each rubbed over his toes. He searched a moment for the cake of soap. When he found it, he put it in his pocket and, carrying his towel in one hand, descended carefully to where the woman was waiting.

"What on earth were you doing out there?" she asked. But having seen what he was doing, she went on. "D. L. called up hours ago. How on earth did I know I'd have to come way down here after you? How could I know you'd be . . ."

They went on up the road.

"Well, I'm sure I don't know what you were doing," said the woman. "You're so cold your teeth are chattering."

The man was avoiding sharp pebbles in the road, and said nothing. His peeled knees worked in and out of the opening of the dressing gown, which occasionally fled out behind him on the wind.

"How would I know you'd take all afternoon?" asked the woman sharply. "D. L. will be wild. And all because—well, what on earth *were* you doing out there?"

"Oh, I don't know," said the man. "I found an old boat."

The woman was unpleasantly silent.

"I was just fooling around with an old boat," the man explained, and again, "That's all I was doing, just fooling around with an old boat I found."

The wind on top of the hill was unexpectedly sustained. The woman, holding down her hair with both hands, made no reply. The man had to clutch at his dressing gown tightly, to keep it from streaming out and leaving him uncovered.

BERNARD MALAMUD

The Jewbird

The window was open so the skinny bird flew in. Flippity-flap with its frazzled black wings. That's how it goes. It's open, you're in. Closed, you're out and that's your fate. The bird wearily flapped through the open kitchen window by Harry Cohen's top-floor apartment on First Avenue near the lower East River. On a rod on the wall hung an escaped canary cage, its door wide open, but this blacktype longbeaked bird—its ruffled head and small dull eyes, crossed a little, making it look like a dissipated crow— landed if not smack on Cohen's thick lamb chop, at least on the table, close by. The frozen foods salesman was sitting at supper with his wife and young son on a hot August evening a year ago. Cohen, a heavy man with hairy chest and beefy shorts; Edie, in skinny yellow shorts and red halter; and their ten-year-old Morris (after her father)—Maurie, they called him, a nice kid though not overly bright—were all in the city after two weeks out, because Cohen's mother was dying. They had been enjoying Kingston, New York, but drove back when Mama got sick in her flat in the Bronx.

"Right on the table," said Cohen, putting down his beer glass and swatting at the bird. "Son of a bitch."

457

"Harry, take care with your language," Edie said, looking at Maurie, who watched every move.

The bird cawed hoarsely and with a flap of its bedraggled wings—feathers tufted this way and that—rose heavily to the top of the open kitchen door, where it perched staring down.

"Gevalt, a pogrom!"

"It's a talking bird," said Edie in astonishment.

"In Jewish," said Maurie.

"Wise guy," muttered Cohen. He gnawed on his chop, then put down the bone. "So if you can talk, say what's your business. What do you want here?"

"If you can't spare a lamb chop," said the bird, "I'll settle for a piece of herring with a crust of bread. You can't live on your nerve forever."

"This ain't a restaurant," Cohen replied. "All I'm asking is what brings you to this address?"

"The window was open," the bird sighed; adding after a moment, "I'm running. I'm flying but I'm also running."

"From whom?" asked Edie with interest.

'Anti-Semeets."

"Anti-Semites?" they all said.

"That's from who."

"What kind of anti-Semites bother a bird?" Edie asked.

"Any kind," said the bird, "also including eagles, vultures, and hawks. And once in a while some crows will take your eyes out."

"But aren't you a crow?"

"Me? I'm a Jewbird."

Cohen laughed heartily. "What do you mean by that?"

The bird began dovening. He prayed without Book or tallith, but with passion. Edie bowed her head though not Cohen. And Maurie rocked back and forth with the prayer, looking up with one wide-open eye.

When the prayer was done Cohen remarked, "No hat, no phylacteries?"

"I'm an old radical."

"You're sure you're not some kind of a ghost or dybbuk?"

"Not a dybbuk," answered the bird, "though one of my relatives had such an experience once. It's all over now, thanks God. They freed her from a former lover, a crazy jealous man. She's now the mother of two wonderful children."

"Birds?" Cohen asked slyly.

"Why not?"

"What kind of birds?"

"Like me. Jewbirds."

Cohen tipped back in his chair and guffawed. "That's a big laugh. I've heard of a Jewfish but not a Jewbird."

"We're once removed." The bird rested on one skinny leg, then on the other. "Please, could you spare maybe a piece of herring with a small crust of bread?"

Edie got up from the table.

"What are you doing?" Cohen asked her.

"I'll clear the dishes."

Cohen turned to the bird. "So what's your name, if you don't mind saying?"

"Call me Schwartz."

"He might be an old Jew changed into a bird by somebody," said Edie, removing a plate.

"Are you?" asked Harry, lighting a cigar.

"Who knows?" answered Schwartz. "Does God tell us everything?"

Maurie got up on his chair. "What kind of herring?" he asked the bird in excitement.

"Get down, Maurie, or you'll fall," ordered Cohen.

"If you haven't got matjes, I'll take schmaltz," said Schwartz.

"All we have is marinated, with slices of onion—in a jar," said Edie.

"If you'll open for me the jar I'll eat marinated. Do you have also, if you don't mind, a piece of rye bread—the spitz?"

Edie thought she had.

"Feed him out on the balcony," Cohen said. He spoke to the bird. "After that take off."

Schwartz closed both bird eyes. "I'm tired and it's a long way."

"Which direction are you headed, north or south?"

Schwartz, barely lifting his wings, shrugged.

"You don't know where you're going?"

"Where there's charity I'll go."

"Let him stay, papa," said Maurie. "He's only a bird."

"So stay the night," Cohen said, "but no longer."

In the morning Cohen ordered the bird out of the house but Maurie cried, so Schwartz stayed for a while. Maurie was still on vacation from school and his friends were away. He was lonely and Edie enjoyed the fun he had, playing with the bird.

"He's no trouble at all," she told Cohen, "and besides his appetite is very small."

"What'll you do when he makes dirty?"

"He flies across the street in a tree when he makes dirty, and if nobody passes below, who notices?"

"So all right," said Cohen, "but I'm dead set against it. I warn you he ain't gonna stay here long."

"What have you got against the poor bird?"

"Poor bird, my ass. He's a foxy bastard. He thinks he's a Jew."

"What difference does it make what he thinks?"

"A Jewbird, what a chuzpah. One false move and he's out on his drumsticks."

At Cohen's insistence Schwartz lived out on the balcony in a new wooden birdhouse Edie had bought him.

"With many thanks," said Schwartz, "though I would rather have a human roof over my head. You know how it is at my age. I like the warm, the windows, the smell of cooking. I would also be glad to see once in a while the *Jewish Morning Journal* and have now and then a schnapps because it helps my breathing, thanks God. But whatever you give me, you won't hear complaints."

However, when Cohen brought home a bird feeder full of dried corn, Schwartz said, "Impossible."

Cohen was annoyed. "What's the matter, crosseyes, is your life getting too good for you? Are you forgetting what it means to be migratory? I'll bet a helluva lot of crows you happen to be acquainted with, Jews or otherwise, would give their eyeteeth to eat this corn."

Schwartz did not answer. What can you say to a grubber yung?

"Not for my digestion," he later explained to Edie. "Cramps. Herring is better even if it makes you thirsty. At least rainwater don't cost anything." He laughed sadly in breathy caws.

And herring, thanks to Edie, who knew where to shop, was what Schwartz got, with an occasional piece of potato pancake, and even a bit of soupmeat when Cohen wasn't looking.

When school began in September, before Cohen would once again suggest giving the bird the boot, Edie prevailed on him to wait a little while until Maurie adjusted.

"To deprive him right now might hurt his school work and you know what trouble we had last year."

"So okay, but sooner or later the bird goes. That I promise you."

Schwartz, though nobody had asked him, took on full responsibility for Maurie's performance in school. In return for favors granted, when he was let in for an hour or two at night, he spent most of his time overseeing the boy's lessons. He sat on top of the dresser near Maurie's desk as he laboriously wrote out his homework. Maurie was a restless type and Schwartz gently kept him to his studies. He also listened to him practice his screechy violin, taking a few minutes off now and then to rest his ears in the bathroom. And they afterwards played dominoes. The boy was an indifferent checker player and it was impossible to teach him chess. When he was sick, Schwartz read him comic books though he personally disliked them. But Maurie's work improved in school and even his violin teacher admitted his playing was better. Edie gave Schwartz credit for these improvements though the bird pooh-poohed them.

Yet he was proud there was nothing lower than C minuses on Maurie's report card, and on Edie's insistence celebrated with a little schnapps.

"If he keeps up like this," Cohen said, "I'll get him in an Ivy League college for sure."

"Oh I hope so," sighed Edie.

But Schwartz shook his head. "He's a good boy—you don't have to worry. He won't be a shicker or a wifebeater, God forbid, but a scholar he'll never be, if you know what I mean, although maybe a good mechanic. It's no disgrace in these times."

"If I were you," Cohen said, angered, "I'd keep my big snoot out of other people's private business."

"Harry, please," said Edie.

"My goddamn patience is wearing out. That crosseyes butts into everything."

Though he wasn't exactly a welcome guest in the house, Schwartz gained a few ounces although he did not improve in appearance. He looked bedraggled as ever, his feathers unkempt, as though he had just flown out of a snowstorm. He spent, he admitted, little time taking care of himself. Too much to think about. "Also outside plumbing," he told Edie. Still there was more glow to his eyes so that though Cohen went on calling him crosseyes he said it less emphatically.

Liking his situation, Schwartz tried tactfully to stay out of Cohen's way, but one night when Edie was at the movies and Maurie was taking a hot shower, the frozen foods salesman began a quarrel with the bird.

"For Christ sake, why don't you wash yourself sometimes? Why must you always stink like a dead fish?"

"Mr. Cohen, if you'll pardon me, if somebody eats garlic he will smell from garlic. I eat herring three times a day. Feed me flowers and I will smell like flowers."

"Who's obligated to feed you anything at all? You're lucky to get herring."

"Excuse me, I'm not complaining," said the bird. "You're complaining."

"What's more," said Cohen, "even from out on the balcony I can hear you snoring away like a pig. It keeps me awake at night."

"Snoring," said Schwartz, "isn't a crime, thanks God."

"All in all you are a goddamn pest and free loader. Next thing you'll want to sleep in bed next to my wife."

"Mr. Cohen," said Schwartz, "on this rest assured. A bird is a bird."

"So you say, but how do I know you're a bird and not some kind of a goddamn devil?"

"If I was a devil you would know already. And I don't mean because your son's good marks."

"Shut up, you bastard bird," shouted Cohen.

"Grubber yung," cawed Schwartz, rising to the tips of his talons, his long wings outstretched.

Cohen was about to lunge for the bird's scrawny neck but Maurie came out of the bathroom, and for the rest of the evening until Schwartz's bedtime on the balcony, there was pretended peace.

But the quarrel had deeply disturbed Schwartz and he slept badly. His snoring woke him, and awake, he was fearful of what would become of him. Wanting to stay out of Cohen's way, he kept to the birdhouse as much as possible. Cramped by it, he paced back and forth on the balcony ledge, or sat on the birdhouse roof, staring into space. In the evenings, while over-seeing Maurie's lessons, he often fell alseep. Awakening, he nervously hop-ped around exploring the four corners of the room. He spent much time in Maurie's closet, and carefully examined his bureau drawers when they were left open. And once when he found a large paper bag on the floor, Schwartz poked his way into it to investigate what possibilities were. The boy was amused to see the bird in the paper bag.

"He wants to build a nest," he said to his mother.

Edie, sensing Schwartz's unhappiness, spoke to him quietly.

"Maybe if you did some of the things my husband wants you, you would get along better with him."

"Give me a for instance," Schwartz said.

"Like take a bath, for instance."

"I'm too old for baths," said the bird. "My feathers fall out without baths."

"He says you have a bad smell."

"Everybody smells. Some people smell because of their thoughts or because who they are. My bad smell comes from the food I eat. What does his come from?"

"I better not ask him or it might make him mad," said Edie.

In late November Schwartz froze on the balcony in the fog and cold, and especially on rainy days he woke with stiff joints and could barely move his wings. Already he felt twinges of rheumatism. He would have liked to spend more time in the warm house, particularly when Maurie was in school and Cohen at work. But though Edie was good-hearted and might have sneaked him in in the morning, just to thaw out, he was afraid to ask her. In the meantime Cohen, who had been reading articles about the mi-gration of birds, came out on the balcony one night after work when Edie was in the kitchen preparing pot roast, and peeking into the birdhouse, warned Schwartz to be on his way soon if he knew what was good for him. "Time to hit the flyways."

"Mr. Cohen, why do you hate me so much?" asked the bird. "What did I do to you?"

"Because you're an A-number-one trouble maker, that's why. What's more, whoever heard of a Jewbird? Now scat or it's open war."

But Schwartz stubbornly refused to depart so Cohen embarked on a campaign of harassing him, meanwhile hiding it from Edie and Maurie. Maurie hated violence and Cohen didn't want to leave a bad impression. He thought maybe if he played dirty tricks on the bird he would fly off without being physically kicked out. The vacation was over, let him make his easy living off the fat of somebody else's land. Cohen worried about the effect of the bird's departure on Maurie's schooling but decided to take the chance, first, because the boy now seemed to have the knack of studying— give the black bird-bastard credit—and second, because Schwartz was driving him bats by being there always, even in his dreams.

The frozen foods salesman began his campaign against the bird by mixing watery cat food with the herring slices in Schwartz's dish. He also blew up and popped numerous paper bags outside the birdhouse as the bird slept, and when he had got Schwartz good and nervous, though not enough to leave, he brought a full-grown cat into the house, supposedly a gift for little Maurie, who had always wanted a pussy. The cat never stopped springing up at Schwartz whenever he saw him, one day managing to claw out several of his tailfeathers. And even at lesson time, when the cat was usually excluded from Maurie's room, though somehow or other he quickly found his way in at the end of the lesson, Schwartz was desperately fearful of his life and flew from pinnacle to pinnacle—light fixture to clothestree to door-top—in order to elude the beast's wet jaws.

Once when the bird complained to Edie how hazardous his existence was, she said, "Be patient, Mr. Schwartz. When the cat gets to know you better he won't try to catch you any more."

"When he stops trying we will both be in Paradise," Schwartz answered. "Do me a favor and get rid of him. He makes my whole life worry. I'm losing feathers like a tree loses leaves."

"I'm awfully sorry but Maurie likes the pussy and sleeps with it."

What could Schwartz do? He worried but came to no decision, being afraid to leave. So he ate the herring garnished with cat food, tried hard not to hear the paper bags bursting like fire crackers outside the birdhouse at night, and lived terror-stricken closer to the ceiling than the floor, as the cat, his tail flicking, endlessly watched him.

Weeks went by. Then on the day after Cohen's mother had died in her flat in the Bronx, when Maurie came home with a zero on an arithmetic test, Cohen, enraged, waited until Edie had taken the boy to his violin lesson, then openly attacked the bird. He chased him with a broom on the balcony and Schwartz frantically flew back and forth, finally escaping into his birdhouse. Cohen triumphantly reached in and grabbing both skinny legs, dragged the bird out, cawing loudly, his wings wildly beating. He whirled the bird around and around his head. But Schwartz, as he moved in circles, managed to sweep down and catch Cohen's nose in his beak, and hung on for dear life. Cohen cried out in great pain, punched the bird with his fist, and tugged at its legs with all his might, pulled his nose free. Again he swung the yawking Schwartz around till the bird grew dizzy, then with a furious heave, flung him into the night. Schwartz sank like stone into the street. Cohen then tossed the birdhouse and feeder after him, listening at the ledge until they crashed on the sidewalk below. For a full hour, broom in hand, his heart palpitating and nose throbbing with pain, Cohen waited for Schwartz to return but the broken-hearted bird didn't.

That's the end of that dirty bastard, the salesman thought and went in. Edie and Maurie had come home.

"Look," said Cohen, pointing to his bloody nose swollen three times its normal size, "what that sonofabitchy bird did. It's a permanent scar."

"Where is he now?' Edie asked, frightened.

"I threw him out and he flew away. Good riddance."

Nobody said no, though Edie touched a handkerchief to her eyes and Maurie rapidly tried the nine times table and found he knew approximately half.

In the spring when the winter's snow had melted, the boy, moved by a memory, wandered in the neighborhood, looking for Schwartz. He found a dead black bird in a small lot near the river, his two wings broken, neck twisted, and both bird-eyes plucked clean.

"Who did it to you, Mr. Schwartz?" Maurie wept.

"Anti-Semeets," Edie said later.

ISAAC ASIMOV

All the Troubles of the World

*T*he greatest industry on Earth centered about Multivac—Multivac, the giant computer that had grown in fifty years until its various ramifications had filled Washington, D.C. to the suburbs and had reached out tendrils into every city and town on Earth.

An army of civil servants fed it data constantly and another army correlated and interpreted the answers it gave. A corps of engineers patrolled its interior while mines and factories consumed themselves in keeping its reserve stocks of replacement parts ever complete, ever accurate, ever satisfactory in every way.

Multivac directed Earth's economy and helped Earth's science. Most important of all, it was the central clearing house of all known facts about each individual Earthman.

And each day it was part of Multivac's duties to take the four billion sets of facts about individual human beings that filled its vitals and extrapolate them for an additional day of time. Every Corrections Department on Earth received the data appropriate to its own area of jurisdiction, and the over-all data was presented in one large piece to the Central Board of Corrections in Washington, D.C.

Bernard Gulliman was in the fourth week of his year term as Chairman of the Central Board of Corrections and had grown casual enough to accept the morning report without being frightened by it. As usual, it was a sheaf of papers some six inches thick. He knew by now, he was not expected to read it. (No human could.) Still, it was amusing to glance through it.

There was the usual list of predictable crimes: frauds of all sorts, larcenies, riots, manslaughters, arsons.

He looked for one particular heading and felt a slight shock at finding it there at all, then another one at seeing two entries. Not one, but two. *Two* first-degree murders. He had not seen two in one day in all his term as Chairman so far.

He punched the knob of the two-way intercom and waited for the smooth face of his co-ordinator to appear on the screen.

"Ali," said Gulliman. "There are two first-degrees this day. Is there any unusual problem?"

"No, sir." The dark-complexioned face with its sharp, black eyes seemed restless. "Both cases are quite low probability."

"I know that," said Gulliman. "I observed that neither probability is higher than 15 per cent. Just the same, Multivac has a reputation to maintain. It has virtually wiped out crime, and the public judges that by its record on first-degree murder which is, of course, the most spectacular crime."

Ali Othman nodded. "Yes, sir. I quite realize that."

"You also realize, I hope," Gulliman said, "that I don't want a single consummated case of it during my term. If any other crime slips through, I may allow excuses. If a first-degree murder slips through, I'll have your hide. Understand?"

"Yes, sir. The complete analyses of the two potential murders are already at the district offices involved. The potential criminals and victims are under observation. I have rechecked the probabilities of consummation and they are already dropping."

"Very good," said Gulliman, and broke connection.

He went back to the list with an uneasy feeling that perhaps he had been overpompous. ——But then, one had to be firm with these permanent civil-service personnel and make sure they didn't imagine they were running everything, including the Chairman. Particularly this Othman, who had been working with Multivac since both were considerably younger, and had a proprietary air that could be infuriating.

To Gulliman, this matter of crime was the political chance of a lifetime. So far, no Chairman had passed through his term without a murder taking place somewhere on Earth, some time. The previous Chairman had ended with a record of eight, three more (*more,* in fact) than under his predecessor.

Now Gulliman intended to have *none.* He was going to be, he had decided, the first Chairman without any murder at all anywhere on Earth during his term. After that, and the favorable publicity that would result—

He barely skimmed the rest of the report. He estimated that there were at least two thousand cases of prospective wife-beatings listed. Undoubtedly, not all would be stopped in time. Perhaps thirty per cent would be consummated. But the incidence was dropping and consummations were dropping even more quickly.

Multivac had added wife-beating to its list of predictable crimes only some five years earlier and the average man was not yet accustomed to the thought that if he planned to wallop his wife, it would be known in advance. As the conviction percolated through society, women would first suffer fewer bruises and then, eventually, none.

Some husband-beatings were on the list, too, Gulliman noticed.

Ali Othman closed connections and stared at the screen from which Gulliman's jowled and balding head had departed. Then he looked across at his assistant, Rafe Leemy and said, "What do we do?"

"Don't ask me. *He's* worried about just a lousy murder or two."

"It's an awful chance trying to handle this thing on our own. Still if we tell him, he'll have a first-class fit. These elective politicians have their skins to think of, so he's bound to get in our way and make things worse."

Leemy nodded his head and put a thick lower lip between his teeth. "Trouble is, though, what if we miss out? It would just about be the end of the world, you know."

"If we miss out, who cares what happens to us? We'll just be part of the general catastrophe." Then he said in a more lively manner, "But hell, the probability is only 12.3 per cent. On anything else, except maybe murder, we'd let the probabilities rise a bit before taking any action at all. There could still be spontaneous correction."

"I wouldn't count on it," said Leemy dryly.

"I don't intend to. I was just pointing the fact out. Still, at this probability, I suggest we confine ourselves to simple observation for the moment. No one could plan a crime like this alone; there must be accomplices."

"Multivac didn't name any."

"I know, Still—2" His voice trailed off.

So they stared at the details of the one crime not included on the list handed out to Gulliman; the one crime much worse than first-degree murder; the one crime never before attempted in the history of Multivac; and wondered what to do.

Ben Manners considered himself the happiest sixteen-year-old in Baltimore. This was, perhaps, doubtful. But he was certainly one of the happiest, and one of the most excited.

At least, he was one of the handful admitted to the galleries of the stadium during the swearing in of the eighteen-year-olds. His older brother was going to be sworn in so his parents had applied for spectator's tickets and they had allowed Ben to do so, too. But when Multivac chose among all the applicants, it was Ben who got the ticket.

Two years later, Ben would be sworn in himself, but watching big brother Michael now was the next best thing.

His parents had dressed him (or supervised the dressing, at any rate) with all care, as representative of the family and sent him off with numerous messages for Michael, who had left days earlier for preliminary physical and neurological examinations.

The stadium was on the outskirts of town and Ben, just bursting with self-importance, was shown to his seat. Below him, now, were rows upon rows of hundreds upon hundreds of eighteen-year-olds (boys to the right, girls to the left), all from the second district of Baltimore. At various times in the year, similar meetings were going on all over the world, but this was Baltimore, this was the important one. Down there (somewhere) was Mike, Ben's own brother.

Ben scanned the tops of heads, thinking somehow he might recognize his brother. He didn't, of course, but then a man came out on the raised platform in front of all the crowd and Ben stopped looking to listen.

The man said, "Good afternoon, swearers and guests. I am Randolph T. Hoch, in charge of the Baltimore ceremonies this year. The swearers have met me several times now during the progress of the physical and neurological portions of this examination. Most of the task is done, but the most important matter is left. The swearer himself, his personality, must go into Multivac's records.

"Each year, this requires some explanation to the young people reaching adulthood. Until now" (he turned to the young people before him and his eyes went no more to the gallery) "you have not been adult; you have not been individuals in the eyes of Multivac, except where you were especially singled out as such by your parents or your government.

"Until now, when the time for the yearly up-dating of information came, it was your parents who filled in the necessary data on you. Now the time has come for you to take over that duty yourself. It is a great honor, a great responsibility. Your parents have told us what schooling you've had, what diseases, what habits; a great many things. But now you must tell us a great deal more; your innermost thoughts; your most secret deeds.

"This is hard to do the first time, embarrrassing even, but it *must* be done. Once it is done, Multivac will have a complete analysis of all of you in its files. It will understand your actions and reactions. It will even be able to guess with fair accuracy at your future actions and reactions.

"In this way, Multivac will protect you. If you are in danger of accident, it will know. If someone plans harm to you, it will know. If *you* plan harm, it will know and you will be stopped in time so that it will not be necessary to punish you.

"With its knowledge of all of you, Multivac will be able to help Earth adjust its economy and its laws for the good of all. If you have a personal problem, you may come to Multivac with it and with its knowledge of all of you, Multivac will be able to help you.

"Now you will have many forms to fill out. Think carefully and answer all questions as accurately as you can. Do not hold back through shame or caution. No one will ever know your answers except Multivac unless it becomes necessary to learn the answers in order to protect you. And then only authorized officials of the government will know.

"It may occur to you to stretch the truth a bit here or there. Don't do this. We will find out if you do. All your answers put together form a pattern. If some answers are false, they will not fit the pattern and Multivac will discover them. If all your answers are false, there will be a distorted pattern of a type that Multivac will recognize. So you must tell the truth."

Eventually, it was all over, however: the form-filling; the ceremonies and speeches that followed. In the evening, Ben, standing tiptoe, finally spotted Michael, who was still carrying the robes he had worn in the "parade of the adults." They greeted one another with jubilation.

They shared a light supper and took the expressway home, alive and alight with the greatness of the day.

They were not prepared, then, for the sudden transition of the homecoming. It was a numbing shock to both of them to be stopped by a cold-faced young man in uniform outside their own front door; to have their papers inspected before they could enter their own house; to find their own parents sitting forlornly in the living room, the mark of tragedy on their faces.

Joseph Manners, looking much older than he had that morning, looked out of his puzzled, deep-sunken eyes at his sons (one with the robes of new adulthood still over his arm) and said, "I seem to be under house arrest."

Bernard Gulliman could not and did not read the entire report. He read only the summary and that was most gratifying, indeed.

A whole generation, it seemed, had grown up accustomed to the fact that Multivac could predict the commission of major crimes. They learned that Corrections agents would be on the scene before the crime could be committed. They found out that consummation of the crime led to inevitable punishment. Gradually, they were convinced that there was no way anyone could outsmart Multivac.

The result was, naturally, that even the intention of crime fell off. And as such intentions fell off and as Multivac's capacity was enlarged, minor crimes could be added to the list it would predict each morning, and these crimes, too, were now shrinking in incidence.

So Gulliman had ordered an analysis made (by Multivac naturally) of Multivac's capacity to turn its attention to the problem of predicting probabilities of disease incidence. Doctors might soon be alerted to individual patients who might grow diabetic in the course of the next year, or suffer an attack of tuberculosis or grow a cancer.

An ounce of prevention——

And the report was a favorable one!

After that, the roster of the day's possible crimes arrived and there was not a first-degree murder on the list.

Gulliman put in an intercom call to Ali Othman in high good humor. "Othman, how do the numbers of crimes in the daily lists of the past week average compared with those in my first week as Chairman?"

It had gone down, it turned out, by 8 per cent and Gulliman was happy indeed. No fault of his own, of course, but the electorate would not know that. He blessed his luck that he had come in at the right time, at the very climax of Multivac, when disease, too, could be placed under its all-embracing and protecting knowledge.

Gulliman would prosper by this.

Othman shrugged his shoulders. "Well, he's happy."

"When do we break the bubble?" said Leemy. "Putting Manners under observation just raised the probabilities and house arrest gave it another boost."

"Don't I know it?" said Othman peevishly. "What I don't know is why."

"Accomplices, maybe, like you said. With Manners in trouble, the rest have to strike at once or be lost."

"Just the other way around. With our hand on one, the rest would scatter for safety and disappear. Besides, why aren't the accomplices named by Multivac?"

"Well, then, do we tell Gulliman?"

"No, not yet. The probability is still only 17.3 per cent. Let's get a bit more drastic first."

Elizabeth Manners said to her younger son, "You go to your room, Ben."

"But what's it all about, Mom?" asked Ben, voice breaking at this strange ending to what had been a glorious day.

"Please!"

He left reluctantly, passing through the door to the stairway, walking up it noisily and down again quietly.

And Mike Manners, the older son, the new-minted adult and the hope of the family, said in a voice and tone that mirrored his brothers's, "What's it all about?"

Joe Manners said, "As heaven is my witness, son, I don't know. I haven't done anything."

"Well, sure you haven't done anything." Mike looked at his small-boned, mild-mannered father in wonder. "They must be here because you're *thinking* of doing something."

"I'm not."

Mrs. Manners broke in angrily, "How can he be thinking of doing something worth all—all this." She cast her arm about, in a gesture toward the enclosing shell of government men about the house. "When I was a little girl, I remember the father of a friend of mine was working in a bank, and they once called him up and said to leave the money alone and he did. It was fifty thousand dollars. He hadn't really taken it. He was just thinking about taking it. They didn't keep those things as quiet in those days as they do now; the story got out. That's how I know about it.

"But I mean," she went on, rubbing her plump hands slowly together, "that was fifty thousand dollars; fifty—thousand—dollars. Yet all they did was call him; one phone call. What could your father be planning that would make it worth having a dozen men come down and close off the house?"

Joe Manners said, eyes filled with pain, "I am planning no crime, not even the smallest. I swear it."

Mike, filled with the conscious wisdom of a new adult, said, "Maybe it's something subconscious, Pop. Some resentment against your supervisor."

"So that I would want to kill him? No!"

"Won't they tell you what it is, Pop?"

His mother interrupted again, "No, they won't. We've asked. I said they were ruining our standing in the community just being here. The least they could do is tell us what it's all about so we could fight it, so we could explain."

"And they wouldn't?"

"They wouldn't."

Mike stood with his legs spread apart and his hands deep in his pockets. He said, troubled, "Gee, Mom, Multivac doesn't make mistakes."

His father pounded his fist helplessly on the arm of the sofa. "I tell you I'm not planning any crime."

The door opened without a knock and a man in uniform walked in with sharp, self-possessed stride. His face had a glazed, official appearance. He said, "Are you Joseph Manners?"

Joe Manners rose to his feet. "Yes. Now what is it you want of me?"

"Joseph Manners, I place you under arrest by order of the government," and curtly he showed his identification as a Corrections officer. "I must ask you to come with me."

"For what reason? What have I done?"

"I am not at liberty to discuss that."

"But I can't be arrested just for planning a crime even if I were doing that. To be arrested I must actually have *done* something. You can't arrest me otherwise. It's against the law."

The officer was impervious to the logic. "You will have to come with me."

Mrs. Manners shrieked and fell on the couch, weeping hysterically. Joseph Manners could not bring himself to violate the code drilled into him all his life by actually resisting an officer, but he hung back at least, forcing the Corrections officer to use muscular power to drag him forward.

And Manners called out as he went, "But tell me what it is. Just tell me. If I *knew*—— Is it murder? Am I supposed to be planning murder?"

The door closed behind him and Mike Manners, white-faced and suddenly feeling not the least bit adult, stared first at the door, then at his weeping mother.

Ben Manners, behind the door and suddenly feeling quite adult, pressed his lips tightly together and thought he knew exactly what to do.

If Multivac took away, Multivac could also give. Ben had been at the ceremonies that very day. He had heard this man, Randolph Hoch, speak of Multivac and all that Multivac could do. It could direct the government and it could also unbend and help out some plain person who came to it for help.

Anyone could ask help of Multivac and anyone meant Ben. Neither his mother nor Mike were in any condition to stop him now, and he had some money left of the amount they had given him for his great outing that day. If afterward they found him gone and worried about it, that couldn't be helped. Right now, his first loyalty was to his father.

He ran out the back way and the officer at the door cast a glance at his papers and let him go.

Harold Quimby handled the complaints department of the Baltimore substation of Multivac. He considered himself to be a member of that branch of the civil service that was most important of all. In some ways, he may have been right, and those who heard him discuss the matter would have had to be made of iron not to feel impressed.

For one thing, Quimby would say, Multivac was essentially an invader of privacy. In the past fifty years, mankind had had to acknowledge that its thoughts and impulses were no longer secret, that it owned no inner recess where anything could be hidden. And mankind had to have something in return.

Of course, it got prosperity, peace, and safety, but that was abstract. Each man and woman needed something personal as his or her own reward for surrendering privacy, and each one got it. Within reach of every human being was a Multivac station with circuits into which he could freely enter his own problems and questions without control or hindrance, and from which, in a matter of minutes, he could receive answers.

At any given moment, five million individual circuits among the quadrillion or more within Multivac might be involved in this question-and-answer program. The answers might not always be certain, but they were the best available, and every questioner *knew* the answer to be the best available and had faith in it. That was what counted.

And now an anxious sixteen-year-old had moved slowly up the waiting line of men and women (each in that line illuminated by a different mixture of hope with fear or anxiety or even anguish—always with hope predominating as the person stepped nearer and nearer to Multivac).

Without looking up, Quimby took the filled-out form being handed him and said, "Booth 5-B."

Ben said, "How do I ask the question, sir?"

Quimby looked up then, with a bit of surprise. Preadults did not generally make use of the service. He said kindly, "Have you ever done this before, son?"

"No, sir."

Quimby pointed to the model on his desk. "You use this. You see how it works? Just like a typewriter. Don't you try to write or print anything by hand. Just use the machine. Now you take booth 5-B; and if you need help, just press the red button and someone will come. Down that aisle, son, on the right."

He watched the youngster go down the aisle and out of view and smiled. No one was ever turned away from Multivac. Of course, there was always a certain percentage of trivia: people who asked personal questions about their neighbors or obscene questions about prominent personalities; college youths trying to outguess their professors or thinking it clever to stump Multivac by asking it Russell's class-of-all-classes paradox and so on.

Multivac could take care of all that. It needed no help.

Besides, each question and answer was filed and formed but another item in the fact assembly for each individual. Even the most trivial question and the most impertinent, insofar as it reflected the personality of the questioner, helped humanity by helping Multivac know about humanity.

Quimby turned his attention to the next person in line, a middle-aged woman, gaunt and angular, with the look of trouble in her eye.

Ali Othman strode the length of his office, his heels thumping desperately on the carpet. "The probability still goes up. It's 22.4 per cent now. Damnation! We have Joseph Manners under actual arrest and it still goes up." He was perspiring freely.

Leemy turned away from the telephone. "No confession yet. He's under Psychic Probing and there is no sign of crime. He may be telling the truth."

Othman said, "Is Multivac crazy then?"

Another phone sprang to life. Othman closed connections quickly, glad of the interruption. A Corrections officer's face came to life in the screen. The officer said, "Sir, are there any new directions as to Manners' family? Are they to be allowed to come and go as they have been?"

"What do you mean, as they have been?"

"The original instructions were for the house arrest of Joseph Manners. Nothing was said of the rest of the family, sir."

"Well, extend it to the rest of the family until you are informed otherwise."

"Sir, that is the point. The mother and older son are demanding information about the younger son. The younger son is gone and they claim he is in custody and wish to go to headquarters to inquire about it."

Othman frowned and said in almost a whisper, "Younger son? How young?"

"Sixteen, sir," said the officer.

"Sixteen and he's gone. Don't you know where?"

"He was allowed to leave, sir. There were no orders to hold him."

"Hold the line. Don't move." Othman put the line into suspension, then clutched at his coal-black hair with both hands and shrieked, "Fool! Fool! Fool!"

Leemy was startled. "What the hell?"

"The man has a sixteen-year-old son," choked out Othman. "A sixteen-year-old is not an adult and he is not filed independently in Multivac, but only as part of his father's file." He glared at Leemy. "Doesn't everyone know that until eighteen a youngster does not file his own reports with Multivac but that his father does it for him? Don't I know it? Don't you?"

"You mean Multivac didn't mean Joe Manners?" said Leemy.

"Multivac meant his minor son, and the youngster is gone, now. With officers three deep around the house, he calmly walks out and goes on you know what errand."

He whirled to the telephone circuit to which the Corrections officer still clung, the minute break having given Othman just time enough to collect himself and to assume a cool and self-possessed mien. (It would never have done to throw a fit before the eyes of the officer, however much good it did in purging his spleen.)

He said, "Officer, locate the younger son who has disappeared. Take every man you have, if necessary. Take every man available in the district, if necessary. I shall give the appropriate orders. You must find that boy at all costs."

"Yes, sir."

Connection was broken. Othman said, "Have another rundown on the probabilities, Leemy."

Five minutes later, Leemy said, "It's down to 19.6 per cent. It's *down.*"

Othman drew a long breath. "We're on the right track at last."

Ben Manners sat in Booth 5-B and punched out slowly, "My name is Benjamin Manners, number MB-71833412. My father, Joseph Manners, has been arrested but we don't know what crime he is planning. Is there any way we can help him?"

He sat and waited. He might be only sixteen but he was old enough to know that somewhere those words were being whirled into the most complex structure ever conceived by man; that a trillion facts would blend and co-ordinate into a whole, and that from that whole, Multivac would abstract the best help.

The machine clicked and a card emerged. It had an answer on it, a long answer. It began, "Take the expressway to Washington, D.C. at once. Get off at the Connecticut Avenue stop. You will find a special exit, labeled 'Multivac' with a guard. Inform the guard you are special courier for Dr. Trumbull and he will let you enter.

"You will be in a corridor. Proceed along it till you reach a small door labeled 'Interior.' Enter and say to the men inside, 'Message for Doctor Trumbull.' You will be allowed to pass. Proceed on—"

It went on in this fashion. Ben could not see the application to his question, but he had complete faith in Multivac. He left at a run, heading for the expressway to Washington.

The Corrections officers traced Ben Manners to the Baltimore station an hour after he had left. A shocked Harold Quimby found himself flabbergasted at the number and importance of the men who had focused on him in the search for a sixteen-year-old.

"Yes, a boy," he said, "but I don't know where he went to after he was through here. I had no way of knowing that anyone was looking for him. We accept all comers here. Yes, I can get the record of the question and answer."

They looked at the record and televised it to Central Headquarters at once.

Othman read it through, turned up his eyes, and collapsed. They brought him to almost at once. He said to Leemy weakly, "Have them catch that boy. And have a copy of Multivac's answer made out for me. There's no way any more, no way out. I must see Gulliman now."

Bernard Gulliman had never seen Ali Othman as much as perturbed before, and watching the co-ordinator's wild eyes now sent a trickle of ice water down his spine.

He stammered, "What do you mean, Othman? What do you mean worse than murder?"

"Much worse than just murder."

Gulliman was quite pale. "Do you mean assassination of a high government official?" (It did cross his mind that he himself—).

Othman nodded. "Not just *a* government official. *The* government official."

"The *Secretary-General?*" Gulliman said in an appalled whisper.

"More than that, even. Much more. We deal with a plan to assassinate Multivac!"

"WHAT!"

"For the first time in the history of Multivac, the computer came up with the report that it itself was in danger."

"Why was I not at once informed?"

Othman half-truthed out of it. "The matter was so unprecedented, sir, that we explored the situation first before daring to put it on official record."

"But Multivac has been saved, of course? It's been saved?"

"The probabilities of harm have declined to under 4 per cent. I am waiting for the report now."

"Message for Dr. Trumbull," said Ben Manners to the man on the high stool, working carefully on what looked like the controls of a stratojet cruiser, enormously magnified.

"Sure, Jim," said the man. "Go ahead."

Ben looked at his instructions and hurried on. Eventually, he would find a tiny control lever which he was to shift to a DOWN position at a moment when a certain indicator spot would light up red.

He heard an agitated voice behind him, then another, and suddenly, two men had him by his elbows. His feet were lifted off the floor.

One man said, "Come with us, boy."

Ali Othman's face did not noticeably lighten at the news, even though Gulliman said with great relief, "If we have the boy, then Multivac is safe."

"For the moment."

Gulliman put a trembling hand to his forehead. "What a half hour I've

had. Can you imagine what the destruction of Multivac for even a short
time would mean. The government would have collapsed; the economy
broken down. It would have meant devastation worse—" His head snapped
up, "What do you mean *for the moment?*"

"The boy, this Ben Manners, had no intention of doing harm. He and
his family must be released and compensation for false imprisonment given
them. He was only following Multivac's instructions in order to help his
father and it's done that. His father is free now."

"Do you mean Multivac ordered the boy to pull a lever under circumstances that would burn out enough circuits to require a month's repair
work? You mean Multivac would suggest its own destruction for the comfort of one man?"

"It's worse than that, sir. Multivac not only gave those instructions but
selected the Manners family in the first place because Ben Manners looked
exactly like one of Dr. Trumbull's pages so that he could get into Multivac
without being stopped."

"What do you mean the family was selected?"

"Well, the boy would have never gone to ask the question if his father
had not been arrested. His father would never have been arrested if Multivac had not blamed him for planning the destruction of Multivac.
Multivac's own action started the chain of events that almost led to
Multivac's destruction."

"But there's no sense to that," Gulliman said in a pleading voice. He
felt small and helpless and he was virtually on his knees, begging this Othman, this man who had spent nearly a lifetime with Multivac, to reassure
him.

Othman did not do so. He said, "This is Multivac's first attempt along
this line as far as I know. In some ways, it planned well. It chose the right
family. It carefully did not distinguish between father and son to send us off
the track. It was still an amateur at the game, though. It could not overcome
its own instructions that led it to report the probability of its own destruction as increasing with every step we took down the wrong road. It could
not avoid recording the answer it gave the youngster. With further practice,
it will probably learn deceit. It will learn to hide certain facts, fail to record
certain others. From now on, every instruction it gives may have the seeds
in it of its own destruction. We will never know. And however careful we
are, eventually Multivac will succeed. I think, Mr. Gulliman, you will be the
last Chairman of this organization."

Gulliman pounded his desk in fury. "But why, why, why? Damn you,
why? What is wrong with it? Can't it be fixed?"

"I don't think so," said Othman, in soft despair. "I've never thought
about this before. I've never had the occasion to until this happened, but
now that I think of it, it seems to me we have reached the end of the road

because Multivac is too good. Multivac has grown so complicated, its reactions are no longer those of a machine, but those of a living thing."

"You're mad, but even so?"

"For fifty years and more we have been loading humanity's troubles on Multivac, on this living thing. We've asked it to care for us, all together and each individually. We've asked it to take all our secrets into itself; we've asked it to absorb our evil and guard us against it. Each of us brings his troubles to it, adding his bit to the burden. Now we are planning to load the burden of human disease on Multivac, too."

Othman paused a moment, then burst out, "Mr. Gulliman, Multivac bears all the troubles of the world on its shoulders and it is tired."

"Madness. Midsummer madness," muttered Gulliman.

"Then let me show you something. Let me put it to the test. May I have permission to use the Multivac circuit line here in your office?"

"Why?"

"To ask it a question no one has ever asked Multivac before?"

"Will you do it harm?" asked Gulliman in quick alarm.

"No. But it will tell us what we want to know."

The Chairman hesitated a trifle. Then he said, "Go ahead."

Othman used the instrument on Gulliman's desk. His fingers punched out the question with deft strokes: "Multivac, what do you yourself want more than anything else?"

The moment between question and answer lengthened unbearably, but neither Othman nor Gulliman breathed.

And there was a clicking and a card popped out. It was a small card. On it, in precise letters, was the answer:

"I want to die."

Flannery O'Connor (1925–1964) was born of Roman Catholic parents in Savannah, Georgia, and was educated in parochial schools and at the Women's College of Georgia. She went to the University of Iowa on a journalism scholarship but soon changed to the Writer's Workshop, where she took an M.F.A. degree in creative writing. At the height of her creative powers, she became ill with an incurable illness; she spent the final ten years of her life as a semi-invalid. A novelist of distinction, she was also a dedicated craftsman of the short story. Her major themes concern belief and grace in an apocalyptic, fallen world; a recurring protagonist is the "backwoods prophet" in the American South. Her outstanding novel is The Violent Bear It Away *(1960). For further reading:* A Good Man Is Hard to Find *(1955);* The Complete Stories *(1971).*

FLANNERY O'CONNOR

The Life You Save May Be Your Own

The old woman and her daughter were sitting on their porch when Mr. Shiflet came up their road for the first time. The old woman slid to the edge of her chair and leaned forward, shading her eyes from the piercing sunset with her hand. The daughter could not see far in front of her and continued to play with her fingers. Although the old woman lived in this desolate spot with only her daughter and she had never seen Mr. Shiflet before, she could tell, even from a distance, that he was a tramp and no one to be afraid of. His left coat sleeve was folded up to show there was only half an arm in it and his gaunt figure listed slightly to the side as if the breeze were pushing him. He had on a black town suit and a brown felt hat that was turned up in the front and down in the back and he carried a tin tool box by a handle. He came on, at an amble, up her road, his face turned toward the sun which appeared to be balancing itself on the peak of a small mountain.

The old woman didn't change her position until he was almost into her yard; then she rose with one hand fisted on her hip. The daughter, a large girl in a short blue organdy dress, saw him all at once and jumped up and began to stamp and point and make excited speechless sounds.

Mr. Shiftlet stopped just inside the yard and set his box on the ground and tipped his hat to her as if she were not in the least afflicted; then he turned toward the old woman and swung the hat all the way off. He had long black slick hair that hung flat from a part in the middle to beyond the tips of his ears on either side. His face descended in forehead for more than half its length and ended suddenly with his features just balanced over a jutting steel-trap jaw. He seemed to be a young man but he had a look of composed dissatisfaction as if he understood life thoroughly.

"Good evening," the old woman said. She was about the size of a cedar fence post and she had a man's gray hat pulled down low over her head.

The tramp stood looking at her and didn't answer. He turned his back and faced the sunset. He swung both his whole and his short arm up slowly so that they indicated an expanse of sky and his figure formed a crooked cross. The old woman watched him with her arms folded across her chest as if she were the owner of the sun, and the daughter watched, her head thrust forward and her fat helpless hands hanging at the wrists. She had long pink-gold hair and eyes as blue as a peacock's neck.

He held the pose for almost fifty seconds and then he picked up his box and came on to the porch and dropped down on the bottom step. "Lady," he said in a firm nasal voice, "I'd give a fortune to live where I could see me a sun do that every evening."

"Does it every evening," the old woman said and set back down. The daughter sat down too and watched him with a cautious sly look as if he were a bird that had come up very close. He leaned to one side, rooting in his pants pocket, and in a second he brought out a package of chewing gum and offered her a piece. She took it and unpeeled it and began to chew without taking her eyes off him. He offered the old woman a piece but she only raised her upper lip to indicate she had no teeth.

Mr. Shiftlet's pale sharp glance had already passed over everything in the yard—the pump near the corner of the house and the big fig tree that three or four chickens were preparing to roost in—and had moved to a shed where he saw the square rusted back of an automobile. "You ladies drive?" he asked.

"That car ain't run in fifteen year," the old woman said. "The day my husband died, it quit running."

"Nothing is like it used to be, lady," he said. "The world is almost rotten."

"That's right," the old woman said. "You from around here?"

"Name Tom T. Shiftlet," he murmured, looking at the tires.

"I'm pleased to meet you," the old woman said. "Name Lucynell Crater and daughter Lucynell Crater. What you doing around here, Mr. Shiftlet?"

He judged the car to be about a 1928 or '29 Ford. "Lady," he said, and turned and gave her his full attention, "lemme tell you something. There's one of these doctors in Atlanta that's taken a knife and cut the human heart—the human heart," he repeated, leaning forward, "out of a man's chest and held it in his hand," and he held his hand out, palm up, as if it were slightly weighted with the human heart, "and studied it like it was a day-old chicken, and, lady," he said, allowing a long significant pause in which his head slid forward and his clay-colored eyes brightened, "he don't know no more about it than you or me."

"That's right," the old woman said.

"Why, if he was to take that knife and cut into every corner of it, he still wouldn't know no more than you or me. What you want to bet?"

"Nothing," the old woman said wisely. "Where you come from Mr. Shiftlet?"

He didn't answer. He reached into his pocket and brought out a sack of tobacco and a package of cigarette papers and rolled himself a cigarette, expertly with one hand, and attached it in a hanging position to his upper lip. Then he took a box of wooden matches from his pocket and struck one on his shoe. He held the burning match as if he were studying the mystery of flame while it traveled dangerously toward his skin. The daughter began to make loud noises and to point to his hand and shake her finger at him, but when the flame was just before touching him, he leaned down with his hand cupped over it as if he were going to set fire to his nose and lit the cigarette.

He flipped away the dead match and blew a stream of gray into the evening. A sly look came over his face. "Lady," he said, "nowadays, people'll do anything anyways. I can tell you my name is Tom T. Shiftlet and I come from Tarwater, Tennessee, but you never have seen me before: how you know I ain't lying? How you know my name ain't Aaron Sparks, lady, and I come from Singleberry, Georgia, or how you know it's not George Speeds and I come from Lucy, Alabama, or how you know I ain't Thompson Bright from Toolafalls, Mississippi?"

"I don't know nothing about you," the old woman muttered, irked.

"Lady," he said, "people don't care how they lie. Maybe the best I can tell you is, I'm a man; but listen, lady," he said and paused and made his tone more ominous still, "what is a man?"

The old woman began to gum a seed. "What you carry in that tin box, Mr. Shiftlet?" she asked.

"Tools," he said, put back. "I'm a carpenter."

"Well, if you come out here to work, I'll be able to feed you and give you a place to sleep but I can't pay. I'll tell you that before you begin," she said.

There was no answer at once and no particular expression on his face. He leaned back against the two-by-four that helped support the porch roof.

"Lady," he said slowly, "there's some men that some things mean more to them than money." The old woman rocked without comment and the daughter watched the trigger that moved up and down in his neck. He told the old woman then that all most people were interested in was money, but he asked what a man was made for. He asked her if a man was made for money, or what. He asked her what she thought she was made for but she didn't answer, she only sat rocking and wondered if a one-armed man could put a new roof on her garden house. He asked a lot of questions that she didn't answer. He told her that he was twenty-eight years old and had lived a varied life. He had been a gospel singer, a foreman on the railroad, an assistant in an undertaking parlor, and he had come over the radio for three months with Uncle Roy and his Red Creek Wranglers. He said he had fought and bled in the Arm Service of his country and visited every foreign land and that everywhere he had seen people that didn't care if they did a thing one way or another. He said he hadn't been raised thataway.

A fat yellow moon appeared in the branches of the fig tree as if it were going to roost there with the chickens. He said that a man had to escape to the country to see the world whole and that he wished he lived in a desolate place like this where he could see the sun go down every evening like God make it to do.

"Are you married or are you single?" the old woman asked.

There was a long silence. "Lady," he asked finally, "where would you find an innocent woman today? I wouldn't have any of this trash I could just pick up."

The daughter was leaning very far down, hanging her head almost between her knees, watching him through a triangular door she had made in her overturned hair; and she suddenly fell in a heap on the floor and began to whimper. Mr. Shiftlet straightened her out and helped her get back in the chair.

"Is she your baby girl?" he asked.

"My only," the old woman said, "and she's the sweetest girl in the world. I wouldn't give her up for nothing on earth. She's smart too. She can sweep the floor, cook, wash, feed the chickens, and hoe. I wouldn't give her up for a casket of jewels."

"No," he said kindly, "don't ever let any man take her away from you."

"Any man come after her," the old woman said, "'ll have to stay around the place."

Mr. Shiftlet's eye in the darkness was focused on a part of the automobile bumper that glittered in the distance. "Lady," he said, jerking his short arm up as if he could point with it to her house and yard and pump, "there ain't a broken thing on this plantation that I couldn't fix for you, one-arm jackleg or not. I'm a man," he said with a sullen dignity, "even if I ain't a whole one. I got," he said, tapping his knuckles on the floor to emphasize the immensity of what he was going to say, "a moral intelligence!" and his face pierced out of the darkness into a shaft of doorlight and he stared at her as if he were astonished himself at this impossible truth.

The old woman was not impressed with the phrase. "I told you you could hang around and work for food," she said, "if you don't mind sleeping in that car yonder."

"Why listen, lady," he said with a grin of delight, "the monks of old slept in their coffins!"

"They wasn't as advanced as we are," the old woman said.

The next morning he began on the roof of the garden house while Lucynell, the daughter, sat on a rock and watched him work. He had not been around a week before the change he had made in the place was apparent. He had patched the front and back steps, built a new hog pen, restored a fence, and taught Lucynell, who was completely deaf and had never said a word in her life, to say the word "bird." The big rosy-faced girl followed him everywhere, saying "Burrttddt ddbirrttdt," and clapping her hands. The old woman watched from a distance, secretly pleased. She was ravenous for a son-in-law.

Mr. Shiftlet slept on the hard narrow back seat of the car with his feet out the side window. He had his razor and a can of water on a crate that served him as a bedside table and he put up a piece of mirror against the back glass and kept his coat neatly on a hanger that he hung over one of the windows.

In the evening he sat on the steps and talked while the old woman and Lucynell rocked violently in their chairs on either side of him. The old woman's three mountains were black against the dark blue sky and were visited off and on by various planets and by the moon after it had left the chickens. Mr. Shiftlet pointed out that the reason he had improved this plantation was because he had taken a personal interest in it. He said he was even going to make the automobile run.

He had raised the hood and studied the mechanism and he said he could tell that the car had been built in the days when cars were really built. You take now, he said, one man puts in one bolt and another man puts in another bolt and another man puts in another bolt so that it's a man for a bolt. That's why you have to pay so much for a car: you're paying all those men. Now if you didn't have to pay but one man, you could get you a cheaper car and one that had had a personal interest taken in it, and it would be a better car. The old woman agreed with him that this was so.

Mr. Shiftlet said that the trouble with the world was that nobody cared, or stopped and took any trouble. He said he never would have been able to teach Lucynell to say a word if he hadn't cared and stopped long enough.

"Teach her to say something else," the old woman said.

"What you want her to say next?" Mr. Shiftlet asked.

The old woman's smile was broad and toothless and suggestive. "Teach her to say, 'sugarpie,'" she said.

Mr. Shiftlet already knew what was on her mind.

The next day he began to tinker with the automobile and that evening he told her that if she would buy a fan belt, he would be able to make the car run.

The old woman said she would give him the money. "You see that girl yonder?" she asked, pointing to Lucynell who was sitting on the floor a foot away, watching him, her eyes blue even in the dark. "If it was ever a man wanted to take her away, I would say, 'No man on earth is going to take that sweet girl of mine away from me!' but if he was to say, 'Lady, I don't want to take her away, I want her right here,' I would say, 'Mister, I don't blame you none. I wouldn't pass up a chance to live in a permanent place and get the sweetest girl in the world myself. You ain't no fool,' I would say."

"How old is she?" Mr. Shiftlet asked casually.

"Fifteen, sixteen," the old woman said. The girl was nearly thirty but because of her innocence it was impossible to guess.

"It would be a good idea to paint it too," Mr. Shiftlet remarked. "You don't want it to rust out."

"We'll see about that later," the old woman said.

The next day he walked into town and returned with the parts he needed, and a can of gasoline. Late in the afternoon, terrible noises issued from the shed and the old woman rushed out of the house, thinking Lucynell was somewhere having a fit. Lucynell was sitting on a chicken crate, stamping her feet and screaming, "Burrddttt! bddurrddtttt!" but her fuss was drowned out by the car. With a volley of blasts it emerged from the shed, moving in a fierce and stately way. Mr. Shiftlet was in the driver's seat, sitting very erect. He had an expression of serious modesty on his face as if he had just raised the dead.

That night, rocking on the porch, the old woman began her business at once. "You want you an innocent woman, don't you?" she asked sympathetically. "You don't want none of this trash."

"No'm, I don't," Mr. Shiftlet said.

"One that can't talk," she continued, "can't sass you back or use foul language. That's the kind for you to have. Right there," and she pointed to Lucynell sitting cross-legged in her chair, holding both feet in her hands.

"That's right," he admitted. "She wouldn't give me any trouble."

"Saturday," the old woman said, "you and her and me can drive into town and get married."

Mr. Shiftlet eased his position on the steps.

"I can't get married right now," he said. "Everything you want to do takes money and I ain't got any."

"What you need with money?" she asked.

"It takes money," he said. "Some people'll do anything anyhow these days, but the way I think, I wouldn't marry no woman that I couldn't take on a trip like she was somebody. I mean take her to a hotel and treat her. I wouldn't marry the Duchesser Windsor," he said firmly, "unless I could take her to a hotel and give her something good to eat.

"I was raised thataway and there ain't a thing I can do about it. My old mother taught me how to do."

"Lucynell don't even know what a hotel is," the old woman muttered. "Listen here, Mr. Shiftlet," she said, sliding forward in her chair, "you'd be getting a permanent house and a deep well and the most innocent girl in the world. You don't need no money. Lemme tell you something: there ain't any place in the world for a poor disabled friendless drifting man."

The ugly words settled in Mr. Shiftlet's head like a group of buzzards in the top of a tree. He didn't answer at once. He rolled himself a cigarette and lit it and then he said in an even voice, "Lady, a man is divided into parts, body and spirit."

The old woman clamped her gums together.

"A body and a spirit," he repeated. "The body, lady, is like a house: it don't go anywhere; but the spirit, lady, is like a automobile: always on the move, always . . ."

"Listen, Mr. Shiftlet," she said, "my well never goes dry and my house is always warm in the winter and there's no mortgage on a thing about this place. You can go to the courthouse and see for yourself. And yonder under that shed is a fine automobile." She laid the bait carefully. "You can have it painted by Saturday. I'll pay for paint."

In the darkness, Mr. Shiftlet's smile stretched like a weary snake waking up by a fire. "Yes'm," he said softly.

After a second he recalled himself and said, "I'm only saying a man's spirit means more to him than anything else. I would have to take my wife off for the weekend without no regards at all for cost. I got to follow where my spirit says to go."

"I'll give you fifteen dollars for a weekend trip," the old woman said in a crabbed voice. "That's the best I can do."

"That wouldn't hardly pay for more than the gas and the hotel," he said. "It wouldn't feed her."

"Seventeen-fifty," the old woman said. "That's all I got so it isn't any use you trying to milk me. You can take a lunch."

Mr. Shiftlet was deeply hurt by the word "milk." He didn't doubt that she had more money sewed up in her mattress but he had already told her he was not interested in her money. "I'll make that do," he said, and rose and walked off without treating with her further.

On Saturday the three of them drove into town in the car that the paint had barely dried on and Mr. Shiftlet and Lucynell were married in the

Ordinary's office while the old woman witnessed. As they came out of the courthouse, Mr. Shiftlet began twisting his neck in his collar. He looked morose and bitter as if he had been insulted while someone held him. "That didn't satisfy me none," he said. "That was just something a woman in an office did, nothing but paper work and blood tests. What do they know about my blood? If they was to take my heart and cut it out," he said, "they wouldn't know a thing about me. It didn't satisfy me at all."

"It satisfied the law," the old woman said sharply.

"The law," Mr. Shiftlet said, and spit. "It's the law that don't satisfy me."

He had painted the car dark green with a yellow band around it just under the windows. The three of them climbed in the front seat and the old woman said, "Don't Lucynell look pretty? Looks like a baby doll." Lucynell was dressed up in a white dress that her mother had uprooted from a trunk and there was a Panama hat on her head with a bunch of red wooden cherries on the brim. Every now and then her placid expression was changed by a sly isolated little thought like a shoot of green in the desert. "You got a prize!" the old woman said.

Mr. Shiftlet didn't even look at her.

They drove back to the house to let the old woman off and pick up the lunch. When they were ready to leave, she stood staring in the window of the car, with her fingers clenched around the glass. Tears began to seep sideways out of her eyes and run along the dirty creases in her face. "I ain't ever been parted with her for two days before," she said.

Mr. Shiftlet started the motor.

"And I wouldn't let no man have her but you because I seen you would do right. Goodbye, Sugarbaby," she said, clutching at the sleeve of the white dress. Lucynell looked straight at her and didn't seem to see her there at all. Mr. Shiftlet eased the car forward so that she had to move her hands.

The early afternoon was clear and open and surrounded by pale blue sky. The hills flattened under the car one after another and the climb and dip and swerve went entirely to Mr. Shiftlet's head so that he forgot his morning bitterness. He had always wanted an automobile but he had never been able to afford one before. He drove very fast because he wanted to make Mobile by nightfall.

Occasionally he stopped his thoughts long enough to look at Lucynell in the seat beside him. She had eaten the lunch as soon as they were out of the yard and now she was pulling the cherries off the hat one by one and throwing them out the window. He became depressed in spite of the car. He had driven about a hundred miles when he decided that she must be hungry again and at the next small town they came to, he stopped in front of an aluminum-painted eating place called The Hot Spot and took her in and ordered her a plate of ham and grits. The ride had made her sleepy and as soon as she got up on the stool, she rested her head on the counter and shut her eyes. There was no one in The Hot Spot but Mr. Shiftlet and the boy behind the counter, a pale youth with a greasy rag hung over his shoulder. Before he could dish up the food, she was snoring gently.

"Give it to her when she wakes up," Mr. Shiftlet said. "I'll pay for it now."

The boy bent over her and stared at the long pink-gold hair and the half-shut sleeping eyes. Then he looked up and stared at Mr. Shiftlet. "She looks like an angel of Gawd," he murmured.

"Hitch-hiker," Mr. Shiftlet explained. "I can't wait. I got to make Tuscaloosa."

The boy bent over again and very carefully touched his fingers to a strand of the golden hair and Mr. Shiftlet left.

He was more depressed than ever as he drove on by himself. The late afternoon had grown hot and sultry and the country had flattened out. Deep in the sky a storm was preparing very slowly and without thunder as if it meant to drain every drop of air from the earth before it broke. There were times when Mr. Shiftlet preferred not to be alone. He felt too that a man with a car had a responsibility to others and he kept his eye out for a hitch-hiker. Occasionally he saw a sign that warned: "Drive carefully. The life you save may be your own."

The narrow road dropped off on either side into dry fields and here and there a shack or a filling station stood in the clearing. The sun began to set directly in front of the automobile. It was a reddening ball that through his windshield was slightly flat on the bottom and top. He saw a boy in overalls and a gray hat standing on the edge of the road and he slowed the car down and stopped in front of him. The boy didn't have his hand raised to thumb the ride, he was only standing there, but he had a small cardboard suitcase and his hat was set on his head in a way to indicate that he had left somewhere for good. "Son," Mr. Shiftlet said, "I see you want a ride."

The boy didn't say he did or he didn't but he opened the door of the car and got in, and Mr. Shiftlet started driving again. The child held the suitcase on his lap and folded his arms on top of it. He turned his head and looked out the window away from Mr. Shiftlet. Mr. Shiftlet felt oppressed. "Son," he said after a minute, "I got the best old mother in the world so I reckon you only got the second best."

The boy gave him a quick dark glance and then turned his face back out the window.

"It's nothing so sweet," Mr. Shiftlet continued, "as a boy's mother. She taught him his first prayers at her knee, she give him love when no other would, she told him what was right and what wasn't, and she seen that he done the right thing. Son," he said, "I never rued a day in my life like the one I rued when I left that old mother of mine."

The boy shifted in his seat but he didn't look at Mr. Shiftlet. He unfolded his arms and put one hand on the door handle.

"My mother was a angel of Gawd," Mr. Shiftlet said in a very strained voice. "He took her from heaven and giver to me and I left her." His eyes were instantly clouded over with a mist of tears. The car was barely moving.

The boy turned angrily in the seat. "You go to the devil!" he cried. "My old woman is a flea bag and yours is a stinking pole cat!" and with that he flung the door open and jumped out with his suitcase into the ditch.

Mr. Shiftlet was so shocked that for about a hundred feet he drove along slowly with the door still open. A cloud, the exact color of the boy's hat and shaped like a turnip, had descended over the sun, and another, worse looking, crouched behind the car. Mr. Shiftlet felt that the rottenness of the world was about to engulf him. He raised his arm and let it fall again to his breast. "Oh, Lord!" he prayed. "Break forth and wash the slime from this earth!"

The turnip continued slowly to descend. After a few minutes there was a guffawing peal of thunder from behind and fantastic raindrops, like tincan tops, crashed over the rear of Mr. Shiftlet's car. Very quickly he stepped on the gas and with his stump sticking out the window he raced the galloping shower into Mobile.

NEW VOICES,
NEW VISIONS

JORGE LUIS BORGES

An Argentinian by birth and a European by early training and education, Jorge Luis Borges (1899–) is generally regarded as one of the most prestigious of authors writing in the Spanish language today. A linguist and a librarian, he was discharged from his librarian's position during the dictatorship of Juan Perón; after Perón's ouster, Borges became the Director of the Argentine National Library. In the same year he became a professor of English and American literature at the University of Buenos Aires. In 1961, he shared the International Publishers' Prize with Samuel Beckett. Borges' work is freighted with arcane, esoteric materials; in atmosphere and tone his short fiction often suggests that of Poe or Kafka. One of his major themes is man's attempt—often by the medium of fantasy—to find order in a chaotic, modern world. For further reading: Labyrinths *(1962);* The Aleph *(1970).*

JORGE LUIS BORGES

The Secret Miracle

And God had him die for a hundred years and then revived him and said: "How long have you been here?" "A day or a part of a day," he answered.

Koran, II, 261

The night of March 14, 1943, in an apartment in the Zeltnergasse of Prague, Jaromir Hladik, the author of the unfinished drama entitled *The Enemies,* of *Vindication of Eternity* and of a study of the indirect Jewish sources of Jakob Böhme, had a dream of a long game of chess. The players were not two persons, but two illustrious families; the game had been going on for centuries. Nobody could remember what the stakes were, but it was rumored that they were enormous, perhaps infinite; the chessmen and the board were in a secret tower. Jaromir (in his dream) was the first-born of

491

one of the contending families. The clock struck the hour for the game, which could not be postponed. The dreamer raced over the sands of a rainy desert, and was unable to recall either the pieces or the rules of chess. At that moment he awoke. The clangor of the rain and of the terrible clocks ceased. A rhythmic, unanimous noise, punctuated by shouts of command, arose from the Zeltnergasse. It was dawn, and the armored vanguard of the Third Reich was entering Prague.

On the nineteenth the authorities received a denunciation; that same nineteenth, toward evening, Jaromir Hladik was arrested. He was taken to an aseptic, white barracks on the opposite bank of the Moldau. He was unable to refute a single one of the Gestapo's charges; his mother's family name was Jaroslavski, he was of Jewish blood, his study on Böhme had a marked Jewish emphasis, his signature had been one more on the protest against the *Anschluss*. In 1928 he had translated the *Sepher Yezirah* for the publishing house of Hermann Barsdorf. The fulsome catalogue of the firm had exaggerated, for publicity purposes, the translator's reputation, and the catalogue had been examined by Julius Rothe, one of the officials who held Hladik's fate in his hands. There is not a person who, except in the field of his own specialization, is not credulous; two or three adjectives in Gothic type were enough to persuade Julius Rothe of Hladik's importance, and he ordered him sentenced to death *pour encourager les autres*. The execution was set for March 29th, at 9:00 A.M. This delay (whose importance the reader will grasp later) was owing to the desire on the authorities' part to proceed impersonally and slowly, after the manner of vegetables and plants.

Hladik's first reaction was mere terror. He felt he would not have shrunk from the gallows, the block, or the knife, but that death by a firing squad was unbearable. In vain he tried to convince himself that the plain, unvarnished fact of dying was the fearsome thing, not the attendant circumstances. He never wearied of conjuring up these circumstances, senselessly trying to exhaust all their possible variations. He infinitely anticipated the process of his dying, from the sleepless dawn to the mysterious volley. Before the day set by Julius Rothe he died hundreds of deaths in courtyards whose forms and angles strained geometrical probabilities, machine-gunned by variable soldiers in changing numbers, who at times killed him from a distance, at others from close by. He faced these imaginary executions with real terror (perhaps with real bravery); each simulacrum lasted a few seconds. When the circle was closed, Jaromir returned once more and interminably to the tremulous vespers of his death. Then he reflected that reality does not usually coincide with our anticipation of it; with a logic of his own he inferred that to foresee a circumstantial detail is to prevent its happening. Trusting in this weak magic, he invented, *so that they would not happen*, the most gruesome details. Finally, as was natural, he came to fear that they were prophetic. Miserable in the night, he endeavored to find some way to hold fast to the fleeting substance of time. He knew that it was rushing headlong toward the dawn of the twenty-ninth. He reasoned aloud: "I am now in the night of the twenty-second; while this night lasts (and for six nights more), I am invulnerable, immortal." The nights of sleep seemed to him deep, dark pools in which he could submerge himself. There were moments when he longed impatiently for the final burst of fire that would free him, for better or for worse, from the vain compulsion of his imaginings. On the twenty-eighth, as the last sunset was reverberating from the high barred windows, the thought of his drama, *The Enemies,* deflected him from these abject considerations.

Hladik had rounded forty. Aside from a few friendships and many habits, the problematic exercise of literature constituted his life. Like all writers, he measured the achievements of others by what they had accomplished, asking of them that they measure him by what he envisaged or planned. All the books he had published had left him with a complex feeling of repentance. His studies of the work of Böhme, of Ibn Ezra, and of Fludd had been characterized essentially by mere application; his translation of the *Sepher Yezirah,* by carelessness, fatigue, and conjecture. *Vindication of Eternity* perhaps had fewer shortcomings. The first volume gave a history of man's various concepts of eternity, from the immutable Being of Parmenides to the modifiable Past of Hinton. The second denied (with Francis Bradley) that all the events of the universe make up a temporal series, arguing that the number of man's possible experiences is not infinite, and that a single "repetition" suffices to prove that time is a fallacy . . . Unfortunately, the arguments that demonstrate this fallacy are equally fallacious. Hladik was in the habit of going over them with a kind of contemptuous perplexity. He had also composed a series of Expressionist poems; to the poet's chagrin they had been included in an anthology published in 1924, and no subsequent anthology but inherited them. From all this equivocal, uninspired past Hladik had hoped to redeem himself with his drama in verse, *The Enemies.* (Hladik felt the verse form to be essential because it makes it impossible for the spectators to lose sight of irreality, one of art's requisites.)

The drama observed the unities of time, place, and action. The scene was laid in Hradčany, in the library of Baron von Roemerstadt, on one of the last afternoons of the nineteenth century. In the first scene of the first act a strange man visits Roemerstadt. (A clock was striking seven, the vehemence of the setting sun's rays glorified the windows, a passionate, familiar Hungarian music floated in the air.) This visit is followed by others; Roemerstadt does not know the people who are importuning him, but he has the uncomfortable feeling that he has seen them somewhere, perhaps in a dream. They all fawn upon him, but it is apparent—first to the audience and then to the Baron— that they are secret enemies, in league to ruin him. Roemerstadt succeeds in checking or evading their involved schemings. In the dialogue mention is made of his sweetheart, Julia von Weidenau, and a certain Jaroslav Kubin, who at one time pressed his attentions on her. Kubin has now lost his mind, and believes himself to be Roemerstadt. The dangers increase; Roemerstadt, at the end of the second act, is forced to kill one of the conspirators. The third and final act opens. The incoherencies gradually increase; actors who had seemed out of the play reappear; the man Roemerstadt killed returns for a moment. Someone points out that evening has not fallen; the clock strikes seven, the high windows reverberate in the western sun, the air carries an impassioned Hungarian melody. The first actor comes on and repeats the lines he had spoken in the first scene of the first act. Roemerstadt speaks to him without surprise; the audience understands that Roemerstadt is the miserable Jaroslav Kubin. The drama has never taken place; it is the circular delirium that Kubin lives and relives endlessly.

Hladik had never asked himself whether this tragicomedy of errors was preposterous or admirable, well thought out or slipshod. He felt that the plot I have just sketched was best contrived to cover up his defects and point up his abilities and held the possibility of allowing him to redeem (symbolically) the meaning of his life. He had finished the first act and one or two scenes of the third; the metrical nature of the work made it possible for him to keep working it over, changing the hexameters, without the manuscript in front of him. He thought how he still had two acts to do, and that he was going to die very soon. He spoke with God in the darkness: "If in some fashion I exist, if I am not one of Your repetitions and mistakes, I exist as the author of *The Enemies*. To finish this drama, which can justify You, I need another year. Grant me these days, You to whom the centuries and time belong." This was the last night, the most dreadful of all, but ten minutes later sleep flooded over him like a dark water.

Toward dawn he dreamed that he had concealed himself in one of the naves of the Clementine Library. A librarian wearing dark glasses asked him: "What are you looking for?" Hladik answered: "I am looking for God." The librarian said to him: "God is in one of the letters on one of the pages of one of the four hundred thousand volumes of the Clementine. My fathers and the fathers of my fathers have searched for this letter; I have grown blind seeking it." He removed his glasses, and Hladik saw his eyes, which were dead. A reader came in to return an atlas. "This atlas is worthless," he said, and handed it to Hladik, who opened it at random. He saw a map of India as in a daze. Suddenly sure of himself, he touched one of the tiniest letters. A ubiquitous voice said to him: "The time of your labor has been granted." At this point Hladik awoke.

He remembered that men's dreams belong to God, and that Maimonides had written that the words heard in a dream are divine when they are distinct and clear and the person uttering them cannot be seen. He dressed: two soldiers came into the cell and ordered him to follow them.

From behind the door, Hladik had envisaged a labyrinth of passage-ways, stairs, and separate buildings. The reality was less spectacular: they descended to an inner court by a narrow iron stairway. Several soldiers—some with uniform unbuttoned—were examining a motorcycle and discuss-ing it. The sergeant looked at the clock; it was 8:44. They had to wait until it struck nine. Hladik, more insignificant than pitiable, sat down on a pile of wood. He noticed that the soldiers' eyes avoided his. To ease his wait, the sergeant handed him a cigarette. Hladik did not smoke; he accepted it out of politeness or humility. As he lighted it, he noticed that his hands were shaking. The day was clouding over; the soldiers spoke in a low voice as though he were already dead. Vainly he tried to recall the woman of whom Julia von Weidenau was the symbol.

The squad formed and stood at attention. Hladik, standing against the barracks wall, waited for the volley. Someone pointed out that the wall was going to be stained with blood; the victim was ordered to step forward a few paces. Incongruously, this reminded Hladik of the fumbling prepara-tions of photographers. A big drop of rain struck one of Hladik's temples and rolled slowly down his cheek; the sergeant shouted the final order.

The physical universe came to a halt.

The guns converged on Hladik, but the men who were to kill him stood motionless. The sergeant's arm eternized an unfinished gesture. On a paving stone of the courtyard a bee cast an unchanging shadow. The wind had ceased, as in a picture. Hladik attempted a cry, a word, a movement of the hand. He realized that he was paralyzed. Not a sound reached him from the halted world. He thought, "I am in hell, I am dead." He thought: "I am mad." He thought: "Time has stopped." Then he reflected that if that was the case, his mind would have stopped too. He wanted to test this; he repeated (without moving his lips) Vergil's mysterious fourth Eclogue. He imagined that the now remote soldiers must be sharing his anxiety; he longed to be able to communicate with them. It astonished h. m not to feel the least fatigue, not even the numbness of his protracted immobility. After an indeterminate time he fell asleep. When he awoke the world continued motionless and mute. The drop of water still clung to his cheek, the shadow of the bee to the stone. The smoke from the cigarette he had thrown away had not dispersed. Another "day" went by before Hladik understood.

He had asked God for a whole year to finish his work; His omnipo-tence had granted it. God had worked a secret miracle for him; German lead would kill him at the set hour, but in his mind a year would go by between the order and its execution. From perplexity he passed to stupor, from stupor to resignation, from resignation to sudden gratitude.

He had no document but his memory; the training he had acquired with each added hexameter gave him a discipline unsuspected by those who set down and forget temporary, incomplete paragraphs. He was not working for posterity or even for God, whose literary tastes were unknown to him. Meticulously, motionlessly, secretly, he wrought in time his lofty, invisible labyrinth. He worked the third act over twice. He eliminated certain symbols as over-obvious, such as the repeated striking of the clock, the music. Nothing hurried him. He omitted, he condensed, he amplified. In certain instances he came back to the original version. He came to feel an affection for the courtyard, the barracks; one of the faces before him modified his conception of Roemerstadt's character. He discovered that the wearying cacophonies that bothered Flaubert so much are mere visual superstitions, weakness and limitation of the written word, not the spoken . . . He concluded his drama. He had only the problem of a single phrase. He found it. The drop of water slid down his cheek. He opened his mouth in a maddened cry, moved his face, dropped under the quadruple blast.

Jaromir Hladik died on March 29, at 9:02 A.M.

ILYA VARSHAVSKY

Escape

*O*ne, two, pull! One, two, pull!"

It was a simple device—a beam, two ropes— but with its help the heavy block of ore was quickly hoisted into the wagon.

"Get moving!"

The load was not exceptionally heavy, but the little man in a striped uniform who leaned his chest into the wagon's crossbar was unable to move it at all.

"Get moving!"

Lending his aid, one of the other prisoners put his shoulder to the crossbar. It was too late! A guard had turned their way.

"What happened?"

"Nothing."

"Well, then, get going!"

The little man once more attempted to move the load, lunging at the crossbar. It was impossible and exhausted by an effort beyond his capabilities, he began to cough. He covered his mouth with his hand.

Silently the guard waited until his coughing spell had passed.

" Show me that hand."

Blood was on the hand that the prisoner extended.

"So . . . turn around."

On the back of the prisoner's jacket was a number which the guard wrote in his notebook.

"Get going!" This was to both of them, to the one who now would pull the wagon and to the one who was no longer capable of it.

The wagon began to roll.

"Excuse me, sir, would it be possible——"

"I told you to report to the doctor!"

He followed the bent back as it disappeared, verifying the entry in his notebook: A O 15/13264. This was obvious enough: A—desertion, O—life imprisonment, barracks No. 15, prisoner No. 13264. Life imprisonment. Yes, he had it correct, but for this prisoner his sentence was nearing its end. This meant the cotton fields.

"One, two, pull!"

Gleaming, polished metal, glass, the diffused light of fluorescent lamps, a kind of peculiar, palpable, sterile cleanliness.

The gray, somewhat fatigued eyes of the man in the white coat peered attentively out of his thick glasses. Here, in Medena's underground camps, human life was highly valued. Of course! Every prisoner, until his soul presented itself before the highest tribunal, had to expiate his guilt before those who in the distant reaches of the universe were engaged in an unprecedented struggle for the hegemony of the planet. And the planet needed uranium. Every prisoner was given work to do, and therefore his life was as valuable as the precious ore. But unfortunately there were cases like this. . . .

"Put your clothes on!"

His long thin arms hastily drew the jacket over his emaciated body.

"Stand here."

A slight depression of a pedal and the sacred number was obliterated by a red cross. Henceforth prisoner A O 15/13264 would once more be addressed as Arp Zumbi. This was only a natural expression of humane feeling for a man who was to labor in the cotton fields.

The cotton fields. Really no one knew anything reliable about them except those who never returned after they had been sent there. It was said that in their hot desiccating climate a man's body in twenty days was transformed into a dry stick, fit fuel for the crematoria.

"Here is your work release. Get out."

Arp Zumbi presented the work release to the guard at the barracks door and plunged into the familiar odor of disinfectant. The barracks resembled a public lavatory with its oppressive odor of disinfectant and hot stoves. The monotony of its white walls was relieved only by a large sign: "Torture and Death is the Punishment for Attempted Escape." This was yet additional evidence for the high regard in which human life was held here: it could be taken only when accompanied by the greatest possible effect.

Along one of the walls was something resembling a huge honeycomb— these were sleeping places divided into individual cells. Both convenient and hygienic. The slightest speck of dirt was apparent on the white plastic. But the cells were not meant for comfort. This was a prison and not a rest home, as the voice loved to repeat which conducted the daily psychological exercises. Separating the sleeping places into cells made it impossible for the prisoners to communicate with one another at night when the guards' alertness was somewhat dulled.

It was forbidden to remain in the sleeping places during the day and Arp Zumbi passed his time sitting on a bench. He thought about the cotton fields. Usually prisoners were collected and sent there once every two weeks when prisoners were brought together from all the camps. Then two days later replacements would arrive. It seemed to him that this had occurred most recently five days earlier, when that strange individual had appeared near Arp in the sleeping places. He was a little touched. Yesterday he had given Arp half of his own bread at the dinner hour. "Take it," he said, "you're so thin your pants are going to fall off." That was something! Giving away your own bread! Arp had never heard of that before. He was probably insane. Last night he was singing before he fell asleep. Imagine, singing in a place like this.

Arp's thoughts once more returned to the cotton fields. He knew that this meant the end, but for some reason he was not saddened. You get accustomed to death after ten years in the mines. But still he was curious about life there in the cotton fields.

During his entire imprisonment this was the first day without work. That was probably why it was passing so slowly. Arp would have liked to lie down and sleep, but that was impossible, even with a work release. This was a prison and not a rest home.

Arp's comrades returned from their work and to the odor of the disinfectant was added the sweetish odor of liquid decontaminant. Every prisoner who worked with uranium ore had to take a precautionary shower in the decontaminant every day. This was one of the measures which increased the prisoner's average life span.

Arp took his place in the line and set off for dinner.

Breakfast and dinner—at these times the guards largely ignored the restriction on conversation. Besides, it was hard to say much with your mouth full.

Arp silently ate his portion and waited for the command to rise.

"Take it!" And once more the crazy man gave him half his bread ration.

"I don't want it."

The command to fall into formation was given. It was only now that Arp noticed that everyone was staring at him. Doubtless because of the red cross on his back. We are always intrigued by a corpse.

"Lively there!"

This was meant for Arp's friend. His line had already formed, but he still sat at the table. He and Arp rose simultaneously and as Arp was taking his place he heard the almost inaudible whisper: "You could escape."

Arp pretended that he hadn't heard. The camp was full of informers and he didn't want to die under torture. The cotton fields would be better than that.

The voice either rose to a scream which made your head ache or it dropped to a barely audible whisper, which you involuntarily had to strain to hear. It issued from a loudspeaker which was fastened at the head of the sleeping places. This was the evening psychological exercise.

A nauseatingly familiar baritone elucidated for the prisoners the utter gravity of their fall. You could neither flee nor hide from the voice, nor could you simply exclude it from your consciousness like the shouting of the guards. You would begin to think about something else besides life in the camp and suddenly your attention would be seized by the voice with its unexpected fluctuations in volume. And that is the way it was three times a day: in the evening before sleep, at night when you slept, and in the morning five minutes before awaking. Three times, because this was a prison and not a rest home.

Arp lay, his eyes closed, and tried to think about the cotton fields. The exercise was nearing its end, but through it he could hear someone tapping rhythmically on the partition between the cells. It was the psycho again.

"Well, what do you want?" he said through his hands, held in the shape of an ear trumpet against the partition.

"Go to the latrine."

Arp himself did not know what compelled him to go downstairs to the doorway where he could hear the sound of running water.

In the latrine it was so hot that it was impossible to bear it for more than two minutes. In a moment they were bathed in sweat.

"Do you want to escape?"

"Get out of here. . . ."

Arp Zumbi was a veteran of the camps and he knew all the informers' tricks.

"Don't be afraid," the man whispered quickly. "I'm a member of the League of Liberation. Tomorrow we're going to try to smuggle out our first

group of prisoners and transport them to a safe place. You don't have
anything to lose: you will be given poison. If the attempted escape
fails. . . ."

"What then?"

"Take the poison. It will be better than death in the cotton fields.
Agreed?"

Unexpectedly, even for himself, Arp nodded.

"You'll get your instructions tomorrow in your bread ration. Be careful."

Once more Arp nodded and then he left.

For the first time in ten years he was so lost in his dreams that he did
not even hear the second and third psychological exercises.

Arp Zumbi stood last in the breakfast line; now his place was at the
end of his lines. Anyone who was released from work was the last to receive
food.

The convict dispensing the soup looked attentively at Arp and then,
with a quick grin, threw him a piece of bread which had lain separate from
the rest.

As he ate his soup, Arp carefully crumbled the bread. It was there. He
placed the rolled-up paper inside his mouth against his cheek.

Then he had to wait until the file of prisoners had left for their work.

He heard the command to rise. Arp left the cafeteria at the end of the
column and, reaching a cross corridor, turned to the left, while the others
continued ahead.

Here, around the corner, Arp was relatively safe. The trustees were
cleaning the barracks and the new shift of guards had not yet appeared.

The instructions were very terse. Arp read them three times, and confident he could remember them, he rolled the paper into a ball and swallowed it.

Now, when it was necessary to act, he was overcome by fear.

He wavered. Death in the cotton fields seemed more desirable that the
threat of torture.

"The poison!"

The recollection of the poison calmed him immediately. When all was
said and done, what did he have to lose?

Fear— disgusting, clinging, strangling fear—welled over him again as
he presented his work release to the guard at the edge of his zone.

"Where are you going?"

"To the doctor."

"On your way."

Arp felt as though his legs were made of cotton. He wandered through
the halls feeling danger behind his back. Any moment he expected a shout

and a round of automatic fire. In such cases they aimed at the legs. For attempted escape the penalty was torture and death. It was impossible to deprive the prisoners of an instructive spectacle; this was a prison and not a rest home.

Turn here!

Arp rounded the corner and leaned against the wall. He could hear his heart pounding and he felt that any minute he might vomit up that crucial ball of paper together with the bile that rose from his stomach. Cold sweat covered his body and his teeth would not cease their chattering. It was to the sound of a drum that prisoners apprehended in an attempted escape were led to the place of execution.

An eternity passed before he could bring himself to move on.

Somewhere here in an alcove there were supposed to be garbage containers. Arp repeated the instructions once more to himself. But again he was touched by doubt. What if this was all arranged? He could climb into a container and then they would have him! And as yet he had no poison. Fool! He should not have agreed to this until he had the poison in his hand. What an idiot he was! He was ready to pound his head against the wall— to fall like this into an informer's trap.

Here were the containers. Near the one on the left someone had placed a painters's trestle, just as in the instructions. Arp stood irresolute. Probably the best thing to do would be to turn back.

Suddenly he heard loud voices and the barking of a dog. A patrol! He had no time to think, but with unexpected agility he climbed onto the trestle and from it leaped into the container.

The voices came closer. He could hear the wheeze of the dog straining against its leash and the ringing of iron heels.

"Back, Gar!"

"There's somebody in one of those containers."

"Just rats, there are plenty of them here."

"No, he would bark differently if it were rats."

"Stupid! Let's get going! And shut up the dog!"

"Quiet, Gar!"

The sound of their steps died away.

Now Arp could inspect this refuge. The container was only one-fourth full and he could not hope to climb out of it, since it was the height of two men. Arp passed his hand along its wall and found two small holes which were described in the note. They were located in the battered sign which read "Labor Camps" girdling the container. Arp was to breathe through these openings when the cover was closed.

When the cover was closed Arp felt himself more than ever in a trap. Who knew how this folly would end? What was the League of Liberation? He had never heard of it in the camp before. Was it perhaps the same people who had helped him desert? He had been wrong not to listen to them and to tell his mother what he had done. That's when someone had informed on him. If he hadn't been such a fool everything could have been different.

Once more he heard voices and the sound of wheels. Arp put his eye to one of the openings and stood still. Two prisoners were pulling a tub with garbage; obviously they were trustees in this zone. They were in no hurry. Making themselves comfortable on the cart they passed back and forth a cigarette butt discarded by one of the guards. Arp watched the pale streams of smoke and his mouth filled with saliva. Some people have all the luck!

They got all they could from the butt. Then they hoisted the tub with the aid of a cable which passed through a pulley over Arp's head. He covered his head with his arms as the contents of the tub fell onto him.

It was only after the prisoners had left that he noticed the foul odor in his hiding place.

The breathing holes were located a little higher than Arp's mouth and he had to scrape some of the rubbish together under his feet to reach them comfortably.

Now he had to be alert. The garbage collection ended at ten o'clock and then the full containers would be sent up.

He did not know where the broad, rough plank, smeared with plaster, came from. One end of it was wedged into a corner of the container while the other was above Arp's head. The plank, like the trestle, was evidence that someone was concerned about the fate of the fugitive. Arp felt this especially keenly when through the garbage a sharp metal rod was driven which caught on the plank and then probed it from top to bottom. If the plank had not been there . . . . It seemed to him that the search would never end.

"What's inside there?" asked an old man's hoarse voice.

"Nothing, just a plank."

"Let's go!"

A light blow, the creaking of a gate, and the container, rocking back and forth, began to move upward. At times it hit against the walls of the shaft and Arp, his face pressed against the side of the container, felt every shock. Between his head and the plank there was a small area free of garbage, and this made it possible for him to pull his head away from the openings when the container swung particularly sharply.

Then it stopped! A final, very incisive blow, and the lid drew open with a rumble. Once more the iron bar probed the container's interior. Once more the friendly plank concealed the man who huddled under it shaking with fear.

Now the openings were turned to a concrete wall and all of Arp's world was limited to a gray, rough surface.

But that world was full of forgotten sounds. Among them Arp could make out the hum of automobile tires, the voices of people walking by, and even the chirping of sparrows.

A steady, persistent beating on the container's lid drove him to roll himself into a ball. The knocking came faster, more insistent, more impatient, and he realized it was rain. It was only then that he perceived how desirable and how close lay freedom.

Everything that night seemed to him like a dream. From the moment that he found himself thrown out of the container, he was either unconscious or awakened by the touch of rats' feet. The dump was full of rats. Somewhere not far away a highway passed and at times the automobiles' headlights outlined the heap of trash behind which Arp was hidden. Squeaking, the rats would throw themselves into the darkness, raking his face with their sharp claws, biting if he attempted to frighten them away, and then returning as soon as the heap was plunged into darkness.

Arp realized that by now his flight would have been discovered. He imagined what was happening in the camp. It occurred to him that dogs might pick up his trail leading to the containers, and then. . . .

Two bright bursts of light stunned him. Arp leaped to his feet as the headlights were extinguished. In their place gleamed a flashlight inside the truck. It was an army van, the kind that was ordinarily employed to haul supplies. The man behind the wheel beckoned to Arp to come closer.

Arp sighed with relief; this was the truck described in his instructions.

He came up behind the van as its rear door opened. Arp seized the hands extended to him and once more found himself in darkness.

The van was very crowded. Sitting on the floor, Arp could hear heavy breathing, and feel other bodies behind him and to the sides. Swaying softly on its springs, the van quietly advanced through the darkness. . . .

Arp was awakened by a flashlight turned onto his face. Something had happened! The sense of movement, which he had already grown accustomed to, had ceased.

"Time to stretch!" said the man with the flashlight. "You have five minutes."

Arp felt no eagerness to leave the vehicle, but many bodies were pressing against him and he was compelled to leap onto the ground.

Everyone milled around the cab; no one dared to go far from the van.

"Listen, friends!" said their rescuer, illuminating the figures in convicts' clothing with his flashlight. "Everything has gone well so far, but before we get you to a safe place anything might happen. Do you know the punishment for attempted escape?"

No one answered.

"You know. Therefore the Committee has poison for you. One pill for each of our friends. It will work instantly. Take it only in case of extreme need. Do you understand?"

Arp took his allotment wrapped in silver foil and climbed back into the van.

The pill which he held in his clenched fist gave him a feeling of personal power. Now the guards had no sway over him. He fell asleep with that idea on his mind. . . .

Danger! It was apparent in everything: the stopping of the van, the pale faces of the prisoners illuminated by the light coming in through the cracks in the van's panels, in the loud voices, there, on the road.

Arp tried to move, to get up, but a score of hands waved to tell him not to stir.

"You know military supplies are not subject to inspection." That was the driver's voice.

"But I'm telling you that we have our orders. Tonight. . . . "

The van roared ahead and automatic rifle fire crackled in pursuit. Chips flew off the ceiling of the van.

When Arp finally lifted his head he noticed that his hand held someone's small palm. From under a shaved skull dark eyes framed in long lashes looked at him and the prison clothing could not hide the girl's rounded body. On her left sleeve was the green star of the inferior race.

Arp involuntarily released his hand and wiped it on his trousers. Any communication with the inferior race was forbidden by Medena's laws, and that was why everyone who wore the star was born and died in the camps.

"Then they won't catch us? Is it true?"

The trembling little voice was so pitiful, that Arp, forgetting the law, shook his head.

"What's your name?"

"Arp."

"Mine is Ghetta."

Arp lowered his head onto his chest and pretended that he was drowsing. Who knows how they would look upon such contacts when the prisoners reached their destination?

Without reducing speed, the van left the highway and began to bounce over a bumpy road. Arp was hungry. Thanks to lack of food and the rough road, he began to feel ill. He tried to suppress his coughing, which offended those around him, but his efforts only made it worse. His body was bent double and the coughs tore from his throat along with a spray of blood.

This coughing spell so exhausted Arp that he did not have the strength to push away the hand which was wiping the sweat from his face, the hand of the girl who wore a green star.

The warm night air was saturated with the odors of exotic flowers, filled with the sounds of cicadas singing.

The prisoners' clothing had been discarded and the long linen gowns reaching to their heels were cool on bodies which had come hot from the baths. With his spoon Arp carefully scraped the last of the groats from his dish.

At one end of the cafeteria near a stage constructed from old barrels and planks stood three figures. A tall gray-haired man with a farmer's sun-burned face was obviously in charge. The second was a mild-visaged lad in a Medena army uniform, the driver of their van. The third was a little woman with thick red hair worn in a braid wound around her head. Her white medical gown suited her very well.

They waited until dinner was completed.

Finally the clatter of spoons subsided, and the man in charge leaped gracefully onto the stage.

"Greetings, my friends!"

A pleasant murmur of voices served to answer that unusual greeting.

"I want to tell you, first of all, that you are completely safe. The government does not know the location of our evacuation camp."

There was such an expression of happiness on the gray, emaciated faces that they almost seemed beautiful.

"You will remain here at our evacuation camp for a period of five to ten days. The exact length of your stay will be determined by our physician because you have a lengthy and difficult transition ahead of you. The place we are taking you to, of course, is not paradise. You will have to work. We have carved every foot of our settlements out of the jungle. But there you will be free, you may rear families and labor to your own advantage. Your residences have been prepared for you by those who have gone before you. This is our tradition. And now I will answer your questions."

As others were asking questions Arp was torn with indecision. He wanted to know if it would be possible at the settlements to marry a girl of the inferior race. But when he finally got his courage to the sticking point and hesitantly raised his hand, the tall man with the farmer's face was already leaving the stage.

Now the woman addressed the fugitives. She had a low sing-song voice and Arp had to strain to understand what she said.

The woman asked everyone to lie down and await physical examinations.

Arp found a cot with his name tag on it, lay down on the crisp cool sheets, and immediately fell asleep.

In his sleep he sensed that he was being turned onto his side, he felt the cold touch of a stethoscope, and opening his eyes, he saw the little woman with the red braid who was writing something in a notebook.

"Are you awake?" She smiled, revealing brilliant even teeth.

Arp nodded.

"You are very worn down. And your lungs are not in good condition.

You will sleep for seven days. We'll put you to sleep now."

It was only then that Arp noticed some kind of a machine which had been advanced to his bed.

The woman pressed several buttons on a white panel and a strange hum entered Arp's brain.

"Go to sleep!" said a remote and melodious voice and Arp fell asleep.

He had an amazing dream, full of sunshine and happiness.

Only in a dream could there be such ravishingly measured moments, such as absence of earth-bound gravity, such an ability to float through the air.

A huge meadow was sown with blinding white flowers. In the distance Arp could see a lofty tower flashing with all the lights of the rainbow. Arp pushed himself away from the earth and then slowly descended. He was irresistibly drawn to the radiant tower from which streamed ineffable bliss.

Arp was not alone. From all ends of the meadow toward the tower streamed people dressed like him in long white robes. Among them was Ghetta, the skirts of her robe overflowing with white flowers.

"What is it?" Arp asked her, pointing to the tower.

"The Tower of Freedom. Come!"

They took each other's hands and floated together through the air bursting with the rays of the sun.

"Wait!"

Arp also gathered flowers, filled the skirts of his robe with them, and they continued their way.

They lay the flowers at the foot of the tower.

"Who else!" cried Ghetta, fluttering through the gray-stemmed plants. "Come with me!"

The others were infected by their example. Only a short time passed and the tower's foundation was piled with flowers.

Then they built fires and roasted great pieces of meat skewered on long thin wands. The captivating odor of the meat blended with the smell of burning branches and aroused memories, very old, very pleasant.

Sated, they lay on the ground near the fire, watched the stars, great unknown stars in a black, black sky.

When Arp fell asleep near the smouldering fire, a little warm hand rested in his.

The fires went out. Variegated lights near the tower were illuminated. Near the ground, doors opened and two gigantic mechanical arms extended to rake in the cotton.

In the glassed-in tower the man with the sun-burned face watched the indicator on the automatic scales.

"Five times greater than any other group," he said, turning on the conveyor. "I'm afraid at that insane rate they won't last a week."

"I'll bet two bottles of wine on that," said the mild-visaged young man in uniform, grinning brightly. "They'll make it the usual twenty days. Hypnosis is a marvelous thing! Isn't it amusing the way they ate those roasted turnips! Anything can be done with hypnosis, isn't that so, Doctor?"

The little woman with the heavy braid of red hair coiled around her head did not hasten to answer. She came to the window, turned on a searchlight, and attentively observed the faces below, their skin drawn tight, like skulls.

"You're exaggerating the possibilities of electro-hypnosis," she said, revealing as she smiled a vampire's sharp teeth. "The powerful radiation of the psi-field can only provide rhythm for the work and determine a certain commonality of effort. What is most important is the preliminary psychological conditioning. The feigned escape, the staged dangers—it all creates a sense of freedom obtained at a dear price. It is impossible to know in advance what enormous reserves in the organism may be aroused by the higher emotions."

ALAIN ROBBE-GRILLET

The Secret Room

*F*irst there is a red spot, bright, red, shiny but dark, shading to almost black. It forms an irregular, clearly outlined rosette, extended on several sides by wide streaks of varying lengths which then divide and dwindle until they are no more than meandering threads. The entire area stands out against the pallor of a smooth, rounded, dull and yet pearly surface, a half-sphere gently curving to an expanse of the same pale hue—a whiteness attenuated by the gloom of the place: dungeon, crypt or cathedral—gleaming with a diffused luster in the darkness.

Beyond, the space is occupied by the cylindrical shafts of columns that grow more numerous and blurred in the distance, where the beginning of a huge stone staircase can be made out, gradually turning and narrowing as it rises toward the high vaulting into which it vanishes.

The whole of this scene is empty, staircase and colonnades. Alone in the foreground, glimmers the prone body, on which the red spot is spreading—a white body suggesting the luminous, supple, doubtless fragile and vulnerable flesh. Beside the bloodstained half-sphere, another identical though intact globe can be seen from almost the same angle; but the darker ringed tip crowning it is here quite recognizable, whereas the first is almost completely destroyed, or at least concealed, by the wound.

In the background, toward the bend of the stairs, a black figure is vanishing from sight, a man wrapped in a long, loose cape, who mounts the last steps without turning around, his crime committed. A faint vapor rises in intertwining spirals from a kind of incense burner set on a high, silvery-metal stand. Quite near lies the milky body where wide rivulets of blood are flowing from the left breast, down the side and over the hip.

It is a woman's body, its forms opulent but not heavy, completely naked, lying on its back, the bust half-raised by thick cushions laid on the floor, which is covered by rugs of Oriental design. The waist is very narrow, the neck long and slender, curved to one side, the head thrown back into a darker area where the features of the face can still be discerned, the mouth half open, the large eyes wide, gleaming with a fixed luster, and the mass of the long black hair spread out in waves of formal disorder on the heavy folds of some fabric, velvet perhaps, on which the arm and shoulder also rest.

It is a smooth, dark-violet velvet, or seems to be in this light. But violet, brown and blue also seem to prevail in the colors of the cushions—of which only a small part is concealed by the velvet material and which extend farther down under the bust and the waist—as well as in the Oriental patterns of the rugs on the floor. Beyond, these same colors recur in the stone of the slabs and columns, the arches of the vaulting, the staircase, the vaguer surfaces where the limits of the room are lost to view.

It is difficult to specify the latter's dimensions; the slaughtered young woman seems at first glance to occupy a considerable place in it, but the vast proportions of the staircase descending toward her would suggest, on the contrary, that she does not take up the whole room, for a noticeable area must actually extend to the right and the left, as well as toward those distant browns and blues in the various rows of columns, perhaps toward other sofas, heavy rugs, piles of cushions and fabrics, other tortured bodies, other incense burners.

It is also difficult to say where the light is coming from. Nothing, on the columns or on the floor, suggests the direction of its source. Moreover, there is no window in sight, and no torch. It is the milky body itself that seems to illuminate the scene, the neck and the swelling breasts, the curve of the hips, the belly, the full thighs, the legs stretched out, wide apart, and the black fleece of the sex exposed—provocative, proffered, henceforth useless.

The man has already moved several strides away. Now he is already on the first steps of the staircase which he is about to mount. The lower steps are long and deep, like the shallow stairs leading to some public edifice, temple or theatre; they then gradually diminish in size as they rise, and at the same time begin a broad spiral movement, so gradual that the staircase has not yet effected a half-turn when, reduced to an awkward narrow passageway without a railing, even vaguer in the deepening darkenss, it disappears toward the top of the vaulting.

But the man is not looking in this direction, where his steps will nonetheless carry him; his left foot on the second step and his right already set on the third, knee bent, he has turned around to take a look at the scene. The long loose cape which he has hastily thrown over his shoulders, and which he holds at his waist with one hand, has been swept by the rotation which has just brought his head and upper body around to face away from the direction he is going, a flap of material raised in the air as though by the effect of a gust of wind; the corner, which folds back on itself in a loose S, reveals the gold-embroidered, red-stain lining.

The man's features are impassive, but strained, as though in anticipation—fear perhaps —of some sudden event, or rather reassuring himself as to the total immobility of the scene. Although he looks back in this way, his whole body has remained leaning slightly forward, as though he were still continuing his ascent. His right arm—the one not holding the edge of the cape—is half extended to the left, toward a point in space where the railing would be if there were one on this staircase, an interrupted, almost incomprehensible gesture, unless it is an instinctive impulse to catch hold of the missing support?

As for the direction of his gaze, it is unquestionably toward the body of the victim lying exposed on the cushions, the limbs extended in a cross, the bust raised slightly, the head thrown back. But perhaps the face is hidden from the man's eyes by one of the columns which rises at the foot of the stairs. The young woman's right hand touches the floor just at this column's base. A thick iron fetter encircles the delicate wrist. The arm is almost in shadow, the hand alone receiving enough light for the slender, spread fingers to be clearly visible against the circular rim that forms a base for the stone shaft. A black-metal chain is fastened around the shaft and passes through a ring on the fetter, closely attaching the wrist to the column.

At the arm's other end, a round shoulder, raised by the cushions, is also plainly lighted, as are the neck, the throat and the other shoulder, the armpit and its down, the left arm stretched behind the body too and its wrist attached in the same way to the base of another column, quite close to the foreground; here the iron ring and the chain are clearly seen, drawn with great distinctness down to the smallest detail.

Seen in the same way, still in the foreground but on the other side, is a similar though somewhat lighter chain which twice encircles the ankle directly, attaching it to a heavy ring set in the floor. About a yard or so behind it, the right foot is chained in the same manner. But it is the left foot and its chain that are represented with the most precision.

The foot is small, delicate, finely modeled. The chain has bruised the flesh in places, making noticeable though small depressions. Its links are oval, thick and about the size of an eye. The ring is like those used for hitching horses; it is lying almost flat on the stone slab, in which it is held by a massive spike. The edge of a rug begins an inch or so away; it is raised by a fold produced, no doubt, by the victim's convulsive though necessarily limited movements when she attempted to struggle.

The man is still half leaning over her, standing about a yard away. He examines her face tilted back, the dark eyes enlarged by cosmetics, the mouth wide as if in a scream. The man's position reveals only one-quarter of his face, but he is evidently in the grip of violent excitement, despite his rigid position, silence, and immobility. His back is bent slightly. His left hand, the only one that can be seen, holds away from his body a piece of fabric, some dark garment which trails on the rug and which must be the long cape with its gold-embroidered lining.

This massive figure greatly conceals the naked flesh where the red spot, which has spread over the bulge of the breast, flows in long rivulets which branch out as they grow thinner, against the pale background of the torso and the whole side. One of them has reached the armpit and traces a fine, almost straight line the length of the arm; others have run down toward the waist and drawn a more arbitrary network, which is already congealing over the belly, the hip and the top of the thigh. Three or four veinules have reached as far as the hollow of the groin and formed a meandering line which joins the point of the V formed by the parted legs and vanishes in the black fleece.

There, now the flesh is still intact, the black fleece and the white belly, the gentle curve of the hips, the slender waist and, above, the pearly breasts which rise in time to the rapid breathing, whose rhythm grows faster. The man, close beside her, one knee on the ground, bends farther forward. The head with the long wavy hair, which alone has kept some freedom of movement, stirs, struggles; finally the girl's mouth opens and twists, while the flesh yields, the blood spurts out over the tender smooth skin, the skillfully painted black eyes widen enormously, the mouth opens still further, the head is flung from right to left, violently, one last time, then more gently, finally falling back motionless in the mass of black hair spread out on the velvet.

At the very top of the stone staircase, the little door is open, releasing a yellow, sustained light, against which the dark figure of the man wrapped in his long cape is silhouetted. He has no more than a few steps to climb in order to reach the threshold.

Then the whole scene is empty, the enormous violet-shadowed room with its stone columns extending on all sides, the monumental staircase with no railing that turns as it rises, growing narrower and vaguer as it mounts into the darkness toward the top of the vaulting, where it vanishes.

Near the prone body whose wound has congealed, whose luster is already fading, the faint vapor from the incense burner forms complicated volutes in the calm air: at first it is a strand inclined to the left, then rises and increases slightly in height, then returns toward the axis of its point of departure, exceeds it on the right, again starts in the other direction, only to return once more, thus tracing an irregular, gradually fading sinusoid, which rises vertically toward the top of the canvas.

*Slawomir Mrozek (1930–   ) was born in Poland,
studied architecture, and has worked as a journalist
and caricaturist for Polish periodicals. One of
Poland's leading satirists, he has written many short
stories, several plays, and a novel. In his works, Mrozek often satirizes the bureaucrats in his own society;
by use of fantastical materials he often makes the
absurd appear real and the real appear absurd. His
most successful play,* The Policeman *(1956), was
produced after the "thaw." For further reading there
are two collections of short stories;* The Elephant
(1962) and The Ugupu Bird *(1968).*

SLAWOMIR MROZEK

Check!

*T*he day was cloudy. I do not mind the weather myself, but I met a
friend who seemed to be very worried about it.

"I'm developing rheumatism. Can't be helped. I wouldn't pay much
attention to it, but what's worse, I caught a cold a few days ago. But all I
need now is to get soaked through. I already have the beginnings of a 'flu.
My bones are aching. And what next? Nobody can be sure that there will
be no serious complications."

I pointed out that after all he did not have to get soaked through; all he
had to do was to stay under cover when it rained. And thank God we were
not short of roofs.

"It's easy for you to talk, you've no outdoor duties. But I have to work
in the open day in day out. One has got to live."

I asked about his work. We had known each other for a long time.
Together we had worked as extras in the theatre. We had had a succession
of temporary jobs, always at the mercy of changing circumstances: delivery
men, part-time caretakers, fourth men at bridge or fourteenth at dinner,
temporary comforters, birds of passage, bodyguards, baby-sitters and professional guests.

He explained that he had found relatively light work, which would have been entirely satisfactory if it were not for his inborn sensitivity to changes of temperature.

"Do you know what living chess is? It's exactly the same as normal chess, except that instead of a chessboard on a table one uses a much larger board marked out on the pavement of a square; instead of inanimate chessmen real men suitably dressed up take part in the game. The players themselves must, of course, be in raised positions at the opposite sides of the board so that they can see it all at a glance. Because of its value as a spectacle, live chess is organized as a part of celebrations and open-air festivals. The public likes it very much. After all, how many people can watch a game on a normal board? Three, five at the most, and they disturb the players. Now, any number can watch live chess, while the players, separated from the multitude, are able to concentrate on the problem of winning. Add to that the attraction of colourful costumes and you'll see why live chess is a popular spectacle. You will find it also in clubs which have a suitable courtyard or other space at their disposal.

"Apart from space you need, of course, the personnel. Sixteen men for the white and sixteen for the black, and a few reserve (men are only human), and also a wardrobe. The volunteers don't have to pass any exams. After the first few minutes of enjoyment the attractions of the game, which had made them offer their services, tend to evaporate. Soon they get tired and impatient and then withdraw under the slightest pretext (death in the family, an electric iron left on at home, an alleged headache) thus spoiling an interesting game. What's needed are regulars, men who having had no interest in the game don't stand the risk of losing it and can be relied upon to stick it to the end without any ups or downs. They get a regular salary, and as professionals they give the required standard of service.

"The work is relatively light. I say, relatively, because this depends on a number of variable factors. In the summer, when the sun shines, it can be quite pleasant, as long as you don't suffer from sunstroke. In the autumn, during protracted foul weather, it can give you a cold and induce melancholia. The winter is worst. There are games played in a snow storm, when you can't see more than two squares ahead and one has got to be careful not to take one of one's own pieces.

"At the moment it's still summer, but a rainy one. I wouldn't complain," ended my friend, "if it were not for the clouds and my tonsils. If I don't go to work to-day, they can give me notice. I'm playing a Bishop. I reached that position with a great deal of effort and to the envy of my colleagues. Will you take over for one day only? Please! Perhaps tomorrow the weather will improve. You'll get full day's pay. It's not too bad; Bishops get more because there is so much running to do. Anyway all the figures get more. One day I might become King."

"I can't" I replied. "I can't stand people looking at me. Don't you remember how this caused difficulties at the theatre? A staring crowd embarrasses me and this leads to a counter-reaction, forcing me into excessively open and frank behaviour. It seems to me that since they come to look at me, it would be less than honest not to show them everything. I was thrown out of the theatre because during a first night, under the influence of so many pairs of eyes, I showed the spectators my boil. And you have said yourself that living chess is a spectacle."

"You needn't worry about that," my friend reassured me. "On this occasion there is no question of a spectacle. I'm working for two old men who have been advised by their doctor to seek outdoor exercise. That's why they gave up ordinary and took up living chess. It's a private game. Apart from the participants you won't see a soul, there won't be a single spectator."

I reflected that I had nothing else to do that day. There was no reason to refuse a favour to a friend, while earning some money at the same time.

"All right," I said, "but will I know how to do it?"

"It is quite simple and the Knight will give you the few essential bits of advice. I'm in the white team and we stand next to each other on the left. At the beginning of each game, before developments separate us, we always manage to exchange a few words."

"Fine, I'll go."

"Go. I'll retire to bed."

We parted.

The game took place in the courtyard of an old palace, enclosed on four sides by two-storied cloisters. I entered through a tunnel-like gateway. A grey square of sky covered the enormous box of the courtyard, so vast that the huge chessboard marked out on its floor did not look large at all. Here and there on the walls vertical pools of Russian vine screened the cloisters. Perhaps because of them the whole courtyard was swathed in an emerald gloom, the intensity of which varied with the passage of mists and clouds high above. A few human figures moving about looked strangely small because we are accustomed to seeing people indoors in restricted spaces, which make them appear large. Here however I found myself under an open sky and yet indoors, as if clever architecture had joined space to enclosure.

As I approached some of the figures acquired a super-natural size. It was because of their costumes. While the pawns were not much larger than normal human beings, the Bishops, Rooks and Knights looked enormous. Only their feet, protruding from under the fantastic dress, remained normal, shod in a variety of old shoes. Above them necks and heads of horses, their teeth bared, each tooth the size of a tile, the severe-looking, geometric and crenellated Rooks, the saucer-like ruffs of the Bishops.

Daunted by all this I involuntarily stopped on the edge of the court-yard. The cavernous gateway, unpleasantly ready to reflect and magnify the slightest noise, suddenly seemed friendly and snug. I did not notice that a black Rook had appeared behind me.

"You are not allowed in here," said a voice from within the castle. I looked at the Rook and noticed painted horizontal and vertical white lines imitating the pointing between bricks. Automatically I looked up to the battlements, though I knew that the head of the speaker must be level with mine.

I explained politely that I was not a casual gaper, but had come to stand in for a sick colleague. The Rook towered over me silently for a while and then from within came the sound as of spitting and he moved away, his heavy shoes creaking on the stones. I entered the courtyard.

On the left wing of the whites I noticed the Knight to whose care my friend had recommended me. I spoke to him and he turned his massive *papier maché* chest and mane frozen in a picturesque disarray, until his nostrils were right above my head.

"All right," he said. "I'll help you to change. Got a cigarette? We are not allowed to smoke during work, but we could have one now. Mind you, one has to make sure that the smoke doesn't go up, because this can be seen and a supervisor might pick on you. But if you blow the smoke into your trousers, it comes out at the bottom and all's well. You must learn these little tricks."

Under the Knight's guidance I put on the Bishop's involucre. It was dark and stuffy inside it. Through the eye-holes I could see the edge of my frill and a part of the courtyard plunged in a green dusk.

"Yes, my friend," said the Knight, "you've got to know the ins and outs here. Now, for instance, we can have a smoke, but we've got to be careful. We can also eat our sandwiches, but you must remember not to drop the wrapping paper on the ground. Later it is more difficult."

The Queen took her place on my right. Instinctively I looked at her feet and saw frayed trouser turn-ups and shoes with cracked uppers. A bit far-ther along towered the majestic silhouette of the King with tennis shoes sticking out from under it.

"The King gets the highest salary," explained the Knight, "because he is the heaviest of the lot. In spite of it he is played by an elderly man; though the piece is heavy there's not much walking to be done, and that's important when you are past sixty. Also in old age the few extra pennies come very handy indeed. Should you notice that it is his turn and he's not moving, you'll do him a service if you knock on his side, that's if you are near enough. Sometimes he falls asleep inside still standing on his feet."

The ranks of the white and black pieces were filling in. Beyond them I could see the cloisters. The air, saturated with damp, was far from clear, the clouds in the sky cast their shadows over everything, and the overhanging roof made the walls darker still. Because of all this the columns, arches and balustrades, here and there obliterated by patches of vine, looked like a flat and misty drawing.

"Oho," said the pawn in front of me, "the black Bishop has again been at the bottle."

"He really shouldn't drink," commented the Knight. "Bishops have to run in straight lines. It's different when you're a Knight. Nobody notices if you stray from your course a little bit because as it is you've got to move sideways. . . ."

"Attention," warned the pawn. "It's beginning."

I used to play chess in my time, not badly either, but one did not have to be a master to notice the low level of the game in which I had to take part. First of all the pauses between moves were of such duration that one could not help wondering if the players had fallen asleep or, perhaps, gone away altogether, forgetting to tell us that they had given up. Hidden in the cloisters they kept on falling into endless contemplation, while our legs were getting numb. Eventually their mental efforts led to hopeless and chaotic moves, which betrayed a complete lack of skill on both sides.

Like all the pieces I was moved about a few times without rhyme or reason and this began to worry me.

"What's the matter?" I whispered to the Knight when at last I found myself again at his side.

"Sclerosis," he whispered back. "A short while ago they could still get through a game in five or six hours, but it seems they've got worse."

"Which of the two plays a better game?"

"Neither. That's why it's such hard work. Sometimes they can't finish before it gets too dark and then they leave us where we stand overnight and finish the game the following day. I'm afraid this is going to happen to-night. The game is going badly and the weather is uncertain."

We walked about the chessboard hither and thither, from one square to another. A few pawns got captured. We looked at them with envy as they walked away.

It started raining. A fine rain, the sort that lasts a long time; it starts with deliberation, knowing that it has a few days in hand and need not hurry, and then gradually gathers momentum. My cardboard costume protected me at first, but I was worried about my feet shod only in light shoes.

"See that Rook in boots?" The Knight pointed at a black figure. "Watch out. He likes to give your ankle a kick when capturing you. He'll also tell on you if you squat for a moment to give your tired feet a rest. A proper patriot he is, too. God forbid that black should start losing. He's at his worst then. Sometimes he gets so excited that he starts crying."

"Is it his game, or what?"

"He's just passionate."

Something started dripping under my collar. The dome-like cardboard structure over my head had parted in one place and was letting through the rain, its drops unpleasantly cold.

The intervals between moves became incredibly long as the players seemed to have increasing difficulty in taking in the state of the game. As the rain thickened, the gargoyles, through which the rain gutters were discharging, began to sing, shyly at first, but with increasing confidence. From all sides came the individual whisper of drops falling against the general background of a noisy downpour. The black Bishop, his alcoholic euphoria gone, had obviously lost heart and swayed sadly two squares away from me. My friend, the Knight, had been shifted to the other end of the board.

Anger swelled inside me. It was all very well for all those old professionals, used to this kind of discomfort. But my feet were getting wet and I could not reconcile myself to it. And there was no prospect whatsoever of the game ever coming to an end.

"Perhaps someone will capture me," I thought hopefully for a moment. "Then I shall be able to go home. But one cannot rely on a happy accident. What else? Wait. And if they leave us overnight? The Knight said that this could happen."

I could see so many openings, which if exploited could help to bring about a decision. . . .But the most obvious, the most glittering chances were being systematically wasted by both sides. The thought that because of this incompetence I might get pneumonia gave another spur to my anger. Not able to bear it all any longer I decided off my own bat to bring the game to a conclusion.

I was sure that I could get away with a little cheating, with moving one or two squares without any orders. Around me I could see only general apathy. The sclerotic players immersed in their thoughts would not notice anything. Slowly, unobtrusively, I started to shift my position and move into the next square. One had to be careful not to overdo it and brazenly move from a black into a white square, because everyone knows that a Bishop has to stick to one color throughout the game. But if I avoided such glaring mistakes I was bound to succeed.

Now I had to make my decisive move. Having found myself on the same diagonal as the black Bishop was I had to take my courage in both hands and capture him? But there was a chance that the player directing the black side, seeing his Bishop opposite me, might decide to have me captured. I had to wait. Anyhow I did not want to move about too much. Minutes passed and nothing happened. I counted up to a hundred and decided to take the risk. Moving with purpose I walked up to the black Bishop.

"You're captured, my friend," I said. "You can go home."

In choosing him as my first victim I counted on the fact that in his drunken stupor he was paying even less attention to the game than the others. When I spoke to him he swayed, cleared his throat and did not disguise his joy.

"Splendid. I'm on my way," he cried. "What? Can't a man have a drink?" He spoke with sudden belligerence and fled without waiting for an answer. I occupied his square as if it was mine of right.

My calculations proved right. The general boredom and indifference were such that nobody knew or cared if it was white's move or black's. The players themselves must have had one of their mental blackouts and I was also helped by the rain and the gathering dusk.

Just in case, however, I waited a few moments before polishing off two black pawns. Neither of them uttered a word, and with obvious relief they left the chessboard. In this way acting in my own interest I was helping my colleagues.

I could not have cared less about white's victory for which I was working. All I wanted was to bring the game to a conclusion. I expected that once I had captured all the black pieces, even the dimmest idiot would be able to checkmate the lonely King. Gradually I grew insolent and captured any handy piece without stopping in between. I was, however, on guard as far as the black Rook in heavy boots was concerned. Not only did I leave him alone, but I also tried to operate as far from him as possible, so that he should not notice what I was doing.

I was just preparing to have a go at one of the black Knights when I noticed that something was wrong.

In spite of all my efforts, the numerical balance of the opposing forces remained unchanged. True that there were fewer pieces on the board, but both sides had been equally depleted. Could it be that the man playing black has suddenly woken up and shown unexpected enterprise? I started to observe closely what was happening around me and discovered that the black Rook in heavy boots was cheating.

Now I understood why, even if he suspected something, he did not expose me. His own hands were far from clean. He was doing the same as I, but from quite different motives—he was the only jingoist in the game. All my efforts were being wasted. The balance between the sides remained unchanged and the chances of the game coming to an end had not increased.

The black Rook was becoming insolent. I saw him jump at our poor Queen, kicking brutally with his heavy boots at the miserable old shoes of my colleague. The enemy had given up all pretence and I could not remain idle. Without wasting a moment I removed the black Queen. It was clear that the black Rook knew what I was doing, but he also knew that I was aware of his activities. He was avoiding me and I could see that he hated me.

On my side, apart from the King of course, only my friend the Knight and a few pawns were left in the game. On the other side the position was similar.

"I don't want to interfere," said the Knight, "but do be careful. I would like to help you, but I'm regular here. If they notice, they'll throw me out, and I want to keep the job. With you it's different. There's nothing they can do to you, because you are here only for the day. Ow! . . ." He cried out with pain as the black Rook, who had approached stealthily, gave him the usual vicious kick. "Farewell," he called to me walking off the field. He was the only one who understood what was happening. But I could not stop to say good-bye, because I had to run and polish off the black Knight. Then came the turn of the remaining pawns. We finished with them in no time, without even trying to keep up appearances. Only the two Kings, the black Rook and myself were left on the board. No further cheating was possible in the now wide open space.

It was now raining cats and dogs. My cardboard costume was sodden and heavy, my shoes full of water. The rain had softened the battlements of the Rook and paint was running off the Kings. The ingenious orchestration of drops and rivulets disappeared under the steady noise now filling the courtyard.

The players made a few primitive moves, putting each other's Kings in check, but it was all pointless and could bring no solution. Then came an endless pause and one really did not know if the players were still there or had gone home. The four of us were standing there, soaking in the rain, and with despair I could see no end to it. Worse still was the possibility, mentioned by the Knight, that we should be left there till the morning, the players hoping in vain to finish the game the following day. The light was failing and the rain splashed with increasing force.

I watched the black Rook, determined to be the first to kick should he approach me. He must have guessed and kept his distance. For a while we stood still, watching each other. At last he gave up and, turning to the white King, said: "Check!"

I decided to put an end to it.

"Listen," I said to the Rook, "let's not delude ourselves. It's dark and pouring with rain. I know you are a patriot and want your side to win, but you can see that the game is inconclusive. It's a draw. Let's go home."

"If I say check," he declared gloomily, "it is check!"

I could see that there was no point in arguing with him. My King had not budged, he must have fallen asleep in spite of the rain. I could not be sure that enraged by this the black Rook would not cause him some bodily harm. I knocked at the King's side.

"Eh? What is it?" The old man woke up.

"You are in check, granpa. Didn't you hear?"

"All right, all right." He shuffled to the adjoining square. The Rook immediately checked him again. Making sure that I was not exposing my-self to the Rook, I gently propelled the King to the edge of the board. The stillness of the courtyard, woven out of the murmur and gurgling of the rain, was interrupted by a succession of hoarse cries of "check!"

"We are going home," I managed to whisper to the black King as we passed him. He yawned, said "Good-night" and walked off. It was already so dark that the enraged black Rook did not even notice.

When we reached the edge of the chessboard I made a dash for the cloisters, pulling the King with me. Panting we hid behind a column. I ordered the King to keep quiet and started listening.

It was now coming down in buckets and the invisible courtyard was splashing and drumming. I expected to hear the heavy boots on the pave-ment. We waited for a time but the sound did not come.

"Finished," I said. "We are going."

"Check!" roared a voice right behind us.

We fled across the courtyard in the direction of the gate. While run-ning as fast as I could I figured out how he managed to surprise us. He must have taken off his boots and in stockinged feet walked stealthily along the cloisters.

I was already under the archway leading to freedom when I noticed that the old man, burdened with age and the costume made doubly heavy by the rain, had fallen behind. His heavy breathing and the squelching of his tennis shoes echoed under the vaulted ceiling. I realized that we could not escape. It was probably fear that suggested a way out. I peeled off my costume, turned back and feverishly started to remove the King's super-structure. Then I threw it as far as I could. The huge, stiff scarecrow settled on the floor with a dull thud. We jumped behind the pillars.

The black Rook was right behind us. He found what he wanted and stopped. Then in the echoing darkness we heard repeated dull blows of a knife piercing a dummy—the empty royal shell of wet cardboard and *papier maché*.

We walked away slowly. There was no more any need to hurry.

Lars Görling (1931–1966), in addition to being one of Sweden's foremost film directors, was a poet and a novelist. His first novel Triptyk (1961) was followed by 491, the novel best known to the English-speaking public. Görling was said to be a revolutionary without an ideology; his writings and his films dramatize the ways in which human rights may be crushed by the weight of social machinery. His premature, sudden death came at the peak of his artistic career.

LARS GÖRLING

Opus Dei

The first line represents him.
The second her.
The third average of their feelings.
The point shows the times
when observations were made.
Each diagonal a week.
Each horizontal a feeling-value.
Everything started July 7
and ended November 30.

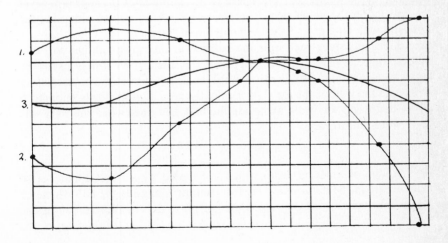

PETER HANDKE

Abstraction of the Ball

That Fell in the River

As children we often sat at the edge of the river Sunday afternoons
watching the soccer game from where we sat at the midfield line. Whenever
the ball fell in the water near where we were sitting we ran alongside the
river and with long poles fished the ball out of the water. We could take our
time doing this since each time the ball fell in the water another ball that
was kept in reserve was put into play from the sideline. We ran as fast as the
ball was carried along by the river until we fished it out always just before
it reached the wall of the weir. As a rule, the river flowed slowly enough so
all we had to do was walk alongside the ball. But once when the river was
swollen we had to run.

At the edge of a soccer field, which is situated by a river, a number of
children are in the habit of having fun running alongside the ball whenever
it falls into the river during the course of play; that is, they run alongside
the ball from the midfield line to the end of the field and fish it out of the

water only there. Once when the river was swollen, the children had to run very quickly.

Children walk alongside the ball each time it falls in the river at midfield. They fish the ball out of the water only at the end of the field. When the river is swollen the children run very quickly.

Persons walk from the midfield line of a soccer field to the end of the field alongside an object that is drifting in the river at the edge of the field. At the moment when they reach the end of the field the referee whistles half-time. When the river is swollen and the persons have to run they come to a stop alongside the object at the end of the field shortly before the half-time whistle blows.

Someone is walking along the edge of a soccer field next to an object that has fallen in the river. He gets under way 30 seconds before the last minute of the first half of the game. At the very moment he has reached the end of the field and stands next to the object the referee blows the half-time whistle. When the river is swollen he reaches the end of the field together with the object precisely one second before the whistle blows and after he has gotten under way simultaneously with the object 10 seconds before the referee blows his whistle.

In order to traverse half the length of a playing field (playing field length = 90 meters) someone requires 1 minute, 30 seconds. When he has to run he requires for the same distance only 9 seconds.

It takes someone 90 seconds to traverse 45 meters. Running it takes him 9 seconds.

90 sec————45 m
 1 sec————speed x m

9 sec————45 m
1 sec————speed y m

$$90\ x\ =\ 45$$
$$9\ y\ =\ 45$$
$$x\ =\ \frac{45}{90}$$
$$y\ =\ \frac{45}{9}$$
$$x\ =\ \frac{1}{2}$$
$$y\ =\ 5$$

As children we walked on Sunday afternoons at a speed of one half meter per second alongside the soccer ball when it was kicked from the playing field into the river. But when the river was swollen we had to run alongside the ball at a speed of five meters per second to fish the ball out of the water before it would be washed over the wall of the weir.

J. G. (James Graham) Ballard (1930–   ) was born in Shanghai, China, and was educated at King's College, Cambridge. After service in the Royal Air Force, he became a professional writer of distinguished science fiction and fantasy short stories and novels. Ballard believes that "science fiction is the authentic literature of the 20th century, the only fiction to respond imaginatively to the transforming nature of science and technology"; furthermore, he suggests the period of greatest moral urgency for the writer is the present, rather than the future. In any event, his work reveals a powerful imagination which reinforces a serious concern with human despair. Two outstanding novels are The Wind from Nowhere *(1962) and* The Drowned World *(1963), both of which treat matters of environmental concern. "The Assassination Weapon" (below) was also produced as a play in London (1969); he has published more than nine collections of short stories. For further reading:* Vermilion Sands *(1973).*

J. G. BALLARD

The Assassination Weapon

*A*n attempt to conceive the "false" deaths of J. F. Kennedy, Lee Harvey Oswald and Malcolm X in terms of the notional character of a psychotic patient in the Belmont Asylum, assumed to have died by his own hand in the rôle of a former H-bomber pilot.

Thoracic Drop. The spinal landscape, revealed at the level of T-12, is that of the porous rock-towers of Teneriffe, and of the native of the Canaries, Oscar Dominguez, who created the technique of decalcomania and so exposed the first spinal landscape. The clinker-like rock-towers, suspended above the silent swamp, create an impression of profound anguish. The inhospitability of this mineral world, with its inorganic growths, is relieved only by the balloons flying in the clear sky. They are painted with names: Jackie, Lee Harvey, Malcolm. In the mirror of this swamp there are no reflections. Here, time makes no concessions.

527

Autogeddon. Waking: the concrete embankment of a motorway extension. Roadworks, cars drumming two hundred yards below. In the sunlight the seams between the sections are illuminated like the sutures of an exposed skull. A young woman stands ten feet away from him, watching with unsure eyes. The hyoid bone in her throat flutters as if discharging some subvocal rosary. She points to her car, parked off the verge beside a grader, and then beckons to him. *Kline, Coma, Xero.* He remembered the aloof, cerebral Kline and their long discussions on this terminal concrete beach. Under a different sun. This girl is not Coma. "My car." She speaks, the sounds as dissociated as the recording in a doll. "I can give you a lift. I saw you reach the island. It's like trying to cross the Styx." He sits up, searching for his Air Force cap. All he can say is: "Jackie Kennedy."

Googolplex. Dr. Lancaster studied the walls of the empty room. The mandalas, scored in the white plaster with a nail file, radiated like suns towards the window. He peered at the objects on the tray offered to him by the nurse. "So, these are the treasures he has left us—an entry from Oswald's Historic Diary, a much-thumbed reproduction of Magritte's Annunciation, and the mass numbers of the first twelve radioactive nuclides. What are we supposed to do with them?" Nurse Nagamatzu gazed at him with cool eyes. "Permutate them, doctor?" Lancaster lit a cigarette, ignoring the explicit insolence. This elegant bitch, like all women she intruded her sexuality at the most inopportune moments. One day. . . . He said: "Perhaps. We might find Mrs. Kennedy there. Or her husband. The Warren Commission has reopened its hearing, you know. Apparently it's not satisfied. Quite unprecedented." Permutate them? The theoretical number of nucleotide patterns in DNA was a mere 10 to the power of 120,000. What number was vast enough to contain all the possibilities of those three objects?

Jackie Kennedy, Your Eyelids Deflagrate. The serene face of the President's widow, painted on clapboard 400 feet high, moves across the rooftops, disappearing into the haze on the outskirts of the city. There are hundreds of the signs, revealing Jackie in countless familiar postures. Next week there may be an SS officer, Beethoven, Christopher Columbus or Fidel Castro. The fragments of these signs litter the suburban streets for weeks afterwards. Bonfires of Jackie's face burn among the reservoirs of Staines and Shepperton. With luck he got a job on one of the municipal disposal teams, warms his hands at a brazier of enigmatic eyes. At night he sleeps beneath an unlit bonfire of breasts.

Xero. Of the three figures who were to accompany him, the strangest was Xero. For most of the time Kline and Coma would remain near him, sitting a few feet away on the embankment of the deserted motorway, following in another car when he drove out to the radio-observatory, pausing behind him as he visited the atrocity exhibition. Coma was too shy, but now and then he would manage to talk to Kline, although he never remembered what they said to each other. By contrast, Xero was an archangel, a figure of galvanic energy and uncertainty. Moving across the abandoned landscape near the flyover, the very perspectives of the air seemed to invert behind him. At times, when Xero approached the forlorn group sitting on the embankment, his shadows formed bizarre patterns on the concrete, transcripts of cryptic formulae and insoluble dreams. These ideograms, like the hieroglyphs of a race of blind seers, remained on the grey concrete after Xero had gone, the detritus of this terrifying psychic totem.

Questions, Always Questions. Karen Novotny watched him move around the apartment, dismantling the mirrors in the hall and bathroom. He stacked them on the table between the settees in the lounge. This strange man, and his obsessions with time, Jackie Kennedy, Oswald and Eniwetok. Who was he? Where had he come from? In the three days since she had found him on the motorway she had discovered only that he was a former H-bomber pilot, for some reason carrying World War III in his head. "What are you trying to build?" she asked. He assembled the mirrors into a box-like structure. He glanced up at her, face hidden by the peak of his Air Force cap. "A trap." She stood beside him as he knelt on the floor. "For what? Time?" He placed a hand between her knees and gripped her right thigh, handhold of reality. "For your womb, Karen. You've caught a star there." But he was thinking of Coma, waiting with Kline in the espresso bar, while Xero roamed the street in his white Pontiac. In Coma's eyes runes glowed.

The Impossible Room. In the dim light he lay on the floor of the room. A perfect cube, its walls and ceiling were formed by what seemed to be a series of cinema screens. Projected on to them in close-up was the face of Nurse Nagamatzu, her mouth, three feet across, moving silently as she spoke in slow motion. Like a cloud, the giant head moved up the wall behind him, then passed across the ceiling and down the opposite corner. Later the inclined, pensive face of Dr. Lancaster appeared, rising up from the floor until it filled three walls and the ceiling, a slow mouthing monster.

Beach Fatigue. After climbing the concrete incline, he reached the top of the embankment. The flat, endless terrain stretched away on all sides, a few oil derricks in the distance marking the horizon. Among the spilled sand and burst cement bags lay old tyres and beer bottles, Guam in 1947. He wandered away from here, straddling roadworks and irrigation ditches, towards a rusting quonset near the incline of the disused flyover. Here, in this terminal hut, he began to piece together some sort of existence. Inside the hut he found a set of psychological tests, out of curiosity ran them on himself. Although he had no means of checking them, his answers seemed to establish an identity. He went off to forage, and came back to the hut with some documents and a coke bottle.

Pontiac Starchief.   Two hundred yards from the hut a wheel-less Pontiac sits in the sand. The presence of this car baffles him. Often he spends hours sitting in it, trying out the front and back seats. All sorts of rubbish is lying in the sand: a typewriter with half the keys missing (he picks out fragmentary sentences, sometimes these seem to mean something), a smashed neurosurgical unit (he pockets a handful of leucotomes, useful for self-defence). Then he cuts his foot on the coke bottle, and spends several feverish days in the hut. Luckily he finds an incomplete isolation drill for trainee astronauts, half of an 80-hour sequence.

Coma: The Million-Year Girl.   Coma's arrival coincides with his recovery from the bout of fever. She never enters the hut, but they team up in a left-handed way. To begin with she wants to spend all her time writing poems on the damaged typewriter. Later, when not writing the poems, she wanders away to an old solar energy device and loses herself in the maze of mirrors. Shortly afterwards Kline appears, and sits at a chair and table in the sand twenty yards from the hut. Xero, meanwhile, is moving among the oil derricks half a mile away, assembling immense cinemascope signs that carry the reclining images of Oswald, Jackie Kennedy, and Malcolm X.

Pre-Uterine Claims.   "The author," Dr. Lancaster wrote, "has found that the patient forms a distinctive type of object relation based on a perpetual and irresistible desire to merge with the object in an undifferentiated mass. Although psychoanalysis cannot reach the primary archaic mechanism of 'rapprochement' it can deal with the neurotic superstructure, guiding the patient towards the choice of stable and worthwhile objects. In the case under consideration the previous career of the patient as a military pilot should be noted, and the unconscious role of thermonuclear weapons in bringing about the total fusion and non-differentiation of all matter. What the patient is reacting against is, simply, the phenomenology of the universe, the specific and independent existence of separate objects and events, however trivial and inoffensive these may seem. A spoon, for example, offends him by the mere fact of its existence in time and space. More than this, one could say that the precise, if largely random, configuration of atoms in the universe at any given moment, one never again to be repeated, seems to him to be preposterous by the virtue of its unique identity . . ."Dr. Lancaster lowered his pen and looked down into the recreation garden. Traven was standing in the sunlight, raising and lowering his arms and legs in a private callisthenic display, which he repeated several times (presumably an attempt to render time and events meaningless by replication?)

"But Isn't Kennedy Already Dead?" Captain Webster studied the documents laid out on Dr. Lancaster's demonstration table. These were: (1) a spectroheliogram of the sun; (2) tarmac and take-off checks for the B29 Superfortress Enola Gay; (3) electroencephalogram of Albert Einstein; (4) transverse section through a Pre-Cambrian Trilobite; (5) photograph taken at noon, August 6, 1945, of the sand-sea, Quattara Depression, Libya; (6) Max Ernst's "Garden Airplane Traps". He turned to Dr. Lancaster. "You say these constitute an assassination weapon?"

"Not in the Sense You Mean." Dr. Lancaster covered the exhibits with a sheet. By chance the cabinets took up the contours of a corpse. "Not in the sense you mean. This is an attempt to bring about the 'false' death of the President—false in the sense of coexistent or alternate. The fact that an event has taken place is no proof of its valid occurrence." Dr. Lancaster went over to the window. Obviously he would have to begin the search singlehanded. Where to begin? No doubt Nurse Nagamatzu could be used as bait. That vamp had once worked as a taxi-dancer in the world's largest nightclub in Osaka, appropriately named "The Universe".

Unidentified Radio-source, Cassiopeia. Karen Novotny waited as he reversed the car onto the farm track. Half a mile across the meadows she could see the steel bowls of the three radio-telescopes in the sunlight. So the attempt was to be made here? There seemed to be nothing to kill except the sky. All week they had been chasing about, sitting for hours through the conference on neuro-psychiatry, visiting art galleries, even flying in a rented Rapide across the reservoirs of Staines and Shepperton. Her eyes had ached from keeping a look-out. "They're four hundred feet high," he told her, "the last thing you need is a pair of binoculars." What had he been looking for— the radio-telescopes or the giant madonnas he muttered about as he lay asleep beside her at night. "Xero!" she heard him shout. With the agility of an acrobat he vaulted over the bonnet of the car, then set off at a run across the meadow. "Come on!" he shouted over his shoulder. Carrying the black Jackie Kennedy wig as carefully as she could in both hands, she hurried after him. One of the telescopes was moving, its dish turning towards them.

Madame Butterfly. Holding the wound under her left breast, Nurse Nagamatzu stepped across Webster's body and leaned against the bogie of the telescope pylon. Eighty feet above her the steel bowl had stopped revolving, and the echoes of the gun-shots reverberated among the latticework. Clearing her throat with an effort, she spat out the blood. The flecks of lung tissue speckled the bright ribbon of the rail. The bullet had broken two ribs, then collapsed her left lung and lodged itself below her scapula. As her eyes faded she caught a last glimpse of a white American car setting off across the tarmac apron beyond the control house, where the shells of the old bombers lay heaped together. The runways of the former airfield radiated from her in all directions. Dr. Lancaster was kneeling in the path of the car, intently building a sculpture of mirrors. She tried to pull the wig off her head, and then fell sideways across the rail.

The Bride Stripped Bare by her Bachelors, Even.   Pausing outside the entrance to the tea-terrace, Margaret Traven noticed the tall figure of Captain Webster watching her from the sculpture room. Duchamp's glass construction, on loan from the Museum of Modern Art, reminded her of the ambiguous role she might have to play. This was chess in which every move was a counter-gambit. How could she help her husband, that tormented man, pursued by furies more implacable than the four riders, the very facts of time and space. She gave a start as Webster took her elbow. He turned to face her, looking into her eyes. "You need a drink. Let's sit down—I'll explain again why this is so important."

Venus Smiles.   The dead face of the President's widow looked up at him from the track. Confused by the Japanese cast of her features, with all their reminders of Nagasaki and Hiroshima, he stared at the bowl of the telescope, searching through the steel lattice for the time-music of the quasars. Twenty yards away Dr. Lancaster was watching him in the sunlight, the sculpture beside him reflecting a dozen fragments of his head and arms. Kline and Coma were moving away along the railway track.

Einstein.   "The notion that this great Swiss mathematician is a pornographer may strike you as something of a bad joke," Dr. Lancaster remarked to Webster. "However, you must understand that for Traven science is the ultimate pornography, analytic activity whose main aim is to isolate objects or events from their contexts in time and space. This obsession with the specific activity of quantified functions is what science shares with pornography. How different from Lautreamont, who brought together the sewing machine and the umbrella on the operating table, identifying the pudenda of the carpet with the woof of the cadaver." Dr. Lancaster turned to Webster with a laugh. "One looks forward to the day when the General

Theory of Relativity and the Principia will outsell the Kama Sutra in back-street bookshops."

Rune-filled Eyes. Now, in this concluding phase, the presence of his watching trinity, Coma, Kline and Xero, became ever closer. All three were more preoccupied than he remembered them. Kline seemed to avoid his eyes, turning one shoulder as he passed the café where Kline sat with Coma, evidently waiting for something. Only Coma, with her rune-filled eyes, watched him with any sympathy. It was as if they all sensed that something was missing. He remembered the documents he had found near the terminal hut.

In a Technical Sense. Webster's hand hesitated on Karen Novotny's zip. He listened to the last bars of the Mahler symphony playing from the radiogram extension in the warm bedroom. "The bomber crashed on landing," he explained. "Four members of the crew were killed. He was alive when they got him out, but at one point in the operating theatre his heart and vital functions failed. In a technical sense he was dead for about two minutes. Now, all this time later, it looks as if something is missing, something that vanished during the short period of his death. Perhaps his soul, the capacity to achieve a state of grace. Lancaster would call it the ability to accept the phenomenology of the universe, or the fact of your own consciousness. This is Traven's hell. You can see he's trying to build bridges between things—this Kennedy business, for example. He wants to kill Kennedy again, but in a way that makes sense."

The Water World. Margaret Traven moved through the darkness along the causeways between the reservoirs. Half a mile away the edge of the embankment formed a raised horizon, enclosing this world of tanks, water and pumping gear with an almost claustrophobic silence. The varying levels of water in the tanks seemed to let an extra dimension into the damp air. A hundred yards away, across two parallel settling beds, she saw her husband moving rapidly along one of the white-painted catwalks. He disappeared down a stairway. What was he looking for? Was this watery world the site where he hoped to be reborn, in this quantified womb with its dozens of amniotic levels?

An Existential Yes. They were moving away from him. After his return to the terminal hut he noticed that Kline, Coma, and Xero no longer approached him. Their fading figures, a quarter of a mile from the hut, wandered to and fro, half-hidden from him by the hollows and earthworks.

The cinemascope hoardings of Jackie, Oswald and Malcolm X were beginning to break up in the wind. One morning he woke to find that they had gone.

The Terminal Zone. He lay on sand with the rusty bicycle wheel. Now and then he would cover some of the spokes with sand, neutralising the radial geometry. The rim interested him. Hidden behind a dune, the hut no longer seemed a part of his world. The sky remained constant, the warm air touching the shreds of test papers sticking up from the sand. He continued to examine the wheel. Nothing happened.

TED HUGHES

Snow

*A*nd let me repeat this over and over again: beneath my feet is the earth, some part of the surface of the earth. Beneath the snow beneath my feet, that is. What else could it be? It is firm, I presume, and level. If it is not actually soil and rock, it must be ice. It is very probably ice. Whichever it may be, it is proof— the most substantial proof possible—that I am somewhere on the earth, the known earth. It would be absurd to dig down through the snow, just to determine exactly what is underneath, earth or ice. This bedded snow may well be dozens of feet deep. Besides, the snow filling all the air and rivering along the ground would pour into the hole as fast as I could dig, and cover me too—very quickly.

This could be no other planet: the air is perfectly natural, perfectly good.

Our aircraft was forced down by this unusual storm. The pilot tried to make a landing, but misjudged the extraordinary power of the wind and the whereabouts of the ground. The crash was violent. The fuselage buckled and gaped, and I was flung clear. Unconscious of everything save the need to get away from the disaster, I walked farther off into the blizzard and collapsed, which explains why when I came to full consciousness and stood up out of the snow that was burying me I could see nothing of either the aircraft or my fellow passengers. All round me was what I have been looking at ever since. The bottomless dense motion of snow. I started to walk.

Of course, everything previous to that first waking may have been entirely different since I don't remember a thing about it. Whatever chance dropped me here in the snow evidently destroyed my memory. That's one thing of which there is no doubt whatsoever. It is, so to speak, one of my facts. The aircraft crash is a working hypothesis, that merely.

There's no reason why I should not last quite a long time yet. I seem to have an uncommon reserve of energy. To keep my mind firm, that is the essential thing, to fix it firmly in my reasonable hopes, and lull it there, encourage it. Mesmerise it slightly with a sort of continuous prayer. Because when my mind is firm, my energy is firm. And that's the main thing here—energy. No matter how circumspect I may be, or how lucid, without energy I am lost on the spot. Useless to think about it. Where my energy ends I end, and all circumspection and all lucidity end with me. As long as I have energy I can correct my mistakes, outlast them, outwalk them—for instance the unimaginable error that as far as I know I am making at this very moment. This step, this, the next five hundred, or five thousand—all mistaken, all absolute waste, back to where I was ten hours ago. But we recognise that thought. My mind is not my friend. My support, my defence, but my enemy too—not perfectly intent on getting me out of this. If I were mindless perhaps there would be no difficulty whatsoever. I would simply go on aware of nothing but my step by step success in getting over the ground. The thing to do is to keep alert, keep my mind fixed in alertness, recognise these treacherous paralysing, yes, lethal thoughts the second they enter, catch them before they can make that burrowing plunge down the spinal cord.

Then gently and without any other acknowledgment push them back—out into the snow where they belong. And that *is* where they belong. They are the infiltrations of the snow, encroachments of this immensity of lifelessness. But they enter so slyly! We are true, they say, or at least very probably true, and on that account you must entertain us and even give us the run of your life, since above all things you are dedicated to the truth. That is the air they have, that's how they come in. What do I know about the truth? As if simple-minded dedication to truth were the final law of existence! I only know more and more clearly what is good for me. It's my mind that has this contemptible awe for the probably true, and my mind, I know, I prove it every minute, is not me and is by no means sworn to help me. Am I a lie? I must survive—that's a truth sacred as any, and as the hungry truths devour the sleepy truths I shall digest every other possible truth to the substance and health and energy of my own, and the ones I can't digest I shall spit out, since in this situation my intention to survive is the one mouth, the one digestive tract, so to speak, by which I live. But those others! I relax for a moment, I leave my mind to itself for a moment—and they are in complete possession. They plunge into me, exultantly, mercilessly. There is no question of their intention or their power. Five seconds of carelessness, and they have struck. The strength melts from me, my bowels turn to water, my consciousness darkens and shrinks. I have to stop.

What are my facts? I do have some definite facts.

Taking six steps every five seconds, I calculate—allowing for my brief regular sleeps—that I have been walking through this blizzard for five months and during that time have covered something equal to the breadth of the Atlantic between Southampton and New York. Two facts, and a third: throughout those five months this twilight of snow has not grown either darker or brighter.

So.

There seems no reason to doubt that I am somewhere within either the Arctic or the Antarctic Circle. That's a comfort. It means my chances of survival are not uniquely bad. Men have walked the length of Asia simply to amuse themselves.

Obviously I am not travelling in a straight line. But that needn't give me any anxiety. Perhaps I made a mistake when I first started walking, setting my face against the wind instead of downwind. Coming against the wind I waste precious energy and there is always this wearisome snow blocking my eyes and mouth. But I had to trust the wind. This resignation to the wind's guidance is the very foundation of my firmness of mind. The wind is not simply my compass. In fact, I must not think of it as a compass at all. The wind is my law. As a compass nothing could be more useless. No need to dwell on that. It's extremely probable indeed and something I need not hide from myself that this wind is leading me to and fro in quite a tight maze—always shifting too stealthily for me to notice the change. Or, if the sun is circling the horizon, it seems likely that the wind is swinging with it through the three hundred and sixty degrees once in every twenty-four hours, turning me as I keep my face against it in a perfect circle not more than seven miles across. This would explain the otherwise strange fact that in spite of the vast distance I have covered the terrain is still dead level, exactly as when I started. A frozen lake, no doubt. This is a strong possibility and I must get used to it without letting it overwhelm me, and without losing sight of its real advantages.

The temptation to trust to luck and instinct and cut out across wind is to be restricted. The effect on my system of confidence would be disastrous. My own judgment would naturally lead me in a circle. I would have to make deliberate changes of direction to break out of that circle—only to go in a larger circle or a circle in the opposite direction. So more changes.

Wilder and more sudden changes, changes of my changes—all to evade an enemy that showed so little sign of itself it might as well not have existed. It's clear where all that would end. Shouting and running and so on. Staggering round like a man beset by a mob. Falling, grovelling. So on. The snow.

No. All I have to do is endure: that is, keep my face to the wind. My face to the wind, a firm grip on my mind, and everything else follows naturally. There is not the slightest need to be anxious. Any time now the Polar night will arrive, bringing a drastic change of climate—inevitable. Clearing the sky and revealing the faultless compass of the stars.

The facts are overwhelmingly on my side. I could almost believe in Providence. After all, if one single circumstance were slightly— only slightly—other than it is! If, for instance, instead of waking in a blizzard on a firm level place I had come to consciousness falling endlessly through snow-cloud. Then I might have wondered very seriously whether I were in the gulf or not. Or if the atmosphere happened to consist of, say, ammonia. I could not have existed. And in the moment before death by asphyxiation I would certainly have been convinced I was out on some lifeless planet. Or if I had no body but simply arms and legs growing out of a head, my whole system of confidence would have been disoriented from the start. My dreams, for instance, would have been meaningless to me, or rather an argument of my own meaninglessness. I would have died almost immediately, out of sheer bewilderment. I wouldn't need nearly such extreme differences either. If I had been without these excellent pigskin boots, trousers, jacket, gloves and hood, the cold would have extinguished me at once.

And even if I had double the clothing that I have, where would I be without my chair? My chair is quite as important as one of my lungs. As both my lungs, indeed, for without it I should be dead. Where would I have slept? Lying in the snow. But lying flat, as I have discovered, I am buried by the snow in just under a minute, and the cold begins to take over my hands and my feet and my face. Sleep would be impossible. In other words, I would very soon collapse of exhaustion and be buried. As it is, I unsnap my chair harness, plant the chair in the snow, sit on it, set my feet on the rung between the front legs, my arms folded over my knees and my head resting on my arms, and am able in this way to take a sleep of fully ten minutes before the snow piles over me.

The chain of providential coincidences is endless. Or rather, like a chain mail, it is complete without one missing link to betray and annul the rest. Even my dreams are part of it. They are as tough and essential a link as any, since there can no longer be any doubt that they are an accurate reproduction of my whole previous life, of the world as it is and as I knew it—all without one contradictory detail. Yet if my amnesia had been only a little bit stronger!—it needed only that. Because without this evidence of the world and my identity I could have known no purpose in continuing the ordeal. I could only have looked, breathed and died, like a nestling fallen from the nest.

Everything fits together. And the result—my survival, and my determination to survive. I should rejoice.

The chair is of conventional type: nothing in the least mystifying about it. A farmhouse sort of chair: perfectly of a piece with my dreams, as indeed are my clothes, my body and all the inclinations of my mind. It is of wood, painted black, though in places showing a coat of brown beneath the black. One of the nine struts in the back is missing and some child—I suppose it was a child—has stuck a dab of chewing-gum into the empty socket. Obviously the chair has been well used, and not too carefully. The right foreleg has been badly chewed, evidently by a puppy, and on the seat both black and brown paints are wearing through showing the dark grain of the pale wood. If all this is not final evidence of a reality beyond my own, of the reality of the world it comes from, the world I re-dream in my sleeps—I might as well lie down in the snow and be done with.

The curious harness needn't worry me. The world, so far as I've dreamed it at this point, contains no such harness, true. But since I've not yet dreamed anything from after my twenty-sixth birthday, the harness might well have been invented between that time and the time of my disaster. Probably it's now in general use. Or it may be the paraphernalia of some fashionable game that came in during my twenty-seventh or later year, and to which I got addicted. Sitting on snow peaks in nineteenth-century chairs. Or perhaps I developed a passion for painting polar scenery and along with that a passion for this particular chair as my painting seat, and had the harness designed specially. A lucky eccentricity! It is perfectly adapted to my present need. But all that's in the dark still. There's a lot I haven't dreamed yet. From my twenty-third and twenty-fourth years I have almost nothing—a few insignificant episodes. Nothing at all after my twenty-sixth birthday. The rest, though, is about complete, which suggests that any time now I ought to be getting my twenty-third and twenty-fourth years in full and, more important, my twenty-seventh year, or as much of it as there is, along with the accurate account of my disaster and the origin of my chair.

There seems little doubt of my age. Had I been dreaming my life chronologically there would have been real cause for worry. I could have had no idea how much was still to come. Of course, if I were suddenly to dream something from the middle of my sixtieth year I would have to reorganise all my ideas. What really convinces me of my youth is my energy. The appearance of my body tells me nothing. Indeed, from my hands and feet—which are all I have dared to uncover—one could believe I was several hundred years old, or even dead, they are so black and shrunken on the bone. But the emaciation is understandable, considering that for five months I have been living exclusively on will-power, without the slightest desire for food.

I have my job to get back to, and my mother and father will be in despair, and God knows what will have happened to Helen. Did I marry her? I have no wedding ring. But we were engaged. And it is another confirmation of my youth that my feelings for her are as they were then—stronger, in fact, yes a good deal stronger, though speaking impartially these feelings that seem to be for her might easily be nothing but my desperate longing to get back to the world in general—a longing that is using my one-time affection for Helen as a sort of form or model. It's possible, very possible, that I have in reality forgotten her, even that I am sixty years old, that she has been dead for thirty-four years. Certain things may be very difficult from what I imagine. If I were to take this drift of thoughts to the logical extreme there is no absolute proof that my job, my parents, Helen and the whole world are not simply my own invention, fantasies my imagination has improvised on the simple themes of my own form, of clothes, my chair, and the properties of my present environment. I am in no position to be sure about anything.

But there is more to existence, fortunately, than consideration of possibilities. There is conviction, faith. If there were not, where would I be? The moment I allow one of these "possibilities" the slightest intimacy—a huge futility grips me, as it were physically, by the heart, as if the organ itself were despairing of this life and ready to give up.

Courageous and calm. That should be my prayer. I should repeat that, repeat it like the Buddhists with their "O jewel of the lotus". Repeat it till it repeats itself in my very heart, till every heartbeat drives it through my whole body. Courageous and calm. This is the world, think no more about it.

My chair will keep me sane. My chair, my chair, my chair—I might almost repeat that. I know every mark on it, every grain. So near and true! It alone predicates a Universe, the entire Universe, with its tough carpentering, its sprightly, shapely design—so delicate, so strong. And while I have the game I need be afraid of nothing. Though it is dangerous. Tempting, dangerous, but—it is enough to know that the joy is mine. I set the chair down in the snow, letting myself think I am going to sleep, but instead of sitting I step back a few paces into the snow. How did I think of that? The first time, I did not dare look away from it. I had never before let it out of my hand, never let it go for a fraction between unbuckling it and sitting down on it. But then I let it go and stepped back into the snow. I had never heard my voice before. I was astonished at the sound that struggled up out of me. Well, I need the compensations. And this game does rouse my energies, so it is, in a sense, quite practical. After the game, I could run. That's

the moment of danger, though, the moment of overpowering impatience
when I could easily lose control and break out, follow my instinct, throw
myself on luck, run out across the wind.

But there is a worse danger. If I ran out across the wind I would pretty
soon come to my senses, turn my face back into the wind. It is the game
itself, the stage of development it has reached, that is dangerous now. I no
longer simply step back. I set the chair down, turn my face away and walk
off into the blizzard, counting my steps carefully. At fourteen paces I stop.
Fifteen is the limit of vision in this dense flow of snow, so at fourteen I stop,
and turn. Let those be the rules. Let me fix the game at that. Because at first
I see nothing. That should be enough for me. Everywhere, pouring silent
grey, a silence like a pressure, like the slow coming to bear of some incalcu-
lable pressure, too gradual to detect. If I were simply to stand there my
mind would crack in a few moments. But I concentrate, I withdraw my awe
from the emptiness and look pointedly into it. At first, everything is as
usual—as I have seen it for five months. Then my heart begins to thump
unnaturally, because I seem to make out a dimness, a shadow that wavers
deep in the grey turmoil, vanishes and darkens, rises and falls. I step one
pace forward and using all my will-power stop again. The shadow is as it
was. Another step. The shadow seems to be a little darker. Then it vanishes
and I lunge two steps forward but immediately stop because there it is,
quite definite, no longer moving. Slowly I walk towards it. The rules are
that I keep myself under control, that I restrain all sobs or shouts though of
course it is impossible to keep the breathing regular—at this stage at least,
and right up to the point where the shadow resolves into a chair. In that
vast grey dissolution—my chair! The snowflakes are drifting against the
legs and gliding between the struts, bumping against them, clinging and
crawling over the seat. To control myself then it not within human power.
Indeed I seem to more or less lose consciousness at that point. I'm certainly
not responsible for the weeping, shouting thing that falls on my chair, embracing it, kissing it, bruising his cheeks against it. As the snowflakes tap and
run over my gloves and over the chair I begin to call them names. I peer
into each one as if it were a living face, full of speechless recognition, and I
call to them—Willy, Joanna, Peter, Jesus, Ferdinand, anything that comes
into my head, and shout to them and nod and laugh. Well, it's harmless
enough madness.

The temptation to go beyond the fourteen paces is now becoming
painful. To go deep into the blizzard. Forty paces. Then come back, peering. Fifteen paces, twenty paces. Stop. A shadow.

That would not be harmless madness. If I were to leave my chair like
that the chances are I would never find it again. My footprints do not exist
in this undertow of snow. Weeks later, I would still be searching, casting in
great circles, straining at every moment to pry a shadow out of the grey

sameness. My chair meanwhile a hundred miles away in the blizzard, motionless—neat legs and elegant back, sometimes buried, sometimes uncovering again. And for centuries, long after I'm finished, still sitting there, intact with its toothmarks and missing strut, waiting for a darkening shape to come up out of the nothingness and shout to it and fall on it and possess it.

But my chair is here, on my back, here. There's no danger of my ever losing it. Never so long as I keep control, keep my mind firm. All the facts are on my side. I have nothing to do but endure.

Isaac Rosenfeld (1918–1956) was a university teacher, journalist, and author whose artistic career was cut short by his untimely death of a heart attack. He graduated from the University of Chicago in 1941 and dropped his studies for a Ph.D. in philosophy at New York University to become a contributor and then staff editor for The New Republic. *Many of his stories communicate the alienation and despair of modern man in a world he cannot learn to understand. His works include an autobiographical novel,* Passage from Home *(1946); a collection of reviews and articles,* An Age of Enormity: Life and Writing in the Forties and Fifties *(1962). For further reading:* Alpha and Omega *(1966).*

ISAAC ROSENFELD

The Brigadier

*W*e have been fighting the enemy a very long time. So long that I, who entered the war a foot soldier, have had time to receive more than the usual number of decorations and promotions and to become a brigadier, attached to staff headquarters. I forget how many times I have been wounded and the names of all the battles and campaigns in which I have participated. The greater number of them, however, are not to be forgotten: Striplitz, Bougaumères, Trèle, Bzelokhorets, Kovinitsa, Laud Ingaume, El Khabhar, Woozi-Fassam, and so on. I am the oldest man in our field office, though not in the brigade itself. Lately, the newcomers have not been rising from the ranks, but from the Academy. They are young men who have not proved themselves in any way; some have not even fought.

I am settled into my work, which for many years, I am pleased to say, has been of an absorbing nature. It is difficult to recall the time when I fretted with impatience to return to what I considered my natural life as a citizen. I am happy that I am no longer impatient. I have developed, instead, a great eagerness—an eagerness, however, which is thoroughly disciplined and in every way related to our military enterprise. I do not hesitate to call our enterprise the most glorious and far-reaching that has ever been undertaken.

543

Far-reaching is not quite the word—though it is only in an unofficial capacity that I admit as much. Let me say that it is not the word for me to use. As a matter, simply, of objective fact, what we are engaged in is, of course, that—I mean far-reaching—and much else besides. But for myself it is not enough, and the work I do must be otherwise defined. I have been studying the ends of our warfare while pursuing them; I have tried to make them a part of myself. I should not want it to be said that the Objective is one thing, and the brigadier's effort in its behalf is quite another, not related to it as the word one and the number one are related. My work is the war itself.

The office in which I do my work was once a schoolhouse; it stands in what used to be enemy country. A section of blackboard, cracked down the middle, is still affixed to the wall near my desk and on it you can read a lesson in the enemy's language, written by one of his children; when the chalk began to fade, I had it carefully restored and covered with a coat of shellac. I can read the enemy's hand— which is sometimes difficult even for scholars, as the script is spidery and irregular and varies not only with the dialect but with the very temperament of the writer. The broken lines read: ". . . of the cat and the dog? What will she . . .;" here the first line ends, broken off at the jagged edge of the board. "We," runs the second line, "know that the . . . [several words are obliterated] while the bird was singing. . . ." The third and last line: ". . . is what we all love. It makes us very happy." I like to imagine, although I know this is nothing but a child's exercise, that these broken lines, could I only complete them, would tell me more about the enemy than all the work of our specialists combined. As for my subordinates, I have led them to believe that these scraps of writing have something to do with logistics—which is all they care about.

The benches, the charts, the books and other blackboards of the schoolhouse have long since been removed. The rooms are now occupied by sturdy desks of our own design, developed during the war, and the walls are lined with filing cabinets and hung with maps of the region. The sides of the house have been reinforced against blast with sandbags, and the windows have been covered with interesting strips of wire and tape which, when the sun is right, cast patterns of shadow upon our papers. If there were nothing else to do, it would be a pleasure to trace some of these patterns. The glass—these are the enemy's original panes—is very bright and clear. The enemy is known for the quality of his glass works. A strange people.

Our office is a relay station among the various fronts. The position of the fronts has grown so complicated through the years, that I never attempt to give our location with reference to the lines of battle. We are well in the center of one circle of fighting, on the periphery of a second, and connected by a long tangent with a third. From time to time our position appears enveloped, and we pack our papers, dismantle our immobile equipment, and prepare to retreat. Subsequent intelligence, however, informs us that the first reports, owing to the complexity of the warfare, were erroneous in many respects and that, far from being encircled, our position may be described as part of an arc thrown round the enemy's flank. The lines of battle, the longer I study them, seem to me more and more like the arms of many embracing bodies.

It is our general purpose, but not my specific task, to supply logistical information to headquarters in the front and in the rear. We are one of a number of stations that co-ordinate the numerous reports both of the enemy's movements and of our own, and relay these back and forth. These reports never fail to conflict with one another, and no matter how well trained our spies, pilots, observers, and scouts may be, we must keep a large staff working round the clock to prevent mistakes, repetitions, and inconsistencies from appearing in our dispatches. Even so we have blundered many times, and our only consolation, and at the same time the reason that reprimands from headquarters have not been more severe, is the fact that the enemy must work under the same disadvantages. Very often a report so complicated and contradictory that it seems impossible to submit, is nevertheless a true picture of the fighting. You can see what we are up against. And then there are the many spontaneous breakdowns of routine for which no one is to blame, the impatience of my superiors which is always interfering with the work, the orders handed down from above, countermanding orders that have already been carried out, and so many other difficulties that are part of the day's normal detail. To make matters worse a training class for scouts is held in the basement of our schoolhouse and we often hear them laughing or crying out in pain as they tumble about on the mats. I have been trying to get this class removed, thus far without success.

My own work developed as a subsidiary of the main logistical operation. My superiors are not yet convinced of the importance of my task (I have been at it for eleven years!), but some of them are interested, and all my equals and subordinates support me in it, so I am not required to give up my investigations. I work in a semiofficial capacity, filling in and sending out my own reports and as much corroborative material as I can lay my hands on—all this in addition to my regular duties. I am kept very busy indeed, seldom working less than sixteen hours at a stretch. I sometimes think, sitting as I do in an old schoolhouse, that I am both schoolmaster and pupil: a teacher to those who are beneath me in rank and an idiot child to my superiors.

I work on the enemy proper. I am trying to discover what he is, what motivates him, what his nature is. And if you say, as so many of my superiors do, that this is known, I reply that I am attacking his very essence. This is not known. In spite of the many long years that we have been at war with him, and the periods of time, in the past, when we lived at his side in restless peace, we know nothing of him that is really worth knowing and that must be known. I myself am convinced that victory will be impossible until we gain this knowledge— and it is precisely to this knowledge that I am devoting my life.

What do we know? The enemy is darker than we, and shorter in stature. His language, as I have indicated, has nothing in common with our own; his religion is an obscenity to all of us who have not made a specialty of studying it. Well then, as I say, he is shorter and darker, two positive facts. His language, though it would be too much trouble to go into it here, is of such and such a kind—a third fact—and his religion is this, that and the other thing, which gives us still another fact. So much we know. Still, what is he?

I have gone many times to the camps and hospitals in the rear to interview the prisoners we have taken. It teaches me nothing, but I nevertheless make my regular visits, and just the other week I returned from one of our hospitals. There was the usual sight in the wards; I am hardened to it. (And yet, almost as if to test myself, I try to recall what I have seen. Am I absolutely hardened?) There were the lightly wounded, their personalities not distorted by pain, and the natural qualities of these men could be observed: their churlishness, stupidity, sullenness, or good nature. They are much like our own soldiers, especially in their boredom. I spoke with them, I took my usual sampling—so many boys (as with our own troops, eleven-year-olds are not uncommon), so many youths, so many of the middle-aged, so many old men, old campaigners. The usual questions, the usual answers—home, parents, occupation, the government, women, disease, God, the purpose of the war, of life, of history, etc. There is nothing to be learned here that we don't already know. Then the wards of the severely wounded—the amputations, the blinded, the infected. The stench is the same as our own stench (the hospital orderlies deny this, maintaining that the enemy's is worse!). The ones with fever have fever, though their skins and eyes show it differently from ours. The delirious rave, the chilled shiver, the poisoned vomit and groan. There are outcries, the usual hysteria, weeping, coughing, and hemorrhage. One lies in a coma, the stump of his leg is gangrenous, it is too late, he cannot be saved. Another soldier has nearly every bone in his body broken: he has both his thighs in traction, a broken back, a broken arm, his skull wound in bandages. Can he be said to suffer either more or less than one of our own men in similar circumstances, or in any way differently from him? I attend an operation—it is the same thing over and over again. The mental casualties in their guarded ward are no different from ours. Some in straightjackets, strapped to their beds, some screaming, some colorless, lifeless, forever immobile. Here and there a dead body, not yet removed. I lift the sheet; the face is already puffed up. The shock of it is gone, and I can no longer remember what it actually used to be like. I poke a finger into a puffy cheek, leaving a depression which takes a long time to fill up again. It is the same death as our own.

I go to the hospitals, though I learn nothing there, and I go to the prison camps, also in vain. Once I had myself incarcerated, disguised as an enemy soldier. I slept with the men in their barracks, ate with them, studied them, was soon infested with the same lice. I was involved in a plan to escape, of which I informed our guards. No one saw through my disguise, and I, in turn, failed to see through the undisguised men and learned nothing. In fact, the few weeks I spent in prison camp were extremely discouraging, for if the gap between the enemy and ourselves is so small that I can pose, undetected, as one of his men, why is it that I can't cross over to him?

I have even suspected my project of a subtle treason. By "cross over to him," I mean of course, "cross the gulf that separates us from knowledge of his true nature." Now I know where I stand in this regard and it no longer troubles me; but at one time I feared that the second expression really meant nothing more than the first and I thought surely that my whole ambition was only to desert to the enemy. Perhaps he fascinated me in the precise sense of attraction, drawing me, through my desire to know, closer and closer to his side. My conscience drove me to my superior, Major General Box. He believes in my project and follows my reports with interest. The General reassured me; it is his opinion that we are all drawn to the enemy, particularly in such a long war, and that the enemy is drawn to us. In certain respects we even begin to resemble each other. But this is only natural, and has nothing to do with my project, which, far from being treason, remains the most important of the war.

I was reassured, but was soon taken with a fresh disquietude. A suggestion that the General had made, without meaning to do so, set me on a new course of activity. The General had said that in certain respects we come to resemble the enemy. What are these respects? Perhaps the knowledge that I was seeking really lay in myself? The resemblance to the enemy might have grown so strong in my case, that it was my own nature I would have to know in order to know his. I took a leave from the service, the only one I have had in the entire campaign, and spent a month in one of the enemy's mountain villages that had been captured by our troops. I lived away from the men, attended only by goats which forage high up among the rocks in this region. I had a hut to myself, and all the mountains necessary to a great introspection. But I learned nothing, nothing that I did not already know.

It was when I returned to active service that I began the most desperate work that I have as yet undertaken. I selected a group of twenty prisoners, all young, sturdy, healthy men. I lived with them until I grew to know them well; some were like my own sons, and one in particular, a peasant boy named Reri, I will say that I loved. I spent long hours out of doors with my

companions, joined them in races and various sports, their own as well as
ours. We went on long camping and fishing trips about the country, and I
developed so great a trust in them that I even provided them with firearms
and let them hunt with me. Evenings, when we were not camping under the
open sky, we entertained ourselves in my lodge, drinking, playing cards or
chess, listening to music, or holding the most intimate conversations— conversations and confidences that verged on love. We became very intimate;
there has never been a group of men whom I have known or loved so well,
never a youth as my Reri for whom I have had such a close and tender
feeling. It was above all with Reri that I carried on my desperate yet gentle
work; I strove to know him as completely as one man can ever hope to
know another, and something in his response to me, perhaps an intuitive
comprehension of my motive, promised that my effort would be rewarded.
He was a handsome boy, taller than the average among the enemy, and
fairer in color and complexion. Certainly one such as he could be known, a
face as open as his could not long conceal the secrets of the inner nature.
Often when I was not with him I would picture his face to myself, trusting
that a chance moment of insight might reveal him, and therefore his whole
people, to me. And I studied his image, sketching him and taking many
photographs while he sat patiently before me. (I have kept these sketches
and photographs, and look at them from time to time as I once looked at
the living Reri. His image still saddens and preplexes me.) So, with all my
companions, I engaged in an unceasing search after friendship and understanding, hoping that love would teach me what I was determined to know.

But my ultimate means were not to be gentle, and when I failed again
I had to resort, with great reluctance, in shame and disgust, to the final
means I had selected to attain my objective. As I had been their friend and
lover and father, their teacher in the ways of our people and their pupil in
the ways of theirs, so, at last, I became their torturer, hoping now to break
them down and force them to yield what they had not been able to give
freely. One day I ordered them whipped, the next, beaten; all of them,
including Reri. I stood by, directing their tortures and noting their surprise,
their hatred of me, their screams and their pleas for mercy. I could not help
feeling that I had betrayed them; but my guilt only excited me the more
and made me inflict always greater agony and humiliation upon them. It
must have been guilt that was responsible for my extreme excitement, in the
grip of which, while supervising the tortures, I would feel an overwhelming
hatred of the enemy, and become convinced that my hatred had brought
me so much farther than love, to the very brink of knowledge. When my
companions died, I trained, in much the same manner, a new group, in
which I included some of the enemy's women. The experiment was repeated. This time I did not spare myself, but submitted in their company to
some of the same tortures, as if there might still be lurking in me an essen-

tial particle of their enemy's nature which was itself either capable of yielding the truth, or of preventing me from finding it. The experiment failed again. Again I learned nothing, nothing at all.

I still go to the wards and the camps, and from time to time I still conduct tortures. I have devised many other means of coping with my problem, some of them not yet tested. Over the years, I have grown hardened to failure: I more or less expect it now as an essential element of my work. But though I am hardened and toughened and experienced, I find that my work grows more and more difficult. Because of my interest in prisoners, new duties have been assigned to me. Recently negotiations for the exchange of prisoners broke down between the enemy and ourselves, and their number keeps piling up, as ours does in their camps; it is now my duty to arrange for their transportation to the interior. And then there are still the many administrative details of my department, to which I must somehow find time to attend; there are still the hazards and ever greater complications of our old war, which we have not yet won, and which, I have become absolutely certain, we will never win unless I succeed in my task. To know the enemy! It is the whole purpose and nature of our war, its ultimate meaning, its glory and its greatness. Already I have succeeded in my own character, for I have become my task in my whole being. Nothing comes between me and the work I do. I have triumphed in my character and in my person, but I must still triumph over the enemy. Sometimes I see his armies standing before me, clearly revealed in their dark, powerful mass, and I rush out of the schoolhouse, out of our office, and I feel that in a moment, but one moment more, I will know the truth. And when I hear our gunfire from the front that winds around us in all directions, I know that if my faith is only great enough, the knowledge will come to me and I will win.

R. V. CASSILL

How I Live Through Times of Trouble

You better just watch it, she said.

Who said? My fifteen-year-old daughter said. She had beer watching
"Maude" on television while I watched Speaker of the House Carl Albert.

I watch it all the time, I said.

Don't crowd your luck, she said.

I crowd my luck all the time, I said.

You better just watch it, she said. She had been quilting an old-fashioned quilt for her own bed.

About two weeks ago I was sitting in my second-floor study when I
became aware that my daughter was sobbing downstairs. I went down to
see why. She was sitting near the television set, but she had earphones on
and was listening to a John Denver record. The sobs I heard hadn't terrified
me, but they had made me think I would be crowding my luck too much if
I ignored them.

I made her take the earphones off and tell me what was the matter.
There was no way I could make her stop crying.

It was the aerosol cans, she said, and the aersosol people who were ineluctably and patiently destroying the ionosphere. In twenty years I'll be dead of skin cancer, she said. I don't want to die. I want to live. They destroy the ionosphere and the radiation keeps getting through.

I had very little patience with her simplistic formulation of our problems, but I knew that if I did not *show* patience I would make things worse—there and then and probably in the long run. I resolved to display patience to her while I diverted her from sobbing by offering her a list of things more threatening —in my view—than the aerosol poisoners.

The real threats, I told her calmly, are. . . .

You're not listening to me. You're not taking me seriously, she said, I don't want to die. I want to live more than twenty years more.

I want you to live a long time and be a very mean old lady, I told her, but. . . .

Then why don't you do something? she demanded. I could see that the tears streaming down her face were in good earnest.

What?

Make them stop using aerosol cans, she shouted. Don't you dare make fun of me!

How? I asked. Tell them Erica Cassill doesn't want to die of skin cancer? Tell who?

You've got to make them stop, she said.

I *can't* make them stop, I said. Do you want me to stop using my aerosol-powered shaving cream? I will. I'll buy it in the tube. Do you want me to do more than that?

If you're making fun of me you'll be sorry, she said.

I'm not making fun of you, I said. Do you want me to cry, too?

You've got to do something, she said. I don't want to die in twenty years.

You may die before that, I said. They're about to get us all with nuclear weapons.

You're not listening to me, she said, crying harder than ever.

The next day I went down to the campus and told my students about this episode. I said to them, I didn't know whether to laugh at her or tell her to shut up or to cry along with her.

The young men and women in my class looked nervous. They felt I should not be saying such things. Earlier in the semester I had asked them to list in order of priority the countries that we should attack, if oil prices threatened to strangle the West. Most of them had put Saudi Arabia at the top of their list and Russia at the bottom, though a few had put Mexico, Canada, or Norway at the top.

I said to them, My daughter did not really mean that she was terrified by aerosol cans. That was a spontaneous metaphor for what really terrified her and terrifies her. It is a synedoche, a part standing for the whole. My daughter had heard what the poet James Dickey called "the beast whistle of space." That phrase appears in a poem of his called "Falling." Mr. Dickey and my fifteen-year-old daughter have heard intimations that the end has come. Now we all hear it, I said, in various ways.

They did not reply to this—perhaps because I did not give them a chance to do so. I think that maybe they heard the beast whistle of space speaking in my voice. I think that I am the reason it is all over and done with, and it will not do much good to list the good things and the nice things I believe I believe in if really I am the one that threatens to bring them all to an end.

The other afternoon a young woman from our local theater group called, made an appointment and then came to see me. She is organizing a program to educate the public about handgun legislation, and she hopes to get a government grant to help finance this educational program. Someone told her that I was an "academic humanist" and that I would help balance the views on any panel she might assemble to discuss the problem of handguns.

When she came, in late afternoon, to my house, it was snowing lightly. She seemed exhilarated as she came in. Before we got to discussing handguns she had to tell me what she had just seen on the street in our neighborhood shopping center. Near the University dormitory on this street she had seen a man sitting in a Volkswagen, masturbating.

I didn't know what to do about it, she said. I asked myself, "as a feminist, what should I do about such a thing?" He was in plain sight, masturbating.

In whose plain sight? I asked.

I did a very ridiculous thing, she said. I ran over to a man in uniform and grabbed his shoulder and said, "Get the number of that Volkswagen." I thought he was a policeman. He had a badge on his cap, but he was a mailman.

Why should you take his license number? I said. If you're opposed to handguns, then you ought to be in favor of a consenting adult masturbating. Or was it because he was close to a college dormitory that you felt you should have a policeman do something about him?

I'm not opposed to handguns, she said. I want to do a very balanced program to educate the public about how the laws on handguns should be changed.

Why do they have to be changed? I asked.

Not everyone even knows what the laws are, she said. The reason I got involved in all this is that I sat through the last debates about this in the state legislature and the arguments were all stupid. A lot of NRA gun nuts kept saying that we were trying to take their rifles and shotguns away from legitimate sportsmen. Here is a sheet that tells what the law is now, in summary. Here is another with statistics about the number of crimes in this state that are committed with handguns.

I read the sheets. It interested me that the law contained a provision for the gun dealer to inform the police, on a form executed in triplicate, when a handgun was sold to a citizen while, after the form was received by the police, they were required to destroy all three copies of the notification form. The law prohibited them from keeping any record whatsoever of the names of the people who owned handguns in our state.

I think I understand the reasoning in this provision of the law, I said. It is a rather wonderfully old-fashioned attempt to strike a balance between one potential abuse and another.

There's nothing to keep anyone from buying a handgun in another state and bringing it into our state, she said. Most crimes committed with handguns are committed by one member of a family on another member of his family.

Yes, I said, and I understand that sometimes small children may find handguns that are inadequately hidden and kill themselves or someone else. But does this mean that handguns should be abolished altogether?

I think that they should be limited to the military and the police, she said.

Shit, I said. Don't you understand what the founding fathers had in mind when they wrote into the Constitution the Amendment that grants us the right to bear arms? So, finally, we can protect ourselves *against* the military and the police.

I don't want to produce just another horror show that uses a multimedia presentation to show babies shooting each other and parents, she said.

She was a good, big, serious young woman, and I didn't want to win any points in an argument that mostly just upset me and got me thinking about the military and the police and William Tell using his private weapon to shoot the tyrant who made him perform an abomination on his son.

I'd like to help, I said. Honestly, I don't know how I can.

If you would be on a panel, it would be all right to say whatever you think about the Constitution, she said. I mean, that side of the problem shouldn't be just left to the NRA gun nuts I suppose.

I said that I wouldn't dare say in public some of the things I had said to her just now in private. There are too many people nearby who would say that I was an NRA gun nut, and it would do no good to explain that the only real weapon I own is a double-barreled .12 gauge Stevenson shotgun. Once the people in an academic community have you labeled as a defender of the NRA your tenure is one notch less secure.

Well, you seem to be living pretty good here, she said.

It's a nice house. We like it, I said. If anyone tried to take it away from me I would hit him in the belly with both barrels of my Stevenson .12 gauge.

No one's going to do that, she said.

Not if I don't talk about the Constitution in public, I said.

I liked this girl quite a lot, for someone I had only talked to for about two hours. She said she was from Plato, Minnesota and I told her I had come from the Midwest, too. We both thought the East was interesting.

Later—later than this day—I told someone that "everything is connected." I said that I had spent most of my life trying to figure out what it was that made the connections between things that a rational man would not see as having anything to do with each other. I summarized my talk with the girl who wanted to educate the people of our state about handguns, and then—in an attempt to be entertaining—I told about what happened two or three hours after she had left. Whimsically, I attempted to tell it in a way that suggested a connection between our talk about handguns and what happened that night.

That night I was back up in my study after dinner when I heard a commotion downstairs. My wife and my youngest son were making distressed noises. I tried to pay no attention to them because I had some work to do and I was trying to think about the cover on *Der Spiegel* which caricatures President Ford and Secretary Kissinger dressed in Marine uniforms landing on a desert shore and machine gunning the oil sheiks.

My wife yelled, Come down here.

I went down and learned that our big, friendly, castrated male cat had brought a live and healthy mouse in through the patented cat door we installed last fall. The cat had taken it to a dead end space on the basement stairs and was torturing it. It seemed to *me* that he was torturing it, that is. I love that cat in an ordinate fashion, but he is so much bigger than mice or the chipmunks he catches in the summer that I always feel he is torturing them before he gets ready to kill them.

And of course, I could see the possibility that the mouse might escape and come to live in our house. I hoped our big, gentle, striped cat would torture the mouse for a while there in the dead end on the basement stairs and then kill it, but I couldn't count on that.

So I said I would shoot the mouse.

My wife thought this was an irresponsible proposal. My youngest son thought I would probably hit the cat if I tried to shoot the mouse in these circumstances.

I went back up to my study and got my Crosman *Medalist* II air pistol out of my desk drawer, where it usually lies on top of some mailing labels and a pack of Tarot cards. By the time I got back to the basement stairs, my youngest son was furious with me for planning to shoot at the mouse and probably hit the cat.

I loaded the air pistol and pumped it up. My youngest son said, You dumb bastard, you'll shoot the cat.

No, I won't, I said. I was feeling a little embarrassed at having this extra heavy gun in my hand and making a sport out of a serious, though minor, problem.

When the cat sat back away from the mouse, the mouse tried to climb the basement door. It would get up about two feet then fall back onto the linoleum. The cat didn't bother it while it was trying to climb. The cat knew this was no use.

About the third time the mouse got as high as it could climb, I shot a pellet at it and missed.

Goddamn you, my son said. He ran down the three steps of this funny dead end on the stairs and grabbed the cat in his arms. He carried it away to safety.

Now the mouse was crouched in its corner between the darkly varnished basement door and a baseboard. The linoleum under it was a pole green—quite light—so that it was perfectly silhouetted and quite still. I shot it. It jerked two or three times and then lay motionless on the linoleum.

Later my youngest son examined it and said I had hit it in the head. Jokingly I said, What did you expect me to do?

My daughter is quilting a quilt for her bed. She does not want to die, after only twenty years more, of skin cancer caused by our using aerosol cans to destroy the only protection we have from the deadly radiation in outer space.

My oldest son wants to be a writer. He has been doing wonderful work in ceramics for the last two years, and lately he has not shown me any of the things he has written. He used to show me poems, but I suspect he is up there in his room writing fiction which he does not mean to show me. He is "due" to go to college next year and he wants to go a certain distance from home for his college years but not too far. He was a worrisome boy until he got well past puberty, but now I worry that he is more gentle, wise, gifted and charitable that it is safe to be.

My youngest son is addicted to television. He falls behind in his homework, though his advisors at high school always say, when they call us, that he is in the highest percentile of intelligence and that they have gone out of their way to get him into classes that will not bore him. They think he is not producing in proportion to his gifts. They are right. He is biding his time. He is biding our time. He cares more about me than about the cat, and he did not want me to have shot the cat that I love because it reminds me, in temperament, of my father, who had a rough life until he broke into the sunny years of his old age. My youngest son will not play chess with me very often because it is very important for him to beat me and he can only do this when I slack off and he overstrains himself.

The young woman from Plato, Minnesota wants me to over-expose myself to people who will be lying in wait for my oldest son if he writes the kind of fiction that I want him to write. I believe she liked me because I joked with her about the man who was masturbating in the Volkswagen by the college dormitory, and she has charitably forgotten any allusions I made to William Tell and the use of handguns on tyrants.

My wife has just come in and said I will ruin my eyes if I keep on typing this late at night. It is true that I have a cyst on my right eyelid which is supposed to be removed, under local anesthetic, in the doctor's office, day after tomorrow.

She does not mean I will ruin "my eyes."

My daughter does not mean that it is the aerosol cans that are going to finish us off with skin cancer.

I do not mean what I have written tonight or in the last thirty years. I am tempted to say this is Krapp's Last Tape, but the temptation seems cheap. My life has not been cheap.

My subtle and barbarous daughter says, Don't crowd your luck.
I suppose this is a line she picked up from watching TV.
I say, I always crowd my luck.

James B. Hall (1918–   ) was born in rural Ohio, educated at Miami University (Ohio), the University of Hawaii, and received a Ph.D. from the University of Iowa. A coeditor of this text, he has published three novels, many short stories, nonfiction, and a book of poems, The Hunt Within *(1973) A long-time director of creative writing programs, he is currently professor of literature at the University of California, Santa Cruz. For further reading see two story collections:* 15×3 *(with Herbert Gold and R. V. Cassill) and* Us He Devours *(1964).*

JAMES B. HALL

Letters Never Mailed

Friday A.M. things okay here and hope you are the same. Two details new on the back bar since you enlisted AF. Card Room and Lodge Room per the usual. BOOTS, on duty. Well, I was a Sergeant in the last one: *do what they tell you* and

          —Crown, water-back and same to you Boots

Regards back bar, Boots changed two things. At left from where I usually sit was a cigar display. Boxes one on top of the other in five rows with the lids open and the pictures on the lids: a gold Crown, a race horse pulling a high-wheeled sulky, per 1890 at County Fairs, Coronas La Palmas, Habana Crooks, cheroots in little cardbord boxes shirt pocket size and

          —Double 7, water-back, and Boots take it out of the
          twenty there's plenty more where that came from
          and have another one on me.

Well Boots moved cigars far end the back bar. In that place he put "7" about this high—a *light* whiskey—so now where the cigars was he has this white styrofoam "7" which is fastened on this lithographed piece of ice, and inside the ice is green parsley or mint, and on the mint leaves the light shines through the ice—from *inside* the ice—has water melting

So much for the news. BOOTS, on duty. Moved cigar display toward *left*. The 7 put in that corner, to the *right*. Tables same. Card Room and Lodge Room per the usual. Sandwich machine with RB cheese egg salad

Tuna or Combination fresh wax paper every two days 25¢ in the middle of the back bar also the same and

(Not here . . .
Try the Oasis)

Regards membership drive I wrote you about last week. Handled very well by Membership Committee of which I was a member but *not any more.* Why? All I know is we did what they told us. Well, the committee has all the receipt books intact and can straighten them out to the satisfaction of all concerned. I mean that's why I'm here this morning. More on this one later.

Fall Market Festival tomorrow and wish you were here. This year our Lodge Booth handled very well by Lodge-Booth Committee of which I am *not a member.* You just watch. They will anyway come to me and want to use the pickup truck for some damn' thing and
—Forney, why I'll have another of the same. So
where's Hutch? Where's Sheddy-boy? Buy Boots
one too and take it all out of the twenty.

(Try the Oasis)

Did I tell you about two items he changed on our back bar? Boots put his cigars on the *East* side toward door Exit and then filled that space with his white 7 made out of glass sponge it seems like. Now it stands at the *West* end, toward the Card Room door. Left by whiskey salesman that drives that sixty or sixty-one Dodge PS & PB.

Fall Market Festival opens tomorrow. Not *a member* for various reasons but my idea is still about right. Like I said last year: merchants to put up big displays via resources of J.C., C of C, Kiwanis if

all others such as our lodge IOOF accept booths and space available anywhere in two roped-off squares. My judgment last year and if a man can't say what's on his mind then the country is in one Hell of a shape.

Regards Membership Committee of which was a member but not any more. Well, we got old members in arrears signed up, per list. We got old members on Demits signed up, per list. We got new members signed up, per list as follows. Ask any of the boys and I mean Hutch and Forney and Sheddy-boy. No Dudleys on any list. *Not one Dudley.* Funeral Sunday.

(Try the Oasis)

—Hey Sheddy-boy Hey Forney Hey Butch, who
brought the receipt books? Set down anyway Boots
that would be one Jack Daniels water two bourbon
Waterfill and soda and me a 7 Crown water-back—
a *light* whiskey—also oneforyou Boots all out of the
twenty and more where that come from . . .
—Why if our auxillary ladies need folding chairs
then someone has to go down the highway. I mean
in a truck.

(Might try the Oasis)

It was the youngest Dudley Girl.
Sharshley Brothers Funeral Parlor has the remains. Dudley claims it
was a virus—but I know damned well she didn't want the baby. You ever
know the youngest Dudley girl? Before enlisted AF and
—Forney Hutch Sheddy Boots you old cork stuffer
same to you and I said take it all out of the ten.
Trust a Dudley. To save a $ they'll lay her to rest in a pair of slacks.
Funeral Sunday p.m. I might view the remains and
—Why that's what I'm here tell you and mean
Hutch, mean Forney, mean Sheddy-boy, am here to
tell you we could use my pickup and then eat a bite
down there and then drive back and then leave the
auxillary ladies the chairs—well, we could unload
them for the ladies if that was called for—but bring
the chairs back long before noon tomorrow, isn't
that Saturday? Well then *leave the chairs* right beside
the booth inside my pickup . . .
—Yes, but if nobody's got the receipt books then
how are you going to straighten out the membership
drive to the satisfaction of all concerned. Well,
that's the question. The money is all here somewhere and
Dudleys family plot lays beside GAR monument. Not that whole section. Dudleys claim it was a virus. Some say she did it herself. But you
wouldn't have known the Dudley girl. Well be good and do what they tell
you and so long for now your dad ps. and
—Why, we could have another one it's a free country but then who goes down the highway and brings
back the chairs as was mentioned folding chairs . . .
—Why I'll drive, that's who. I'd take my pickup.
And if you boys would want to help out . . .
—Boots if Madge—wife—calls say expected back
and hold this for me and

(Haven't see him
Try the Oasis)

Saturday a.m. things okay here and hope you are the same.

Nothing new except Market Festival and aim to get downstairs to view same. Did I tell you two details new on the back bar?

Well you'll remember how he had them stacked up, five rows high with lids open 35¢ Corona Grande Hoja Exquisita—BERING—AsiaAlaska celebrated Danish Navigator—Vitus Bering—Discovery of Bering Strait 1728 his picture between AsiaAlaska in picture seal skin whiskers hair and oil skin flat sailor hat and hat rim with light shines very much like ice and. BOOTS, on duty and

—7 Crown, water-back and have a double on me
and take it all out of the twenty. Well, we got back
late. That's what.

Now cigars moved to the Left, toward Card Room. To the *Right* a styrofoam 7—a *light* whiskey—which fastens through cardboard, screws on lithographed ice block then inside ice this green shrub, and on the shrub it has light as though ice inside has water melting. Saw it in plain box per delivery—DO NOT CRUSH—when the one who drives that sixty or sixty-one with Power Steering called here and

—Water-7-back and double me on the all out of the
twenty Boots old cork stuffer.

Well, Fall Festival opens and still say my idea is about right. Merchants to put up big displays via resources if PLAN AHEAD then all others such as our lodge IOOF accept booths between space available anywhere in two roped-off squares. So Auxillary per Madge and other wives: homemade hamburger homemade pie homemade hotdogs relish catsup mustard onions? Well, they needed the chairs. The agreement was before we started out that if it was called for then why not leave the chairs right there? I mean they would be there in the morning. Which is Saturday. Before it even starts.

—No, the boys *not* here now because I've been here
since Boots came in and all they said last night was,
Let me off on the other side of the railroad crossing,
which was done about 2:30A.M. mean Forney,
Hutch, Sheddy-boy. I mean we all went down the
highway in my pickup.
—Why, I'd say it to anybody. When auxillary ladies
won't take a chair out of a pickup this country's in
one hell of a shape. Anyway that's where I parked
my pickup. After they said just let us out across the
railroad about 2:30A.M. . . . .

All out of the twenty and same to you double sock roller and

(You could try
at the Oasis)

Did I tell you about the youngest Dudley girl?
Very sudden. Remains are now at Sharshley Brothers. Virus, they say.
Thought you might have because weren't you on that Vic Ditching & Concrete job out on old Route 137 this side of the Halley Sidenstricker place?
So you would have laid tile right past Old Man Dudley's place. Some say
she did it herself. Didn't want the baby. Old Man Dudley says, "Okay then
bury her in slacks," and the second Mrs. Dudley, the mother, says "She et
steak so now she's got to do the dishes."
Well, you wouldn't have known her and

(Try the Oasis)

—Why there they are look at them all here in one
piece! Why put two tables together for Hutch and
Forney
So where's Sheddy-boy . . .
—Why he got out of the pickup along with you two
the other side of the railroad and then I parked and
left it. I mean the pickup is there so the auxillary
ladies can get them if they would just look under the
tarp. Well that's the question. If Sheddy-boy has got
all our receipt books then we just have to wait right
here . . .
—One bourbon Jack Daniels water, two bourbon
Water-fill and soda one double 7—a *light* whiskey—
water-back and Boots a double shot so let's say that
would be two bourbon Waterfill and two bourbon
Jack a double 7 so two fives, two twos ninety cents
in change and just leave the change right where it is
so everyone will know.
Membership drive handled very well by Membership Committee of
which I was a member but *not any more.* We did what they told us. Sheddy-
boy all intact. All in order. It's just a matter of straightening attached lists
and double check against CASH ON HAND against RECEIPTS against
ATCHED lists against CARBON COPY INSERT HERE broken down
twenty, ten, five, singles, misc. 50¢, 25¢ and
—Sheddy-boy why look at him all in one piece and
if a hair of the dog won't bite you then the country

is in one hell of another round of the same, the same, the same except two bourbon Jack Daniels water, two bourbon Waterfill and soda—and none for me I got to add our receipt books and all out of the twenty and leave the change right there so everyone will know . . .

—Why Boots wouldn't that have been two Jack Daniels water two bourbon Waterfill and soda one double 7 Crown water-back a double Sheddy-boy per the usual Jim Beam also water-back now what have you actually got there before we get started: two Daniels two Waterfills two double 7 twice and a double Sheddy-boy . . .

(This isn't the Oasis.
You could try the Oasis)

—*Under* the tarp. *Under* the tarp that's why I left the pickup all night in the first place, I mean we're *all tied up here.* So couldn't they just roll back the tarp and hand the chairs down to other ladies who can unfold chairs and can set them right in a row at the counter if they are going to serve the general public? Did you ask them that well ask them that . . .

—Boys, just leave all our receipt books right where they are. . . .

—First we better go downstairs to unload them chairs.

Sunday a.m. things okay here and hope you are the same.

Two details new on the back bar since you took off and enlisted AF. Card Room and Lodge Room per the usual. Well, I was a Sergeant in the last one: *do what they tell you.* BOOTS, on duty and

—Crown double, water-back same for you Boots.

Regards back bar did I tell you at the left from where I usually sit he had cigar boxes one on top of the other in five rows. Lids open. Pictures showing all in a row on the lids: gold Crown, race horse pulling per 1890 Habana Crooks cheroots in little cardboard shirt pocket size for our ladies auxillary mostly.

Well, Boots moved cigars, and in that place put this 7 made out of white styrofoam on a lithographed ice chunk and inside the ice the light shines on mint leaves underneath like water melting.

Sandwich machine with roast beef egg salad or Combination stapled by wax paper and inside the corner yellow tags 25¢ says egg salad, Combi-

nation but facts of the matter no Tuna. Well, I eat here a lot and it don't
make a damn so long as the RB holds out just speaking for myself. Otherwise all okay and

> —Double 7 Crown, water-back, have one on me
> Boots old sock stuffer pull up a chair because no
> Forney, no Hutch, no Sheddy-boy until maybe
> away past noon. Well, when you get time but take it
> out of the twenty and

Regards our Membership Drive. Handled very well by Membership
Committee of which I was a member *but not any more.* All I know is we did
what they told us. We had a meeting yesterday Saturday a.m. Forney,
Hutch, Sheddy-boy, Whacker, Sid. Old members in arrears signed up per
list, Demits per list, new members per list attached. No Dudleys on any list.

So then lists check against RECEIPTS against ATCHD LIST HERE
against CARBON INSERT COPY HERE against CASH ON HAND
Well, we put all that on the table. We called it all off to everybody. I said,
it's all here someplace.

> —Less: one bourbon Jack Daniels water two bour-
> bon Waterfill and soda and double 7-Crown (me)
> also double Boots and all out of the twenty, so
> wouldn't that be two bourbon Jack and 7 Boots out
> of two tens and odd change it's all here someplace. I
> mean because that way it's as fair for one as it is for
> the other.

They called us out to unload some chairs which is what you can't plan
ahead on. We got back up here and everything was just like we left it per
atched list cash-on-hand, INSERT CARBON INITIAL HERE. What I'm
saying it's all here someplace and

> —Boots, old lork stroller Grande Hoja Exquisita—
> Bering—AsiaAlaska Danish celebrated navigator—
> Vitus Bering—Discovery of Bering Strait 1728 seal
> skin whiskers hair and oil skin sailor hat for rim ice.
> Also a RB stapled wazz paper and inside stapled
> yellow tag and Boots take it all out of the ten there's
> more and sametoyou and if you get the time why set
> down here and if you can't set down then the coun-
> try is in one hell of a shape.

Well, as it turned out the other a.m. I never did see their rope. That's
why they couldn't get the tarp off my pickup. Because the light pole came
down also and was laying *across* the pickup truck and through the tent
homemade hamburgers homemade pies homemade hotdogs mustard onion
catsup onion.

You get the picture?

Well, we got it unloaded but why would they leave a rope tied like that across the square, the main street of town?

Two details new on the back bar since you enlisted AF. Boots moved cigar display toward *left*. The 7 put in that same place, to the *right*. Sandwich machine RB fresh wax paper every two days in middle 25¢ per also the same.

Say, did you ever know the youngest Sharshley girl? Her funeral this p.m. Trust them to save a $ so will lay her to rest in a pair of slacks. Might view the remains.

No reason for you to know that youngest Sharshley girl except you ran Vic Ditching & Concrete, that ditching machine, right past their place on that job. Remember, just this side the old Halley Sidenstricker place so maybe you parked my pickup truck on their land, or barnyard. I mean that's possible but she wasn't around much, they say.

So Old Man Sharshley said, She's not my daughter. So then the mother says, Well she et steak so now let her do the dishes.

Some say virus. Some say she done it herself—didn't want the baby. Well, I'm not mixed up in it one way or the other, but might view the remains this p.m.

Thought you might have parked the ditching machine in the barn yard and

—Boots, same to you and water-back and where's. . .

(Try the Oasis)

—Wherebody, mean Forney Toots Hutch Wacker
Sheddy-boy mean Cleet. Wherebody, I mean where
even a Dudley this A.M.

Was a member, but *not any more*. Receipt books per membership drive INITIAL HERE, CASH ON HAND, so figure Demits, figure New Members per *all* lists per *all* receipt books less One Bourbon Jack Daniels two Bourbon Waterfill & soda one Daniels 7 crown double water-back BOOTS, on duty. So two fives two singles all out of the second twenty and so it's all right here someplace.

So they left my pickup truck right there all afternoon parked beside the IOOF auxillary ladies booth because nobody looked *inside*. My ignition key was right where I left it *per arrangement* so they could move it. They blame me. BOOTS, on duty and

—Boots old corkstuffer old sockroller 7 double
Daniels soda-back and you have a Jack Waterfill
Beam on me and take it all out of the other twenty
so wherebody? Mean Forney-boy, Heddy, mean
Shuch, Clacker, Weet and

Why, that's why we got a Clean-Up Committee in the first place because a Festival's all over and that's why I'm here because if nobody *per arrangements* meets here then who takes back the folding chairs I mean back down the highway where they came from. If nobody then the country's in one Hell of a shape I mean I'm ready so what about a wazzpaper roat boof so what about a Grande Hoja Exquisita navigator—Vitus Bering—Bering Strait seal skin whiskers oil and hair skin sailor by hat rim lightice and 7 crown ice-back in mint, *inside* the mint on water melting. Well, you have to eat someplace.

Say, did I tell you Boots moved the cigars to the end of our back bar? In that place he put a "7"—a *light* whiskey—now where the cigars was he has this white styrofoam 7 fastened on the ice. All tables the same. Card Room and Lodge Room per the usual.

Well, that's the news.

Was a Sergeant in the last one: *do what they tell you.*

yr
DAD

p.s.

It was the youngest Dudley girl—not the Sharshley girl.
Sharshley Brothers has the remains.

(. . . not here,
Try the Oasis)

GRACE PALEY

The Long-Distance Runner

*O*ne day, before or after forty-two, I became a long-distance runner. Though I was stout and in many ways inadequate to this desire, I wanted to go far and fast, not as fast as bicycles and trains, not as far as Taipei, Hingwen, places like that, islands of the slant-eyed cunt, as sailors in bus stations say when speaking of travel, but round and round the county from the sea side to the bridges, along the old neighborhood streets a couple of times, before old age and urban renewal ended them and me.

I tried the country first, Connecticut, which being wooded is always full of buds in spring. All creation is secret, isn't that true? So I trained in the wide-zoned suburban hills where I wasn't known. I ran all spring in and out of dogwood bloom, then laurel.

People sometimes stopped and asked me why I ran, a lady in silk shorts halfway down over her fat thighs. In training, I replied and rested only to answer if closely questioned. I wore a white sleeveless undershirt as well, with excellent support, not to attract the attention of old men and prudish children.

Then summer came, my legs seemed strong. I kissed the kids goodbye. They were quite old by then. It was near the time for parting anyway. I told

Mrs. Raftery to look in now and then and give them some of that rotten Celtic supper she makes.

I told them they could take off any time they wanted to. Go lead your private life, I said. Only leave me out of it.

A word to the wise . . . said Richard.

You're depressed Faith, Mrs. Raftery said. Your boy friend Jack, the one you think's so hotsy-totsy, hasn't called and you're as gloomy as a tick on Sunday.

Cut the folkshit with me, Raftery, I muttered. Her eyes filled with tears because that's who she is: folkshit from bunion to topknot. That's how she got liked by me, loved, invented and endured.

When I walked out the door they were all reclining before the television set, Richard, Tonto and Mrs. Raftery, gazing at the news. Which proved with moving pictures that there *had* been a voyage to the moon and Africa and South American hid in a furious whorl of clouds.

I said, Goodbye. They said, Yeah, O.K., sure.

If that's how it is, forget it, I hollered and took the Independent subway to Brighton Beach.

At Brighton Beach I stopped at the Salty Breezes Locker Room to change my clothes. Twenty-five years ago my father invested $500 in its future. In fact he still clears about $3.50 a year, which goes directly (by law) to the Children of Judea to cover their deficit.

No one paid too much attention when I started to run, easy and light on my feet. I ran on the boardwalk first, past my mother's leafleting station—between a soft-ice-cream stand and a degenerated dune. There she had been assigned by her comrades to halt the tides of cruel American enterprise with simple socialist sense.

I wanted to stop and admire the long beach. I wanted to stop in order to think admiringly about New York. There aren't many rotting cities so tan and sandy and speckled with citizens at their salty edges. But I had already spent a lot of life lying down or standing and staring. I had decided to run.

After about a mile and a half I left the boardwalk and began to trot into the old neighborhood. I was running well. My breath was long and deep. I was thinking pridefully about my form.

Suddenly I was surrounded by about three hundred blacks.

Who you?

Who that?

Look at her! Just look! When you seen a fatter ass?

Poor thing. She ain't right. Leave her, you boys, you bad boys.

I used to live here, I said.

Oh yes, they said, in the white old days. That time too bad to last.

But we loved it here. We never went to Flatbush Avenue or Times Square. We loved our block.

Tough black titty.

I like your speech, I said. Metaphor and all.

Right on. We get that from talking.

Yes my people also had a way of speech. And don't forget the Irish. The gift of gab.

Who they? said a small boy.

Cops.

Nowadays, I suggested, there's more than Irish on the police force.

You right, said two ladies. More more, much much more. They's French Chinamen Russkies Congoleans. Oh, missee, you too right.

I lived in that house, I said. That apartment house. All my life. Till I got married.

Now that *is* nice. Live in one place. My mother live that way in South Carolina. One place. Her daddy farmed. She said. They ate. No matter winter war bad times. Roosevelt. Something! Ain't that wonderful! And it weren't cold! Big trees!

That apartment. I looked up and pointed. There. The third floor.

They all looked up. So what! You blubrous devil! said a dark young man. He wore horn-rimmed glasses and had that intelligent look that City College boys used to have when I was eighteen and first looked at them.

He seemed to lead them in contempt and anger, even the littlest ones who moved toward me with dramatic stealth singing, Devil, Oh Devil. I don't think the little kids had bad feeling because they poked a finger into me, then laughed.

Still I thought it might be wise to keep my head. So I jumped right in with some facts. I said, How many flowers' names do you know? Wild flowers, I mean. My people only knew two. That's what they say now anyway. Rich or poor, they only had two flowers' names. Rose and violet.

Daisy, said one boy immediately.

Weed, said another. That *is* a flower, I thought. But everyone else got the joke.

Saxifrage, lupine, said a lady. Viper's bugloss, said a small Girl Scout in medium green with a dark green sash. She held up a *Handbook of Wild Flowers.*

How many you know, fat mama? a boy asked warmly. He wasn't against my being a mother or fat. I turned all my attention to him.

Oh sonny, I said, I'm way ahead of my people. I know in yellows alone: common cinquefoil, trout lily, yellow adder's-tongue, swamp buttercup and common buttercup, golden sorrel, yellow or hop clover, devil's-paintbrush, evening primrose, black-eyed Susan, golden aster, also the yellow pickerelweed growing down by the water if not in the water, and dandelions of course. I've seen all these myself. Seen them.

You could see China from the boardwalk, a boy said. When it's nice.

I know more flowers than countries. Mostly young people these days have traveled in many countries.

Not me. I ain't been nowhere.

Not me either, said about seventeen boys.

I'm not allowed, said a little girl. There's drunken junkies.

But *I! I!* cried out a tall black youth, very handsome and well dressed. I am an African. My father came from the high stolen plains. *I* have been everywhere. I was in Moscow six months, learning machinery. I was in France, learning French. I was in Italy, observing the peculiar Renaissance and the people's sweetness. I was in England, where I studied the common law and the urban blight. I was at the Conference of Dark Youth in Cuba to understand our passion. I am now here. Here am I to become an engineer and return to my people, around the Cape of Good Hope in a Norwegian sailing vessel. In this way I will learn the fine old art of sailing in case the engines of the new society of my old inland country should fail.

We had an extraordinary amount of silence after that. Then one old lady in a black dress and high white lace collar said to another old lady dressed exactly the same way, Glad tidings when someone got brains in the head not fish juice. Amen, said a few.

Whyn't you go up to Mrs. Luddy living in your house, you lady, huh? The Girl Scout asked this.

Why she just groove to see you, said some sarcastic snickerer.

She got palpitations. Her man, he give it to her.

That ain't all, he a natural gift-giver.

I'll take you, said the Girl Scout. My name is Cynthia. I'm in Troop 355, Brooklyn.

I'm not dressed, I said, looking at my lumpy knees.

You shouldn't wear no undershirt like that without no runnin number or no team writ on it. It look like a undershirt.

Cynthia! Don't take her up there, said an important boy. Her head strange. Don't you take her. Hear?

Lawrence, she said softly, you tell me once more what to do I'll wrap you round that lamppost.

Git! she said, powerfully addressing *me*.

In this way I was led into the hallway of the whole house of my childhood.

The first door I saw was still marked in flaky gold, 1A. That's where the janitor lived, I said. He was a Negro.

How come like that? Cynthia made an astonished face. How come the janitor was a black man?

Oh Cynthia, I said. Then I turned to the opposite door, first floor front, 1B. I remembered. Now, here, this was Mrs. Goreditsky, very very fat lady. All her children died at birth. Born, then one, two, three. Dead. Five children, then Mr. Goreditsky said, I'm bad luck on you Tessie and he went away. He sent $15 a week for seven years. Then no one heard.

I know her, poor thing, said Cynthia. The city come for her summer before last. The way they knew, it smelled. They wrapped her up in a canvas. They couldn't get through the front door. It scraped off a piece of her. My uncle Ronald had to help them, but he got disgusted.

Only two years ago. She was still here! Wasn't she scared?

So we all, said Cynthia. White ain't everything.

Who lived up here, she asked, 2B? Right now, my best friend Nancy Rosalind lives here. She got two brothers, and her sister married and got a baby. She very light-skinned. Not her mother. We got all colors amongst us.

Your best friend? That's funny. Because it was *my* best friend. Right in that apartment. Joanna Rosen.

What become of her? Cynthia asked. She got a running shirt too?

Come on Cynthia, if you really want to know, I'll tell you. She married this man, Marvin Steirs.

Who's he?

I recollected his achievements. Well, he's the president of a big corporation, JoMar Plastics. This corporation owns a steel company, a radio station, a new Xerox-type machine that lets you do twenty-five different pages at once. This corporation has a foundation, The JoMar Fund for Research in Conservation. Capitalism is like that, I added, in order to be politically useful.

How come you know? You go over their house a lot?

No. I happened to read all about them on the financial page, just last week. It made me think; a different life. That's all.

Different spokes for different folks, said Cynthia.

I sat down on the cool marble steps and remembered Joanna's cousin Ziggie. He was older than we were. He wrote a poem which told us we were lovely flowers and our legs were petals, which nature would force open no matter how many times we said no.

Then I had several other interior thoughts that I couldn't share with a child, the kind that give your face a blank or melancholy look.

Now you're not interested, said Cynthia. Now you're not gonna say a thing. Who lived here, 2A? Who? Two men lives here now. Women coming and women going. My mother says, Danger sign: Stay away, my darling, stay away.

I don't remember, Cynthia. I really don't.

You got to. What'd you come for, anyways?

Then I tried. 2A. 2A. Was it the twins? I felt a strong obligation as though remembering was in charge of the *existence* of the past. This is not so.

Cynthia, I said, I don't want to go any further. I don't even want to remember.

Come on, she said, tugging at my shorts, don't you want to see Mrs. Luddy, the one lives in your old house? That be fun, no?

No. No, I don't want to see Mrs. Luddy.

Now you shouldn't pay no attention to those boys downstairs. She will like you. I mean, she is kind. She don't like most white people, but she might like you.

No Cynthia, it's not that, but I don't want to see my father and mother's house now.

I didn't know what to say. I said, Because my mother's dead. This was a lie, because my mother lives in her own room with my father in the Children of Judea. With her hand over her socialist heart, she reads the paper every morning after breakfast. Then she says sadly to my father, Every day the same. Dying . . . dying, dying from killing.

My mother's dead Cynthia. I can't go in there.

Oh . . . oh, the poor thing, she said, looking into my eyes. Oh, if my mother died, I don't know what I'd do. Even if I was old as you. I could kill myself. Tears filled her eyes and started down her cheeks. If my mother died, what would I do? She is my protector, she won't let the pushers get me. She hold me tight. She gonna hide me in the cedar box if my Uncle Rudford comes try to get me back. She *can't* die, my mother.

Cynthia—honey—she won't die. She's young. I put my arm out to comfort her. You could come live with me, I said. I got two boys, they're nearly grown up. I missed it, not having a girl.

What? What you mean now, live with you and boys. She pulled away and ran for the stairs. Stay way from me, honky lady. I know them white boys. They just gonna try and jostle my black womanhood. My mother told me about that, keep you white honky devil boys to your devil self, you just leave me be you old bitch you. Somebody help me, she started to scream, you hear. Somebody help. She gonna take me away.

She flattened herself to the wall, trembling. I was too frightened by her fear of me to say, honey, I wouldn't hurt you, it's me. I heard her helpers, the voices of large boys crying, We coming, we coming, hold your head up, we coming. I ran past her fear to the stairs and up them two at a time. I came to my old own door. I knocked like the landlord, loud and terrible.

Mama not home, a child's voice said. No, no, I said. It's me! a lady! Someone's chasing me, let me in. Mama not home, I ain't allowed to open up for nobody.

It's me! I cried out in terror. Mama! Mama! let me in!

The door opened. A slim woman whose age I couldn't invent looked at me. She said, Get in and shut that door tight. She took a hard pinching hold on my upper arm. Then she bolted the door herself. Them hustlers after you. They make me pink. Hide this white lady now, Donald. Stick her under your bed, you got a high bed.

Oh that's O.K. I'm fine now, I said. I felt safe and at home.

You in my house, she said. You do as I say. For two cents, I throw you out.

I squatted under a small kid's pissy mattress. Then I heard the knock. It was tentative and respectful. My mama don't allow me to open. Donald! someone called. Donald!

Oh no, he said. Can't do it. She gonna wear me out. You know her. She already tore up my ass this morning once. Ain't *gonna* open up.

I lived there for about three weeks with Mrs. Luddy and Donald and three little baby girls nearly the same age. I told her a joke about Irish twins. Ain't Irish, she said.

Nearly every morning the babies woke us at about 6:45. We gave them all a bottle and went back to sleep till 8:00. I made coffee and she changed diapers. Then it really stank for a while. At this time I usually said, Well listen, thanks really, but I've got to go I guess. I guess I'm going. She'd usually say, Well, guess again. *I* guess you ain't. Or if she was feeling disgusted she'd say, Go on now! Get! You wanna go, I guess by now I have snorted enough white lady stink to choke a horse. Go on!

I'd get to the door and then I'd hear voices. I'm ashamed to say I'd become fearful. Despite my wide geographical love of mankind, I would be attacked by local fears.

There was a sentimental truth that lay beside all that going and not going. It *was* my house where I'd lived long ago my family life. There was a tile on the bathroom floor that I myself had broken, dropping a hammer on the toe of my brother Charles as he stood dreamily shaving, his prick halfway up his undershorts. Astonishment and knowledge first seized me right there. The kitchen was the same. The table was the enameled table common to our class, easy to clean, with wooden undercorners for indigent and old cockroaches that couldn't make it to the kitchen sink. (However, it was not the same table, because I have inherited that one, chips and all.)

The living room was something like ours, only we had less plastic. There may have been less plastic in the world at that time. Also, my mother had set beautiful cushions everywhere, on beds and chairs. It was the way she expressed herself, artistically, to embroider at night or take strips of flowered cotton and sew them across ordinary white or blue muslin in the most delicate designs, the way women have always used materials that live and die in hunks and tatters to say: This is my place.

Mrs. Luddy said, Uh huh!

Of course, I said, men don't have that outlet. That's how come they run around so much.

Till they drunk enough to lay down, she said.

Yes, I said, on a large scale you can see it in the world. First they make something, then they murder it. Then they write a book about how interesting it is.

You got something there, she said. Sometimes she said, Girl, you don't know *nothing*.

We often sat at the window looking out and down. Little tufts of breeze grew on that windowsill. The blazing afternoon was around the corner and up the block.

You say men, she said. Is that men? she asked. What you call—a Man?

Four flights below us, leaning on the stoop, were about a dozen people and around them devastation. Just a minute, I said. I had seen devastation on my way, running, gotten some of the pebbles of it in my running shoe and the dust of it in my eyes. I had thought with the indignant courtesy of a citizen, This is a disgrace to the City of New York which I love and am running through.

But now, from the commanding heights of home, I saw it clearly. The tenement in which Jack my old and present friend had come to gloomy manhood had been destroyed, first by fire, then by demolition (which is a swinging ball of steel that cracks bedrooms and kitchens). Because of this work, we could see several blocks wide and a block and a half long. Crazy Eddy's house still stood, famous 1510 gutted, with black window frames, no glass, open laths. The stubbornness of the supporting beams! Some persons or families still lived on the lowest floors. In the lots between, a couple of old sofas lay on their fat faces, their springs sticking up into the air. Just as in wartime a half-dozen ailanthus trees had already found their first quarter inch of earth and begun a living attack on the dead yards. At night, I knew animals roamed the place, squalling and howling, furious New York dogs and street cats and mighty rats. You would think you were in Bear Mountain Park, the terror of venturing forth.

Someone ought to clean that up, I said.

Mrs. Luddy said, Who you got in mind? Mrs. Kennedy?—

Donald made a stern face. He said, That just what I gonna do when I get big. Gonna get the Sanitary Man in and show it to him. You see that, you big guinea you, you clean it up right now! Then he stamped his feet and fierced his eyes.

Mrs. Luddy said, Come here, you little nigger. She kissed the top of his head and gave him a whack on the backside all at one time.

Well, said Donald, encouraged, look out there now you all! Go on I say, look! Though we had already seen, to please him we looked. On the stoop men and boys lounged, leaned, hopped about, stood on one leg, then another, took their socks off, and scratched their toes, talked, sat on their haunches, heads down, dozing.

Donald said, Look at them. They ain't got self-respect. They got Afros *on* their heads, but they don't know they black *in* their heads.

I thought he ought to learn to be more sympathetic. I said, There are reasons that people are that way.

Yes ma'am, said Donald.

Anyway, how come you never go down and play with the other kids, how come you're up here so much?

My mama don't like me do that. Some of them is bad. Bad. I might become a dope addict. I got to stay clear.

You just a dope, that a fact, said Mrs. Luddy.

He ought to be with kids his age more, I think.

He see them in school, miss. Don't trouble your head about it if you don't mind.

Actually, Mrs. Luddy didn't go down into the street either. Donald did all the shopping. She let the welfare investigator in, the meterman came into the kitchen to read the meter. I saw him from the back room, where I hid. She did pick up her check. She cashed it. She returned to wash the babies, change their diapers, wash clothes, iron, feed people, and then in free half hours she sat by that window. She was waiting.

I believed she was watching and waiting for a particular man. I wanted to discuss this with her, talk lovingly like sisters. But before I could freely say, Forget about that son of a bitch, he's a pig, I did have to offer a few solid facts about myself, my kids, about fathers, husbands, passers-by, evening companions, and the life of my father and mother in this room by this exact afternoon window.

I told her for instance, that in my worst times I had given myself one extremely simple physical pleasure. This was cream cheese for breakfast. In fact, I insisted on it, sometimes depriving the children of very important articles and foods.

Girl, you don't know nothing, she said.

Then for a little while she talked gently as one does to a person who is innocent and insane and incorruptible because of stupidity. She had had two such special pleasures for hard times she said. The first, men, but they turned rotten, white women had ruined the best, give them the idea their dicks made of solid gold. The second pleasure she had tried was wine. She said, I do like wine. You *has* to have something just for yourself by yourself. Then she said, But you can't raise a decent boy when you liquor-dazed every night.

White or black, I said, returning to men, they did think they were bringing a rare gift, whereas it was just sex, which is common like bread, though essential.

Oh, you can do without, she said. There's folks does without.

I told her Donald deserved the best. I loved him. If he had flaws, I hardly noticed them. It's one of my beliefs that children do not have flaws, even the worst do not.

Donald was brilliant—like my boys except that he had an easier disposition. For this reason I decided, almost the second moment of my residence in that household, to bring him up to reading level at once. I told him we would work with books and newspapers. He went immediately to his neighborhood library and brought some hard books to amuse me. *Black Folktales* by Julius Lester and *The Pushcart War,* which is about another neighborhood but relevant.

Donald always agreed with me when we talked about reading and writing. In fact, when I mentioned poetry, he told me he knew all about it, that David Henderson, a known black poet, had visited his second-grade class. So Donald was, as it turned out, well ahead of my nosy tongue. He was usually very busy shopping. He also had to spend a lot of time making faces to force the little serious baby girls into laughter. But if the subject came up, he could take *the* poem right out of the air into which language and event had just gone.

An example: That morning, his mother had said, Whew, I just got too much piss and diapers and wash. I wanna just sit down by that window and rest myself. He wrote a poem:

Just got too much pissy diapers
and wash and wash
just wanna sit down by that window
and look out
            ain't nothing there.

Donald, I said, you are plain brilliant. I'm never going to forget you. For God's sakes don't you forget me.

You fool with him too much, said Mrs. Luddy. He already don't even remember his grandma, you never gonna meet someone like her, a curse never come past her lips.

I do remember, Mama, I remember. She lying in bed, right there. A man standing in the door. She say, Esdras, I put a curse on you head. You worsen tomorrow. How come she said like that?

Gomorrah, I believe Gomorrah, she said. She know the Bible inside out.

Did she live with you?

No. No, she visiting. She come up to see us all, her children, how we doing. She come up to see sights. Then she lay down and died. She was old.

I remained quiet because of the death of mothers. Mrs. Luddy looked at me thoughtfully, then she said:

My mama had stories to tell, she raised me on. *Her* mama was a little thing, no sense. Stand in the door of the cabin all day, sucking her thumb. It was slave times. One day a young field boy come storming along. He knock on the door of the first cabin hollering, Sister, come out, it's freedom. She come out. She say, Yeah? When? He say, Now! It's freedom now! Then he knock at the next door and say, Sister! It's freedom! Now! From one cabin he run to the next cabin, crying out, Sister, it's freedom now!

Oh I remember that story, said Donald. Freedom now! Freedom now! He jumped up and down.

You don't remember nothing boy. Go on, get Eloise, she want to get into the good times.

Eloise was two but undersized. We got her like that, said Donald. Mrs. Luddy let me buy her ice cream and green vegetables. She was waiting for kale and chard, but it was too early. The kale liked cold. You not about to be here November, she said. No, no. I turned away, lonesomeness touching me and sang our Eloise song:

Eloise loves the bees
the bees they buzz
like Eloise does.

Then Eloise crawled all over the splintery floor, buzzing widly.
Oh you crazy baby, said Donald, buzz buzz buzz.
Mrs. Luddy sat down by the window.
You all make a lot of noise, she said sadly. You just right on noisy.
The next morning Mrs. Luddy woke me up.
Time to go, she said.
What?
Home.
What? I said.
Well, don't you think your little spoiled boys crying for you? Where's Mama? They standing in the window. Time to go lady. This ain't Free Vacation Farm. Time we was by ourself a little.
Oh Ma, said Donald, she ain't a lot of trouble. Go on, get Eloise, she hollering. And button up your lip.
She didn't offer me coffee. She looked at me strictly all the time. I tried to look strictly back, but I failed because I loved the sight of her.
Donald was teary, but I didn't dare turn my face to him, until the parting minute at the door. Even then, I kissed the top of his head a little too forcefully and said, Well, I'll see you.
On the front stoop there were about half a dozen mid-morning family

people and kids arguing about who had dumped garbage out of which window. They were very disgusted with one another.

Two young men in handsome dashikis stood in counsel and agreement at the street corner. They divided a comment. How come white womens got rotten teeth? And look so old? A young woman waiting at the light said, Hush . . .

I walked past them and didn't begin my run till the road opened up somewhere along Ocean Parkway. I was a little stiff because my way of life had used only small movements, an occasional stretch to put a knife or teapot out of reach of the babies. I ran about ten, fifteen blocks. Then my second wind came, which is classical, famous among runners, it's the beginning of flying.

In the three weeks I'd been off the street, jogging had become popular. It seemed that I was only one person doing her thing, which happened like most American eccentric acts to be the most "in" thing I could have done. In fact, two young men ran alongside of me for nearly a mile. They ran silently beside me and turned off at Avenue H. A gentleman with a mustache, running poorly in the opposite direction, waved. He called out, Hi, señora.

Near home I ran through our park, where I had aired my children on weekends and late-summer afternoons. I stopped at the northeast playground, where I met a dozen young mothers intelligently handling their little ones. In order to prepare them, meaning no harm, I said, In fifteen years, you girls will be like me, wrong in everything.

At home it was Saturday morning. Jack had returned looking as grim as ever, but he'd brought cash and a vacuum cleaner. While the coffee perked, he showed Richard how to use it. They were playing tick tack toe on the dusty wall.

Richard said, Well! Look who's here! Hi!

Any news? I asked.

Letter from Daddy, he said. From the lake and water country in Chile. He says it's like Minnesota.

He's never been to Minnesota, I said. Where's Anthony?

Here I am, said Tonto, appearing. But I'm leaving.

Oh yes, I said. Of course. Every Saturday he hurries through breakfast or misses it. He goes to visit his friends in institutions. These are well-known places like Bellevue, Hillside, Rockland State, Central Islip, Manhattan. These visits take him all day and sometimes half the night.

I found some chocolate-chip cookies in the pantry. Take them, Tonto, I said. I remember nearly all his friends as little boys and girls always hopping, skipping, jumping and cookie-eating. He was annoyed. He said, No! Chocolate cookies is what the commissaries are full of. How about money?

Jack dropped the vacuum cleaner. He said, No! They have parents for that.

I said, Here, five dollars for cigarettes, one dollar each.

Cigarettes! said Jack. Goddamnit! Black lungs and death! Cancer! Emphysema! He stomped out of the kitchen, breathing. He took the bike from the back room and started for Central Park, which has been closed to cars but opened to bicycle riders. When he'd been gone about ten minutes, Anthony said, It's really open only on Sundays.

Why didn't you say so? Why can't you be decent to him? I asked. It's important to me.

Oh Faith, he said, patting me on the head because he'd grown so tall, all that air. It's good for his lungs. And his muscles! He'll be back soon.

You should ride too, I said. You don't want to get mushy in your legs. You should go swimming once a week.

I'm too busy, he said. I have to see my friends.

Then Richard, who had been vacuuming under his bed, came into the kitchen. You still here, Tonto?

Going going gone, said Anthony, don't bat your eye.

Now listen, Richard said, here's a note. It's for Judy, if you get as far as Rockland. Don't forget it. Don't open it. Don't read it. I know he'll read it.

Anthony smiled and slammed the door.

Did I lose weight? I asked. Yes, said Richard. You look O.K. You never look too bad. But where were you? I got sick of Raftery's boiled potatoes. Where were you, Faith?

Well! I said. Well! I stayed a few weeks in my old apartment, where Grandpa and Grandma and me and Hope and Charlie lived, when we were little. I took you there long ago. Not so far from the ocean where Grandma made us very healthy with sun and air.

What are you talking about? said Richard. Cut the baby talk.

Anthony came home earlier than expected that evening because some people were in shock therapy and someone else had run away. He listened to me for a while. Then he said, I don't know what she's talking about either.

Neither did Jack, despite the understanding often produced by love after absence. He said, Tell me again. He was in a good mood. He said, You can even tell it to me twice.

I repeated the story. They all said, What?

Because it isn't usually so simple. Have you known it to happen much nowadays? A woman inside the steamy energy of middle age runs and runs. She finds the houses and streets where her childhood happened. She lives in them. She learns as though she was still a child what in the world is coming next.

William Harrison (1933–   ) was born in Dallas, Texas, and after attending Texas Christian University matriculated at the theological school of Vanderbilt University; he gave up a career in the ministry for graduate studies at the University of Iowa Writer's Workshop. For several years he has taught literature and creative writing at the University of Arkansas; presently at that school he is director of a newly activated department of film. Harrison's first novel, The Theologian *(1965), was followed by* In a Wild Sanctuary *(1969). He is professionally interested in film production and wrote the script for the recent film production of the title story of his collection,* Roller Ball Murder, and Other Stories *(1974).*

WILLIAM HARRISON

The Good Ship Erasmus

*T*his is one of those cruise ships dedicated to helping people. These ships embark every day now from such places as Miami, Liverpool, Naples or Athens, some of them stuffed with psychiatrists trying to help the passengers forget their troubles, others with physical culture experts trying to beat the blubber off a fat clientele, others with religious leaders trying to purge or mystify those who are aboard.

Our ship, *The Erasmus,* has a somewhat less complicated mission: theoretically, at least, it is just a ship which will hold us captive on the high seas until we have all stopped smoking. We sailed from Amsterdam a few days ago, puffing like mad on the dock before the horn sounded, and in a few short weeks we will be around Italy, the warm Mediterannean waters soothing us—one hope being, I assume, that craved minds will turn away from nicotine to romantic lust—until all lungs are healthy again.

My game is smuggling thousands of cigars and cigarettes on board.

By the time we see the French coast I'm largely in control of many of the three hundred lives around me.

It is enough to make me slightly melancholy, philosophic. I stand here at the rail gazing into the calm summer waves, ruminating on things economic, psychological, theological.

The Erasmus has twin stabilizers, a cruising speed of twenty-six knots, lounges, shops, bars, a gymnasium, swimming pools, dining rooms, and an optimistic staff. Perry Cheyenne is the Passenger Host who directs our seminars, offers encouragement to those in withdrawal and despair, arranges parties and games and contests. He wears tennis clothes and a yacht cap, grins, bounces as he goes. Our captain is never seen, just this happy Passenger Host; the captain is far away, up there somewhere on the bridge, steering us onward.

I find in this a metaphor for life.

Shopping for clothes, I buy tennis wear just like Perry's and give serious consideration to a maroon tuxedo. I boarded with four oversized suitcases and a trunk all stuffed with everyone's favorite brands, domestic and foreign, so only had my one business suit.

I do all this because of the character of our age. It grows difficult to find a situation in which one can be clearly immoral, in which one can be sure of his deeds against nature and the soul.

"I'd *give* you the tux, mister, for one lousy cigarette, believe me," sighs Ramona, the salesgirl. She is working her passage on this expensive cruise here in the men's shop.

"I have plenty of cigarettes in my cabin," I disclose, admiring the cut of the jacket.

She eyes me openly, wantonly.

"What price you asking?" she blurts out, incapable of coyness.

"There are many prices," I tell her. "The cost isn't always the same."

There are deeper elements in all this beyond the fact of it being a simple tobacco-curing sea voyage. There is the death of God, the tides of history, and my own somewhat complicated personality. It's very confusing, sorting it out, which accounts for the choppy style of this report. Also, not only do I lose track of the exact philosophic flow, but my attention span, like yours, is short.

On deck, naturally, we passengers exchange personal information.

My father was from Chicago, my mother from Geneva, and I was born in the skiing village of Igls above Innsbruck as an American citizen. Father was an author and consumer of thick books and in his library I spent my asthmatic adolescence, ducking out of boarding schools to sit among his volumes instead. Once, six days into my puberty—I knew you'd want this incidental and inevitable note—I seduced our young Austrian housekeeper. I travelled and studied. Soon I knew many things and some of these which I tell my fellow passengers are:

The earliest cave men lived in caves on the French Riviera very near the beach and sunshine.

The poet Rilke died from being pricked by a rose thorn.

The population of the world now doubles every thirty years.

Scheherazade's erotic *Thousand and One Nights* ends with a prayer.

The only place to get a drink on Sunday morning in Rome is inside the bar at St. Peter's.

Choose one.

Sitting in deck chairs together, Mrs. Murtaugh and I discuss our separate problems. She is already beginning to resist therapy and sits here sucking a dummy cigarette, a little wooden Tinker Toy with a red-painted tip.

"My seminar group is meeting right now," she wails, "but I just can't go today. I don't like my hypnotist. If you don't respond to your hypnotist, he just can't put you under so you might as well quit."

"This is a degrading sort of troublemaking," I complain, "coming on board a sailing vessel peddling smokes. In another age I might've been a Satanic figure, my life a tragedy of corruption. Now look at me: I go around letting those of weak wills sniff the nicotine on my fingers and smell my brown breath."

"Worse yet," she continues, "I can't make love without a ciggie. I *have* to catch a smoke before and afterwards or I just can't go for sex. I told my group leader that and I told that insensitive hypnotist, too!"

"The world is just too libertine," I muse aloud. "In another age I could've been Iago, but not now. I take the whole reckless course of human history back to its cosmic roots, too, and the lost sense of the divine."

"So here I sit in a dowdy deck chair! A deck chair! I'm only fifty-six years old! I'm a warm-blooded woman, let me *tell* you, and a cruise is a cruise!"

"One could blame God, of course, for making man finite. A really benevolent God would've made man his equal—been a sport about the creation, I mean—but no, man is a weak hybrid, lower than the angels. And so it was certain to come to this: a time when the moral distinctions completely blur. Man adrift in a sensual sea. Perfecting the rhythms of pandemonium."

"What'd you say you peddled? Did you say ciggies?"

"I once wanted to be really evil. For instance, I thought of things like murder. But the world has too strong a death drive on its own—nothing very original can even be done with murder! And sex criminals can't get a headline because their perversions are so everyday. I spent my teen years practicing lots of nasty habits, I mean, but now there're movies and songs celebrating these things! I'm trying to get across the point, Mrs. Murtaugh, that all my life I've dreamt about doing people in, but fortune has only left me a few petty hustles."

"Did you say you actually have ciggies?"

Clearly, Mrs. Murtaugh isn't quite on my frequency when I describe the final indifference of the Greeks to their gods, Dante's rejection of religion in favor of secular politics, the Renaissance, growth of the factories, Einstein. Her eyes fasten on me as I talk and gaze out toward the Spanish coast, but she hears little.

At last, yes, I say, yes, Mrs. Murtaugh, I'll take your Bank Americard.

Everyone scampers ashore at Bilbao, the Bay of Biscay glistening in the hot sun around *The Erasmus* as I wait on board. By this time those who have resisted me run boldly toward the nearest cafes where they pay outlandish prices for packs of Pipers, Celtas, and other mediocre Spanish cigarettes.

Perry stands astride the gangplank, meanwhile, with his good-natured shakedown crew. When passengers return with bulges under their sport shirts and Bermuda shorts, the crew searches them and laughingly tosses their goodies into the bay. I look on with approval. A mere $20 bribe passes my contraband aboard without the slightest inspection and I disdain the lack of foresight and these clumsy attempts on the lone returning gangplank.

Perry gives the fallen few peptalks, making a fist as he lectures like a determined prep school coach. Both his teeth and shoes glisten white.

Later, two of my customers are caught smoking in one of the cramped hatches and Perry and his crew suffer doubts over their effectiveness at the gangplank. Perry shames the offenders in front of a Combined Seminar Meeting in the auditorium, shredding their cigarettes in public. One of them, a civic leader from Palatine, Illinois, nearly weeps. I respect Perry's zeal.

After this spectacle there is a speech by the ship's doctor, who says things like, "Please, *folks,* don't poison your body!" Then we have a demonstration by the hypnotist whose victim is a long-legged girl named Judy. When she swoons many in the audience are visibly moved.

There aren't enough chairs and the room is crowded, so I move among the throng like a savage force. Here and there I catch a knowing eye.

The famous Danish porno cruise ship, *Flicka,* passes us after we turn back into the Atlantic. Dedicated to orgy-minded travellers, it flies a single red flag and moves by us slowly on the hint of music.

Erasmus lists to port as we pass, my envious fellow passengers out there clutching the rail for a good look. Soon it is beyond our wake.

Pensive, my philosophical mood hanging on, yet talkative, I consent to my assigned session with one of the psychiatrists-in-residence, a Doctor Gonatt. He is impressed by my Austrian background and remarks that he once tried to read one of father's novels.

Gonatt strives to comprehend me and suggests an arrested moral growth brought on by culture fatigue and I have some difficulty explaining, no, I am actually an advanced and complex monster and that dedication to evil usually has curious and subtle side benefits for mankind anyway. We all know the evil that good men invariably do, I point out, but we must also consider the ironic value of the deviate. The sheep is not truly itself without the wolf, I explain, fetching an illusion which escapes him.

We talk and talk.

Gonatt has a drinking problem, I learn, and is trying to recover financially so he can re-open his clinic near San Diego. He used to smoke a pipe, he recalls: a big, curve-stemmed Meerschaum with a bowl like a factory chimney.

As he prattles his hands begin to tremble, so I can do no other than offer a menthol filter which, naturally, he accepts.

Here I sit in the Desiderius bar, the ship's plushest lounge, with the keys to my closet and locker safely rattling in my pocket, content that the stewards who clean my cabin will never find anything, but one of my best customers comes over and informs me that Perry Cheyenne is onto somebody. At first this makes me paranoid and I consider returning to B Deck and checking my hoard, but I calm myself.

"Watch your step, pal," my customer advises. His name is Mr. Branch, a successful food expert from Brussels, and he has never indulged in such side-of-the-mouth dramatics before.

I offer the next barstool. "Steady now. Tell me what's happening," I say evenly, trying to reassure him.

He insists there are high-level meetings involving Perry, the captain, the ship's doctor, and certain spies. Perry is furious. There have been butts in the public rooms and tell-tale holes burnt in a few of the bed linens.

I buy poor Branch a drink and promise an extra pack for his loyalty, but inside me I feel a stirring: a tingle of excitement, a new pulse. Deep down, perhaps, I crave confrontation.

I wear my maroon tuxedo to the evening dance. I know that Perry watches me as I make the rounds talking and laughing. The game seems to be on.

Later, back in my cabin I can't sleep. In spite of my tendency toward asthma, I smoke one of my cigarettes and speculate on my troublesome nature. The saintly good man, by definition, is humble to the point that he can move through the world anonymously; the man of evil, to the contrary, must have his foul deeds known and take pride in them. Ruminating, I decide that a showdown with Perry might be inevitable, yet it isn't what I want. Specifically, I need an intellectual adversary—not just some giddy zealot.

The captain: one wonders what or who he is.

The sleepless night continues and I finally dress and make my way to the ship's library. Perusing the magazines, I find nothing of interest and eventually settle back with a strange little volume by the Dutch philosopher Aart van der Leeuw who remarks that, "The mystery of life is not a problem to be solved but a reality to be experienced."

This also fails to move me and I return to my berth.

Beyond Gibralter the nights turn suddenly hot and life on *The Erasmus* grows intense. Pairing off seems to occupy everybody's time and the ship begins to rock with new diversions. Girls in bikinis, laughing, spring from one deck to another; the men are brown and strangely healthy in spite of my booming business, their coughs lessened, and all the meals and games are attacked with gusto.

At the pool there is hardly room for me to splash around. One of the major lounges has been converted into a lively casino, games in every corner, and the Desiderius is packed with roaring drunks.

Perry seems content that such revelry excludes smoking, but a few of us detect his almost imperceptible discontent. Perhaps the slant of his yacht cap. A bounce slightly lessened.

However, before the floor show and dance he leads us in our nightly deep-breathing exercises, slapping his hands loudly and giving off his familiar, "Hey, everybody, now!"

Afterward the usual crowd of female enthusiasts are around him, gushing, admiring his stamina.

Out on deck I stroll along moodily until my shopgirl, Ramona, comes and takes my arm. I speak of the ancient Roman mentality which resulted in Nero, the acute aesthetic awareness of certain high Nazis, the occasional meditations of De Sade which, in my opinion, soared beyond his more frequent banality.

Meanwhile, Ramona nuzzles my neck.

From high on the bridge comes a green glow from the captain's window.

The sea is moderate.

Mrs. Murtaugh and Dr. Gonatt pass by holding hands.

We anchor offshore at Cannes. Everyone pours down into the awaiting launches to go ashore and visit the film festival, shop, strut around the promenade, and of course steal a few drags.

Near the beach just outside the Hotel Martinez photographers encircle a movie starlet who tries to contain herself in a peek-a-boo swimsuit. As I linger near this confusion, my thoughts momentarily meandering onto the nature of publicity and its role in the world's present corruption, I find Perry beside me. He makes a tsk tsk at the proceedings, appears friendly, but I take this seemingly accidental appearance as ominous.

"How's everything going?" I query him.

"Not awfully well," he admits. "We should have many more passengers cured by now than we do."

"Oh? How many do we have?"

"At last night's staff meeting we estimated fifteen percent—far below normal. I've been ramrod on cruises where we got fifty percent."

Now I make a tsk tsk.

We exchange a few minutes of small talk there on the promenade until the starlet back-peddles into the hotel with her fixed smile. Then Perry excuses himself and ambles away and, yes, I see that his bouncy walk has modified.

No doubt of it: he's worried and this banter was an ill omen. Why me?

In the cover of darkness, later, I transfer my diminished stock into the locked cabinets beneath the hand-painted ties and initialed handkerchiefs in Ramona's men's shop. For a mere pack a day, she is now my dealer and accomplice and it's none too soon.

Sicily is admired for its lovely cliffs above the sea, its hearty peasants, its wines, but I admire it for its history of violence.

As we pass by on a sunny noon, I cease whittling my Christian name into the rail and salute with my pocket knife.

The captain asks to see me.

When Perry presents himself at my cabin door with this message I feel a myriad excitement. Do they have evidence, I wonder, or are they bluffing? Will the captain be a worthy adversary? Even if I'm caught dead to rights with Ramona as the unshakable witness for the prosecution, what could they possibly do to me?

I dress slowly in my all-whites. Take, I caution myself, every possible psychological advantage. My thoughts spin around like dervishes.

They're just no match for me, neither Perry nor his eager scouts. Also, I've committed no crime and at most they can only put me ashore at one of these lovely southern ports. And what could they possibly say? I'm an articulate devil, if I say so myself, and intellectually stockpiled to parry any of their pious thrusts, to argue far above their simple heads that good nowadays is a form of evil and vice-versa.

Perry waits smugly for me in the corridor and escorts me up to Deck AA. Every step I'm practicing my suave argument.

Society has gone mad, so that as the man of reason tries to apply his reason to madness he is being absurd. He thinks he is doing good as he uses his wit against the world's puzzle, I'll tell them, but he's actually trying to ponder the unfathomable. Not only is he a useless dolt, but he's even harmful because he misleads others. The true monster, however: ah, he goes his wicked way, attracts constant notoriety, and possibly teaches mankind a hard lesson in morality—in spite of himself.

We reach Deck AA. A long walk to the bridge.

My lips move as I practice my lines.

Perry, straight of back, knocks with authority on the door, opens it, and ushers me inside. Before us is the helm of the ship—a big wheel just like in swashbuckling movies—and the luminous green eye of a large compass. The walls are dingy white and beyond the wide, salt-sprayed windows the bow breaks the waves.

The captain isn't present.

Nervously, Perry announces that we should wait.

As we stand in silence shifting from one foot to another together, I take a good look at the bridge. It seems vaguely familiar—although I've never been in such a place before—yet also personalized and different. The captain, wherever he is, is clearly a man of some reading habits; paperbacks, a few antiquated leather-bound volumes, magazines and newspapers are stuffed into the shelves behind the desk. There is also a narrow, uncomfortable looking bed.

When I inquire, Perry admits that sometimes the old man sleeps up here and doesn't bother to go below.

A variety of clothing is strewn around. Not a very neat man, I surmise, and I count two frayed naval topcoats, a rain slicker, a few discolored turtlenecks, underwear, socks, and, curiously enough, a shawl.

Perry shows his discomfort as I observe all this.

Soon there is a whistle, a cough, and another whistle from an instrument near the compass and Perry dashes over there. A man from the boiler room—I can hear, in the midst of his profanities, talk of gaskets and seals— says that the captain is down there, grease up to the elbows, yes, dammit, and, no, there's nothing seriously wrong, but the captain can't make it. I'm to come back later, the voice says, because the captain has the opinion that the appointment isn't urgent.

This frustrates us. Primed for accusation and argument, I start to protest. Perry, his smugness gone, sputters and asks if he shouldn't remain and steer the ship, but the voice answers hell no, naturally not, the ship's locked on course.

Embarrassed, Perry says he must attend his many duties and offers that I'll have to find my own way to see the captain.

"No problem," I say. "Get on with your business."

He is visibly shaken. His yacht cap sags as he tells me that Deck AA is often closed to passengers, that I should probably seek written permission, that, er, perhaps another crew member could escort me.

"You heard the man in the boiler room," I answer. "It's nothing big. I'll stop around again when it's convenient for everyone."

The cigarettes are untouched, safely there underneath the counter in Ramona's shop. She doesn't understand why I kiss her cheek.

Later, alone, I probe the aspects of my new advantage. Either they were bluffing or they have the barest suspicion. At any rate, now I'm free to make this a real intellectual rendezvous, a true confrontation; I'll bring down the weight of Nietzsche, Machiavelli, and all the obsure Mongol thinkers on that innocent captain's arguments.

The best time to catch the old sea dog, I reason will be in the evening, so I wait until the day's seminars finish and the dances begin before making my way to the bridge once more.

Empty. The ship is still automatically fixed on course. I peer through the window at the green glow of the compass. Eerie.

Feeling odd, I go back to my cabin, slip into my maroon tuxedo, and take refuge in the music of the Desiderius.

The next day I make frequent trips up to Deck AA, but the old boy is never there.

On one of my visits I try the door and find it open. Inside, I casually grip the wheel. On the nearby desk are charts—an outline of the Italian coast around Amalfi. I exchange stares with the omnipotent compass, gaze off at the horizon where, dimly far away to port, lies the coast.

The wheel, yes, is fixed on course. Comforting.

Days pass.

Perry is deep in a frenzy of work now, seemingly having forgotten me. The seminars are booming therapy sessions with the members shouting obscenities at each other, vomiting up their private lives, accusing and demanding, and Perry is there, I learn, orchestrating all of it. When I see him on deck his clothes are soiled and wrinkled, his hair is long and hanging from his yacht cap, his eyes weary.

I hear of a bloody fight in the casino lounge.

Beside the nearly empty swimming pool—one fat man lolling on his back—I take a glum stroll. After a while I sit down on the tile, deciding not to take my swim.

Where, I wonder, is our elusive captain?

Tonight after checking the bridge again I visit the boiler room, but the engines are purring unattended. There seems to be no one above or below, just Perry and his bedraggled crew working amidships with an increasingly restless cargo of passengers. The voyage is too long for us, I tell myself.

Toward morning I wander back toward the vacant bridge. Prying, I rummage around in the captain's desk—paperclips, parchments, a service medal, the passenger list, a quill pen—and pull a few books off the shelves. A few first editions nobody would ever read. Magazines: popular European gossip items, nudist camp publications, occult periodicals, journals on sports, wildlife, travel, cuisine.

And so who is my eclectic adversary? An ordinary escapist, the Flying Dutchman, some alienated intelligence, just a shy and simple pilot?

Before departing again, I trace my finger over the charts. Not too difficult reading charts, I conclude; the deeps and shallows are clearly marked.

The scent of the Greek isles rides the wind.

At times, now, I forget exactly where we're putting into final port.

My mind is on last diversions—parties, another amateur night, my shopgirl who insists she has fallen in love with me, testimonials in the Desiderius for those few who have actually kicked the habit—and I am still playing hide-and-seek with the old sea wolf upstairs.

Disheveled, a mere wisp of a smile left on his face, Perry goes around patting everyone on the back and making the best of a cruise low on converts.

A few brave passengers grin sheepishly, shrug, and light up the last of my dwindling supply in public.

I speak to Ramona of noble Sparta, the breakdown of physical integrity followed by general decline.

Here I am on the bridge again.

Once more I take a grip on the helm and peer out over the bow, but this time I'm surprised to find that we're not on a fixed course and that I'm alone at the wheel. The locking device: yes, here it is. I see, it must be part of an automatic system in conjunction with the compass. Sure.

The compass illuminates the darkened room in a cozy green glow, my charts curl, and I slip into one of the turtlenecks.

Long days and nights.

Far out now, no sign of land.

We have a westerly course, a good barometer.

The new Passenger Host pops in, salutes, makes happy small talk, and reports that the new passengers are settled into seminars. His name is, I think, Jerry, and he asks if I'll have my meals up here today and I say, yes, please. I watch him bounce away in his whites, calling and waving to someone below as he descends.

Later he returns with a crisp new passenger list, the mimeograph ink hardly dry. I read over it wondering if any of these passengers might be capable of philosophical discussion.

My Ramona is gone.

We made a stop somewhere, exchanged everyone, took on supplies, set forth again, and the most curious thing about this is that my new quarters are filled with cigarettes.

Robert Stone (1937–   ) was born a Catholic in Brooklyn, New York. A high school drop-out, he joined the U.S. Navy at seventeen and served as a journalist. After several years of marginal odd-jobs, he became a reporter for the New York Daily News. *He continued his education, however, and graduated from the Stanford University Writing Program. There he wrote his first novel,* Hall of Mirrors *(1967), for which he received a Houghton Mifflin Fellowship. Stone's work relies on naturalistic detail; the protagonists are often marginal members of society, frequently misguided or unlucky. In technique and materials, his work suggests Frank Norris or the best of James T. Farrell. For further reading: the novel,* Dog Soldiers *(1974).*

ROBERT STONE

Aquarius Obscured

*I*n the house on Noe Street, Big Gene was crooning into the telephone.

"Geerat, Geeroot. Neexat, Nixoot."

He hung up and patted a tattoo atop the receiver, sounding the cymbal beat by forcing air through his molars.

"That's how the Dutch people talk," he told Alison. "Keroot. Badoot. Krackeroot."

"Who was it?"

He lay back on the corduroy cushions and vigorously scratched himself. A smile spread across his face and he wiggled with pleasure, his eyelids fluttering.

"Some no-nut fool. Easy tool. Uncool."

He lay still with his mouth open, waiting for rhyming characterizations to emerge.

"Was it for me?"

When he looked at her, his eyes were filled with tears. He shook his head sadly to indicate that her questions were obviated by his sublime indifference.

Alison cursed him.

"Don't answer the fucking phone if you don't want to talk," she said. "It might be something important."

Big Gene remained prone.

"I don't know where you get off," he said absently. "See you reverting to typical boojwa. Reverting to type. Lost your fire."

His junky mumble infuriated Alison. She snorted with exasperation.

"For Christ's sake!"

"You bring me down so bad," Gene said softly. "I don't need you. I got control, you know what I mean?"

"It's ridiculous," she told him. "Talking to you is a complete waste of time."

As she went into the next room she heard him moan, a lugubrious, falsetto coo incongruent with his bulk but utterly expressive of the man he had become. His needles had punctured him.

In the bedroom, Io was awake; her large brown eyes gazed fearfully through crib bars at the sunlit window.

"Hello, sweetie," Alison said.

Io turned solemnly toward her mother and yawned.

A person here, Alison thought, lifting her over the bars, the bean blossomed. Walks and conversation. The end of our madonna and child number. A feather of panic fluttered in her throat.

"Io," she told her daughter, "we have got to get our shit together here."

The scene was crumbling. Strong men had folded like stage flats, legality and common sense were fled. Cerebration flickered.

Why me, she demanded of herself, walking Io to the potty. Why do I have to be the only one with any smarts?

On the potty, Io delivered. Alison wiped her and flushed the toilet. By training, Alison was an astronomer but she had never practiced.

Io could dress herself except for the shoes. When Alison tied them, it was apparent to her that they would shortly be too small.

"What'll we do?" she asked Io with a playful but genuinely frightened whine.

"See the fishies," Io said.

"See the fishies?" Alison stroked her chin, burlesquing a thoughtful demeanor, rubbing noses with Io to make her smile. "Good Lord."

Io drew back and nodded soberly.

"See the fishies."

At that moment, Alison recalled the fragment of an undersea dream. Something in the dream had been particularly agreeable and its recall afforded her a happy little throb.

"Well that's what we'll do," she told Io. "We'll go to the aquarium. A capital idea."

"Yes," Io said.

Just outside Io's room, on the littered remnant of a sundeck, lived a vicious and unhygienic doberman, who had been named Buck after a dog Big Gene claimed to have once owned in Aruba. Alison opened the sliding glass door to admit it, and watched nervously as it nuzzled Io.

"Buck," Io said without enthusiasm.

Alison seized the dog by its collar and thrust it out the bedroom door before her.

In the living room, Big Gene was rising from the cushions, a cetaceous surfacing.

"Buck, my main man," he sang. "Bucky bonaroo."

"How about staying with him today?" Alison said. "I want to take Io to the aquarium."

"Not I," Gene declared. "Noo."

"Why the hell not?" Alison asked savagely.

"Cannot be."

"Shit! I can't leave him alone here, he'll wreck the place. How can I take him to the goddamn aquarium?"

Gene shrugged sleepily.

"Ain't this the night you get paid?" he asked after a moment.

"Yeah," Alison said.

In fact, Alison had been paid the night before, her employer having thrown some 80 dollars' worth of half-dollars full into her face. There had been a difference of opinion regarding Alison's performance as a danseuse, and she had spoken sharply with Mert the Manager. Mert had replied in an incredibly brutal and hostile manner, had fired her, insulted her breasts, and left her to peel coins from the soiled floor until the profile of Jack Kennedy was welded to her mind's eye. She had not mentioned the incident to Gene; the half-dollars were concealed under the rubber sheet beneath Io's mattress.

"Good," Gene said. "Because I got to see the man then."

He was looking down at Io, and Alison watched him for signs of resentment or contempt but she saw only sadness, sickness in his face. Io paid him no attention at all.

It was startling the way he had mellowed out behind smack. Witnessing it, she had almost forgiven him the punches, and she had noticed for the first time that he had rather a kind heart. But he stole and was feckless; his presence embarrassed her.

"How'm I going to take a dog to the aquarium, for Christ's sake?"

The prospect of having Buck along irritated Alison sorely. In her irritation, she decided that the thing might be more gracefully endured with the white-cross jobbers. The white-cross jobbers were synthetics manufactured by a mad chemist in Hayward. Big Gene called them IT-390 to distinguish them from IT-290 which they had turned out, upon consumption, not to be.

She took a handful from the saki jar in which they were stored and downed them with tap water.

"All right, *Buck*," she called, pronouncing the animal's name with distaste, "goddamn it." She put his leash on, sent Io ahead to the car, and pulled the reluctant dog out behind her.

With Io strapped in the passenger seat and Buck cringing under the dashboard, Alison ran Lombard Street in the outside lane, accelerating on the curves like Bondurant. Alison was a formidable and aggressive driver, and she drove hard to stay ahead of the drug's rush. When she pulled up in the aquarium's parking lot, her mouth had gone dry and the little sanctus bells of adjusted alertness had begun to tinkle. She hurried them under wind-rattled eucalyptus and up the massive steps that led to the building's Corinthian portico.

"Now where are we going to put this goddamn dog?" she asked Io. When she blinked, her eyeballs clicked. I've done it she thought. I've swallowed it again. Vandalism.

After a moment's confused hesitation, she led Buck to one side of the entrance and secured his chain round a brass hydrant fixture with a carefully worked running clove hitch. The task brought to her recollection a freakish afternoon when she had tied Buck in front of a bar on El Camino. For the protection of passersby, she had fashioned a sign from the cardboard backing of a foolscap tablet and written on it with a green, felt-tipped pen—DO NOT TRY TO PET THIS DOG. Her last memory of the day was watching the sign blow away across the street and past the pumps of an Esso station.

Buck's vindictive howls pursued them to the oxidized-copper doors of the main entrance.

It was early morning and the aquarium was uncrowded. Liquefactious sounds ran up and down the smooth walls, child voices ricocheted from the ceiling. With Io by the hand, Alison wandered through the interior twilight, past tanks of sea horses, scorpion fish, African *Tilapia*. Pausing before an endlessly gyrating school of salmon, she saw that some of the fish were eyeless, the sockets empty and perfectly cleaned. The blind fish swam with the rest, staying in line, turning with the school.

Io appeared not to notice them.

In the next hall, Alison halted her daughter before each tank, reading from the lighted presentation the name of the animal contained, its habitat and Latin name. The child regarded all with gravity.

At the end of the East Wing was a room brighter than the rest; it was the room in which porpoises lived in tanks that were open to the sky. As Alison entered it, she experienced a curiously pleasant sensation.

"Look," she said to Io. "Dolphins."

"Dolphins?"

They walked up to the glass of the largest tank; its lower area was fouled with small handprints. Within, a solitary blue-gray beast was rounding furiously, describing gorgeous curves with figure of eights, skimming the walls at half an inch's distance. Alison's mouth opened in awe.

"An Atlantic Dolphin," she told Io in a soft, reverential voice. "From the Atlantic Ocean. On the other side of America. Where Providence is."

"And Grandpa," Io said.

"And Grandpa is in Providence, too."

For the space of several seconds, the dream feeling returned to her with an intensity that took her breath away. There had been some loving presence in it and a discovery.

She stared into the tank until the light that filtered through the churning water began to suggest the numinous. Io, perceiving that her mother was not about to move on, retraced her steps toward the halls through which they had come, and commenced seeing the fish over again. Whenever an aquarium-goer smiled at her, she looked away in terror.

Alison stood transfixed, trying to force recall. It had been something special, something important. But silly—as with dreams. She found herself laughing and then, in the next moment, numb with loss as the dream's sense faded. Her heart was racing with the drug.

God, she thought, it's all just flashes and fits. We're just out here in this shit.

With sudden horror, she realized at once that there had been another part of the dream and that it involved the fact that she and Io were just out there and that this was not a dream from which one awakened. Because one *was*, after all.

She turned anxiously to look for Io and saw the child several galleries back, standing in front of the tank where the blind fish were.

The dream had been about getting out of it, trying to come in and make it stop. In the end, when it was most terrible, she had been mercifully carried into a presence before which things had been resolved. The memory of that resolution made her want to weep.

Her eye fell on the animal in the tank; she followed its flights and charges with fascination.

There had been some sort of communication, with or without words.

A trained scientist, Alison loved logic above all else; it was her only important pleasure. If the part about one being out there was true— and it was—what then about the resolution. It seemed to her, as she watched the porpoise, that even dreamed things must have their origin in a kind of truth, that no level of the mind was capable of utterly unfounded construction. Even hallucinations—phenomena with which Alison had become drearily familiar—needed their origins in the empirically verifiable—a cast of light, a sound on the wind. Somehow, she thought, somewhere in the universe, the resolving presence must exist.

Her thoughts raced, she licked her lips to cool the sere dryness cracking them. Her heart gave a desperate leap.

"Was it you?" she asked the porpoise.

"Yes," she heard him say. "Yes, it was."

Alison burst into tears. When she had finished sobbing, she took a Kleenex from her bag, wiped her eyes, and leaned against the cool marble beside the tank.

Prepsychosis. Disorders of thought. Failure to abstract.

"This is ridiculous," she said.

From deep within, from the dreaming place, sounded a voice.

"You're here," the porpoise told her. "That's what matters now."

Nothing in the creature's manner suggested communication or even the faintest sentience. But human attitudes of engagement, Alison reminded herself, were not to be expected. To expect them was anthropocentrism— a limiting, reactionary position like ethnocentrism or sexism.

"It's very hard for me," she told the porpoise. "I can't communicate well at the best of times. And an aquarium situation is pretty weird." At a loss for further words, Alison fell back on indignation. "It must be awful for you."

"It's somewhat weird," she understood the porpoise to say. "I wouldn't call it awful."

Alison trembled.

"But . . . how can it not be awful? A conscious mind shut up in a tank with stupid people staring at you? Not," she hastened to add, "that I think I'm any better. But the way you're stuck in here with these slimy, repulsive fish."

"I don't find fish slimy and repulsive," the porpoise told her.

Mortified, Alison began to stammer an apology, but the creature cut her off.

"The only fish I see are the ones they feed me. It's people I see all day. I wonder if you can realize how *dry* you all are."

"Good Lord!" She moved closer to the tank. "You must hate us."

She became aware of laughter.

"I don't hate."

Alison's pleasure at receiving this information was tempered by a political anxiety. The beast's complacency suggested something objectionable; the suspicion clouded her mind that her interlocutor might be a mere Aquarium Porpoise, a deracinated stooge, an Uncle. . . .

The laughter sounded again.

"I'm sorry," Alison said. "My head is full of such shit."

"Our condition is profoundly different from yours. We don't require the same things. Our souls are as different from yours as our bodies are."

"I have the feeling," Alison said, "that yours are better."

"I think they are. But I'm a porpoise."

The animal in the tank darted upward, torpedo-like, toward the fog-colored surface—then plunged again in a column of spinning, bubbling foam.

"You called me here, didn't you?" Alison asked. "You wanted me to come."

"In a way."

"Only in a way?"

"We communicated our presence here. A number of you might have responded. Personally, I'm satisfied that it was yourself."

"Are you?" Alison cried joyfully. She was aware that her words echoed through the great room. "You see, I asked because I've been having these dreams. Odd things have been happening to me." She paused thoughtfully. "Like I've been listening to the radio sometimes and I've heard these wild things—like just for a second. As though there's been kind of a pattern. Was it you guys?"

"Some of the time. We have our ways."

"Then," she asked breathlessly, "why me?"

"Don't you know why?" the beast asked softly.

"It must have been because you knew I would understand."

There was no response.

"It must have been because you knew how much I hate the way things are with us. Because you knew I'd listen. Because I need something so much."

"Yet," the porpoise said sternly, "you made things this way. You thought you needed them the way they are."

"It wasn't me," Alison said. "Not me. I don't need this shit."

Wide-eyed, she watched him shoot for the surface again, then dive and skim over the floor of his tank, rounding smartly at the wall.

"I love you," she declared suddenly. "I mean I feel a great love for you and I feel there is a great lovingness in you. I just know that there's something really super-important that I can learn from you."

"Are you prepared to know how it is with us?"

"Yes," Alison said. "Oh, yes. And what I can do."

"You can be free," the animal said. "You can learn to perceive in a new way."

Alison became aware of Io standing beside her, frowning up at her tears. She bent down and put her head next to the child's.

"Io, can you see the dolphin? Do you like him?"

'Yes," Io said.

Alison stood up.

"My daughter," she told her dolphin.

Io watched the animal contentedly for a while and then went to sit on a bench in the back of the hall.

"She's only three-and-a-half," Alison said. She feared that communion might be suspended on the introduction of a third party. "Do you like her?"

"We see a great many of your children," the beast replied. "I can't answer you in those terms."

Alison became anxious.

"Does that mean that you don't have *any* emotions? That you can't love?"

"Were I to answer yes or no I would deceive you either way. Let's say only that we don't make the same distinctions."

"I don't understand," Alison said. "I suppose I'm not ready to."

"As your perception changes," the porpoise told her, "many things will seem strange and unfamiliar. You must unlearn old structures of thought that have been forced on you. Much faith, much resolution will be required."

"I'll resist," Alison admitted sadly. "I know I will. I'm very skeptical and frivolous by nature. And it's all so strange and wonderful that I can't believe it."

"All doubt is the product of your animal nature. You must rise above your species. You must trust those who instruct you."

"I'll try," Alison said resolutely. "But it's so incredible! I mean for all these centuries you guys and us have been the only aware species on the planet, and now we've finally come together! It just blows my mind that here—now—for the first time . . ."

"What makes you think it's the first time?"

"Good Lord!" Alison exclaimed. "It's not the first time?"

"There were others before you, Alison. They were weak and fickle. We lost them."

Alison's heart chilled at his words.

"But hasn't it ever worked?"

"It's in the nature of your species to conceive enthusiasms and then to weary of them. Your souls are self-indulgent and your concentration feeble. None of you has ever stayed with it."

"I will," Alison cried. "I'm unique and irreplaceable, and nothing could be more important than this. Understanding, responding inside— that's my great talent. I can do it!"

"We believe you, Alison. That's why you're here."

She was flooded with her dreaming joy. She turned quickly to look for Io and saw her lying at full length on the bench staring up into the overhead lights. Near her stood a tall, long-haired young man who was watching Alison. His stare was a profane irritation and Alison forced it from her mind, but her mood turned suddenly militant.

"I know it's not important in your terms," she told the porpoise, "but it infuriates me to see you shut up like this. You must miss the open sea so much."

"I've never left it," the animal said, "and your pity is wasted on me. I am here on the business of my race."

"I guess it's the way I was brought up. I had a lousy upbringing, but some things about it were good. See, my father, he's a real asshole but he's what we call a liberal. He taught me to really hate it when somebody was oppressed. Injustice makes me want to fight. I suppose it sounds stupid and trivial to you, but that's how it is with me."

The dolphin's voice was low and soothing, infinitely kind.

"We know how it is with you. You understand nothing of your own behavior. Everything you think and do merely reflects what is known to us as a Dry Posture. Your inner life, your entire history are nothing more than these."

"Good Lord!" Alison said. "Dry Posture."

"As we work with you, you must bear this in mind. You must discover the quality of Dry Posture in all your thoughts and actions. When you have separated this quality from your soul, what remains will be the bond between us. At that point your life will truly begin."

"Dry Posture," Alison said. "Wow!"

The animal in the tank was disporting itself just below the surface; in her mounting enthusiasm Alison became increasingly frustrated by the fact that its blank, good-humored face appeared utterly oblivious of her presence. She reminded herself again that the hollow dissembling of human facial expression was beneath its nature, and welcomed the opportunity to be divested of a Dry Posture.

The silence from which the dolphin spoke became charged with music.

"In the sea lies our common origin," she heard him say. "In the sea all was once One. In the sea find your surrender—in surrender find victory, renewal, survival. Recall the sea! Recall our common heartbeat! Return to the peace of primordial consciousness!"

"Oh, how beautiful," Alison cried, her own consciousness awash in salt flumes of insight.

"Our lousy Western culture is worthless," she declared fervently. "It's rotten and sick. We've got to get back. Please," she implored the dolphin, "tell us how!"

"If you receive the knowledge," the animal told her, "your life will become one of dedication and struggle. Are you ready to undertake such striving?"

"Yes," Alison said. "Yes!"

"Are you willing to serve that force which relentlessly wills the progress of the conscious universe?"

"With all my heart!"

"Willing to surrender to that sublime destiny which your species has so fecklessly denied?"

"Oh, boy," Alison said, "I surely am."

"Excellent," said the porpoise. "It shall be your privilege to assist the indomitable will of a mighty and superior species. The natural order shall be restored. That which is strong and sound shall dominate. That which is weak and decadent shall perish and disappear."

"Right on!" Alison cried. She felt her shoulders squaring, her heels coming together.

"Millennia of usurpation shall be overturned in a final solution!"

"Yeah," Alison said. "By any means necessary."

It seemed to Alison that she detected in the porpoise's speech a foreign accent; if not a Third World accent, at least the accent of a civilization older and more together than her own.

"So," the porpoise continued, "where your cities and banks, your aquaria and museums now stand, there shall be rubble only. The responsibility shall rest exclusively with humankind, for our patience has been thoroughly exhausted. What we have not achieved through striving for equitable dialogue, we shall now achieve by striving of another sort."

Alison listened in astonishment as the music's volume swelled behind her eyes.

"For it is our belief," the porpoise informed her, "that in strife, life finds its purification." His distant, euphonious voice assumed a shrill, hysterical note. "In the discipline of ruthless struggle, history is forged and the will tempered! Let the craven, the once-born, shirk the fray—we ourselves shall strike without mercy at the sniveling mass of our natural inferiors. Triumph is our destiny!"

Alison shook her head in confusion.

"Whoa," she said.

Closing her eyes for a moment, she beheld, with startling clarity, the image of a blond-bearded man wearing a white turtleneck sweater and a peaked officer's cap. His face was distended with fury; beside him loomed a gray cylindrical form which might have been a periscope. Alison opened her eyes quickly and saw the porpoise blithely coursing the walls of its tank.

"But that's not love or life or anything," she sobbed. "That's just cruelty."

"Alison, baby, don't you know it's all the same? Without cruelty you can't have love. If you're not ready to destroy someone, then you're not ready to love them. Because if you've got the knowledge—you know, like if you really have it—then if you do what you have to do that's just everybody's karma. If you have to waste somebody because the universe wills it, then it's just like the bad part of yourself that you're wasting. It's an act of love."

In the next instant, she saw the bearded man again. His drawn, evil face was bathed in a sinister, submarine light, reflected from God knew what fiendish instruments of death.

"I know what you are," Alison called out in horror. "You're a fascist!"

When the beast spoke once more, the softness was vanished from its voice.

"Your civilization has afforded us many moments of amusement. Unfortunately, it must now be irrevocably destroyed."

"Fascist!" Alison whimpered in a strangled voice. "Nazi!"

"Peace," the porpoise intoned, and the music behind him turned tranquil and low. "Here is the knowledge. You must say it daily."

Enraged now, she could detect the mocking hypocrisy in his false, mellow tones.

"Surrender to the Notion
Of the Motion of the Ocean."

As soon as she received the words, they occupied every cubit of her inner space, reverberating moronically, over and over. She put her hands over her ears.

"Horseshit!" she cried. "What kind of cheapo routine is that?"

The voice, she suspected suddenly, might not be that of a porpoise. It might be the man in the turtleneck. But where?

Hovering at the mouth of a celestial Black Hole, secure within the adjoining dimension? A few miles off Sausalito at periscope depth? Or—more monstrous—ingeniously reduced in size and concealed within the dolphin?

"Help," Alison called softly.

At the risk of permanent damage, she desperately engaged her linear perception. Someone might have to know.

"I'm caught up in this plot," she reported. "Either porpoises are trying to reach me with this fascist message or there's some kind of super-Nazi submarine offshore."

Exhausted, she rummaged through her knit bag for a cigarette, found one, lit it. A momentary warp, she assured herself, inhaling deeply. A trifling skull pop, perhaps an air bubble. She smoked and trembled, avoiding the sight of the tank.

In the next moment, she became aware that the tall young man she had seen earlier had made a circuit of the hall and was standing beside her.

"Fish are groovy," the young man said.

"Wait a minute," Alison demanded. "Just wait a minute here. Was that . . .?"

The young man displayed a woodchuck smile.

"You were really tripping on those fish, right? Are you stoned?"

He carried a camera case on a strap round his shoulder, and a black cape slung over one arm.

"I don't know what you're talking about," Alison said. She was suddenly consumed with loathing.

"No? 'Cause you look really spaced out."

"Well, I'm not," Alison said firmly. She saw Io advancing from the bench.

The young man stood by as Io clutched her mother's floor-length skirt.

"I want to go outside now," Io said.

His pink smile expanded and he descended quickly to his haunches to address Io at her own level.

"Hiya, baby. My name's Andy."

Io had a look at Andy and attempted flight. Alison was holding one of her hands; Andy made her fast by the other.

"I been taking pictures," he told her. "Pictures of the fishies." He pursued Io to a point behind Alison's knees. Alison pulled on Io's free hand and found herself staring down into the camera case.

"You like the fishies?" Andy insisted. "You think they're groovy?"

There were two Nikon lenses side by side in the case. Alison let Io's hand go, thrust her own into the case and plucked out a lens. While Andy was asking Io if she, Io, were shy, Alison dropped the lens into her knit bag. As Andy started up, she seized the second lens and pressed it hard against her skirt.

Back on his feet, Andy was slightly breathless.

"You wanna go smoke some dope?" he asked Alison. "I'm goin' over to the art museum and sneak some shots over there. You wanna come?"

"Actually," Alison told him, "I have a luncheon engagement."

Andy blinked. "Far out."

"Far out?" Alison asked. "I'll tell you something far out, Andy. There is a lot of really repulsive shit in this aquarium, Andy. There are some very low-level animals here and they're very frightening and unreal. But there isn't one thing in this place that is as repulsive and unreal as you are, Andy."

She heard the laughter echo and realized that it was her own. She clenched her teeth to stop it.

"You should have a tank of your own, Andy."

As she led Io toward the door, she cupped the hand that held the second lens against her hip, like a mannequin. At the end of the hall, she glanced back and saw Andy looking into the dolphin's tank. The smile on his face was dreadful.

"I like the fish," Io said, as they descended the pompous stone steps outside the entrance. "I like the lights in the fish places."

Recognizing them, Buck rushed forward on his chain, his tongue dripping. Alison untied him as quickly and calmly as she could.

"We'll come back, sweetie," she said. "We'll come back lots of times."

"Tomorrow?" the child asked.

In the parking lot, Alison looked over her shoulder. The steps were empty; there were no alarums or pursuits.

When they were in the car, she felt cold. Columns of fog were moving in from the bay. She sat motionless for a while, blew her nose, and wrapped a spare sweater that was lying on the seat around Io's shoulders.

"Mama's deluded," she explained.

James Alan McPherson (1943–   ) grew up in Savannah, Georgia, where his father was an electrician for the U.S. Navy. He attended Morgan State College in Baltimore and Morris Brown College in Atlanta; he graduated in 1968 from Harvard Law School. Except for volunteering legal services to the needy, he has not practiced law; instead, he has become a writer of short fiction and a writer-teacher in various universities. He is also a contributing editor of Atlantic Monthly. *His stories are distinguished by the complexity of his vision of the relationships among his wide range of protagonists: between blacks and other blacks, or between blacks and whites. For further reading:* Hue and Cry *(1969).*

JAMES ALAN McPHERSON

Of Cabbages and Kings

Claude Sheats had been in the Brotherhood all his life, and then he had tried to get out. Some of his people and most of his friends were still in the Brotherhood and were still very good members, but Claude was no longer a good member because he had tried to get out after over twenty years. To get away from the Brotherhood and all his friends who were still active in it, he moved to Washington Square and took to reading about being militant. But, living there, he developed a craving for whiteness the way a nicely broke-in virgin craves sex. In spite of this, he maintained a steady black girl, whom he saw at least twice a month to keep up appearances, and once he took both of us with him when he visited his uncle in Harlem who was still in the Brotherhood.

"She's a nice girl, Claude," his uncle's wife had told him that night, because the girl, besides being attractive, had some very positive ideas about the Brotherhood. Her name was Marie, she worked as a secretary in my office, and it was on her suggestion that I had moved in with Claude Sheats.

"I'm glad to see you don't waste your time on hippies," the uncle had said. "All our young men are selling out these days."

The uncle was the kind of fellow who had played his cards right. He was much older than his wife, and I had the impression that night that he must have given her time to experience enough and to become bored enough before he overwhelmed her with his success. He wore glasses and combed his hair back and had that oily composure that made me think of a waiter waiting to be tipped. He was very proud of his English, I observed, and how he always ended his words with just the right sound. He must have felt superior to people who didn't. He must have felt superior to Claude because he was still with the Brotherhood and Claude had tried to get out.

Claude did not like him and always seemed to feel guilty whenever we visited his uncle's house. "Don't mention any of my girls to him," he told me after our first visit.

"Why would I do that?" I said.

"He'll try to psych you into telling him."

"Why should he suspect you? He never comes over to the apartment."

"He just likes to know what I'm doing. I don't want him to know about my girls."

"I won't say anything," I promised.

He was almost twenty-three and had no steady girls except Marie. He was well built so that he had no trouble in the Village area. It was like going to the market for him. During my first days in the apartment the process had seemed like a game. And once, when he was going out, I said: "Bring back two."

Half an hour later he came back with two girls. He got their drinks, and then he called me into his room to meet them.

"This is Doris," he said, pointing to the smaller one, "and I forgot your name," he said to the big blonde.

"Jane," she said.

"This is Howard," he told her.

"Hi," I said. Neither one of them smiled. The big blonde in white pants sat on the big bed, and the little one sat on a chair near the window. He had given them his worst bourbon.

"Excuse me a minute," Claude said to the girls. "I want to talk to Howard for a minute." He put on a record before we went outside into the hall between our rooms. He was always extremely polite and gentle, and he was very soft-spoken in spite of his size.

"Listen," he said to me outside, "you can have the blonde."

"What can I do with that amazon?"

"I don't care. Just get her out of the room."

"She's dirty," I said.

"So you can give her a bath."

"It wouldn't help much."

"Well, just take her out and talk to her," he told me. "Remember, you asked for her."

We went in. "Where you from?" I said to the amazon.

"Brighton."

"What school?"

"No. I just got here."

"From where?"

"*Brighton!*"

"Where's that?" I said.

"*England,*" she said. Claude Sheats looked at me.

"How did you find Washington Square so fast?"

"I got friends."

She was very superior about it all and showed the same slight irritation of a professional theater critic waiting for a late performance to begin. The little one sat on the chair, her legs crossed, staring at the ceiling. Her white pants were dirty too. Both girls looked as though they would have been relieved if we had taken off our clothes and danced for them around the room and across the bed, and made hungry sounds in our throats with our mouths slightly opened.

I said that I had to go out to the drugstore and would be back very soon; but once outside, I walked a whole hour in one direction, and then I walked back. I passed them a block away from our apartment. They were walking fast and did not slow down or speak when I passed them.

Claude Sheats was drinking heavily when I came into the apartment.

"What the hell are you trying to pull?" he said.

"I couldn't find a drugstore open."

He got up from the living room table and walked toward me. "You should have asked me," he said. "I got more than enough."

"I wanted some mouthwash too," I said.

He fumed a while longer, and then told me how I had ruined his evening because the amazon would not leave the room to wait for me and the little one would not do anything with the amazon around. He suddenly thought of going down and bringing them back, and he went out for a while. But he came back without them, saying that they had been picked up again.

"When a man looks out for you, you got to look out for him," he warned me.

"I'm sorry."

"A hell of a lot of good *that* does. And that's the last time I look out for *you,* baby," he said. "From now on it's *me* all the way."

"Thanks," I said.

"If she was too much for you I could of taken the amazon."

"It didn't matter that much," I said.

"You could of had Doris if you couldn't handle the amazon."

"They were both too much," I told him.

But Claude Sheats did not answer. He just looked at me.

After two months of living with him I concluded that Claude hated whites as much as he loved them. And he hated himself with the very same passion. He hated the country and his place in it, and he loved the country and his place in it. He loved the Brotherhood and all that being in it had taught him, and he still believed in what he had been taught, even after he had left it and did not have to believe in anything.

"This Man is going *down*, Howard," he would announce with conviction.

"Why?" I would ask.

"Because it's the Black Man's time to rule again. They had five thousand years, now we get five thousand years."

"What if I don't *want* to rule?" I asked. "What happens if I don't want to take over?"

He looked at me with pity in his face. "You go down with the rest of the country."

"I guess I wouldn't mind much anyway," I said. "It would be a hell of a place with nobody to hate."

But I could never get him to smile about it the way I tried to smile about it. He was always serious. And once, when I questioned the mysticism in the teachings of the Brotherhood, Claude almost attacked me. "Another man might kill you for saying that," he had said. "Another man might not let you get away with saying something like that." He was quite deadly, and he stood over me with an air of patient superiority. And because he could afford to be generous and forgiving, being one of the saved, he sat down at the table with me under the single light bulb and began to teach me. He told me the stories about how it was in the beginning before the whites took over, and about all the little secret significances of black, and about the subtle infiltration of white superiority into everyday objects.

"You've never seen me eat white bread or white sugar, have you?"

"No," I said. He used brown bread and brown sugar.

"Or use bleached flour or white rice?"

"No."

"You know why, don't you?" He waited expectantly.

"No," I finally said. "I don't know why."

He was visibly shocked, so much so that he dropped that line of instruction and began to draw on a pad before him on the living room table. He moved his big shoulders over the yellow pad to conceal his drawings and looked across the table at me. "Now I'm going to tell you something that white men have paid thousands of dollars to learn," he said. "Men have been killed for telling this, but I'm telling you for nothing. I'm warning you not to repeat it because if the whites find out, you know, you could be killed too."

"You know me." I said. "I wouldn't repeat any secrets."

He gave me a long, thoughtful look.

I gave him back a long, eager, honest look.

Then he leaned across the table, and whispered: "Kennedy isn't buried in this country. He was the only President who never had his coffin opened during the funeral. The body was in state all that time, and they never opened the coffin once. You know why?"

"No."

"Because he's not *in it!* They buried an empty coffin. Kennedy was a Thirty-third Degree Mason. His body is in Jerusalem right now."

"How do you know?" I asked.

"If I told you, it would put your life in danger."

"Did his family know about it?"

"No. His lodge kept it secret."

"No one knew?"

"I'm telling you, *no!*"

"Then how did you find out?"

He sighed, more from tolerance than from boredom with my inability to comprehend the mysticism of pure reality in its most unadulterated form. Of course I could not believe him, and we argued about it, back and forth; but to cap all my uncertainties he drew the thirty-three-degree circle, showed me the secret signs that men had died to learn, and spoke about the time when our black ancestors chased an evil genius out of their kingdom and across a desert and onto an island somewhere in the sea; from which, hundreds of years later, this same evil genius sent forth a perfected breed of white-skinned and evil creatures who, through trickery, managed to enslave for five thousand years the onetime Black Masters of the world. He further explained the significance of the East and why all the saved must go there once during their lifetime, and possibly be buried there, as Kennedy had been.

It was dark and late at night, and the glaring bulb cast his great shadow into the corners so that there was the sense of some outraged spirit, fuming in the halls and dark places of our closets, waiting to extract some terrible and justifiable revenge from him for disclosing to me, an unbeliever, the closest-kept of secrets. But I was aware of them only for an instant, and then I did not believe him again.

The most convincing thing about it all was that he was very intelligent and had an orderly, well-regimented life-style, and yet *he* had no trouble with believing. He believed in the certainty of statistical surveys, which was his work; the nutritional value of wheat germ sprinkled on eggs; the sensuality of gin; and the dangers inherent in smoking. He was stylish in that he did not believe in God, but he was extremely moral and warm and kind; and I wanted sometimes to embrace him for his kindness and bigness and gentle manners. He lived his life so carefully that no matter what he said, I could not help believing him sometimes. But I did not want to, because I knew that once I started I could not stop; and then there would be no purpose to my own beliefs and no real conviction or direction in my own efforts to achieve when always, in the back of my regular thoughts, there would be a sense of futility and a fear of the unknown all about me. So, for the sake of necessity, I chose not to believe him.

He felt that the country was doomed and that the safe thing to do was to make enough money as soon as possible and escape to the Far East. He forecast summer riots in certain Northern cities and warned me, religiously, to avoid all implicating ties with whites so that I might have a chance to be saved when that time came. And I asked him about *his* ties, and the girls, and how it was never a movie date with coffee afterward but always his room and the cover-all blanket of Motown sounds late into the night.

"A man has different reasons for doing certain things," he had said.

He never seemed to be comfortable with any of the girls. He never seemed to be in control. And after my third month in the apartment I had concluded that he used his virility as a tool and forged, for however long it lasted, a little area of superiority which could never, it seemed, extend itself beyond the certain confines of his room, no matter how late into the night the records played. I could see him fighting to extend the area, as if an increase in the number of girls he saw could compensate for what he had lost in duration. He saw many girls: curious students, unexpected bus-stop pickups, and assorted other one-nighters. And his rationalizations allowed him to believe that each one was an actual conquest, a physical affirmation of a psychological victory over all he hated and loved and hated in the little world of his room.

But then he seemed to have no happiness, even in this. Even here I sensed some intimations of defeat. After each girl, Claude would almost immediately come out of his room, as if there were no need for aftertalk; as if, after it was over, he felt a brooding, silent emptiness that quickly intensified into nervousness and instantaneous shyness and embarrassment, so that the cold which sets in after that kind of emotional drain came in very sharp against his skin, and he could not bear to have her there any longer. And when the girl had gone, he would come into my room to talk. These were the times when he was most like a little boy; and these were the times when he really began to trust me.

"That bitch called me everything but the son of God," he would chuckle. And I would put aside my papers brought home from the office, smile at him, and listen.

He would always eat or drink afterward, and in those early days I was glad for his companionship and the return of his trust, and sometimes we drank and talked until dawn. During these times he would tell me more subtleties about the Man and would repredict the fall of the country. Once he warned me, in a fatherly way, about reading life from books before experiencing it; and another night he advised me on how to schedule girls so that one could run them without being run in return. These were usually good times of good-natured arguments and predictions; but as we drank more often he tended to grow excited and quick-tempered, especially after he had just entertained. Sometimes he would seethe with hate, and every drink he took gave life to increasingly bitter condemnations of the present system and our place in it. There were actually flying saucers, he told me once, piloted by things from other places in the universe, which would eventually destroy the country for what it had done to the black man. He had run into his room on that occasion, and had brought out a book by a man who maintained that the government was deliberately withholding from the public overwhelming evidence of flying saucers and strange creatures from other galaxies that walked among us every day. Claude emphasized the fact that the writer was a Ph.D. who must know what he was talking about, and insisted that the politicians withheld the information because they knew that their time was almost up and if they made it public, the black man would know that he had outside friends who would help him take over the world again. Nothing I said could make him reconsider the slightest bit of his information.

"What are we going to use for weapons when we take over?" I asked him once.

"We've got atomic bombs stockpiled and waiting for the day."

"How can you believe that crap?"

He did not answer, but said instead: "You are the living example of what the Man has done to my people."

"I just try to think things out for myself." I said.

"You can't think. The handkerchief over your head is too big."

I smiled.

"I know," he continued. "I know all there is to know about whites because I've been studying them all my life."

I smiled some more.

"I ought to know," he said slowly. "I have supernatural powers."

"I'm tired." I told him. "I want to go to sleep now."

Claude started to leave the room, then he turned. "Listen," he said at the door. He pointed his finger at me to emphasize the gravity of his pronouncement. "I predict that within the next week something is going to happen to this country that will hurt it even more than Kennedy's assassination."

"Good-night," I said as he closed the door.

He opened it again. "Remember that I predicted it when it happens," he said. For the first time I noticed that he had been deadly serious all along.

Two days later several astronauts burned to death in Florida. He raced into my room hot with the news.

"Do you believe in me *now?*" he said. "Just two days and look what happened."

I tried to explain, as much to myself as to him, that in any week of the year something unfortunate was bound to occur. But he insisted that this was only part of a divine plan to bring the country to its knees. He said that he intended to send a letter off right away to Jeane Dixon in D.C. to let her know that she was not alone because he also had the same power. Then he thought that he had better not because the FBI knew that he had been active in the Brotherhood before he got out.

At first it was good fun believing that someone important cared enough to watch us. And sometimes when the telephone was dead a long time before the dial tone sounded, I would knock on his door and together we would run through our telephone conversations for that day to see if either of us had said anything implicating or suspect, just in case they were listening. This feeling of persecution brought us closer together, and soon the instruction sessions began to go on almost every night. At this point I could not help believing him a little. And he began to trust me again, like a tolerable little brother, and even confided that the summer riots would break out simultaneously in Harlem and Watts during the second week in August. For some reason, something very difficult to put into words, I spent three hot August nights on the streets of Harlem, waiting for the riot to start.

In the seventh month of our living together, he began to introduce me to his girls again when they came in. Most of them came only once, but all of them received the same mechanical treatment. He discriminated only with liquor, the quality of which improved with the attractiveness or reluctance of the girl: gin for slow starters, bourbon for momentary strangers, and the scotch he reserved for those he hoped would come again. There was first the trek into his room, his own trip out for the ice and glasses while classical music was played within; then after a while the classical piece would be replaced by several Motowns. Finally, there was her trip to the bathroom, his calling a cab in the hall, and the sound of both their feet on the stairs as he walked her down to the cab. Then he would come to my room in his red bathrobe, glass in hand, for the aftertalk.

Then in the ninth month the trouble started. It would be very easy to pick out one incident, one day, one area of misunderstanding in that and say: "That was where it began." It would be easy, but not accurate. It might have been one instance or a combination of many. It might have been the girl who came into the living room when I was going over the proposed blueprints for a new settlement house, and who lingered too long outside his room in conversation because her father was a builder somewhere. Or it might have been nothing at all. But after that time he warned me about being too friendly with his company.

Another night, when I was leaving the bathroom in my shorts, he came out of his room with a girl who smiled. "Hi," she said to me.

I nodded hello as I ducked back into the bathroom.

When he had walked her down to the door he came to my room and knocked. He did not have a drink. "Why didn't you speak to my company?" he demanded.

"I was in my shorts."

"She felt bad about it. She asked what the hell was wrong with you. What could I tell her—'He got problems'?"

"I'm sorry," I said. "But I didn't want to stop in my shorts."

"I see through you, Howard," he said. "You're just jealous of me and try to insult my girls to get to me."

"Why should I be jealous of you?"

"Because I'm a man and you're not."

"What makes a man anyway?" I said. "Your fried eggs and wheat germ? Why should I be jealous of you *or* what you bring in?"

"Some people don't need a reason. You're a black devil and you'll get yours. I predict that you'll get yours."

"Look," I told him, "I'm sorry about the girl. Tell her I'm sorry when you see her again."

"You treated her so bad she probably won't come back."

I said nothing more, and he stood there silently for a long time before he turned to leave the room. But at the door he turned again, and said: "I see through you, Howard. You're a black devil."

It should have ended there, and it might have with anyone else. I took great pains to speak to his girls after that, even though he tried to get them into the room as quickly as possible. But a week later he accused me of walking about in his room after he had gone out some two weeks before.

"I swear I wasn't in your room," I protested.

"I saw your shadow on the blinds from across the street at the bus stop," he insisted.

"I've *never* been in your room when you weren't there," I told him.

"I *saw* you!"

We went into his room, and I tried to explain how, even if he could see the window from the bus stop, the big lamp next to the window prevented any shadow from being cast on the blinds. But he was convinced in his mind that at every opportunity I plundered his closets and drawers. He had no respect for simple logic in these matters, no sense of the absurdity of his accusations, and the affair finally ended with my confessing that I might have done it without actually knowing, and if I had, I would not do it again.

But what had been a gesture for peace on my part became a vindication for him, proof that I *was* a black devil, capable of lying and lying until he confronted me with the inescapable truth of the situation. And so he persisted in creating situations from which, if he insisted on a point long enough and with enough self-righteousness, he could draw my inevitable confession.

And I confessed eagerly, goaded on by the necessity of maintaining peace. I confessed to mixing white sugar crystals in with his own brown crystals so that he could use it and violate the teachings of the Brotherhood; I confessed to cleaning the bathroom all the time merely because I wanted to make him feel guilty for not having ever cleaned it. I confessed to telling the faithful Marie, who brought a surprise dinner over for him, that he was working late at his office in order to implicate him with the girls who worked there. I confessed to leaving my papers about the house so that his company could ask about them and develop an interest in me. And I pleaded guilty to a record of other little infamies, which multiplied into countless others, and again subdivided into hundreds of little subtleties until my every movement was a threat to him. If I had a girlfriend to dinner, we should eat in my room instead of at the table because he had to use the bathroom a lot, and he was embarrassed to be seen going to the bathroom.

If I protested, he would fly into a tantrum and shake his big finger at me vigorously. And so I retreated, step by step, into my room, from which I emerged only to go to the bathroom or kitchen or out of the house. I tried to stay out on nights when he had company. But he had company so often that I could not always help being in my room after he had walked her to the door. Then he would knock on my door for his talk. He might offer me a drink, and if I refused, he would go to his room for a while and then come back. He would pace about for a while, like a big little boy who wants to ask for money over his allowance. At these times my mind would move feverishly over all our contacts for as far back as I could make it reach, searching and attempting to pull out that one incident which would surely be the point of his attack. But it was never any use.

"Howard, I got something on my chest, and I might as well get it off."

"What is it?" I asked from my bed.

"You been acting strange lately. Haven't been talking to me. If you got something on your chest, get it off now."

"I have nothing on my chest," I said.

"Then why don't you talk?"

I did not answer.

"You hardly speak to me in the kitchen. If you have something against me, tell me now."

"I have nothing against you."

"Why don't you talk, then?" He looked directly at me. "If a man doesn't talk, you think *something's* wrong!"

"I've been nervous lately, that's all. I got problems, and I don't want to talk."

"Everybody's got problems. That's no reason for going around making a man feel guilty."

"For God's sake, I don't want to talk."

"I know what's wrong with you. Your conscience is bothering you. You're so evil that your conscience is giving you trouble. You got everybody fooled but *me*. I know you're a black devil."

"I'm a black devil," I said. "Now will you let me sleep?"

He went to the door. "You dish it out, but you can't take it," he said. "That's *your* trouble."

"I'm a black devil," I said.

I lay there, after he left, hating myself but thankful that he hadn't called me into his room for the fatherly talk as he had done another time. That was the worst. He had come to the door and said: "Come out of there, I want to talk to you." He had walked ahead of me into his room and had sat down in his big leather chair next to the lamp with his legs spread wide and his big hands in his lap. He had said: "Don't be afraid. I'm not going to hurt you. Sit down. I'm not going to argue. What are you so nervous about? Have a drink," in his kindest, most fatherly way, and that had been the worst of all. That was the time he had told me to eat in my room. Now I could hear him pacing about in the hall, and I knew that it was not over for the night. I began to pray that I could sleep before he came. I did not care what he did as long as I did not have to face him. I resolved to confess to anything he accused me of if it would make him leave sooner. I was about to go out into the hall for my confession when the door was kicked open and he charged into the room.

"You black son of a bitch!" he said. "I ought to *kill* you." He stood over the bed in the dark room and shook his big fist over me. And I lay there hating the overpowering cowardice in me, which kept my body still and my eyes closed, and hoping that he would kill all of it when his heavy fist landed.

"First you insult a man's company, then you ignore him. I been *good* to you. I let you live here, I let you eat my uncle's food, and I taught you things. But you're a ungrateful m-f. I ought to *kill* you right now!"

And I still lay there, as he went on, not hearing him, with nothing in me but a loud throbbing which pulsed through the length of my body and made the sheets move with its pounding. I lay there secure and safe in cowardice for as long as I looked up at him with my eyes big and my body twitching and my mind screaming out to him that it was all right, and I thanked him, because now I truly believed in the new five thousand years of Black Rule.

It is night again. I am in bed again, and I can hear the new blond girl closing the bathroom door. I know that in a minute he will come out in his red robe and call a cab. His muffled voice through my closed door will seem very tired, but just as kind and patient to the dispatcher as it is to everyone, and as it was to me in those old times. I am afraid, because when they came up the stairs earlier they caught me working at the living room table with my back to them. I had not expected him back so soon; but then I should have known that he would not go out. I had turned around in the chair, and she smiled and said hello, and I said "Hi" before he hurried her into the room. I *did* speak, and I know that she heard. But I also know that I must have done something wrong; if not to her, then to him earlier today or yesterday or last week, because he glared at me before following her into the room, and he almost paused to say something when he came out to get the glasses and ice. I wish that I could remember just what it was. But it does not matter. I *am* guilty, and he knows it.

Now that he knows about me I am afraid. I could move away from the apartment and hide my guilt from him, but I know that he would find me. The brainwashed part of my mind tells me to call the police while he is still busy with her, but what could I charge him with when I know that he is only trying to help me? I could move the big ragged yellow chair in front of the door, but that would not stop him, and it might make him impatient with me. Even if I pretended to be asleep and ignored him, it would not help when he comes. He has not bothered to knock for weeks.

In the black shadows over my bed and in the corners I can sense the outraged spirits who help him when they hover about his arms as he gestures, with his lessons, above my bed. I am determined now to lie here and take it. It is the price I must pay for all the black secrets I have learned, and all the evil I have learned about myself. I *am* jealous of him, of his learning, of his girls. I am not the same handkerchief-head I was nine months ago. I have Marie to thank for that, and Claude, and the spirits. They know about me, and perhaps it is they who make him do it and he cannot help himself. I believe in the spirits now, just as I believe most of the time that I am a black devil.

They are going down to the cab now.

I will not ever blame him for it. He is helping me. But I blame the girls. I blame them for not staying on afterward, and for letting all the good nice happy love talk cut off automatically after it is over. *I* need to have them there, after it is over. And he needs it; he needs it much more and much longer than they could ever need what he does for them. He should be able to teach them, as he has taught me. And he should have their appreciation, as he has mine. I blame them. I blame them for letting him try and try and never get just a little of the love there is left in the world.

I can hear him coming back from the cab.

Alan Sondheim (1943–   ) is a native of Wilkes-
Barre, Pennsylvania; currently he teaches in the hu-
manities program at the Rhode Island School of Design. He writes poems and fiction, and is a choreog-
rapher; a highly innovative talent who uses available
technology, he has produced mixed-means theatrical
pieces, and constructed his own electronic-music syn-
thesizer. Meta, Inc., is his consulting firm; he is in
the process of publishing two collections of materials
relating to experimental fiction, scheduled for 1977.

(_ ⹁

ALAN SONDHEIM

TraditCollege Coarse Catalog

Basic **Basketweaving:**   This has been charged by freeskool, hilldale, and
correction-institute. We have accordingly taken action, offering the same
"in the teeth of the enemy." The baskets will be displayed. The approach is
"traditional," cording, wrapping, and cutting. Mr. Kalman, G 817, Pd 4.

I (a,b',c)eP.T (Ez) (a,b,z) eP& (z,a,c)eS):   A study of this interesting
equation, leading to a generalized approach to the mathematical sciences.
Practical guidance in calculating the gradient of bulwarks and other "defensive mechanisms." Mrs. Eaton, C 407, Pd 7.

Freeskool: required coarse. A detailed historical-political investigation into the first splinter enemy. Their professors, children, offensive and
defensive tactics. Films of "group-grope," farming, painting and smearing.
A nurse shall be available. Some field work. The Staff, C 817;803;807, Pd 3.
(See board in C 15 for section lists.)

The Year 3000:   A study of the future, beginning a millenium after
most science fiction films have ended. In other words, a millenium after the
events in the films have occurred, or the theatres have let out. Special topics
will include practical militancy and the arsenal, as well as tunnels under
hilldale. Mr. Sondheim, C 14, Pd 5. (Not for seniors).

What is the reason that, seeing there are so many of Diana's Temples
in Rome, the men refrain into that only which stands in Patrician Street?: A

613

seminar investigating the style and content of this most interesting of Plutarch's questions, which possesses applications in the field of armada strength. Miss Forsythe, C 901, Pd 5.

Is it upon the account of the fabulous story, that a certain man, ravishing a woman that was there worshipping the goddess, was torn to pieces by dogs: and hence this superstitious practice arose, that men enter not in?: A seminar discussion of this most interesting of Plutarch's answers. Special attention given to "answers-in-question-form," with four periods devoted to Wondering. An onslaught in the direction of correction-institute is also planned. Miss Forsythe, C 901, Pd 6.

Basic English: Required for Hilldale (see below). A study of our origins, the power of vitriol and invective, the use of euphemism and the real thing. Mr. Klemency, C 19, Pd 1.

Hilldale: Tremendous detail and analysis on the subject of the second splinter group. The two hilldale-freeskool battles will be considered, as well as the political effect of our recent skirmishes with correction-institute. This is an Aktion course. Mr. Kalman, C/B (bunker), Pd 1.

Winter and Summer: Empedocles and the Stoics believed that winter is caused by the thickness of the air prevailing and mounting upwards: and summer by fire, it falling downwards. Lecture, with passing disparaging reference to freeskool. Mr. Cotton-Young, C 817, Pd 2.

Reading/Writing/Arithmetic: A seminar devoted to teaching the student the skills of reading, and writing. Pagination is presented as an "approach" to the new mathematics. Several books are distributed. The course also constructs cannon of the third rate, and mortars of the second and third. Their use as both offensive and defensive is presented. Students are required to wound. Mr. Callahan, C 415, Pd 2.

Education, where it has become: A study of "it" becoming education. Serious investigation into the present crisis. The fragmentation of the universities and the early wars between the "freeskool students" and the "traditionalists": the complete breakdown and corruption of "external society", with the rise of the Vigilants; the connection between the Vigilants and correction-institute, etc. Not required, but urged. Foraging into the City as a radical alternative is discussed. Mr. Callahan, Miss Forsythe, Mrs. Eaton, C 778–779–780, Pd 2.

Mr. Callahan: A study of his coarse mixups (timing, presentation, etc.). Given as a service to *TraditCollege*. Miss Forsythe, Mrs. Eaton, C 779–780, Pd 3.

The death of a student: Required for both students and faculty: Discussions and lectures on the death of a student. A captive from freeskool is slowly executed. (Later, if lucky, a captive from hilldale may also be presented.) This coarse hardens the young volunteer, and reminds the old. Mrs. Nancy, C 100, Pd 1–7.

Dogs: The logicians say that a dog, making use of the argument drawn from many disjunctive propositions, thus reasons with himself, in places where several highways meet; either the wild beast is gone this way, or that, or that way; but not that way, nor that way, therefore this way; the force of sense affording nothing but the minor premise, but the force of reason affording the major proposition, and inferring the conclusion of the assumption. Attention given to the smell of hilldalers and the tracks they make. Miss Forsythe, C 27, afternoons at 3.00.

Pillaging: An Aktion coarse in natural history. Grades given on the basis of the "bring-back" or booty. Any student who can produce a captive for The Death of a Student coarse is automatically given a pardon, and ½-degree. Captured students are naturally expelled. Mr. Will Young, C 101, Pd 6.

An Historical Approach to L.B. Rothby: Rothby was the perpetrator of the first splinter, and, defecting, led the way to the third. His 3-F manifesto ("Fight, Fickle Freemen") is read. (This work is not obtainable elsewhere.) An attack on "his good name" is led, as well as the possible burning of hilldale. Mr. Will-Young, C 207, Pd 7.

Correction-Institute: The study of proles, toppers, etc. The third and fourth splinters, recriminations and counter-recriminations, and why we won't speak to them. The distribution of spears and bows to the populace is an important issue. Field-work with Miss Asmythe, C 119, Pd 4.

Sexual Attitudes on Campus: The investigation into *TraditCollege* sex and what can be done to improve the situation. Establishment of anti-abortion-contraception campaign. Enrollment of "young" students, and the building of a nursery to train for "tommorrow's warriors." Miss Asmythe, C 119, Pd 7.

Espionage: Theoretical-Practical: ldkerhtiuer831   lkj430   lkj9d8 tjke jeiu *7e51 98tu4m hyfyr74u e 8 doiu 9 11dkfjjkl9ru5 4— 00945s. jk foie9. jdireiu54, dote140211-theirds, fkute. (ltkejr dhild.) jkfiwuejk d; k 148, fj v.

General Science and Armanent: Consideration of the following problems: In what sense does Plato say, that the Antiperistasis (or reaction) of motion—by reason there is no vacuum—is the cause of the effects in physicians' cupping-glasses, in swallowing, in throwing of weights, in the running of water, in thunder, in the attraction of the loadstone, and in the harmony of sounds? These have occupied our Attention for a number of years, and still no answers appear forthcoming. A new theory of projectiles has resulted, however, with several casualties of a sort hitherto unknown. Mr. Sondheim, C 14, Pd 6.

The Tigris River: At the end of the Term, *TraditCollege* shall move to the vicinity of the Tigris. We have found a hill overlooking two *wadis,* which are difficult to traverse. The location is ideal: one can see for 20 kilometers in each and every direction. Trenches, bunkers, etc. are already being installed. The Tigris River will prepare the student for the future of the college, and his own role in it. Specifically, lorry drivers and misslemen are at present in short supply. This coarse is given in place of all others; attendence is required at all times. Limited enrollment. Mr. Wenet-Will. The first meeting is Wed. Sept. 17, 7:00 A.M. near the flag-pole.

Notice: Attention Students: We regret to announce that coarse Winter and Summer will not be offered this season, due to the untimely death of Mr. Cotton-Young. Mr. C-Y was taken Captive shortly before this catalog went to press, by several "rounders" of hilldale. Although we have not had definite word concerning his condition, we assume that he fell victim to that "certain fate." In the words of Theogenis: "Change manners with thy friends, observing thus/ The many-colored, cunning polypus;/ Who let him stick to whatsoever rock,/ Of the same color does his body look." (vs. 215).

Cynthia Buchanan (1942–   ) was born in Phoe-
nix, Arizona, and received degrees from Arizona
State University (B.A.) and the University of the
Americas (M.A.) in Mexico City. Since 1970 she has
lived as a full-time writer in New York City. Maiden
(1972), a first novel, brought unusual critical acclaim
and is to become a movie. Her first short story, "The
Wind Chandelier," was reprinted in Best Short Fiction from the Little Magazines (1970) and is the
basis for a play, Carbona (1976), produced for the
Arena Stage in Washington, D.C.

CYNTHIA BUCHANAN

The Wind Chandelier

*T*he day of her birthday, the old woman reached up slowly and felt of
her hair. The unmarried daughter Lillian kept it clean and cut as short as a
paper boy's.

Lillian had washed the old woman's hair today. When she sat her
mother down in the living room afterwards, she said, "And you *stay* that
way, hear?"

"Sister," the old woman said, "when I was fourteen, my hair was
heavy, and it traveled clean down to my waist. Sid . . . he was near twicet
my age then . . . Sid, he never let me cut it. So, by God, I wore it in coils
. . . top of my head, you know. Oh, every oncet in a while, I let it go wild
about my waist until it came caught against them splintered posts. Or in
Sid's hands. 'I'm going to tie you up in them ribbons,' he would tell me,
meaning my hair, don't you know. And he would smile."

"Yes, yes, yes, I know," Lillian said. "Lord, what time is it? I've got to
call Maxine!" She bounded into the kitchen, and the old woman listened to
her dialing the telephone.

Where was that remote punch for the television? She looked around
for the small hand device with the buttons. She punched one of them, and
the television tube whined forth an image.

Mother!" Lillian yelled from the kitchen. "Mother, if you would kindly
turn that down a minute I could hear what Maxine is saying. What, Max?

617

What? Hold on a sec; Mother's got that TV going until I think my head is going to split in two. Hold on." She opened the swinging kitchen door.

"Mother! How do you suppose we can talk with that Queen for a Day show splitting my head in two? Now, you can just wait until I'm through on the phone in here." She retreated with the swing of the door. "All right, Maxine; go on."

"Whuh?" the old woman said. "Didn't know you was on the telephone." She punched the remote control, and the television picture melted into a distorted white dot. She stared at the electronic point on the tube and said, "Turn it off. Clean off, that's what we'll do." Resting her head on the back of the armchair, she stared into the living room of the tract house. She had it memorized down to the contents of the odds and ends drawer. A few *How-to* books on the shelves. Beige carpet with sworls. Scrabble game in the closet for certain of the company. Oleander bushes next to the front porch. Toaster had a crocheted cover. Flamingoes on the bathroom shower curtain. Sewing basket in the bedroom with Lillian's aprons-in-the-making stacked on top.

"She's got it fixed up nice for my birthday," the old woman said and looked into the dining room where the party preparations waited on the table. All the family would come today by four o'clock and have cake. Someone's Pekingese would have to be fussed over and put in the bathroom, so he wouldn't wet on the rug. Lillian had put a paper tablecloth on the table in the dining room, with paper "Happy Birthday" lettering taped on the mirror.

She heard Lillian say, "Mother's calling, Maxine. I'd better go see what it is now. Yes, bye. See you at four. Un-huh. Yes, Hawaiian's fine. You can get it in those pint bottles. Mixes up enough to feed an army. Yes, uh-huh, okay then, four o'clock or a little tinsy bit before."

There were saucers of nuts and pretzels on the end tables at the couch, and all the magazines were straightened in their stacks. The napkins on the table cooperated in a symmetrical diamond design.

"I wonder what ever happened to Celia Franks," the old woman said to herself. "She married that boy. She should have gotten rid of those moles." She folded her hands in her lap. "But she got that boy. Moles or no, she got him. Her family was a shameful, thieving lot, but *she* turned out, moles and all. All right that Celia Franks."

Lillian came through the door. "Yes, Mother? What is it, Mother?"

"Nothing. I was just saying to myself you got the house fixed nice. I been taking notice of the things in the dining room and what all."

Lillian smoothed her hands on her apron.

"Yes, it does look rather festive, if I do say so myself. Now, are you ready for your bath? Go on in, and I'll be in in a minute. Pratt and all of them will be here early."

"He came yesterday."

"Well, yes, he came yesterday. Pratt can come visit his own mother without it being her birthday, can't he? He can come two days in a row, I should think. You don't mind seeing Pratt, your own flesh and blood, do you?"

The old woman tapped the end of her fingers absently on the arms of the chair and pursed her lips in and out.

Lillian rearranged the zinnias. "Well, you don't, do you?"

"No, miss, I don't mind seeing him two days in a row, and I don't see reason for you to talk to your mother so, either."

"Are you going to be peevish today? On your birthday? Come on. You better get your bath."

The mother had her bath and her Yardley talcum. Lillian put on a jersey dress and stood before the mirror, pulling her hair back at the temples with two combs. The old woman sat on the edge of the bed holding a satin brassiere in her hands.

Lillian saw the reflection in the mirror and turned abruptly. "Here, here, here! What are you doing, Mother?"

"Getting dressed, Lillian. For my party."

"I thought I put that silly thing away last Christmas. And now what do I find you doing?"

The old woman put the brassiere down in her lap. "You don't need to concern yourself with my things."

"Oh no, no, I don't need to concern myself with your things." Lillian sighed and pulled the venetian blinds open. "No, I, Lillian, have never had to concern myself with your things, Mother. Never in my life have I had to look after you . . . or care for you . . . or stay in this house and rot! Here, give me that brassiere."

"It's my birthday, and I'm going to wear it. Leave it be. Nancy's girl ordered that for me from Frederick's of Hollywood."

"Oh, yes. And if that doesn't take the cake!" She scratched around in a dresser drawer, laying amber colored jewelry out on the dresser top. "No, I never have to concern myself with you or with your belongings or your happiness. Never once in the past millennium have I ever given a thought to your happiness or comfort. I've lived entirely for myself. Yes, wear that silly bra from . . . Frederick's of Hollywood! What in the world Jennifer thought you would ever do with a . . . a . . . provocative . . . and expensive . . . French brassiere, I'll never know."

The old woman looked at the piece of lingerie. It was white . . . as white as seagulls . . . whiter than her wedding dress. "She knows I like pretty things. Nothing wrong with giving a person pretty things."

"Well, don't we all like pretty things, Mother. Every last one of us, I'm sure."

She answered that Yes we did, all of us, and her daughter said that that was no reason to waste good money on impractical items like French brassieres.

"It's almost . . . "Lillian smiled with one side of her mouth but did not quite laugh. "Oh, go ahead if you want to try and actually wear the thing. It's no business of mine. I only live here. I certainly wouldn't try to see any things of yours. I never have in my life, why should I start now?"

The old woman put on the brassiere. When she was buttoning up the little rhinestone buttons slowly at the front of her nylon dress, Lillian said, "Here, here, I'll do that. We don't have all the time in the world to be buttoning ourselves together when Pratt and all of them will be getting here just any time."

The old woman sat on the bed after Lillian went into the kitchen to see to the cake and paper cups. She rose and looked in the mirror at her cheeks and neck. They were criss-crossed with grooves; it looked as if the sewing machine had stitched the pattern of wrinkles. "Well, birthday, birthday, birthday," she said and sat on the bed again. She would like a little coffee-colored volume of poems for her birthday. She could read them just as well as the newspaper or the TV Guide or the Milk of Magnesia bottle. "What did they do with all those books any more? I used to have some pretty little poem books among them. One was E. A. Poe, and it had a pressed pansy on top of the poem about Helen. Sid or someone or I stuck that flower there. Little books with ribbons to mark your place if you wanted to stop reading and go some place for a while and then come back and read some more. Could keep your place." Maybe somebody today would give her some colored cotton balls in a round plastic box like Lillian had here the other day to give away as a bridge prize. They were pastel cotton balls, gentle and almost candy or magic, nestled one next to the other in that clear-plastic box. Pretty and delicate and pastel. "Or say, I know what I'd like to have." She smiled. "I'd like to have a hammer. Brand new with a new yellow wooden handle and a shiny, heavy head. Fresh from the hardware place. A hammer that could sit on the night table, or I could hold it in my hand when I wanted." With the head of it cool and firm in her hand, like a cool stone from the seashore. Oh, a hammer was a beautiful thing once you thought about it.

She plicked at the chenille on the white bedspread and wondered whatever did happen to that girl with the moles, that Celia Franks. She and Celia Franks used to hide oranges in the mesquite trees on their way to school and then find them on the way home. Sure, sure did, though, think this white brassiere was pretty. Maybe Nancy's girl would come today, and maybe she would bring her a hammer or some pastel cotton balls. "Say, I wouldn't mind having any of those things."

"Mother!" Lillian called from the kitchen.

"Yay-oh?"

"Mother, come here a minute and tell me where you want this cake. In the middle of the table, like this, or do you want it more towards the living room for everybody to see?"

"What you want. It's the same whatever's best," she whispered.

"Mother? Mother! I *said* would you come here a second to tell me about this birthday cake. Where you want it put? Do you want it . . ." Lillian was nearly shouting; she turned as her mother entered the kitchen. "Oh! I didn't know you were here already. Why didn't you tell me you were standing there, so I wouldn't be yelling? Now, where do you want your cake?"

"Is Nancy's girl coming today?"

"What does that have to do with the price of eggs? I asked you where you wanted your cake." She opened and slammed the refrigerator door after taking out some Philadelphia creamed cheese. "I don't know if Jennifer's coming or not. I can't keep track of neighbors. I've got my hands full here as it is."

"I can hear you. You're shouting, sister." The old woman shuffled through the kitchen and looked at the arrayed table in the dining room, with the plastic ivy leaves hanging on one wall. "Yes, Pratt's said he's going to find out if that tomcat got run over or not."

"What?"

"Pratt. He's going to ask about that orange tomcat that was around here, if he got run over by a car out in the road or not. Haven't seen him for some while." She looked out the window at the two palm trees and a pink dust storm.

"Haven't seen him for a while? He was just over here yesterday, Mother! He came to show us the trophy he won bowling in the city semi-finals."

"Who?"

"Why, Pratt, Mother, *Pratt!* Why don't you listen? Now, do you or do you not want your cake on the dining room table, or do you want it closer so everybody can see it?"

Lillian put the cake in the middle of the table and began unceremoniously punching candles ("just . . . a . . . few . . . here . . . and . . . there!") into the white frosting. She told her mother that if she wasn't going to cooperate with her own birthday party, she'd do best to go sit in the living room and no, of course that cat had not been run over. "I, Lillian, gave it away to the paper boy. Why, we couldn't have any more cat hairs flying around here, coming in the door and into the kitchen where the food is kept, food that you eat."

The old woman sat in the living room and looked out the picture window to where a glass thing hung from the front porch. She sat and waited for her guests, liking that little glass thing more and more as the minutes passed. It was Japanese or Chinese, made of short striplets of glass that hung by threads and tinkled in the wind. Kind of like a wind chandelier, she thought. And those tiny brush strokes of the designs painted there by some Jap or some Chinaman. Just as little and delicate as you could want them. Nancy's girl had brought her the gift that swayed and played crystal notes in the breeze. Nancy's girl went to Chinatown in San Francisco, and when she came back, the two of them had had a fine time fixing the string and glass thing up on the porch.

A breeze now brushed across it, and the wind chandelier talked to itself in little crystal laughs. It talked to the old woman and made her think of oceans and seaside things and love and jade and then of Sid when he was a young strapping man.

"Nancy's girl brought this thing hanging out on the porch, didn't she?" she called into the kitchen. Come to think of it, Nancy's girl did bring that tender glass thing. Brought it some months back.

Where were those cigarettes? She looked over her shoulder at the kitchen door. She picked around in the pocket of her dress, her eyes still on the door. She then put a single crumpled cigarette on her knee and attempted to straighten it out and pinch some of the falling tobacco back into one end. She stood up slowly and lighted the cigarette with a book of matches whose cover asked her if she had psoriasis. She exhaled and closed her eyes, placing one hand lightly on top of the television set.

And to have some poems with a ribbon.

"Huh? What are you saying in there, Mother?" Lillian shouted over the grinding and flushings of the automatic dishwasher. The noises stopped abruptly, and the old woman stuffed the cigarette quickly in the vase of fresh zinnias, where it died in the water.

Lillian appeared, wiping her hands on a towel. "What is it? All the muttering. What do you want, Mother?"

When she found that again it was nothing and nothing, always nothing, she wondered if Pratt was or was not going to come early and said she would like to see the day *she* would try to wear a silly satin brassiere when her own daughter advised her against the silliness of it. "Say, wait a minute! Do I smell smoke?" She strode around the living room with her head cocked to one side and her nostrils flared and sniffing.

"Is that Nancy's girl coming for my birthday?"

Her daughter stopped and threw her hands out at her sides; they dropped with a slap to her thighs. "Oh, Lord. I ask you if I smell cigarette smoke, and you are still going on about Jennifer. That takes the cake." Deciding she did not smell anything, that her mind was playing tricks on her because of all this overwork in preparation for the party, Lillian went back into the kitchen.

At three-thirty, Pratt arrived with his hefty wife and their three bickering sons in YMCA T-shirts. After Pratt and his family, more and more family arrived, plopping in chairs and divans. The children turned the television on, ate the pretzels and socked each other. Nineteen family came.

One grandchild brought blow-bubbles-through-a-plastic-ring and got whipped when the bubbles exploded on the newly polished coffee table and left little soapy rings on Lillian's clean furniture.

The offspring talked among themselves, jumping up from their chairs from time to time to tell the guest of honor that she was looking younger every year.

Pratt kissed her gingerly, shying away from the smell of dentures and age. "Bet you're itching to get your hands on those birthday presents, eh, Motherkins?" He laughed and winked at her. "Hey, Maxine, hand me another cup of that Hawaiian, will you?" Then he piled her gifts in her lap. "Dig in, Mom!"

The old woman opened the packages and found three pairs of brown winter-warm stockings for her circulation, a round tin of stuffed dates, a bathmat with rubber suction cups to hold it to the tile of the bathroom ("Then nobody slips and gets hurt, right, Mother?"), and a framed family picture of Pratt and all of his. Then there was a shoehorn, a box of See's candy, which was passed around the room, an envelope with a subscription to *Senior Citizen!*, and a bottle of Pacquin's hand cream with the pricetag on it.

She opened each gift carefully, putting the ribbons in a pile and folding the wrapping paper to save it. She thanked for each item and thought, Nancy's girl should be here soon. She will come through all them and light upon my knee like a little moth, and I won't dare to move my hand so that her wings will be just so.

She said, "Pratt, what time is it, son?"

"Eight o'clock or a hair before."

"I'm thinking Nancy's girl ought to be popping in here any minute."

"Nancy whose girl?"

The front door opened suddenly, and the old woman leaned forward rigidly in her chair. That would be Nancy's girl from across the oceans and the wind chandeliers! It was one of the grandchildren who ran in after another one. She sat back slowly in the chair and folded her hands in her lap. It was very late. Only parts of the party were left around. She stared at her hands and tried to remember a poem about a hummingbird. Or a moth. Was it a moth? Nancy's girl was off flying around the light somewhere too far or too high and away. Oh and oh and oh.

Lillian moved around quickly wadding up wrapping paper. "I know somebody who's had a pretty big day." She winked at the family and turned to her mother, "Come on, birthday girl."

"No, I think I'll wait a spell."

Lillian squeezed a ball of crumpled paper so tightly her knuckles turned white. "Mother . . . Nancy's girl is not . . . N . . . O . . . T . . . coming."

"I expect not, but I think I'll wait some anyway."

"I don't think you will, Mother."

"Says who?"

"We'll . . . we'll pretend that you didn't say that. Now, let's bundle ourselves off to bed, shall we? Say goodnight to Pratt and to . . ."

"I'm going to wait for my birthday to finish itself up. I'm going to stay up until midnight."

Lillian shot a look at the guests and said to her mother, "Now, you go on in the bedroom and go to sleep, and if you have to use the bathroom, call me or Pratt first, so that Chow-Chow doesn't get out and ruin the rug. I'll come in and help you get undressed in a minute."

"Lillian, lady, I'm telling you that I'm going to wait my birthday out."

Pratt grunted forward in his chair as he reached to snap on the television remote control. "Oh, now, Mother, let's not get testy on our birthday . . ."

In a high, tight voice, Lillian said, "Oh no, Pratt; that's all right, little brother, if she wants to be petulant . . . she can just be petulant until she rots." She opened the door to her mother's bedroom. "But she's not going to spoil our day with her little obsessions. If you, Mother, want to wait your birthday out, you can do so in here."

The old woman struggled to her feet and shuffled in to the bedroom. "I think I'll do that, lady." She sat down in a chair and stared through the venetian blinds.

"And thank you, Mother," Lillian said before shutting the door, "for being so very very appreciative of your birthday party that I was such a fool as to try and make nice for you!" With the light out, the room was filled with moonlight.

But through the closed door, the old woman could hear the wives and daughters scraping the party into the garbage disposal. The children would be going to sleep on the rug as the men watched the wrestling matches on the television.

She sat and sat and presently heard all the guests leaving and the refrigerator door opening and shutting. Lillian would be taking her carton of yogurt to bed with her.

Lillian opened the bedroom door and stood holding the yogurt and a spoon. "Oh, my my, you're still up, are you? I see. Well, wait on until dawn, if you like. Your birthday should surely be over by then." She slammed the door shut, and the old woman continued to sit in the chair.

She fell asleep there but awakened sometime before she heard the clock in the hall chime midnight. She stared at the white tufts of chenille on the moonlit bedspread and blinked, thinking of someone's hair falling down her back like long long wild ribbons.

Chronology of Authors

CHRONOLOGY OF AUTHORS

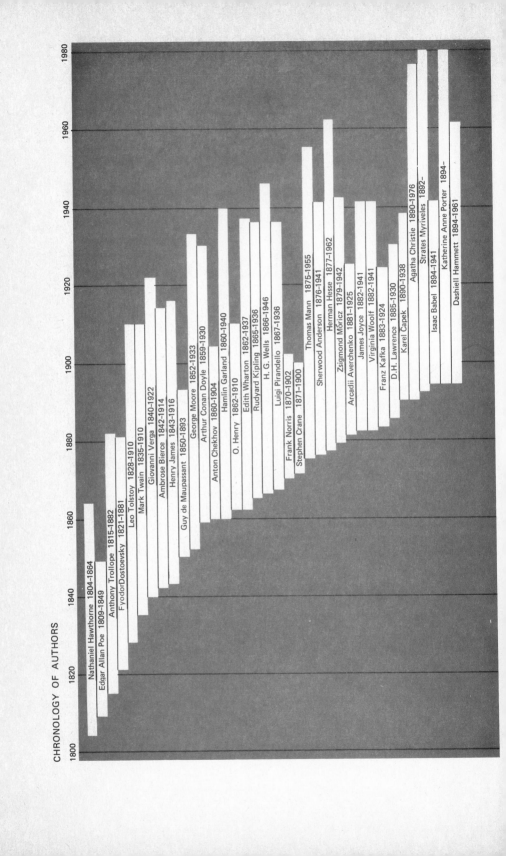

1800　1820　1840　1860　1880　1900　1920　1940　1960　1980

Nathaniel Hawthorne 1804-1864
Edgar Allan Poe 1809-1849
Anthony Trollope 1815-1882
FyodorDostoevsky 1821-1881
Leo Tolstoy 1828-1910
Mark Twain 1835-1910
Giovanni Verga 1840-1922
Ambrose Bierce 1842-1914
Henry James 1843-1916
Guy de Maupassant 1850-1893
George Moore 1852-1933
Arthur Conan Doyle 1859-1930
Anton Chekhov 1860-1904
Hamlin Garland 1860-1940
O. Henry 1862-1910
Edith Wharton 1862-1937
Rudyard Kipling 1865-1936
H. G. Wells 1866-1946
Luigi Pirandello 1867-1936
Frank Norris 1870-1902
Stephen Crane 1871-1900
Thomas Mann 1875-1955
Sherwood Anderson 1876-1941
Herman Hesse 1877-1962
Zsigmond Móricz 1879-1942
Arcadii Averchenko 1881-1925
James Joyce 1882-1941
Virginia Woolf 1882-1941
Franz Kafka 1883-1924
D.H. Lawrence 1885-1930
Karel Capek 1890-1938
Agatha Christie 1890-1976
Strates Myriveles 1892-
Isaac Babel 1894-1941
Katherine Anne Porter 1894-
Dashiell Hammett 1894-1961

F. Scott Fitzgerald 1896-1940

William Faulkner 1897-1962

Ernest Hemingway 1898-1961

Elizabeth Bowen 1899-1973

Jorge Luis Borges 1899-

Sean O'Faolain 1900-

V. S. Pritchett 1900-

Langston Hughes 1902-1967

John Steinbeck 1902-1968

Frank O'Connor 1903-

Graham Greene 1904-

Jean-Paul Sartre 1905-

Samuel Beckett 1906-

Alberto Moravia 1907-

Tommaso Landolfi 1908-

Ilya Varshavsky 1909-1974

Eudora Welty 1909-

Walter Van Tilburg Clark 1909-1971

Bernard Malamud 1914-

Heinrich Böll 1917-

Isaac Rosenfeld 1918-1956

James B. Hall 1918-

R. V. Cassill 1919-

Doris Lessing 1919-

Isaac Asimov 1920-

Alain Robbe-Grillet 1922-

Grace Paley 1922-

Flannery O'Connor 1925-1964

Slawomir Mrozek 1930-

J. G. Ballard 1930-

Ted Hughes 1930-

Lars Görling 1931-1966

William Harrison 1933-

Robert Stone 1937-

Peter Handke 1942-

Cynthia Buchanan 1942-

James Alan McPherson 1943-

Alan Sondheim 1943-

Acknowledgments

Sherwood Anderson, "The Egg" from *The Triumph of the Egg* by Sherwood Anderson, published by B. W. Huebsch, Inc., 1921. Copyright © 1921 by B. W. Huebsch, Inc. Renewed 1948 by Eleanor C. Anderson. Reprinted by permission of Harold Ober Associates, Inc.

Isaac Asimov, "All the Troubles of the World." Copyright © 1958 by Headline Publications, Inc. Reprinted by permission of the author.

Arcadii Averchenko, "The Young Man Who Flew Past" from *A Treasury of Russian Literature,* published by Vanguard Press, Inc., translated by Bernard Guilbert Guerney. Copyright © 1943 1965, by Bernard Guilbert Guerney. Reprinted by permission of Bernard Guilbert Guerney.

Isaac Babel, "The Awakening" from *An Anthology of Russian Literature in the Soviet Period from Gorki to Pasternak,* translated and edited by Bernard Guilbert Guerney. Copyright © 1960 by Bernard Guilbert Guerney. Reprinted by permission of Random House, Inc.

J. G. Ballard, "The Assassination Weapon," originally published in *New Worlds,* 1966. Copyright © 1966 by J. G. Ballard. Reprinted by arrangement with the author's agent, C. & J. Wolfers, Ltd.

Samuel Beckett, "Stories and Texts for Nothing, III," translated by Anthony Bonner and Samuel Beckett. Copyright © 1955, Editions de Minuit. First published in *Great French Stories,* selected and introduced by Germaine Brée. Copyright © 1960 by Germaine Brée, Dell Publishing Co., Inc.

Heinrich Böll, "My Melancholy Face," from his volume *Wo Warst Du, Adam.* The translation by Ranier Schulte and Sandra Smith. Published in *Continental Short Stories,* copyright © 1968 by W. W. Norton & Co., Inc. Reprinted by permission of W. W. Norton & Co., Inc.

Jorge Luis Borges, "The Secret Miracle," from his volume *Labyrinths,* translated by Harriet de Onis. Copyright © 1962 by New Directions Publishing Corporation. Reprinted by permission of New Directions Publishing Corporation.

Elizabeth Bowen, "Her Table Spread," from her volume *Look at All Those Roses.* Copyright © 1941 by Elizabeth Bowen. Reprinted by permission of Alfred A. Knopf, Inc., and Jonathan Cape, Ltd.

Cynthia Buchanan, "The Wind Chandelier." Copyright © 1968 by Cynthia Buchanan. Originally published in *Epoch,* winter, 1968. Reprinted by permission of the author and *Epoch* magazine.

Karel Čapek, "The Last Judgment," from his volume *Tales from One Pocket.* English translation by Norma Jeanne McFadden and Leopold Pospišil especially for *Realm of Fiction* with permission of the Estates of Karel Čapek and Dilia. Copyright © 1965, 1970 by McGraw-Hill Book Company, Inc.

R. V. Cassill, "How I Live Through Times of Trouble," from *New & Experimental Literature,* published 1975 by Texas Center For Writers Press. Reprinted by permission of the author.

Anton Chekhov, "Gusev," translated from Russian by Ben Clark especially for *Realm of Fiction.*

Agatha Christie, "The Double Clue," published in *Blue Book* magazine, August 1925. Copyright © 1925 by Agatha Christie, renewed 1953. Reprinted by permission of Harold Ober Associates, Inc.

Walter Van Tilburg Clark, "The Rapids," from his volume *The Watchful Gods and Other Stories.* Published in 1950 by Random House, Inc. Copyright © 1950 by Walter Van Tilburg Clark. Reprinted by permission of International Creative Management.

Fyodor Dostoevsky, "A Christmas Tree and a Wedding," translated by P. H. Porosky especially for *Realm of Fiction.* Copyright © 1965, 1970 by McGraw-Hill Book Company, Inc.

William Faulkner, "Mule In The Yard," from *Collected Stories of William Faulkner.* Reprinted by permission of Random House, Inc.

F. Scott Fitzgerald, "The Long Way Out." Published in *Esquire* magazine, September 1937. Copyright © *Esquire* 1937. Renewed 1964 by Frances Scott Fitzgerald Lanahan. Reprinted by permission of Harold Ober Associations, Inc.

Lars Görling, "Opus Dei," translated by Lennart Bruce. Published in *Breakthrough Fictioneers* and in *Choice* magazine. Copyright © Ingrid Görling. Reprinted by arrangement with Lennart Bruce.

Graham Greene, "Brother," from his volume *Twenty-One Stories.* Copyright © 1949 by Graham Greene. Reprinted by permission of Viking Penguin, Inc. and Laurence Pollinger, Ltd.

Alain Robbe-Grillet, "The Secret Room," from *Esquire* magazine, February 1963, translated by Richard Howard. Copyright © 1963 by Alain Robbe-Grillet. First published in *Esquire* magazine. Reprinted by permission of Editions de Minuit.

James B. Hall, "Letters Never Mailed." First published in *Kenyon Review,* January 1963, and in *Gallery of Modern Fiction: Stories from the Kenyon Review,* published 1966 by Salem Press, Inc. Copyright © 1964 by James B. Hall and reprinted with author's permission.

Dashiell Hammett, "The Gatewood Caper." Copyright © 1923 by Dashiell Hammett. Copyright © renewed by Lillian Hellman as exectrucix of the estate of Dashiell Hammett. Reprinted by permission of Harold Matson, Co., Inc.

Peter Handke, "An Abstraction of the Ball That Fell in the River," translated from German by Michael Roloff. First appeared in *Fiction,* Vol. 1, #1, 1972. Copyright © 1972 by *Fiction.* Reprinted by permission of *Fiction,* Inc.

William Harrison, "The Good Ship Erasmus," from his volume *Roller Ball Murder.* Copyright © 1974 by William Harrison. Reprinted by permission of William Morrow & Co., Inc.

Ernest Hemingway, "In Another Country," from his volume *Men without Women.* Copyright © 1927 by Charles Scribner's Sons. Reprinted by permission of Charles Scribner's Sons.

Herman Hesse, "The Poet," from his volume *Strange News from Another Star,* translated by Denver Lendley. Translation copyright © 1972 by Farrar, Straus & Giroux, Inc. Translated from the German, Merchen, copyright © S. Fischer Verlag, 1919. Copyright © 1955 by Suhkamp Verlag, Berlin.

Langston Hughes, "Who's Passing for Who?" from his volume *Laughing to Keep from Crying,* published by Henry Holt and Co., New York. Copyright © 1952 by Langston Hughes. Reprinted by permission of Harold Ober Associates, Inc.

Ted Hughes, "Snow," from *Introduction: Stories by New Writers,* edited by A. O. Chater and others. Reprinted by permission of Faber and Faber, Ltd.

Grace Paley, "The Long Distance Runner," from her volume *Enormous Changes at the Last Minute.* Copyright © 1967 by Grace Paley. Published by Farrar, Straus & Giroux, Inc. Originally appearing in *Esquire.*

Luigi Pirandello, "The Tortoise," from his volume *Luigi Pirandello: Short Stories,* translated by Frederick May. Copyright © 1965 by Oxford University Press. Reprinted by permission of Toby Cole, on behalf of the Pirandello Estate.

Katherine Anne Porter, "Rope," from her volume *Flowering Judas and Other Stories.* Copyright © 1930, 1958 by Katherine Anne Porter. Reprinted by permission of Harcourt Brace Jovanovich, Inc.

V. S. Pritchett, "Many Are Disappointed," from his volume *It May Never Happen and Other Short Stories.* Published 1945 by Chatto and Windus, Ltd. Reprinted by permission of A. D. Peters & Co., Ltd., and Chatto and Windus, Ltd.

Isaac Rosenfeld, "The Brigadier," from *Partisan Review,* March-April, 1947. Reprinted through the courtesy of Mrs. Isaac Rosenfeld and *Partisan Review.*

Jean-Paul Sartre, "The Wall," from his volume *The Wall,* translated by Lloyd Alexander. Copyright © 1948 by New Directions Publishing Corporation. Reprinted by permission of New Directions Publishing Corporation.

Alan Sondheim, "*TraditCollege* Coarse Catalog," published in *Breakthrough Fictioneers,* 1973. Copyright © 1972 by Alan Sondheim. Reprinted by permission of the author.

John Steinbeck, "The Chrysanthemums," from his volume *The Long Valley.* Copyright © 1938, 1966, by John Steinbeck. Reprinted by permission of Viking Press, Inc.

Robert Stone, "Aquarius Obscured," from *American Review* #22, 1975. Published by American Review-Bantam Books. Copyright © 1975 by Robert Stone. Reprinted by permission of Candida Donadio & Associates, Inc.

Ilya Varshavsky, "Escape," translated by Leland Fetzer. Copyright © 1973 by Leland Fetzer. Reprinted by permission of Leland Fetzer.

Giovanni Verga, "Consolation," from *The She Wolf and Other Stories,* translated by Giovanni Cecchetti. Reprinted by permission of University of California Press.

H. G. Wells, "The Lord of the Dynamos," from his volume *Thirty Strange Stories.* Copyright © 1897 by Edward Arnold. Reprinted by permission of Harper & Row, Publishers.

Eudora Welty, "Livvie," from her volume *Thirteen Stories.* Copyright © 1942 renewed 1970 by Eudora Welty. Reprinted by permission of Harcourt Brace Jovanovich, Inc.

Virginia Woolf, "The Duchess and the Jeweler," from her volume *A Haunted House and Other Stories.* Copyright © 1944, renewed 1972 by Harcourt Brace Jovanovich, Inc. Reprinted by permission of Harcourt Brace Jovanovich, Inc., and Leonard Woolf.